FINDING DEVO

A NOVEL ADVENTURE

SEVE VERDAD

Devo's Diversiones, Inc.
P.O. Box 261998
Encino, CA 91426

ISBN: 978-0-9889566-0-5 (ebook)
ISBN: 978-0-9889566-2-9 (ebook)
ISBN: 978-0-9889566-1-2 (Pbk)

For my Parents

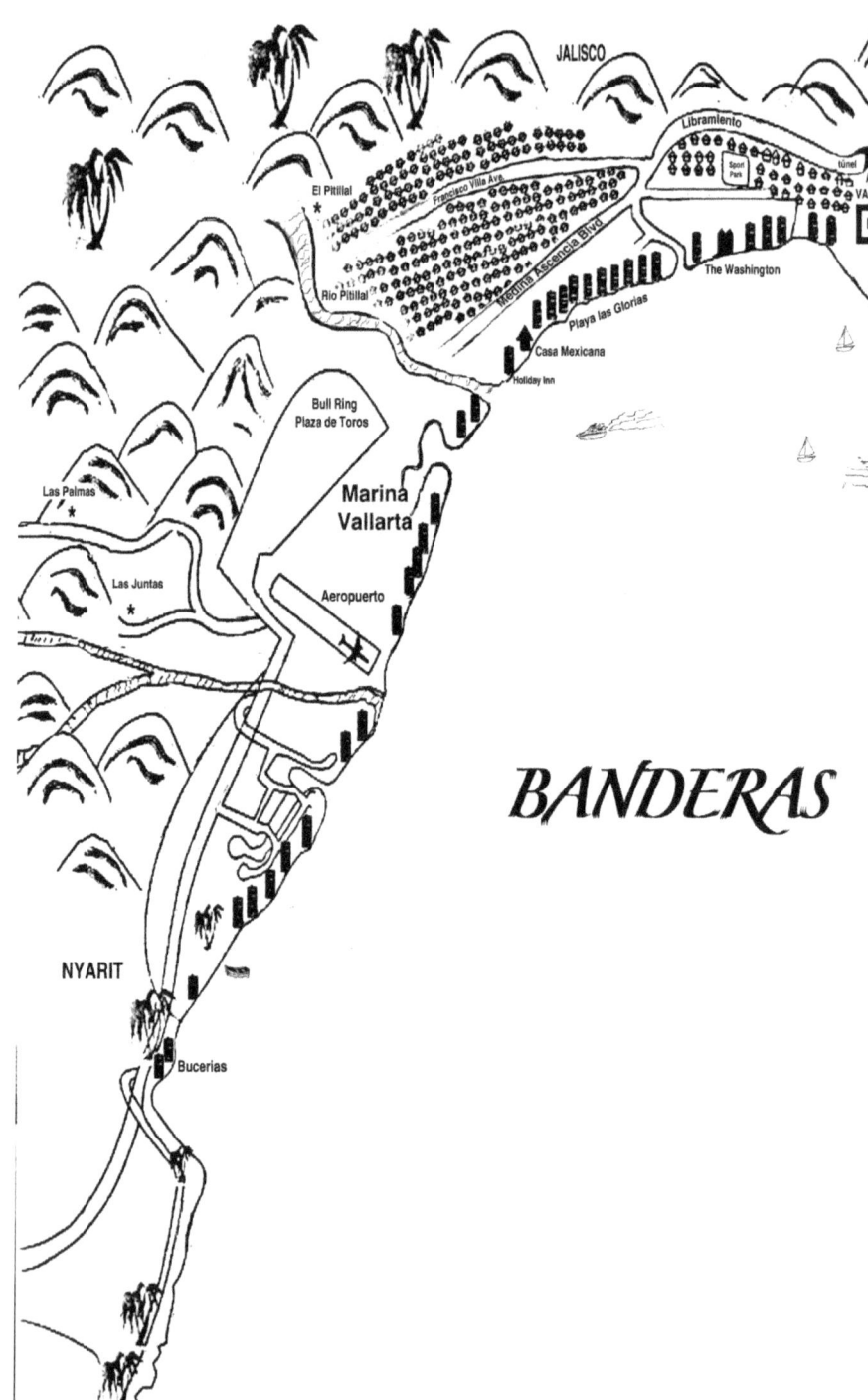

Prologue

Horns added panache to the big man's villainous persona. With horns spiking out his hooded mask, Masked Apocalypse closed ranks with the *rudos*—dirty fighters disrespectful of the public and rivals alike. Wrestling fans despised him accordingly, with boos and hisses, spit and curses. Epithets echoed his every move with a ferocity that matched the cheers for the (usually) victorious *técnicos*—the honorable, fair-fighting heroes of Mexican professional wrestling. But when teams of wrestlers flooded the ring for a melee, as they often do, and spilled out amongst the spectators, you never knew when Masked Apocalypse might take a volatile turn. Unlike many wrestlers, he'd never been unmasked in the ring; yet in response to a sleight from a fellow rudo, it wasn't uncommon for him to rip his horns from his head like offending appendages, toss them into the stands to the delight of fans, and convert himself into the lesser of evils—a dirty-fighting antihero. Masked Apocalypse never sided with the heroic técnicos, they were always subject to his wrath, but he did win over the crowd every now and then by attacking and vanquishing ugly vampires and goblins, gorillas and cavemen...any and all species of malevolent monster and beast.

Masked Apocalypse had a good bit—theatre—going for him; at least I thought so when I saw him wrestle in Guadalajara. He wasn't a huge star but just might figure in a story about Mexican wrestling I planned to write for New World Sports magazine someday soon...

That was before I discovered how Masked Apocalypse lived up to his name outside of the ring, before I came to the conclusion that my name would have to be changed, before the name *Playa de los Muertos*—Beach of the Dead—gained renewed significance... And before I met Devo.

Playa de los Muertos is in Puerto Vallarta where I met Devo, about two hundred miles west of Guadalajara... Hell of a name for a lively playa—*Beach of the Dead*. Bones and ceramic artifacts discovered there suggest it's an ancient burial ground, or sacred battle ground; yet you'd think that once Puerto Vallarta became a big tourist attraction, those in charge of such things would have changed the beach's macabre appellation to something romantic and alluring. But they didn't. Funny how a name will stick. It's almost as if they knew the name was appropriate, that a place can't shake its name so easily, or its past. And the past repeats itself.

That might be an unfair assessment, for ground zero of the great tragedy that befell Vallarta didn't occur at Playa de los Muertos but a few miles up the coast. Body parts did wash up on Los Muertos beach however. And other than the beach where the attack took place, Playa de los Muertos was the only beach where an intact corpse was found; ocean currents delivered three of them. So like I said, funny how a name will stick; though during my ill-fated journey I only considered the significance of the name once, days before the bombing, shortly after I arrived in Vallarta from my home in the States.

It was April and spring break—a time to party...for most. Therapy was the way I looked at it, like learning to dance again after losing your leg and your dance partner—your lover—in a car crash, except my appendages were all intact and she hadn't died in a car crash. Her family and I had laid her to rest in Old Vallarta over six months ago. I hadn't been back since. Upon my return, I visited Rosalita's grave and placed flowers on her headstone. Afterwards, while wandering the streets towards the Los Muertos shoreline, the name *Playa de los Muertos* suddenly struck me as an obscene irony, like naming your child Lucifer. What kind of destiny does a name like that portend? Had I married a local girl in Vallarta under the specter of death? Why did she die instead of me?

The words, the name—*Playa de los Muertos*—seemed a direct reference to me and my grief. An absurd notion that suggested I was the center of the universe or something. The name was not all about me, or Rosalita.

I didn't ponder the significance of the name again until well after I escaped Vallarta...even while strolling the Los Muertos shoreline the following evening, Friday—the night I witnessed the first of Devo's many outlandish tricks I would see him perform over the next three or four days.

He was causing an uproar in Ándale Bar and Grill. Devo sported an eye patch and, from what I could gather from across the bar, he lifted the patch and squirted a false eyeball into a patron's beer. The patron, a square-faced blond fellow with a weak chin, was apoplectic, shocked beyond words. As he struggled to raise his voice in protest, Devo laid some pesos on the bar for the beer, drank it down, spit up the eye and popped it back into his head for all to see. A few girls screeched in disgust amidst a clamor of displeasure and applause. Devo's display might have caused a row but for his imposing stature. He looked to be a head taller and twice as broad as me or anyone else in the joint. That didn't stop the manager of Ándale from cutting him off at the bar though. Devo accused him of bigotry and cursed him in

2

a string of beautifully profane guttural Spanish. Apparently he felt the manager held something personal against rangy, half-drunk, bearded white men who couldn't keep their eyeballs out of other people's cervezas. Cops arrived and took Devo away in handcuffs. He left with them quite agreeably, as if happy to see them. A few hours later, I ambled back into Ándale and saw Devo, eyes beaming and full of life (no sign of his eye patch or false eyeball), buying drinks for the chief of police and a boisterous round for everyone in the house...except the manager who was nowhere to be seen.

I rather enjoyed Devo's "eye" trick, but the way he returned to Ándale shortly after getting arrested was truly impressive. When the bartender told me Devo was entertaining the police chief—el comandante—I had to laugh. It's one thing to bribe the cops to get out of jail (if that's what Devo did), quite another to have them accompany you back to the crime scene to help sanctify and enrich your evening shenanigans.

Devo's performance in Ándale stuck with me. The following evening I mentioned it to Johnny in Rudy's Sports Bar in Old Vallarta, five or six blocks inland of Playa de los Muertos. I had never personally met Devo but Johnny had. He'd pointed him out to me at the Vallarta marina about a year ago, after one of our fishing trips. "A notorious grower from Mendocino County," he called him.

"What do you mean *notorious*?"

"Psycho, according to some."

"And according to you?"

"Not sure. I've met him but don't know if I wanna actually get to know him."

Reasonable. Why get to know a psycho pot farmer if you don't need to? The subject was dropped and in the months that followed, as I visited Rosalita with greater frequency, I saw Devo around Vallarta from time to time but avoided meeting him.

Or was *he* avoiding *me* all along, waiting for the proper moment for me to *find* him?

Whatever the case, the man had now piqued my interest, and news of his antics in Ándale provided Johnny an opportunity to expound on Devo's "notorious" reputation over beers in Rudy's.

Johnny and I often meet up south of the border to go fishing. And that's what we had in mind this trip as well, but we never got the chance.

Book I

Fiesta

It is as easy to dream a book as it is hard to write one.

Honoré de Balzac

Man is vile, I know, but people are wonderful.

Peter de Vries

1

COMANDANTE Héctor Diamante Pasqual was furious. He had been exasperated for weeks over his teenage daughter's involvement with an Indian boy who had shown little respect for his exalted position as Comandante of the Puerto Vallarta Police Department. The boy had a future darker than his pimply naco skin. Barely sixteen years of age, he'd already been picked up three times by police—twice for drunken brawling and once for shoplifting. In general, el comandante had nothing against Indians—los indios. After all, like most every Mexican, he himself was part Indian. But the boy was trouble. This was as clear as a January day in Vallarta, at least to el comandante. His wife was another matter. Her stance on the issue was as baffling as a Jaliscan snow storm, if there ever were such a thing. She insisted that the relationship between their daughter and the Indian boy wasn't anything more than passing infatuation. "Like tears shed at a wedding," she told him, "it will soon pass." Héctor didn't care for the analogy but cared even less for arguing with his wife. Despite the machismo he demonstrated on the job, his wife was la ama de la casa—master of the house. So Héctor Diamante Pasqual, el comandante, let his ill feelings over the Indian boy simmer, taking solace in his work where he was the master and could better channel his animosity (especially if he caught that pinche naco mocoso up to no good again), and soothing himself every now and again off duty with drink.

Today, however, his work had offered him no solace at all. In fact, it had terminated in utter humiliation. And he was furious about it.

El comandante's pock-marked, Creole face flushed and twitched as he balled his fists upon his desk. "It all started with that puta madre gangster we arrested this afternoon," he growled at the lieutenant standing before him. "This *Paco* we have locked up."

Lieutenant Benito Cuevas Romero held el comandante's inflamed gray eyes with a quiet gaze. "Let me and my men work on him some more," he said. "We suspected the duplex was a drug house and he confirmed as much. But he had to know the place would be empty when we raided it. It looked to have been vacated some time ago, maybe even last night. And the pinche chingón lied about who was renting the duplex...has lied about his identity, his nationality and—"

El comandante interrupted, "His identity? We have his Venezuelan passport. And once you got his shirt off this afternoon those tattoos told the truth about the sin madre gangster. Mara Salvatrucha are his people, his pueblo, his gang."

"And gangsters must have been renting that duplex instead of Arab terrorists as he claimed. I think he mentioned Hezbollah to cover for his gang and buy himself some time. He probably knows about that arrest up at the border in Tijuana and figured we would take his claim of Arab terrorists operating in Vallarta very seriously."

"Yesterday's police advisory is confidential, Lieutenant. How would he know about the arrest?"

"A story like that does not remain confidential for long, señor. *Paco* could have heard about the arrest of a Hezbollah leader in Tijuana secondhand, presumed we knew about it, and then lied about terrorists in that duplex to conceal the fact that gangsters had really been renting it."

El comandante frowned in thought, a hand to his chin. Lieutenant Romero shook his head imperceptibly, chiding himself. In hindsight, the idea of Arab terrorists in Vallarta seemed farfetched. They were rarely encountered outside of the nation's border regions and the crime-infested Mexico City barrio of Tepito. "We have never come across foreign terrorists in Vallarta," he said, his voice toneless, "or domestic ones for that matter, other than Los Zetas narco gangsters; but they have yet to gain much of a foothold here."

"We had never come across MS-13—Mara Salvatrucha—in Vallarta either Lieutenant, until today."

"Perhaps the Zetas drug cartel has formed an alliance with MS-13 in a renewed effort to gain ground in Jalisco and Vallarta."

El comandante cursed with a throat clearing grunt, *"Carajo,"* and lowered his gaze, mindful that, even if his raid had allowed gangsters to escape instead of Arab terrorists, it remained a dangerous failure. He raked his lower teeth over his mustache and looked a question at the lieutenant. "The prisoner was in possession of a Venezuelan passport when arrested, but you have doubts about his nationality?"

"He may have dual citizenship. He denies he is Mexican and we have yet to match his fingerprints, but I am certain the pinche güey is Mexican. Probably chilango. Stupid naco. His slang and accent give him away, especially when prodded with Paulo's nightstick."

"Stupid naco," repeated el comandante; his mind's eye glimpsed the Indian boy courting his daughter. "They have no respect. Better to send them all north. Let the gringos deal with them, fill their jails with them."

"The gringos might be interested in *Paco* once we are done with him." Lieutenant Romero paused, his collected aplomb belying the contempt he held for the prisoner. "He probably crosses the border regularly; they could have his fingerprints on file. MS-13 is—"

"Yes Lieutenant," el comandante intervened with forbearance, "North American. But they are also Salvadorian. And Mexican...and Honduran. Do we have to name every country in the entire maldito continent where you can find these filthy gangster pigs?"

"No, señor. But MS-13 is involved in human as well as drug trafficking. They cross the northern border illegally all the time which, as you know, is why they are usually associated with the Juárez and Tijuana cartels."

El comandante snorted, "Puta." He planted his elbows on his desk, his expression strict and aggravated. "They have also operated in the nation's capital, Lieutenant, and Michoacán...and in Sinaloa. And now that we have found one of them here in Vallarta..." he allowed Lieutenant Romero a concordant nod, "...you may be right about an alliance between MS-13 and Los Zetas." El comandante crossed his arms and sucked in his breath. "Narco-gang violence is on the rise in Vallarta," he said. "We cannot allow the putos to establish a cartel infrastructure here."

"Agreed, señor."

Héctor clenched his teeth as he locked onto the lieutenant's polished figure: black hair slicked back and parted off center, razor sharp; heavy dark brow and smooth flawless features but for a neat scar under the jaw; blue uniform snug and tidy over his taught, slender frame; cap tucked under an arm. He had declined to sit in the chair at his side upon entering el comandante's office. Lieutenant Romero looked like he'd just arrived for duty, though Héctor knew he'd been on the job for over twelve hours, including well over two hours of rather stressful work organizing and conducting the raid, a botched raid that, despite his icy confidence and guarded disposition, had to infuriate the lieutenant as much as it infuriated him. The cabrón was harder to read than a politician's smile.

Unlike the lieutenant, who often opted to wear his uniform, el comandante rarely wore his, and today was no exception. Uniforms were optional for ranking officers (depending on their day's field duties) and he afforded himself this concession to comfort. Héctor tucked in the tail of his shirt and slouched in his chair, feeling somewhat disheveled. He should. He'd been on the job for over twelve hours as well. "And now we have a dead man to contend with," he said. "A body discovered at the marina, fairly close to the raid. What do you make of that, Lieutenant?"

The lieutenant's eyes flickered with uncertainty. "Inexplicable, señor."

11

SEVE VERDAD

"How could anyone get away with murder at the marina? Security is tight and there were lots of tourists around."

"Yet the victim must have been killed there. I cannot imagine why anyone would risk dumping a dead body at the marina." The lieutenant relaxed his posture and dropped his police cap onto the chair by his side. "The victim may have been associated with the occupants of the duplex we raided, señor. We discovered his Jeep around the block from there... And the three passports found on the body are Venezuelan, like the passport confiscated from our prisoner, which suggests a connection between our prisoner and the dead man."

"And since you seem convinced that our prisoner is lying about his nationality..."

"All the passports may be false, señor. Immigration—Sandra—should have a full report on their authenticity completed by the day after tomorrow, Monday."

"Make sure that copies of all fingerprints are faxed to Guadalajara. Their automated fingerprint-identification system should speed up the investigation... Anything to indicate that the dead man was a member of MS-13? tattoos on his body? Those fucking culeros always mark themselves with tattoos."

"No. But considering the cocaine and cash we found on him and in his vehicle, he may have been supplying drugs to those in the duplex."

"Did gangsters kill him?"

"Maybe... They kill each other all the time—"

"Why would his killers leave drugs and cash on the body?"

Lieutenant Romero offered his commander a minute shrug, "Perhaps vengeance was the motive...or—"

"And the disc discovered on the victim? Anything on that yet?"

"Pedro has had trouble decoding it."

"The disc must be what the killer or killers after, Lieutenant. It was secured to the dead man's thigh and they did not take the drugs or money we found on the body, or the keys to the victim's Jeep, a Jeep which contained more drugs and money."

A sort of vapid eagerness flitted across the lieutenant's face. He'd already considered this. "The disc was accessible, señor," he said. "I discovered it upon simply frisking the body. And the man was killed with brutal efficiency. His neck, ankle and arm were broken without leaving any signs of a struggle. A killer, or *killers* of that caliber would not have missed the disc or the cash and drugs on the body."

Héctor's irritation resurfaced, his voice piqued: "That does not prove it was a vengeance killing, Lieutenant! Someone probably

12

scared the killers away before they could grab the disc. It may have been *accessible* but...*híjole*. It was stuffed down his pants! The disc must have some special value and could help us discover who committed the murder."

"Perhaps, señor, but—" Lieutenant Romero shifted his weight from foot to foot, his dark eyes leveled on el comandante. "No witnesses to the homicide have come forward, Security at the marina could not identify the dead man, and no one in the vicinity recognized the victim from his passport photo. It is not clear who, if anyone, frightened off the killers."

"Yet in all likelihood, Lieutenant, someone did."

"The killers might have made off with something else they were after...a laptop or briefcase..."

They lapsed into a contemplative silence; Héctor modulated his tone: "How the hell anyone could get away with murder inside the marina gates is a mystery. But this murder was committed in close quarters, Lieutenant. So even if vengeance was the principal motive and/or the killers managed to steal something, I find it hard to believe that they would purposely leave drugs and money on the body...or the disc. Someone spooked them."

Lieutenant Romero shook his head in befuddled agreement. El comandante had a point.

El comandante massaged his temples. This was a troubling case. Troubling because it had the potential to get worse, had been getting steadily worse since the arrest of that puto Paco after his brakes failed and he broadsided a Toyota, injuring a child. The piece-of-shit naco gangster was clearly at fault; and police found several grams of cocaine in his pickup, though he didn't appear intoxicated...

And that maldito raid. No less than a week ago police had fingered the duplex as a possible drug house, and now... It was bad enough that the place was empty when they raided it, but state federales had been included in the operation. Who knew when they would exercise their authority, take a sudden interest in *Paco*, report the botched raid to their superiors, and inform the mayor of Vallarta that gangsters...or *terroristas* had escaped?!? Humiliating! or worse. The mayor could slap Héctor with a reprimand, maybe even have the Jalisco Police Ministry in Guadalajara put him on probation...

El comandante absently flipped through the file on his desk pertaining to *Paco's* arrest. "We have a dead body on our hands yet to be positively identified," he said, "a distinct possibility of forged Venezuelan passports, and a kilo or more of cocaine. But no arrests, except for this naco Paco."

The lieutenant measured el comandante with his fiercely large dark eyes. "We also have cash," he reminded him, "and the Jeep where we found cash and drugs under its backseat."

Héctor pawed at his front pocket, feeling for the car keys found on the dead man. The Jeep was a late model Grand Cherokee Laredo in excellent condition. Leather interior. Officer Talla was in the process of verifying the car's paperwork and ownership but, for now, the Jeep belonged to el comandante. He straightened himself in his seat and rifled through the file once more. "Yes, of course," he said. "I will have to pay off Lazarito—keep this puta madre embarrassment out of the news. But you will receive your share of the cash."

"Perhaps later this evening, after my next interrogation of the prisoner and you are finished with Lazarito."

El comandante ran an exasperated hand through his thinning hair. "Chíngaderas. We do not need these problems now. Governor Palacio will be in town for the dedication of Arena Vallarta tomorrow and all branches of the department have to help manage security."

"Sí señor."

"Try not to inflict too much more *visible* damage on the prisoner, Lieutenant. This *Paco*...puta." Sharp disdain seeped into el comandante's voice. "Federales were involved in that raid and it may only be a matter of time before we have to hand him and any evidence pertaining to his arrest over to them."

"The federales... Do they know about the dead man found at the marina?"

"Not yet," Héctor replied quickly. "And I will keep his file separate from the prisoner's. Everything associated with the dead man is solely under our jurisdiction. That could change, however." El comandante shared a quiet, conspiratorial gaze with the lieutenant. "But until it does, we will keep as much of this business as possible within the department."

"Muy bien, señor."

"We should receive a preliminary autopsy report on the dead man tomorrow. In the meantime, we need to investigate any possible links between him and the prisoner in an effort to identify and find the killers."

Lieutenant Romero retrieved his cap from the chair beside him. "Understood, señor," he said. "I will have Paulo and los chicos get started on the prisoner right away." He pulled an about-face. El comandante detained him. "Lieutenant," he said.

Lieutenant Romero faced his commander. "Sí señor?"

"Push Pedro on decoding that disc. I want to know its contents as soon as possible."

"I will call him immediately, señor. He should be working on it at home right now."

Lieutenant Benito Cuevas Romero exited the office. The botched raid had frustrated him but he remained about as disheartened as a tiger whose prey has escaped. He was on the hunt and would continue to follow his instincts. Those instincts had helped him streak up the ranks of the department. This was an opportunity to shoot to the top, perhaps with a little help from his friends—influential friends in the Mexico City Police Department as well as CISEN (Mexican Intelligence)—friends who might be able to lend him a hand in identifying *Paco* and the dead man discovered at the marina should his own investigations bog down. Might Los Zetas be colluding with MS-13 in an effort to gain ground along this relatively peaceful strand of the pacific coast? If he uncovered as much, the lieutenant could find himself in command of a small army to rid Vallarta of the sin madre killers.

Héctor swiveled around in his chair and stared blankly out the barred window at the illuminated streetlamp across the street below. Should he attend the lieutenant's next interrogation of the prisoner? He discarded the idea. A meeting with Lazarito had to take precedence. El comandante didn't generally conduct a lot of business with Puerto Vallarta's Media Minister (Minister of Propaganda). Gang violence was on the rise in Vallarta yet the municipality retained a small beach-town atmosphere, without the preponderance of scandal, egregious graft and violent crime that had infected the larger Mexican pacific-coast resort cities of Acapulco and Mazatlán. Only on occasion did el comandante find it necessary to grease Lazarito's palms for favorable publicity or to muzzle the media on his behalf. But the press must have gotten wind of the raid and, with a foul-up of this magnitude, Héctor's reputation was on the line. A story about how police let terrorists or gangsters slip through their fingers could kill him. Best to be sure Lazarito was on his side on this one.

2

RUDY'S Sports Bar, Puerto Vallarta. Not exactly a clean well-lighted place but, who cares? It's got all the necessities—a couple of dining rooms, three TVs, decent food, a jukebox, pool table, well-stocked bar, and the occasional gaggle of hookers. And let's not forget the proprietor, Rudy, a fortyish man with a well-rounded figure, a raucous twinkle in his chestnut eyes, graying temples, and a love of sports. Rudy's is decorated with sports memorabilia. Everything from worn boxing gloves and old wooden tennis rackets to photos of Mexican soccer teams, posters of American football players, and pinups of the Dallas Cowboy cheerleaders adorn the walls of Rudy's Sports Bar.

The afternoon's big Mexican League soccer matches had ended some time ago and the bawdy late-night crowd wasn't due to begin heating the joint back up for a while yet. Overhead fans enlivened the boozy air. Festive Mexican voices and trumpets came from the jukebox. Rudy's had settled into a lyrical early-evening lull in sync with several low-key stragglers—men playing dominos, others gnashing antojitos and drinking beer in the adjacent dining room, a couple more smoking cigarettes and playing bar dice at the bar. The Mariners and Royals were playing on one TV above and behind the bar, the Suns and Clippers on the other. I was seated at a table with Johnny, my fishing buddy.

"I'm only tellin' you this," he said, " 'cause your story about him was so good. It's strictly off the record."

"*Strictly* off the record...? You never talk to me *strictly* off the record."

Johnny pushed his gray fedora off his forehead. "Just don't quote me directly."

"Never have and don't plan to. Your account's probably not good enough to publish anyway."

Johnny's spaniel eyes narrowed reproachfully. A couple of years ago he figured in a piece of mine published in New World Sports about deep sea fishing off the coast of Costa Rica. He got a real kick out of that. Johnny's always looking for a part in one of my stories and always careful to remind me not to use his real name. His profession isn't given to publicity.

"You wanna hear it or not?"

"Get on with it."

He dropped his chin, voice confidential, as if offering me a big scoop. "Word is," he began, "that Devo was growing on government as well as private land and cops ripped him off. Not sure if it was the feds or state or both, but he managed to escape the choppers and disappear." Johnny took a drink from his beer. "He never got busted, arrested or even wanted. Pigs just took everything, made their killing and forgot about him."

I stroked my goatee. "So the cops are thieves," I shrugged. "That's an old story."

"At the time, police didn't know who he was. But get this..." Johnny leaned forward and drew me in with a covert nod. "A couple

16

months or so later, someone tried to give Devo up. Some canary bird the cops got their hands on." He bounced his eyebrows. "And Devo resurfaced, cut the motherfucker up, and disappeared again. I mean he slit his throat, and...uh—"

"Stuffed his genitals in his mouth?"

Johnny jerked his head at me, like he hadn't thought of that. "Yeah," he said. "Somethin' like that." His voice caught an edge. "Can you believe it? How can Devo not be fingered by the cops, feds, or *someone* after slicin' and dicin' that canary?... Shit." He took a deep breath and relaxed his posture. "Too good to be true. Takes more'n ability to pull that off. Guy must be connected..." Johnny folded his hands on the table. "So now he's back down here but, considerin' your story about his antics last night, it sure don't seem like he's on the run."

"Sure doesn't." I kept my tone dispassionate, mindful that, more often than not, Johnny's embellished stories have lots of gravy and little meat. "You read about this stoolie's death?"

"Oh yeah. And I got my sources. The guy was found sliced to pieces in the woods outside a Willits." Johnny grabbed his beer mug, sat it back down, and regarded my dubious expression as if it gave off a disgusting odor, his face pinched and offended. "Look it up if you don't believe me," he said. "Google it."

"Police talk to any witnesses?"

"To the murder? There were no witnesses. Said so in the paper."

"So how the hell do you—"

"Jesus Russ." Johnny ran an indignant hand over his face. "Can't you just listen to me for once 'stead of fuckin' up the story? Like I told ya. I got my sources."

"Doesn't everybody?"

"If you don't wanna believe me," he flipped me the bird, "that's your problem."

"Hey," I smiled lightly, "don't take it so personally. Just doin' my job. Tell me more."

Johnny waved me off and turned his attention to the bar across the room. He raised his voice to Rudy: "Where're all the women, Rudy?"

English doesn't faze Rudy but he rarely answers in kind. "Busca en tu culo," he said as he dumped lime wedges into a bowl. "Han dicho que hay bastante espacio." Look up your ass. They've said there's plenty of space.

Rudy sauntered back into the kitchen. Johnny chuckled, "I knew he was gonna say that."

"But the only word you understood was *culo*," I said.

Johnny snorted, "Least I don't take it up there."

"Whatever you say." I grabbed a handful of nuts from the bowl between us. "You ready to continue your story?"

Johnny sipped his beer languidly, making me wait—pay for forcing him to digress.

"Go on," I said. "Tell me more about Devo. Promise not to interrupt."

"Well," he began again, "only met him a few times before the cops ripped him off last year. He talks a good game, you know? Pound some booze with ya and bullshit about sports, chicks, politics. Could be a regular guy, 'cept for that *psycho* rep he's got. Heard he used to be a big time smuggler, a *treetop flier*. And could he tear another motherfucker up again? Ha! Why not?" Johnny tugged on the brim of his fedora, a crooked, envious grin creasing his lips. "Like to think I could do the same under those circumstances. I mean, hell, that canary was ripe for killin'. He obviously gave Devo's name to the pigs without ever having met him or knowin' much if anything about him. How idiotic is that? I don't care what kinda trouble the guy thought he was in. You can't be long for this life if you go blurtin' out someone's name, the name of a man you don't even know, to the police. There're plenty of people roamin' around who are more dangerous than cops."

"No shit."

"Yeah, no shit." Johnny took a disdainful slug of beer. "It's common sense. And, as far as Devo goes, I guess he feels that if he's stupid enough to get ripped off by the cops it's best to disappear and live to fight another day. But if an idiot goes blurting his name to the cops, well..." Johnny glanced over his shoulder, like someone might be eavesdropping. Nobody paid us the slightest bit of attention. "It's one thing," he advanced, "to fuck up and get ripped off by pigs you can ultimately fool, long as you live to fight another day. But you can't let a fool live who can kill ya."

"Good refrain. You come up with that?"

Johnny ignored my question and raised his chin at something over my shoulder. Two girls cruised by—a brunette Venus and a peroxide-blond Twiggy; they took a seat at a table behind him. Tough choice. Johnny eyed them, debating the option—the cost for each and the cost for both. Venus fished a cigarette out of her purse and cooed at him through plump plum-red lips. Johnny bummed a smoke off her. Thick mascara flared like oiled wings around her almond eyes; the strap of her blouse hung loosely off a fleshy shoulder. You could lose a keg of beer down that cleavage and drown yourself trying to find it. Johnny said something to her in broken Spanish that made her squeal like a piglet. Twiggy crossed her legs and massaged her ankle. Johnny was putting her feet to sleep. Or maybe the drugs were.

Johnny faced me with the grin of an insurance salesman at my door. "She'll give me a Spanish lesson later."

I downed my beer and signaled the waitress for two more. Loose dice went rolling across the bar and fell behind it. One of the men playing asked Rudy to retrieve them. Three guys sat down at the table with Venus and Twiggy. Johnny looked them over surreptitiously. Someone cranked up the jukebox. A Vicente Fernández ballad. Rudy couldn't find one of the die, told the men playing to look up their culos for it. The waitress attended our table with a rabbity smile, two frozen mugs and cervezas. We poured the beers ourselves. A skinny kid in polyester sitting across from Venus broke into song. He didn't have Vicente's voice but the drunken harmony was appropriate for the Mexican lament of unrequited love: "Lástima que seas ajena!" Venus and Twiggy giggled, their heads bobbing up and down. A pair of bobblehead dolls. I told Johnny that he was in danger of losing his Spanish lesson for the evening.

He scanned the tavern and waved his cigarette dismissively. "Gettin' a little crowded all of a sudden. Not enough women."

"More'll show up. Working sluts if nothin' else."

A heavy sigh straightened his slight frame and slouched him over his beer. "They only want me for my money."

"At least you got somethin' they want." I washed some nuts down with beer. "There'll be plenty of girls where I'm headed tonight."

"Chicks really dig chickens pecking each other's eyes out?"

"Cocks. Gallos. Roosters."

Johnny pointed his cigarette at me. "Can you eat 'em?"

"Somebody does."

"Then they're chickens."

I flicked a bead of sweat from my brow. "There's lots of gambling at cockfights, Johnny. You know how that excites girls. Plus, there's the musical entertainment...some famous mariachi singer will be performing tonight."

Johnny pondered this, beer clutched between his hands. The door behind me was held open and fresh, tepid air caressed the back of my neck. A couple of drunks lumbered by our table, leaned on each other with a mutual "compadre" and made for the bar.

I pounded most of my beer and slapped some pesos on the table. "I'm outta here."

SEVE VERDAD

A tightness wrenched down upon my shoulder, a familiar iron grip. I cranked my head up and found a finger pointed at my nose. "Me debes." You owe me.

"Paid you last night."

Enrique Santos let a small smile play across his face. "You did? Oh. Pues, maybe Johnny will buy me a cerveza then. Cómo te va, Johnny?"

"Muy bien." Johnny crushed his cigarette under foot, reached for Enrique's outstretched hand and squeezed with all his might. He lasted less than five seconds before shaking free from the former journeyman boxer. "Shit. Never can outlast you."

Enrique responded to Johnny's English in earthy, burly Spanish: "The skinny fucking mule still has the grip of a chicken. It would be less painful if you were to drink beer and practice your Spanish with me, *Juanito*, like the last time."

Johnny snuffed blandly.

Enrique, a stout twenty pounds and equal number of years over his one-fifty fighting weight, never boasted of his boxing career. Not much to brag about, except he never got knocked out. Had that twisted nose of his busted a few times though, and his scarred brows indicated he was something of a bleeder. When pressed, Enrique would deny he was a bleeder; he just found his impregnable jaw to be his best defense at times and, as a consequence, his eyes often took a beating. But Enrique Santos retired from the ring well before suffering any serious permanent damage. A smart move. Smarter still how he kept his stocky frame in condition with construction work, went back to school, and seized upon an opportunity to become President of Puerto Vallarta's chapter of the Obreros Unidos labor union.

I lost a bet to Enrique on a prizefight we saw on TV here at Rudy's last night and had told him he might find me and Johnny here tonight.

Johnny hailed the waitress. Enrique called out to her for a shot of Herradura tequila and adjusted his tie, told us he was running late for a meeting and didn't have time to sit for a beer. "Only wanted to remind Russell he was a loser last night."

"One of those cigars I paid you with would better refresh my memory," I said.

"You can try again next Friday. Good match up. Hernández versus that Panamanian, Meléndez. Meet me here. Better hope your man hits harder."

"And takes a better punch," I added in English with an eye to Johnny. He'd been straining to follow our Spanish.

Enrique thanked the waitress for his tequila. I proposed a toast to Arena Vallarta, Enrique's all-consuming pet project the last several years. It was to be dedicated tomorrow. Enrique knocked back his tequila without lime, salt or grimace. "Nos vemos," he said and was gone.

I idly wondered why the hell he was in such a hurry to attend a meeting on a Saturday night. A fairly benign question that would gain considerable significance in the coming days. I would not see Enrique again.

"That guy's grip seems even stronger than the last time," Johnny said.

"Best for a skinny *buey* like you to keep on his good side then." I stood from the table and slapped down more pesos for Enrique's tequila. "Well? Like I said, I'm outta here."

Johnny checked out Venus again. She was involved in a five-way conversation that mixed and garbled the lyrics emanating from the jukebox. I gave him an extra incentive to accompany me: "Mountain said he'd meet us at the cockfights."

"Really?" Johnny got a spark in his eye, like I'd just offered him free tickets to a big ball game which, given Mountain's celebrity around these parts, wasn't far off base.

He rose from his seat as I made for the door. "Might as well tag along. Could be better than bar hoppin' for tourist girls."

"And there's nothin' in here that won't keep."

"Unless she's already spoiled."

"Or a transvestite."

"Pinches putos."

3

MEDIA Minister Lazarito Charlado was not in the habit of gloating over the misfortunes of others. Yet he was in the habit, the business, of determining which misfortunes (or fortunes, as the case may be) were reported in the news. Naturally, an element of self-preservation prevailed in making such determinations—he wasn't about to place his job or his benefactors in the Socialist Reform Party in jeopardy. As Vallarta's Media Minister (as well as an attorney) he was an expert in manipulating and sidestepping Mexico's nascent transparency laws to his advantage. Lazarito Charlado was also quite adept at recognizing when he had the upper hand; and this evening, the misfortunes of some were about to advance the fortunes of Lazarito Charlado.

SEVE VERDAD

Four televisions dominated Lazarito's sparsely furnished office—three against the wall opposite his large mahogany desk and one mounted up on the wall behind. All were on but muted so he could better communicate with Comandante Héctor Diamante Pasqual, the man seated in the rather uncomfortable vinyl chair before him.

Lazarito's deep leather armchair creaked and lifted his feet off the carpet as he leaned back and folded his hands upon his ponderous belly. His unctuous, fleshy face—usually an agreeable if not outright jolly appendage (he rarely missed an opportunity to dress up as Santa come Christmas)—currently wore an expression of concerned perplexity. He addressed el comandante apologetically, as though asking for help:

"I might be able to postpone the story. I am not certain though, Comandante. It is already in the works for tomorrow's Sunday edition of the Vallarta Diario. And there is the art to think about. Nothing has been posted on the Internet...as far as I know. But I do believe that the managing editor has access to photos, and maybe some video."

"Local media publicity..." responded Héctor haltingly, "...is what concerns me. I think you can understand...that the timing of a story like this...with the governor due in town tomorrow for the dedication of the arena and all...well... It would certainly be in the interest of everyone concerned to have the focus of tomorrow's news be the governor and the dedication and not..." Héctor released a light-hearted laugh, "...some insignificant raid."

"Hardly insignificant," Lazarito said with a high-pitched sigh. "Any time federales are involved in something like this it is indeed a significant story. Indeed it is. I should think you would not be here otherwise. And from what I gather, you may have let some dangerous people slip through your fingers. That, señor, is news. Indeed."

Héctor had begun to sweat through the fresh dress shirt he'd slipped on before coming to the Media Minister's office, The Bureau; it stuck to the vinyl chair as he uncrossed his legs, smoothed his tie and sat forward. Somehow he had to conceal his desperation, a difficult task considering he was prepared to grease Lazarito's palms with more money than he had ever offered him before.

El comandante lowered his voice in a show of intimacy as he advanced his offer of a bribe to keep the raid out of the news...and obfuscated the misinformation he was about to impart about the raid:

"You are right, señor, this was not an insignificant raid. It did in fact yield vital clues in a current investigation and, as soon as we gather more evidence and are prepared to make a public statement, I will come to you first. But, for now, I can only share with you my sincerest hope that this investigation will not be hindered at this time by premature publicity. Furthermore, as a gesture of goodwill and gratitude for your assistance in this matter, I am prepared to offer you some of the proceeds gathered thus far from the investigation."

Comandante Héctor Diamante Pasqual pulled an envelope from his back pocket, placed it upon Lazarito's desk, and resumed his position in his chair.

Lazarito creaked forward in his leather armchair and reached for the envelope. He fingered through its contents. "Always a pleasure to receive dollars," he said. Lazarito stroked his double chin and reclined. "But the sum does not appear adequate. Indeed not. The cost of keeping a story like this out of the news will certainly exceed five hundred dollars. Indeed it will."

"I assure you the sum will be doubled in a matter of days, a week at most. And I am not requesting you keep this affair out of the news permanently but for a postponement of the story so we can continue our investigation without undue publicity. When the time comes we will all look forward to headlines that reflect positively on the police department and Vallarta."

"Why not have that story now? If you give me a few more details I am sure we can spin this little debacle to your, *our* mutual advantage...at very little additional expense."

El comandante uncrossed his legs and attempted another light-hearted laugh. The effort resulted in a nervous chuckle. He knew that absolutely nothing about today's botched raid could be spun advantageously until arrests were made. "Well...uh...Lazarito, for the moment it is advisable to wait. Like I said, the sum you see on the table will be doubled within a week, at which time more details will be forthcoming, I promise you."

Lazarito took satisfaction in el comandante's switch to an informal, familiar form of Spanish, a sure indication that he, the Media Minister, held some strong cards. The raid had surely been a debacle, a failure. How much of a failure Lazarito couldn't be certain. "Clues" aiding a police investigation were likely garnered, including, perhaps, the money in the envelope. But Héctor needed him on his side and was playing to their supposed friendship, a dubious tactic as they enjoyed each other's company infrequently, usually at formal gatherings or an occasional fiesta to which they were both invited.

The Media Minister passed a hand over his balding pate and scratched the back of his head, guarding the posture of a befuddled academic when, in actuality, like a chess master, he was thinking several moves ahead. "Seems to me there is at least one other issue to be considered here," he said.

El comandante frowned incoherently. "I cannot imagine—"

SEVE VERDAD

"A little matter of a man found dead at the marina at approximately the same time as the raid. Not too far from where the raid took place. Quite a coincidence, indeed it is."

"There is no evidence—" El comandante bit his lower lip to keep himself from an emotional outburst, his heart punching inside his chest.

The Media Minister's reserved tone gained strength: "Are you denying the accuracy of the story?"

El comandante held his short, sharp breath between his teeth and cursed himself. He should have suspected Lazarito had heard about the dead man at the marina despite the absence of media at the scene and precautions taken by police not to cause commotion or release information. Was there a leak in the department, someone on Lazarito's payroll? Did federales also know about the dead man? Héctor couldn't concern himself with these questions right now. The only thing that mattered was that Media Minister Charlado knew about the dead man and seemed to think he could use this information to leverage him by connecting the body to the raid...and...

Was it possible Lazarito thought that the dead man discovered at the marina was killed by police after escaping the raid? Would he actually threaten to publish such an outlandish story?

El comandante sensed a trap and knew it was best to keep quiet under such circumstances. Yet this was a sensitive negotiation requiring some give and take. The standard, "No comment," could worsen his position... And to top things off, the accuracy of the story could not be denied, it's overall import reaffirmed by Héctor's hasty, defensive reaction to Lazarito's disclosure. In effect, the Media Minister had already ensnared him.

El comandante shook his head with a smile and let his voice acquire a touch of irony: "I will not deny anything, Lazarito. Nor will I confirm anything at this time. There is not enough evidence to confirm or deny anything with respect to the raid or the dead man. And any story you release to the media connecting the two will be at your own risk for it will be based on pure speculation. *That* is accurate."

Lazarito remained reclined, the steeple of his hands before his double chin. He tapped his fingers in a gesture of deep thought, or mock applause at el comandante's prudent posture. "Yes," he said, "indeed. However, I do believe the odds are in my favor here, Héctor, with respect to assuming a connection between the dead man and the raid. But I am feeling generous and as anxious as you to bring this session of ours to a swift and just conclusion. So let us compromise. You say the sum in that envelope will be doubled within a week?" Héctor assented. Lazarito cleared his throat, "Indeed. Well, for a moderate additional price of...let us say...two hundred dollars—payable at once of course—I will postpone the story about the raid and bury news of the dead man in tomorrow's paper, far from page one. Dead bodies found in Vallarta generally merit a headline and I have a feeling that this one—"

"Spare me your feelings, Lazarito." El comandante stood, retrieved a roll of bills from his pocket, counted out fifteen-hundred pesos, and tossed them onto the desk with a flourish that brought Lazarito forward in his deep leather chair.

"Now señor, in pesos that would be—"

El comandante added another two hundred pesos. "We have a deal."

"I must say, señor, you drive a hard bargain. Indeed you do." Lazarito pushed himself up from his desk and extended a fleshy stub of a hand. El comandante shook it without distaste; their eyes locked in good faith. A deal had been struck, but the closing handshake was cut short by a startling buzz echoing through the open door to the adjoining office. Someone wanted into The Bureau from the street below.

Lazarito locked the cash into his desk drawer and muttered something about it being an odd hour for uninvited guests. "The Bureau is closed and my secretary left for the day hours ago."

He hitched up his slacks, waddled past el comandante into the adjoining office, and pressed the button to the intercom on his secretary's desk. "Sí?"

An austere, feminine voice answered: "You cannot hide, Lazarito. And neither can you, Héctor. Buzz me in."

"Puta madre," whispered Lazarito.

El comandante concurred, "Híjole. I knew she was quick and informed but..."

Lazarito said, "Right away, señora," and unlocked the door to the stairwell with the push of a button.

El comandante adjusted his tie and tucked in the tail of his shirt. He shot Lazarito a conspiratorial glance that didn't linger. The Media Minister dropped his head, lost in thought, his mind racing through the platitudes and pleasantries necessary to placate this woman.

Lazarito waddled to the door, paused, and opened it at the sound of a knock.

La Señora didn't wait for an invitation but stepped right in. The Media Minister stammered, suffering a rare loss of words, momentarily taken aback. Gloria had impressed him in formal dress before but it had always been just that, in a dress, at a couple of weddings and a few receptions. Her understated elegance in this beige charro suit—the formal trousers, coat and bow tie of the Mexican cowboy—put him off his game. He examined the woman for a second as though he didn't recognize her. Gloria's shoulder-length corn-silk hair, golden loop earrings, light makeup, finely lined umber eyes, and bronzed tropical complexion all played off her sporting costume and gave her the air of an action figure—a woman somewhat younger than her forty years prepared to take on the world with a six shooter and a bull whip. Her beauty was as understated as her elegance, and generally so was her authority, but not this evening. Throughout this evening Gloria's authority would be well stated.

Lazarito, never one to be put off his game for long, assumed a fawning demeanor and reached for her hand with two of his. "Señora Infante Velázquez, que placer." A pleasure.

She blunted his advancing fingers with an open palm below her breast. "Save it, Lazarito. Have a seat at your secretary's desk. I am on my way to meet my husband at Pelanque El Pitillal and time is of the essence."

Lazarito shuffled over to the desk. "Off to the cockfights? A splendid idea indeed. The mariachis are going to be excellent tonight." He took a seat. "And how is the mayor?"

Gloria's eyes glazed over at the question. "You should know, Lazarito. Keeping tabs on the mayor comes with your job. And so does taking bribes or, if you prefer, extortion, which makes you no different than the rest of México." Her eyes flicked at Héctor. "Long day, Comandante?"

El comandante stepped into the secretary's office. "Sí, señora. We were just discussing some details—"

"I can imagine. If you got anything less than a postponement of the story on this raid fiasco from our Media Minister here I could have saved you the trouble. He would have moved it off the front page to the Local section at my request." She shifted her pointed gaze back to Lazarito. "After all, we do not want to upstage Governor Palacio's arrival tomorrow, do we Lazarito?"

Lazarito ran a finger over his brow where a slight perspiration had broken out. "Indeed not, señora. And I was going to ask you about that very—"

"In fact, I did get a postponement of the story, señora."

"Very good, Héctor." Gloria glanced at her watch. "I did not see a squad car or your car outside, Comandante, but as you were not at police headquarters or at home I assumed you were here. I left a message on your cell phone requesting you contact me... I also assume you have a vehicle at your disposal?"

Lazarito shot Héctor a curious stare that said, "Whose car are you driving?" El comandante ignored it, resigned to placing himself in the hands of Señora Velázquez, a meeting he had hoped to postpone along with the story about the raid. Behind a calm veneer, Héctor Diamante Pasqual cursed himself once more. This time for having the temerity to drive the dead man's Jeep to Lazarito's office. The temptation offered by the midnight-blue, fully equipped V8 had overcome him and, as a result, he would not only have to give Señora Velázquez details about the raid and his deal with Lazarito but reveal information about the dead man found at the marina as well...

"Yes I do have a car, señora," he said. "And I left my cell phone in it, which is why I have yet to receive your message."

"Very good. You and I are going to take a short drive in your vehicle. We should not be long."

El comandante held the entry door open for la señora; she paused to tell Lazarito that she looked forward to seeing him at the dedication of Arena Vallarta tomorrow. He smiled through the folds of his veal-colored lips, said it would be a huge success indeed.

4

AN April shower had freshened the evening, leaving murky puddles on the sidewalks and cobblestone streets. The cobblestones were fist-sized baubles reflecting diffuse light from streetlamps and headlights. Johnny sniffed the lush air and swung his gaze across the mountains to the full, partially obscured moon. Thunderheads growled and crawled over the mountain tops like bridled spectral beasts—threatening, but unable to break free and let loose. Johnny and I shared a concordant nod. We knew the unseasonable weather would clear by morning.

A bus roared and lurched across the street. Traffic moved at a leisurely pace, as did the pedestrians. I skipped over a familiar hole in the sidewalk and we hoofed it down to Olas Altas Street, just beyond Playa de los Muertos. One of my favorite taco stands was there, under a pitched tarp tonight.

Pepe is a magician with the machete. If he were an executioner, he could lop off five heads at once with it. When he needs to, Pepe can make eight tacos al pastor simultaneously, four on each of the two plates in his left hand as he wields his machete with his right. Thin slices of skewered pork fall evenly over the tortillas, followed by pineapple wedges he flicks from a pineapple atop the skewer onto each and every taco with the speed and accuracy of a fencing champion.

And he can do it all while managing a grill of carne asada. Pepe will add cilantro, beans and onions if you like, but it's up to you to choose your salsa from one of the ceramic receptacles on the counter. Careful of those salsas. Pepe will tell you which is más picante (hottest) if you ask. Johnny was feeling cocky and took no such precaution. Johnny often feels cocky—winks and clucks at himself in the mirror every day.

"Careful of that salsa," I advised. "It can be sneaky."

Johnny dumped two ladles of crimson liquid onto his plate, folded one of his carne asada tacos and dipped it into the salsa picante. "Whaddaya think I am, a rookie?" Salsa dribbled from his mouth as he bit into the taco. I garnished my tacos al pastor with salsa verde.

Johnny washed the last of his taco down with Coke. "Pretty damn good." He repeated his dipping procedure with his next taco.

I savored each bite and studied Johnny's face for signs of picante overdose. He kept a brave appearance but couldn't hide the tears in his eyes. Something akin to a severe allergy attack was about to overcome him.

Johnny forced a feral whisper: "I like 'em hot." He didn't dip his last taco in salsa before biting into it. His face was acquiring the color of his picante sauce. He downed his Coke and gulped like a goldfish, eyes a bulge. He motioned for another Coke. Pepe twisted his mouth into a culpable half-grin. He refilled Johnny's cup. His white coveralls were splattered with myriad chili colors and he sported a blue Los Angeles Dodgers baseball cap. The evening before, we'd discussed the Dodgers' improved pitching and hopes for the season. Pepe was very optimistic, said the Dodgers would win the World Series. I told him they could only do it if the team moved beyond steroids to gene therapy. "Sometimes it seems like professional sports are as corrupt as the Mexican and United States governments when it comes to drugs," I added. Pepe said that was impossible.

Pepe's moon-shaped face and arched eyebrows do not conceal emotion. If not for his talents with the machete, he'd make a fine clown. He clearly took satisfaction at the sight of another gringo lighting himself aflame with too much salsa picante. Hot sauces and prizefighters are two things Mexicans take deserved pride in. Pepe laid out a plate of grated cheese. Johnny frowned at it and sucked ice cubes between sips of Coke. "Cheese softens the picante blow," I said.

Johnny stuck a pinch of cheese into his mouth and sucked air. A burst of pineapple flooded my palate. I extended a ladle full of salsa casera to him. Johnny attempted a smirk. I dumped the salsa onto my taco, took a giant bite, and offered him some. Johnny grimaced, belched, and dumped ice into his mouth. I winked at Pepe, told him that Johnny reacted similarly to hot women. We laughed and were suddenly distracted by rude voices behind me. A flicker of recognition crossed Pepe's face. Two Mexicans sat down at the opposite end of the counter and began speaking to him in rapid-fire Spanish garnished with traditional Mexican niceties: "motherfucker," "little sons of bitches," "fucking sons of whores," "cocksuckers," and "fucking assholes." Colorful language but not necessarily hostile. Mexican men in casual conversation can spread it thicker than a syrupy love song; and these two were singing harmony. I retreated into my food and regained that saucy pineapple tingle on my tongue, ears tuned in to the chatter. A pretty good story. Federales had raided a house a couple of hours ago on the other side of town, not far from the marina. Policía y federales. Pepe said to them, "Drugs?" Maybe. But they were really after—

Johnny asked me where he could get some ice cream. "That bloody salsa should be banned," he said. I told him to stop whimpering and go buy some beer.

Johnny's cheeks looked about ready to blister. "Beer work better than Coke?"

"No."

"Fuck you."

Pepe said, "Híjole," as much to me as the two new arrivals. His face retained a quizzical expression, as if digesting an outlandish rumor (rumors abound in Vallarta). I eyed the newcomers and asked them what was up. "Qué onda? Are the policía raiding houses and stealing drugs and money again?"

"They were after more than drugs," replied the one nearest me. "It was a big raid. Policía y federales." He was probably eighteen years old but looked on the edge of puberty. Like Pepe, he sported a billcap, black and ragged around the edges, with an Oakland Raiders logo on it.

Pepe drew a big breath that rounded out his pear-shaped figure. "And the place was empty?" he asked. "No arrests?"

"No arrests," said the other fellow on the far-corner stool. He was a bit older than the kid in the Raider cap, darker complexioned, and showed no signs of the acne that plagued his friend. "I heard that someone tipped the Arabs off to the raid and they escaped."

I nearly choked on my taco. "Arabs?!? Foreign Arabs?"

The kid in the Raiders cap shrugged. "Islamistas," said his friend. Islamists. I took his answer to mean that he didn't know if they were foreign or not. Yet if they were Islamists...

There are many Mexicans of Arab descent and about a million Arabs populate Mexico, most in Mexico City. But I'd never heard of a

29

Mexican police raid targeting Arab Islamists before. The notion suggested one of two things: either this was a tremendous scoop about Islamic terrorists at large in Vallarta, or a baseless rumor sparked by a botched police raid aimed at drug traffickers and embellished by imaginative Vallarta locals.

Pepe served the locals their tacos. Johnny asked me what the hell was going on. He mopped sweat from his forehead and face with a fistful of napkins as if under hot lamps and receiving the third degree.

"Not sure what the hell's goin' on," I said. "Sounds like an outrageous rumor to me." I took a swig of Fanta and raised my voice to Pepe, "Cunden muchos rumores en Vallarta, Pepe." Lots of rumors are spread in Vallarta.

The kid in the Raiders cap jerked his head up from his food. "Es la verdad," he said as though offended. It's the truth.

"What is? There are terrorists in Vallarta?"

"They escaped," said the older fellow with a hasty bite of his taco. "Probablemente al norte."

And the rumor grows. Terrorists on the march north, towards the US from Vallarta.

Pepe approached me. "You know there are always rumors," he said in a flat voice, "especially here in a beach town like Vallarta. But there cannot be many reasons for such a large raid as this."

"Are you saying you believe this crap?" I retorted, my tone a whispered roar. "Islamic terrorists here in Vallarta?"

"Maybe I believe it, maybe not. But this is not a good rumor to spread around. Nobody wants to scare away dollars. And who knows anyway? After all, the house was empty."

Pepe returned to his grill. I back-handed Johnny's shoulder in a show of contempt for the question I proceeded to ask him: "What in the hell are terrorists doing here?"

"Get outta town. Did a bomb go off or what?"

"No. A house was raided. But no arrests. These locals here," I quickly surveyed the Mexicans on their corner stools, "they say the place was empty and Arab terrorists got away."

Johnny glanced at them over my shoulder and fanned himself with his fedora, ample brown hair matted over his ears. "Sounds like a buncha bullshit to me."

"Sure as hell does."

Pepe's grill sizzled and steamed as he sliced and diced meats and onions upon it. He turned to the locals and asked them a question I was wondering about myself: "Why did they raid the house in the early evening instead of surprising them in bed in the morning?"

"Quién sabe?" they chimed. Who knows? "They must have raided the house as soon as they could," added the older one, "but too late to prevent the Arabs' escape."

"The policía y federales probably robbed the place," proffered the kid, "made off with drugs, money, electronics, maybe even weapons."

"A big raid with a big payoff," Pepe said, his head cocked in my direction. The reference to Mexican corruption added verisimilitude to the story... There probably was a raid but...

An anxious twinge tickled the back of my neck. My journalistic instincts were stirring. I needed to get to the bottom of this. "Pero por qué?" I gestured to no one in particular. "Why would Arab terrorists be in Vallarta?"

The guy on the corner stool stared at me over his buddy's cap. "Maybe they were casing hotels."

"Or nightclubs," suggested his friend.

"Or dealing drugs and waiting for an opportunity to cross the border."

"Maybe they were on vacation," Pepe suggested. His vaulted eyebrows were askew. Somehow this gave him a serious expression. "Terroristas need vacations too, do they not?"

The four of us guffawed: "Claro que sí, señor!" "Certainly!" "Desde luego." "But of course!"

Johnny flared his nostrils at me. "Sounds like a buncha bullshit to me."

"You don't understand a damn thing we're talking about."

"That's what I said. It all sounds like a buncha bullshit." Johnny downed his last gulp of Coke and chewed ice. One partially eaten taco was left to the side on his plate, a healthy distance from the generous quantity of salsa that remained.

"You know, Johnny" I said, "I believe you're right. These guys don't know any details and we gotta get goin' to the cockfights." I polished my plate with the last of my tacos, washed it down with Fanta, and paid Pepe.

As Johnny and I strolled down the street to hail a cab, I resolved to look for information on the raid in the newspapers, maybe ask around town about it. I'm not entirely sure why. My stories (the ones I get paid for) revolve around sports, and this was not a sports story. It also had all the earmarks of an overblown rumor, especially the part about Arab terrorists. On the other hand, I'm always interested in a good scoop, sports or otherwise, and since I was on vacation for the next week or so, why not spend time snooping around a bit? I couldn't think of a reason why not.

IF Media Minister Lazarito Charlado and el comandante acted as though Gloria had them under her thumb it's because she did. El comandante answered to her husband, the Mayor of Puerto Vallarta. And Lazarito owed his job as Media Minister of Vallarta to Gloria, which meant she could probably have him fired.

Gloria had never been particularly close to Lazarito but he was acquainted with her father, and she appreciated his work when he was managing editor of the Guadalajara newspaper, La Jornada. She had important connections in Guadalajara, not the least of whom was her father, Alexis Hidalgo Infante, a wealthy landholder and personal friend of Governor Palacio's. Gloria, an astute power broker for her husband, the mayor, recommended Lazarito to the governor for the position of Media Minister because he struck her as a man she could manipulate. Governor Palacio, grateful for her father's contributions to his campaigns and taken with Gloria's charms, barely questioned her recommendation. Lazarito jumped at the opportunity. The new position offered a larger salary as well as control over the printed media, television...*all* the news and publicity emanating from Vallarta and surrounding areas. As a consequence, however, he had to be careful not to cross Gloria, as did most everyone within her sphere of influence.

Gloria Infante Velázquez might have become mayor of Puerto Vallarta herself, or perhaps Guadalajara, her hometown, but, like most good power brokers, she found she was most effective working behind the scenes. Gloria wasn't averse to the spotlight. Quite the contrary. She just preferred to pick and choose the times when the light shined on her, a luxury not afforded politicians.

As is generally the case, the source of Gloria's power resided in money. However, the vast family fortune at her disposal—ranch holdings and distilleries of blue agave, the plant used to make tequila—was not her only asset. Gloria was also blessed with endless charm and an ability to conceal her intentions even as she twisted arms to achieve her goals. Furthermore, she knew how to adapt her goals to her needs. Gloria had exhibited these talents (referred to by her parents as an independent streak) throughout her life, including at the University of California Berkeley where, much to her father's chagrin, she changed her major from Business Administration to Political Science. Gloria returned to Guadalajara well versed in left-wing politics but without a grounding in how to administer the family's lucrative tequila business.

FINDING DEVO

Gloria's father could not remain disappointed in the eldest of his two daughters. Gloria had always been headstrong and he decided early on it was best to let her find her own direction. He took grudging pride in his daughter's diploma, especially as she convinced him that her hopes and dreams could dovetail quite nicely with the family business. In the political arena, Gloria would make business contacts, be an emissary for Infante Distilleries while her father and brothers ran the enterprise.

Gloria left Guadalajara for the wide open political waters of Puerto Vallarta where her dreams began to blossom with her vision of building a grand tourist attraction. A monument distinct from any building in Vallarta. A monument to the rich Jaliscan culture and a focal point for entertainment. A project that would bring her into close working relationships with labor unions, politicians, and ordinary people: Arena Vallarta.

And Gloria's dreams fully bloomed after she met Juan Pacífico Velázquez.

Juan was a coddled only child; not all too common in Mexico, but his mother had suffered greatly during his delivery and a hysterectomy followed. Unlike Gloria, but typical of a great many Mexicans, Juan followed his family's advice instead of his dreams. He took a stab at his dreams—enrolled in some acting and drama classes at the Universidad Nacional Autónoma de México (UNAM) in Mexico City and landed bit parts for no pay in a few low-budget local plays—but was easily discouraged. Juan was not accustomed to rejection and quickly discovered that the acting profession was full of it. As was dating. Both the women he dated at UNAM abandoned the swarthy hirsute Juan to become engaged to other men. In essence, Juan's confidence level at UNAM never grew beyond that of a dwarfed sapling in the woods. So he opted for a profession that garnered his father's support and guidance. Juan finished college closer to home, at the University of Guadalajara, and became a lawyer.

Father and son shared office space in Vallarta...and that could have been the end of it for Juan. He resigned himself to living a mundane life of managing contracts and settling tort cases, even planned to ask for the hand of his girlfriend from la prepa (high school). Then one day a woman walked into his office, without an appointment. A young, oddly attractive woman about his age. Oddly attractive because little in her narrow-set eyes, small inquisitive nose and rather sharp chin held a suggestion of beauty...until she began talking. Her husky, vivacious enunciation of the romantic Spanish language lit up her face, her supple mouth fluid as fingers on a harp. Juan was dumbstruck. This plain girl with mousy brown hair had somehow been transformed into an attractive young woman. And she certainly had some curves beneath that knee-length black skirt and paisley blouse. Petite with somebody to it. Juan had forgotten her name. Gloria apologized and handed him her card. A family business, tequila, she explained in reference to her card. She lived in Vallarta now and handled some business out here for Infante Distilleries, perhaps he'd heard of it? Juan said the name rang a bell. Would he be kind enough to look over a couple of contracts? That's what we do at Velázquez y Velázquez. Juan returned Gloria's smile. She thought him good looking, apple-brown eyes heavy and vulnerable, suave jaw and manner. It would be best to have that unruly black mop on his head cut short though, and his mustache kept trim above the lip. He could improve his posture as well... Yet most importantly, from what she knew about Velázquez y Velázquez, Juan's father could put her into contact with some of Vallarta's most influential businessmen and politicians...

After reviewing the contracts with Juan, Gloria set them aside and mentioned another reason for her visit. Juan replied that he might sign her petition for a public-works grant to build a cultural center in Vallarta but would need more details first.

Juan Pacífico Velázquez signed that petition and, soon after, a marriage license. He loved her because she was many things he aspired to be: decisive, ambitious, elegant and passionate. Gloria loved Juan because she recognized within him a reservoir of untapped potential aching to be released and channeled by her. His dreams had been unfulfilled yet could be adapted to hers, and their dreams would come true.

Their courtship was brief, their honeymoon in Rio torrid. Juan's new bride completely altered the course of his life. He kept his hair and mustache trimmed short, practiced standing straight (nearly five foot eleven when he did so), and immersed himself in politics.

As an attorney, Juan had learned to manage his fear of rejection in the courtroom (mostly by plea-bargaining instead of going to trial). As a politician, he would have to learn to overcome it in the public arena. Gloria accurately surmised that his fear was due to a lack of confidence—doubts about his ability to bounce back from setbacks, failures, and "defeat." She built his confidence by carefully stroking his ego and lecturing him on the absurdity of his fear of rejection. Rejection and failure weren't necessarily bad. In fact, they could make you stronger once you learned how to rally and overcome them. As a team they could overcome anything. Gloria's effect on Juan was like a healthy portion of sunshine and fertilizer for the sapling that was his confidence, and his confidence grew. He didn't exactly brim with confidence but he learned to play the part, the *role* of a confident man. Gloria appreciated his talents and cultivated his acting ability, an ability which had remained largely dormant since his college days at UNAM. Juan already knew how to enter a room and listen without speaking, understand without imposing himself on others. But thanks to Gloria (as well as his own experience as an actor) he gained presence, charisma, and a talent for assuming any number of impressive attitudes ranging from doubtful and concerned to supportive and carefree. And inspiring. Always inspiring. *"Inspire people,"* Gloria emphasized. "Only dwell on the negative long enough to have your public begging to be inspired. Then inspire them."

Gloria's advice, guidance and financial backing made Juan Pacífico Velázquez mayor of the largest tourist attraction in the Mexican state of Jalisco, the third largest in all of Mexico behind Acapulco and Cancún: Puerto Vallarta. He and Gloria were rubbing elbows with some powerful people. None were more powerful than Governor Palacio who was expected tomorrow, Sunday, for the dedication of Arena Vallarta, the culmination of that petition Juan had signed for Gloria over fifteen years ago. The dedication was certain to be a highlight of Juan's inaugural term as mayor and his wife impressed upon him the need to ensure it was a peaceful celebration. Political demonstrations were expected, "And political demonstrations can get out of hand," she reminded him. "Vallarta had some problems of this nature before your term as mayor and we cannot allow it to happen on your watch, especially at the dedication of Arena Vallarta. This is the dedication of a cultural center, not May Day at el zócalo del DF" (Mexico City's town square).

Mexico City—el DF (the Federal District). One of the most populace cities in the world and hundreds of miles away. Gloria was speaking euphemistically. Nothing that ever occurred in Vallarta resembled May Day in Mexico City. On May Day, el DF is a magnet for those who want to demonstrate, protest, or, on occasion, riot. Everything is on the table, from depressed teacher's salaries and "inflated" student tuitions to global warming, globalization, gay rights, workers' rights, indigenous rights, animal rights, abortion rights, Palestinian rights, drug legalization, NAFTA, capitalism and Yankee imperialism. And the activists themselves run a fair gambit of Mexican society. Students, teachers, campesinos, Zapatistas, anarchists, pacifists and labor unions are all represented, though their demands and methods of protest are, as often as not, mutually exclusive.

The number of activists expected for the dedication of Arena Vallarta was nowhere near the thousands who descend on el zócalo del DF on May Day. Puerto Vallarta had a fraction of Mexico City's population and, as opposed to el DF, had never been a hotbed of political activism. And nationwide, the dedication of a cultural center in this coastal resort town simply wasn't controversial; it didn't suddenly make Puerto Vallarta a natural magnet for protesters. Before Juan's term as mayor however, problems with political activists had occasionally impacted negatively on tourism. Nothing on a grand scale, but there were troublemakers around, some of whom had already voiced their displeasure with the building of Arena Vallarta by picketing the construction site.

With the governor due in town and May Day approaching, activists far and wide were bound to look upon the dedication of Arena Vallarta as a warm-up for the big show in Mexico City on May first. In and of itself, Arena Vallarta was not the issue with these people. Their demands and grievances were about as diverse as those you'd find aired in el DF on May Day. They would denounce Gloria's cultural center as "a symbol of corporate greed and government waste" but, in reality, the dedication of Arena Vallarta merely represented an opportunity for them to gain exposure as they did what came naturally: voice their opinions, grievances and demands.

Gloria had considered postponing the dedication because of the date's proximity to May Day, but a post May Day dedication ran the risk of attracting undesirable demonstrations from those hot off their DF rallies. After over fifteen years of leaping hurdles and overcoming setbacks, the arena was finally ready to be dedicated and Gloria was not about to be intimidated into a postponement, not when she felt she could thwart any possible disruptions by activists before they got started.

She could not prevent activists from showing up, but Gloria had a strategy on dealing with them. She was acquainted with the handful of leaders who exercised influence over possible troublemakers and all of them (with the exception of union leader and foreman of the Arena Vallarta project, Enrique Santos) had at least one thing in common: an insatiable desire to voice their opinions, grievances and demands anytime, anywhere. So on the eve of the dedication, Saturday night, before she and her husband appeared at the cockfights, Gloria saw to it that the activist leaders had an opportunity to do just that...directly to her and the mayor, in Arena Vallarta's dining hall. An offer none could refuse, not just because they couldn't resist a chance to express themselves and their demands directly to the mayor and his wife but because they felt they had nothing to lose. Gloria had given them a false sense of security by leaving them in the dark as to her motives and nature. She knew they considered her a mere extension of her husband, and knew they thought of him as an affable man with experience in local politics but an untested mayor who could be intimidated. Gloria had studied and knew her enemy, talked with them individually and informally. The activist leaders poised to meet her and the mayor in Arena Vallarta had no clue who they were dealing with and the lengths she would go to protect her interests.

6

ALTHOUGH I never saw Enrique Santos again after he left me and Johnny in Rudy's to attend a Saturday night meeting, he wasn't off to meet his end in some dark alley, nor was he in imminent danger. In fact, Enrique was at the top of his game and would receive much deserved accolades for his work at the dedication of Arena Vallarta tomorrow. That was a huge project he supervised, a formidable challenge. There are lots of obstacles to overcome in a construction job like that and he took care of business.

He intended to take care of business Saturday night as well. The activist leaders gathering in Arena Vallarta planned to disrupt its dedication the following day and Enrique, President of Vallarta's chapter of the Obreros Unidos labor union, had been called upon by the mayor and Gloria to make it clear that demonstrators would not receive any labor union support. There is strength in numbers and the activist leaders just might lose resolve at the meeting once they saw their numbers thus reduced. Enrique wasn't privy to the overall strategy Gloria and Juan had devised for dealing with them but, as foreman of the Arena Vallarta project, he was happy to be of assistance. He didn't want to see the dedication tarnished by demonstrations any more than they did.

Enrique knew damn well which of the activist leaders posed the biggest threat. Trouble was, he didn't know much at all about a couple of others expected to attend Saturday evening's pre-dedication affair. So he asked his son Pedro, a junior officer in the police department, to do some investigating and give him the dirt on them. Pedro gave his report to his father and big brother Alejandro (a union member and Enrique's right-hand man during the Arena Vallarta project) Saturday afternoon, well before the meeting at Arena Vallarta that night.

I never got a chance to meet Alejandro, or his youngest brother Eduardo, or two of their three sisters, Eva and María Luz. Eventually, Pedro and I got to know one another, though when we first crossed paths a couple of days after the dedication I had no idea who the hell he was.

37

SEVE VERDAD

Unlike his father and siblings (including his sisters), Pedro Santos never showed much interest in boxing. This was fine with Enrique. He'd been drawn to the sweet science more out of desperation than love for the sport. Boxing was his ticket out of the Guadalajara ghetto. When his kids wanted to roughhouse, Enrique taught them to box as a matter of self-defense and fitness; and when his eldest, Alejandro, gave the amateur ranks a try for a spell, Enrique encouraged him. But deep down he hoped none of his kids would follow his footsteps into the ring and cared not a whit that Pedro wasn't drawn to the sport, especially since he did well in school, exceptionally well when he applied himself.

Alejandro ended up working with his father in construction and became a mason, a skilled mason. Enrique couldn't have been prouder if his son had won a title. Enrique was proud of all his kids, from Alejandro to his youngest, twelve-year-old Angélica, whose pigtails never needed to be curled because they were naturally curly. "Natural as her dimples," Enrique told me the one time I visited his home. His wife Beti confirmed this by running her fingers through her own ample curls. Little Angélica was the only sibling home at the time. I played some baseball with her and she smashed a line drive past my ear with enough power to suggest that she might one day possess the knockout punch her Daddy lacked (Enrique actually threw a pretty fair right hand in his prime and had more than a few knockouts to his credit). All the Santos children took after their parents in one way or another, including Pedro, though he was somewhat of an anomaly. Eduardo got a kick out of pounding nails and cutting boards. And the girls enjoyed sticking their hands in concrete, kind of like Alejandro and Enrique. But Pedro was more cerebral and introspective, and, as it turned out, unpredictable when it came to his future. A computer whiz bored with school and with little aptitude for construction work or athletics, Pedro opted out of college and did something quite unexpected: he joined the Puerto Vallarta Police Department where, as part of his training, he finally did learn to box some.

As the resident computer expert at police headquarters, Pedro held a pretty secure and cushy position within the department. Enrique held out hope that his son would go to college but, in the meantime, he wasn't beyond taking advantage of the junior officer's talents and position. And Pedro, a twenty-two year old with thoughtful doe eyes, curly ebony hair that never stayed, and a dimpled smile easy as an endless summer day, he always accommodated his old man, provided the department wasn't compromised. So on the Saturday afternoon in question, after the traditional Mexican comida (the day's biggest meal), Pedro provided the information his father had requested.

38

FINDING DEVO

Beti served coffee, kissed her husband's scarred brow, and began clearing the table. Two of the teenagers, Eduardo and Eva, were off to the beach; the third, María Luz, stuck around to help ma in the kitchen. Angélica sat at the PlayStation in the living room while Enrique conferred with his two eldest at the dining table, sons Alejandro and Pedro.

The box air conditioner purred; a fan whirled gently overhead. Enrique had built himself a cozy home and spoke with all the ease of a man lounging at the dining table with his sons. "So tell me about this Pati Redondo, Pedro," he said. "Pati and...what was her name?"

Pedro flipped through his hand-written notes. "Antonia Pantiblanca."

"Sí. The two on the mayor's list I have not had the pleasure of meeting."

"Both are student activists," said Pedro, "from the University of Guadalajara—Pati from the University proper and Antonia from the University's extension here in Vallarta. Pati was arrested last year in the capital during the May Day demonstrations but released that same day."

"Details?"

"She was arrested with some North Americans—American and Canadian exchange students who were demonstrating and shouting anti-government slogans... Let me see here... The foreigners were arrested because Mexican law prohibits them from demonstrating in México. Pati Redondo was caught in the middle. She demonstrated with them but, because she is Mexican, she could not be held. The gringos, North Americans, were all deported."

"Anything else?"

Pedro looked up from his notes. "Remember that demonstration in Vallarta a year and a half ago in support of the teachers-union strike?"

"Sí."

"It seems that Pati and Antonia collaborated in organizing the students to demonstrate along with the teachers." Pedro scanned his notes once more. "Both signed a petition for higher wages for teachers and lower student tuitions. Their signatures appear one right after the other." He paused for a sip of coffee. A burst of laughter and the clanking of pots and pans could be heard from the kitchen. "It would not be surprising," Pedro added, "if Pati has formed an alliance with Vallarta student activists, such as Antonia, who probably join her for protests and demonstrations in Guadalajara on occasion." Pedro returned to his notes. "There is something more... Here. Pati was detained in Guadalajara six months ago for destruction of private property. Detained with one of your favorite Zapatistas who is also due at the meeting tonight." Pedro tilted an ironic stare at his father.

"Javier," Enrique said, his tongue lathering the name with contempt.

"Javier Menticlaro. He was arrested with Pati and jailed for three days. But Pati Redondo was released almost immediately."

"Why?"

"Money," said Alejandro. "She must have paid someone off."

Pedro nodded. "No doubt. Naturally, there is no record of a bribe but the girl has money. Her family is pretty well set in textiles and artesanías."

Enrique felt the blood rush to his temples. "*Javier.* That hijo de la chingada has fucked with us too many times. His maldito Cora and Guerrero Zapatistas tried to shut down the Arena Vallarta project with their demonstrations." He sipped coffee and modulated his tone, "What is the connection between Pati and that pinche—?"

"Javier," Alejandro interceded, his tan eyes growing dark and hard. "If this Pati Redondo is associated with that fucking communist then she probably knows who you are, papi. Javier—"

"I know, mijo." Enrique rolled his shoulders as if preparing to shadowbox. He'd like nothing more than to put Javier in the hospital and eliminate him from tomorrow's dedication altogether. "I am the foreman so he directs his threats and insults at me. I will be ready for him...and this...Pati Redondo."

Pedro shrugged, unfazed by the growing tension around the table. "The connection between Pati and Javier is unclear. The mayor invited both of them to the meeting at Arena Vallarta tonight so he must be expecting them at the dedication tomorrow. Javier and Pati may have formed a loose alliance and probably plan to disrupt the dedication with demonstrations."

"We know that is what the mayor is concerned about," Enrique said. "The purpose of the meeting tonight in Arena Vallarta is to preempt any planned disruptions of the dedication." He relaxed his posture, his voice quiet and crushing. "Puta madre. Under no circumstances will Javier be allowed to spoil our celebration with his protests."

"And what about your union?" Pedro said. "They have been known to demonstrate with Zapatistas in el DF."

"Not exactly." Enrique drew a weary breath. He needed some rest before the meeting tonight; a siesta and a shower. "Zapatistas are always around when grievances are aired in el DF. But they will not be allowed to disrupt the dedication of Arena Vallarta tomorrow."

UPON his arrival at Arena Vallarta Saturday night, Mayor Juan Pacífico Velázquez received some disconcerting news from his wife over his cell phone. She would be unavoidably delayed with Comandante Pasqual. A matter of "vital importance" had popped up. A security issue for tomorrow's dedication that could have a direct impact on the meeting tonight at Arena Vallarta. She would fill him in later. "Practice your powers of persuasion with our guests, Juan," she said, a cheerful note to her voice, "as well as your listening skills. That group always has plenty to say. I will not be delayed long."

Gloria's detour had also prevented her from taking their daughter to a quinceañera party (Mexican sweet fifteen, as opposed to the American sweet sixteen). Juan dispatched their driver, Felipe, to their house in the upscale Vallarta suburb of Conchas Chinas to pick up Sofía and deliver her to the fiesta. This left Juan on his own to begin the meeting. No problema. He could handle it. Surely these people could understand that tomorrow's dedication was to be a peaceful celebration and not an occasion for disruptive demonstrations. They were expecting a tour of the arena and he could probably get them to listen to reason before they even sat down together in the dining hall.

Unfortunately, there would be no tour of the arena.

The foreman of the Arena Vallarta project, Enrique Santos, had arrived ahead of Juan and met him in the lobby. "Nice outfit," he said, referring to Juan's elegant blue charro suit he'd donned for his appearance at the cockfights later this evening. "Leave your sombrero behind?"

"In the car," Juan replied, his eyes steady on the flickering overhead lighting. "What—"

"Power outage," Enrique said. "A junction box I can have fixed well before tomorrow's dedication. A generator is powering enough circuits to accommodate tonight's meeting."

Aside from the dining hall and lobby, most of the rest of Arena Vallarta was in the dark and without ventilation. A tour was out of the question. As the guests gathered in the lobby, the copiously figured student activist, Pati Redondo, made a snide remark on the inconvenience: "So, I suppose the arena is still unfinished."

Juan assured her that Arena Vallarta was completed. Glitches were to be expected with a project of this size but all would be in order for the dedication. Pati said, "Vamos a ver," we'll see, and introduced Carlos Mansalva to the mayor, her "advisor and confidant. Knowledgeable in Indigenous affairs and Mexican-North American relations." The unexpected guest shook the mayor's hand. Carlos was missing an arm, his left, the stump just barely concealed beneath its short shirtsleeve.

Juan attempted a bit of small talk with Carlos as he guided his guests into the dining hall for coffee: Did he study at the University of Guadalajara with Pati? What was his major?

Carlos fingered his wispy mustache. "I expect to be back in school soon," he responded curtly. Juan had his doubts. The guy was at least thirty years old, seven or eight years Pati's senior. If he hadn't gone back to school by now he likely never would. Carlos smoothed his glossy anthracite hair and pushed his eyeglasses up along the concave ridge of his nose. A bespectacled toad, Juan thought. At least he wore a collared shirt with his baggy jeans. Pati wore black, as she had the few other times he'd met her. Black polyester pants; the ruffle collared blouse and pleated vest combo did little to mask her enormous breasts—important assets for a girl with the shape of a beach ball. Pati wasn't showing cleavage tonight but had her wild black mane pulled back in a ponytail to better accentuate two more distracting assets— enormous mahogany eyes, windows to a mind Juan had found in the past to be as bloated as the rest of her body.

Juan remained standing as Carlos, Pati, Javier Menticlaro, Antonia Pantiblanca, teachers' union representative Teodoro Viareal, and Enrique Santos took their seats at the roundtable. Javier immediately asserted himself with a light-hearted joke regarding the mayor's outfit: "Ehh hombre, al irse a la charreada no se le olvide el sombrero."

The twenty-three-year-old Zapatista had reminded the mayor that one shouldn't forget his sombrero when attending a Mexican rodeo. Javier got some decent laughs with the line.

Enrique Santos, the burly voiced union leader, had to add his two cents along with a jab at Javier who was seated by Pati and Carlos opposite him: "You make us all feel underdressed, Señor Mayor. Javier has on his *finest* clothes—slacks and a button-down shirt—and has done his hair in a natty braid for the occasion. But me, pues, I could have brought my trumpet and worn my mariachi suit with its many silver buttons."

Nervous chuckles. Javier tightened the natural curl of his lip. Everyone at the table understood the wiry, hard-eyed Javier and robust Enrique to be at odds with one another. Enrique's florid, oval cheeks contained a carnivorous grin that matched his short crop of iron-gray hair. He loosened his tie and served himself more coffee from the pot in front of him. His shirt sleeves were rolled up a couple of notches around formidable forearms; he looked as though he might break into a sweat at any moment, though the temperature in the dining hall was comfortable.

The meeting had barely begun and the tension between Javier and Enrique was already palpable. Juan attempted to lighten things up with a pleasantry: "Bring your trumpet to the cockfights, Enrique. Perhaps the mariachis will allow you to sit in. And you are all invited to the cockfights as well, once we are finished here."

Juan never was a fountain of original quips and ideas, but his comment did ease him into his role as speaker. Pati and Javier lit cigarettes. Juan adjusted his white moño (wide flowing bow tie of the Mexican charro). "Now to the business at hand."

Teodoro Viareal, the teachers' union representative, agreed: "Yes, let us talk business." He laid his briefcase on the table but didn't open it.

Teodoro was a small-boned bookish man in his early fifties with thinning salt-and-pepper hair, thick owlish glasses, a walnut complexion, and the voice of an excitable Chihuahua. Tieless, he wore a navy blue button-down shirt and gray slacks and often, but not always, displayed his current air of haughty disdain. "My contacts tell me that the name of Arena Vallarta is to be changed to Arena Infante after the dedication," he said. "Arena Infante, as in *Infante Distilleries*. Tell me, Señor Mayor, is this arena a cultural center or a way for Infante Distilleries to gain publicity? And how much—"

Antonia Pantiblanca, the student activist from Vallarta who had twice demonstrated with Pati, interrupted: "I thought it was also a sports arena."

Juan shifted his attention to the attractive twenty-one-year-old Vallarta native seated opposite him, the youngest of the group. He'd been pleased to see Antonia arrive in a printed summer dress that complemented her slender figure and highlighted hair.

Antonia took it as a compliment when mistaken for North American though she wasn't sure how she felt about gringos in general, or Canadians for that matter.

"It is a museum that can accommodate sporting events," said Juan with a smile he hoped was paternal, "as well as concerts and conventions."

Javier blew smoke from his cigarette straight up into the air. "Yes, but who pays for it?"

"We do," said Pati in a lofty tone. "Whether we use it or not."

"How do you pay?" Enrique snorted. "Because money used to build and maintain the arena is not handed over to you instead?" He shifted his glare between Pati and Javier. "Since you want something for nothing, it might please you to know that the general public will be able to enter the museum at no charge."

"There will be a charge for concerts and sporting events and the like," Teodoro said. "And as far as the museum goes, Señor Mayor, I am sure that you will follow the example of other museums and require a public donation for entry."

"Donations to the museum will be voluntary, Teodoro," replied Juan. "And most museums charge for entry."

"But a donation to whom?" said Teodoro. "Infante Distilleries? If Infante Distilleries is going to ask for public donations, that is *outrageous*."

"The donations will go into a fund for care and maintenance of the museum, Teodoro."

Teodoro raised a slender finger. "A museum which is part of a *private* institution."

The mayor sensed a need to quell this rumor immediately: "Arena Vallarta is *not strictly* a private institution, Teodoro. Where the hell do you get your information?"

"I have my sources, contacts."

"Arena Vallarta merely needed an infusion of private funds to be completed and—"

"Does that make Arena Vallarta *private* property?" Antonia looked past Teodoro, addressing the question to Enrique. She'd only just met him here at the arena but his uncommon views and authority piqued her interest.

Pati blew fierce plumes of smoke from her nostrils. "Most certainly private."

"Really?" Antonia questioned her with a pretty lift of her young eyebrows.

Javier offered a straightforward, original Marxist thought on the subject: "Private property is theft."

"My workers are well paid," said Enrique. "If that is theft I prefer it to what your Zapatistas offer. Can you even borrow on your Indian lands, your *ejidos*? Reinvest the capital? I suppose not, since the government actually owns the ejidos and we know how corrupt they are."

Teodoro exclaimed, "Outrageous! That is an outrageous slander on the ejido system and indigenous communities and not at all pertinent to our...*discussion*. The question here pertains to Arena Vallarta and Infante Distilleries who I maintain are one in the same."

"Just what are you insinuating, Teodoro?" Juan was beginning to feel outraged himself.

Javier snarled under his breath, "I do not live on an ejido."

FINDING DEVO

Javier lived in Tepic, a bustling town northeast of Vallarta in Jalisco's neighboring state, Nyarit. He wasn't exactly a city boy but Javier had been Mexicanized, more or less—a full-blooded Cora (Huichol) Indian battling an identity crisis.

"Would you like to make a declaration Teodoro?" The first words from Carlos *El Manco* Mansalva, words intended to inflame the growing discord around the table. Incitement was one of his specialties. Pati concurred with her confidant: "Yes Teodoro. Make a declaration. All those in favor..." She raised her hand, as did Javier and Carlos. "Raise your hand Teodoro. That gives us a majority."

Teodoro shook his head mulishly. "I do not need a majority to speak."

Juan's feelings of outrage stabilized into controlled frustration. The meeting was getting out of hand. He had hoped to sit down with these people and reason with them. He didn't dare sit now, a sure sign of capitulation. "We are not here to vote on anything. We are here to come to an under—"

"Then I shall make a declaration," said Javier with a hasty puff on his cigarette. "Expel capitalists from México and take back the means of production."

"Has that not been tried before?" asked Antonia in all seriousness.

Enrique thought this a hilarious thing to say and burst out in neighing laughter.

Pati snuffed out her cigarette in a gesture of finality. She had all the answers. "Not exactly. Not in this country, and not the way a united *People's Republic of México* can do it."

"No need to vote on that declaration," Enrique said. "The first vote is always the same as the last for communists."

"That is an outrageous thing to say. Outrageous!" Teodoro couldn't hold Enrique's contemptuous stare and spoke to the group as a whole as if he had called the meeting. "Labels like that have no bearing on the issues in question and are intended to impugn a person's motives. And besides, communists vote their conscience all the time on a variety of issues."

"And always with the same despotic result." Enrique shifted his stare back across the table at Javier. It was evident to Juan that Enrique felt threatened, perhaps for good reason. Javier, along with his Zapatistas and other Huichol Indians, had demonstrated in an attempt to halt construction of Arena Vallarta, claiming that government funds used to build the cultural center would be better invested in ejidos. Their efforts were unsuccessful and Enrique wasn't about to let him tear the arena down now, disparage the accomplishment and make a mockery of it. The union leader was proud of the finished product; Javier's remarks (not to mention those of Pati and Teodoro) insulted his work as well as the work of his men.

If Juan were in Enrique's position, he'd feel the same, did feel the same, though he could not afford to choose sides and risk alienating most of those present. He had to put his feelings aside and recalled Gloria's sage political advice on such matters: "You can often best achieve your goals by acting in a manner contrary to your personal opinion or feelings on a particular issue or controversy."

The politics of subterfuge. Part and parcel of appealing to the masses. Within those masses none had a more enduring influence in Mexican politics than left-wing activists like the ones Juan was facing now, a fair representation of those who would descend on el zócalo del DF on May Day. Over the years, Gloria had drilled him on their demands and methods. "Many of their demands," she explained, "never change. Others appear new and of our time. They can be diverse and you may agree with some, all, or none of them. But one aspect of their demands remains consistent: the *means* to their ends. The route they see as most expedient to having their demands met is via bigger government, either through nationalization of industry and property or by keeping private citizens and industry perpetually indebted to and dependent on the State. Call these two policies—*philosophies*—and the political parties that continue to implement them to varying degrees on the local and national level whatever you like: Socialist Reform, Institutional Revolutionary, Democratic Revolutionary, Christian Democrat, National Action, Socialist Progressive, Green, Yellow, Orange, or Purple. It all boils down to the same thing: communism and fascism. Two sides of the same coin and always popular. Popular because the rhetoric sounds egalitarian and the policies are for the good of the *volks*. Naturally the policies or philosophies are rarely if ever identified for what they are, so Mexicans do not recognize that those who gain power have been flipping that same coin throughout the country's history, since well before the revolution a century ago. The rhetoric espoused by every political party sounds as though it signifies change, and el pueblo laps it up. Yet what el pueblo ends up getting is the same communism and fascism. And when Mexicans see that nothing has changed, that penury and stagnation still reign, what do they blame? The same thing they have been conditioned to blame for decades: the corrupting influence of capitalism; as if the country has suffered the ideals of economic and political liberty rather than communism and fascism, as if corruption were not particularly endemic to communism and fascism, philosophies el pueblo and power-hungry elites embrace."

FINDING DEVO

Gloria never suggested revolution as the solution but to work within the system, to manipulate and take advantage of the system and establish their own niche of power. The Socialist Reform Party (PSR) was on the rise and, though it wouldn't reform a thing, it could provide a springboard for Juan's political career. So he mastered the mantras of the party: "México for Mexicans"; "The state will put the poor first"; "Down with imperialist capitalism"; "The collective shall overrule the classes"; and "One México without corruption or lies", amongst others. Simple lines to regurgitate, and they dovetailed nicely with promises to redistribute the wealth produced by tourism in Vallarta and create jobs. Gloria kept Juan well-grounded in practical realities in this regard. She never failed to remind him that, despite the popularity of communist, socialist, and fascist rhetoric (and contrary to much of her formal education on the subject), communists, socialists, and fascists needed capital as much as capitalists or anyone else. "Work the system," she expounded. "As long as the right bureaucrats are paid off, Vallarta will continue to attract foreign and domestic capital and enough jobs will be created to placate the masses as we invest our own capital in you and our future."

Juan racked his brain for a platitude, an appeal that would dampen the flaring animosity around the table. He came up with one along the lines of Arena Vallarta as an investment in the future, and tapped his coffee cup with a spoon in an effort to gain everyone's attention. It didn't work. Javier said something about Enrique and Mexico being at the mercy of foreign and domestic neoliberal capitalists. Carlos agreed. Enrique said it was typical of Mexicans like them to blame the whole world for Mexico's problems. Teodoro exclaimed, "Outrageous!" and added that nobody said the *entire* world was to blame for Mexico's problems. Antonia mentioned that "it is easy to blame others but that does not mean others are not to blame." Enrique assured her that "looking for scapegoats never accomplishes anything. If we looked to blame others every time we had a problem building Arena Vallarta, we never would have finished it." Pati said it still wasn't finished.

"Yes it is." Juan was surprised at the explosive crack in his voice. All eyes were upon him. "You will see for yourselves tomorrow. Arena Vallarta is an accomplishment we can all be proud of, an investment in our future, and I want assurances from each of you that nothing will be said or done to detract from the celebration of its dedication."

"Stifling free speech is nothing to celebrate," Pati said. "And if that is what you propose it only gives us something more to protest."

SEVE VERDAD

Javier glowered at Enrique through billows of smoke, his voice harsh with anger. "Why spend money on an arena when Mexicans are going hungry? Who really benefits?"

"Infante Distilleries," said Teodoro. "I propose we dispense with this charade and ask the mayor to divulge all information pertaining to all investments Infante Distilleries has made in this arena and what their projected profits are."

Juan drew a cool, collected breath. He couldn't afford to lose his composure and allow Teodoro to get the best of him. The teachers' union representative was trying to lure him into a trap, get him to incriminate himself by admitting an eternal truth: in Mexico, big-money government projects like Arena Vallarta are always fraught with corruption.

"Just what do you mean by *all* investments, Teodoro?" he asked innocently. "The contributions of Infante Distilleries to this facility are a matter of public record."

"My contacts say otherwise."

Enrique drew a smoldering breath. Big beads of sweat appeared on his temples as he balled his fists and leveled a low pit bull growl at Javier:

"Mexicans starve in a land of plenty because people like you produce only enough to sustain yourselves. You pretend to care about others but are unwilling and incapable of investing in a future that extends beyond your own ignorant naco nose."

"Another outrageous, inflammatory comment." Teodoro sounded resolute but his heart had begun skipping beats from fear of a physical confrontation between Enrique and Javier.

Antonia carefully considered Enrique, her waifish tone a sharp, pensive whisper: "I never thought of it that way."

Javier gnashed his teeth; the fire in his eyes leapt into plain view as he stabbed out his cigarette. He thought about the switchblade in his pocket, heard Pati and Carlos accuse Enrique of selling out Mexico to corporate interests, and vaguely recognized Juan's voice pleading for calm. He also heard Enrique's insult, "ignorant naco nose," echo in his ears. Fighting words. There was no pacifying Javier's wrath, but an honest appraisal of his adversary and probable allies in a brawl did restrain him. Enrique, a former prizefighter from the rough barrios of Guadalajara, was likely prepared for his switchblade and, though well into his forties, could squash the one-armed Carlos instantly, flat as a bug under his shoe; the frail Teodoro, now on his feet ready to flee, would be of no use to Javier at all; Pati and Antonia were inconsequential; and the mayor, while no threat to him personally, just might intervene enough to give Enrique the opening he needed to land a devastating blow to Javier's jaw.

Then a voice entered the fray which changed the entire course of the meeting.

I see you all have been missing me." Gloria stood at the entry to the dining hall. No one had noticed her, not even Juan who faced that direction but was distracted by the growing threat of violence between Javier and Enrique. Teodoro sat back down as though nothing had been amiss in his racing pulse; everyone fell still and silent, eyes upon her, listening to each other's breathing. Gloria headed for the table, her boots clicking across the tile floor, and stood next to Juan. She cut a finer figure than he in her beige charro suit. A General looking over her sorry excuse for troops. "Lose your powers of persuasion my dear Mayor?" she said, her tone light.

Juan was relieved to finally have a seat. "It appears I never quite had them this evening."

Gloria swept her gaze around the table. "Sorry for the delay muchachos but I have just come from an unavoidable meeting that might have a bearing on this one." Gloria leaned forward, palms on the table, and had a close look at the challenge before her. "How many Huichol Zapatistas are you expecting tomorrow, Javier?"

Javier cleared his throat, inexplicably cowed. He'd met Gloria twice before but had forgotten the graceful authority of her voice, didn't recognize the sound of her voice at all. Like some kind of ancient Huichol harvest chant. He did his best to meet her unyielding yet somehow accommodating eyes. "Zapatistas? Uh...maybe ten. Other Huichol will be there."

"Ten? Any Zapatistas expected from other states besides Jalisco and Nyarit?"

"Maybe. I think...a few from Guerrero."

"Fine. Pati? Sorry, I do not recognize the gentleman seated beside you."

"This is Carlos my...uh...advisor." Pati tried to make it sound as though her "advisor" lent her status. The effect was lost.

Gloria shot Carlos a dignified stare. "Carlos?" She didn't bother to introduce herself. Carlos pointed a questioning thumb at his chest, surprised that this woman who so easily commanded respect would address him. Why did she command respect? He wasn't sure. Perhaps her sudden entrance, her confident air, her elegant charro suit, or— "How many student activists are you and Pati expecting from Guadalajara tomorrow, Carlos?"

Carlos and Pati exchanged thoughtful expressions. "Hundreds," Pati said.

"Hundreds, Pati?" Gloria smiled knowingly. She saw right through this ruse and Pati too.

"The whole university knows about it."

"You will be lucky if thirty show up."

Carlos and Pati gaped at her and, like sullen children, snapped their jaws shut. A sure sign Gloria was right. And she was. Twenty-three showed.

Gloria next questioned Antonia and Teodoro. Teodoro expected all Vallarta teachers to be at the dedication and Antoina expected most all students as well. But when pressed on the number of "activists" they could not come up with a number higher than fifteen or twenty between them.

Gloria linked her tidy blonde locks behind her ears and faced Enrique.

"Nice to see you again, Gloria." Enrique had his hands folded on the table and was no longer perspiring.

"The pleasure is mine, Enrique. A fine job your workers have done here though there seems to be a problem with the electricity."

Enrique purred like a lion lounging in the shade: "All will be in order by tomorrow morning."

"Expecting many out-of-town guests tomorrow, Enrique?"

"Dozens from Guadalajara, and more from el DF. Many arrived today and yesterday."

"All to enjoy our beautiful weather, beaches and, naturally, to admire your excellent work."

"That is the understanding, Gloria." Enrique stared imperatively around the table. "None will be joining any political demonstrations."

Javier and Carlos were unmoved by the news. Pati, Antonia, and Teodoro shared darting, feeble glances.

Gloria said, "I think it best you go now to see what you can do about this vexing problem with the electricity, Enrique. We will talk more tomorrow."

"Certainly." Enrique rose from his chair, shook hands with the mayor and Gloria, and left the scene without another word. He gave Antonia a friendly nod as he passed.

Gloria stood at ease before the roundtable. She was now ready to take advantage of her windfall. Today's botched police and federale raid was an unfortunate foul-up but, as is often the case when mistakes are made, it had provided her with an unanticipated opportunity. She and el comandante had requested and would receive extra security forces from Tepic and Guadalajara. The number of troops and equipment at Gloria's disposal for tomorrow's dedication had doubled. Now she could cut to the chase, no bullshit.

"There will be no signs," she began pointedly, without bravado, "posters or banners allowed at the dedication except those provided by Arena Vallarta. Anyone caught with a banner, sign or poster not provided by the arena will be immediately arrested, as will anyone shouting anti-government slogans." Pati opened her mouth to speak, her enormous eyes quivering with the effort. "You will be allowed to call a lawyer from jail, Pati. Even if you and Javier gather an army and mount an invasion of Vallarta, I guarantee there will be plenty of police and federales to thwart any plans of disrupting the dedication and plenty of trucks to haul off agitators. I do not expect Teodoro or Antonia to present as much of a threat as the two of you but the same goes for them." Gloria gave Teodoro and Antonia a courtesy glance. Her eyes had darkened, become bland, almost dead. Shark eyes.

Javier said, "Is that a—"

"This is not a threat, Javier, but a fact. If you want to join your Zapatistas in Chiapas, Guerrero, Oaxaca or el DF, you are more than welcome to. No one here will stop you. But if you threaten Vallarta or tourism in Vallarta at any time, and most specifically tomorrow, your ass and the ass of everyone associated with you will be in jail. Of course you may consider it a great honor and sacrifice to get arrested, so I have reserved a special cell for you and your *compadres*...in Guadalajara where you will be charged with terrorism for threatening Governor Palacio. Federales there have special methods of inter-rogation reserved for terroristas and they are anxious to practice them on you."

Javier clenched his jaw in dull resentment, and dipped his chin in a rare display of acquiescence.

Gloria drove her point home: "You can show up with Zapatistas if you like. After all, we will not know you are Zapatistas because no Zapatista banners, leaflets, clothing, proclamations or shouting of slogans will be permitted. Eyes will be upon you, Javier. This is not May Day in el DF."

Carlos shifted nervously in his seat. He thought maybe he had misunderstood who the mayor of Vallarta was. This woman was clearly in charge. It would take more than a rabble of activists to do battle with her. Busloads of anarchists? An army of anarchists? Even if he were capable of gathering such a force it looked as though this woman might be prepared for it. On the other hand, a person this sure of herself could get caught off guard, if he bided his time, waited for an opening—

Gloria's eyes flashed unexpectedly. "Something else on your mind Carlos?"

"No."

Teodoro almost raised his hand to ask permission before speaking. "I will have to inform my union of your intransigence on the issue of free—"

"Incitement to riot is not free speech, Teodoro. Your union can get away with blocking streets and businesses and protesting, destroying the so-called *bourgeoisie* in Oaxaca but not here. Make your arguments in a court of law."

Teodoro swallowed the thickness in his throat. He wanted nothing more than to get the hell out of there. He would not show up for the dedication and would not be missed.

Gloria clasped her hands at her waist. "Now, since there are no more questions, I assume we have a clear understanding of what is expected of you tomorrow, if you choose to show up. If you decide against joining the festivities, I wish you well. There will be plenty in attendance without you. Good evening."

WHILE on their way to the cockfights in their Range Rover early that evening, Gloria told Juan that her meeting with Comandante Héctor Diamante Pasqual concerned a botched police and federale raid—an unfortunate foul-up that nevertheless facilitated a request by her and el comandante for extra security from Tepic and Guadalajara. They would now have a security force well beyond that previously planned for the dedication of Arena Vallarta. "Trouble is," Gloria added in a tone of absent frustration, "gangsters who escaped the raid may still be in town."

Juan huffed scornfully, "Los pinches Zetas. Vallarta had been free of any significant gangster violence for years before they showed up."

"One of the gangsters was arrested this afternoon before the raid," Gloria said. "He is not a Zeta but a member of an obscure gang—Mara Salvatrucha or some such."

Juan looked a question at his wife beside him in the passenger seat. "Mara...Salvatrucha...? Qué diablos does that mean?"

Gloria placed a reassuring hand on her husband's leg. "It means, cariño, that we will have plenty of security for the dedication tomorrow."

"If word of a botched police raid on the eve of the governor's arrival gets out, Comandante Pasqual will have hell to pay."

"It might be in the news eventually," Gloria said, "but not until after the dedication"—and who knows what other news will come out? she thought to herself. The terrorist rumor she'd heard before encountering Héctor with Lazarito at The Bureau earlier this evening was the most disconcerting, but el comandante had assured her that there was no hard evidence to support the rumor other than the testimony of a jailed gangster with ulterior motives. Gloria agreed that the rumor was farfetched and was not to be repeated. She followed her own advice, for the time being. And the dead man found at the marina? Pues, he would be buried in tomorrow's Vallarta Diario. She might mention him to Juan after the dedication.

8

WHEN I awoke in my hotel room Sunday morning the hammer pounding my brain nearly punched out my eyeballs. I clutched a pillow and tried to think pleasant thoughts. There were a few to recall from the cockfights. Missed the mariachis. Johnny and I were kicked out before we had a chance to see them...

I pictured Brenda flipping her streaked hair over a shoulder and fiddling with my pocket camera. Fair skinned for a Mexican. Her skinny cropped jeans tapered down to just below the knee and bared shapely calves bronzed a shade darker than the sliver of cleavage exposed beneath her floral summer blouse. Freckles adorned her button nose above full lips painted a rare violet color. Green eyes suggested French descent, ancestry from Maximilian's occupation of Mexico.

Brenda was Mountain's date. She still had my camera... My temples ached. Mountain appeared, his face smooth and large as a ham shank; short jet-black hair squared off around rectangular ears and a forehead the size of a snowplow. His malleable mouth, brawny black eyebrows and rugged factions readily render an overwrought, defensive expression, or a defiant offensive expression, but rarely an aggressive one. And the way he grew somber when...

That old welling pain worked its way up from my diaphragm. Sickening, guilt-ridden pangs. The pain in my head was preferable.

The lack of facilities in Vallarta was to blame. An ambulance had to take Rosalita all the way to Guadalajara. "Shitty Vallarta hospitals," I told Mountain. "Stupid fucking abortion laws."

"As long as you do not blame yourself," he said.

I buried my face in my pillow. *Easy for him to say...*

I winked at myself in the bathroom mirror. As far as shiners go, it wasn't all that bad. It magnified my hangover and stung when I touched it but wasn't all that bad. A shapely eclipse under my left eye that would get uglier, but I've had 'em worse. It's always worse when you don't see the punch comin', and I'd seen that cheap shot comin' a mile away...just wasn't in a position to defend myself.

The last guy who gave me a black eye wound up with a broken nose and a few missing teeth. That was years ago. I didn't retaliate last night. A silly altercation really. The result of an accident. I'd slipped on tequila lime wedges and fell across his girlfriend's lap.

Maybe I deserved it.

What a buncha bull. The sonuvabitch had wanted a piece of me and was waiting for an opportunity to clobber me.

I downed some Advil and made my way to the balcony. A sparkling morning. There was swell up the shoreline. A thin off-shore breeze held the surf motionless for an instant before waves broke in long, languid curves. I grabbed my fin off the table and my swim trunks hanging from a chair.

Perfect hangover-bodysurfing waves. Barely noticed I was getting exercise. After a breakfast of huevos rancheros, I bought a Sunday Vallarta Diario and hauled myself back to the beach into the shade of a palapa. A kind waiter, Chevy, recognized the soldiers marching through mud between my ears and brought me a beer and a cup of ice for my eye. In no time at all a siesta was in order. I assumed the position, facedown on my towel in the sand.

"Hey gringo. Fighting's for cocks, gringo. You really that big a prick gringo? Look at you. We drink to you and you pay the bill." Waves crash on ice cubes. But the cubes don't melt, they grow. How can they grow in this heat? Brenda offers me a margarita on the rocks. It's strong...and huge. I can dive right in. So refreshing.

I was losing shade, my legs beginning to roast. A bucket full of ice, beer and bottled water was on the table. Johnny lounged in a chair under the palapa, beer in hand between his legs, head back, an Oakland Athletics baseball cap pulled down over his sunglasses.

"How's your head?" I asked.

Johnny took a deep breath and ignored the question. I pushed myself to my feet. The heat landed solid shots to my temples and sent me staggering into the ocean.

After cruising with the white water for a round or two, I was ready to mix it up a little. I posed over Johnny's slumbering form, dukes up. He snored, his head listing, beer bottle upright. Johnny knows how to hang on to a beer, and a football.

Johnny Miles, All City 5A Varsity Football, so they say...so they told me when I first laid eyes on the skinny little shit about fifteen years ago, not long after arriving in northern California from Los Angeles on my motorcycle.

At five-feet-nine-inches tall (he calls it five-ten) and 155 pounds soaking wet, it didn't seem possible. But there he was: Johnny Miles, All City San Jose, California. Johnny Miles, playin' beach football in Santa Cruz where he should've been surfing on that agile, springy frame of his, or spiking volleyballs instead of taking and dishing out punishment. Turns out he's AAA beach volleyball, a hell of a surfer, and a one-man fast-break/full-court press on the basketball court. Kicks plenty of ass in tennis and Ping-Pong too. But my first impression of Johnny Miles was of him sprintin' on soft sand like a greyhound and swingin' and swivelin' his hips over, under and around everyone who tried to tackle him. I've got over three inches on him and forty pounds of gym-hardened muscle yet never could knock him out of a game, mostly 'cause he's so damn elusive, but also due to his toughness. Wasn't long before I made sure Johnny was on my team every time, whatever the sport or occasion.

Came to appreciate the weed he grows too.

The shallow minded would condemn Johnny as just another scumbag drug dealer. They condemned his father, Bertrand Miles, for his habitual use of marijuana to relieve the deadly throes of nausea brought about by chemotherapy. Bertrand Miles did time in an Arizona prison for possession of three ounces of grass... A few years after his father died, Johnny marched in the streets with pro-pot demonstrators as the feds raided state-licensed medical-marijuana distributorships in LA and made off with millions upon millions of dollars in cash, weed, and equipment. Two years later, he marched with demonstrators in San Francisco shortly after the feds made off like bandits again. He's also escaped the cops and choppers a few times. His licensed and unlicensed farms have been raided in northern California and southern Oregon. Ask him why he does it and he'll claim he's a libertarian activist, "a freedom fighter battling for the *re-legalization* of consensual consumption." Suggest he's in it for the money and he'll admit that most things worthwhile are worth getting paid for, but he's also quick to remind you that the corrupt bastards who invented drug prohibition steal billions and "have imprisoned millions for *consensual crimes*."

SEVE VERDAD

What Johnny lacks in a formal college education he definitely makes up for in street smarts and solid cojones. Plus, he's a good reader; books I mean, not just the Sports page.

"Pot farming can get scientific at times," he's told me on occasion. "So best to keep up on reading of all kinds and not let the mind mold."

My formal college education, both at home and abroad, has exposed me to innumerable elitist intellectual pinheads far less stimulating than Johnny. Our friendship defies a singular explanation but I suppose at its basest it has provided me a link to the activities, product, and mindset of contemporary bootleggers—modern-day cowboy outlaws supplying the demands of the masses.

I slapped on my wayfarer sunglasses and relaxed in the lounge chair opposite him with the Sunday Vallarta Diario. The front page announced the arrival of Governor Palacio for the dedication of Arena Vallarta that afternoon and included a photo of Mayor Juan Pacífico Velázquez and his wife, Gloria, beaming proudly in front of the arena. I read the caption to the photo aloud, "Sí se puede." Yes we (you) can. A trite phrase signifying change and progress that's always been popular with politicians and the general public in Latin America. My experience in Mexico and Latin America had taught me that "sí se puede" was actually a roundabout third-world way of saying "goddamn it, I can never get anything done." In this case, however, it more or less meant "see, I told you we could do it." But I knew the foreman of the Arena Vallarta project. A pretty good friend of mine. The caption to the photo really should have read "Sí *Enrique* Puede."

I flipped to La Nación (The Nation) section. The leading headline quoted Presidente Cárdenes de Ortega of the Socialist Reform Party: "México will not be held hostage." The article centered on the drug cartels and gangs that had taken over Ciudad Juárez and other northern border regions as well as Sinaloa... *Let's not forget el DF, Veracruz, Michoacán, Acapulco and...* On the opposite page, Zapatistas and Magonistas reaffirmed their solidarity in Chiapas with a pledge to march together in Mexico City on May Day. *Always endearing to see communists and anarchists joining hands, preparing the ground for strongmen to restore order.* El Mundo (The World) section contained a picture of Venezuelan strongman, Husmo Marqués, greeting Cuban strongman, *Más Fidel*, in Venezuela. Iran's president, *Ali Must-a-be-loco*, and Chinese envoy, *Cha-ching*, were to join them in Venezuela Saturday evening. *Time to choose sides and divide up the world.*

The European Union was choosing sides—condemning Israel for responding violently to violence from Hezbollah and Hamas...*and The*

FINDING DEVO

Muslim Suicide/Homicide Brigade, and Islamic Martyrs on Parade, and Allah's Cult of Death Replayed, again and again and again and...

Another article blamed America's war on terror for the rise in terrorism around the world. *Amazing how the enemy's ranks swell once you declare war on them.* The editor also printed a column about the beheadings of Christian school girls by Islamists in Indonesia...*also America's fault...*

The final article in El Mundo was devoted to the downing of American Airlines Flight 3356 in Lima, Peru, two years ago. Yesterday, Saturday, United States investigators were expelled from Peru for the second time since the tragedy, and for the same reason: conspiring with the conservative opposition party to overthrow the government.

How in the hell does concluding that the plane was shot down by an Iranian portable surface-to-air missile constitute conspiring to overthrow the Peruvian government?

I brushed off my query as rhetorical. Conspiring to overthrow the government is the standard explanation given by Latin American leaders for the expulsion of undesirable foreigners, be they diplomats, the media, investigators, or even protesting students. And the true motive behind the expulsion was clear: *Those damn Peruvian politicians in charge must have something to hide.*

I perused the Local section. Violent crime and homicide rates had dropped in Vallarta the last three months. Ironically disturbing. Good news but, little more than a year ago, there wasn't much of a violent-crime rate to speak of in Vallarta, let alone a homicide rate...

Los pinches Zetas. Re-legalize *drugs and fuck 'em...*

The Delitos section reported that a couple of adolescents were busted for running marijuana on the road to Tepic. The pictures always make the accused look guilty as sin. I wondered if the guns and dope were really theirs or if the kids were patsies for the famously corrupt Mexican police...

Not a word about a police raid. Did it happen too late to be in the paper? Maybe it'll be in tomorrow's edition.

At the very bottom of the page, an inch of print reported that the corpse of an unidentified male had washed up on shore by the marina docks yesterday evening. He was moreno—dark hair and skin—and in his mid-thirties. An apparent drowning. The report struck me as curious for a few reasons. First of all, an apparent "drowning" wouldn't normally appear in the Delitos section unless a crime was involved. That's what "delitos" means—crimes (other than murder). There was no mention of an assault, robbery, or any other crime associated with the "apparent drowning". Secondly, there is no "shore" to wash up on at the marina. Sand skirts the lawn in areas but, barring a hurricane, a drowned, dead body floating around the harbor would end up bouncing off of the rocky seawall and never make it up onto the sand or lawn. The report's brevity was also strange. Dead bodies found in Vallarta usually merit a headline.

Discovered in the early evening at the marina. Not far from where those locals said the raid occurred last night... The raid happened at about that time. Why wasn't it reported as well?

I made a mental note to look for news of the raid in a different paper and scanned the Sports section. Chivas, from Guadalajara, and Toluca, from just outside Mexico City, were scheduled to play a big soccer game late this afternoon. A local basketball tournament had its final round today. And the Dodgers and Giants were slated to play a doubleheader in an important early-season Major League Baseball matchup in Los Angeles. Saturday's game had suffered a rare LA rainout. I flipped to the Comentarios section, perused some editorials and letters, and found a story, a reminiscence about Elizabeth Taylor and Richard Burton in Vallarta... After a party at director John Houston's house on the other side of the bay, the two of them returned to Vallarta by boat in the early morning hours. They were drunk and got into one of their infamous fights at their new house in the rain forest. Valuable household articles were broken and Liz was left alone—

"Did we make the news?"

I faced Johnny and removed my sunglasses. "Not yet. Guess we have to try harder."

"Nice shiner. Try any harder and you'll be difficult to look at."

"How's your head?"

"Fine. But I was shittin' flames this morning. That was some damn *hot hot hot* sauce."

"You got your own bathroom in that dive you're at?"

"A TV too. Why ask for more when I can horn in on you here at Casa Mexicana? And you owe me. I saved your ass last night."

"Mighta made the paper had you let me tumble into the cockfighting pit. I'll sign for the beer and water."

Johnny stuck his half-full beer bottle in the bucket of ice, pulled out a small bottled water, and drained it in three gulps. "You'd rather find news of terrorists in Vallarta," he belched, "than news about us. You find anything?"

We'd spoken little of the terrorist rumor since we heard it at Pepe's taco stand. But Johnny knows me too well to think I'd forgotten about it...knew it had to be on my mind. I'm always on the lookout for a scoop.

"Not yet," I said. "But at the cockfights last night, Mountain confirmed there was a raid. A botched police and federale raid. He wasn't sure who the cops were after, so I'll have to do a little more digging."

"Come visit for an Oregon outdoor harvest and I'll show you some terrorists."

I flashed him a bemused smile. "You looking forward to running from choppers again this year Johnny?"

"Keeps me in shape."

I reclined with my paper. We were quiet for a small time. I reread that blurb about the dead guy found at the marina. "You goin' to Mountain's party tonight?" I said.

"Sure. Same place as last year, right?"

"Yep."

"Is it a housewarming party? He finally gonna buy the place?"

"Not sure," I said abstractedly. Johnny and I had gotten kicked out of the cockfights for fighting (though neither of us threw a punch) before Mountain had a chance to tell us the reason for his party. I flipped the page. "Mountain's heard about Rosalita."

Johnny blanched. My casual voice didn't fit the subject matter. We'd spoken about Rosalita some over the phone but I'd only seen Johnny once since her death six months ago. Yesterday he offered brief condolences; now seemed as good a time as any to broach the subject with a little more candor.

His tawny color was back. Over the years I've seen Johnny Miles banged up after beach football games, hammered at wild parties, thrashed from a night in the drunk tank and, once, nearly killed in a scrape with a guy twice his size (a couple of us had to break that one up and save his ass). Johnny always recovers quickly. A tribute to a tough constitution that belies his narrow build and boyish countenance.

"Well," he said, "it's been several months. You knew word would get around. You would've mentioned Rosalita to Mountain anyway, eventually."

"Yeah, sure. Just thought I'd let you know in case he brought it up to you at some point. Didn't want you to be surprised."

"When you gonna visit her family?"

"Soon. I'll try to get in some vacation time first."

"Much deserved. Gotta say, looks like you've bounced back pretty well. I...uh..." Johnny's voice faded. He put a hand to his sunglasses and looked out over the sea as if it could remind him of something he'd intended to say but had forgotten. "I'd never seen you depressed like that before," eyes on me again, "when I saw you last."

I forced air from my lungs and tossed the paper onto the table. "It was rough going for a while," I said. "Eventually anger took over the depression and then..."

"Yeah?"

"Nothin'. Empty, I guess. And pissed...and sad...sometimes...too much of the time."

A trio of pelicans glided along the peak of a wave. Were they surfing, searching for food, or both? *What a life. Surf and fish.* Two little boys roughhoused in a tide pool. They began throwing wet sand at one another, and the smaller one was getting the worst of it. A female voice from behind us told them to calm down. A couple of shapely young women walked by in their skimpy bikinis. My gaze followed them down the shore until it met up with another pretty girl heading our way in a single-piece suit that accentuated her athletic legs and firm bust line. I fixed on her figure as she passed by.

Johnny stood with a growl, reached for the sky and bent for his toes. Then he straightened and did some twists with hands on hips. "Nice to see you can still get your head in the ballgame, Russ. Plenty more rears like that one around this town."

"Loosening up for a big afternoon?"

Johnny did some deep knee bends. "Figured I'd head down to Los Muertos and check out the spring-break babes on la playa."

"Good call. How's the garden coming along?"

"Called this morning. On schedule for some May hikin' and transplantin'." He reached for his toes again and brought his head to his knees.

"Good teamwork."

"We all get time off."

"Got any medication for me?"

Johnny fished around in his knapsack and handed me a joint. "You hangin' here for the day?" he said.

"You walkin' to Los Muertos?"

"It's pretty far. Maybe walk a mile or so south then hop a bus."

"Think I'll ice the eye and rest up. Like to see some of that dedication this afternoon."

"If I don't get lucky on the beach maybe I'll see ya at the arena..." He surveyed my hotel behind us. "They still allow me in the pool at this joint?"

"Long as you don't cause trouble."

Johnny shouldered his pack, wrapped his towel around his neck and headed for the pool.

LIEUTENANT Benito Cuevas Romero had honed his interrogation skills while in the Guadalajara police force where he became well-schooled in the value of deprivation—sensory, sleep, food, water, oxygen, you name it—to gain information and force confessions from prisoners. Most significantly, he learned to appreciate the rewards that come with inflicting physical and mental agony on detainees. He championed torture as a means of breaking a man. Lieutenant Romero missed that about Guadalajara, all the opportunities to break a man—a drug dealer, kidnapper, gangster or killer. Vallarta would never offer near the number of such opportunities that a big city like Guadalajara did... What he didn't miss about Guadalajara though was the suffocating city life...and his ex-wife.

She actually grew to be more unstable and domineering than her mother, fatter too. After their marriage, nearly ten years ago now, her figure seemed to gain kilos from the moment she got out of bed in the morning; every time she opened her mouth it was full of food and whiney, nagging vulgarities. How could her breasts sag and tumble and her waist become riddled with stretch marks without even having bared a child? Her transformation was astonishing. Benito was grateful to be rid of her, grateful she hadn't borne him children...even grateful for her miscarriage two months after their wedding. The less tying him to her the better. Why have a baby with a woman you can't stand? Why stand women at all, but for one thing...?

Lieutenant Romero divorced his wife eight years ago at the age of twenty-six and left Guadalajara for Vallarta. He proceeded to streak up police ranks. His big breakthrough came within two years when a Canadian tourist was shot and killed in the Vallarta suburb of Gaviotas. A clear case of a drug deal gone bad. Cocaine. The lieutenant paid off and extorted informants, combined brutal interrogations with smart detective work, and initiated a timely police raid on a drug house in El Pitillal, Puerto Vallarta. The raid was carried out to near perfection. Only two shots fired—BANG! BANG! To this day his only kill. A head shot that brought instant justice to the crack and powder dealer responsible for murdering the Canadian tourist. Benito gracefully accepted a commendation, though the shooting hadn't been nearly as satisfying to him as breaking a man.

In the ensuing years, Benito received regular promotions. He had a talent for investigative work, extorting suspects, and extracting confessions. Despite his kill, he didn't become trigger happy. Vallarta wasn't the place for that. There had been an upsurge in gang violence the last eighteen months or so but, overall, Puerto Vallarta remained far removed from Mexico's hotspots, places like Tijuana, Culiacán, and Ciudad Juárez where the government was engaged in an outright war with drug cartels; a trigger-happy cop could be put to good use in places like that, if he wasn't corrupted by the lure of drug money. Since his kill, the lieutenant had only discharged his weapon twice while on duty, both warning shots. By comparison, his infrequent interrogations of drug dealers, armed robbers, and gangsters were plentiful.

Lieutenant Benito Cuevas Romero never bruised his knuckles during his interrogations of prisoners, never even sullied himself. He left that to his lackeys in the Puerto Vallarta police force. And his two interrogations of the current prisoner, Paco, were no different. For the most part, the lieutenant remained seated in his chair behind a table, his slender figure immaculate in his uniform (or plain clothes, as the case may be), dark soap-opera eyes impassive, while los chicos did the dirty work—followed his every verbal and nonverbal command.

Pain was a marvelous ally, a marvelous tool. Pain inflicted by fists, boots, the butt of a rifle, truncheons...the slice of a knife. A single blow to the ribs, an elbow, knee, or kidney and you could see the radiant pain explode in a man's face and come screaming out his mouth. He would confess to all, everything, if you only stopped the pain. The tool needed to be used intelligently though. Joaquín 'Garras' de Jesús, the lieutenant's CISEN (Mexican Intelligence) confidant stationed in Guadalajara, had stressed this to him on occasion, usually over a beer. "You need to know something about the answers you are looking for," Garras would advise. "A prisoner might confess to any crime, real or imagined, to stop the pain, so you must educate yourself on his background, criminal history, associates, and habits to better formulate your questions and prevent him from leading you astray. And if you go too hard on him too rapidly, delirium sets in and the prisoner is worthless until he recuperates. This can be a fine line to follow. Sometimes you may find it advantageous to make your man suffer until he loses consciousness but it needs to be your choice. You have to know when to ease off before your man becomes worthless and you are forced to let him recuperate."

Lieutenant Romero had to admit that he hadn't faithfully followed Joaquín's advice when he interrogated his prisoner yesterday. In hindsight, Paco's initial claim to have consorted with Arab terrorists was obviously a case of him admitting to an "imagined" crime to stop the pain; and that hasty, infuriating botched raid resulted.

Last night, once as many holes had been punched in Paco's internal organs as his story about terrorists in Vallarta, the prisoner was stripped and forced up against a wall where he proceeded to collapse and pass out from sheer agony. The lieutenant had no choice but to end the interrogation prematurely so Paco could recuperate overnight. He hadn't followed that fine line of knowing when to ease off. At least Paco had finally admitted to being chilango (from Mexico City) and to sharing that raided duplex with MS-13 gangsters. Today, Sunday morning, Lieutenant Romero planned to grill him on his connections to Zeta cartel gangsters and the dead man found at the marina before tending to his security detail at the dedication of Arena Vallarta...

A telephone call he received at police headquarters changed everything.

"DF federales are coming to retrieve the prisoner, Lieutenant," Juan said. "Mara Salvatrucha has been operating in the capital with the Mano con Ojos cartel. Arrests have been made and our federale friends believe that your gangster's presence will facilitate their interrogations."

Lieutenant Romero was taken aback. He had expected the lack of publicity surrounding Paco's arrest and the ensuing raid to give Vallarta police at least a three-or-four-day window to work on the prisoner before federales intervened... And Jalisco federales had been involved in Saturday's raid, not DF federales. Did his contact in the Mexico City Police Department investigating copies of the fingerprints and passports he faxed him leak word of the captured gangster in Vallarta? Or perhaps Jalisco federales reported the arrest of Paco to counterparts in el DF. Pinches federales, he thought. Give them half a chance and they assert their authority.

The lieutenant quickly collected himself. "I will be happy to oblige," he said, his voice measured. "And I presume the federales will also require all evidence pertaining to our prisoner's arrest."

"They will require more than that, Lieutenant."

Lieutenant Romero's heart skipped a beat. Had DF federales also heard about the dead man discovered at the marina? Would they demand *all* the evidence Vallarta police had gathered yesterday, including all that money found in the Jeep? maybe even question him about any connection between the raid and the dead man? But there wasn't a connection between the raid and the dead man, or Paco and the dead man. No *discernible* connection. Not yet at any rate...

The mayor's next words allayed his fears: "They also require el comandante's presence in el DF. He has some questions to answer about that botched raid yesterday."

The lieutenant stifled a sigh of relief. Better that el comandante be subjected to questioning from DF federales than him. "I am sure that el comandante will be happy to oblige, señor. Is there anything specific required of me?"

"It is my understanding, Lieutenant, that you were to have a report ready for Héctor this morning on yesterday's interrogations of the prisoner."

"Sí, señor. I have it here."

"El comandante has been instructed to meet the federales at the airport, Benito," said the mayor. "Leave a copy of the report for him there at headquarters and meet me at Arena Vallarta in half an hour. You are now acting Comandante of the Puerto Vallarta Police Department."

10

NONE of the TV stations in my hotel room carried a Major League Baseball game. Most unfortunate. Napping during baseball games can be very therapeutic. I managed to nap through basketball instead. Tried to write some about the cockfights as well. Before I knew it, it was too late to make it to the dedication of Arena Vallarta. A couple hours before sunset, ESPN en Español reported that the Dodgers had lost the first game of their doubleheader against the Giants 3-2.

Not a single Mexican news cast reported a police raid in Vallarta or the discovery of a dead man found at the marina.

After a shower and a close trim of my goatee, I caught a cab for the malecón (seawall), Vallarta's long promenade that skirts attending shops, restaurants, and night spots. I had the cabby drop me off several blocks short of the malecón, across the street from a pair of sleek octagonal structures astride a domed axis large enough to house a basketball court and a few thousand fans: Arena Vallarta.

A throng of people crowded the steps leading up to the arena. I recognized the mayor and his wife, Gloria, standing under the arched entry pressing palms and making small talk. Enrique was nowhere to be seen. I imagined him inside the arena celebrating, buying drinks for his union pals at the bar. Joining him was out of the question. No way was I gonna battle the crowd. If police hadn't been there for crowd control, forcing people to form a line before taking the steps up to the arena, the mayor and his wife would have been smothered under a mass of humanity. I crossed the plaza towards the far end of the arena to simply observe. That's when I first laid eyes on Ara.

She was talking to Gloria under the arched entry to the arena. A toffee-colored china doll; porcelain profile, generous mouth, dark smiling eyes. Black hair, like Rosalita—raven tresses draped down over her bare back like layers of satin linen. Tight jeans hugged her slender, grindy body. She reminded me of Rosalita, but her skin was a lighter brown, her features not as sharp... I sagged inwardly. *Sweet, Dulce Rosalita...*

"You cannot enter from here." A snub-faced police officer with a dented nose held out a hand to stop my progress. I'd been drifting, skirting the cordoned edge of the arena toward Gloria and that raven-haired china doll.

"Sí. Lo siento." I'm sorry. "I am a journalist and would like to ask the mayor a couple of questions." I gave the cop a tight grin and adjusted my sunglasses. He widened his eyes—the thin dull slits in his face.

"Credentials?"

That did it. My ID and credentials as a journalist for New World Sports were in my room. A standard precaution to guard against losing them. I hadn't expected they would be of use since my destination was Mountain's party. This made me feel pretty stupid, like I'd been caught pissing in an alley or somethin'. Under circumstances like these, with all the cops around, you should never mention you're a member of the media without having your credentials handy. Just raises suspicions. Guess I'd been distracted. The china doll with smiling eyes nodded at Gloria, giving her assurance of some sort.

A short frumpy man with a bow tie stuffed under his double chin placed a hand on the cop's back. "There a problem officer?"

"He says he is a journalist, Señor Charlado, and wants to ask the mayor a few questions."

Señor Charlado scratched his balding melon head. "Is that so?" he hummed. "I thought I knew all the reporters here today. How well do you speak Spanish, young man?"

My khaki cargo shorts, printed rayon beach shirt and sun-tinged fair skin made me look like a typical gringo tourist, so he assumed I didn't speak much Spanish. "Fluently," I said. "I studied quite a bit here in México and other parts of Latin América, as well as Spain, but am from the United States." My Spanish retains a singsong central-Mexico (Puebla) accent. Señor Charlado lifted a rumpled brow at the sound of it.

"Indeed," he said. "Well, we have a Canadian reporter here from the Associated Press. She will be handling the press releases in North América." Señor Charlado canted his head from one side to the other, eyes narrowed, viewing me skeptically. "You are welcome to take a tour of Arena Vallarta, indeed you are, but will have to wait your turn like everyone else. And if you wish to interview the mayor, I suggest you make an appointment through his office tomorrow."

Señor Charlado's mannerisms and the natural squeal to his voice lent him a pompous air, a pompous bearing I presumed was due, as least in part, to more than a modicum of authority. I thanked him, noticed my china doll had disappeared, and turned to go. But something held me back, an instinct, recognition of an opportunity all journalists jump on. "Excuse me, Señor Charlado?"

Señor Charlado had advanced towards the entrance to the arena with the snub-faced police officer. He waved off the cop and waddled in my direction, his gut toppling over the belt beneath his white dress shirt. With a figure like his, one should always wear suspenders instead of a belt. He hiked up his trousers to keep from losing them. "Yes young man?"

"Can you confirm that there was a police raid last night, early evening, in the vicinity of the marina?"

Señor Charlado frowned, cheeks puffed. Prick him with a needle and he'd explode. He regained his composure and let the air escape his mouth with only a hint of rancor. "Young man, rumors abound in Vallarta. If you are interested in rumors, write fiction, but do not ask me to confirm them."

Nice non-denial denial.

"What is your name?" he asked sharply.

"I write for—"

"Do you have credentials?"

"In my hotel room. Why was the raid not reported on television newscasts or in the Vallarta Diario?"

Señor Charlado scrutinized me with a look that drew lines in his face. "You will be denied access to the mayor," he said delicately, careful not to raise his voice and cause a scene. "And if you persist with your—"

"Is it true that police and federales raided an empty house?"

"I am afraid I will have to ask you to—"

He wanted to say "leave" (or get your puta madre culo the hell outta here) but my catty smile forced him to swallow the word(s). He knew that I knew he was being far too defensive for someone who had not been attacked. His black eyes shifted beneath heavy swags of flesh as he calculated his next move.

He's hiding something.

Señor Charlado found some spring to his step and made for a couple of cops like a fat old goose scooting from a hound. I beat it around the nearside of the arena. The first cab I hailed stopped for me.

THE anarchist and the Zapatista stewed as they sat on a bench under a palm tree, smoking cigarettes and scoping out Arena Vallarta from across the plaza.

The Cora Zapatista, Javier Menticlaro, huffed, "Puta. What a bunch of sheep. You would think they were going to meet the pope."

Carlos 'El Manco' Mansalva absently massaged his tricep—the stump hanging from his left shoulder—and pulled the cigarette from his lips. "The pope would attract more sheep. And if we are to join those in the arena, we will have to behave like lambs."

Carlos and Javier were natural allies thrown together by fate, circumstance, and jail—a nine-day stint in a common cell in Mexico City last May, for incitement to riot and destruction of private property on May Day. With the help of cohorts on the outside, they were able to make bail. Shortly thereafter Javier introduced Carlos to student activist Pati Redondo. She was immediately smitten. Carlos seemed a romantic, worldly figure, having practiced his specialties during political conventions and rallies, immigration marches, and free-trade summits in places like Seattle, Chicago, Miami, New York, Los Angeles, San Diego, Toronto, Oaxaca, and Cancún. Carlos appreciated Pati's enthusiasm, though she wasn't cut out for rioting. Pati preferred relatively peaceful methods of protest like marching, blocking streets and yelling slogans. But she was supportive, gave great head, and was easy to find at the University of Guadalajara when the urge struck him.

Javier lengthened the natural curl of his lip into a half-smile, half-sneer. "Let Pati behave like a lamb. She must be playing the role well since she is still inside the arena."

"And what role did she play when she was arrested with you in Guadalajara six months ago?"

"Pati just got caught up in the fray. The girl can be inspiring but her hands are clean."

A white pickup loaded with police racketed along the cobblestone street in their direction. At the far end of the plaza, a squad car pulled up to the curb—a sentry on the lookout for troublemakers.

Javier placed his elbows on his knees and surveyed the scene before him—the elegant lines of the arena, all the "sheep" flocking at the foot of the steps leading up to the arched entry, and police working crowd control. His gaze clouded over, dulling his chiseled Indian features. "Carajo," he grumbled. "We would have needed an army today to disrupt the dedication."

SEVE VERDAD

"A May Day army." Carlos sighed with reverie. "And Molotov cocktails, ammonium-nitrite bombs loaded with nails, live CS canisters..."

"So you say. But do we have to wait until May Day to stop talking and take action? Just hanging around like this can be as frustrating as working the tobacco plantations in Nayarit."

The Zapatista paused and leveled a sardonic gaze at the anarchist's bespectacled eyes. Carlos bared his teeth. "Chinga las plantaciones de tabaco," they said in unison. Fuck the tobacco plantations.

"Chinga las plantaciones de tabaco" was something of a rally cry between them. The phrase was taken literally but also meant "fuck the corrupt bourgeois government" and sprang from a slice of Javier's life as a Cora Indian.

Javier's father had died of pesticide poisoning working tobacco plantations. Worked them for years before his periodic bouts with headaches and nausea suddenly became acute and were accompanied by tremors, blurred vision, loss of coordination—symptoms that had preceded the deaths of two other Cora tobacco laborers.

Convulsions left Javier's father in a comatose state and subsequently paralyzed his respiration. Tepic doctors all said the same thing: natural causes.

Javier's account of his father's death bridged the war stories he and Carlos had shared while getting to know each other in jail. "I always saw my father through a child's eyes," he said, his obsidian eyes flaring in the meager cellblock light. "He seemed a superman—tireless and strong. To watch him waste away like that was like watching the sun and the moon and the stars fall from the sky. What can survive that? What could it mean but my own death, the death of my family and everything I cherished? He struggled heroically and it was not long before I understood his death to be a barbaric crime. But when the truth finally came out, when it was discovered that the doctors had lied, dozens, hundreds had already been poisoned and we, the Cora and Huichol were too weak to fight for justice—for more than the pinche healthcare and meaningless quantity of cash offered us by the government and the *puta madre mestizo* landowners."

Javier paused imperatively, as though challenging Carlos to take offense. Carlos' lighter complexion suggested European heredity and characterized him as mestizo.

Carlos spat out the word "mestizos" like a vulgarity. He had disowned his European heritage long ago. "Fucking mongrels."

Remote speculation suffused Javier's expression. "So you are not—"

"Not mestizo," Carlos said, his voice venomous, "mixed bloods who do not embrace their indigenous heritage. If they would embrace their heritage and refuse to buy into the colonial, neoliberal system, there would be no corporate tobacco plantations but only fields, forests and seeds of *our* nation."

"*Our* nation?"

"The entire continent belongs to us, those of indigenous blood."

"Nyarit and Jalisco are Cora," Javier insisted with unmistakable pride, "and Huichol."

"Of course," Carlos agreed expansively, as if to bequeath North America unto Javier. "Just like always."

Thus the anarchist and the Zapatista constructed a foundation on which to build an alliance. Both bitterly resented how government appropriation of Cora Indian lands had allowed "mestizos" to gain corporate ownership of plantations. This resulted in much higher productivity but left the comparatively less educated Cora and indigenous cultures elsewhere in Mexico in poverty. They had few options to sustain themselves outside of living on ejidos (reservations) and working plantations or peddling artesanías.

Productivity to sustain the nation of Mexico was not the issue. The government was corrupt, the lands stolen from their rightful owners.

Like many Cora and Huichol, Javier's family left the ejido for a large population center in search of a better life. They settled in Tepic, in their home state of Nyarit. Yet Javier's father still worked the plantations, his only marketable skill.

Javier refused to end up like his old man. When he died it was not going to be from pesticide poisoning but in a fight for his rights. Carlos responded to this declaration by coining the phrase "chinga las plantaciones de tabaco."

Carlos drew inspiration from Javier's story, a story replete with further struggles and family tragedy, and often revisited it with him, as he was right now at Arena Vallarta.

Carlos 'El Manco' Mansalva crushed his cigarette underfoot. "It is frustrating to have to act like lambs, Javier," he said. "But for now we need to have patience. Acting like lambs is the only way to get inside the arena, so we have an idea of its layout in case an opportunity ever arises—"

"Check out the gringo." Javier's obsidian eyes had alighted on a lone figure separated from the flock of sheep at the entrance to the arena. Was this a ram or a wandering lamb butting headlong into a police officer? The Zapatista bared his teeth into a grimacing smile.

"Did he try to sneak in?" Carlos said.

"Maybe. Wonder why...?"

"Drunk...or..."

"He has attracted the attention of the fat man."

Carlos chuckled wryly. He stood from the bench, eyes fixed on the gringo. "Vámanos," he said. "We can check him out as we join the sheep."

12

THE malecón's boardwalk was active with pedestrians, foreign and Mexican, drifting through the expiring day and its gentle on-shore breeze: couples holding hands, a family sharing ice cream next to a planter of blooming begonias, and festive students on spring break. I paused to listen to a guitarist under a palm tree. A flower woman approached, said that if I didn't have a girl I could pick one out with one of her roses. I politely declined and continued on my way. There was the pleasant feeling of relief that a sunset brings after a hot day. Along the horizon, clouds displayed bulbous hues of purple, silver and red beyond the slanted billows of a half-dozen sailboats. Two of the boats tacked starboard in the near distance, a heading that would take them past my hotel to the marina. A car horn bleated amidst the methodical street traffic. Across the street, restaurant balconies were filling with people, as were the cafes and bars below. Their voices and laughter mixed happily with a variety of music—rock and roll, ranchera, hip-hop—and emptied out over the malecón. Some of the restaurants provided live mariachi music and every now and again trumpets dominated the cornucopia of sounds. I bought a cup of shaved ice with lemon syrup from a street vendor and took a seat on a bench next to one of the bronze sculptures that trim the malecón's seaside—a seahorse mounted by a naked imp. I finished my lemon icy as the sunset dissipated.

The street was lit. I joined a rather large crowd mulling around the amphitheater towards the end of the malecón where artists sell their wares by a fountain of bronze dolphins and local women sell pastries and cook corn on charcoal braziers. The corn is sold toasted on the ear or as boiled kernels in cups seasoned as you like with lime, salt, mayonnaise and powdered chili. I opted out this time. At the amphitheater, clowns performed on an illuminated stage with children chosen from the audience. The antics were universal. The two lone English-speaking tourist kids on stage excited as many laughs and received as many balloon animals as the Mexican children.

70

Rather than follow the malecón's bend along the coast to the footbridge and Playa de los de Muertos, I kept to the street and its sidewalk. A solicitor for guided tours tried to get my attention. I ignored him and nearly stumbled over two old Indian women huddled together in the thinning light. They were wrapped in traditional Mexican serapes and held out plastic cups begging pesos, hands gnarled as driftwood. I gave them several pesos each. "Que Dios le bendiga," they said. Suddenly I was surrounded by five barefoot kids in soiled clothes, their stained, pleading palms reaching for me. Two little girls were selling gum. I patiently explained that I didn't give money to children but would buy some gum. I bought enough gum to go around and gave the lanky bright-eyed boy a stubby pencil from my pocket. That satisfied them. I crossed the traffic bridge with long strides. More children selling gum reached out to me on the other side. A pregnant woman sat in obscurity at the head of the steps that led down to the Rio Cuale. She held out an empty cup. I waved them all off with a polite "mañana" and slipped into a corner market to buy an evening paper.

WAS that my china doll speaking to Pepe at his taco stand? Thought it was but I arrived too late to catch her. Sure looked like her satin hair and grindy body disappearing around the corner.

Pepe had a member of his family helping out at the taco stand this evening—one of his daughters or a niece, I couldn't remember which. Patrons occupied every stool, all fixated on a small flickering color television on a shelf opposite them above an ice chest. I stood at the corner of the counter and slapped on my wayfarers. Pepe was busy over his grill; I got the girl's attention. Pepe's niece, she reminded me. Her buxom teenage body tallied with Pepe's pear-shaped figure. I ordered two dorado tacos and a Fanta and focused on the TV. The soccer match featured the two teams I'd read about in the paper this morning—Chivas versus Toluca. To make conversation, I asked the man sitting next to me how Chivas was doing. He complained that Toluca was lucky. Chivas should have scored at least two goals by now. Chivas missed another scoring opportunity and the men at the counter groaned. The game was over. A zero-zero tie. A couple of stools were now available. I took a seat opposite Pepe. His niece delivered my tacos. I added salsa casera to them.

"Who was that beautiful doll I saw you chatting with, Pepe?"

Pepe piled up onions, chilies and meats, scraped the grill and toweled off his hands. "You would love to know, try to make her yours, eh cabrón?"

"So she is yours. How many mistresses does that make for you now?"

"If she were mine, I should not need another."

"Is that what she told you?"

Pepe smiled. The smile of a man with a wish to be granted and a secret to keep. "She keeps me informed."

"I bet she does." I bit into a taco. "She know the mayor? Think I saw her at Arena Vallarta today with the mayor and his wife."

"Many people were with the mayor and his wife today." Pepe took hold of his machete, scraped it with a spatula and threw me a curve all at once: "Dodgers are playing the Giants tonight."

But for his clownish arched eyebrows and guileless grin, the abrupt change in subject might have made me think Pepe was hiding something about my china doll. His expression held the genuine emotion of a fan who paints his face for a ballgame. The image of Pepe with his face painted Dodger blue and white made me forget my china doll for the moment.

I adjusted my sunglasses thoughtfully. "That cocky new rookie from the rich family is pitching for the Dodgers," I said. "Preen. Josh Preen."

"The one who says he has no need for the money."

"He still managed to get a multi-million dollar contract from the Dodgers."

"Claro. But he is rich already."

"Rich family. But the idea that his contract and the money are unimportant to him sounds like a pretext to stick that hundred-mile-an-hour rápido wherever the hell he wants to, including in Bobby Stock's ear."

"Qué lástima! I do not have cable here and must stay and make a living for a few more hours."

Pepe took an order from a new arrival. I removed my shades and thumbed through the paper as I ate. It was replete with delitos and crímines of all kinds. One of Mexico's popular shock tabloids. Sensationalized versions of regular news with an emphasis on hard, macabre crime. It's unlikely that Puerto Vallarta figures much in this type of hype but you never know. The bullet-ridden bodies of two dead drug traffickers in Tijuana adorned the front page. Pages three and four contained the story of a man in Culiacán hacked to death by a jealous husband wielding a machete. Photos of the bloodied corpse were strewn across the pages like strips of his shredded clothing. The middle section revealed before and after pictures of two police officers found dead in Ciudad Juárez. They were killed mob style—a single bullet between the eyes. Someone had taken the time to clean them up for their pictures—close-ups with eyes closed in peaceful grace, as though embalmed. The article said drug gangs killed them which, to my mind, didn't exclude corrupt fellow officers. Towards the end of the paper it was reported that two suspected kidnappers were beaten by an angry neighborhood mob in Mexico City and left in the street to die. They survived but their faces resembled the spoiled remains of stuffed pomegranates. There was no mention of a big police raid anywhere. I chased down the last of a taco with Fanta; an article on the last page with a nondescript photo caught my eye. The picture was of a male corpse lying facedown in the sand. *That picture could have been taken of anyone most anywhere.* The article said that the thirty- to thirty-five-year-old man had a broken neck, arm and ankle and was discovered south of the Regina Hotel, Puerto Vallarta. *Sounds like the marina to me. Could be the same body I read about in this morning's local paper.* In the popular style of the rag, there was plenty of speculation as to motive—drugs, a jealous husband, a drunken brawl—but robbery seemed the likely reason for the murder as nothing was found on the body. In the picture the victim's clothes appeared dry, but the article said they were damp and mentioned that drownings don't usually produce that kind of physical damage. An autopsy was pending and the victim remained unidentified.

Must be the same body. There couldn't have been two *unidentified dead bodies found in Vallarta yesterday. This is probably the only unidentified victim in the entire paper.*

I began scouring the paper for unidentified dead bodies. Pepe spoke up: "What happened to your eye?"

"Fell off my bicycle."

"You have a bicycle?"

"My girlfriend bit me."

"Told you about hot-blooded Latin girls."

"I was beaned in a baseball game."

"You were fighting."

"Got kicked by a horse. Un caballo muy bravo. Why do I always get the spirited bruto...?"

"So how does the other guy look?"

"I was too busy stealing his girlfriend to care."

"Oh. Claro. So you deserved it."

"She was worth it. How come no one reported last night's raid?"

Pepe snorted, "Aye cabrón. Always looking for a story. Maybe that is why you have a black eye. Pues...let me tell you something. When the policía want it in the news you will read about it."

I gibed: "There really was no raid..."

"Ask him." Pepe nodded at the man standing at the counter four stools down from me. "Oye, Fernando," Pepe motioned with his hand.

Fernando laid pesos on the counter and stepped on over. He was an older man, early fifties, of medium build with a full crop of groomed hair a shade lighter than his gray off-the-rack suit. His white, pinstriped shirt had been relieved of a tie. Fernando's austere bearing slackened when Pepe asked him to repeat his story for us.

"Híjole," Fernando said. "Such a waste. They disturbed the entire neighborhood for nothing. I was driving home when I see these flashing lights in front of me blocking traffic, so I decide to take a different route to my house when I see lights behind me. 'Hijo de la chingada,' I said to myself, 'They are after me!' But I could not imagine for what. Then I thought maybe my wife and family were in trouble and said a prayer. I pulled over and those hijos de puta drive right by me. 'Aye cabrón,' I said to myself, 'Why are you so nervous? You have done nothing and your family is fine. They cannot arrest you for simply *thinking* about killing your mother in law!' "

We laughed at his punch line.

"You live out there?" I asked. "Did you see the place they raided?"

"I live close by. The apartment, duplex, was empty. Policía, they like to make a big show. But all they got was a Jeep..." I proffered him a skeptical smirk. "I passed by when they were searching it," he added.

"The Jeep or the duplex?"

"The duplex. But I heard that a Jeep was confiscated a block or so from there."

"Was it a duplex or a house? What were they looking for?"

"A duplex. Nobody knows. Drugs, dealers...maybe."

I nodded knowingly, "Cartel gangsters."

"Maybe. But this is not Mazatlán or Acapulco. The cartels do not have an infrastructure here."

"Did you ever see the people who lived in the duplex?"

"Sometimes. But I never spoke to them. The policía, they asked everyone about them but nobody knows anything."

"Did you talk to the policía? How many lived in the duplex?"

Fernando leveled a wary stare at Pepe. Pepe winked at it. "Careful. He is a writer."

"A writer?!?" Fernando glared at me. "Puta madre," he said under his breath.

"No se preocupe," I reassured him. Don't worry. "The raid has nothing to do with what I write about. I am a sports writer. But when I heard about the raid it made me curious."

"I am also curious." Fernando spit behind me into the street. "But I know that, like food, drink, and women, too much curiosity can kill you... What happened to your eye?"

"I sliced up some Arab terrorists last night."

Fernando shot Pepe a startled glance, as though offended rather than surprised at my glib remark. Had he heard the terrorist rumor? I couldn't tell. The thin smile creasing his softened expression was unrevealing.

"No, I did not speak to the policía," he said, eyeing me now, "or the federales. But with a story like that, the policía may want to talk to *you*, amigo."

Fernando saluted abruptly and left.

So federales were *there also.*

I quickly pondered Fernando's response to my bluster about Arab terrorists. He wasn't giving up any information at all about the identity of those in the duplex so I'd hit him with some glib bravado to needle him, maybe force a hasty, revealing response. A cute journalistic trick on my part but he sure seemed to get defensive about it. Practically threatening. Yet I couldn't deduce much from his posture, certainly nothing to refute or support the terrorist rumor. "That guy is a lot more serious than I first thought," I said to Pepe.

"He is chief of the work crew at the Washington Hotel." Pepe shook his head with a smirk. "Try to be careful, Russell. If that terrorist rumor spreads, it will be bad for business."

13

IT was well before nine p.m. and Lieutenant Benito Cuevas Romero had already made a Sunday killing. Police payouts (entres) to Comandantes are always made in cash and the lieutenant accepted nothing less from both the preventativa (petty crime/public security) and investigativa (serious crime) branches of the department. In exchange for desirable shifts and promotions, cops are required to pay up a portion of the daily money extorted from pimps, whores, johns, smugglers, illegal liquor vendors, drug dealers, drug addicts, drunk and disorderly tourists, drunk and disorderly locals, drunk and disorderly drivers, sober drivers who may not have broken any law, and general scum. The dedication of Arena Vallarta had gone smoothly enough but, as it was spring break, Vallarta was packed with tourists in addition to your usual riffraff and those in town for the dedication. Vallarta police had more than their usual opportunities to extort money this Sunday. Financially speaking, the timing of Lieutenant Romero's unexpected temporary promotion to Comandante (he was still officially a lieutenant) could only have been better had he taken over for the entire weekend, but he still made a Sunday killing.

And the evening had just begun.

Extra security forces in town for the dedication had left Vallarta. The department remained on high alert however, not only on the lookout for opportunities to extort money but for gangsters who escaped Saturday's raid...and the killer responsible for a homicide at the marina. Police headquarters was abandoned to Lula at dispatch, a handful of drunk and disorderlies in a holding tank, two officers, and Lieutenant Romero.

Despite his burgeoning Sunday windfall, Lieutenant Romero was unnerved. Something in the coroner's preliminary autopsy report of the dead man found at the marina raised more questions than answers. So he called on the best man available to help him sort things out. The best man period. A junior officer who was involved in the investigation.

"Thank you for coming in on your day off, Pedro," he said. "Sunday is usually my day off as well but not all Sundays are equal and the department has been under unusual stress this weekend, as you know. And since your expertise has already been required in this particular investigation, I thought you might help me clarify a few details tonight."

Pedro Santos leaned forward in his chair, his face bright and eager. Beat officers tossed him a bone—ten, twenty, fifty pesos—most every day for routine research. But when ranking officers like the lieutenant or el comandante asked him for special assistance he knew an extra hundred, two-hundred pesos or more could be coming his way.

The lieutenant had surprised Pedro with his Sunday evening phone call. The junior officer was further surprised to find him sitting behind el comandante's desk here at police headquarters. The lieutenant offered a brief explanation—something about el comandante being on an indefinite leave of absence—but in Pedro's station as the department's unofficial Investigative Analyst, police politics were none of his concern. He never had to pay entres because nobody in the department could manage a computer like him. His job and work shifts were pretty much guaranteed, and his promotion to the currently vacant rank of Sergeant On Duty *En Casa* (In House—headquarters) all but secured, if Pedro chose to dedicate himself to the police force for another couple of years. He'd been told as much by el comandante.

FINDING DEVO

Sounds good, Investigative Analyst. As if Pedro examined evidence from conspiracy cases and homicides on a daily basis. He examined crime evidence on occasion, weekly sometimes, but Vallarta simply didn't have the high-crime rates of Mexico's major cities. Aside from the research individual officers requested, Pedro's duties basically consisted of editing and uploading police reports into the department's database and updating the computers at headquarters when needed. Yet Pedro also had a couple of other things going for him. Two indispensable natural assets: an incisive mind and affable personality, each of which made him invaluable when his superiors needed someone to bounce ideas off of or to offer insights into an investigation.

Via the Internet and books, Pedro educated himself in a variety of subjects, including criminal investigation and forensic pathology. He also augmented his studies with regular viewings of the television program CSI. He got a kick out of how CSI's endoscopy camera transported viewers through the damaged bodies of murder victims. And the science, mitochondrial DNA analyses and the like, fascinated him.

Right up until Pedro got a chance to visit the county coroner, Antonio Infunto, in action and up close, he had considered forensic pathology as a future career. The vomit he left on the floor of the morgue and the loss of his healthy appetite for a day convinced him otherwise. Antonio could snack on a sandwich in the midst of the deathly stench of blood and guts; Pedro couldn't even hold down breakfast.

At times, Pedro also fancied himself a detective. This wasn't necessarily due to watching CSI or any other television program but his reading. Throughout his young, largely autodidactic life (school was a bore), he entertained himself with all kinds of books, often times detective books. Mario Vargas Llosa, Ignacio Taibo, as well as Spanish translations of old-time North American authors—Raymond Chandler and Mickey Spillane—all occupied space on his bookshelves at home, as did the Englishman, Conan Doyle.

Pedro identified most with Doyle's Sherlock Holmes. This wasn't an intellectual sleight at private eyes such as Mike Hammer or Héctor Belascoarán Shayne, it was just that, as he put himself in the hero's shoes, Pedro saw himself as better suited to the refined techniques of Sherlock Holmes rather than the bust-their-heads-and-balls approach employed by the likes of Spillane's Mike Hammer. Logic was always paramount with Holmes. Brains over brawn. He was prepared to kill but never fooled into brawling, never had to get himself bloodied to solve a crime.

77

The exciting fictional lives of detectives rarely matched reality though. Pedro understood this intuitively and from his interactions with police during his tenure in the department. In reality, he knew that detectives fought boredom at every turn—endless stakeouts, and a hundred dead-end leads for every one that amounted to anything. And in Vallarta, despite a spike in gang-related crime over the past year or so, few cases required authentic detective work. Police in the field were more apt to be occupied with mundane law enforcement or extorting suspects and criminals. On a personal level, extortion didn't agree with Pedro. It seemed a slippery slope that led to greater corruption throughout Mexico, especially in big cities and Mexico's drug-war hotspots where police consorted with drug cartels and gangsters and turned against one another, killed one another, or simply killed drug dealers for their drugs and money and then wound up dead themselves, murdered in a vengeance killing. A police officer had yet to be killed on duty during Pedro's short tenure in the Vallarta police force. And he hadn't come across a case of an officer killing a gangster or drug dealer for his drugs and money either, but that didn't mean it couldn't or didn't happen. So to keep himself from sliding down that slippery slope, Pedro shied away from fieldwork and only allowed his palms to be greased on the up-and-up—honestly and right out front—for information he provided as an investigative analyst; information he knew from memory, discovered with the help of a computer, and/or came upon through reasoning, like Sherlock Holmes! And as a young bachelor living with his parents (as most young adults do in Mexico), Pedro felt very well compensated for his work. So if the twenty-two-year-old doe-eyed junior officer with a dimpled smile and ebony curls that never stayed appeared happy to be of assistance to the lieutenant on a Sunday evening, in all probability he was. Other than el comandante, no one could boost Pedro's income like Lieutenant Romero.

"Happy to be of assistance, señor," Pedro said. "As you requested, I have been at work trying to decode that disc. Unfortunately, my home computer has given me the same negative results as the computers here."

"That is unfortunate, Pedro," said Lieutenant Romero. "The sooner you break that code the better. I will give you a couple more days before sending the disc to Guadalajara for analysis. But that is only one reason I called you here." The lieutenant extended the coroner's preliminary autopsy report to Pedro. "Have a look at this. It was delivered to dispatch a couple of hours ago."

Pedro accepted the folder, his nut-brown face cracking a grin. "With pleasure, señor." He quickly scanned the first page of the report. "What in particular concerns you, señor?"

"Time of death."

Lieutenant Romero appreciated the young man's enthusiasm almost as much as his intelligence. Pedro acted like a teenager with a new computer game whenever the lieutenant made a request of him. But the kid needed direction and seasoning. If his office work weren't so invaluable, the lieutenant would insist he get more field experience, maybe find the time to take him out in the field himself on occasion.

"Let me have a look here," Pedro said. "This must be the dead man who had the disc—"

"On whose person the disc was found, yes. I am expecting a full autopsy report within the week."

Pedro looked up from the report. "An *unidentified* male? I thought he was found with—"

"*Three* passports, Pedro. They may be forgeries. I have a police report for you to review after we take a look at this preliminary autopsy report."

"Still no suspects, señor?"

"Not yet, Pedro."

"Híjole. Who could get away with murder at the marina?"

"No one," the lieutenant said, a sharp edge to his voice. "Not if we can help it." He pointed his chin at the report in Pedro's hands.

Pedro read the report carefully, speaking up at intervals: "Broken neck as probable cause of death... No sign of asphyxiation or drowning..." he flipped a page. "Broken...broken... Absence of...absence of... Body temperature...rigor mortis...livor mortis." Pedro raised his eyes to the lieutenant. "Death probably occurred between three and six p.m. yesterday, señor."

"Yes Pedro. I have read it and know what it says but..." The lieutenant paused to get his thoughts in order...he'd spent most of the last hour immersed in the implications of this preliminary autopsy report...

"This was not a drowning or an accident, Pedro" he began academically, as though reciting a philosophical theory. "The victim suffered extensive damage: broken neck, arm and ankle. All the breaks are clean. No splintered bones or partial fractures. And there are no signs of blunt-force trauma or excess bruising. Not a single abrasion or laceration was left on the body. His clothing was not ripped or torn, and no skin tissue, blood, hair, or fibers were discovered under the dead man's fingernails or anywhere else on his person. No signs of a struggle at all. The victim appears to have been killed instantly,

79

without having been restrained, and there are no indications that a weapon, other than the killer's bare hands, was used to commit what I and the Vallarta Police Department have officially classified as a murder."

Pedro had his eyes on the report. "Bare hands..." he muttered. "By the looks of things..." Pedro flipped back to the top of the report. "I have to admit, señor," he said, eyes lifted to the lieutenant, "since there is no evidence that a weapon was used, all that remains are the killer's bare hands."

"What do you think of that, Pedro?"

Pedro pursed his lips studiously. "Extraordinary, señor," he said. "The absence of any signs of a struggle suggests that death occurred quickly. And the nature of the injuries..." Pedro stared back down at the report. "...no signs of blunt-force trauma or even a punch being thrown...and the victim was a grown man in apparent good health." He looked up at the lieutenant. "Sounds like something you might see in the movies—the killer takes a man's head in his hands and simply snaps his neck."

"Why break the man's arm and ankle as well?"

"Perhaps to immobilize the victim. But I would expect signs of a struggle to accompany those injuries." Pedro paused with a small shrug. "It almost seems like the arm and ankle were broken after the kill, for show, to confuse our investigation."

Lieutenant Romero leaned forward, hands folded on el comandante's desk. "Yes it does," he agreed, "and perhaps to make it appear as if more than one killer committed the murder."

Pedro hesitated... "You think a single assassin committed the murder, señor?"

"It takes an awful lot of strength and skill to break a man's neck," the lieutenant said pointedly, "especially like this, with such apparent alacrity. And if more than one killer were *needed* to inflict this kind of damage, signs of a struggle would be expected, at the very least restraining marks. Naturally, a single killer can produce indications of a struggle as well but, as there are *no* signs of a struggle or that the victim was restrained, I believe we may be dealing with a single, exceptionally dangerous individual who used the element of surprise and struck with great speed."

Lieutenant Romero regarded the junior officer's pensive expression. Pedro brought a hand to his chin, eyes narrow and calculating. "Have you a question, Pedro?"

Pedro straightened his posture. "If the victim knew his killers, señor, was friendly with them, it seems to me that more than one person could have attacked and killed him without leaving signs of a struggle."

The lieutenant had considered this. "Perhaps, Pedro," he said. "But even if you know your attackers or are friendly with them, you will sense danger and try to defend yourself once they close in on you, which would leave signs of a struggle. And the element of surprise diminishes as the number of people involved increases. It is much easier for one man to sneak up on another than two or three. As you said, this death happened quickly. I think instantly. The victim probably never saw his attacker coming. He was caught completely off guard. In my opinion this was a barehanded murder committed by a single assailant."

The lieutenant tilted his head at Pedro, an invitation to respond.

A little twinge in Pedro's chest quickened his pulse. Lieutenant Romero's analysis produced a sense of danger and excitement. Could a single man really have killed another in this fashion? Who might they be dealing with? "That sounds reasonable, señor," he said at length. "Once a victim is alerted to the danger we must expect him to fight for his life. Yet with perfect coordination and timing, I think two or more killers could have accomplished this murder, whether or not they were friendly with the victim or had to sneak up on him."

The Lieutenant reached for his pack of cigarettes on el comandante's desk. "Anything is possible, Pedro," he said. "But if more than one killer got their hands on the victim, pues, that is a lot of bodies, arms, legs, heads, hands and feet. Our victim would have been much more likely to have sustained excess bruising, had his clothing torn, or, at the very least, ended up with hair, skin, blood or fibers under his fingernails or somewhere on his person."

Pedro's cheeks dimpled as he mulled this over.

The lieutenant pulled a golden lighter from his breast pocket; smoke curled his lips as he spoke: "I believe we are dealing with a single killer but..." He waved his cigarette dismissively, "For all we know the victim was with acquaintances when one or more of them struck and killed him from behind. So let us set aside the question of a single assassin for now and consider the time of death again, Pedro. Is it consistent with the information contained in the report?"

Pedro replied as he reviewed the report once again: "It is very difficult to determine an exact time of death under these circumstances, señor, especially here in the tropics where a body's cooling rate is often impossible to measure accurately. Antonio, the coroner, made his estimate according to rigor and livor mortis which—"

The lieutenant interrupted in a forbearing tone: "Excuse me, Pedro. I know you have studied the subject and am sure it is fascinating. But without getting into too much detail, can you please just confirm for me that the report is consistent and accurate with regards to the time of death?"

Pedro frowned in concentration as he thumbed over a couple of pages in the report. "It certainly appears to be," he said.

"So death did in fact occur between three and six p.m. yesterday."

Pedro looked up from the report with a confident nod. "In all likelihood. Sí señor."

The lieutenant contemplated the ceiling for a moment. "What do you recall about the circumstances surrounding the body's discovery, Pedro?"

"Only what you told me last night when you gave me the disc to examine, señor: you and Officer Sánchez arrived at the scene in response to an anonymous tip received right after the raid at the duplex. The disc, drugs, money, and passports were found on the victim. No witnesses to the...what appeared to be a murder had come forward, and a suspect had yet to be apprehended or identified... You said Harbor Security had no idea who the victim was, and that no one in the general vicinity recognized the picture of the victim—the photo in one of the passports found on the body... Has a witness come forward?"

"Not yet, Pedro. Do you recall where at the marina the body was discovered?"

"Through the gates and across the lawn. Not far from the docks."

"And how populated is the marina at that time? Are there people around that area at that hour on a Saturday?"

"Most certainly, señor. Aside from Security there are fishing boats, tour boats. Tourists in general, señor... Are you asking why we have yet to find a witness to the homicide? Tourists walk across the lawn to get to and from the marina docks but do not generally congregate inside the gates once they are through the turnstiles... But it does seem strange that Security or—"

The lieutenant interrupted: "Hold that thought, Pedro. I am not specifically concerned with the lack of witnesses but you are on to something we need to explore." The lieutenant raised his voice in quiet reflection. "Police arrived immediately after receiving that anonymous tip—about seven thirty. Harbor Security also called police at about that time and when we arrived only the harbor master and Security knew that there was a dead man just out beyond the docks. Now, think about this. If death occurred between three and six...?"

FINDING DEVO

Pedro quickly grasped the lieutenant's meaning. "Why was it not reported between those hours? Someone should have stumbled across the body, or seen it from the docks."

"Unless?"

Pedro let the tingle of comprehension course through his brain and down his neck. The deduction could not be missed. He should have come to it right away! Pedro slapped a chastening hand to his forehead. "Unless the murder happened somewhere else," he said emphatically and fisted his hand at his ear, like he'd caught a fly. "The body was probably moved, señor, planted there at the marina after the murder took place. The marina was a crime scene, since the body was dumped there, but not the murder scene."

Lieutenant Romero flicked an ash from his cigarette into the ashtray on el comandante's desk, an ashtray for guests as el comandante didn't smoke. "A very astute way to put it, Pedro," he said, cigarette aloft. "But that leaves open another question. The disc, drugs, money, and passports were found on the body. And if the killer had time to move and plant the body, it seems there would be time to rob it as well. Naturally, the victim may have been robbed of something when he was killed, but were these other items planted on the body or already on the body and purposely left where they were?... Is it likely that the killer would have missed them or left them by mistake?"

Pedro laid the coroner's report upon el comandante's desk. "I doubt the killers...or...the assassin would have missed the items police found on the body, señor, or left them by mistake. He may not have cared what the victim had on his person but, well...he must have figured the body had *something* on it."

Lieutenant Romero took a long drag on his cigarette and considered another question: "Why did the assassin plant the body at the marina, Pedro?"

Pedro shook his head with a befuddled grimace. "Not just why, señor, but how? At that hour, it would seem nearly impossible to get away with murder at the marina or plant a dead body there without being seen."

The lieutenant stabbed out his cigarette in the ashtray and exhaled a steady stream of smoke. He'd been thinking about Pedro's question in one form or another since the body was first discovered. "The body was found seaside," he said, "on a patch of sand bordering the lawn above the seawall, about twenty meters from the docks. The entrance to the marina is well manned daily at that hour and there is no evidence that anyone cut through the razor-wire fencing surrounding the marina. It is possible that the killer was somehow able to pick the lock to the Harbor Master's gate, cross the lawn, leave the body, and then escape without being witnessed, but it seems highly unlikely, especially at that hour. It seems more likely that a boat was used to transport the body to the marina and as an escape craft. The murder may even have taken place on a boat. How the assassin was able to deposit the body up onto that patch of sand and then escape without being seen when it was still light out is a mystery. Evidently though, he managed it. The killer took one hell of a risk delivering the body to the marina like that and what I want to know is, why bother?"

"Why not just leave the body anywhere?"

"Exactamente. What did the killer gain by taking such a risk?"

Pedro slouched into a question mark. "He must have wanted us to find the body when and where we did for some reason," he said.

Lieutenant Romero leveled his large brown eyes on Pedro's. "The marina is a secure location," he said, "especially inside the gates and behind the fence where the docks are. The assassin must have known that, once planted there, the body would not be disturbed *or robbed* until we found it."

Pedro leaned back in his chair, doe eyes searching. "If that is the case then..."

"If all the assassin wanted was for us to find the body, Pedro, he could have left it just about anywhere."

Pedro ran a hand through his curls and let the lieutenant's insight sink in. "So he wanted us to find all that *evidence*," he intoned. "But was it planted on the body or simply left where it was on the body?"

"*That*," replied Lieutenant Romero, "is a good question. No fingerprints were found on the disc or its case but those on the passports and the bag of cocaine belong to the dead man." The lieutenant cocked an eyebrow at Pedro. "Why were no prints found on the disc and the victim's prints found on the passports and bag of drugs?"

Pedro answered without hesitation: "It suggests that the disc was planted, señor, and the other items left on the victim." He shook his head skeptically. "But we cannot be certain."

"Of course not, Pedro. But whatever evidence was planted or simply left on the body, one thing is certain: the killer wanted us to find the body when and where we did as well as the disc, passports, drugs and cash found on the victim; not to mention the keys to a Jeep...a Jeep found around the block from the raided duplex with more drugs and money inside."

"Really?" Pedro's eyes widened. "Any fingerprints in the Jeep?"

"The victim's fingerprints were all over the inside of the Jeep along with others we have yet to identify."

Pedro huffed in disbelief. "Whoever killed that man certainly left us a lot of evidence."

"And on purpose, Pedro. Someone risked life in prison by committing murder and then risked discovery by dumping the body at the marina, and it was done so we would find precisely what we found when we found it. But to what purpose? Why would the killer want us to find all these items along with the corpse?"

Pedro crossed his arms in a show of resolve. "We may not know the answer to that until we discover the motive for the murder."

Lieutenant Romero reposed in el comandante's chair. "It is possible," he said, "that evidence was left on the corpse so we would waste time examining useless clues like those passports and trying to decode that disc." He brought a pensive hand to his chin. "But I have a feeling there is much more to it than that. I doubt this assassin of ours has underestimated us. This was a well-calculated homicide. Whoever killed in that fashion and planted the body at the marina knows we are thinking of these things."

They fell silent for a short time. Lieutenant Romero reached for his pack of cigarettes but left them on the desk. Pedro mused, "It would help if we could confirm the victim's identity."

"Once Sandra at Immigration has completed her examination of the passports, we may have more to go on in that regard." The lieutenant planted his forearms on the desk and drew Pedro in with a confidential tone: "Leaving aside motive and the victim's identity, who do you think could have killed this man, planted the body at the marina, and escaped?"

Pedro shrugged, "Harbor Security?"

"Possible," the lieutenant said dubiously, "but unlikely. I know those people and cannot imagine—"

"The same man who could effectively break another man's neck, arm and ankle with his bare hands and not leave signs of a struggle?"

Lieutenant Romero held Pedro's inquisitive stare. "Yes," he agreed. "I do believe we are looking for a *man*, and maybe an accomplice or two who helped move the body and pilot a boat. Yet I am not convinced that this assassin needs accomplices. It looks to me as though he is a brutal, efficient killer of considerable strength and training capable of carrying out this operation on his own. He is probably accustomed to working alone. Fewer variables to deal with, and one man can act with greater stealth than two or three... He could be a hired killer." The lieutenant leaned back in el comandante's chair, a distant look in his eyes. "Your typical cartel gangster would have used a gun or a knife. This man could be a hired independent contractor; or maybe he killed for personal motives and gain... And he used his bare hands to kill..." The lieutenant refocused on Pedro. "That is extremely personal, though as of yet we cannot presume that the assassin had something personal against his victim or that he even knew him personally... And he toys with us for some reason—this business of planting the body at the marina and leaving the disc and other *evidence* to be found on the victim; the killer does not hesitate to take chances. He has no fear. He may even have left that anonymous tip about a dead man at the marina, a man he himself murdered."

Pedro stroked the thin stubble on his chin, nearly two-days growth. "Do you think there is a connection between the dead man and those who escaped the raid, señor? The murder might have occurred at approximately the same time as the raid, and the Jeep was parked around the block from the raided duplex."

The lieutenant nodded slowly. "Could be," he said. "And if there is a connection, then the dead man is likely a gangster, or associated with gangsters like that puto gangster *Paco* police arrested and I interrogated before and after the raid yesterday."

"The gangster, can we—"

"Federales took him to el DF. Apparently they feel he can be of use in a separate investigation. There is no connection that we know of between him and the dead man, so each case has its own file. Federales have yet to inquire about the murder and may not know about it yet."

Pedro's eyes shied away from the lieutenant's. He had a nervous hunch that the prisoner's departure was somehow related to el comandante's and might have been politically motivated—tied to federal, state, and local law enforcement power plays...and payoffs. He always kept himself removed from police politics and had absolutely no desire to delve into the sordid subject now.

Lieutenant Romero slouched in his chair. "Puta," he muttered. "Should the victim turn out to be a gangster..." He buried his fists in his armpits, a vacant look of resignation on his face. "He may very well be a gangster and, if federales had not taken the evidence and copies of the reports pertaining to the raid along with the prisoner, we could claim he was killed during the raid. At least we would have something to show for our efforts..."

The lieutenant's words struck an uneasy chord in Pedro's mind and disparate threads of the case were suddenly joined by a disturbing hypothesis. Pedro's insight went to motive. He shifted uneasily in his chair, unsure how to go about expressing it.

"Something else on your mind, Pedro?" the lieutenant asked.

Pedro hesitated, and qualified his thoughts with the self-evident: "Even if we could take credit for killing him, señor, there is still a killer or killers at large."

"Sí, Pedro. It was just an idle musing."

"Excuse me, señor. I hope you do not think this an impertinent observation."

"You are an exceptionally bright young man, Pedro. Any observation you have is certain to aid in the investigation."

Pedro steeled himself, smoothed his trousers and placed the palms of his hands over his knees. "Maybe the assassin is setting us up, señor."

The lieutenant's large brown eyes shrank behind a befuddled frown. "How so?"

"The timing of the murder is beginning to bother me, señor, and the timing of the anonymous tip. With our police needing something to show for the raid and all I...well... Maybe the killer knew about the raid, knew that the duplex was empty, and that police would either take credit for killing that man found at the marina...or...uh...be blamed for it, señor."

"Blamed for it? You think police can be framed for this murder?"

"Just a thought, señor. It seems the killer could have waited an hour or two to deliver the body to the marina. The conditions are about the same with regards to security, the number of tourists, and the probability of the body being robbed, but the cover of darkness would have made it easier to carry out the operation without being witnessed. Yet he chose a time that coincided with the raid. The window for the time of death even coincides with the raid. And if he purposely left evidence for us, he may have also kept evidence, concealed evidence that could come to light and implicate—"

The lieutenant raised a hand, cutting Pedro off in mid-sentence. He brought his hand to the bridge of his nose, eyes closed, as though battling a sudden wave of fatigue.

Pedro shrank into his chair and silently cursed himself. He'd always vowed not to get involved in police politics and had just blundered into the subject with his "observation." Federales and police were often at odds, and who else but federales would try to "blame" police for killing the victim found at the marina? Who else but federales would the assassin leak evidence and information to in order to frame police? Or... Pedro shuddered and fought to keep his anxious hands squeezed together in his lap. Had he just suggested that federales might have murdered the man found at the marina? Could federales be planning on framing police for the murder? Had they yet to inquire about the murder because they already knew about it?

SEVE VERDAD

Pedro bunched his fingers, his pulse quickening in his throat. This was no time to panic, lose himself in unsubstantiated assumptions. One thing was not an assumption however: he'd gone too far with his observation, almost an accusation. Borderline insubordination, Pedro thought, fearing that his suggestion of a setup would obligate the lieutenant to respond with a reprimand in defense of himself and the department...

But Lieutenant Romero was merely taking a few seconds to digest the simplicity of Pedro's idea. The horrifying truth to it. Could federales, once they found out about the homicide, possibly make some sort of connection between the dead man and the raid that would implicate the lieutenant and el comandante in murder, the killing of a gangster for his drugs and money? No, not murder. He and el comandante had, at the very least, plausible alibis. Accessory to murder? Maybe, if federales received information, clues into the case that the lieutenant didn't have. Was this assassin that smart? Why not? His timing had certainly been perfect. Police were already in the vicinity raiding a duplex. Maybe the assassin could leak further evidence and information that would finger police for killing the victim and dumping his corpse at the marina.

Was the assassin a police officer? A military man? A federale? Mexican Intelligence—CISEN? Was he out to get him and the department for some insane reason? Lieutenant Benito Cuevas Romero fought off a fierce desire to find the killer at once, a sense of urgency and paranoia he knew did him no good. With patience he would get his man, and when he did...

The lieutenant blinked his eyes open and folded his hands upon the desk, his Latin-lover looks a flawless dispassionate mask. "Now that I think about it, Pedro, I have to admit that your observation has merit."

Pedro released a small sigh of relief. Lieutenant Romero was a reasonable man and would not reprimand him for an innocent observation. "I just thought it seemed like a possibility, señor," he said.

"Anything is possible, Pedro, until you uncover the truth. Then the truth is all that is left. And I must say, the possibility that this murder could be some sort of frame-up makes it all the more important to solve it quickly."

"Sí señor."

Lieutenant Romero retrieved a folder of reports from a desk drawer and handed it to Pedro along with a two-hundred-peso note. "These police reports and that preliminary autopsy report will be of assistance. A little more investigative experience for you, Pedro. This case is a puzzler... And keep at that disc. I remind you that it is your personal responsibility. You are not to seek outside help, for now. That goes for the case in general."

"Sí señor." Pedro stuffed the two-hundred-peso note into a pocket as he stood to leave, reports in hand. "Gracias señor."

Before Pedro left el comandante's office, Lieutenant Romero told him to report back to him tomorrow morning to review the case further. They could not allow it to grow cold.

14

A fat orange moon hung over the mountains. There was a fiesta up in those hills. Mountain's fiesta at a house he rented six months out of the year. The higher you climb into the lush forest above Old Vallarta the higher the value of the home, many worth well over a million dollars. I considered taking a cab to the party but it seemed a splendid evening for a hike up into the woods. I found fortification for the journey through the swinging saloon doors of El Cabezón (The Big Head), a fairly popular local dive in Old Vallarta not given to much tourist traffic.

El Cabezón is named for an old-time Mexican outlaw who may or may not have carried a big head on his shoulders but did, as legend has it, heft an oversized helmet on the nightstick beneath his trousers. El Cabezón met his demise when he was shot in that legendary big head, a target that, apparently, could not be missed. Details about his life of crime are sketchy. He is supposed to have been a species of Robin Hood who specialized in robbing trains and banks and may have partnered-up with Pancho Villa during the Mexican revolution. Jorge, the owner of El Cabezón, has never been able to validate El Cabezón's legend to my satisfaction and I've yet to uncover any evidence to suggest that he is anything more than a maudlin Mexican invention.

To advance the legend of El Cabezón, the walls of El Cabezón are decorated with crooked images of gangsters, outlaws, and notorious heroes: a fresh-faced sketch of Joaquín Murrieta on horseback, dark hair flowing and raised fist clutching a dagger; Butch Cassidy and the Sundance Kid (a black and white shot of Paul Newman and Robert Redford sprinting and shooting into a Bolivian fusillade); Pancho Villa ensconced in the Mexican Presidential Chair, brimming with laughter and wild overconfidence (an absurd buffoon compared to the sullen, suspiciously handsome Emiliano Zapata seated next to him); Alfonso Bedoya as the smiling bandit Gold Hat in 'Treasure of the Sierra Madre', his cunning eyes and toothy grin angered in the midst of his famous line, "We don't need no stinking badges"; the Ochoa brothers (drinks all around at a fancy restaurant); a color, double-breasted portrait of Al Pacino as Scarface; Pablo Escobar pointing an accusatory finger at the hijo de puta photographer; and, of course, Al Capone mug shots—profile and full-face—, as well as a frontal full-length portrait of him in an immaculate pearl gray fedora and fine Italian threads.

A colorful framed caricature of a mustachioed man in a bandolier and sombrero holds a place of honor above and behind the bar. It's said to be a rendition of El Cabezón but doesn't convince me of the truth of his legend. Many stills, sketches, and portraits hang on the walls of El Cabezón, none of which are definitive renditions or agreeable proofs of El Cabezón himself. But that doesn't stop patrons of El Cabezón from insisting that El Cabezón did in fact exist before, during, or after the invention of the camera. Debate on the subject is usually lighthearted, though some take it downright personal if you don't believe in El Cabezón. An obvious response is to grab your crotch and exclaim, "I do believe!" I got some laughs that way once, yet such behavior could prove risky in the company of rough customers should they take the joke seriously and force you to prove your faith.

El Cabezón has overhead fans and lighting, a jukebox, bar, tables, chairs, and three booths against the wall as you enter. Prices are Mexican. Women generally occasion the joint accompanied by men, but a few work there.

The place was in good spirits tonight. Not too crowded but festive. A trio of guitarists played music for patrons at one of the tables. Two couples danced behind them. I took a seat at the bar and got the barmaid's attention. A pleasant-looking brunette with a terse mouth. I asked her if Jorge was around. She said he didn't work Sundays and was out of town until Tuesday. I ordered a Cuba libre. The drink was gone the moment it touched my lips.

Not enough rum.

As the term Cuba libre literally means "free Cuba," I asked for another with "más Fidel."

"More rum?" She held up the bottle.

"Sí... Poor Cuba..."

She rounded out the refrain, "Has never been free," and averted her eyes.

"So add more Fidel and let it all go to hell," I clucked.

FINDING DEVO

She sat my drink on the bar with a reluctant half-smile and turned to rinse out some glasses in the sink.

Be cute if she was friendly.

I drank, swiveled on my stool, and was ensnared by my reflection in the mirror behind the bar. My black eye seemed to darken by the second. I refocused on the familiar visage staring back at me. The bruise maintained its color. A notable crescent shadow. It would've added panache to my banal poetry if I was heavyweight champion of the world. Applause rang out in response to the music. I chugged my drink and laid sixty pesos on the bar. The guitarists belted out a ballad as I reached the saloon doors: "Yo soy un hombre sincero..."

There would be no music the next time I visited El Cabezón.

THE moon had become an immaculate silver saucer suspended over Vallarta like a masterpiece hung in a museum. Thoroughfare traffic was thick so I walked the side streets. The shops were all closed but a handful of restaurants and bars remained open as well as a few small stores selling sodas and snacks. Sections of plaster walls were dull and peeling, others freshly painted in varying shades of gray and white. Rich aromas from the occasional taco stand attracted me. There would be plenty of food at the party so I resisted the temptation. I passed numerous family dwellings. All the windows were barred but curtains were drawn and doors left open. I idly observed families dining, watching TV, and lounging in their living rooms. Some family members had brought chairs out onto the uneven sidewalks where they socialized and minded half-naked children.

A scrawny stray dog slunk away from me at the foot of the steps that led to the highway. I paused and recalled that the climb up to Mountain's place was excellent, if you enjoy lots of reps and working up a sweat. I took off my shirt, hung it from my khaki cargo shorts at the hip, and began a leisurely ascent. Two gringo couples greeted me up at the highway with a "buenas noches" before beginning their descent. I marched south along the highway and looked out over Old Vallarta. The rustic town hummed with lights, traffic, and faint timbres of music. Looming condo and hotel edifices partially obstructed the glistening waters of Banderas Bay. I crossed the highway and climbed another set of stairs up into the forest. The stairs crested at a plateau just off a residential road. I took in the view once again. A phalanx of deep-purple clouds made the horizon out beyond the bay; a few yachts dotted the moonlit waters. The colonial style pirate ship built for tourists cruised the coast in my direction—from the malecón towards Old Vallarta's Los Muertos shoreline. Its high masts were decorated with lights. The ship was much larger than the yachts and loaded with spring breakers. Beyond the malecón, a thick shimmering line of upscale hotels tapered north several miles to the marina. The pueblo Bucerías glittered halfway up the coast; above that I could make out the silhouette of Punta de Mita, the northern point of the bay. My gaze dropped back down to Vallarta and settled on the illuminated crown atop the bell tower of Nuestra Señora de Guadelupe Temple—Vallarta's most recognizable feature.

My eye didn't hurt so much when I dabbed sweat from my forehead and face with the tail of my shirt, just enough to remind me how easy it is to get into trouble, how suddenly life can change and that I was lucky to only have a black eye...

That seemed like a bunch of crap, like when you're down and out and someone tells you things could be worse. Is that supposed to make you feel better? Does it actually make things better? Fuck no! *Things can always be worse, shithead!* What would've been better is if the other guy got the black eye and I stole his girlfriend.

I walked up the street and thought about Rosalita. Nobody told me things could be worse when she died. Could things get any worse than that?

Is that what I'm supposed to think about when I'm down to make me feel better? how bad things can get?

I resolved to punch the next sonuvabitch who said "things could be worse" to me.

A block up the street more stairs deposited me onto a path that snaked amongst the woods to Mountain's pad. I took a short breather on the darkened trail, not because I was tired but to dim the flaring anger in my chest—a pernicious feeling I'd been suffering since Rosalita died. The anger was preferable to hideous depression but could be equally destructive...and I'd learned how to tame it. After about thirty seconds my pulse and mind steadied.

I continued up the trail and paused when Mountain's place came into view; an unassuming structure nestled neatly in the forest on a one-acre parcel. Once you're invited inside and walk the grounds, it quickly becomes clear that it's far from a modest cottage. From my vantage point below the clearing and chain-link fence, I could see smoke from the barbecue and people milling about on the deck in front of the dining room's sliding glass doors. I'd been a guest of Mountain's in that house. The place was divided into about five primary sections with the garage and front entrance on the far side facing a road. I followed the trail and perimeter fence, passed Mountain's house to my left, rounded the seven-foot hedge trimming the near edge of the lawn, and crossed the lawn to the front door.

There was female laughter and a bass rhythm. Someone broke a glass in the kitchen. I put on my shirt and sunglasses and punched the doorbell.

15

PEDRO was confused. For one thing, he wasn't a professional computer nerd or hacker but simply a guy with a high degree of computer smarts. He was a decent computer technician and had significantly increased the power and capacity of his own computer along with those at police headquarters. But he had no doubt that Lieutenant Romero could find someone more qualified to crack the encrypted disc found on the dead man, both in Vallarta and Guadalajara. He could recommend someone to him right here in town, as well as two computer experts in the Guadalajara Police Department with access to computers more powerful than any in Vallarta. Why was he sticking with him? For some reason Lieutenant Romero wanted the case of the dead man found at the marina to remain within the Vallarta department for now. That was fine with Pedro, he just couldn't figure out why? It must have something to do with that embarrassing botched raid and el comandante's mysterious leave of absence. Police politics. Best not to think about it.

Another reason Pedro was confused had to do with the disc itself. The disc had demanded "keys" (in English) when he first tried to gain access to it yesterday on a computer at police headquarters. Pedro understood this to mean that the disc was encrypted and required a password or phrase to access. In order to gain access to the disc Pedro needed to break the encryption or code—the algorithm. Given modern encryption technology, this was a daunting task even for a professional computer expert with access to the most advanced and powerful computers designed to crack algorithms. If Pedro could get a hold of the computer on which the disc had been encoded—its hard drive and algorithms—he stood a better chance. And if he had more information, personal data on the person who had encoded the disc, he might get lucky and guess the password or phrase. Pedro could also get lucky with the brute-force number-and-sign-crunching technique he was currently employing in search of the algorithm. This technique (represented by a number count at the bottom of his computer screen) is akin to trying to break a combination lock by going through all the possible combinations of numbers—a long shot for success against encrypted discs even with a computer far more powerful than Pedro's.

All this Pedro understood very well. What confused him, however, was a message that had begun flashing in the center of his computer screen: La invasión empezó hace años... México siempre llega tarde a las fiestas.

(The invasion began years ago... Mexico always arrives late to parties.)

A message from the disc. But the number count at the bottom of his screen—numbers changing and shifting like a haywire car odometer—indicated that the disc's code hadn't been broken. They would stop and set once the code was broken. Clearly, the code had not been broken; so why, after twenty-four hours, did the disc suddenly decide to reveal a message? And what did the message mean?

The reference to Mexico always arriving late for fiestas was a common refrain. Pedro understood it as a cute turn-of-phrase expressed by Mexicans to acknowledge that their country lags far behind much of the world when it comes to technological, economic, even athletic achievement. A poetic way of saying that a country with Mexico's resources and population should not be so screwed up with poverty and corruption. Simple enough. An accepted truism. But what was this about an invasion? The world is always full of invasions and wars involving dozens and hundreds of tribes and countries. Which did it refer to? and how did it relate to Mexico always arriving late for fiestas?

The message seemed meaningless and muddled Pedro's thoughts. He cleared his head, let his mind stray from his computer and drift out the screened window to the almond tree reflected in the moonlight, its pale trunk spitting distance from his unvarnished confines—his home office. The office he shared with his father, Enrique Santos. It had been constructed by his father and older brother, Alejandro, almost as an afterthought once the house was completed. The office soon became Pedro's favorite refuge, though his father often occupied it as well. They'd work their own projects together at their respective desks, the overhead fan a whirl and the window open, each respectful of the other's space, showing interest in one another's work without intruding, like they were constructing distinct pillars of the same monument—home and family.

Family. Alejandro had his own now. Pedro was in no hurry to start one but knew he would one day. That's the way of the world, isn't it?

Now he began thinking about girls. An old girlfriend, two girls he was dating... Marriage? Pedro shuddered. The mere thought of marriage was enough to snap him back to reality. He'd rather think about the incessant blinking on his computer screen. A veiled message...left by an assassin?

One assassin or multiple assassins? Pedro wasn't convinced of the lieutenant's lone-assassin theory, but whoever killed that man at the marina could be deranged and might have left a deranged message. Yet the killer had demonstrated a great deal of cunning. What had the lieutenant said about him? Pedro heard his dispassionate candor: "Whoever killed in that fashion and planted the body at the marina knows we are thinking of these things... He also toys with us for some reason... The killer has no fear." Was the killer toying with Pedro right now? Did he know who had the disc?

A stray dog. That's what snapped twigs outside. And the rustling? Birds in the almond tree. Pedro gulped the stark breeze wafting through the window and took hold of his desk, steadying himself against an unfamiliar, foreboding shiver. A door opened from beyond the office walls behind him. The front door to the house! He swiveled his chair around and instantly froze, his mind reeling in disbelief, stunned by inexplicable fear. Fear of the unknown. Fear of...?

His brother, Eduardo. Home before ten on a Sunday evening. Pedro could hear him talking with their mother, Beti, in the living room. Eduardo asked where papi was. Ma said she expected him soon. He was out with union workers from el DF who had come to town for the dedication of Arena Vallarta. They both agreed that the dedication had gone exceptionally well.

Pedro shook his head, chiding himself for his paranoia. The house was secure. Locked up tight. Even his office window, open to the evening air, was barred. And the killer wasn't after him anyway... What nonsense.

Like that blinking message.

What invasion? Which? Had Mexico been invaded? Maybe. Many parts of the country seemed to be in a perpetual state of war against narco gangs and cartels. And the militarized Zapatistas in Chiapas were always a thorn in the government's side. But weren't these groups homegrown? Foreigners probably only accounted for a small percentage of their numbers and by definition "invasion" meant a foreign incursion, like when the gringos chased Pancho Villa from New Mexico across Chihuahua, the last time Mexico had literally been invaded. But that was during the Mexican Revolution a century ago. The disc couldn't be referring to that, could it?

Perhaps Mexico was the victim of a different kind of invasion. An economic and cultural invasion...perpetrated by the American colossus to the north? Is that why Mexico lagged, was late for fiestas?

But this was an old message, a convenient explanation, an excuse for Mexico's shortcomings. If it wasn't the oldest message in Mexico it was certainly one of the most repeated.

Pedro mumbled, "Pobre México, tan lejos de Dios y tan cerca de los Estados Unidos."Why would someone design an encoded disc in order to deliver a message everyone in Mexico had already received?

Could "invasion" refer to Mexicans crossing the border illegally into the United States? No. That was one fiesta Mexico wasn't late for. To Pedro's mind, the message made no sense. And why did the disc reveal a message when it hadn't been decoded? He made some clicks and shifts on his keyboard in an effort to get his taskbar or toolbar to appear, so he could try to fast forward the disc's images.

Nothing.

A spasm of irritation washed over his concentration. Pedro glared at his computer sitting on the corner of his desk, at the slot containing the disc. Had the disc taken control of his computer somehow? Did it contain a virus? Should he remove it? If he did, would he have to wait another twenty-four hours for it to begin revealing its contents again...?

He stared at the message, stared at the number count, stared at the time in the bottom corner, and stared at the message again. The message wasn't there an hour ago. As far as he knew, the disc hadn't revealed anything else since he stuck it into his computer, unless something had appeared and disappeared on the monitor when he wasn't in his office to see it. The message—white block lettering against a gray backdrop—flashed in his eyes. On and off, on and off...in perfect cadence. One second on, the next off. One second on, the next off. As if...keeping time?

Pedro rose from his desk and shifted his attention to the computer behind him on his father's desk. He would go online and learn more about disc decryption...*timed* disc decryption.

16

MI amigo Armando *La Montaña* (Mountain) Montoya was a helluva football player. American football—fútbol americano. A certifiable beast who tore up the Canadian league and then wreaked havoc in the NFL for a couple of seasons. Yet he claimed to never really care for the sport. Mountain preferred soccer but his tremendous girth had prevented him from excelling at it. He was a natural athlete—shot-putter, wrestler, baseball catcher—and played Mexican fútbol americano at the University of the Americas (UDLA) outside of Puebla, Mexico, before transferring to San Diego State University in southern California and NCAA college ball. After his senior season, the NFL passed on him so he opted for the Canadian Football League. He gained a tidy sum as well as two Defensive Player of the Year awards playing defensive tackle for the pro team in Ottawa and finally made it to the NFL. A guaranteed contract. Five million for three years with the Miami Dolphins. Then he blew his knee out in the last game of his second season, ending his career at the ripe old age of twenty-eight. That was about four years ago. He returned to his roots in Guadalajara shortly thereafter. His injury made him somewhat bitter and increased his apathy for the sport, but that didn't stop him from frequenting sports bars when big fútbol americano games from the States were on TV.

Though his athletic career had given him more than a measure of prestige, Armando Montoya remained a bit self-conscious of his physical enormity and over compensated with an aloof, sometimes irascible bearing, especially around those he didn't care for. Those to his liking, however, would encounter a surprisingly good-natured fellow with a sharp, wry wit. We'd met a few years ago at a bar here in Vallarta when I bought him and his friends, Mario and Miguel, a round or two during a televised soccer match between two teams from the Mexican League. I awoke the next day on his couch, in this same house where he was now throwing a party.

A lanky adolescent male with spiked green hair answered the door. He wore a small loop earring and yellow sunglasses with lenses shaped like American footballs.

"Nice shades," I said.

His face lost some luster within a questioning frown. I repeated myself in Spanish.

"Gracias. Yours too. Come in. You are a friend of Armando's?"

"Sí." I stepped into the foyer. Mambo music came from the living room stereo. I introduced myself. We shook hands. He told me his name was Sergio, "Armando's nephew." Sergio twirled car keys on a finger, like he was ready to get rollin' somewhere.

"Help yourself to anything you like," he said. "Drinks over there," he nodded to the wet-bar in the living room where I recognized brothers Mario and Miguel on the brocade couch. They were sitting with several others around Mountain's hand-hewn oak coffee table, "and food and wine in the kitchen," Sergio pointed off to his right.

"You going somewhere?" I asked him distractedly. Through the living room's expansive window a young woman was sitting poolside playing guitar amongst four or five guests. A dead ringer for my china doll; out of those tight jeans and into a mauve dress.

"Sí," Sergio said. "Some friends are waiting for me. Nos vemos."

Sergio shut the door behind him. Beyond the partition wall to my left, two girls were giggling over a round chopping block in the middle of the kitchen. One bent over and swept up remnants of a broken glass, but the blond saw me. I shot her a smile, wagged my fingers at her. She raised her glass of wine to me and said something to her friend. I considered joining them but was detained by an abusive burst of Spanish from the living room.

"Campéon!" Mario chortled at me. Champion! "You really kicked the hell out of that cabrón at the cockfights last night."

His brother, Miguel, chimed, "A pathetic performance. Bring me a margarita, Russell, so we can drink to forget it."

I stepped down onto the living room carpet. The brothers beamed at me. Miguel, with his long, more plentiful hair and ever present brown stubble of a beard, was the wild one. In his mid-twenties, he was into surfing, soccer, beer and, of course, chasing women. His blue jeans, sneakers and polo shirt were in accord with my knee-length shorts, button-down rayon shirt and teal-blue running shoes. Miguel works with his brother (according to Mario, not enough). Mario, the elder, is married with children, runs a boutique with a number of employees, and exhibits a natty wardrobe along with a nascent potbelly and balding pate. He wore pleated navy blue slacks with matching loafers, and a tan silk shirt open at the collar to reveal he still had plenty of hair. A braided gold chain around his neck and silver Rolex on his wrist divulged his financial status. But most of his wealth is old money; the boutique has never been a huge moneymaker.

"I refused to fight because I only fight for love and money," I told the brothers. "Make me an offer."

Miguel dug a peso out of his pocket and flipped it to me. I let it fall to the carpet. "I can be bought," I shook my head gravely, "but I am not cheap." The remark elicited a few wry chuckles from around the table. I asked if anyone else wanted a drink. A round girl in a black pants suit informed me that margaritas were already made in the wet bar refrigerator. "All you have to do is add ice and blend it."

I installed myself behind the bar and got to work. The music switched to Latin pop—Shakira. Through the window, Brenda, Armando La Montaña Montoya's date at the cockfights last night, was talking to the woman with the guitar. I flipped off the blender and poured a couple of margaritas. Three separate conversations were in swing around the coffee table. I sipped my margarita, carefully carried both across the living room, and headed out past the kitchen and dining room to the veranda. Music from the living room issued through an open window. Four or five groups of people were scattered around the cement perimeter of the pool, some standing, others in deckchairs at tables outfitted with dark-blue umbrellas, most of which had been left open. Shorts and beachwear were the norm, with a smattering of more elegant attire. There looked to be almost as many women as men, all eating, drinking and talking. Lampposts that resembled relics from a 1950's Hollywood movie set were planted along the pool area's periphery where neatly trimmed grass sloped down into the woods. The party was bigger than I expected for a Sunday night but not at all overwhelming. Plenty of space to get around. Montoya probably figured that a Friday or Saturday night party would have attracted too many uninvited guests. He was nowhere to be seen yet had to be around somewhere, evidently in the house; I didn't see Johnny either but was confident in his inability to miss out on a party. Brenda stood with her back to me several paces off to my right with her friend, my china doll, cradling the guitar. Definitely my china doll. A fellow approached them. Their energetic conversation dissuaded him and he passed me as he retreated. I eased my way towards the girls. Brenda's brown hair, slightly teased and streaked, shimmered down the back of her cotton lime-green short-sleeved top cut above white cuffed shorts that flared delectably around smooth cinnamon-brown thighs. The heels of her sandals were short yet her legs looked rather long, though she isn't much over five-feet-five, about seven inches shorter than I. My china doll laid her guitar down on a lounge chair and nodded at Brenda. I bided my time under the umbrella of an unoccupied table opposite theirs.

There was a sigh and pause in their conversation. I advanced from the flank.

"Así es," said my china doll.

"Sí, así es," Brenda agreed.

"Y aquí está." I offered Brenda the margarita.

"Russell! So glad you could make it. This is for me? Gracias. Allow me to present my sister, Araceli."

My china doll swung her long black locks over a shoulder. "Ara," she said with a pleasant smile. Ara reached for Brenda's margarita, took a sip and handed it back. Rings, none of which were a wedding or engagement ring, shone on their fingers.

"Would you like me to get you a margarita as well, Ara?"

"No gracias, Russell. I will get one."

Ara stood, smoothed her dress and held out her hand to me. I considered kissing her hand but gently squeezed it instead. "Encantado." Enchanted.

SEVE VERDAD

"Un placer." She walked off. A pleasure.

"Where was she last night, Brenda?"

"Ara flew in from Guadalajara this morning. Armando picked her up at the airport."

"Is everyone in your family so attractive?"

Brenda's lips fluttered and smiled. "When you meet them all you can let me know. But I warn you, even our pets are adorable, though sometimes they bite."

"Really? You have a dog that bites?"

"Only unfriendly strangers. But you are not a stranger, and you must be friendly because you did not punch that guy who hit you last night. You might be attractive as well but I can no longer see your eyes. I think they are green like mine, no?"

"Purple, actually." I removed my shades.

Brenda caught her breath. "Aye por Dios. Is it very painful?"

"Only when I look at it."

"Have you something to treat it with?"

"I iced it most of the day."

"No, I mean for the bruise. I have some balm in the house that may lighten it."

"Maybe later." She brought a hand to my chin and turned my head slightly. Somehow her lavender eye shadow matched her auburn lips. *How do girls know how to match colors?* I sensed a small essence of jasmine, or maybe rosewater.

"No other marks?" she asked.

"Only the dimple under your thumb."

Brenda traced her thumbnail through my trim goatee. "Oh yes, I see," she mused and pressed her lips together. "Does that hurt as well?"

"Depends on how you use your hands."

She gave me a gentle slap on the cheek. "Now I understand why you got hit. Perhaps you are lucky it is not worse."

Yes, things could be much worse than this. "I may look like an easy mark at times but usually manage to dodge punches. I would much rather watch a fight than participate in one."

"Smart of you not to retaliate."

"Glad you were impressed," I said with a modest sip from my margarita. "Get a picture of it with my camera?"

"I think so. Right after you got punched."

"Really?" I stuck my shades into my pocket. "Can we have a look?"

"Follow me."

We headed for the house. Brenda glided across the veranda, her hips bouncing to a samba beat. Last night I learned she was tapatía—from Guadalajara—and had studied at UCLA in southern California. A dance instructor and artist. The woman had the sleek curves of a classic guitar. I pounded my margarita. *Mountain can't possibly be dating* both *sisters*. She guided me into the living room, sat her unfinished margarita on the bar, and told me she'd be right back with my camera.

Behind the bar stood a fellow with an unkempt beard and a thinning shock of blond hair sure to completely disappear at least a decade before any gray could set in. He sported a gold loop in his nose and a loose-fitting hockey jersey with a Canadian maple leaf on the chest.

"Still enough margaritas?" I asked

"Just checking." He opened the refrigerator under the counter. "Are all those containers...?"

"Full of margaritas. I'll help." I put some ice in the pitcher. He filled it with margarita.

"I think I'll have mine on the rocks," he said and prepared his drink separately.

"Good idea. Let's add a bit more tequila," I grabbed a bottle, dumped some into the pitcher, and sparked the blender for a second or two, "blend it a bit less and give it a try."

I poured the chunky liquid into my cup and freshened Brenda's drink. I sipped from mine and shuddered, "Perfect. You from Vancouver?"

"How'd you guess?"

"Well, your shirt... Most Canadians down here are from BC or Montreal. How do you know Montoya?"

"I don't. I came with a friend, Carlos, the guy sitting over there on the end of the couch."

And there he was, Carlos Mansalva. Also known as El Manco. A bespectacled badger smoking cigarettes with the round girl in black. His greasy hair and dark T-shirt blended with her outfit. I'd soon meet him and then wish I hadn't. Manco's missing arm wasn't apparent at the moment but the red-block lettering on his shirt caught my eye right away: Viva la Raza.

"How long you known Carlos?"

"Quite a while... You're from the States, eh?"

"But can you guess which one?"

The Canadian stared at me cockeyed.

"Oregon. I'm Russell. I've known Armando Montoya for three or four years now."

SEVE VERDAD

We shook hands but he didn't introduce himself, said he had to "visit the head, eh," and left.

Brenda appeared. She handed me my pocket camera. "Your scuffle's in there somewhere," she said in English. We had been conversing in Spanish. "It's a pretty good shot." Her English retained the light, musical quality of her Spanish. I scanned through a few pictures. Brenda coughed, "What happened to my drink?"

I shrugged sheepishly. She gave me a sardonic smirk and added margarita mix to her drink. I refocused on my camera's view screen; a face leapt out at me like a drunken cowboy in a barroom brawl.

"You know this guy?"

Brenda squinted at the view screen. "Which one?"

I clicked zoom and handed her the camera. "The bearded guy with the bandanna on his head."

"Oh, sure. That's Devo. A friend of ours."

"What's he doing in the cockfighting pit?"

"Helping a gallero manage a few birds."

"He train the birds too?"

"Sometimes. Why? You know him?"

After the stories Johnny and I had shared about Devo last night in Rudy's, I found the idea of him training fighting cocks in Mexico humorously ironic. What was next? Devo the matador? "Can't say as I know him," I said. "Seen him around town though."

"He's here tonight."

My voice leapt with surprise, "Devo?" I would have never expected him at Mountain's party. My pulse quickened at the prospect of meeting Johnny's "treetop flier" who had sliced and diced a "canary".

"Yeah." Brenda stared about the house. "Where did they go anyway? They must be in the—"

A tenuous roar rose from the far end of the house. Brenda and I frowned at each other. "Game room," she nodded.

"Of course." I grabbed my margarita and made a move to head over there. "You comin'?"

"I'll be out by the pool," Brenda said.

I passed through the kitchen into the hallway at the far end of the house and entered a brightly lit salon large enough to equip a Ping-Pong table, pool table, sofa, lounge chair, and flat-screen TV. Devo wasn't in there. Two guys at the pool table had stopped their game to stare at the HD television up on the wall to my left where Armando Montoya and four other guys stood in front of the sofa. At six-foot-two, Mountain Montoya isn't overly tall, but his wide back, shoulders and head, as well as the absence of a neck, make him stick out like a fire plug in the middle of a desert road. They were watching a baseball game turned Sunday Night Fights. I approached for a closer look at the TV. The Dodger and Giant teams had flooded the field; it was evident that there had been a melee in front of the pitcher's mound, though at this point most all the players and coaches were restraining one another instead of fighting. But then, between third base and home, a punch was thrown and everyone on the field converged to the spot. Rowdy cheers arose from fans in the game room. A guy off to my left griped that the punch hadn't even connected.

The Giants started it!" exclaimed another. "Hit him again!"

"What do you mean? Preen threw at him! The Dodgers started it!"

Mountain punctuated everyone's Spanish in a gravelly English/Spanish combo: "Me lleva la...ya terminó. Deyz done figh'en." He sat himself down on the sofa with a heavy grunt.

Mountain's English has always struck me as a unique hybrid of Mexican and African American accents worthy of a unique label. I dubbed it American Football Gangsta Spanglish.

Up on the TV, cooler heads had prevailed, the angrier players completely separated from one another. A commentator remarked that the pitcher, Josh Preen, would surely be tossed from the game as he had no doubt thrown at Bobby Stocks with intent. The fat guy from the pool table bumped me as he leaned over the back of the sofa to ask Mountain what was being said. The satellite dish was picking up an English feed of the Fox channel. Mountain translated with disgust and added that it wasn't Preen's fault.

A replay on the TV showed a Preen heater drilling Stocks squarely on his enormous elbow pad.

"Looks like it was Preen's fault to me," I said. "The kid has incredible control as well as a tremendous fastball."

Mountain twisted around on the couch and greeted me with wild eyes and a flurry of raucous Spanish: "You made it! Thought you might be in jail. Que cabrón. You get hit last night and say it is not your fault and now Stocks gets hit by a pitch and you say it is not *his* fault? Pinches putos los dos."

Under the right circumstance the word "puto" will get a laugh, and it got a good one now. I was pleased that my presence had Montoya juiced up.

"Preen threw at him," I said.

Mountain let loose with a derisive chortle. "Of course he threw at him! Stocks stands all over the plate with his sin verga elbow wrapped in that huge chinga su madre armor hanging in the strike zone! Preen is the only one in the pendeja league with the cojones to do it."

"Many players wear armor nowadays," I retorted lightly.

We had everyone's attention, and Mountain was on a roll: "Not that big. Add the drugs, steroids, the broken records, and you have the greatest cheater in all of sports! The greatest cheater of all time! What a bunch of pure mierda. If you are too puto to go to bat without using a shield in the strike zone then get off the puta madre field."

"Are you only bitter about American football and baseball or are you disgusted with American sports altogether?"

Mountain growled thoughtfully. "The NBA has gotten better... I guess vólibol is okay too." He folded his arms and inflated his chest to forge a massive shelf over his billowing trunk. The man's about as tractable as a tree stump sometimes. That linen shirt he was wearing didn't look like it could support those pylon biceps of his for many rounds before tearing at the seams. He stared back at me with a flexed jaw, his brawny black eyebrows burrowed deep into the ridge of his nose. "Owyouz doyn buddy?" he said in his inimitable English. "Guapo ojo morado." Handsome black eye.

PREEN was indeed ejected from the game, along with two other players of little renown. Stocks was spared. He'd charged the mound but didn't throw a punch. It was late in the game though, 8th inning, and the Dodgers easily held their four-run lead to win.

A couple of new arrivals to the game room—a guy and a gal— were playing pool. The fat muchacho had the remote and was flipping around the channels from a recliner.

A fellow lying in a bean-bag chair beyond the coffee table opposite him said, "Oye Gordo, déjalo en ESPN en Español." Hey Fatso, leave it on ESPN in Spanish.

Two other guys started playing Ping-Pong.

I was seated on the sofa with Mountain Montoya. He stretched his arms over the cushions and said it was about time to join the party. It came out, " 'Bout tang ta joyen dee paddy."

"Really," I said. "Some kind of host you are."

"Ony bean heya haf ouwa."

"You been in here for an hour at least."

"Youz shuya? De veras?"

The TV was showing a replay of Stocks getting drilled by Preen's fastball. "You know," I said abstractly. "Stocks has a doctor's note for that armor he wears."

A startling falsetto rose from behind me: "You mean a note from his mommy?"

Mountain leapt from his laid-back position like a giant bull frog and landed facing the opposite direction, no small athletic feat for a man of his proportions. He pointed at Devo theatrically, like he'd crashed the party, and looked from side to side as if expecting an ambush. "Corrrrrrrecto Errrrrrrnesto!" he exclaimed.

This meant he agreed with you, or "good comeback."

Devo and Mountain bumped fists over my head.

I said, "Am I in the middle of an anti-Stocks party? Can I change the channel?" Gordo extended the remote to me from the recliner. Apparently he did understand some English. I told him to put it on ESPN en Español.

"Commercial," he said and began clicking the clicker again.

Devo tossed Mountain one of the Modelos he was cradling and handed me one as well; he was going to chuck a beer to Gordo but Gordo wasn't paying attention so he dropped it on the sofa. An argument surged over at the Ping-Pong table and resolved itself.

I thanked Devo for the cerveza and cracked it.

"Germán told me I missed a fight," he said.

"From what I've seen," I proffered with a hint of admiration, "you win 'em without throwing a punch."

Devo looked quite a bit different from his picture on my camera screen or the guy I'd seen take over Ándale Bar and Grill with the chief of police Friday night. A shave and haircut had changed his image from swashbuckler to vacationing Manhattan Beach high school teacher. Straight, sandy-brown hair flopped to one side of his forehead; sun-splashed, hallowed cheeks embraced a hardened chin. His nose resembled a hawk's beak and was skirted by predatory aqua eyes. On a rangy frame he wore appropriate party attire for a man accustomed to teaching surfers how to read and write: a faded black Hawaiian shirt printed with green bamboo and scant rose-colored flower petals, belted knee-length tan shorts, and leather Topsiders, without socks.

"And what did you see?" Devo asked.

"Your performance in, out, and back into Ándale the other night."

"Oh, that." He shucked his shoulders. "Sometimes I get lucky." Devo offered me his hand. "Name's Devon. Devo."

Mountain rounded the sofa. "Wheyaz Bizco?" Where's Cross Eyes?

"Russell," I said and shook Devo's hand over the back of the sofa. His grip was mild but his hand seemed to swallow mine up. "Who's Bizco?"

"My puppy," Mountain said.

"He wanted to stay out by the pool," Devo stated blithely. "There's a party out there." He gestured at me with his beer. "Russell. Figured it was you. Heard about your scuffle last night. Your eye doesn't look that bad. Montoya must've exaggerated the punch you took."

"He does that."

"I don' zagerate. Youz guyz unda-azzimate." Mountain stomped off, presumably to go look for his puppy. The draft he created closed the door on his way out of the game room.

Devo shot me a direct, rather presumptuous question: "Is it true that writers write what they can't live?"

"Good ones should be able to," I responded without missing a beat. "But only poets can write without living much at all, with possible exceptions like Shelly, Morrison, and Dylan. 'Course Shelly and Morrison died quite young, didn't they."

"Jim's still alive, somewhere. Montoya said your stuff was shitty but then I read your piece on Mexican fútbol americano and it wasn't bad at all... Must spend a lot of time down here."

I pounded most of my beer in two gulps and sat it next to the reading lamp as I got up. Devo straightened his posture. He struck me as quite tall, but then immediately contracted into a slight slouch that shrank him to about Mountain's height, as if he'd pulled a release valve. The effect was disorienting for a second, like glimpsing an image in a distorted mirror.

"For Mountain," I said, "reading is like taking a shit. He does it when he has to. Sports section, maybe the Classifieds. So if he said my stuff was shitty it could be a compliment. Meant he had to read it for some reason or another."

"Good metaphor."

I circled the sofa. "Simile."

"Un-huh."

"Guess we should join the party."

Devo followed me towards the exit. The Ping-Pong table fell silent; the couple at the pool table slowly embraced. Party noises from behind the game-room door had been reduced to a low drum beat. A startling, familiar gravel voice from behind stiffened me: "I reedz youz on dee tylit."

FINDING DEVO

I glanced over my shoulder at the sound, expecting to see Mountain, and found Devo standing between me and the sofa, his grin exposing a gold bicuspid.

I faced him. "What the hell? That was so good I thought Mountain had snuck back into the room somehow. You practice him often?"

"Sometimes I can't resist." Devo sharpened his tone. "Wanted to ask you about the invasion."

"The what?" My astonishment at Devo's impression of Mountain deepened into confusion. What was he talking about?

"The invasion," he repeated with equanimity, like it was a subject we often discussed. Devo retreated backwards to the sofa and stared over his shoulder. I followed the point of his gaze to the TV; a clamorous sound invaded my ears. On the screen a turbaned imam pumped his hands, exhorting what looked to be thousands of frenzied Muslims—contorted faces, throngs of enraged voices and thrusting fists. The Imam faded within whirling cries of "al-Mawt Li Israil! al-Mawt Li America!" and footage of goose-stepping Muslim soldiers in black berets and checkered scarves. The images shifted as Gordo clicked through the stations; the Ping-Pong game resumed off to my right.

Devo reposed on the back of the sofa, his voice detached and dry. "Pulled up an op-ed piece of yours on the Internet."

I jerked my head at him. *Op-ed piece?* "Which...? Don't write many of those..." I considered Devo as if seeing him for the first time and flashed on the piece he must have been talking about. It wasn't about sports.

Devo's voice grew sonorous: "The one you wrote for the third anniversary of 9/11, Martell, that appeared in the LA *Blinds*. Nice piece of word play and satire, yet you still managed historical perspective. You accurately identified the perpetrators of 9/11 as Islamist descendants of Hitler's old ally, Amin Al Husseini. So I figured you were hip to their invasion of the New World, from Canada to Argentina."

I shook my head minutely, unsure why Devo wanted to delve into a subject like this at a party, or if I did. "Know somethin' about it..." I said slowly, "...but it's not exactly my area of expertise."

" 'I call 'em like I see 'em,' you said in that op-ed piece." Devo released a thick molasses chuckle, "Like you're an umpire or something. Pretty clever." He stood off of the sofa. Devo appeared taller, a full head taller than me now, his eyes as calm as windless ocean waters. "In typical Arab fashion, Hitler's Muslim allies switched sides once the Nazis were in retreat. Can't pull that off when you're playin' a ballgame, can you Martell...?"

"No." I felt an immodest smirk form on my face. Devo had just invited me to quote my op-ed piece, and I obliged: "But this ain't a ballgame. And things haven't changed, just gotten more dangerous at home."

"Damn good," Devo nodded, "like you were talkin' baseball—*home plate*. And you showed some balls by coming right out and naming the enemy. Called 'em like you saw 'em, with your own twist on the politically incorrect term. No better way to describe the enemy than—"

"I know what I called them," I intervened, surprised at my defensiveness, an unnatural feeling for a fairly seasoned journalist employed in the mostly benign field of sports. And I had nothing to be defensive about anyway. The op-ed piece had appeared a number of years ago and was well received. Yet Devo had unnerved me somehow. I wasn't sure why. After all, he seemed to be complimenting my work. But this topic didn't appeal to me at all right now so I offered him a concurrence of sorts I hoped would bring it to a close: "If I ever get inspired on the subject again I'll be sure to focus on the Islamist invasion of the New World."

Devo released another molasses chuckle and spoke dully from beneath lowered eyelids: "Sure you will. You can include it in a New World Sports piece about armor in the strike zone and the end of the world as we know it."

"The end...?" *Did he just insult sports writing?*

Devo downed his beer and made for the door. "Margarita?"

I stammered, unsure of what to make of my first personal exchange with Devo: "Uh...sure."

"Meet ya by the pool."

Music entered the game room as Devo opened the door and left. The games were in full swing at the Ping-Pong and pool tables. I checked out Gordo. He and his buddy in the beanbag chair were snoring to ESPN en Español.

17

PEDRO drum rolled his fingers before his computer keyboard. That blinking message had disappeared fifteen minutes ago, replaced by a slow-developing outline of what looked to be a map of South America. The encoded disc seemed to be revealing itself, and taking its time about it. About five minutes ago, a semblance of his taskbar appeared unexpectedly, but he still couldn't fast forward, reverse, or pause the disc's image. The damn thing had taken over his computer. He could access the time, mouse movement, and hookup an external hard drive to record the disc's images, but that was about it. Couldn't even connect to the Internet. Once again he considered removing the disc from his computer. It could contain a virus. But what if he had to wait another twenty-four hours for it to begin revealing its contents again?

Unless his computer suddenly (and miraculously) decoded the disc, there was nothing left to do but wait and see what the pinche güey had to say.

Pedro wasn't sure what to make of this. From his limited experience with encoded and locked programs and discs, you either gained access with a code or password or you didn't gain access at all. An encoded disc with a time-delayed self-decryption (a self-decryption on a fixed schedule with a time delay of twenty-four hours!) seemed a pretty sophisticated piece of technology. Either that or it was merely a virus. Both?

And might the disc's programmer also be an assassin?

His computer screen flashed a couple of times. Pedro sat up in his chair with renewed anticipation. What else did the maldito disc have to say? All at once, a complete map of South America appeared. Color was added—shades of brown and blue for land and water, and red in a few countries.

Pedro was seeing red. Red in Argentina. Red in Brazil. Red in Paraguay. A triangle of red at the intersection of those three countries, right there in the groin of South America. A deeper red than was evident in the rest of the map. What did it mean? Bits of Central America were added. Then the screen split into separate panels, two side-by-side panels. Two black and white political maps delineating countries, most of which were labeled. South and Central America were on the left, Europe, northern Africa and the Middle East on the right. Color was added—green and brown for land, blue for water, and varying shades of red in numerous countries signifying...?

Pedro retrieved his cell phone on his desk. It was time to call the lieutenant. The disc might be on the verge of revealing its contents. He paused and studied the maps again, his brow wrinkled indecisively. What would he tell the lieutenant? that the disc was giving him a geography lesson? He rang him up, got his voicemail, and left a message. The disc was revealing itself but nothing of significance had appeared yet. He would call back if something did.

Pedro crossed his arms in restrained resolve, eyes focused on the maps and their shifting shades of red. "Puta," he grumbled.

"Geografía." Not exactly his favorite subject. What he needed was another perspective, another person to help him decipher the meaning of all those red zones...

Voices in the living room again. His father, Enrique, was home. Pedro could hear him exchange pleasantries with ma. Laughter. Pedro heard his mother say, "En la oficina." He swiveled around in his chair, anticipating his father's knock on the office door, a courtesy to announce entrance rather than to ask permission to enter.

The knock sounded. Enrique stepped inside the not altogether tidy office. "Qué onda, mijo?" What's up, son? his voice kind and a tad beery. "Mucho trabajo?" Lots of work?

Pedro greeted his father with a brawny congratulatory hug. The hug he'd learned from him. A hug he initiated whenever the opportunity presented itself. A bump of chests and thumping embrace. "Not too much work to miss the dedication today," he said. "You made us all proud, papi."

Enrique mussed Pedro's curls. A paternal gesture he'd been missing for a time. "The mayor exaggerated my efforts. I was only one of many."

"And it was only one job of many, like you have said many times. But a special one."

"Another starts this week. But we enjoyed the fruits of our labor today." Enrique glanced at his son's computer screen. "Giving yourself a geography lesson?"

Pedro cranked his head around and sat at his desk, his face retaining a pleased smile. "Appears that way."

Enrique gave his son a pat on the back. A familiar signal of "adiós". Pedro said, "Stick around for a minute or two, papi. Maybe you can help me see something in these maps."

"This is police work?"

"Yes. But... Geography has never been a strong suit of mine and—"

"Two heads are better than one."

"Sí." Pedro stared up at his father's wise tan eyes. Lieutenant Romero had ordered Pedro not to seek outside help in decoding the disc...yet, at this point, the disc was decoding itself; and its images seemed disconnected and without relevance. Papi's fresh perspective should be harmless and could help Pedro see something of significance in these maps. "I am not sure what to expect from this program, papi; something sensitive might pop up."

"Give me the word and I will leave without having seen a thing." Enrique regarded the two panels of maps on his son's computer screen. "Is this a puzzle of some sort?"

Pedro said, "Maybe. Actually, I believe it *is* a puzzle."

"Colorful maps. And they look accurate. The red certainly sticks out. What do those different shades of red mean?"

"You tell me."

"More red in Europe and the Middle East than in the Américas." Enrique leaned over his son's shoulder, his gaze shifting between the two panels. "Surinam, Guyana, and that triangle at Brazil, Paraguay, and Argentina are redder than any other spot in South and Central America, almost as red as the Middle East in the other panel. A little darker than Spain, England and France." Enrique pointed at the Middle East, his finger tracing a line from Iran through Iraq, Saudi Arabia, Yemen, and into the horn of Africa. "These sections here must have something in common. They are reddest of all...crimson."

"Maybe everything in red has something in common," Pedro ventured, "but to different degrees according to the shade of red."

Enrique retreated, sat on the edge of his desk and pondered the puzzle. He had discussed his son's work with him before, usually minor details about crimes committed in the county, but it had been a while since he had helped him with anything resembling academics. Yet Enrique prided himself in being well read. Far from your ordinary palooka, he'd gone back to school after his boxing career and had always been active in union politics, often helping script publications. Enrique made a habit of scouring newspapers, reading books and magazines, and, thanks to Pedro's coaching, he was adept at surfing the Web.

Though his formal education amounted to little more than a high school diploma, all in all Enrique was a fairly well-educated guy. He hadn't been elected President of the Vallarta Chapter of Obreros Unidos for nothing. And he also had a talent for getting to the nuts and bolts of a question, recognizing the roots of a dispute, dilemma or problem. This often entailed stating the obvious, a basic fact or necessary starting point others may have missed or glossed over as unimportant. Invariably, Enrique's insights not only exposed the crux of a problem but the beginnings of a solution as well. And this is what he offered now. "You know, Pedro," he said, "the reddest countries are all Muslim."

"Yes they are." Pedro considered the significance of this. "I wonder if..." his voice trailed off in quiet reflection. "If that is the significance here, you would think all Muslim countries would be that same deep red. Kuwait...well...almost as red. What about—"

"Morocco is a lighter red, and a Muslim country. Maybe—"

"Israel is pink, surrounded by deep red." Pedro ran a hand through his hair. "You think the intensity of red has to do with Muslim populations? the percentage of Muslims in a given country or territory?"

"Could be, or the type of Islam practiced... Europe certainly has its share of Muslims. But why so much red in Central and South América? Muslims live there but only a fraction of the number who live overseas... And look at Surinam and Guyana. Are there that many Muslims in Surinam and Guyana...? and in that triangle down at Brazil and Argentina?"

"And Paraguay." Pedro's mind began to race. Was the red somehow connected to that message about an invasion and Mexico arriving late for fiestas? Was the disc highlighting a Muslim invasion of the Americas? Europe?...Mexico? If it was, was it true? And why did it matter? It might matter if "invasion" referred to a *radical Islamist* invasion. Yet, how the hell did an invasion of any sort relate to Mexico always arriving late for fiestas?

Pedro needed more clues from the disc, at the very least a map of Mexico and North America.

"I think you have some research to do, mijo." Enrique slid off the edge of his desk. "Can you search the Internet while that program is running?"

"No."

"Investigate Muslim—Islamic—demographics and the accuracy of these maps on my computer. You might want to consider political sympathies and alliances amongst the red countries as well. Venezuela is getting red, the whole country."

"I just noticed that."

"Pues, Venezuela is not Islamic, and I doubt many Muslims live there. It is an ally of Iran though. That pinche clown Marqués in Venezuela...thinks he is the next Bolívar, greater than Bolívar. Marqués would strike a deal with the devil himself for the power he craves."

Enrique was ready to join his wife in bed but had one last question, as well as more advice: "Is this police work for Immigration?"

Pedro murmured, "No," red countries reflected in his eyes.

"I never believed your work to be so far reaching," Enrique said. "You better ask for a raise."

18

ARMANDO La Montaña Montoya was reposed in a lounge chair in the pool area, interacting with guests as if holding court. Ara sat in a deckchair at his side, bare feet in his lap. A woman leaned in and exchanged pecks on the cheek with her. Johnny was at a nearby table chatting with a blond girl. I snuck up behind him and tickled the back of his neck. "You two arrive together?"

Johnny looked up at me, his expression bright as the full moon. "Hey Russ. Qué tal? Splendid party, isn't it?" He raised his margarita. "This is Gail. She's from Texas and has the sexiest accent."

"Ge-or-gia, silly," said Gail. "Ah'm from Ge-or-gia and *study* at the Uni-ver-sity of Tex-as."

She had a charming, southern-belle accent, not the kind that makes you sound dumb or uneducated. I tipped my head to her. "Nice to meet you. I'm Russell. Hook 'em horns." I flashed her the Texas Longhorn sign, index finger and pinky extended, two middle fingers tucked under my thumb.

"Woo hoo!" Gail pumped double-fisted Longhorn signs back at me. "Hook 'em horns. They-as four of us heya from the uni-ver-sity, and we all a-gree."

"All girls?"

"You bet," said Johnny. "I met 'em at the beach. Then we went over to their hotel for a swim in the pool. Stripped down naked and danced till dusk. You missed out."

Gail slapped Johnny's shoulder. "We weren't nay-ked, you silly..."

"Where are your friends now, Gail?" I really wanted to know.

"They-ah day-an-cin' on tay-bles at the Zoo. But ah say-ed to mah say-elf, 'lord girl, you need a chay-ange of pay-ace.' So here ah yam with Johnny. Sure glad ah did come! Bee-u-ti-ful place. Have you seen the view from the deck?"

My eyes day-anced over the no-frills banded top draped over the most bountiful portions of Gail's fleshy body. "Not tonight," I said.

"Well hells bells, Chili!" Gail swigged from her margarita. "Have a look. It's a ma-aah-ve-lous view. Just the gah-randest view you evah did see. You can see the whole town from they-ah, not to mention the bay."

Gail said something to Johnny about the view of her hotel from the deck. She sure was a talker. Her accent was less fetching the more she prattled on. After another margarita or two her words were bound to slur. She was a big girl, maybe fifteen pounds shy of Johnny's 160 or so, and fairly attractive despite a thick coat of makeup. Johnny bobbed his head up and down at her as she talked.

SEVE VERDAD

My attention meandered amongst the guests gathered around Mountain and Ara. Johnny gave me a nudge. "I'm goin' fishin' tomorrow," he said.

"Where?"

"Only around the bay so I don't have to get up too early. Gonna stick some snapper, maybe dorado. We leave at eight a.m. from the Washington Hotel. Wanna come?"

"Maybe. You goin' Gail?"

She smacked her lips. "Well ah jus' don' know. Ah'll pro-bably sleep in. Aftah all, this fiesta could go on for-evah. The en-ty-ah town is quite a pahty, isn't it? Almost ne-vah ends! And this he-ah is an en-gay-gement pahty, isn't it gah-RAND?"

My jaw fell to my toes. "An engagement party?!?"

Johnny said, "Yeah. Mountain just told us. Didn't you know?"

I pivoted and took a couple steps toward Mountain and Ara. They were occupied with others, but I caught Mountain's eye. He leg pressed himself to his feet, allowing those around him time to make space; his double-stitched, double-extra-large gabardine slacks stretched thin over his massive thighs. He approached and laid an arm around me, one of those sides of beef draped in linen hanging from his shoulders. I asked him why the hell he didn't tell me he was getting married.

"I was going to wait until later," he said, "and tell everyone at once. Guess it slipped out early."

I'd have given him a congratulatory hug but he had my shoulder pinioned to the grille of a Mack truck—his chest. "What woman could possibly handle you, Montoya?"

A woman's touch on his arm loosened his grip about me. I met Ara's smiling eyes. "I am a lot tougher than I look," she said. "Vámanos, Armando. Now we must tell the rest of the party."

Mountain and Ara headed for the house along with most everyone else. I shouted out to him: "Montaña! Where is your puppy?"

Mountain yelled back, "He must be down on the hill! Call him!"

Johnny stood from Gail and yelled out over the hillside, "Bizco! Ven Bizco!" Gail brushed by me on her way to the house.

"Don't you wanna see the puppy?" I asked.

"Oh ah've seen enough of him, Chili." Gail paused, fingertips grazing her rounded cheek, her eyes a blameless summer blue. "Think ah'll help mah say-elf to a-na-thah mah-gah-rita."

I swung around from Gail in response to what sounded like a small stampede down on the hillside. A beast akin to a pony came rumbling up to Johnny like he'd been cracked by a whip. Johnny stood his ground, anticipated Bizco's lunge, and took hold of his front legs. The animal tried to lick his face but Johnny kept him out of range.

Johnny puckered his lips. "That's a good boy."

"Christ almighty," I remarked. "That's gotta be the biggest puppy I've ever seen."

"Mountain says he's barely a year old."

Bizco pawed for Johnny's shoulders as if to embrace for a dance. Johnny cajoled him in a husky voice: "You're a big baby aren't you Bizco...?" He released Bizco's legs. Bizco pranced happily about him. Johnny whistled, got him to sit, and scratched him behind his cropped ears. You could lay bricks on that animal's head.

"Looks like he needs to fill out some," I observed.

"Oh the big kid's gonna get even bigger, aren't you Bizco?"

Bizco panted. His fangs were the length of six-penny nails. "Charming smile," I said.

"Oh he's a pretty boy. See his tie?"

"His tie?"

"Check out his chest."

The spots adorning Bizco's short beige pelt merged under his spiked collar to form what looked like a black bow tie. I patted his head and looked into his yellow-rimmed eyes, his pupils aimed at his prodigious nose. He was, as his name suggested, cross-eyed. "A cross-eyed Great Dane, or is he a Mastiff?"

"Probably a mix."

"How many of us do you think he sees?"

"Who knows? But he must think he has lots of friends. Mountain had him chasing a plastic ball a little while ago and he didn't get mixed up. Guess he's adapted." Johnny shot me a sardonic stare. "*Devo* was out here playing with him when I arrived. You meet him?"

I scratched Bizco under his chin. "Yeah. I met him."

"Get any good stories out of him?"

"None I'd tell you," I teased.

"How the hell does he know Mountain?"

"Through a gallero, a cockfight trainer."

"Really? Small world."

"Especially around Vallarta."

We walked over to the veranda with Bizco in tow. A guy was there hooking up stereo speakers. I helped untangle the wires while Johnny went inside to get us some drinks. One of the wires doubled over and wiggled around on the ground like a pair of snakes. Bizco stomped it and barked. I took hold of his collar and patted his shoulders. The guy thanked me, said he could handle the rest of the job. I decided to take Gail's advice and check out the view from the deck. Bizco followed me. The deck had been abandoned; a single light illuminated the barbecue. In the far corner, a stand of hillside palm trees cast moon shadows. Bizco and I strolled over to the corner and gazed at the city lights below. A Luis Miguel romance sounded from the veranda's newly connected stereo. Never was a big fan of his but Rosalita sure loved him...

"**B**IZCO! Bizco! Ven Bizco!" Bizco galloped across the deck towards the call. The music shifted to a lively Caribbean calypso. Somebody opened the sliding glass door from the dining room and stepped out onto the deck.

"Cálmate Manco, no seas tan chingón." Calm down Stumpy, don't be such a hard ass (motherfucker).

"La pendeja no sabe nada de lo que dice," countered Manco. The dumbfuck doesn't know what she is talking about.

Three guys walked out onto the deck followed by the round girl in black who I remembered seeing when I arrived. I also remembered Carlos in the Viva la Raza T-shirt, but hadn't noticed his missing left arm until now. This explained his nickname, Manco (Stumpy). The Canadian I'd run into at the wet bar was with him, as was a thin fellow I didn't recognize, the one trying to mollify Manco. He said, "She is just a dumb *güera* on vacation. You cannot expect gringos like her to think about these things."

"Mira Flaco." Look Skinny. "There is no need for them to think. They only have to get off their fat asses and have a look around to see the result of their *manifest destiny*. Reality is all around them."

"She's a self-centered bitch," said the Canadian in English.

"That's not unusual for un estadounidense." Manco pushed his glasses up the ridge of his nose with his middle finger. He had combined his English and Spanish, spitting out estadounidense (United States citizen) like a vulgarity.

I kept to my corner in the moon shadows, a secret observer wondering if this heated dialogue might lead to something more than foolishness—perhaps a bit of entertainment. I wasn't disappointed.

A voice in strict, measured Spanish surged from the dining room: "That is no excuse to ruin the party with your stupid opinions."

Brenda stepped out onto the deck from the dining room and planted her feet in a balanced athletic position, hands on hips. "If Armando had heard you in there you would be kicked out of here this instant. Just because your family in Guadalajara is close with his does not give you the right to—" Brenda stiffened, her flaming green eyes fixed on Manco. "—be rude and insulting."

"Yehee," Manco squealed. "*La Malinche* is taking the side of the gringa, eh? No wonder México is so fucked up."

"Yes it is fucked up," Brenda agreed. "And if you had your way América would be just as fucked up with Mexicans like you who refuse to take responsibility for your own corrupt state of affairs. Well, I have news for you. There are plenty of Mexicans living in América who do not wish to turn it into México and plenty of Americans who like to visit beautiful México without listening to your bullshit."

Manco's voice acquired an even, threatening tone: "When you have nothing to eat, terror results."

Another voice swelled, from behind Brenda; English with a baritone Chicano accent: "If thas trrue, Stumpy, weys all thee sueecide bommas en Chiapas? Wha happem to 'em? Tha' how you lose thee arm, eh 'mano? Nobody wanna 'elp you wit' thee car bomb?"

Devo. He towered behind Brenda, his blithe expression obscured by the moon shadow cast by the eves of the roof. Brenda barely reacted to him, her flaming eyes boring into Manco.

Manco fidgeted on his feet. "Who the hell—"

Devo stepped out from behind Brenda and planted himself in front of her, arms spread like giant wings. "I be your worst nightmare laddy," he said in a succinct Irish twang. "A drunk Eye-rishman who knows verily well all ye want is power...an I'm na a gonna give i' ya."

Brenda peered around Devo. His broad back blocked her view; she couldn't quite see what I saw. Certainly she saw Devo's size but I'm not so sure she saw his breadth. From my vantage point, he looked positively enormous. Manco and his clan stared up at him like a pack of cornered mice hypnotized by a looming cobra. Even compared to Mountain, Devo looked enormous. He's taller than Mountain but, at the moment, he also appeared just as massive. His V-shaped torso and widening reach radiated unassailable strength and density, as if forged from solid-steel crossbeams. Heavy enough to support or topple a house. And his eyes were mesmerizing. Snake eyes—dull with a flash. Each pulsing flash seemed to suck the will right out of his prey...

Manco culled his strength. "Crazy fucking gringo," he said. The Canadian staggered back towards the handrail. Flaco joined him, his jaw hanging by a thread.

The round girl took hold of Manco by his stump. "Come on Carlos. Come on and dance."

Brenda placed a hand on Devo's back. "Okay. That's enough Devo."

"Crazy fucking gringo," Manco muttered. The round girl guided him away, towards the veranda and pool area. Flaco and the Canadian followed. Manco glanced back with a stiff frown that didn't linger.

Devo lowered his arms. Brenda released a hefty sigh. "Glad that's over," she said in English. "But I just had to say something to the pinche...shithead."

"Don't blame you," said Devo. "Oh, almost forgot." He stepped into the dining room and was back with two margaritas and two shot glasses of tequila—a pair of drinks in each hand. He walked past Brenda in my direction. "Who are those for?" she asked.

Devo swiveled around at her. "Us...and Russell." He nodded towards my corner draped in moon shadows. "I promised him a drink."

"Russell?" Brenda joined Devo and stared my way. I waved. "You been standing there the whole time?"

I stepped out from the shadows. "Sure was," I said with a chuckle. I accepted a margarita from Devo. "Wanted to applaud at several intervals but didn't dare spoil the production."

"Well I hope you enjoyed yourself," she chided.

"It was exceptional. Especially Devo's role. But I have to say, you cut an awfully imposing figure yourself, Brenda."

"Too bad you didn't get it on film," Devo said.

"My thoughts exactly. How'd it start?"

Brenda worked her jaw; I thought I heard her teeth grind, but it was just her voice, harsh with anger. "*Carajo*," she cursed. "That pinche Manco... I was giving Gail a tour of the house and we ended up in the game room. Carlos—*El Manco*—and his clan were there, playing pool and horsing around. She went on about the house and how lovely Mexico is. Then outta the blue Manco spouts off, in English, tells her all is not what it seems...says she should visit the slums of Guadalajara to see how her culture's illegal *colonial conquest* has destroyed the *Mexica* people. Same old trash, blaming her and her *paisanos*—gringos—for his grievances, Mexico's and the *world's* grievances." Brenda's nostrils flared. "Can you believe it? insulting a friendly girl like that at a party like this for no reason at all? Poor Gail was at a loss for words, near tears. I told Manco to shut the fuck up, in Spanish so Gail wouldn't totally get it, and escorted her back to the living room for a drink." Brenda drew a deep breath, a renewed poise lending her carriage the charm of an elegant hostess. "I apologized to Gail. And your friend Johnny had her giggling when I left but..." She pursed her lips, staving off another throe of anger. "I just couldn't let Manco get away with that."

Brenda's empathy for Gail was contagious, had me itching to punch that little shit Manco myself. "How long has Manco been calling you *La Malinche*?" I asked her.

"Who cares what *he* calls me. I'd rather be Cortez's Mexican girl than one of Manco's any day."

Devo proposed a toast: "Let's drink to an appreciative audience. To Russell." He handed Brenda a shot of tequila.

I raised my cup. "To both of you and a fine performance. Salud!" "Salud." "Salud."

Devo and Brenda downed their tequilas. Devo had made my margarita nice and strong.

"The play's the thing," Devo rejoined with a Piccadilly flair.

"Indeed," I said. "You're a natural."

Devo relieved Brenda of her empty shot glass. "Think I'll show Johnny and Gail how to play pool." He vanished into the house.

"That guy sure has timing," I observed. "He appears and disappears right on cue."

"Sure does...did. Didn't know he was behind me till he spoke up. Guess he overheard Manco's attack on Gail from the hall."

"This is the second time tonight he's performed for me." I took a sip from my margarita. "How tall is he?"

Brenda shrugged. "Seems pretty tall, doesn't he?"

"Sometimes."

"I suppose he did show up at a fortuitous moment."

"Fortuitous? You learn that word at UCLA?"

Brenda allowed my comment a small smile. "My experience there wasn't always so— Oh look!"

I heard distant gunfire—*pop pop pop*—and swung around to see a fireworks display down on the coastline. The colonial pirate ship loaded with spring breakers had begun its nightly show. We approached the handrail to view the spectacle.

"So how did Manco really lose his arm?" I said.

Brenda put a hand around my margarita. I gave it to her. She took a sip, coughed, and handed it back. "You always make them so strong?"

"It's Devo's fault. He made it."

Brenda sniggered, "*Men*," and brushed a wisp of hair from her eyes. Two other couples walked out onto the deck to watch the fireworks.

"So?"

"Well..." Brenda twisted her mouth into a thoughtful smirk. "Several years ago Carlos entered the US illegally. He started out picking fruit, I think. He worked some farms anyway. I guess he was a real good worker. Plus he studied and practiced his English daily, which is kind of rare for a migrant worker. Then—"

"He became indispensable."

"I don't know about that. But he did get more responsibility. He got to work some of the heavy equipment."

"Oh my God. Don't tell me..."

"I can't remember what kind of a machine it was...some kind of reaper or something like that. Anyway, he took a spill. There's a rumor he was drunk..."

"So he got his arm caught in a reaper? That's fu—" I cut myself short with a gulp from my margarita, "...gruesome. I can see why he's bitter."

"Well, that's not all. Apparently the state took care of his medical and his employer helped him get an education. He received some sort of workman's compensation and went on to study a couple years at a Junior College in San Diego."

"At least he got something out of it."

"Yeah but that's where he got caught up in all that MEChA crap."

"Viva la Raza."

"Right."

"For those of Manco's race everything, for those outside it, nothing."

"Exactly. So you know about that stuff?" she asked.

"Not too complicated. Manco thinks the entire continent belongs to *La Raza*, the race of saints."

"There's a bit more to it than that."

"We should all live like Indians?" I raised a suggestive eyebrow.

Brenda hummed a chuckle. "Devo gave you the answer."

"Devo?"

"Sure. In his Irish accent. I thought you were listening."

"That's pretty funny."

"What?"

"You understood Devo's Irish twang."

"Fully. Did you?"

The fireworks ceased. My mind wandered. "Sorry," I said. "I've forgotten the question."

Brenda's tone acquired an edge. "At UCLA, the Chicano Student Movement of Aztlán—MEChA—passes out their pamphlets right alongside those charming Hezbollah Arabs and anti-anti-communists."

"Anti, anti...?"

"Communists."

I passed my margarita under my nose. "And they are?"

"Communists. Don't you get it?"

I really didn't but said the first thing that came to mind: "Sure... I get it. Manco's after power...like Devo said."

"The power to destroy those he perceives as more fortunate in order to elevate himself and leave everyone else equal—equally hopeless and stagnant." A flurry of whistling rockets exploded in the distance. Brenda helped herself to another sip of my margarita. She had the same fire in her eyes I'd seen when she reprimanded Manco. In close quarters like this, her fire sparked a little flame in my loins.

I teased her with a bit of sarcasm to keep the flame burning: "The abuse of power in the name of egalitarian principals. How exquisitely elitist. I am sure Manco knows best. Sounds like he'd make a fine American politician or judge."

Brenda snickered humorlessly. "And Mexican politician or judge," she said.

"You really sore about this or just trying to show me another side of yourself?"

"Show you another side of myself."

"And which side is that?"

"The real me that isn't motivated by power, doesn't care to have power over others, and refuses to be dominated by those who do."

"Too bad. I was looking forward to being dominated by you."

Brenda winked at me, a flicker of flame alive in her eyes. "You'll have to try harder."

"Can't you go ahead and dominate me anyway, for egalitarian purposes? You know, for my own good and everyone else's?"

"You mean like a politician?" she said innocently. "Sorry, I'm not devious or dishonest enough."

"I see... But you do have power."

Brenda tempted me with a catty sneer. "Clearly."

"Yet somehow you resist abusing it, even against those *charming* Hezbollah Arabs, communists, MEChA and La Raza."

"Why stoop to their level? My power is personal power. They're way too militant for me." The fire in Brenda's eyes went bland. A couple of bombs burst in air. Her gaze passed over them like the explosions didn't exist, her voice small: "Sometimes I wonder if anyone's motives can be distinguished from theirs." Brenda shook her head cynically. "People are brutal, Russell. The whole lot of us."

I sat my margarita on the handrail and leaned in close to her. "I'm feeling rather tender at the moment."

Her eyes glittered within slivers of moonlight. "That might make you an easy target, like Gail."

"If Manco wants to try his gringo-bashing shit with me, I'll be ready for him."

Brenda tensed; I thought she might tell me to avoid trouble with Manco, but she had something else on her mind:

"His rhetoric is so old it never dies. I got sick of that kinda crap at UCLA. *Viva la Raza*...I refuse to consider myself a victim like they do... I just concentrated on my studies, and grew rather fond of your country. In fact..."

Brenda showed me the back of her head. The fireworks appeared to be over on our side of the bay. We were alone on the deck. Her profile reached for the pirate ship, a tear in her eye. I had no idea we'd touched on a sensitive subject and put an apologetic arm around her. "I'm sorry. You don't need to explain or defend—"

"I'm...it's okay." She snuffled. "It's just that... Uh...I also fell in love with a young man at UCLA."

I dropped my arm from around her shoulders. "I see."

Brenda drew a saddened breath. "He died a young man."

"Died...?" I groaned, dropped my head and pressed the heels of my hands into my eyes.

Brenda's lips grazed my ear. "Tranquilízate Russell." Take it easy. "We have something in common."

I raised my head, and caught her lips with a kiss just long enough to empty my mind.

"You know about Rosalita," I said.

She nodded, head down. I rested my head upon hers. We were quiet for a small time.

"How did your...uh...boyfriend die?"

"My fiancé. In a plane crash a couple of years ago. In Lima, Peru."

I felt the blood rush from my face. Brenda tucked her head under my chin, her breath shallow and hushed, as though listening to my pulse hop at this news. I stammered, "Not...was it?"

"Sí," she said levelly. "American Airlines Flight 3356."

My mind stuttered over a flurry of questions, each a threat to spoil this tender moment, drown us in a common past too heartbreaking to share at a lively party. Salsa music wafted over us from the veranda. Brenda looked up at me. "Vamos a bailar," she said. Let's dance.

19

PEDRO blew out an exasperated breath as he lifted his gaze from the latest information he'd pulled up on his father's computer. He stared at the map of South and Central America on his computer screen a few paces across the office and asked himself a critical question: Qué diablos does any of this have to do with the dead man found at the marina?

The map, replete with swaths, speckles and colorings of red, had appeared shortly after papi left the office to join ma in bed nearly an hour ago. Initially, Pedro immersed himself in its implications: Did the red in the map indicate the spread of Islam as papi's insight suggested? Did the disc's message about an "invasion" refer to a radical Islamist invasion of the Americas? On the face of it, this evoked a vision of Muslim hordes overrunning the continent and seemed absurd, yet Pedro knew that radical Islam had left its mark in the Americas. Six months ago a bomb exploded just outside the Israeli Embassy in Ecuador killing a number of people. Hamas claimed responsibility. And Pedro had a clear recollection of the 9/11 attacks in the United States. He was still in grade school at the time. Images of the attack on New York's twin towers were replayed on television with such frequency they resembled reruns of a Hollywood disaster movie...

And then there was the case of American Airlines Flight 3356 bound from Lima, Peru, to Los Angeles, California.

It was all over the news when it happened two years ago. No survivors. Available footage of the plane's decent into the Pacific Ocean proved inconclusive as to the cause of the tragedy and no one had claimed responsibility for a terror attack. Speculation about what brought the aircraft down had been recurrent in the media and World Wide Web ever since. Was mechanical failure to blame as the Peruvian government alleged? or was there evidence to suggest that a terror attack—an Iranian portable surface-to-air missile—was responsible as the Americans claimed? Pedro hadn't given the dispute much thought before, yet if the Americans were right, that might lend support to the idea of an Islamist invasion of the Americas. A quick review of the case on papi's computer revealed that United States investigators had been expelled from Peru yesterday—Saturday—for the second time since the crash after concluding (also for the second time) that an Iranian surface-to-air missile had downed the aircraft. They claimed that witnesses had been silenced and evidence lost—a missile ejector-motor the Americans had examined a few weeks after the plane crashed into the ocean. Furthermore, the reassembled fuselage in a Lima hanger remained largely incomplete, and the Peruvian government disputed the results of American lab tests on seat fabric that (supposedly) revealed rocket fuel residue. Thus far, the American government had not officially classified the plane crash as a terror attack, but the dispute begged the question: did the Peruvian government have something to hide? North American Peruvians for Justice sure thought so. Their website accused the Peruvian government of withholding information that would expose the guilty parties: Maoist pressure groups and guerillas—Horozonte Iluminado, Túpac Amaru, and the Revolutionary Left Movement—linked to Jamaat al-Fugra, an Islamist terror organization known to have training camps in the United States as well as South America. The website also chastised the American government and media for dragging their feet: "Why are you so afraid to refute the Peruvian government outright and call this a terror attack? After two years of delays it is now time for the American government to act forcefully and bring international pressure to bear on Peru until the perpetrators of this heinous act of terror are brought to justice."

Jamaat al-Fugra? Pedro had never heard of them. How many different Islamist terror organizations were operating in the Americas? He expanded his investigation and googled *el islamismo radical en las américas*. Pedro was so astonished by what he discovered he began to wonder if this didn't in fact constitute an invasion of the Americas. Five months ago multiple members of Jamaat al-Fugra were arrested in both Surinam and Guyana for plotting government takeovers in the name of Islam. And the red zone revealed by the disc at the intersection of Brazil, Argentina and Paraguay was known as "El Triángulo Musulmán". The Muslim Triangle was a hotbed of Islamic terror organizations like Hamas, Hezbollah, al Qaeda, and the Albanian Mafia. The IRA was there too, as well as Aryan Nations and Asian Mafia types, but several websites identified that tri-border region as the heart of radical Islamist activity in South America. Over the past couple of years, numerous arrests had been made of radical Islamists smuggling everything from drugs and counterfeit dollars to arms and uranium into and out of the Muslim Triangle...

Pedro found that all the different shades of red dotting and coloring the disc's map of South and Central America corresponded to pockets of Muslim populations and/or concentrations of Islamist terror organizations...with the exception of Venezuela.

Burnt orange—a unique shade of red—colored Venezuela. Why highlight Venezuela like that? According to Pedro's research, Muslims made up less than .5 percent of that nation's population, though Caracas was home to Latin America's second-largest mosque. And Margarita Island, where a sizable portion of Venezuela's Muslims lived, didn't appear in the disc's map at all. Perhaps, as papi suggested, Venezuela was highlighted due to its alliance with Iran. But could the country's leader (that "clown" Marqués, as his father called him) also have ties to Islamic terrorists operating on the continent? Pedro considered surfing the Web to investigate this angle but had a funny feeling he was getting sidetracked. You can't believe everything you read on the Internet, and what did the disc's maps have to do with the dead man found at the marina anyway?

Qué diablos did any of this have to do with the dead man?

Pedro reposed in papi's chair, received the ceiling fan's gentle air on his face, and contemplated the question... Was the disc suggesting that the victim was an Islamic terrorist? Was the killer an Islamic terrorist? Pedro thought this unlikely but not out of the realm of possibility. Over the last year or so, radical Islamists had been arrested in the Mexico City barrio of Tepito, as well as in the nation's northern border regions where they were suspected of consorting with drug cartels. One was arrested in Tijuana a few days ago. Might they be involved in this homicide somehow?

Pedro had briefly reviewed the police reports on the botched raid and the interrogations of that gangster *Paco*. Gangsters were now presumed to have escaped the raid but Arab terrorists were the anticipated target, thanks to Paco's testimony, the testimony of a gangster who could not be trusted... Was the disc any more trustworthy?

Pedro slouched over his father's desk. "Y México siempre llega tarde a las fiestas," he muttered.

And Mexico always arrives late for parties.

None of it made any sense. Not even the idea of an Islamist invasion made much sense. Millions of Muslims populated Latin and North America. Did the actions of a small minority warrant labeling them all invaders? Of course not.

Was he misinterpreting the disc's revelations? Maybe. And maybe the disc's message and maps were designed to distract him from the investigation, get him to think about issues unrelated to the murder. The disc had to have *some* purpose. The assassin had taken a big risk in planting the body at the marina with the disc and all that other evidence and, as the lieutenant said, he did it "...so we would find precisely what we found when and where we found it."

But to what purpose? Was the assassin simply deranged? The more Pedro thought about it the more the disc and perhaps the murder itself appeared to be the work of a deranged man obsessed with delivering a bigoted message about Islam.

A deranged *man*, or had there been more than one killer?

Pedro returned to his desk. "Pinche tramposo," he remarked derisively at his computer screen and the disc. He took his seat and retrieved the preliminary autopsy report. The maldito disc had been distracting him from studying the case forensically. One killer might have been able to inflict those injuries on the victim but—

Pedro's computer screen went blank. He regarded the screen with patient anticipation. "Diga," he said, as though answering his telephone. The disc responded with another message in white block lettering. A steady message this time, without the incessant blinking: Era un buen día para una lapidación.

(It was a good day for a stoning.)

20

ARMANDO La Montaña Montoya leaned back in his lounge chair by the pool and hugged his right knee. Perspiration seeped through his shirt, his jet-black hair smooth and glistening, as if painted over his vast cranium. "Puta madre," he cursed. "Ahora me chinga la rodilla." Now my knee is fucking me.

Mountain had tweaked his knee dancing with Ara, though he'd demonstrated extraordinary coordination. My gaze bounded over his mammoth figure and I wondered, "How much you weighin' in at now Montoya? Three-thirty?" His playing weight had fluctuated between 280 and 300 incredibly quick pounds.

"Huna-tuyty kilos."

"Don't believe it. Sounds good in kilos though."

"Corrrrrrecto Errrrrrnesto!"

I was seated next to him on the concrete, in a puddle of water, stripped down to my swim trunks. An insolent female laugh rose from the pool and someone jumped in, sprinkling us with water. Mountain recoiled, but I didn't mind. I'd just come from the pool after a dance session with Brenda.

Did she mean to hurt me? Probably not, just dominate me some. My lower back had rebelled unexpectedly in the midst of a salsa dip but I played through the pain, until my wind abandoned me. My sweat-soaked shirt and socks were hanging from a chair, my shoes in a pile with my shorts below. Brenda danced with Johnny now, down towards the shallow end of the pool. She had lightened her pace to teach him some salsa steps. Her skin had a fine sheen, not quite perspiring. I knew she had some sweat on the back of her neck. I couldn't tell if Johnny was missing so many steps because he was drunk or wanted Brenda to lay her hands on him again and again to steady his gyrations. Probably both. He could dance better. She twirled and slide-stepped behind him, hips bouncing like a belly dancer's.

Mountain asked me if I'd get him a fresh shirt from his bedroom so he didn't have to get up.

FINDING DEVO

"I could use a fresh shirt myself," I said.

"Don' haf no'en da fi' ya."

"Sergio might," Ara interjected. She set a tray of margaritas and water down on the table and handed me a towel. "Sorry I take so long. I made many more margaritas."

"Sergio, 'ez too ezkinney," said Mountain. "Ruzzell, 'ez a big un."

Ara squeezed my bicep. She wore a modest engagement band I hadn't noticed before. "Strong too, aren't you Russell."

I flexed my bicep for her, "Keep talking Ara. Your English is getting better all the time."

Ara smiled, her teeth a lovely contrast to her toffee-brown skin. A shade darker than her older sister, Ara has the same cute button nose, oval face and gentle chin.

Mountain flexed and stretched his leg as he stood. "Got something for my knee in my room," he said with a wink at me.

I quickly toweled off and grabbed a margarita along with my shorts. Ara accompanied us around the pool to the near end of the house where slate footstones led into a hedged corridor. The ridged slate massaged the soles of my feet and kept me from slipping as we headed for the thin light cast by a lamp above a door on the exterior wall. Mountain inserted a key into the door, opened it and flipped on a light. We wiped our feet on the mat and entered the master bedroom.

Ara walked straight into the bathroom. Mountain limped for the closet directly to our left. Six Mountains could fit in there. To my right, through the blinds on a large square window, I could make out the action around the pool. Salsa was still the dance. I set my margarita on the carpet, dropped my swim trunks, threw on my shorts, and hung my wet trunks on the door handle. I retrieved my margarita and ran a hand over the sleigh bed frame. Quality Mexican oak stained cherry red. A Gauguin print hung above the colonial style dresser opposite me. Somehow the dark colors made the tropical animals and people bright. I looked at myself in the mirror. The eye had to be as dark as it was going to get. It didn't hurt at all. *Must be the margaritas*. I took a sip, pulled my shades from my pocket and slapped them on.

The dresser was cluttered with personal knick-knacks—a man's watch, lady's hand bag, cologne, a thin wallet, a Bic lighter, two pens, a notepad, comb, hair brush, a book that had to belong to Ara: *Arráncame la Vida*, by Ángeles Mastretta, and an issue of New World Sports en Español that contained a story of mine; next to that was a plate with a pile of cocaine on it. I removed my wayfarers and set them on the dresser. It looked like cocaine. A white straw lay on the plate as

127

well. I dabbed the edge of the pile with my pinkie and took a little taste, just to be certain. It was coke.

The toilet flushed inside the bathroom. Mountain tossed a shirt at me. It draped around my neck. "Try that," he said. "It never fit me."

I threw it on. Ara emerged from the bathroom, took one look at me and released a burst of laughter. "What is that?!?"

I scrutinized the geometric design and poker-chip buttons in the mirror. "Looks like a night gown."

Mountain chuckled, "You can keep it." He had changed into blue shorts, a collard short-sleeve shirt with sailboats on it, and huarache sandals. His legs could squat a fire truck.

Ara said, "There is a shirt around here that will fit you, Russell. Un momento." She walked behind me and out the door into the hall. Mountain stood next to me and looked in the mirror. He adjusted his collar and grabbed the comb. "Really, you can keep the shirt."

"Prefer the four hundred pesos you owe me from the cockfights." Johnny and I had been kicked out before I could collect my winnings.

Mountain slipped on his watch, slipped it off and put it back on the dresser, adjusted the fat studded ring around his middle finger, and pulled a joint from his breast pocket. "Have some of this instead," he said. He grabbed the Bic lighter on the dresser and sparked it up.

I took a hit. Next to Johnny's herb it tasted like moldy tortillas. I passed the joint back to Mountain. "A two-hundred-peso bet wins two hundred. That makes four hundred you collected for me."

"Three-eighty. The house keeps ten percent of the winnings." He took another hit off the joint and sat it in an ashtray on the dresser. "How about some of this?" Montoya held up the plate of coke. "I saw you take a taste."

I took up the straw and had a jolt from the edge of the pile. My forehead instantly expanded. I was now taller than Montoya. "Save me some for later and we'll discuss it."

Ara entered holding up a red T-shirt with a bull on the front charging through a Plaza de Toros Guadalajara insignia. "My uncle gave this to me. I use it as a night shirt."

It fit snug, but I liked the bull. "Gracias. I promise to return it nice and clean."

Ara had a freeze of coke from the plate but didn't snort any. My margarita had melted enough to chug. The room pitched portside; a figure appeared at the door to the hall—Devo—leaning against the door frame, hands in pockets, his head cocked as if inspecting some rare species of insect.

"When do you close escrow on this place?" he inquired in fluid Spanish.

"Thursday," Montoya said. "And we are married in June."

"So you *are* buying this house," I said with feigned surprise. Last year he'd mentioned he might to both me and Johnny.

Mountain shrugged, "Sí. Por qué no?" Why not?

Ara got up on her toes and kissed Mountain's jaw. "Vámanos," she said. "We should join the party."

Devo stepped inside the room to let Mountain and Ara pass. He approached the dresser, and seemed focused on the plate of cocaine at my side but reached for the issue of New World Sports next to it instead. Devo flipped the magazine open to my article. "This the only stuff you write?"

"For the most part." I took up the plate of coke and had another jolt to see if it would make me taller than Devo. "You want some?"

"Don't do the product."

My stature shrank. *Doesn't do the product.*

"But go ahead. Someone has to."

"Think that's enough for now."

I set the plate of coke back on the dresser and studied Devo as he leafed through my article. His unblemished countenance elongated and stretched a feathery pallor over his sun-splashed face. Was he turning into a bird right before my eyes? I might have looked away so he wouldn't catch me staring but couldn't resist the possibility of witnessing a metamorphosis. A quick glance at me with those avian eyes of his broke the spell.

"What else do you write," he said, "besides the rare op-ed piece?"

"Translation work for journals on occasion." I shifted my weight self-consciously. Devo's tone suggested I should produce something more substantial, something most all journalists consider themselves capable of writing: a book. I'd often thought about writing a book of course, just hadn't settled on whether it would be fiction, nonfiction, fantasy or... "I've given short-story fiction a shot," I said. "Haven't had much luck publishing though."

"That's 'cause you haven't really tried."

"Yes I have," I retorted.

Devo deadpanned me.

"I've made a few bucks publishing on the Internet. And I've had eight short stories rejected by three magazines."

"Eight?" Devo nodded gravely. "Sounds like one helluvan effort. Running short on material or ambition?"

"Neither." I shot him a leery stare. "You lookin' for a story or got one for me?"

"Lookin' for the one you have."

SEVE VERDAD

"You a publisher or somethin'?"

"Whadda you think?"

Our eyes held in a show of measured respect. No way was Devo a publisher, not from what I knew about him. But it's gratifying when someone shows an interest in your work and, unlike in the game room where we were discussing an old op-ed piece of mine I didn't care to relive, Devo's renewed interest sparked my imagination this time, almost like I'd just been "discovered" and had "great expectations."

"Are you trying to inspire me?" I chided.

A thin smile creased Devo's lips. "Do you need inspiration? Thought you said you weren't running short on material or ambition."

"I've got a story or two germinating."

"About sports, or something more inventive?"

The remark struck me as a challenge, like he didn't believe I had a story about something other than sports. Well, I did have a story, had done some investigative work on it, asked around about it, and was resolved to keep digging. So why not do some digging right now with Devo? You never know where a source of information will come from or who might add an unexpected twist to your plot, a new perspective.

I stuck a couple of fingers in my back pocket and whipped out the picture of the dead guy and attending article with a flourish that unfolded the page. "Know anything about him?"

Devo's face was blank as a slug's belly. "Looks familiar. But I've seen many a man in his condition."

"Dead?"

"Is he dead? Looks plastered, ready to get up and party after his siesta. Why should this interest you?"

" 'Cause no one else seems to take an interest in him. The guy hasn't gotten much publicity at all even though he was found dead right here at the marina. Vallarta isn't exactly a hotbed of murder and mayhem. Dead bodies discovered around town always get plenty of publicity."

Devo took the article from me. "La Estrella Nocturna. Evening Star. Kind of a trashy rag, doncha think?"

"Yeah. But for some reason or another the Vallarta Diario found the story so routine they buried the poor bastard in the Delitos section."

"So it's not murder."

"Depends on which paper you read. The Star makes it sound like it could be murder, the Diario a probable drowning. The Diario said he was found up by the docks, which could agree with that picture of him facedown in the sand. Yet if he drowned, his body would have been discovered down at the water line below the seawall, not up on the sand skirting the lawn. And drownings as well as murders usually merit a headline in the Diario instead of just an inch or two on a back page."

Devo's eyes were on the article. "Sounds like he was busted up pretty good," he said. "Also says 'injuries not consistent with a drowning.'" Devo looked a question at me. "You gonna weave a story around the victim or the Diario glossing over the death of a man written up in a trashy rag like the Estrella?"

"I'm still piecing things together. There's another fragment or two that could add some intrigue."

Devo handed the article back to me. "Lemme guess," he said mundanely. "The cops did it."

"You hear about the federale and police raid yesterday evening?"

"As a matter of fact, I did." He had a seat on the edge of the bed.

"Pretty big raid, wasn't it?"

"I suppose. What's your point?"

"Well, I haven't found a single report of it; at least the dead guy got a touch of publicity."

"Don't see—"

"The marina's not too far from the duplex that was raided. And according to my investigations, both events—the discovery of the body and the raid—occurred at approximately the same time. Plus, that body couldn't have been laying at the marina very long before being discovered. Not at that hour. Too many people around. So his actual death, or at least the body's appearance up there by the docks, also occurred at about the same time as the raid."

"So you think—"

"Not sure what to think. But considering the timing and proximity of the two events, they could be related. Yet the dead guy got reported in the paper and the raid didn't. The raid might get a write-up tomorrow but I don't think so. It hasn't even been reported on TV. And neither has the dead guy for that matter."

"Where's your story?"

I leaned back on the dresser and contemplated my bare feet. The Doors were playing 'Light my Fire' outside. "Uh... Well, I heard a rumor," I said. "I know there are always rumors but this one might explain why the raid wasn't reported."

"The raid wasn't reported because they didn't find anyone or anything."

I jumped on his comment like he was witness to a crime. "How do you know?"

"Rumors." Devo grinned. It must have been a wide grin to fit all those leaden teeth in there. "What exactly *did* they find, Russell?"

"Heard that the cops made off with a Jeep parked around the block from the raided duplex. Bet they found something more. But whatever they found..." The significance of the terrorist rumor had been lost within Devo's take on why the raid hadn't been reported. So I backtracked to regain my bearings. It was important to get my story straight, for myself rather than Devo. "...a big raid in Vallarta is difficult to keep out of the news. And here in Mexico the feds have a tendency to trump up stuff like that."

"Trump?"

"Sí señor! Even if it's a failure, why keep it quiet when you can always bullshit and say it was a big success? I mean, it's not like they raided a public place—a restaurant or somethin'. It was a duplex; they could've claimed they found most anything inside... Over half the world around here knows there was a raid anyway so why not play it up? The feds, policía, their shit always floats. And people are expecting to see their crap floatin' by. They're used to it. But when there is no crap at all, well...someone took a shit somewhere."

"So you're saying—"

"Somebody must have been paid off to keep the raid under wraps when under normal circumstances there is no reason whatsoever to keep something like that out of the news. In fact, there is every reason in the world to play it up."

Devo leaned back on his hands in patient repose. "Maybe the raid was kept out of the news so tourists wouldn't find out about it."

"I know about it. Mountain knows about it. Johnny knows about it. *You* know about it. Tourists might get nervous if the truth about the raid came out, whatever that truth may be, but the raid could be played in the media any way the feds and cops want. Yet it hasn't been played at all!"

Devo rolled his jaw, eyes distant, digesting my train of thought. Was there a story here somewhere? I thought so, and perhaps others would too. "Look," I said, a pragmatic hand tilted at him, "I can't be the only one who's thought about this. Keeping a big federal and police raid like that out of the news is risky...could raise suspicions. *Does* raise suspicions."

"Only amongst an imaginative few."

"Somehow that raid was an enormous fuckup that had to be kept quiet. And I can't figure out why... Unless some very dangerous people got away. Or maybe," I held up the dead guy, "someone was killed who wasn't supposed to be."

"Killed during the raid or at the marina?"

"Probably during the raid. Hard to believe there wouldn't have been witnesses to the crime at the marina."

FINDING DEVO

Devo raised a brassy eyebrow. "So the cops couldn't kill him at the marina without being witnessed but they could have killed him at the duplex and then planted the body at the marina without being seen? Pretty shaky reasoning, Martell. You'll have to do better than that to make your story believable."

I puzzled over his logic for a moment.

Devo stood from the bed, languid as a man off to make his morning cup of coffee. "You could be on to something with respect to the raid but connecting it to the dead body has muddled your thinking. The raid was botched, plain and simple. They were obviously after *someone*, perhaps some very dangerous people as you suggest. And it's much tougher to lie about arrests made than, say, evidence found. So with no arrests to their credit, cops have reason to keep the raid under wraps. Especially a large raid like that. Must be quite embarrassing to walk away empty handed." Devo drifted towards the window and turned to face me again, a scholarly finger raised above his shoulder. "And as far as the dead guy found at the marina goes," he said, "I can do much better than your take on it. He didn't get it accidentally. He ended up dead and facedown in the sand because he was supposed to die." Devo stuffed his hands in his pockets. "The guy was intentionally murdered but it wasn't the cops or feds who killed him and they have no clue who did kill him. And since the body was dumped at the marina, a fairly busy place at that hour, word got out, so the federales and policía couldn't take credit for a kill made, for example, during the raid... They missed their man, or men, again— those at the duplex and whoever killed that guy found at the marina— and they are damn pissed and humiliated about it, pissed and humiliated enough to keep both the dead man and the raid out of the news as much as possible."

Devo sauntered out of the room and down the hallway. I took his place on the bed. *He was* supposed *to die? The body was* dumped *at the marina?*

"Hehya! What's goin' on in here?" Johnny entered and had a look around. "You doin' drugs without me?"

"Don't worry Johnny. Indoors or out, your weed's still the best."

"Better be. But what's this?"

"Das mine," said Mountain. He lumbered through the doorway and took the plate of coke from Johnny. "Youz can hafa li'l bu' if youz wan' moe youz godda pay." Mountain separated a rail from the pile with the straw; Johnny accepted the invitation.

"Pinches cabrones. Poze I godda lock dee doe?"

"That's okay Mountain," I said. "We were just leaving. But I might get some from you later."

Mountain grunted and slid the plate into a drawer. I heard him lock the door from the inside when Johnny and I left.

On our way down the hall Johnny took hold of my arm. "Guess what?" he said. "The mayor's here!"

I stopped short and stepped back into the shadowy light of the hall as Johnny strolled into the living room. Someone was in the living room who might have a direct impact on my story, and it wasn't the mayor. I recognized his frumpy figure and melon head. The man I had a run-in with at Arena Vallarta before sunset today. He stood with Brenda and another fellow by the wet bar. I wanted to question him again but...how to approach him?

Brenda introduced Johnny to Lazarito Charlado and Captain Bob. Lazarito poured Johnny a margarita. Captain Bob, a fortyish lanky fellow in a white yachting cap and blue guayabera shirt, said he was surprised at the size of Arena Vallarta: "Impressive yet unimposing from the outside, but seems like a cruise ship could fit inside the stadium."

Lazarito tipped his head to that. "Indeed," he said. "And thee museeum, it is also unimposing but at thee same time ver-ry accessible and...uh...amplio..." Lazarito gave Brenda a questioning glance and caressed his graying comb-over hairdo, searching for the right English word. Brenda helped him out. "Spacious," she offered

Lazarito's black eyes twinkled within heavy swags of flesh, his thick lips stretched in a smile. Lascivious lips the color of rare veal; they appeared pasted to his face, the brown face of a weasel. "Yes, my dear," he said. "My but your English...it is ver-ry good. Spacious. Thee museum is quite spacious with an extensive collection of cultural displays. It weel be a fine tourist attraction. Indeed it weel."

I shuddered. Lazarito was flirting with Brenda. He could have just said "large" and probably already knew the word "spacious". Charlado's English squealed and wheezed from his mouth with a pomp equal to his Spanish. What the man lacked in elegance he made up for in pomp. He sported a rumpled green dress shirt with a bow tie stuffed under his double chin. Unlike the black bow tie I'd seen him wearing that afternoon at the arena when I questioned him about the raid, this red one looped and had tails. His casual-wear bow tie. Baggy white slacks rounded out his outfit, an outfit lending him all the colors and flutters of a Mexican flag flapping in the wind.

Brenda told Lazarito she was sorry to have missed the dedication. Lazarito said he would be at the arena tomorrow afternoon and would be happy to give her a tour. Brenda was gracious; she doesn't need to turn on the charm to be charming, and she looked positively ravishing.

Brenda held my attention now. How could she not? Ripened from dancing, her body exuded sexual energy: breasts in full blossom beneath a sheathe of lime-green cotton; tasseled mane wild about her radiant oval face and slender shoulders; a bare sliver of her stomach accentuated shapely hips. Sleek, balletic legs. Her toenails were painted party pink. Brenda has plenty of sex appeal but, unlike many attractive women, she is remarkably unpretentious—her beauty as natural and unobtrusive as a fountain in your garden, or the subtle melody of a flute or harp. I approached and caught her eye. Brenda went on addressing Lazarito: "I'll see if I can squeeze it into my schedule."

I placed a hand on Lazarito's back. "I can vouch for Señor Charlado. He is a most accommodating tour guide." Lazarito swung his head up at me and froze like an animal caught in my headlights. "You certainly were with me this afternoon, weren't you Lazarito?"

A wave of surprise and anger passed over Lazarito's face, a bilious expression of recognition. He puffed out his cheeks, his eyes small and defensive, bereft of the authority he wielded during our encounter at the arena. I sensed an advantage but quickly decided not to question him directly about the raid. Such a tack could easily prove fruitless once again and put an embarrassing, needless damper on the party. Harmless banter was the prudent course. A bit of needling to see what I could deduce from his reactions.

I offered Lazarito a warm handshake, like an old friend. "Russell Martell," I said. "Have you forgotten already?" Lazarito shook my hand with a look of befuddled relief. His palm felt like a shucked oyster—squishy and moist. "Yes," I added and released his hand, "Lazarito here has the answers to all your questions, even those not pertaining to the arena. Isn't that right Lazarito?"

Lazarito responded with an unconvincing chuckle, his gaze scampering over Johnny, Brenda, and Captain Bob. "Pues, I...uh. I weesh to be of help, sí..." He frowned at me, eyes narrow, nearly threatening. "To thee tourists."

I smiled disarmingly. "Well Lazarito, I suppose I qualify."

"Me too," said Brenda, "as a tapatía."

Johnny didn't understand. "Tapatía?"

"From Guadalajara." I fixed on Lazarito. "Where are you from, Lazarito?"

"Guadalajara as well," he said with a nod to Brenda. "I came...uh—" Lazarito cut himself off and sipped from his margarita, taking time to gather his thoughts. He clearly distrusted me, which suggested he had something to hide. Lazarito remembered me, knew I was a journalist, and was preoccupied with the motive behind my earlier inquiries into the raid.

I prodded him with a solicitous smile. "You came to Vallarta for work. Well, not a bad place to work. Are you the Mayor's press secretary?"

Captain Bob spoke up: "What makes you say that?"

"At the arena today, Lazarito offered to make an appointment for me to interview the mayor. He claimed to know every journalist at the dedication and seemed to be in complete control. Even the police looked to him for orders, didn't they Lazarito?"

Lazarito stretched his neck as though his tie irritated his double chin; the edgy glow of sweat beading up at his temples confirmed for me that the control and power he had exercised at the dedication of Arena Vallarta did not apply here. Apparently, Señor Lazarito Charlado's power was severely limited outside of media events like the dedication. He figured to be no threat to me whatsoever as long as I remained friendly, despite my cutting undertone.

I had already forgotten how quickly life can change.

Lazarito took a deep breath as though preparing to meditate. Then he grinned, first at Brenda and then at me. The broad, affable grin of a man comfortable at parties. Lazarito had gotten over his initial shock at finding me by his side and was determined not to let me fluster him. "I weesh I was in complete control, young man," he said. "If I was I weel be mayor."

Polite laughter all around. Then I saw the mayor, Juan Pacífico Velázquez. He was right in my line of sight, through the expansive living room window, poolside chatting with Mountain. I gestured toward him. "Guess you're never too far from the mayor, Lazarito. Are you his press secretary or bodyguard?"

"Bodyguard," Johnny chirped blithely. "Looks pretty tough to me."

"Me too," I agreed without a hint of sarcasm.

"Maybe the mayor guards *him*," said Captain Bob. "They arrived together and at first Lazarito seemed to attract more attention."

"He must make news," I winked at Lazarito, "or decide who does. Us men of the press have to be careful how we wield our power, don't we Lazarito? lest we upset or upstage those who pay our salaries."

Lazarito regarded me cynically, a nervous twitch in his eye. He wasn't about to reveal anything to me, least of all his profession or who paid his salary. Yet he did realize I knew he had pull with the mayor. "Yes, *you* haf to be careful," he said. "As for me, pues, I weel also advise thee mayor to be careful should you be permitted to interview him." Lazarito finished his margarita and bowed to Brenda. "A pleasure meeting you my dear. And thee two of you." He bowed to Johnny and Captain Bob.

Lazarito narrowed the gap between us before taking his leave, came close enough for me catch a whiff of his stale cologne and hear his teeth grind as he hissed quietly: "Or maybe thee mayor weel haf someone interview *you.*"

Señor Lazarito Charlado hitched up his trousers and waddled off to join the mayor.

"I say," said Captain Bob, "are you really with the press, Russell?"

Brenda answered for me: "Yes he is. I read a story of his on Mexican fútbol americano this morning. Pretty good, Russell."

"Thanks," I said, my eyes fastened on Lazarito's frumpy backside. *Awfully defensive. Wouldn't be surprised if he was the one paid off to keep the raid out of the news.*

21

THE images appeared one right after the other, each filling Pedro's computer screen for a couple of seconds before another took its place. Photos of young men, many with faces hidden behind masks, throwing stones at uniformed adversaries. Several of the images looked familiar, like snippets from news casts he had seen on television. Some recalled a recent wave of riots in London and Madrid—cars overturned amidst bonfires in the streets; a phalanx of shielded troops advancing on agitators. A few others looked to be of Palestinians taking on Israelis—flags portraying the blue Star of David were clearly visible in each. The disc flashed its pictures for thirty seconds or so and froze on a shot Pedro thought he recognized but wasn't sure why. Four males, eyes black with defiance, looked to be running circles around two uniformed officers with their backs to the camera, one in the process of drawing his gun. Two of the young men gripped stones, their arms cocked. The other two had just released their stones in tandem, side-armed and on the run, like baseball shortstops. And they may have played some baseball, for at the left edge of the photo loomed an infamous landmark—the North American border fence—that marked the four guys throwing stones as Mexican.

Pedro stared at the photo until his throat went dry and tight; his eyes watered in anger and shame—anger at seeing armed gringos threatening his countrymen, and shame at seeing his countrymen, his paisanos, attack border guards in such a fashion. Pedro knew that border skirmishes were all too common, often involving drugs and firearms. These four Mexicans didn't strike him as drug runners however but desperately poor campesinos in search of a better life. And ultimately, it wasn't they who were abandoning their country but their own country that had abandoned them and tens of millions of others to poverty and acts of desperation like this; and it was shameful.

He remembered his father's words on the subject at the dinner table on occasion over the years: "There is no shame in protecting one's home or border. And there is no shame in you leaving to find a better life, maybe crossing another's border if you have to. But *I am* ashamed if my negligence forces you to do so."

Pedro released a hapless sigh. The image on his computer screen faded into a postcard blue sky, the kind of sky you might see in Vallarta during the dry season, except this sky seemed cold and heartless, like it could suck the air right out of you. A ramshackle fútbol stadium withered beneath the sky, its wooden stands occupied by what looked to be a couple-thousand spectators, some of whom were sheltered under tarps strung up between tall pillars. Pedro couldn't quite make out what the crowd was viewing out on the frozen dirt field skirted by a thin layer of snow. The camera zoomed in on the field; Pedro blinked in surprise as the still photograph became a silent video. A diminutive figure kneeled at midfield shrouded in a long gray headdress, robe, and veil. The attire suggested this to be a woman. The others swarming around her, perhaps two dozen, were clearly men, many with beards, all in pants and jackets, some wearing turbans. The stones they hurled at her appeared no larger than Ping-Pong balls; the ground was littered with them, an endless supply, none large enough to effect a merciful, quick death.

Pedro felt his stomach shrivel up inside, his heart sickened in his chest. He wanted to look away, save himself from viewing this needless barbarity, but something held his attention. The woman, slouched in agony, shuddered with every blow. Why didn't she try to escape? What was holding her down on her knees like that? As if to answer his question, the camera zoomed in a little closer. The woman's shoulders and head collapsed, yet she remained upright, like a wilted flower. Pedro shaded his eyes in anguish. The woman was not kneeling. She had been planted in the ground, nearly up to her chest, her hands bound behind her back.

He turned from his computer, took a long sip of water, and let his eyes fall blindly upon his desktop. What was the disc trying to say? What the hell was this all about? Pedro drew a deep breath against a convulsive ache in his diaphragm. Out the corner of his eye he saw a white flash from the disc. He looked up at his computer screen. Another message: Un buen día para una decapitación.

(A good day for a beheading.)

22

ARA was playing guitar and singing to the stereo music issuing into the living room from the veranda. The popular Mexican standard 'Volver'. On the couch, Miguel played the attentive student while Johnny's date, Gail, gave him an English lesson. He sat close to her, feigning ignorance as he repeated words he'd learned years ago. The song ended. There was some applause, a Jaliscan yell, and another song. Johnny helped himself to some nuts on the coffee table and eavesdropped on the English lesson Gail was giving Miguel. I ambled over to the bar and struck up a conversation with a couple making margaritas: "So Armando Montoya is getting married. Quite a surprise."

"Not really," replied the woman holding the pitcher of ice.

"We could see it coming," said her companion. He added the proper amount of tequila and margarita mix to the pitcher. "He fell pretty hard for Ara about four months ago."

"No kidding? Only four months?"

She turned on the blender. He kissed her forehead. She had big hair and a tiny body. He wasn't much larger but sinewy with vascular arms.

"Oh they have known each other longer than that." She turned off the blender, peeked inside, and flipped the switch again. We waited and in a moment or two she had it right.

He poured margaritas into Styrofoam cups. "When Ara got back from Europe four months ago, Armando got serious."

I graciously accepted a margarita and introduced myself. Tomás and Teresa were newlyweds. I congratulated them.

"Good strategy by Ara," I said.

Teresa wiped imaginary lint from the sleeve of her pink blouse. "What do you mean?"

"Going to Europe like that. Must have finally gotten Armando's attention."

"I doubt Ara planned it that way," Teresa said. "I think it was a surprise for both of them."

"I never thought about it like that, Russell," said Tomás. "You may have a point. After all, women can be very sneaky."

We touched cups. Teresa gave him a playful slap on the shoulder and parried with the typical "aye los hombres son cabrones, todos iguales!"

Tomás kissed her forehead. "Teresa is right."

"All men are cabrones?" I said.

"Pues, that too. I mean Ara and Armando were not seriously dating before she went to Europe. They both just matured while she was away. Armando started wrestling when she left and—"

"Wrestling? Professionally? He finally did it?" My eyebrows must have shot up around my hairline. I wanted to know all about it. Tomás opened his mouth to speak but I went on: "I thought his knee was holding him back."

"He has not made a lot of money at it yet," Teresa said.

"But he has made something of a name for himself," Tomás advanced. "He was already a well-known Mexican athlete—a fútbol americano star."

"I only see Armando a few times a year," I confessed, "so this is all news to me. A new career, house, and wife. All since I last saw him six or seven months ago? Wow!" My eyes danced about the living room. "Where is he anyway?"

"Maybe the game room," said Tomás. "Or the office."

El Manco and El Flaco approached the bar, followed by their Canadian friend. Teresa introduced me to Carlos (El Manco) and Ramón (El Flaco). I pretended I was pleased to meet them and shook their hands. A burning desire to lash out at Manco for his treatment of Gail and the way he disrespected Brenda out on the deck rose in my chest, but I kept it at bay. With a little patience, this encounter might provide an opportunity for me to put him in his place without causing a scene.

The Canadian lingered in the background, hands in pockets. I reminded him we'd met here at the bar earlier in the party but, "I didn't catch your name."

"Eric."

"We were just talking about Armando's wrestling career," said Teresa.

"Armando *La Montaña* Montoya," Tomás announced as he distributed margaritas to the new arrivals.

"Guess there is no reason to change his nickname," I said, "unless we call him El Gorila. How about King Kong Montoya?"

"Yehee...El Gorila." Manco's stilted laugh was that of a wounded hyena. "Or maybe La Bestia." The Beast.

"I think there already is a Bestia," said Flaco, "Gorila too. Gorila Two Face. King Kong might be good."

"Call him El Grizzly Warrior," I suggested, "like the bear."

"Yehee." Manco repeated the exchange in English to Eric who had been nodding and smirking without understanding our Spanish. Manco's translation elicited a weak chuckle from him.

"Or maybe El Toro Bravo," Manco said.

"I think there already is a Toro," Flaco replied. "El Toro Negro."

Manco adjusted his glasses, his expression hardened. "I said El Toro *Bravo. Bravo.*" He sat his margarita on the bar and slid the palm of his hand over his slick coiffure. "Why not call Armando El Gordo?" he said to Flaco, "then he can wrestle El Flaco."

"I think I met El Gordo around here already," I said. "In the game room."

The newlyweds giggled. Manco ran the back of his hand across his wispy mustache, then held two fingers out to Flaco. Flaco planted a cigarette there and lit it for him. Manco blew smoke past me. I pointed at the red *Viva la Raza* lettering printed across his shirt. "Qué signífica eso? What does that mean?"

"Oh," Teresa said, "that is Carlos' hobby."

"A hobby he is always anxious to share with others," added Tomás. The newlyweds excused themselves and strolled across the living room to Ara who had set aside her guitar to socialize.

"*Viva la Raza* means he's proud of his race," Eric expounded as if revealing an ultimate truth.

"Really?" I said, my tone the essence of sincerity to disguise my contempt for Manco. The memory of his menacing exchange with Brenda out on the deck remained fresh in my mind, as was Brenda's account of how he had bullied Gail. The guy was a punk, a bitter scum-of-the-earth leech whose only purpose was to drain the life blood from those he imagined responsible for his pathetic existence. If his family hadn't been close to Montoya's, I couldn't imagine Mountain being associated with him. "Well, I'm proud of his race too...and proud of my race...and yours as well, Eric. Where can I get a shirt like that?"

"Don' hab one to fit you," said Flaco. He had the long face of a horse, his dark hair stringy, like a horse's mane.

Manco's expression held a grimacing smile. "Yehee," he snickered, "it weel fit him, but 'ee wone fit thee shirt."

I sipped from my margarita and added a note of triumphant irony to my voice: "But I could change—narrow my horizons and become more single-minded."

Manco's naturally flared nostrils enlarged to the size of silver dollars. He furrowed is brow, not in anger but as though pondering over whether or not he'd just been insulted.

Eric took a step forward and jabbed a thumb at Manco's shirt. "You have to be one with the race to wear the shirt," he said with decision, "and sympathetic to the cause."

"So it's an exclusive club," I shrugged. "How much for a membership?"

"I don' thing you comprendas, Russell." Flaco's face acquired some breadth.

"Oh 'ee understan'." Manco fixed me with a menacing scowl; it gave me great pleasure to see that my invective wasn't lost on him. "You wanna make a conreebution to thee cause, Russell?"

"Do I have to give you my house or will you be happy with my car? Don't tell me you require the entire state of Oregon as well as the other western American states. I only live there, I don't own it."

"It's not about cars or money," Eric said, "it's about justice."

"If I make a contribution can you guarantee I won't be found guilty of injury and injustice to *la raza* and the cause?"

Flaco's fingers skipped down his open collar to the thin silver cross dangling from his neck. "I thing you buy foe, five shirrs."

"Shut up Flaco," said Manco.

Eric jeered at me, "It's all about attitude and what's fair."

"I must be in the wrong life," I clucked, " 'cause it sure ain't fair. That's my attitude anyway."

Manco sneered, "Thee policía at thee arena today, were they fair?"

"Police?"

"You lef' in a rush so I suppose no."

Manco's sneer stiffened as though ironed on his face. He had me confused for a second. But only a second. Evidently, he'd seen me beat a retreat from Lazarito and that cop at Arena Vallarta. "At the arena?" I said coolly, conscious that Manco had probably had more than his share of run-ins with cops. "I did my best to cover for you. The police know nothing of your plans."

Manco's eyes darted to and fro behind his glasses and his head twitched from side to side as though afraid someone besides his trusted cohorts had overheard me. Did he have something up his sleeve? Was he really planning something that might interest the police?

"What happem to yo' eye?" said Flaco.

"Been brawling with the Aryan Brotherhood over shirts like Carlos'. I tried to steal one of their Master Race versions."

142

FINDING DEVO

Eric's nose ring quivered. I aimed a broad, knowing grin at Manco. He stabbed out his cigarette in an astray on the bar, took off his glasses, and cleaned the lenses with his vacant sleeve. He could tie fishing line with those five dexterous fingers and, judging from the outline of the stump beneath his shirtsleeve, clasp a fishing rod there at the armpit. His black eyes had been enlarged by his glasses. They were actually those of a medium-sized rodent.

Flaco switched to mostly Spanish: "What does *Ar-yan Brotherhood* mean?"

Manco put his glasses on. "It means he thinks he is funny and we are fools. You think we are fools Russell?"

"Not exactly. More like lingering testaments to the absolute *brilliance* of Generalísimo Santa Anna during the Mexican-American War."

Round Girl arrived with a bowl of ice cream. She offered Manco some. He declined, magnified eyes holding on me. Despite my hostile feelings, I maintained a sociable posture and addressed him in guileless Spanish: "When you finally establish Aztlán in the United States, what is it you will import from México first? Parasites in the water? dilapidated infrastructure? Illiteracy, penury, corruption?"

Round Girl intervened on Manco's behalf: "Does the United States need more corruption? Thought they had enough."

I acknowledged her with a pleasant smile. "Can always use a little more. Nothing like learning from the best."

Round Girl dripped a spot of ice cream on her blouse. She dabbed at it with a napkin. I introduced myself.

"Pati," she said cordially. Pati ladled ice cream into her mouth. "Yes," she rejoined with a *slurp*, "I suppose México is best when it comes to corruption. Or worst. A result of colonialism, not to mention North American conquest."

"So you will be importing lack of personal responsibility too," I said. "I thought the United States had enough of that as well." Pati's big mahogany eyes swelled and circled in her head as she digested my words. Like an indoctrinated schoolgirl, she wasn't used to having her premises on "colonialism" and "North American conquest" challenged and couldn't quite determine if they had been. I resolved to remove all doubt on the subject and treat her with the same irreverence due any member of Manco's clan. I reverted to English, my eyes smirking at the four of them, "Yearn for Monteczuma's urns full of human hearts, huh?" I repeated the phrase in Spanish. It's poetic timbre in the language surprised me so I stuck with Spanish and added a rough edge before withdrawing: "Original hijos de la chingada, you Aztecas. Best to be careful what you wish for. Monteczuma's revenge will leave you

143

more bloodied than Santa Anna, Sam Houston, and Winfield Scott did."

23

FELIPE wasn't one to listen in on other people's conversations, yet as the mayor's driver, he often couldn't help but overhear what was being said in the backseat of the Range Rover, or in the backseat of the Lincoln Continental, the car of choice Sunday night when he drove the mayor and Media Minister Charlado to and from Armando Montoya's party. His presence in the car rarely if ever hindered the conversation, even when a sensitive subject came up. Felipe frequently doubled as the mayor's personal secretary and was privy to confidential information anyway. So while he didn't habitually follow every word being said, he was dutifully prepared for the mayor (or Gloria) to prompt him into the dialogue with an occasional "what do you think about that, Felipe?" or "make a note of that, Felipe." And tonight, en route from Montoya's party to dropping off Lazarito at home, the mayor's tenor resonated restrained joy and excitement, so Felipe paid close attention, expecting to be drawn into the discussion.

Mayor Juan Pacífico Velázquez was in exceptionally high, unabashed spirits. He had come away from the party with an important commitment, a commitment in need of publicity. "I want this on the front page tomorrow, Lazarito," he said. "You need not make it the headline but I want it on page one."

Lazarito stared up at the full moon sliding into view out his backseat window, sorting out a few work-related issues as Felipe took the curves down into Old Vallarta. Foremost on his mind was el comandante's leave of absence and the debt due within a week for postponing that story about the raid...yet, as always, he remained attentive to the mayor. "Too late for that," he said. "It is after midnight and I—"

"Rayos," the mayor cursed. "Long day with the dedication and all...forgot how late it was... Pues, the next day's paper then. Tuesday's paper. But make sure it is given high priority on television and radio tomorrow. We need plenty of exposure. And Felipe?"

Felipe glanced at the mayor through the rear view mirror. "Sí?"

"I want flyers posted all around town before the end of the day tomorrow. And see to it that news of the match is posted on my website. This is our first major attraction at Arena Vallarta and now that we have star power we can no longer delay in giving it all the publicity it deserves."

"I will get started first thing in the morning, señor."

"We have given publicity to the other matches being held at the arena on Saturday," Lazarito said. "And we could have given Armando Montoya's match publicity as well—"

Juan's temper flared uncharacteristically: "*Carambas*, Lazarito! That is no way to deal with Armando. He told us he would give us his answer tonight and he has. If you had publicized the match without his consent he would have taken it as an insult, made another commitment and left us looking like fools. La Montaña is an honorable man who is strong of will as well as body. Sometimes I wonder qué chingados you are thinking... Puta."

Lazarito remained silent but Juan doubted he was sufficiently chastened. Behind Lazarito's admirable social skills and media savvy lurked a conniving nature. Media Minister Lazarito Charlado's talents were well suited to the political arena but Juan often found them lacking when it came to dealing with individuals honestly.

"And after he agreed to the match I did not even consider your proposal to make an announcement at the party, Lazarito. Montoya's party is his affair and has no bearing on our negotiations with him."

"Just a harmless suggestion," said Lazarito blandly, "to garner witnesses. Difficult to back out once so many know about—"

"Montoya would have seen right through such a ploy and taken it for what it was: a strong-arm tactic and an affront to his honor since he had just given us his word. A man like him has no fear of public opinion when his honor is at stake, Lazarito. And the only way he would *ever* back out on his word would be in response to a personal insult, such as making a scene at his party intended to leverage him." Juan ran an exasperated hand through his hair. "*Garner witnesses...*pinche cabrón. We were *negotiating*, Lazarito, not *litigating*. Híjole. When you negotiate you have to get to know a man before adopting a strategy on how to deal with him. Dios mío, es el sentido común." It's common sense. "Right Felipe?" Juan searched for Felipe's eyes in the rearview mirror.

"Sí señor." Felipe remained fixed on the road. But Juan caught a glimpse of his own shadowy eyes in the mirror. Invulnerable eyes, a trait he wasn't accustomed to seeing in himself. He flashed on last night's meeting—the curious, intractable, violent, seething faces at the round table in Arena Vallarta's dining hall; the way his wife, Gloria, left them tamed, cowed, vanquished; broken and beaten as whipped dogs; dismembered and scattered like vulture food, carrion in the desert. He truly admired Gloria's fearless ability to utilize the power at her disposal and blurted out his next remark as if to lend himself that same fearlessness: "And if you cannot deal with a man, shoot him."

Felipe wondered if he had heard right and wasn't sure he wanted to know if he had. Media Minister Charlado raised his rumpled brows at the mayor and searched his face. A swarthy expressive face, the twisted smile and mustache distorted by the moon shadows rolling through the car. Lazarito loosed a dry cough against a cold shudder in his chest, apprehension choking his tongue. He'd never heard the mayor say such a thing. Shoot the man if you cannot deal with him? He couldn't possibly be serious. Juan sensed Lazarito's uneasiness and pointed a gun finger at him, thumbed the trigger, and cut into the tension with a genial laugh. "Fortunately," he said, "*you* can be dealt with, Lazarito."

Lazarito allowed himself a small chuckle at his own expense. He caught a glint in the mayor's eye challenging him to find his ever present tongue and come up with a retort. "Gracias, Señor Mayor," he said, pausing to gather his wits. "But if we shoot Montoya because we cannot deal with him, we have nothing to gain. The arena still loses his star power and the money he might bring in. Best to keep him alive and hope we can deal with him later."

A smile exploded across the mayor's face. "That," he chortled, "is exactly what my wife would say."

A deep belly laugh relieved Lazarito of his remaining apprehension and set him off into a peal of cackles. Felipe stopped at a red light, peaked over his shoulder, and joined in the laughter. He couldn't help himself, not because laughter is contagious but because of a sudden image he had of Lazarito turkey waddling to his plump turkey cackle. Lazarito laced his hands under his ample belly, got a grip on himself. "I imagine she would say that, señor," he said. "Yes indeed..." Felipe accelerated through the intersection. "So I suppose," Lazarito surmised with lingering mirth, "we must find alternatives to shooting a man we cannot deal with."

"Fortunately," said Juan, "Armando is only difficult to deal with, not impossible. For the most part, what you see is what you get with La Montaña. I took the time to watch him wrestle in Guadalajara and have gotten to know him. Met his trainer as well. Montoya is true to himself above all else and will always fulfill his promises and obligations, whether you like it or not."

Juan grew sober, lost in self-reflection. He drew a pensive breath, "Politics," he exhaled, "law, the media, these are the sources of our power, Lazarito, our status confirmed by the diplomas, titles, and licenses we hold. But our status does not work to our favor with a man like Montoya. He will give us the respect we require but, if he does not receive respect in return, he is not afraid to treat us with the same disregard. And given our positions of power, he mistrusts our motives much more than he mistrusts the motives of others without such power. He knows he is popular, imposing and talented, knows he can be utilized to great benefit in a variety of venues, not just Arena Vallarta. And," Juan proffered Lazarito a hardened stare, "he is also well aware that there are plenty of chingones around looking to screw him over. He will not be taken advantage of, especially by men like me and you." Juan's gaze drifted out the windshield. "Due to my position, political contacts and the like, he will go to great lengths to make sure I do not get him under my thumb. And I have no desire to have him under my thumb. But I do wish to do business with him."

Lazarito nodded absently, a distant look in his eye, calculating what he stood to gain should the mayor strike a long-term business deal with Armando Montoya... Exclusive interviews with a future wrestling champion? A piece of the action as a promoter? Bigger pieces as Manager *and* Promoter...?

Juan saw the wheels turning in Lazarito's brain and raised his voice to snap him out of his musings: "And I will not have you spoiling my negotiations with him, Lazarito. I brought you along tonight to meet Montoya, the man to whom you will be giving quite a bit of publicity this week, *not* to have you meddle in the deal with idiotic ideas about how to make sure he keeps his word. But now I see it may have been a mistake to bring you along. You need not have met him at all. Nowadays you *pinches periodistas* spend much of your time writing about subjects you know nothing about anyhow."

Lazarito released a throat-clearing grunt. "Negotiations," Juan added deliberately, "are not like reporting or inventing news, Lazarito, where you can and do disassociate yourself from your subject." He waved off Lazarito's muted protest. "There may be exceptions, personal interviews and the like, but you do generally have the luxury of disassociation, or of invention, or of simply pleading ignorance to a person's motives and goals, however ugly or honorable they may be."

"That is because a person's motives and goals are not always relevant to the news, señor."

"Perhaps not, Lazarito. But they *are* always relevant when negotiating. And thanks to my informed and tactful approach, Armando promised to sign a contract in my office tomorrow afternoon. For one match and one match only. We now have a most popular opponent for Masked Apocalypse."

Felipe was a wrestling fan and curious about a detail: "Will La Montaña unmask Apocalypse?"

SEVE VERDAD

"Armando La Montaña Montoya will win the match," declared Mayor Velázquez with gusto, "and we will see how much money Apocalypse requires to have his mask removed." He shifted his weight and faced the Media Minister. "But I want that rumor spread, Lazarito. A juicy rumor about the true identity of Masked Apocalypse and how it might be revealed this coming Saturday night at Arena Vallarta's *Wrestling Extravaganza*."

"Most certainly," the Media Minister agreed eagerly. "Rumors are my specialty." Lazarito felt inspired by the mayor's renewed enthusiasm, inspired enough to risk changing the subject so he could forge ahead with his own agenda. "And speaking of rumors," he said, "I recently managed to quiet one or two."

The mayor gave Lazarito a reassuring pat on the knee. "Yes Lazarito. Gloria told me of your little deal with el comandante. Too bad he has taken an extended leave of absence. But have patience. My wife has not forgotten you. She will be in touch tomorrow. You will get your just due."

Lazarito cringed. He would much rather deal with police or the mayor than Gloria. But the mayor was right. He would get his just due.

24

SEVERED heads planted on wooden stakes. Heads adorning a spiked fence. Four more impaled on roadside pikes. The three panels on Pedro's computer screen were titled: Ciudad Juárez, Nogales, Culiacán...the heads brazenly displayed in all their gory splendor for public viewing.

Pedro snorted caustically and stared at the screen as though viewing stills from a horror movie he'd seen a hundred times. This type of gore was all too common in Mexico. The mainstream media didn't generally splash photos of severed heads and decapitated bodies across television screens, magazine covers and newspapers, but such images could often be found in trashy tabloids as well as on the Internet. And police databases throughout Mexico had them on file. Typical gangland casualties. The decapitation of rival gangsters had become a popular method of intimidation for Mexican narco gangs and cartels, and police and federales were often killed (if not beheaded as well) for no other reason than to mark a gang's territory. The drug-war's death toll of police, federales, military troops, gangsters, and innocent civilians was staggering. Thousands upon thousands had died over the past couple of years alone. And the more troops and treasure the government sacrificed to fight the drug war, the more powerful and vicious the drug lords became. In some parts of the country, the drug war resembled a civil war.

The disc flashed to a single shot of two bloodied heads staining a car hood in Ciudad Juárez. A particularly gruesome photo. The grimacing faces seemed to stare right at Pedro, the heads planted on the hood like ornaments. He averted his eyes and asked himself the same dispassionate questions he'd been asking since he began viewing the disc's contents: what was this all about? what was the disc trying to say? and what did this have to do with the dead man discovered at the marina? Drugs and cash (as well as the disc) were found on the corpse. Was he connected to all this butchery somehow?

Was the disc suggesting that it was just a matter of time before relatively peaceful tourist towns like Vallarta, Cabo San Lucas, and Cancún were engulfed in bloodshed? Were these images intended to scare him, cause panic, fear of a *nationwide* civil war?

A nationwide civil war over what? Drugs? The idea seemed as absurd as a radical Islamist invasion of Mexico and the Americas. Yet...

Pedro settled his eyes back on his computer screen and the image of the heads atop the car hood. Terror certainly had come to Mexico. The country hadn't experienced such widespread violence since the revolution a century ago.

He felt himself growing morose and dropped his chin to his chest. This sin madre drug war, he thought, causes more pain and suffering than all the drugs ever invented by God and Man. Best to just legalize them, as Mexico's former president Vicente Fox had suggested... Or *re-legalize* them. Why, when and how were they ever made illegal—prohibited—in the first place?

A low murmur tingled Pedro's ears and curled the hair on the back of his neck. His eyes darted out the barred window, his ears straining to capture another sound. He heard the murmur again, but it didn't come from outside the window. Pedro's eyes flicked back to his computer screen and a new picture—a video of eight hooded men armed with automatic rifles standing behind a bound and gagged prisoner on his knees. This time audio accompanied the video, the first sounds from the disc. The man standing directly behind the prisoner raised a finger to the heavens. His voice grew louder, and Pedro could see his lips move from behind his mask. The language was incomprehensible but he thought he recognized the words "Koran," "Jihad," "Islam" and, as the man drew a knife from his belt, the unmistakable phrase "Allahu Akbar" echoed amongst those gathered around him.

SEVE VERDAD

Pedro froze at his desk, doe eyes wide and pulse quickened. One of the hooded men gripped the prisoner's hair, straightening his posture. Singular grunts and groans escaped from the bound and gagged victim as the man with the knife pierced his jugular and sawed through his neck. Blood flowed inexorably, the decapitated torso collapsed on the floor, the head held up triumphantly on the point of the knife.

Pedro gasped, and choked down the bile rising in his throat with a gulp of water from a trembling glass. "Pinche rechingado," he cursed turning away from his computer. He squeezed his eyes shut and covered them with a hand as if to block the vision of the decapitation from reentering his mind. Qué demonios did it all mean? He uncovered his eyes and jerked them open in a fit of lucidity. A distinction; the assassin had forced him to see a distinction between gangster brutality and fanatic Islamist brutality. Wasn't that it? But why? And what exactly was that distinction...? Gangsters usually beheaded their victims after killing them, the fatally wounded bodies often found nearby. But the bloodlust of these terrorists...they relished the ceremony. Bloodthirsty savages! *Re-legalize* drugs and the cartels would be depleted, disbanded and destroyed. But what would stop these Islamic terrorists? Even a world converted to their twisted religious ideology would only serve to sanctify and multiply their atrocities.

Overall though, were these really valid distinctions? Cartel gangsters were known to have performed live beheadings; countless innocent victims fell prey to both cartel gangsters and Islamic terrorists daily, so perhaps the live beheading and those stills of severed heads were meant to point out the *similarities* between gangster brutality and Islamist brutality—fanatic brutality. The brutality of religious fanatics and fanatic drug lords... And what about the brutality and destruction perpetuated by anti-drug zealots—prohibition *jihadists*?!? They must relish the drug war, and war in general. Why else wouldn't they just re-legalize drugs and be done with it?

The whole world had gone mad! Was that the point the disc was trying to make?!?

Pedro stiffened and chanced a look at his computer screen. Another message had appeared against a dark background: La vida corta y trágica de Sasha.

(The short and tragic life of Sasha.)

150

MEXICO'S next wrestling sensation was somewhere around the house and I made it my job to find him and chastise him for keeping his new profession from me. The only way he could pay for the insult was with free ringside tickets to his matches and personal interviews whenever the hell I wanted...for a story germinating in my head right now... A story he just might like...

All Pro NFL beast La Montaña *looms south of the US border...making his comeback...poised to terrorize cities across the globe... Better hide your women and children...*

Something like that.

Mountain wasn't in the game room so I followed the hallway to the end where a door swung open and I came face to face with El Gordo and his extraordinary gut. He could balance a bottle of tequila on his belly while standing—the bottle he held in his hand. He greeted me with a pat on the back and a tilt of the bottle. I raised my margarita. He added a shot. "A shot of sanity," he said and made his way down the hall. I wasn't sure what he meant by that but it sounded cheerfully ironic. I stepped inside the office. Before me, a bay window the size of a drift boat broadcasted a partial ocean and city view. Below the window a wooden counter littered with several Styrofoam cups ran the length of the wall. Mountain was off to my right, sitting on an iron-legged barstool and chomping the end of an extinguished cigar. He was immersed in conversation with someone but acknowledged my presence with a shallow lift of his chin. At the opposite end of the counter a man and a woman occupied two more stools. They were chatting with Devo who stood with his back to me. I took a healthy swig from my margarita, shuddered, and immediately grasped the meaning of Gordo's parting irony... He hadn't added a shot of "sanity" to my margarita but *insanity*—mezcal, tequila's crazy cousin. Despite the similar name, mezcal does not contain mescaline or other *identifiable* psychotropic substances, but it sure feels like it does sometimes, especially if you drink enough to get to the worm at the bottom of the bottle. I ate that worm once. Don't remember exactly what happened afterwards but I do remember having the most colorfully exotic dreams of my life that night.

I was already tipsy and the pungent, loamy taste of mezcal swelled my palate and set my head afloat. Space seemed to expand; the vaulted ceiling gave me a sensation of having entered a cathedral. I felt out of place and forgot why I had entered "la oficina". Devo's head swiveled around and pierced me with mica eyes. His gaze guided

me to an empty stool between him and Mountain. I installed myself
there and took in the view out the window. I couldn't see the moon but
it sure did shine somewhere overhead. Its reflection streaked the ocean
far below. Stars dotted the sky and faded into city lights. Lights are
attractive but I was drawn to the darkened woods off to the left. Purple
figures were in the darkness. Recognizable forms growing shapeless as
I deciphered them.

I sipped my mezcal-laced margarita and settled into a comfort
zone all my own. My ears, habitually tuned to gossip, reveled in the
office chatter as my eyes deciphered the changing forms in the forest.
To my right, an encouraging deep voice spoke to Mountain in Spanish,
told him he'd meet him at the airport in Guadalajara on Wednesday.
Mountain said he still wanted to think about it. The woman to my left
addressed Devo in smug English, said one needn't think much at all to
know that everything was blown out of proportion. Devo said that
everything had been *settling* out of proportion for some time now.
Deep Voice reminded Mountain that everything was settled. The
contract conformed to all legal standards. Mountain reminded *him* that
this is Mexico. When you're screwed it doesn't matter what's fucking
legal. Smug Voice impressed upon Devo that these were legal matters
to be handled through proper channels according to the law. Devo said
this is war and war has its own rules. The victor will decide what is
legal. Smug Voice's partner had a squeamish voice thick with the
hubris of a reform-minded professor. He feared that an attitude like
Devo's only incited violence, there really was no terror war. Deep
Voice told Mountain it was war, the competition fierce. Time was of
the essence and he needed to make a decision. Mountain said he would
make up his mind in a few days. Devo's forbearing tone was light as a
breath of air tickling my ear. He submitted that the enemy's mind was
made up, their motives unchanged over the last thousand years. You
couldn't avoid war any more than you could convince rapists in a dark
alley not to rape you. He also joked that it might be a good idea to treat
war as a legal matter, bring the battlefield into the courtroom, and kill
all the judges and lawyers. Smug Voice found Devo's quip trite,
Shakespearean but unconvincing. Progressive, liberal thinking and
policies would win the hearts and minds of our "supposed enemies"
without bloodshed. Mountain told Deep Voice that blood and theatre
were part of the spectacle, but winning was what mattered most. How
long would it be before he, La Montaña Montoya, won all his matches
and became champion? Deep Voice said it might take some time. He'd
have to twist some arms. He had a promoter or two by the balls. Devo
said that when you get the enemy by the balls, hearts and minds
follow. But the only people *progressive thinkers* ever got by the balls

were government dependents. Progressive, *liberal* ideology could only rally a fraction of the warriors who rally to the enemy's message of religious conquest. *Progressive thinkers* would have to adapt to circumstances or never live to see any progress at all. Smug Voice said he was exaggerating and asked for a definition of progress. Mountain said he needed to make some progress, and progress means win, *now*, right away. Every match. Deep Voice assured him that he had a clear strategy in the works to advance his career. Squeamish Voice insisted that terror sprang from ill-advised strategies and a lack of understanding for those who hate us. Smug Voice agreed and added that there was still time for self-evaluation as no real, imminent terror threat existed. Devo said it should be easy for them to feel that way from their perch at the Washington Hotel. Smug Voice sniggered, said she was unimpressed with the Washington. They would stay at Dreams the next time.

My gaze had been drifting between purple figures in the darkness and a bank of lights from what I presumed was the Washington, Vallarta's largest hotel. I swung my gaze around to the smug voice a few paces off my left shoulder. A pinkie extended out from underneath her wineglass, a sparkling bracelet hanging loose from the wrist, her lace blouse draped loosely about her shoulders. Graying Dutch-cut blond hair cradled her sanguine profile—her face singed from the tropical sun, an upturned confrontational nose, thin chin and lips frozen in a moist, beatific smile. Her older (middle-aged) well-groomed and manicured companion sat in the corner contemplating his thumbs, immersed in self-evaluation and the question of why terrorists hate us.

Mountain aimed his gravelly tone at the back of my head: "Oye Ruzz, you think I should sign a contract with this güey?"

I shot him an exceedingly sober stare. "I would not sign anything until I had the opinion of a trusted, disinterested third party."

"You are that party."

"Your friend Tomás told me you are wrestling, not you. Does that sound like you trust—"

"Pues, I am telling you now."

"Where is the contract?"

"In my bedroom."

I scrutinized Deep Voice, his narrow eyes and scheming lips. "Now is not the time to sign anything," I said. "Maybe tomorrow after a swim and sober breakfast."

Deep Voice glanced at his heavy watch. "Very good. Good advice. I will be in touch Tuesday morning. Now I must get some sleep. Early flight tomorrow." He shook Mountain's hand and left.

"Pinche fucking güey," Mountain said.

"If you feel that way about him, don't sign with him."

"Deyz odda optionz, datz fo' shuya."

"He a prospective agent?"

"Fucking pinche cabrón is what he is."

Mezcal may be distinct from mescaline but, as opposed to tequila and other hard liquor, it can sharpen your senses as well as drug them, just like a small dose of mescaline. And I suddenly felt sharp, completely focused on why I'd entered the office in the first place: "Why the hell didn't you tell me you were wrestling? Whaddaya think I am? some scumbag newspaperman out to destroy your reputation? I can help make you famous. When are you gonna sign with an agent? Better have an attorney review all prospective contracts. Who do you have in mind to promote your matches? When is—"

Mountain cut me off with an abrupt raise of his hand. He hopped off his stool to greet Smug Voice. "Youz leafen Lezlie?" She met him in the center of the office, lips thawed and puckered to bid adieu to Mountain cheek to cheek. He said he was glad they came. Her companion extended his thumbs and clasped Mountain's hand in both of his. "We are always happy to see you," he said, "and take a break from cold Montreal."

"Mi casa es su casa," Mountain assured them graciously. They thanked him and trundled out of the office.

"Where'd you meet them?" I asked.

"Oh, deyz frienz fom dee fooball daze en Oddawa. Dey livz en Monreal now."

"Her husband, Oscar, is from the United States," said Devo.

"Minnezoda." Mountain moved his stool closer to mine, took a seat and lit his cigar. The scar on his right knee was a neat silver zipper over the kneecap. Armando 'La Montaña' Montoya's speed and quickness, unusual in an athlete his size, had been his greatest asset as a football player, giving him a wide range of moves to beat larger offensive linemen and make more than his share of tackles, sacks, and forced turnovers. After his surgery, it soon became evident that no amount of rehabilitation could regain his edge. So rather than risk ending up a cripple with an attempted comeback, he retired. A smart move. Especially since, according to my estimates, between his CFL and NFL careers he'd pocketed over six-million dollars plus endorsements, endorsements from companies like Nike, McDonald's, and Pharmaton Vitamins that do business in Mexico where his popularity peaked during his football heyday. Given his savvy conservative nature, he had likely banked a good deal of that money in secure investments, eventually allowing him to buy this house.

FINDING DEVO

(Mountain is always circumspect about his financial status. But part of my job is to know the business end of sports and, as I've reminded him when we banter on the subject, sports contracts and attending endorsements are most always a matter of public record. Naturally, I have respect for his privacy and only pry into how he's grown his fortune since his retirement from football when our banter leaves me the opening, an opening he invariably blocks with Mountainous ease.)

Devo said, "Leslie's with the Associated Press, Martell."

"No kidding. That might explain some of that conversation you had with her and, uh, Oscar... You don't seem to share Oscar's preoccupation with why terrorists, hate us."

"Religious Islamic fanatics, to be precise."

"Right. I think I understood that."

Devo gave me a careless grin with a shrug attached. "There's always some sort of justification for brutality. The Nazi's were justified in their hatred and aggression because the treaty of Versailles was unjust. Tojo and his fascists were justified in their hatred and aggression 'cause Roosevelt cut off fuel supplies to Japan. The South was justified because Lincoln wanted to destroy their way of life. Who gives a shit *why* Islamic fanatics hate us? The question is a distraction, empowers the enemy and implies we're to blame for their behavior."

"Someone always has a reason," Mountain growled in succinct Spanish, "an excuse to fuck you." He frowned, his great brown eyes fierce. La Montaña was not about to let *anyone* fuck up his new-found wrestling career.

Devo concurred: "That's right. And when you give 'em what they say they want, they'll want more. Never fails...*ever.*"

I focused on Mountain. "Unless you sign an ironclad contract."

Devo moved a stool closer to me and took a seat at the counter. "No such thing," he said.

Mountain held my gaze and repeated Devo's words in Spanish: "No hay tal cosa." He swiveled around to take in the view out the window. I took in the view as well, one eye on Mountain. "There are limits to acting on your own behalf, Montoya. You will need to hire an agent, like you did for football."

"Not before I am ready."

He slid a talavera ashtray over. Devo offered me a cigar. I accepted with a "thanks." Light flared at Devo's fingertips. Smoke gathered above his head as he lit his cigar. He tossed a box of matches onto the counter.

The tip of my cigar already had a hole punched in it. I lit up and blew smoke past Montoya. "When's your next match?"

"Saturday night at Arena Vallarta."

SEVE VERDAD

"Arena Vallarta?... Perfect. I expect free ringside seats."

"No problema. You can go with Brenda and Ara, and Johnny if he wants."

"I also expect a personal interview with you after."

Mountain tossed me a wry smile and winked at Devo. "Bueno," he said. "But youz godda pay."

I was about to jump all over him for that, remind him that he was a public figure and as such I didn't have to pay him a dime to write about him, that it was up to him to get on my good side if he wanted good publicity, that he was lucky to have a friend like me as a journalist, someone he could trust to advance his career, but Devo intervened: "Thought you had other, new ideas to write about, Martell."

I cast Devo a wary glance. "Why do you care?"

He took a languid puff from his cigar, as if listening to music in his robe and slippers.

"Ja! Wha' kina bull youz woykin' on now, Matell? Ecuadorian llama razin'?"

Mountain's glib grin required a glib retort: "How do you get a llama to run faster? Do they run after something like the bone dogs chase in dog races? How do you train a llama? Are there llama jockeys? Can you bet on llama races?"

"You can bet on anything," said Devo. "And I'll bet you've come up with another angle on that dead guy you told me about."

"Qué?" Mountain's tone grew alarmed. "What dead guy?"

Devo studied his cigar. "Tell'm what ya got, Martell."

Devo could never have met Mitch Broadrick, Assistant Managing Editor at the home office of New World Sports in Seattle. He'd never heard Mitch's nasal drone pronounce, "Tell'm what ya got, Martell," seen his eyes squint and lower lip extend as he massaged his chin, or witnessed an ash at the end of Mitch's stogie maintain its figure between his fingers. But somehow Devo had Mitch's mannerisms down pat, right down to the cigar ash and nasal drone.

I shook the déjà vu from my head, but couldn't shake a needling uncertainty I had about Devo's uncommon interest in me. Was it a genuine interest in my writing or was he simply toying with me for his own amusement? I could feel Mountain's inquisitive stare boring into the back of my head as I regarded Devo. I'd have to tell him about the dead guy. And I did have another angle on the story, one Devo might have heard something about, since his conversation with Leslie and Oscar had reminded me of it.

"Well," I began slowly, my attention split between them. "You both know about the raid yesterday."

156

Mountain nodded. "Policía y federales fucked it up. The place was empty, though they likely robbed it."

"Well," I reached for the article in my back pocket, "I thought this might be connected somehow." I showed Mountain the dead guy.

"Loo' li' 'eez oba dozed."

"Yeah, he's over dozed all right," Devo said.

"He was put to sleep permanently, at the marina. About the same time as the raid. Suffered a broken neck along with a couple other appendages."

Mountain frowned at the photo. "The Vallarta marina?"

"Yep. Found up by the docks." I laid the dead guy on the counter and took a hasty puff from my cigar. "At least he got a little media attention, unlike the raid, enough to deduce it was probably murder. Who were the cops after at the raid? Drug dealers?"

"Pobly. Deyz odda posabileez. Rateros, youz know. Teebz, hoodlumz, tugz."

"I was thinking of another reason, something that would explain why such a large police and federale raid hasn't been reported in the media." I had lowered my voice a tad and their heads tilted at me.

"Sí?" Mountain said.

"Go on," said Devo.

"Well, Devo, when you and Leslie were talking about terrorism...were you thinking there might be terrorists here in Vallarta?"

Devo snorted. "That's a good one Martell. Keep that imagination working."

"I heard a rumor yesterday that Arab terrorists were renting that duplex that was raided."

"Jah-umff!" Mountain stared at his cigar with an overwrought scowl. Apparently, neither one of them had heard the rumor. Had it been kept quiet? Was there any truth to it? Maybe not, according to Devo and Mountain.

"You heard the rumor on Saturday?" Devo inquired, smoke curling the faint smile on his lips, "the evening of the raid?"

"Yeah. After the raid. At a taco stand after the raid."

Mountain slouched and hooded his eyes as if preparing to attack, or take a siesta.

"Sorry if rumors bore you Mountain. And they always seem to stop short of scaring tourists. You never hear rumors about *terrorists* in Vallarta. But if the raid was aimed at terrorists and missed, well, that could explain the rumors and why the raid wasn't reported."

Devo's voice was tranquil, almost feminine: "What does that hypothesis have to do with the dead guy?"

"If terrorists killed him, that would be a good reason to keep him outta the news as well. I had to scour the papers to find him."

"Killed him for what?"

I flicked an ash into the ashtray and let my imagination go: "Maybe he was a gangster who was dealing drugs to the terrorists, or buying drugs from them. Maybe he owed them money, or ripped them off. Or maybe the terrorists were holding him prisoner and he escaped but they killed him at the marina... Maybe the cops found the body at the marina *before* the raid, connected the victim to the duplex, but were too late to catch the terrorists..."

Devo blew smoke rings. "I knew you had a few more angles to this," he said.

I took that as a compliment. There *was* a story here somewhere...

"But I still think the cops have no clue who killed him."

"Maybe not," I had to admit. "And I'm not sure how the guy could have been killed at the marina or the body *dumped* there without witnesses to the crime. Of course there might be witnesses we don't know about, witnesses who have been silenced for some reason. And if the body was *dumped* at the marina it was probably from a boat... But I can't figure why anyone, even the cops, who might be able to get away with it, would risk dumping a body there."

Mountain extended a paw in my direction and snuffed out his cigar in the ashtray. He crossed his arms and smirked, half at me and half out the window. The man's chest was refrigerator thick, his head solid as a wrecking ball, and he spoke in the tone of a guy who wants the radio station changed 'cause he's heard that shitty little tune too many times: "Gangstaz, terroristas, fucking corrupt policía. Why don' youz juz' keel dem all en dee eztoyie? Sounz li' dey needz a goo' keelen."

"Yeah. Kill everyone, Martell. Good and bad. Start with the cops and feds since they've fucked up so much... And after they're gone, you can be the hero!"

"Corrrrecto Errrrrnesto! So daz i', eh buddy? Youz gowyen a be a 'ero!"

My cigar got bitter all of a sudden. I laid it in the ashtray. "Maybe I'll make you the hero, Montoya."

Mountain jumped off his stool and slapped me on the back. "Sounz goo'. Youz godda pay dough." He lumbered out of the office with powerful strides belying any knee injury.

Devo stood from his stool and held up the dead guy. "Can't anyone come up with a better photo? Or is this all you need for a good story? I'll pay you a thousand pounds sterling to find his killer!"

"You carry British pounds?"

FINDING DEVO

Devo dropped his cigar in the ashtray. Then he tore the article in half, slapped one half over the other, made a bindle, and held it in front of my nose. "You wanna see a pound?"

"Only if it's coke."

He sniggered, hid the bindle in his left hand, cupped his hands together and shook. He flashed his empty palms at me, reached behind my left ear with his right hand, and produced an old silver English pound, a glistening portrait of the queen (Victoria?).

My tone was flat, as though unimpressed by Devo's trick: "I said coke." I noted Devo's unadorned hands. Like me he wore no jewelry at all, not even a watch.

Devo put the coin between his hands, rubbed them together, flashed his palms and pulled the bindle from behind my right ear.

I said, "That doesn't look like a pound."

"Open it up."

I opened the bindle. Nothing.

"Go ahead and unfold it completely. Be careful. Do it slowly."

The article was in one piece and had the same angular edge from where I'd torn it from La Estrella Nocturna. A generous portion of powdered cocaine covered the photo of the dead man—a white sheet leaving only his feet exposed. The sight of it gave me a jolt equal to huffing a couple of rails.

"If it...uh...weren't for your short sleeves..." I stammered, surveying Devo's bare arms, "...I'd say you have plenty up them."

"Check it out," he said, eyes grinning. "The cocaine."

I stuck a pinkie on the dead-man's shins and had a tiny taste. "It's coke. That was some trick." It really was. My eyes were still blinking in amazement. "What'd you do? find a copy of the same article to rip in half? How'd you manage to get the drugs into—"

"You know a good magician never reveals his secrets."

I held the coke out to him. "Keep it," he said with a quick wave of his hand. "You said you might want some later."

"Did I? That's 'cause Mountain owes me."

"You can have this then."

"I dunno. Looks like double the legal amount for personal use."

"Give half to Johnny."

"Well... Since you put it that way, thanks." I carefully folded the article up and slipped the cocaine into my back pocket. Devo headed for the door.

"I thought you were gonna produce a pound."

Devo pivoted. "I did."

"Not of coke."

"You have enough there, doncha?"

159

SEVE VERDAD

I released a begrudging chuckle. "Oh yeah."

Devo paused and stroked his chin. "You know El Cabezón?"

"Sure. Big Head. I stopped by there before the party."

Devo's gray, smiling eyes were those of an old man who'd never lost his sense of humor. Paternal eyes. He can't be too much older than I am yet at that moment he recalled an image of my grandfather. "Buy ya a beer there tomorrow evening," he said. "Around eight o'clock. You can let me know how your story is developing."

26

Sasha ve la navaja
La resplandeciente garra de la luna
deciende en el crepúsculo y apaga el alba
su sexo florido bañado en sangre sagrada

THE poem held its position in the center of Pedro's computer screen. He studied it, unsure if he grasped its meaning. Was this the short, tragic life of Sasha the disc had referred to? She sees the blade, the sparkling moon's claw descends in the twilight and snuffs out the dawn, her flowering sex bathed in sacred blood? What interpretation could be drawn from that? Had Sasha been cut down in the prime of life, gutted like a fish, sliced open through her sex (vagina?) just as she had begun to flower and bloom? Or was the entire poem a metaphor? Did it refer to a woman's plight in general? the sacred blood of her menses and the suffering of her sex—her gender? How her spirit, her light, her flowering dawn is snuffed out?

Pedro mumbled, "Su sexo florido bañado en sangre sagrada," and felt an acrid shudder deep in his diaphragm. More blood must be coming, he thought. Another gruesome spectacle from the disc. The poem inched its way up his computer screen. Pedro braced himself for a grizzly display. But as quickly as his body tensed he relaxed, for taking the poem's place were more words, small print crawling up from the bottom of the screen and filling it with a short story. Pedro began reading:

> But she falls in love anyway. At least Sasha thinks she might be in love. And that is where love begins, in the mind which, for Sasha, remains intact, unlike her genitals, stripped from her as she bloomed into adolescence.

160

Pedro whispered, "Que poca madre," and clamped his thighs together against a sharp ache in his testicles, the poem's imagery of a female circumcision suddenly crystal clear. He continued reading:

> Sasha only sees the boy when in the company of her mother, on Sundays, in the market where they often stop at his fruit stand. He always smiles at her, and she smiles back, beneath the veil. But her almond eyes are skittish, meeting his radiant gaze in fleeting moments of intimacy, an intimacy her mother must never be allowed to discover. When he speaks to Sasha in his tender voice, she bows her head and waits for her mother to reply for her or prompt her to respond "sí," "no," "gracias," or "de nada."
>
> At home in prayer she asks forgiveness for her sins, for allowing her heart to flutter when in the boy's presence, for not keeping her gaze lowered, for wishing to take off the veil and return his smile, for dreaming of removing her robes and feeling the sun on her skin as they walk a beach together. She promises Allah, the most gracious and merciful, that she shall please Him, regain her modesty and always be obedient to her father and mother.
>
> Yet the following Sunday she sins again. This time it is discovered. Her eldest brother, Sobhi, finds a pear hidden in her room. Their mother didn't buy pears today and since Sasha would not have stolen the pear from the fruit stand, it must be a gift. A gift from the boy. A kafir boy. A native of their adopted home, Ciudad del Este, Paraguay, and a Catholic.
>
> Sasha is forbidden to leave the house. One Sunday, she is alone when a cousin arrives to fix the kitchen plumbing. He's more interested in Sasha's plumbing. She is raped, her scars torn, her painful screams gagged, her sin and shame multiplied a thousand times.
>
> Sobhi is the first to notice the bulge beneath his sister's robes, the evidence

confirmed by their mother. Father has gone north to fight the jihad so it is left to the eldest son to restore honor in the family. The whipping is brutal, Sasha's cries that their cousin raped her met with scorn. She has no witnesses, much less the four male witnesses required by Islamic law, so she is beaten further for dishonoring a cousin.

Sasha's miscarriage is judged Allah's will as the child was certainly kafir. And before Sobhi's own pilgrimage north to join his father in jihad, he sees to it that honor is fully restored to his family. Sasha is bound in chains, hooded in black, and drowned in the river.

Sasha's story froze on Pedro's computer screen. He scowled at it, benumbed by the succinct cruelty. Is that it? He recoiled. What about Sobhi? and the cousin who raped Sasha? Did they get away with their crimes? This can't be the end of the story. Someone has to avenge Sasha's death! What the hell kind of story is this?!?

"A story to make me sick," Pedro muttered to himself. Just like the video of that beheading...and the stoning of that woman. Was Sasha's story true...? He imagined it was as true and real as the beheadings and stonings.

Pedro slumped in his chair in blackened disgust and sorrow. Sasha's story struck him as particularly barbaric and cruel. He had three sisters and wouldn't dream of...if anyone tried to hurt them in any way...

A subtle fury invaded his spirit and dissipated within a wave of fatigue. Pedro suddenly realized that he was taking Sasha's story awfully personally. He buried his face in his hands and rubbed his eyes. He needed a break, a night's sleep, but couldn't get Sasha out of his mind. The traditions of her family seemed more tribal than religious, ancient traditions still followed by those of many faiths. Despicable, hateful traditions. And what did her story have to do with the dead man found at the marina? Did the assassin expect the disc to justify his murder by revealing crimes the victim had had a hand in? Was the dead man Sobhi? Sobhi and Sasha's cousin?...or maybe their father?

Useless speculation. It was getting him nowhere... Perhaps that was the disc's purpose—to wear him down and get him to engage in useless speculation. Pedro glanced at the external hard drive copying the disc's images and stood from his desk. Anything else the disc had to say tonight could wait until he viewed the copy on his father's computer tomorrow morning. He blinked sleepy-eyed at the last paragraph of Sasha's story, as if to say good-bye to her; it slowly faded away as another map took its place. South America again. This one titled *La Ruta de Sobhi* (Sobhi's Route). South America contained the same smatterings and colorings of red as in previous maps, Venezuela that odd burnt orange. But this time Ciudad del Este was highlighted with a yellow star in the red Muslim Triangle at the intersection of Brazil, Argentina and Paraguay. A black trail bisected the continent from the Muslim Triangle right up through the border of Colombia and Venezuela where the map ended.

Pedro glowered at the map. "Y entonces?" he asked. And then? "A dónde se fue Sobhi?" Where did Sobhi go?

As if in response, Venezuela began blinking.

"Pinche cabrón," Pedro said. Venezuela again, and that clown Marqués. The disc was leading him in circles! If the disc wasn't intended to distract him from the investigation into the dead man found at the marina, what *was* its purpose? Really, what possible motive could drive any of this, *anybody* involved in the disc's revelations—the assassin, Marqués, radical Islamists, gangsters? It all seemed so absurd!

Pedro stiffened and said exactly that, "Es absurdo," to his computer, the disc, the assassin...

South America vanished, gave Pedro a start, like the disc really *was* answering him. He stood there, doe eyes fixed on his blank computer screen, arms folded, waiting. Waiting to go to bed, waiting for an image to appear on the screen, daring the assassin to keep him up...waiting for another message.

And there it was. In block white font against a dark background. The answer to a question, his last question. Something for him to sleep on: el poder. Utilízalo o lo pierdes a los que te destruyen.

(Power. Use it or lose it to those who destroy you.)

Pedro thought this very clever and probably true. Power was the motive, for the assassin, terrorists, cartel gangsters, prohibition *jihadists*, Marqués...perhaps everyone.

Pedro left his office. Without some sleep, he'd be powerless in the morning when the lieutenant called him back about that tramposo disc.

MASKED Apocalypse was in good spirits for a change. The last thirty hours or so had been dicey, ever since that police raid. But now his confidence was back in force. His confidence began making a comeback late Saturday night when he received confirmation that no one had been arrested in that raid. And now, by one a.m. Monday morning, after taking more than his usual liberties with a filthy motherless whore, he was his old self.

She had protested. They always do when you slip like that, stick it in the wrong hole. Except he hadn't slipped and it was in the right hole, for him. Masked Apocalypse crushed her with the titanic ease of a monster wave pounding an unsuspecting tourist, her screams easily stifled, raspberry red mouth buried beneath his grappling claw of a hand as he forced his turgid girth right on through. He could see the stunned fear in her eyes, the disbelief and terror. She thought she knew him, had serviced him three times in the last three days, why this outrage now? Why had his brown eyes lost their warmth? Why was his amiable, scrupulous face suddenly stamped with deadly fury? He wanted to tell her why. Why she was powerless. Why she was destined for the inferno. Why she was godless. But in this respect Masked Apocalypse restrained himself. She would never know why or have any recourse. Her destiny had been sealed. The only thing she did know was that she was outweighed by fifty kilos and might end up disgorged, gaffed and gutted like a fish.

When he finished and she lay unconscious, Masked Apocalypse spared her life. Left her money too. What the hell. She was a whore and suffered her station in life, would suffer more in the afterlife. And by the time she recovered enough to remember him he would be gone, never to be seen in Vallarta, or Mexico, again.

"And now?"

"Three blocks and to the left," Ahmed said to the cabby; Masked Apocalypse gave an intersection to drop them. He was rarely without Ahmed, his Lebanese bodyguard and first contact in Mexico when he arrived five years ago from the tri-border region of Brazil, Argentina and Paraguay. The tortuous journey over what American Intelligence dubbed the "Terrorist Highway" brought him from his home base of Ciudad del Este, Paraguay, through the Brazilian jungle, into Venezuela (with an extended stay in neighboring Colombia), Central America, and then, finally, to Mexico.

They passed El Pitillal's littered main plaza on the right, a bench or two occupied by indigent drunks. Masked Apocalypse would not miss Mexico, a country trapped in self-imposed indigence. Corrupt of mind, body and, most importantly, soul—spirit. The five years he'd spent here proved this to him. The people were mongrel, more so than anywhere else in the New World, or the Old World for that matter. A slovenly mix of pagan Indian and blasphemous Catholic cultures that left them bereft of identity, always in search of masks—Aztec, Mayan, Olmec, European, Christian—and incapable of recognizing their own corrupt, indigent faces. Bastard faces. No. Orphan faces, without father or mother. Even their blessed Virgen de Guadeloupe only served as a delusion, a false assurance that they weren't mongrel, weren't indigent, weren't fatherless and motherless but sons and daughters of that gran puta madre. As if such a superstition could mask Mexican indigence, offer guidance and give the country an honorable, genuine identity. As if such a superstition could alter the course of history—truth—the inescapable truth that identity is only found through the book of Allah and the guidance of His prophet, Mohammed, may Allah's peace and greetings be upon him. The inevitable, glorious truth that godless, apostate regimes will be destroyed the world over as surely and righteously as he, Masked Apocalypse, had conquered that whore.

Conversion of Indians and infidels was left to others. Masked Apocalypse used other methods.

Masked Apocalypse paid the cabby, stepped out into the moonlight and padded down the sidewalk with Ahmed as though in a clutch of Manhattan foot traffic. But there was no foot traffic or anything resembling big-city skyscrapers and bright lights. Just an apartment complex, several houses (two under construction), a parking garage where Ahmed had stashed their car, a hardware store, family grocery store, and an office building. They were headed for the alley behind the office building, a backdoor that would lead them down a stairwell and into their rented office space.

Masked Apocalypse looked the part of a hard-working Mexican, a hotel manager or clerk returning home from a late night shift or business meeting—light briefcase, his suit a dark polyester blend unencumbered by a jacket or tie. Nothing too snappy. And Ahmed, similarly dressed but empty handed and without the authoritative stature of Masked Apocalypse, was perhaps a relative who worked with him, a cousin returning to his house in the same neighborhood. In reality, however, neither expected to return home until Paradise beckoned. Their work was an endless crusade.

Masked Apocalypse didn't have too many complaints about this particular part of Mexico—Vallarta and surrounding areas. It wasn't nearly as dirty and crime ridden as Mexico City or Guadalajara. In those cities even criminals had to beware of crime. Few places on earth could match the scope of Mexico City when it came to filth, corruption and crime. Ciudad del Este could be a contender, if it had another ten to fifteen million inhabitants. Yet despite his distaste for the country and its people, he had had little trouble adapting to Mexico. He'd spent most of his life—twenty out of his thirty years—in Latin America, spoke fluent Spanish, Portuguese, and Arabic (as well as passable English), and the lessons he had learned in the tri-border region and on the Terrorist Highway made him adaptable to every country in the Americas, most any country in the world. From pirating software, money laundering, forgery, and covert operations, to drug trafficking, assassination, mass murder and jungle warfare, Masked Apocalypse had been nurtured and trained by the world's greatest terror outfits right here in the New World: Hezbollah, Hamas, and al Qaeda. Whatever grievances these organizations harbored against one another in the Old World, they certainly could come together for jihad against a common enemy here in the New one. A testament to the power of Allah.

Ahmed muttered something about the time. It was well after one a.m. and Ali the Persian still hadn't called or texted them; they had been out of contact since Saturday afternoon. Masked Apocalypse dismissed Ahmed's remark with an audible grumble, "Tranquilízate," a weighty reassurance of his command over the task at hand, his understanding of its details and particulars. Ali the Persian was their Iranian moneyman, a terror mastermind nearly as capable as Masked Apocalypse. Masked Apocalypse and Ahmed were supposed to have escaped Vallarta on Ali's heals Saturday night in anticipation of Monday morning's blessed operation. But the circumstances had changed, and Ali no longer mattered anyway. For all intents and purposes, his job was over. No one could call off the mission now, unless the imam called at the last minute. The ordained day had finally arrived and the morning hours would be truly glorious. A morning never seen before in these parts. As if all other mornings had been shrouded in clouds, this morning would bring the brightest flames of the sun... One last duty remained and Masked Apocalypse was right on time for it. And afterwards, his personal star would rise with those flames.

Like his father before him, Masked Apocalypse guarded his hostility behind a quiet, aloof bearing that belied his intentions, talents and ambition. Should you by chance meet him, the dark, clean-cut, mild-mannered man would not strike you as anything more than gentle and quite large. Yet behind this façade lurked an aching rage waiting for an opportunity to be released with a spectacle worthy of his ambition.

His rage grew exponentially when his father died. A Mexican intelligence—CISEN—sting (carried out with the help of the CIA) had forced his father to sacrifice his life before the infidels could capture him. One of his bodyguards had done the deed for him, executed him like the honorable Muslim general he was. One bullet between the eyes. Within eighteen months, the martyred general's eldest son, Sobhi Khalil Aal, fresh off of campaigns alongside FARC rebels in Colombia, entered Mexico with Venezuelan documents and began to meticulously carve out his own niche in Mexican society.

Now the time had come for Sobhi, alias Masked Apocalypse, to strike his mightiest blow yet for Islam and avenge his father's death.

The barrel-chested Ahmed strode ahead of him to have a look down the alley. His specialty was knives but he also had an affinity for explosives and guns. A naturally suspicious man, as a good bodyguard should be, he never left anything to chance, and now was no exception. The moonlight made them conspicuous but would also reveal any danger, give them time to react to intruders. There were none. The alley was as deserted as the street. Ahmed yielded to his charge with the proper respect, guarding Sobhi's back as they marched down the alley.

Sobhi certainly merited respect. A large man by any measure— over six feet tall, a solid two hundred and thirty pounds, shoulders wide as an axe handle—and his reputation preceded him. Due to his father's martyr status as well as his own personal exploits, Sobhi Khalil Aal commanded power and respect amongst the entrenched Hezbollah cells in Mexico City when he arrived. He solidified this respect with a stroke of genius: a wrestling career as *Masked Apocalypse*. A convincing, ideal cover. A brilliant deception worthy of a CIA operative that allowed him to travel much of Mexico (and to Los Angeles, California, on two occasions) completely undetected as the terror master he was. Wrestling fans rooted against him but rarely loathed him, rooted for him but never loved him. Masked Apocalypse was careful to nurture a modest wrestling career. As a villainous *rudo* given to turn on fellow rudos, he always lost more matches than he won and never sought undue fame or fortune. And all the while he facilitated connections for dozens of trained jihadi warriors to enter the head of the serpent, the USA, through a network of MS-13 coyotes. Ever true to his stage name, Masked Apocalypse also spent his five years in Mexico contriving to unleash apocalyptic events on the continent, not the least of which was a hastily abandoned (according to him) suicide-bombing mission intended to slaughter the president of

Mexico, his cabinet members and much of the senate. The missed opportunity left the bitter taste of defeat in his mouth, as if the mission had ended in humiliating failure rather than inglorious abandonment.

Yet as the death of infidels on a grand scale is a goal in and of itself for the true believer, Allah, in his infinite wisdom, had delivered unto Masked Apocalypse the means for an even greater triumph. The pieces were all in place. A bus load of Jewish-American tourists had arrived in Vallarta at one of the designated targets. The mission was going forward and, Allah willing, would compare favorably to the attacks of 9/11 in the United States and make the downing of AA Flight 3356 look like a child's fireworks display.

The irony of his self-anointed name was not lost on Sobhi. Praise Allah, for He would guide and protect Masked Apocalypse.

AHMED unlocked a backdoor to the office building, flipped on the light, and locked the door behind them. He led the way down the stairs to another dead-bolted door. Their office. A bunker really—concrete floor and windowless, unadorned white walls. A naked light bulb in a ceiling socket beside a grated metal vent. All was in order: two lone suitcases against one wall, two office chairs by the desk at the near wall, and a clock-radio on the desk. Ahmed sniffed the stale air and grew suspicious again. The office smelled dank, thick and rancid. Reminded him of the air in a prison cell he'd spent some time in a decade ago.

"A problem with the air conditioner?" asked Masked Apocalypse, his tone gruff. He spoke Arabic now, their native tongue, reserved for times when they were out of earshot from an unsuspecting public.

"A minor one late this afternoon." Ahmed reached for the metal grating in the middle of the ceiling, a vent little wider than his head, and felt for fresh, cool air. Nothing. "Something, a power surge maybe, caused the air conditioning to labor, rattle quite a bit. Not working at all now though."

"Clearly not working now... No matter." Masked Apocalypse laid his briefcase on the desk, removed his laptop computer, and connected it to the receptacles on the wall. This would be the second employment of his computer from this location, one of three secure communication headquarters he had reserved for this glorious strike against the infidel West. "We will not be long and never be back."

Ahmed paced the office floor. "The imam should have contacted us from Guadalajara by now."

"Not necessarily. He called this afternoon from Tepic to give us his blessings... Perhaps he was delayed." Masked Apocalypse sat at the desk as his computer booted up. He glanced over his shoulder at his bodyguard. "Relax, Ahmed. Everything is now going as planned."

"Not entirely. Ali the Persian has not contacted us either."

"Ali will be available when we need him again."

"May Allah guide and protect him. But—"

"You still worry about that raid?" Masked Apocalypse flicked sweat from his brow, a quaver of irritation entering his voice, "or all the police at the dedication of Arena Vallarta this afternoon?" He clicked an icon on his computer screen.

"Not the dedication. We knew security would be tight." Ahmed stared vacantly at the computer screen. "There were more police and federales than we anticipated but," he added with a scowl, "they are long gone and with the false sense of security of a job well done..." Ahmed began pacing again. "Saturday's raid was unexpected though. We should have left that evening. It was all arranged months ago."

Masked Apocalypse balled his fists upon the desk, chiseled chin and stubbled cheek aquiver. He quickly regained his patience (something he rarely lost) and flattened his hands upon the desk. "We acted in accordance with the imam's wishes," he said tonelessly. "May Allah cherish his servitude." He shifted his bulk in his seat and faced his bodyguard. "Our allies are resourceful, Ahmed. They all escaped the raid."

"Someone tipped them off, and I would like to know who that someone was. None of our contacts seem to know and, if it was an outsider, we should find out who he is connected to."

Masked Apocalypse raised his voice a notch in a show of powerful restraint. "Have no fear but that which you have for Allah," he proclaimed. "All shall go as planned."

Ahmed stopped pacing and clasped his hands as if in prayer, or silent resolve. Masked Apocalypse rolled the remaining office chair over to him. "Sit down and relax," he said, his voice empty and lyrical in the cramped office air, "if only for a moment, please."

Ahmed grudgingly took a seat in the middle of the office. "After that raid..." He paused, raised a restless hand and smoothed his lanky brown hair. He'd been letting it grow of late, his beard as well. "We cannot afford any mistakes," Ahmed said quickly. He folded his arms.

Masked Apocalypse made some clicks and shifts on his computer, slackened his great volumes of muscle, and faced Ahmed again, abundant brow arched and nonchalant. "Mistakes and accidents happen, Ahmed. Bombs explode at the wrong time, or fail to explode. Boats sink and cars crash." Masked Apocalypse loosened a shirt button and took a miasmic breath. The air had become oppressive, the office more and more stifling with each passing minute. "However, in approximately seven hours, Allah willing, there will be no mistakes or accidents."

Masked Apocalypse turned to his computer and the desired image. He sent his message: a subtle change of color in the eyes of the Virgen de Guadeloupe—from black to brown—in the collage on the encrypted webpage. Allah's illustrious martyrs needed this one last signal before embarking on their journey to Paradise. This signal was for the most important target. The biggest target. The target where the Jewish-American tourists were located. An added bonus. He had learned of the Jewish-Americans' anticipated visit to Vallarta only a month ago. Their arrival at his previously selected target had to be a sign that nothing could go wrong. Allah was indeed willing and just.

Masked Apocalypse rose from his desk and opened the door to the back stairwell from which they had entered. The office was positively suffocating. He gestured across the room. "Unlock and open that door to the front stairwell, Ahmed," he said. "See if we can get some air flow through here."

As Ahmed stood from his chair, the air conditioning came to life with squeaks and sputters through the vent directly overhead. Then it began rattling as though ball bearings had been scattered within the ducting beyond the ceiling.

Perplexed, Masked Apocalypse approached Ahmed and the vent, head aloft. "Is that the noise it made this afternoon?"

"Something like that." Ahmed rolled his chair back towards the wall, reached up, fingers extended just short of the ceiling, and felt for fresh air escaping the vent. "I think I feel some...what the...?" He rubbed trickles of moisture between his thumb and fingers and gaped at his hand as though he didn't recognize it. "That looks like... Feels...blood?!?"

Plaster drizzled from the ceiling as Masked Apocalypse blinked incomprehensively at his bodyguard's fingers. And in the blink of an eye, his life was over. The door to the front stairwell flew open, the ceiling vent came crashing to the floor, and two Buck knives cleaved the air with masterful speed and accuracy, one with deadly accuracy. In the instant it takes to flip a switch, Ahmed found himself flat on his back, paralyzed, head hooked upward, his face a character of horrified astonishment. He could see the knife embedded in his right nipple, half its eight-inch blade ripping his flesh and muscle with each shortened, gasping breath; but that wasn't what had him paralyzed. No, what paralyzed Ahmed, kept him motionless, stiff as a corpse in full rigor, was another knife, this one aimed between his eyes. A knife

170

held by a giant standing over him, straddling his body; a man in black, long sleeves and gloves, his head and face covered with...in...a mask? A red mask with thin golden stripes... Masked Apocalypse? What was he doing with that knife?

"Ironic, is it not, Ahmed," said the giant, "that a man with your knife skills should find himself in this position?"

Ahmed gasped, "Allah help me," a kind of lumbar whistle. The giant sounded just like Masked Apocalypse, had the same baritone Lebanese accent to his Arabic, but...he couldn't be! Most definitely not! This man was taller, much taller than Masked Apocalypse...and bigger, massive. And his eyes! Masked Apocalypse had brown eyes, but these eyes were lasers of shifting light the color of burning gas—blue, some yellow and...green? They splintered his mask, adding color to it...depth...like...like they were part of the mask itself! Ahmed was certain those eyes could cleave him as cleanly as that knife aimed at his head. The giant stooped to relieve him of the pistol tucked under his belt and the switchblade in his pocket. He slipped the weapons into a pouch at his hip and sharpened his Arabic to that of a Saudi native: "As you can see, Ahmed, I also know how to handle knives. But you missed some of my handiwork."

He adjusted the angle of his blade, shifted the tip and pointed it off of Ahmed's right ear towards the front stairwell. "Have a look at what fell from above like a gift to you from Allah."

Fell from above...? Ahmed thought... What...? and remembered his blood-stained fingers. He stared at the hole in the ceiling left by the vent that had crashed to the floor, and slowly turned his head, followed the point of the knife with his gaze, careful to avoid a hasty movement that could be his last. But all the care in the world could not have prepared him for what he saw. A sight so unexpected, so horrifyingly familiar he had to recoil with a guttural scream. Yet the scream never sounded and he couldn't recoil because the giant was upon him, his enormous octopus hand wrapped around his throat, a knee thrust against his ribs pinning him to the floor. Ahmed Mehri Fayed, bodyguard for Masked Apocalypse, master of knives and explosives, author of unspeakable crimes, was completely impotent, powerless, unable to utter the barest whimper, barely able to shiver.

"Shocked, Ahmed? Alarmed? At Koranic justice? I thought by now you would be accustomed to such sights. Your breed certainly makes a habit of producing and recording enough of them." The giant leaned into Ahmed and hissed barrio Spanish into his ear. Spanish from the gutters of Mexico City: "Hijo de la gran rechingada puta madre. Vales verga. Worried about your pig imam? Wondering why he has not contacted you this evening? Pues, imam has la verga del

171

diablo stuffed up his culo now. Have a good look at your imam's pig head. I saved it just for you."

His broad grip synched around Ahmed's jugular and jaw and extended up beyond his ear. Ahmed's breath came in writhing grunts as his skull was twisted to force the terrifying vision upon him. Resistance was impossible so he took refuge within himself, shut his eyes and prayed. The giant loosened his grip ever so slightly; Ahmed felt a tacky, viscous liquid pooling around his cheek, smelled the sublime grit. Blood! His eyes shot open at the thought of bleeding to death, and leapt from their sockets as he found himself nose to nose with the anguished, contorted face, the marbled white eyes and grimacing mouth, the blood stained beard, of the imam. The giant's knife hand gripped the imam's head by its matted hair and lifted it off the floor to expose the neck's sliced edge. A clean cut. "I try to make a quick job of it," he said with academic finesse, a surgeon describing a surgical procedure. "You might be pleased to know that Ali the Persian still has his head. I did break his neck though."

Ahmed squeezed his eyes shut, the imam's agonized grimace imprinted on the darkness. Hadn't he called from Tepic just this afternoon and given his blessing? How could things have gone so horribly wrong?

He realized then that he was in the clutches of an assassin. A practiced, skilled assassin. This man had killed the imam, and Ali the Persian, and now...

Ahmed felt himself losing consciousness. He hadn't the strength to fight it and relaxed his body in anticipation of the relief a blackout would bring. The assassin was having none of it. There would be no relief for Ahmed, not yet. He released him from his grip, got up off his ribs, and snatched the blade from his chest with a swipe of his hand. Ahmed gasped and rolled into a fetal position, his back to the imam's head, and retched a bile through the singeing pain.

"Hell is too good for you, all of you," said the assassin, his Spanish sharp as a nail through Ahmed's ear. "In life and death."

Blood seeped through Ahmed's fingers as he clutched his chest wound. The pressure he applied did a decent job of stanching the blood. It was a neat wound, not nearly as bloody as he had imagined. And he was in much better condition than the imam...and another Islamic warrior felled by the assassin. A victim Ahmed hadn't been in position to see until this moment: Masked Apocalypse.

The assassin stepped back to the desk and computer without so much as a glance at Sobhi—Masked Apocalypse. But Ahmed took an interest in this new vision. A strangely detached, academic interest. Sobhi's profile had already begun to gray. Red spittle drained from the corner of his flagging lips. His open eye captured the light from the naked bulb above and the iris fluttered and twitched as if amazed by what it had just witnessed. The knife in Sobhi's chest was buried to the hilt, bisecting his heart. This assassin did like to make a quick job of things. Sobhi Khalil Aal had died instantly. Struck by lightning, he'd tumbled to the ground a corpse, couldn't even attempt to pull the knife from his chest, his face a blank slate, arms at his side. The vision represented more than his fallen comrade and leader—Sobhi Khalil Aal, alias Masked Apocalypse—slain with a sniper's calculated efficiency, more than an indomitable, righteous Islamic soldier who had lived and died by the sword. Above all, Ahmed recognized this vision as that of a tragic fate he had thus far escaped, and wondered why he had been spared. There must be a reason. This assassin did not make mistakes.

"Curious as to why you remain alive, Ahmed?" The assassin stood over him again, knives holstered at his belt, eyes ardent, his voice light and carefree, as though reciting a Spanish sonnet, an ode to spring. "Pues, because you still have a part to play. Now everything *will* go as planned, but not as *you* planned, Ahmed.

28

JUST watching Brenda dance will take your breath away. When we danced salsa together earlier in the evening she left me breathless...and winded. There was a fluid fervor to her movements I was unfamiliar with, a sensual electricity to her expression and touch that forced me to cool off in the pool. I felt as though she was trying to teach me a lesson, could almost hear her say, "See Russell, this is how you let go of a dead lover—dance your heart out." Seemed like good advice, especially if I could keep up with her. We had connected...and there was one sure way to keep up with her: slow dance.

She came along willingly when I took her by the hand. "Party's thinned out," I observed. "And this is the song I've been waiting for." Two couples were dancing, both on the near side of the pool. I led Brenda to the far side with a twirl and deep dip. The song was 'Bésame' (Kiss Me), a standard romance. A slow dance can require technical steps but Brenda was content to keep astride of me, head beneath my chin, arms around my neck. I asked if she preferred slow dancing. She said it depended on the partner, but in general a rapid pace was more fun. Dancing was sport she added, the sport she practiced most. She asked what my favorite sport was. I said I liked to

173

watch American football but was never much good at it. Brenda stopped and looked at me incisively. "To participate in," she said, as if challenging me to come up with a physical activity we could enjoy together. Something in her eyes startled me, a reflection of myself perhaps, stripped of my emotional defenses. Brenda's tragic loss of her lover allowed her an intimate understanding of my grief, gave her window into my soul, my most vulnerable parts. A sudden anxiety invaded my spirit...like I'd unwittingly confided in a stranger who might abuse my trust. I inflated my chest and quickly regained our rhythm, leery of further exposure. She held me close, as if to draw strength from me, as if to remind me that she was vulnerable too. I felt that connection to her again, stronger this time. My anxiety evaporated like dew under a luxurious sun. "I love to sail...fish, and swim," I said, and invited her for a swim at the beach tomorrow. She said she'd love to. I gave her a twirl. She came to rest in the crook of my arm and I obliged with another dip. A shallow one this time. Our bodies melded. Brenda nuzzled my neck, her breath moist beneath my ear. A twinge of guilt creased my chest. Our intimacy was unsettling, like I was cheating on Rosalita! An inexplicable feeling really, but this was the first time since her death that my sexual impulses had deepened into anything more meaningful than lust. I stiffened apprehensively. Brenda wrapped herself around me with the comfort of a cashmere sweater. My apprehension abated, replaced by a burgeoning hard-on. I remembered my swim trunks hanging in the master bedroom. Without them I had little support. Except for Brenda. I gave her a half spin and embraced her from behind. Her soft breast heaved above my forearms in response. My mind emptied, like when we had kissed out on the deck. Brenda and I were the only ones left in the universe. I grazed her ear with my mouth, said that dancing was my favorite sport as well, given the right venue and partner. She laid her arms over mine and raised her head. We were cheek to cheek gazing across the pool. Brenda asked which venue I had in mind. A crescendo brought the corners of our lips together. She turned her head for a full kiss, and then another that allowed our tongues a languid twirl and dip. The song was over. I kissed the freckles on her nose. I'd been wanting to do that since I first saw them.

"You kiss as well as you dance," I said.

"You kiss better than you dance," she replied. "But you dance very well."

The music changed to ranchera—a sort of wild, sentimental polka. Brenda twirled from me and quickened her pace. I felt a firm tap on my shoulder. Johnny handed me a margarita and asked if I would "cut in on Gail and Miguel."

"Are you nuts? I'm at the top of my game here."

"You can have Brenda right back. I'll cut in on you right after...as soon as Miguel goes in the house for a drink."

"Do your own dirty work. You're goin' fishin' in the morning anyway. Go to bed. I'm busy." Brenda swiveled her hips at us and danced in a circle.

Johnny gripped my shoulder. "It's late," he said. "Most everyone's left. No more girls. Miguel won't let me cut in. But you—"

"Go to bed."

Johnny deadpanned me, like he couldn't believe I'd deny him this small favor. He settled doleful eyes on Brenda. I scowled at him mockingly, "You'll pay for this."

A catty smile creased his face. "Thanks pal," he said. "Promise to getcha back." Johnny two stepped over to Brenda. She returned my wink and took Johnny by the waist. Her smile is stunning. A beautiful morning every day.

I strolled between tables and chairs to the other side of the pool. Miguel and Gail were the only ones left over there. Gail was doing more talking than dancing. Her strapless blouse hung loosely from an elastic band running under her arms and a sliver of bountiful cleavage was revealed as she hunched and bent over. I asked Miguel if I could cut in.

"Nice try Russell," he said.

"Qué?"

"I know you prefer Brenda. You want to hand Gail over to Johnny. You can do better than that old trick."

"Hey Chilies," said Gail, "Cain't yall include me in on the conversayshun? I don't unda-stay-and espang-yall."

"I was just asking Miguel if I could cut in."

"Oh honey cain't ya wait? He owes me a day-ancen lesson for the English I been a teachin' he-um."

"Nice old trick," I said to Miguel in Spanish.

Miguel's leonine eyes grinned at me. "My English needs some help. And at least my tricks work." He bounced on his toes to the rhythm. Gail pranced and wiggled her torso.

"Great moves you have been teaching her too," I said in all honesty.

"Both you Chilies wanna day-ance with me?"

"I was just telling Miguel I'd be right back with margaritas." I offered Miguel a shrug of surrender. He hadn't fallen for my "old trick" and I had no desire to press the issue on Johnny's behalf...he could do his own dirty work.

SEVE VERDAD

When I reached the veranda Gail called out, "Make myan on the rocks, Chili!"

I pounded my margarita before reaching the bar and pounded a small bottled water when I got there. The blender was half-full. Melted margarita. Didn't look worth the hassle of freshening up so I left it and reconsidered—one margarita on the rocks would be enough to share with Brenda; Johnny could make his own if he wanted, and a couple for Miguel and Gail as well. That would give him an excuse to nose in on their "day-ancen lesson". But since I was at the bar, to be polite I asked if anyone else wanted a drink. There was no response because the living room was empty. I tittered and once again reconsidered. A bottle of Patrón Silver whispered to me. My favorite tequila. A very popular export to the United States but difficult to find in Mexico for some reason. I uncorked the bottle and held the mouth under my nose. The bouquet brought tears to my eyes, a memory of the last time I drank Patrón in Mexico—with Rosalita. A clean shot glass shouted at me from under the bar like a guy hailing a cab. I filled it up, pounded the tequila, and slammed the shot glass on the bar. *Sweet.* I steadied myself against the taste of Rosalita's lips, both hands on the bar. *Dulce Rosalita.* Even in death, she'd never left me. I saw her in my dreams and often felt her near, like right now. And I knew precisely where to take her.

I grabbed a large bottled water by the throat and plodded out to the deck. A padded lounge chair sat alone and empty beyond the glare of the light shining on the barbecue. I reposed in it, tugged on the lever to recline a bit more, and studied the stars. The music was cut off. Voices merged at the veranda. Stars held my attention. They increased in number by the second, emboldened by the descending moon. I read once that there are more stars than grains of sand on every beach in the world. It didn't seem possible. Even through a telescope on a moonless night in the desert it didn't seem possible. I thought about all that sand. Sand in your swim suit, sand in your hair. Rosalita and I tore off all our clothes one evening at about this time and swam naked in the ocean...rolled around in the sand and surf like Burt Lancaster and Deborah Kerr in 'From Here to Eternity', except we didn't get sand trapped in our swim suits like they must have in the movie. We were still washing the sand from our hair the next day. I thought about that. Then I thought about a dead man lying in the sand, his neck broken. You have to hit soft sand pretty damn hard and awkward to break your neck on it. Difficult to do unless you dive off a pier, or someone picks you up and drops you on your head. Taking a nose dive into harder wet sand would do the trick. Surfers on a beach break run that risk, less risky than surfing over shallow reef though. I knew a guy who

176

dove under a wave and broke his neck on a sandbar. He didn't die, but his legs were paralyzed. A couple of years later he joked that his erection had compensated for his legs... Rosalita came to mind again, and an umbilical cord wrapped around the neck of our premature baby girl. My eyes swelled with biting tears. I choked them back and cursed myself. A couple hits from the water bottle calmed me. I shut my eyes.

A lumbering shadow clawed at the deck and snorted at me. Bizco's jowls opened and dropped a ball on my lap—a chewed plastic orb the size of a bowling ball. He sat, stared at it and licked his chops. I put the ball under my lounge chair and scratched him behind the ears. He swung his head at me. I leaned back to avoid his anaconda tongue.

"Play time's over pal," I said with an eye to the stars. A perfect evening to sleep under them. "Time for us dogs to get some rest."

Arms slithered around my neck, accompanied by a kiss on the top of my head. "Time for puppies to get some sleep," said Brenda.

I nuzzled her chin. "Is that an invitation?"

She patted Bizco on the shoulder and sat down beside me on the lounge chair. "Where are you staying?"

"Here if you like."

"I mean your hotel."

"Casa Mexicana. Wanna come over?"

Brenda stroked my cheek with the back of her hand. Her eyes were dark and looked over my face like she was trying to memorize it. Bizco flopped down on the deck with a heavy sigh that rolled him onto his side.

"I'm going to tell you something I don't want you to repeat," Brenda said.

"I'll only repeat it to you."

"Very good. You remember when I was talking to Ara and you gave me that margarita? When you first arrived at the party?"

"Yes. It looked kinda serious, the conversation."

"It was. Ara is pregnant."

"Oh... Maybe you shouldn't tell me."

"Well it's too late now." Brenda furrowed her brow. I kissed her forehead. "She doesn't seem unhappy about it," I said.

"It was kind of unexpected so..." Brenda pursed her lips, "...she's pleased but a little upset."

"I thought it was natural for women to feel that way about most anything anyhow," I teased.

Brenda scowled at me with the cutest nasty look I'd ever seen. I apologized and took her hand.

"May I continue?" she asked.

"Absolutely."

"Well, that's really why I came to Vallarta. Saturday was Ara's last day of work in Guadalajara and I flew in early with a couple of her suitcases to help her get settled..." Brenda paused for a response.

"Yes. Go on."

"How long are you staying in Vallarta?"

"Another week. I have a few personal responsibilities... Rosalita...her family I mean."

Usually the subject of Rosalita caused me to look away out of grief or guilt. This time I was trapped inside Brenda's eyes with no desire to escape.

"That's great," she said and caught herself. "Uh...god that sounded awful... I mean it's great you have another week. So do I."

"And we're going swimming tomorrow."

"Yes. Definitely. But I... Oh hell. What I'm trying to say is, let me give priority to Ara." She ran a hand over my chest. "That's why I'm here."

"Is this a polite way of kicking me out?" I prodded with a provocative smile. "I was planning on spending the night out here with Bizco."

"He has a bed by the veranda."

"Big enough for two?"

Brenda giggled and rested her head on my shoulder. I stroked her hair. "Johnny still here?"

"They left."

"He left with both Gail and Miguel?"

"The three of them walked downtown."

I released a wry sigh and closed my eyes. "Guess that means no one gets the girl."

"Both could, but you're probably right."

Brenda snuggled her head beneath my chin. Bizco's snoring subsided. I could feel the ocean in the silence, hear its beating surf...no, not beating surf...a tender breeze rustling the woods. Then I caught the temperate air and smelled the ocean. The unmistakable fragrance of the sea mixed well with Brenda, though I wasn't sure I could distinguish the two...

A motorcycle warming up broke the spell. Bizco in dreamland. We laughed. Bizco snored louder. Brenda nudged him with her foot. "Ven Bizco," she said as she stood from my side. "Time for bed."

Bizco stood with a yawn wide enough to stifle an orchestra. He followed Brenda over to the veranda. When she sat back down beside me I placed a little something in her hand.

She examined the card. "What's this?"

"A key to my room. They used to have the old style there. You know, like the ones we use for houses. They've made some improvements."

"Casa Mexicana is a beautiful old hotel. But...?"

"If I'm not here tomorrow when you get up, come on by. Room 1163. Or look for me by the pool. Or under a palapa on the beach. If anyone asks any questions just smile and flash the key."

"You have another key."

"In my room. But they know me. I'll have no problems. And neither will you, with your charm and the key."

I pulled the lever on the lounge chair and got horizontal, on my side, Brenda's hips snug in my stomach. "Good night mi amor."

"Don't you think you'd be more comfortable on one of the couches inside?"

"Don't you think you'd be more comfortable out here with me on such a lovely night?"

Brenda looked up at the stars and moon as though considering the invitation. I caressed her back. She dropped her gaze to mine. Something fragile shone in her eyes as she came close. "Soon," she whispered. I rose to her mouth and we shared a lingering kiss.

"I'll be right back with something to make you more comfortable," she said.

Brenda was gone before I could tell her that she was all I needed to feel comfortable. I kicked off my shoes.

The light on the deck went out. Brenda was back. She gave me a blanket and pillow. "Is this your pillow?" I asked suggestively.

She pecked me on the cheek. "I've been sleeping with it," she said with a pretty lift of her eyebrows.

The moon was still high above the horizon when I fell asleep.

Book II

Rain

Human beings can be awful cruel to one another.

Huckleberry Finn
(Mark Twain)

No one who has not sat in prison knows what the State is like.

Leo Tolstoy

I'M sitting on the carpet in the office at Mountain's house, knees drawn up to my chest, arms wrapped around them, bathed in hard sunlight. I get up and look out the window. Brenda is down on the hillside below but I can't open the window and get her attention. I yell for her. She leans and strains against a giant boulder and rolls it down the hill. Bizco chases after it into the woods. I pivot and head for the door. The handle turns but the door won't budge. I return to the window. Brenda rolls another boulder down the hillside. I lean into the hull of the window and yell for her again. The glass breaks and I'm falling. This is going to hurt. Thunder rakes my body.

I awoke to a mild rumble...*thunder?* rolled onto my back, and glimpsed the blue early-morning sky. *Must have been a dream.* I curled up with Brenda's pillow; a volley of barks echoed up from the hillside. Deep cavernous barks followed by pitched yelps. There was a short pause and the barking began again, sharper this time, with a sense of urgency. An annoying sound that made it impossible to sleep.

Bizco. What the hell was all the commotion about? Sounded like he'd treed a wild animal or an intruder down on the hill. My irritation abated. Bizco was just doing his job, being a good watchdog. I massaged a dull ache in my head and made my way to the handrail in time to see him charge up the hillside like a bull released from his toril. I shuffled over to the veranda. Bizco streaked by me onto the deck, barking over the handrail. Mountain opened the door to the veranda and lumbered outside. He was draped in a black robe and held a bowl of kibble. Bizco wheeled and ran past us toward the pool. Mountain shouted, "Bizco...! Bizco!" Bizco banked around the far end of the pool. Mountain took a knee and, with tongue pressed between his teeth, let out a piercing whistle. "Bizco! Ven! Qué te pasa? Ven!"

Bizco yelped, wiggled up to him and sat. The dog shivered as though pulled from a snow bank. Mountain massaged him all over and whispered in his ears.

I shuffled back onto the deck and looked down on the property in search of an intruder. All quiet.

Probably another dog outside the fence.

I looked up, and down to the ocean horizon. Not a cloud in the sky. Another beautiful morning. The sun had yet to rise above the mountain behind us. It figured to be about seven or eight a.m.

Thought I heard rumbling...thunder?

SEVE VERDAD

I found a cloud. One cloud. North up along the coast. Strange place for a cloud. It wasn't high in the sky but hovered over the shore like exhaust from a lumber mill.

When did they build a mill? That's a huge mill. Am I dreaming?

I rubbed my eyes and refocused. The exhaust belched plumes of smoke, dark and angry. A frog croaked in my throat as I called to Mountain. I spit it over the handrail and blinked at the spectacle below. A tawny brume stretched beyond the dark billows and enveloped the Washington Hotel. The Washington had two towers. I saw one. Only one. "Oh my fucking god."

"Qué pasa Ruzz? Whaz down deya?" Mountain joined me at the handrail. Bizco whimpered behind us.

"I think..." I stammered, "...the Washington is on fire."

A gaseous gray cocoon smothered the visible tower while thick soot and smoke expanded beside it. Mountain murmured, "Santísima Madre de Dios." Our eyes met in bewildered angst and immediately returned to the Washington. Mountain took a big strangled breath and grunted as if in preamble to speaking, but said nothing. My mouth felt like I'd been puffing on the smoldering end of a cigar. I retreated and drank from the water bottle beside my lounge chair. A siren wailed from somewhere not too far away. The phone rang in the kitchen. Mountain and Bizco abandoned the deck. I approached the handrail, my head and vision steadily clearing within an insipid hangover. Black smoke down at the Washington reached for the sky, grew taller and fatter, the cocoon around the south tower thickening to a smoggy grizzle. The customary off-shore morning breeze prevailed and confined most of the smoke to the hotel and its beach. While the Washington burned, Vallarta remained clear. The contrast was astonishing. Buildings, houses, and greenery were vibrant, alive with color. I stared at the Washington again. The hotel was several miles away and remained a chimeric vision, like my eyes were playing tricks on me. I dropped my gaze south a couple of miles, to the malecón. The street was lined with traffic. People scurried along the promenade and between cars like bugs. They headed in all directions, pushing ahead in a panic. Some barely moved at all, as if in shock. Traffic on the one-way street crept south, in my direction, towards the Rio Cuale and Old Vallarta. I took another fix on the Washington. The protracted view and sheer volume of smoke prevented me from determining the extent of the damage. I couldn't make out any flames or the north tower but somewhere beneath that smoke there had to be...

A lump formed in my jugular... *The Washington is on fire! and packed with spring breakers!*

186

FINDING DEVO

I swung my gaze out over the bay. The violet sea remained an impassive, indestructible void, so close yet so far removed from the fire. A sailboat was out there...and a couple of small fishing boats heading for the malecón... I felt the blood rush to my ears.

"Johnny!" I cried at the Washington, willing him to hear me, demanding his presence by my side. His fishing boat was due to leave from the hotel this morning! I clutched the handrail to keep from taking a flying leap to save him.

I threw on my shoes. Brenda walked out onto the deck from the dining room. She wore a pink nightgown and pressed a cell phone to her ear. She hooked her arm around mine and pierced me with a look of severe composure as she guided me to the handrail. She spoke Spanish into her phone: "Sí, ahora lo veo." Yes, I see it now. "There is a lot of smoke... There must be but I do not see any flames...we are far away and... It looks horrible..."

I leaned back against the rail, Johnny's image flashing before my eyes—lounging on the beach, playing football, dancing, laughing, fishing.

Brenda's voice spiked: "A what?!? How do you know...? You heard it? Aye por Dios... Pues, we will find out for ourselves... Now. Right now... I will call you back and..."

Ara approached the deck from the dining room, Mountain close behind. He was in jeans, boots, and a blue pullover, ready to roll, Ara in jeans and a white bathrobe. She was barefoot and stutter stepped around me as I crossed the deck, my heart doing the samba on a trampoline. I had to call Johnny. Brenda headed for the veranda, said she'd be right back. From the handrail Ara said, "Santa María madre de Dios." I told Montoya in passing that I needed to use his phone and made for the kitchen.

I left a message on Johnny's cell phone. The fact that he didn't pick up was no cause for alarm. Last time we were in Vallarta he mentioned that his cell didn't work south of the border. I didn't bother calling my pricy new satphone charging in my hotel room to see if he'd left a message, he didn't have my new number. I pawed through a couple of drawers in a vain attempt to locate a phonebook. I needed to call Johnny's hotel and, if he wasn't there, my hotel to see if he had left me a message. A computer would get me those numbers. There had to be a laptop or two in the house. I joined Montoya and Ara out on the deck to ask for a smartphone or laptop. Before I could get a word in, Mountain handed me my wayfarer sunglasses, his brow set in a hard line. "Me voy al Washington," he pronounced, like an order for me to accompany him. "And you and the girls can come along. But my nephew, Sergio, has my truck."

187

"No way we could drive down there anyhow," I said. "Traffic is bound to be horrible. Is Sergio okay?"

Mountain nodded, "Sí."

Mountain was all eye of the tiger. He had told me once how, unlike so many of his teammates in college and the pros, he'd never felt the need to scream and yell to psych-up for a big game, or to relieve big-game jitters with a violent puke. I'd never seen him play live but have been around athletes like that, calm before game time with the eye of the tiger, born to leave it all on the field. That's how Mountain was now. All eye of the tiger.

"Sergio was stuck in traffic at the marina," Mountain intoned. "I told him to go back north to Bucerías and wait for my call."

"Where are the flames?" Ara had her hands cupped around her face, focusing her vision.

"There may have been an explosion." Brenda was back, out of her nightgown and into jeans, a light sweatshirt, and a green and orange UDLA (University of the Americas) Aztecas billcap, her hair twisted up underneath.

Ara faced her sister, her eyebrows up at her hairline. "No me digas. An explosion?!?"

"Gabriela told me they heard an explosion down there," Brenda said.

"Maybe a gas line or something," Mountain proffered.

Brenda pursed her lips dubiously.

"Johnny was supposed to be at the Washington this morning," I said. "To go fishing. He never misses a fishing trip."

We stared at one another and time froze, like we were trapped in a photograph.

Mountain broke the spell: "Lezlie is at the Washington. Vámanos."

30

MOST days Lieutenant Benito Cuevas Romero was up by seven. He made his bed, laid out his uniform or plain clothes, chose his shoes (to be shined that morning by a shoeshine boy down the street), prepared himself a sparse breakfast of cereal or eggs and tortillas (never too much to clean up immediately afterwards), and was showered, shaved and looking movie-star slick at police headquarters by nine o'clock. A man of ordered, you might say fastidious disposition and habits.

FINDING DEVO

Happenings in Puerto Vallarta, a relatively tranquil tourist town, rarely required him to work long hours or drastically change his routine. This last weekend had been quite the exception however. Between *Paco's* arrest and interrogations, the raid, and security detail for Arena Vallarta's dedication (not to mention the time the lieutenant spent on his investigation into the dead body found at the marina) the last two days had been hectic; hectic and, in Lieutenant Romero's new position as Comandante, profitable.

His appointment as Comandante (temporary though it might be) had greased the lieutenant's ego nearly as much as Sunday evening's police entres (pay-outs) had greased his palms. So, notwithstanding his concerns about an assassin at large who might frame police for the murder of the dead man found at the marina (he was beginning to attribute his worries about a frame-up more to paranoia than any real threat to him or the department), the lieutenant afforded himself a bit of Sunday night revelry. Revelry that compelled him to sleep in a little Monday morning.

It was nearly seven thirty when Lieutenant Romero rolled out of bed.

She hadn't been all that good, not nearly good enough to inspire him to spend the night with her. The cunt rarely was anymore. Worn like a hole in your carpet. Can't help but abuse it until you get a new one. She was hardly any better than taking his impulses out on a bitch transvestite...pinches putos...

The lieutenant wasn't hung over, just a little groggy and running late, which led him to reverse part of his morning routine. Breakfast would come first, before making his bed and laying out his clothes. He shrugged into his robe and headed for the kitchen to prepare a cup of instant coffee and a bowl of cereal.

The kitchen was immaculate, like the rest of his apartment. His twice-a-week maid service was indispensable.

Lieutenant Romero didn't read during breakfast, watch television, review his e-mails, or listen to music. He simply savored this quiet time to reflect on yesterday's implications for today's work. He downed the last of his coffee, readied for today's first piece of business: a call to Pedro. The message Pedro left on his voicemail last night had sounded promising. The disc might even be decoded by now. But would it provide clues as to the identity of the assassin? That maldito killer was a crafty one. The lieutenant resisted a sense of urgency, a rabid desire to find the assassin immediately, the same desperate gnawing in his chest he experienced after Pedro suggested that the assassin might be setting up police. He reminded himself to be patient. He would get this killer. And when he did...

SEVE VERDAD

The fax machine on his desk in the living room came to life. This could be an enlightening start to the day, perhaps information from his contact in the Mexico City Police Department in response to copies of fingerprints and passports he'd received from the lieutenant Saturday night. Lieutenant Romero cleared the table, sat the dishes in the kitchen sink, and strolled into the living room as the fax transmission was completed. Maybe now he'd get some solid leads into the true identities of that gangster Paco and the dead man found at the marina. He expected Sandra at Immigration here in Vallarta to have a report ready today on the passports, as well as results from the automated fingerprint-identification search in Guadalajara. Yet, who knew how complete her information would be or precisely when she would share it? The lieutenant's man in el DF was resourceful and expedient; and it never hurt to have independent sources of information.

He switched on his desk lamp, took a seat, and retrieved the pages from his fax machine, his brow furrowed in concentration.

His man in el DF had garnered some fascinating information on the gangster, information from a most reliable database—the United States Immigration and Customs Enforcement (ICE) Criminal Database. The information he turned up suggested that the prisoner, "Paco", was indeed in possession of a false Venezuelan passport.

The lieutenant released a snide chuckle. Just as he'd suspected all along: that chinga su madre gangster was chilango (from Mexico City). But his name wasn't Paco (Francisco) and he didn't live in Mexico. His name was Vicente—Vicente Luis Rojas—a Mexican with a Los Angeles, California, address. Apparently, Vicente had avoided trouble, or at least had avoided getting fingerprinted before he crossed the US border as an undocumented young teenager six years ago. Consequently, regardless of the technology at hand (like the automated fingerprint-ID systems in Guadalajara and Mexico City) his fingerprints could not be matched without accessing the ICE Criminal Database.

Lieutenant Romero wondered if Sandra had accessed the ICE criminal database and discovered the gangster's true identity.

Although Vicente never applied for a passport or government-issue photo ID while living in Mexico (it wasn't clear from the fax if the kid had carried any identification at all when he entered the United States), somehow he obtained a matrícula consular card (Mexican identification card) through a Mexican consulate office in Los Angeles. A few years later he was arrested and fingerprinted in San Francisco, California, for transporting undocumented immigrants in a stolen van (and driving without a license). Released on bail, he never appeared for his court date. A few years after that—about a year ago—

Vicente was arrested and fingerprinted again. This time the arrest was made by the US Border Patrol, for smuggling human cargo across the border. The Border Patrol identified him by his matrícula consular card as one *Julio Paloma de Mayo.*

Julio received a stay of deportation and skipped out on bail once again. That's when ICE finally initiated an investigation. The agency determined that the name and ID number assigned to Julio Paloma de Mayo didn't match any *legal* matrícula consular card and, with the help of an informant, matched his fingerprints to those of Vicente Luis Rojas and an arrest record that had been sealed in San Francisco.

The lieutenant made a note to have a search done for Vicente's Mexican birth certificate (a rather ordinary task his contact hadn't gotten around to. He couldn't be expected to do everything) and for the time being attributed this new alias of Vicente's—Julio Paloma de Mayo—to a counterfeit matrícula consular card he must have obtained on the black market. But why had Vicente's arrest record been sealed in San Francisco? Is that what prevented ICE from getting involved in the case in the first place? Did gangster coyotes stealing cars and trafficking in human cargo merit special constitutional protection north of the border? Surely if ICE and the border patrol had known who they had in custody—a coyote who had already skipped out on bail once—Vicente would never have been released from jail a second time, would he? Did law enforcement have its hands tied by a twisted political agenda? corrupt judges and politicians? a lack of funds? Or perhaps a mistake had been made.

A mistake had clearly been made.

The lieutenant scanned the third and last page of the fax. His jaw dropped as he neared the end. Increíble! Could all this be true...? Positively astounding intelligence on the dead man found at the marina. The lieutenant reread several sentences and took a moment to digest them—information from a United States National Security Agency database. Had Sandra and Immigration turned up *this* information yet? He'd have to consult with her about it. First though, he'd meet with Pedro at headquarters to discuss this development right away.

Suddenly Lieutenant Romero's morning began moving exceedingly fast. Before he could grab his cell phone charging on the desk next to his fax machine, it rang. A call from Linda at police dispatch. The mayor had ordered all officers on duty immediately. Why? An explosion, a disaster of immense proportions! Where?!? The Washington Hotel. When? Not ten minutes ago! Linda had heard the thunderous crack and BOOM! right there at headquarters. It felt like an earthquake! Calls were flooding in about it. The lieutenant said he was on his way.

He'd never heard Linda so alarmed, her voice so panicked, penetrated with fear...

Lieutenant Romero's cool was impenetrable.

It usually took the lieutenant some time to make it to headquarters from his suburb of Las Juntas. He'd break all records, have a squad car escort him if necessary.

The dishes would have to wait today, and he'd wear his uniform instead of plain clothes.

Lieutenant Romero took the time to shave though, get himself looking and feeling sharp, his mind right.

31

SHOCKWAVES from the explosion shook Pedro out of a deep sleep. The explosion didn't wake the rest of the family though; they were already downstairs in the kitchen having breakfast, except for his father who was off to work.

At first Pedro thought big brother Alejandro was shaking his bed. He even called out, "Papi! Tell Alejandro to stop shaking my bed!" but as he stirred to consciousness, he realized it couldn't be Alejandro. He'd moved out of the house three years ago. He rolled over in a dreamy fog and saw that his younger brother, Eduardo, wasn't the one shaking his bed either... Eduardo's empty bed was also shaking, and rumbling! Something shattered in the kitchen downstairs; little Angélica screamed. Pedro was wide awake now, eyes as big as saucers. He leaped from his bed as if it were in flames. The shaking subsided and he heard Eduardo yell for him, nearly stumbled into him on his way down the stairs. "Terremoto," (earthquake) they said to each other and hustled to the kitchen.

Beti called out for Pedro as he appeared in the kitchen in his pajamas with Eduardo, both displaying wild expressions of embattled determination...and fear. A look she wasn't unfamiliar with. Beti hadn't seen her husband, Enrique, box much, but she remembered his indomitable expression and wild, calculating eyes when the bell sounded, his rock-solid jaw setting a determined visage. She found this look appropriate for the brutal sport but incongruous with his personality, until her husband explained to her the fear he had, that all boxers have and must learn to channel. "A fighter who denies his fear, refuses to accept it for what it is and turn it to his advantage, is a loser, a *bum,*" he'd told her. Beti never could fully discern the fear in Enrique's face when he was in the ring but she saw it now, as well as the indomitable determination, in both her sons' expressions.

Pedro locked onto his mother's figure—her arms wrapped around his sisters, Eva and María Luz; Angélica hugged ma's waist. His eyes met his mother's. "Terremoto," they said in unison. "Vámanos."

Vallarta wasn't a stranger to earthquakes. Beti and her family knew an aftershock might be coming. Twelve years had passed since the last earthquake and at the time only Beti (pregnant with Angélica) was home. After that, Enrique often reviewed with everyone in his family what to do in case of an earthquake and how to respond if they were home when another hit: get out of the house and go the park—the wide open spaces of Los Jardines across the street.

Beti raised Angélica to her breast and Pedro held the door open as everyone scrambled out of the house. Then he made a split-second decision and darted into his office to retrieve his cell phone. He'd call police headquarters for information on the quake.

Pedro's computer screen caught his eye. He didn't take but a brief moment to look at it but that was all he needed to memorize the map on its screen. A new map from the disc. A map of Mexico and the United States with a swath of copper red extending from the southern border of Chiapas into the North American heartland.

Banderas Bay, Puerto Vallarta, was painted blood red.

32

THE last great disaster to hit Vallarta was Hurricane Kenna in 2002, and Juan Pacífico Velázquez was not the mayor. The hurricane caused over 100 million dollars in damage but, miraculously, no deaths.

In cases of disaster, the death toll is what counts, and shortly after 8:00 Monday morning Mayor Juan Pacífico Velázquez found himself faced with a disaster that just might count amongst the deadliest in the history of the state of Jalisco.

The mayor and his family lived in the sumptuous suburb of Conchas Chinas, south of Old Vallarta, their home isolated within forested hills. No one, not Juan, Gloria, their two children or the nanny, Catalina, had heard or felt the explosion. And the property's southwest ocean view, pristine as this April morning's crystalline sky, did not include Vallarta to the north and the blackening tragedy at the Washington Hotel. Nevertheless, on Monday morning Juan's household suffered shockwaves from the disaster. Breakfast came to a halt as telephones rang and trilled with calls from friends and relatives in Vallarta, police dispatch, the fire department, and the military base out by the airport. Puerto Vallarta was in a state of emergency. The town's largest hotel, the Washington, was on fire! There had been an earth-shattering explosion! An earthquake, plane crash or bomb! Juan and Gloria fisted telephones at their ears in the living room, voices raised in shock. They moved toward each other and fell back, eyes filled with awe and uncertainty. Instinctively, they muted their cries. The shockwaves from an unimaginable catastrophe had reached their household but they refused to amplify them in front of their children.

Gloria paced the living room, cordless phone in hand and her eye on the television. The images on TV were too horrendous to be believed. Smoke. Cascades of rubble. The north tower of the Washington Hotel was shrouded in a great gray cloud, its face shorn and decimated. Fire trucks had arrived; a commentator said there were reports of what sounded like a bomb going off. Gloria froze and cringed upon hearing the word "bomb" coming over the public airwaves.

Ten-year-old Juanito, seated on the floor before the television, turned to his older sister Sofía beside him. "This looks more like a movie than the news," he said quizzingly.

Gloria gripped the cordless telephone white knuckled. She was on hold for Governor Palacio and spoke softly despite the hammering of her heart in her ears: "A movie you do not need to see, Juanito"—a sickening movie that could very well get even sicker, she added to herself with a shudder.

Gloria had Catalina take Juanito to the playroom.

On the living room phone, Juan stood before the couch in his robe, a hand habitually running through his hair as he spoke with police dispatch on a landline. The governor clicked on the line for Gloria. "My secretary has been trying to get through to you and the mayor for five, ten minutes, Gloria."

Gloria whispered a shriek: "Are you watching this?"

"Yes I am." The governor's voice cracked, not out of panic but as if to slow his flow of thought. "I have been in contact with Military Camp 41-A there in Vallarta and have received clearance from el DF to order units to the scene to assist in any way possible with Search and Rescue and damage and crowd control. I assure you that the state and federal government will see to it that Vallarta receives all the support it requires. But, Gloria..." The governor's voice acquired a strict and measured tenor, "...we cannot have the media acting irresponsibly. I just heard a word over the airwaves that I do not want to hear again, at least not until a full investigation has been initiated. Speculation about a *bomb* going off causes unjustified panic. There is absolutely no need for reporters to bandy that word about as if this were a Hollywood disaster movie."

"I fully agree, señor."

"I want you to get a hold of that Media Minister of yours and..." The governor groaned, "Aye no. What the... Who the hell authorized *that*?"

Gloria blanched at her television—an aerial view of the Washington from a helicopter; coiling black smoke, a blizzard of dust and destruction. Sofía gasped, "Que enorme," and Gloria, "Dios mío." Gloria felt the blood rush to her face. "God damn that Lazarito," she cursed in English. "He—"

The governor cut her off in a gruff, stabbing tone: "*Carajo.* Straighten out that Media Minister of yours at once, Gloria. Tell him to get a handle on the media, specifically that güey in the helicopter. And inform Lazarito that I have given you the authority to fire him on the spot and hire someone else if he fails to do so."

"You bet I will. Right away, Governor."

"Malditos images like this from that helicopter result in wild, baseless speculation and panic. And can we *please* come up with other plausible explanations for the explosion reported besides a ruptured gas line or— Hijo de... Did you hear that? What was that he said? 'Looks like an erupting volcano'?"

Gloria stifled a curse. "I believe so."

"A volcano?!? Are we to have everyone in Vallarta running from an erupting volcano?!? What kind of...?" The governor spit a muffled expletive. "We cannot put up with...under no circumstances will I put up with sloppy journalism like this. I want that man in the helicopter drawn and quartered! Comprendes?"

"Perfectamente."

Governor Palacio cleared his throat and excused himself. The man was worked up, more worked up than Gloria had ever heard him. She visualized the governor regaining his composure, assuming the affected sincerity—a twinkle in the eye, or a tear, depending on the circumstance—that won him the election. And he didn't disappoint, his voice renewed with his patented, forbearing vigor: "I have known you and your family a long time, Gloria. Twenty-five years now. Since your quinceañera."

"Sí." Gloria massaged the back of her neck, searching for the innocence of those days, an irretrievable innocence that seemed altogether alien in the face of the inconceivable guilt overwhelming her.

SEVE VERDAD

That rumor of terrorists in Vallarta, why hadn't she given it the attention it deserved? Because, like el comandante, she found it too hard to believe? Or was it because she couldn't allow anything disrupt the dedication of her precious arena? Was the destruction at the Washington the work of terrorists...and her fault? Could she have done something to prevent it...? The governor continued: "Let me be frank, Gloria. This may have been an accident. I sincerely hope to God it *was* an accident and not some twisted act of war. But accident or not *someone* did not do their job to prevent it and is going to be held responsible. Heads are going to roll, Gloria, and I will be damned if one of them is going to be mine."

Gloria nodded, "I understand, Governor," in complete agreement and with the full knowledge that one of those heads might very well be her own.

"However," added the governor, "I *will* take responsibility for finding out what the hell happened down there and *anyone* found negligent in their duties *before or after* the fact will pay a heavy price. We must do everything in our power to rescue survivors, control and limit the damage and..." the governor lowered his voice to a growl, "control the media. There will be no talk at all of a bomb going off, not until a full investigation is well underway... But... If it *was* a bomb..." The governor's voice trailed off and they remained silent for an anxious second or two.

"Steps have been taken..." Gloria paused to curtail the dry quiver in her throat. "Roadblocks are up, Governor, and vehicles are being searched. And all vessels at the marina will be searched as well."

"The federal government will coordinate its effort with state and local authorities, Gloria. Ten minutes ago the navy was ordered to blockade the bay as well as the marina and search all vessels; and air traffic has been restricted. Fucking—" the governor cleared his throat once more. "Excuse me, Gloria... Gangsters, drug cartels, Maoists...who knows who could have been behind this? if it was indeed a bomb. And you have my go-ahead to begin a preliminary investigation into this...this tragedy yourself. Demonstrate some leadership. Federale investigators from el DF will probably arrive in Vallarta this afternoon and you can get things started for them. Now pass me to your husband."

Juan barked an order, "get a police escort, Lieutenant," and rang off as Gloria passed him the cordless phone. She took a seat in the armchair and punched numbers on the living room line. The governor told Juan that the Vallarta police and fire departments would be reinforced by men from both Tepic and Guadalajara and to expect local military troops to arrive at the Washington in short order. Juan

196

tried to keep the tremor from his voice yet couldn't help but sound a pleading tone: "We need reinforcements as soon as possible, señor. Initial reports from police and the fire department indicate that the damage is incalculable." Governor Palacio assured him that Vallarta would receive all the help it required, "But it will take time to mobilize the manpower, Juan. I expect you to rise to the occasion. Coordinate every resource at your disposal—the police department, fire department, Search and Rescue. Make the necessary calls and get your ass down to the Washington and demonstrate some leadership."

Juan was momentarily taken aback by the admonition. He wondered if he needed to steady himself, his voice. Did he sound panicked? incapable? He couldn't be sure. He'd never faced anything like this before. The mayor stood at attention, playing the part of an army corporal from his days in the theater. "Sí señor" he said, mostly satisfied with his resolute tone. "Ahora mismo, señor."

"Federal assistance has been cleared in el DF," said the governor. "I have another call into the president and will be in contact with you throughout the day."

Click.

Juan glanced at his wife seated on the couch. She kept her voice down but spoke on the phone in the strict tone of an officer reprimanding an AWOL soldier. Sofía turned from the TV and asked if there would be school today. Juan said, "No corazón," and suggested she play a computer game with her brother.

"Can I go see the fire papi?"

Juan replied, "No," a little too tersely and brought a hand to the sudden pain behind his eyes.

Sofía's voice grew meek and hesitant. "Be careful at the fire, papi."

Juan approached his daughter and stooped to kiss her troubled brow. "I will," he said.

"Can I call Carmen back?"

Juan ignored his trilling cell phone behind him, on the kitchen counter beside Gloria's. "Ma will return your phone to you soon, cariño. But no calls right now. And we can talk about the fire later, when I get home, okay?"

Sofía pouted, "Bueno."

Juan's cell phone quieted; he caressed his daughter's head. "Now go on and play."

Sofía obediently retreated from the living room. The mayor dialed up his driver, Felipe, on the cordless phone. Felipe said he had been delayed. Northbound traffic between his home in Mismaloya and Vallarta was horrendous. "What about your motorcycle?" suggested the mayor. "That should help beat the traffic." Felipe said he was on his way back home to retrieve his Yamaha. The mayor rang off and answered his trilling cell phone. Rodrigo Ortiz, Chief of the Puerto Vallarta Fire Department. Search and Rescue were undermanned. The mayor asked Rodrigo if the fire had been contained. "Contained to what remains of the Washington's north tower, sí," replied the fire chief huskily. He raised his voice over a screaming siren, "Search and Rescue is the priority!"

Gloria's cell phone sounded. Juan said, "The governor has assured me that reinforcements are on the way, Rodrigo," and spied Gloria's caller ID. Her father. "Enlist volunteers until help arrives." Rodrigo agreed and rang off. Juan answered Gloria's cell as the cordless phone rang again.

33

THE morning the Washington blew, Media Minister Lazarito Charlado found himself multitasking like he'd never multitasked before. He was in contact with beat reporters, journalists, TV monitoring stations, news castors, editors, cameramen, a broadcast relay station, a political heavyweight and his deputy, political lightweights and their secretaries...you name it, and many simultaneously. Lazarito was e-mailing, text messaging, talking on his cell phone, talking on his home phone, giving orders, requesting help, asking for details, and, as needed (and if he had it), doling out information about the disaster at Vallarta's Washington Hotel.

For Lazarito, information was the most valuable commodity, and from the time he lethargically rolled out of bed Monday morning he received loads of it—from startling phone calls to unbelievable reports and images on TV he struggled mightily to control. It seemed like Armageddon! Lazarito broke out in a prickly sweat right there in his living room, his insides doing backflips beneath his cotton robe as he paced his ponderous belly back and forth in front of the TV. The Vallarta news editor on Lazarito's cell phone spoke of a bomb going off, maybe two. Lazarito barked into the phone: "There will be no more talk of a bomb going off on the news! Not until I authorize it!" His wife bleated at him from the couch, said he was getting too excited. "Anger is not good for your blood pressure." She lit a cigarette between trembling fingers and whimpered, "Dios mío, how can this be happening?" Lazarito's respiration had become accelerated, like he was performing strenuous athletic feats, his head turgid and flushed as if in a strangle hold. He rang off his cell as the living room phone sounded. Gloria. Was he watching TV?!? Yes he was watching! Unbelievable! Gloria told him to gain control of the media, the images on television, "Starting with that outrageous footage from a helicopter. Who the hell authorized that?!?"

"Not me," Lazarito said. "But it has been blacked out and there will be no repetition of it."

"The images on television say too much. The reporters are saying too much. There is to be no more talk of a—"

"*Bomb*," Lazarito interjected with an angry hiss. "I have already taken steps to ensure that reporters will not repeat the word over the airwaves without my authorization."

Gloria kept her tone short of a shriek. "Do you know what this means, Lazarito?"

"Clearly." Lazarito's anger ebbed, his hot blood numbed by a tingle of fear at the base of his skull. "Some rumors are true, Gloria."

"There cannot be any talk of..." she forced a feral whisper, "bombs or terrorism in the media for at least twenty-four hours, until an investigation is well underway."

"Agreed. And that maldito reporter in the helicopter is from Guadalajara. I—"

"The language used on the air can cause panic, Lazarito."

"We already *are* panicked, Gloria."

Both Gloria and Lazarito instinctively knew that a bomb had gone off. The botched raid, rumors of terrorists, the destruction at the Washington...it all pointed to a terror attack. They didn't have to say it, didn't have to share their common thoughts and insights, they knew.

Gloria's somber words sounded like a prayer: "Dios mío, Lazarito. Our lives are all in danger. Another attack could be imminent. But we cannot allow the general population to panic. Get a handle on this thing right now. Get a grip on the public, the media."

"I am, señora."

"And we need another explanation for the *alleged* explosion besides a ruptured gas line."

"I have already taken care of that. A report from Hotel Krystal Vallarta should be coming on at any moment. I got in touch with Guadalajara's channel 13 news crew. An underground explosion in a sewer line flooded with fuel will be a suggested explanation. Something similar happened in Guadalajara in 1992."

"Muy bien." Gloria measured her next words with authority. She and Lazarito were on the same page and she had to make sure it would stay that way. "Governor Palacio has instructed me to keep you in line,

Lazarito, and to replace you if you are not up to the job. I will be in touch."

Click.

Media Minister Charlado grumbled derisively. It was no secret that Gloria had the power to fire him. She recommended him to the governor for the Media Minister position. But he didn't like being reminded of it, having her breathe down his neck like this, something she rarely did. Nonetheless, he completely agreed with her about the need to preserve calm; there was absolutely no reason to add to the panic by broadcasting anything about bombs or a terror attack. Yet Lazarito also had ulterior motives for quelling rumors about terrorism. A terror attack (rather than a freak accident) cast dispersions upon local law enforcement, not to mention the federal government, and then payoffs, bribes, favors...corruption in general would become a major issue. It had to! Under normal circumstances, bribes paid or received by media ministers, police comandantes, senators, judges, CEOs...or the president of the country were no big deal, unless you bankrupted the nation to line your pockets, like President Salinas did in the early 90s. That was a scandal. Yet in general, corruption is an accepted practice in Mexico. A time-honored tradition Lazarito practiced with great alacrity and finesse. But under these circumstances, everyone was going to come under the magnifying glass... The trail of corruption leading up to the attack on the Washington passed straight through the Media Minister...and Gloria knew it! El comandante had admitted as much to her when she showed up at The Bureau to find him and Lazarito there after they had just completed their little deal on postponing the story of the botched raid, a raid that may very well have missed terrorists...terrorists who bombed the Washington Hotel! Lazarito also suspected that Gloria knew he had buried the story about the dead man found at the marina, a man brutally murdered and whose death was probably tied to the raid somehow...and maybe tied to the disaster at the Washington!...

These were far from normal circumstances. The north tower of the largest hotel in Vallarta had been blown to pieces. Dozens, perhaps hundreds of people were dead. Had Media Minister Charlado declined el comandante's bribe, ran the story of the botched raid and given the dead man found at the marina his due publicity, the public would have known some very dangerous people were on the loose; police and the mayor would have been under tremendous pressure to protect the citizens and tourists of Puerto Vallarta. A catastrophe might have been avoided.

The mayor and Gloria were not beyond reproach in this debacle but Lazarito felt their position to be much stronger than his. He had nothing on them. They may have strolled the trail of corruption and ineptitude into a terrifying abyss and turned a blind eye to those cutting the trail, but they hadn't cut the trail themselves. To Lazarito's knowledge, Gloria and the mayor had not taken or paid bribes to anyone, not recently anyway...not since some of the shady dealings surrounding the construction of Arena Vallarta. But Lazarito had. Business as usual.

Business as usual would not cut it this time. Given the gravity of the situation, the mayor and Gloria were apt to hold Lazarito hostage to his abuse of power. As pressure mounted to find scapegoats in this blood bath, el comandante, Lieutenant Romero, the entire police force was going to have hell to pay. Lazarito envisioned any or all of them bringing him down with them.

Jail was a possibility. Prison time. The mere thought filled him with anxious pangs of gloom. A feeling of despair and helplessness that rivaled his grief and anger over the destruction at the Washington. And fear of another attack, an "imminent" attack, only served to numb his spirit and deepen his gloom. But Lazarito Charlado had a deep reservoir of panache, pomp and confidence. As he would throughout the day, he dipped into this reservoir and found the strength to focus on the job at hand. Heads were going to roll and one of those heads might be the Media Minister's if he didn't get a firm grip on this story and spin it to his advantage. His cover story about a sewer line blowing up would only last so long (unless, by some impossible coincidence, this had actually occurred); if a terror attack was indeed responsible for what had happened at the Washington, Lazarito needed to be the one to publicize it. On his terms. There had to be a way for him to elevate his status by helping to bring the terrorists to justice while obfuscating any claims linking him to the corruption and ineptitude that led up to the bombing.

After speaking with Gloria, Media Minister Charlado redoubled his efforts at gaining control of the media and called the man he knew to be ultimately responsible for the aerial footage. A friend of his. Ignacio Mirador, Director of Guadalajara's Channel 13 News. Ignacio had come to town to cover the dedication of Arena Vallarta. The cabrón must have authorized network helicopter footage of the disaster. Ignacio denied he had given any such authorization and promised to reprimand the guilty parties. "All too often journalists work on their own initiative," he added. "And the government has now restricted Vallarta airspace to emergency aircraft and personnel, so there will not be any more such footage." This satisfied Lazarito. He moved on. Ignacio was someone he could work with and manipulate so he offered him a deal. Ignacio could be in charge of a broadcast crew with exclusive coverage of this catastrophe (a team that included media members from both Vallarta and Guadalajara so as not to ruffle too many feathers) if he corralled his people, stationed them and all members of the team no closer than two to three blocks from the Washington Hotel, and started reporting responsibly, "without any speculation about bombs or terrorism."

"You see my people on television broadcasting from Hotel Krystal right now?" said Ignacio.

"Indeed I do."

"Before they went on the air they told me you leaked this story about an exploding sewer line to them."

"I most certainly did."

"Did you *leak* it or *plant* it?"

"As you wish."

"Shrewd tactic, Lazarito."

"Indeed. I hope the president's Media and Communications Director sees it the same way. His deputy and I have coordinated a few transmission details and I expect the Director himself to be in contact with me sometime this morning. We are sure to come under his thumb, Ignacio. If your team performs satisfactorily, he just might have you stay on the story and sweeten the deal for you."

Ignacio had no desire to lock horns with the Media and Communications Director, a member of the president's cabinet, especially if he could end up in his good graces by playing along. He agreed to Lazarito's terms and promised there would be no "undue speculation" in his broadcasts. Lazarito gave him the go-ahead to organize his broadcast team.

Next he called Leslie Hinot, from the Associated Press. Lazarito had met her in 2002 when they were both in Vallarta to report on the aftermath of Hurricane Kenna. Leslie was more acquaintance than friend. A fine journalist. She had covered the dedication of Arena Vallarta and to Lazarito's knowledge was the only foreigner in town with both AP and international press credentials. She should be a valuable ally as he spun this story. He'd offer her a leading role in all press releases, if she was alive. She had told him she was staying at the Washington, the south tower as he recalled—the one still standing. Lazarito got her voicemail, left a message, and jotted her name down in his notepad so he'd remember to call her back.

Satisfied with his early morning gymnastics, Lazarito shaved, had a bite to eat, and headed to his office, The Bureau, where he would continue his morning workout with the media before visiting the Washington Hotel himself.

FINDING DEVO

AT The Bureau, Media Minister Lazarito Charlado got plenty of help in his multitasking from his secretary, Esmeralda, who wasn't nearly as pretty as her name or the secretary who preceded her but compensated admirably with graceful efficiency. Lazarito was never more grateful to have made a concession to efficiency than when he arrived at The Bureau to find her fielding telephone calls and e-mails. Before he could get a word out she informed him that an important call from el DF had been holding for the last two minutes.

Lazarito waddled into his office to take care of this urgent piece of business. There was no way on earth he could hope to control the flow of local news, stem the tide of domestic and international media poised to invade and take over Vallarta, and comply with Gloria's request (and his own desire) to stifle media as well as public speculation about a terror attack without the help of the federal government and the man he had left two messages for this morning: the president's Media and Communications Director, Francisco Panza de León.

Lazarito had never met the Media and Communications Director, never even spoken to him. But when Señor Panza de León came on the line personal introductions were thrown by the wayside:

"Everyone from your governor's office to the presidential palace here in el DF is in complete agreement, Señor Charlado. Vallarta will be declared a disaster area and there is to be a thorough investigation before any public statement is made confirming or denying that the explosion heard this morning was the result of a bomb, in essence a terror attack. Media access to Vallarta will be restricted and foreign media forbidden to enter the town for at least thirty-six hours. Much of the personnel needed to accomplish this are already on duty in Vallarta and surrounding areas and reinforcements are on their way. The maintenance of calm is a top priority, Señor Charlado, which means we must control the media to the best of our ability."

The Media and Communications Director didn't sound angry or upset, didn't raise or drop his voice perceptibly or manifest any signs of stress. But his strict, commanding tone came through loud and clear. He sounded like a general following orders and giving a briefing to an officer, and Lazarito responded in kind. "Sí señor," he said.

The Media and Communications Director then asked if Señor Charlado had planted that story about an exploding sewer line. Without too much hesitation, Lazarito admitted he had. The Director responded agreeably, "Decent cover story," and observed that, according to what he was witnessing on television, Lazarito had also chosen a single news station—Guadalajara's channel 13—to transmit live broadcasts picked up around the nation and the world along with those originating in el DF. "A very judicious move. But my deputy has just informed me that there have been some recent glitches somewhere on your end as the transmissions are routed through the Media and Communications Center here in el DF to insure quality control. Trouble that may be originating right there at the Vallarta transmission station. This is causing relay delays for editors reviewing your work before broadcasting, Señor Charlado." Lazarito thanked him for bringing this to his attention and gave his assurance that he would rectify the problem immediately.

"I am sure you are aware," the Director continued, "that the international media will not be satisfied with our government's initial line on the story. Fortunately, none are stationed in Vallarta. Vallarta is not a major city with a significant international media presence and the government will see to it that the place is not suddenly overrun by international journalists. Many will likely depend on the Internet to get their information however, which makes everyone in Vallarta with access to the World Wide Web a potentially valuable international, not to mention national, media source. Your mayor has been informed that federales will be on the lookout for any unauthorized use of cameras and electronics. These items shall be confiscated and turned over to you. Yet we need not be overzealous on this issue. Shocking footage accompanied by unfortunate language on television early this morning were inconclusive as to the true nature of the disaster and I expect any unauthorized images appearing on the Internet to prove similarly inconclusive. And overall, unauthorized live interviews on the Internet with *ear and eye witnesses*, as well as unauthorized blogs, will not be credible as the Web is always filled with wild speculations and outlandish claims." The Media and Communications Director added an edge to his voice, "Just make sure none of your people contribute to that trash."

"Sí señor. You can count on me, señor."

"I certainly hope so. In the meantime, el pueblo mexicano and the world at large will remain in the dark as to the nature of this disaster until we study results from a thorough investigation and are prepared to make a public statement. A personal envoy of mine, Pablo de Vega, shall be on the scene shortly with a small team instructed to identify and weed out errant and *non-credentialed* journalists. You will be hearing from him. And you can expect me in Vallarta tomorrow afternoon for a briefing. I will be arriving with Presidente Cárdenas de Ortega on Presidential Transport 02. Mayor Velázquez and Governor Palacio have been so advised and will meet us at the airport. In the meantime, I expect you to keep the lid from blowing off this story, Señor Charlado."

"Sí, señor. I am honored to—"

"Do not disappoint us."

Click.

Lazarito released a self-satisfied hum. He was now officially at the helm of the biggest news story on the continent. Even federales and a personal envoy of the Media and Communications Director would be reporting to him! Lazarito had all the power he required to divert attention from any corruption charge and spin this story to his liking, if he acted quickly. His position of power remained tenuous, subject to the whims of his superiors; but if he came upon evidence or information to make him a major player in bringing terrorists to justice, if he could publicize any information at all of this nature before his briefing with the Media and Communications Director tomorrow afternoon, Lazarito Charlado just might find himself a member of the president's cabinet someday.

By late Monday evening, Media Minister Lazarito Charlado would have his information, critical information from a most unexpected source.

34

I'D walked the grounds of the Washington Hotel before but never stayed there. The place was huge. Its two towers composed the largest hotel in Puerto Vallarta. Six hundred rooms plus condos. Yet the towers were not imposing skyscrapers. The architecture blended with the skyline. Each tower was thirty-five stories tall and approximately that same width. The north tower contained hotel rooms, the south tower condos as well as hotel rooms. Every room had an ocean view and there were four swimming pools, the largest with a swim-up bar. There weren't enough palm trees, palapas en la playa, or shade in general for my taste, but the hotel was very popular, especially with Americans, and regularly booked solid during peak seasons like spring break.

The Washington came into view as we approached Stadium Sport Park across the street from the hotel. Car traffic, which had been impossibly thick during our hour-long hike down here, was nonexistent due to roadblocks. Foot traffic remained scattered. It looked as though just as many people were anxious to put distance between themselves and the Washington as were intent on getting to the scene to find out what had happened. The four of us gathered together opposite the park with Bizco and stared at the distant hotel in horrid fascination. The wind was at our backs allowing for decent visibility, though the air smelled chalky and rancid. If not for the off-shore breeze, the smoke and ash and dust would have completely blocked out the sky. The Washington's north tower was shrouded in a veil of sallow dust, an ocher mushroom cloud above it. The tower resembled a giant ridged clam shell half-buried in boulders and rubble. Streams of water rocketed into the sky and down upon the ruins. I imagined emergency vehicles surrounded the area but could only make out the tops of a few fire trucks peeking above the throngs of spectators bordering the boulevard. Pedestrians heading for the Washington passed us by, their harried voices fading and swelling within sirens that one moment seemed close and the next far away. Glass littered the street and sidewalk, glass from blown-out storefront windows and parked cars.

A hollow pain expanded in my stomach. Somehow I had to find Johnny. I'd been unable to get through to his hotel or mine. Busy signals. Phone lines were jammed. There was no way of knowing if he had tried to contact me...or if he was out on a fishing boat...or if he was trapped somewhere at the Washington...or if he had even made it to the hotel for his fishing trip...

Johnny rarely misses a fishing trip.

Mountain had called his friends Leslie and Oscar a couple of times and left voicemail messages.

Bizco sat, nose aloft. I caught the acrid scent of death and destruction. Mountain and I removed our sunglasses and stared about, as if uncertain of our next move. "We're gonna need something to cover our faces," I said.

Mountain grunted in agreement, his expression calm and severe. He handed me Bizco's leash and tore off his blue cotton pullover, leaving himself in a white T-shirt. He shredded the pullover and handed out bandannas to us. Brenda's cell phone at her belt trilled and immediately fell quiet. Smoke reflected in her sunglass and tiny beads of sweat dotted her forehead below the bill of her UDLA cap. Her moist lips glistened like cherries picked fresh in the morning dew. "Que disastre," she said and hooked her arm under mine, cherries between her teeth.

"Un disastre enorme," replied Ara solemnly. An enormous disaster.

Bizco fidgeted. I handed his leash back to Mountain. We secured our bandanas over our faces and Bizco led us to the Washington.

THE Santos residence was empty. Ma had taken the girls to grandma and grandpa's house, Enrique was at the Washington with sons Alejandro and Eduardo, and Pedro was on his Honda 250 motorbike, scooting back home after a shocking visit to the Washington and a brief meeting with Lieutenant Romero at police headquarters.

Pedro skidded to a stop in the driveway, hopped off his motorbike and sprinted to the front door. Inside, he pulled off his helmet and hustled into his office. He stopped short, eyes fastened on his computer screen. The map he'd seen this morning of North America—Banderas Bay painted blood red—had been replaced by a black and white one of Africa. He cursed the disc, "Maldito seas," the lieutenant's words to him not twenty minutes ago flooding his thoughts: "That dead man found at the marina has been identified as an Iranian terrorist.."

Lieutenant Romero gave him the news at headquarters, took him aside at dispatch, his voice strict and reserved. "This information is confidential, Pedro," he said as he thrust a sealed envelope into his hand. "You are directly involved in the investigation of the dead man found at the marina and the only man in the department I have shared this information with thus far. Its implications will likely impact on an investigation into today's events, but I remind you that the standing order to all officers is to comment on nothing except a fire which may have caused an explosion..."

Pedro gaped at him, and brought a hand to his forehead with such force the lieutenant asked him what was wrong.

"I have to return home, señor," Pedro said. "The disc...I may have missed something very important. I will report back to you right away."

Now that Pedro was home in his office, he wondered with quiet alarm what he would report to the lieutenant. Had the disc made a prediction? Did it represent more than disconnected ramblings, indecipherable messages, riddles and images? It was found on the body of a dead terrorist; were its revelations a portent of a coming *terror attack*?!? a terror attack on the Washington?!? If the disc had indeed predicted this morning's tragedy, wouldn't that prove that the destruction at the hotel was the result of a bomb instead of some sort of freak accident?!?... Were more predictions to come?

Pedro took a sharp gulp of air and quickly connected the external hard drive copying the disc's images to his father's computer. At what time did he feel an "earthquake"? Eight a.m.? Was that the time of the reported explosion? He'd have to double check with police dispatch. Pedro clutched the mouse and sifted through the copied images until the clock in the bottom right-hand corner read 7:45 a.m. That looked something like the map he had seen this morning—Mexico and the United States—but it was black and white, without any red. He clicked fast-forward and the clock ticked off the minutes. At 7:50, brown and green colors were added to the map; at 7:55 a copper-red swath appeared, extending from the southern border of Chiapas into the North American heartland. The map looked very familiar now. Pedro held his breath as he ticked off a few more minutes: ...7:56...7:57... He sucked in a strangled gasp at 7:58, his blood singing in his ears, eyes transfixed on the red stain targeting Banderas Bay.

"Ni el diablo," he breathed, "chingá." His eyes flinched past papi's computer screen to his own and the nondescript map of Africa, the current image displayed by the disc. "Increíble."

A cold shudder raked his body. Pedro refocused on the screen before him and clicked fast-forward, held it fast through the remaining hour-and-a-half or so of the recording. He saw it all in about a minute, his frantic gaze anticipating another painted target... Nothing more. Just black and white Africa...

But what was to come?

He pulled his cell phone from his pocket. First he'd contact police dispatch to confirm the time of the explosion. If it had occurred at eight, he'd alert Lieutenant Romero that the disc needed to be monitored at all times. The damn thing was predictive.

36

JOAQUÍN 'Garras' de Jesús had been a wiry youth. Wiry in his early thirties as well. Rangy and big boned. Compact, thick wrists. Compact, thick ankles. A broad brow embedded brawny, blistering blue eyes beneath a shock of black hair. Garras wasn't exceptionally tall at six-foot-one but possessed the lean, wide reach of a man quite a bit taller. He didn't have to jump too high to dunk a basketball, but basketball wasn't his sport. Garras excelled at martial arts, a skill he augmented with weightlifting as he grew older. By his mid-to-late thirties, Garras had added a great deal of substance to his frame—muscled up. Wiry no longer described his physique. He'd acquired the deep definition and raw power of a light-heavyweight Olympic wrestler, along with a little something else besides muscle, a natural consequence of the aging process. Garras could still dunk a basketball but...now he had a slight paunch to lift, a bit of extra weight to throw around; a penny-roll of fat he knew he could lose if he cut out his evening cervezas. He didn't drink them every night but did tend to imbibe extras if and when he had a day off. Working for Mexico's Center of Investigations and National Security (CISEN—something like the FBI and CIA all in one) could be demanding and dangerous. Cervezas helped him unwind. He never drank on the job though. Rarely drank on the job. It depended on the type of work, work that varied from the exceptionally sobering covert or clandestine operation (which might require a drink or two to keep up appearances) to what had become his specialty: interrogation. The meticulous physical and mental subjugation of prisoners (which allowed for a beer between shifts).

Garras wasn't the easiest of men to work with. Difficult with a tedious disposition. Socially, if he talked to you at all, it might be to argue the color of the sky. A man who liked things his own way. This might account for why the interrogation of prisoners became his specialty. It required him to work with others but only in a specific, predictable environment where, for the most part, he was free to employ his talents as he saw fit. And not the least of these talents were his hands, his *garras*—claws.

Joaquín's garras were large but not huge, his overall body strength impressive but not extraordinary. Yet his grip was legendary. His fingers and wrists seemed forged from blocks of steel. No one in CISEN could best him wrist wrestling and he was known to have literally ripped out the throat of a drug lord in a Tijuana nightclub; ripped it right out, tendons and guts, one handed.

There were plenty of witnesses to that one, including CISEN witnesses. His most infamous bare-handed throat ripping.

Garras didn't keep many partners or often work with large teams of men. As Chief Interrogator he didn't have to, and in the field he didn't care to. He knew he was a fearless asset in the field, knew how to guard a partner's back as well as his own, knew that his legendary *garras*, skill, and taciturn nature inspired as much fear as respect amongst his peers, and he knew that none were exactly eager to work with him, which suited Garras perfectly. Tough shit. He didn't particularly enjoy working with others either, but always got things done. A fact not lost on his superiors who allowed him a great deal of latitude in his work.

The morning the Washington Hotel blew Garras felt like ripping some throats. That routine on the news about an exploding sewer or gas line made a good cover story but didn't wash here at CISEN headquarters, Guadalajara. So he called an acquaintance of his in the

Puerto Vallarta Police Department to get a reliable firsthand account: Lieutenant Benito Cuevas Romero. "Qué diablos pasa allá en Vallarta?" he messaged.

Garras was in his office stewing over floor plans of the Washington on his computer screen when Benito finally returned his call. "CISEN has a tendency to believe the worst, Benito. Did a bomb go off or what?"

Garras heard the lieutenant grip his cell phone tight against his chin, a siren in the background. "We cannot be certain," he said. "But an explosion was reported, and felt at headquarters. And I have been to ground zero. Hijo de puta. It sure as hell looks like a bomb went off, which means this may very well have been a terror attack."

"No me chingues cabrón," replied Garras, like he'd known all along.

"No public statement will be made as to the cause of the disaster until an investigation is well underway." Lieutenant Romero let his regular, cool pitch gain the urgency of a man with untold responsibilities in the midst of dire circumstances, which he was. This would be a short conversation. He didn't want to give Garras an opportunity to prod him for information that might be revealed in an investigation, information he preferred to keep to himself, for now. Was there a connection between the dead terrorist found at the marina, Saturday's botched raid, and the disaster at the Washington? Maybe. But recriminations were bound to fly soon enough and he had no desire to have CISEN breathing down his neck in the nascent hours of this catastrophe, not before the department had a chance to round up suspects. "We have no definitive evidence and the town is panicked enough as it is."

Garras grabbed the rubber ball on his desk and squeezed it into his hand. The exercise strengthened his grip and kept his angry blood from clouding his thinking. "How in the hell," he grumbled rhetorically, "could CISEN allow this to happen?"

He and Benito knew the answer to that question: the restructuring program. The restructuring program recommended by the president's cabinet and approved by congress required CISEN to do all the restructuring—thin its ranks in Jalisco as well as other relatively tranquil states for integration into the military and redeployment to the nation's hotspots in the drug war. In many quarters, both inside and outside the agency, this seemed an outrageous waste of government resources. The idea that operatives from Mexico's most powerful intelligence agency should be integrated into the military was akin to forcing sharpshooters to trade in their weapons for wrenches and become mechanics.

FINDING DEVO

Lieutenant Romero stated his opinion on the subject as plainly as a middle finger flipped at those truly responsible for this morning's tragedy in Vallarta:

"Fucking DF bureaucrats and politicians. They expect you to keep the army from colluding with drug cartels but have forgotten that CISEN is an intelligence agency, not a branch of the military. What the hell do they think the agency is made up of, mobile units of trained watchdogs?"

Garras responded in a low growl: "Those corrupt bureaucrats and politicians are the ones who need restructuring, and all their fucking throats ripped out."

The lieutenant spat, "That might be the only way to change anything in el DF," and abruptly rang off with a promise to be in touch.

Garras was right. Lieutenant Romero knew it, Garras knew it...the whole world knows it. It's common knowledge—corrupt bureaucrats and politicians really should have their fucking throats ripped out. In Mexico, the problem was particularly severe. Endemic corruption permeated nearly every branch of the civil service, from elected officials to the military and police, but it began at the top, with powerful DF politicians and bureaucrats. And those expected to keep the peace were woefully underpaid, so drug money and personal threats were potent incentives for police, city officials, army officers, federales, and foot soldiers to collude with the enemy, even supply them with arms.

One hell of a way to fight a war—the interminable drug war that often flared and blazed and was now in full conflagration. Thousands upon thousands were killed annually, the dead spilling over borders to the north and south of Mexico. A clear threat to Mexican, continental, international security.

Up until the restructuring of CISEN began in earnest early last year, the agency's participation in the bloodshed had been limited to its usual work along and behind enemy lines: covert operations, gathering intelligence, and spearheading assassinations. CISEN operatives had also played a part in arresting army officers as well as federales and police suspected of protecting and running arms for drug lords. Yet like most any intelligence agency, be it Great Britain's MI5, Israel's Mossad, or the FBI and CIA in the USA, CISEN was not developed as a branch of the military. It had always enjoyed autonomy from the armed forces. The agency had no problem with military-style Special-Ops or working in conjunction with the army. That was part of its job; CISEN Special-Ops and operatives had slaughtered and brought to justice an abundance of Mafiosos, gangsters, would-be revolutionaries, drug lords, assassins, spies, and terrorists since its inception in 1989, both inside and outside of Mexico. Individual CISEN operatives had even infiltrated branches of the Mexican military on occasion to root out traitorous corruption. But parsed agency sections had never been fully *integrated* into a standing army in the field before, and for good reason. CISEN ranks consisted of highly skilled intelligence operatives, not foot soldiers trained to keep an eye on military troops like a species of government watchdog.

Diverting and converting CISEN resources in an attempt to satisfy this absurd national defense strategy was insane. Most every CISEN operative agreed. The effort diminished its capacity to fulfill its most important duty: to gather, investigate, and act on intelligence. That's how CISEN protected the nation from enemies at home and abroad. And if the disaster in Vallarta turned out to be a terror attack, CISEN would shoulder the blame, though the government's restructuring program clearly prepared the ground for just this kind of intelligence failure.

Whenever your boss (in this case the Mexican federal government and Interior Ministry) prevents you from doing your job, it's not good for morale. Grumblings of discontent were growing in CISEN ranks. Operatives, including Joaquín 'Garras' de Jesús, couldn't stand to watch the government eviscerate its most powerful domestic and international intelligence agency. As would be expected, any intelligence failure resulting in a domestic terror attack (Maoists struck an oil pipeline seven months ago) served to fuel their discontent... Maybe now, with what appeared to be a deadly terror attack in Puerto Vallarta, the agency would finally rebel, reassert its power and authority.

Garras was acutely prepared for such a reassertion of CISEN power.

He crushed his rubber ball from hand to hand as he walked down the hall to his section chief's office to inform him of the intelligence he'd just received from his eyewitness police source in Puerto Vallarta: It sure as hell looked like a bomb went off...

37

WE marched down the street towards the Washington Hotel in what had, by happenstance, become our coordinated positions: Bizco and Mountain leading, followed by the girls walking together and me guarding the rear. Sweat trickled down my sunglass lenses. It didn't matter. All had become a blur anyhow, like a grainy old black and white sport short in which everything—the players and fans—move in flickering fast motion. Even the parked cars—blown out windshields and flattened tires—were fidgety and blinking. And I could hear the tape rolling, the movie running through the projector with a rapid *click click click*. A distant helicopter tapped out this particular sound effect. I spied it out the tops of my eyes as it banked around the mushroom cloud staining the sky.

Bizco nosed his way through the crowd and guided us to wooden barricades manned by police at the boulevard. A panorama of destruction loomed off to our right across the street, a football field away. Mounds and mounds of obliterated concrete and jutting stalks of twisted steel. Cascades of rubble flattened out at the boulevard where a long, dissembled line of assorted emergency vehicles were parked on whitened pavement. Forest-green fire trucks held a central position and shot arching streams of water hundreds of feet into the middle of the ruins; smoke rose in response like waves of heat and steam rising from a quiet lava dome. I cleaned my wayfarers with my bandana and strained to see flames but couldn't make any out through the chalky air.

Brenda and Ara were asking questions of those around us, many of whom were similarly clad in bandannas or nuisance masks. Little doubt remained that an explosion had occurred. I heard the nervous, weighty words "explosion," "gas explosion," "underground explosion," and even "bomb." This last uttered as a tentative simile: "Looks like a bomb went off."

I flashed on that terrorist rumor...again. I'd reminded Mountain about it not long ago, out of earshot of the girls. He told me that anyone who spread a rumor like that at a time like this just might find himself being questioned by police. "Keep it between us," he said. And that's what I did, and continued to do, though a reckless journalistic impulse needled me to ask around about it.

Mountain had advanced with Bizco beyond the barricades. He spoke with three men—a fireman and two armed men clad in fatigues—who looked to be in charge of crowd control on this end of Stadium Sport Park. They were clearly undermanned. Over at the hotel I could see people in street clothes who had breached Crowd Control from somewhere and were combing through the ruins. Or were they lending a hand to undermanned Search and Rescue crews?

The disaster had indeed left Search and Rescue severely undermanned and Armando Montoya, recognized by the men he spoke with beyond the barricades, had volunteered his services for what would turn out to be an excruciatingly long and heroic effort on his part (aided, naturally, by Bizco). The girls and I were thus granted permission to also lend a hand. We were all warned to stay clear of the unstable remnants of the north tower and told that the use of electronic devices was prohibited. If we were caught using a phone, handheld computer, camera or any such device it would be seized.

As we approached the emergency vehicles parked directly across from the north tower, I half expected to see a mountain of dead bodies, but the vast majority of dead must have been buried beneath the ruins. I did see two dead however, two fully sheeted bulging gurneys being loaded into white ambulances. Red ambulances and lime-green pickups were reserved for the injured who gathered around them in all manner of carriage that a state of shock can afford. Some slouched and leaned against vehicles, some slouched and collapsed; others sat in bundles or were stretched out on the ground. Most of the injured were receiving care from paramedics, firemen, personnel clad in fatigues (army, National Guard, some kind of *federale*), or police. The injured seemed expressly calm, as though going through an evacuation drill. Suddenly panicked shrieks and cries pierced the air; four children were held aloft and loaded into the bed of one of the pickups. A sobbing woman tried to climb aboard with them but was held back as a bloodied body was laid in the bed of the pickup as well. I heard Ara blurt out, "Que horror." At that instant my senses sharpened to the point where my very being was dulled to insignificance. What could I possibly accomplish in the face of such pain and anguish, suffering and despair? Should I abandon my search for Johnny and try to lend a hand? *Abandon Johnny? No way!* Yet...did I stand a chance of finding him in the midst of this devastation? Could any particular person be found here? And if I did not find him or receive word about him, should I stick around and try to help out or make a mad dash for his hotel in search of him?

Mountain and Bizco skirted the emergency vehicles. We ambled onward, towards what used to be the hotel's parking lot. A sulfurous gas and fumes from materials that don't normally burn—cement, insulation, asbestos—added a noxious stench to the alien environment. Looming through a hazy fog, the frayed and tattered south tower held the forsaken, shattered look of a twin who had just lost her sister. The north tower was unrecognizable, its face completely devastated—a façade of sheer cantilevered cliffs and leaden toothy tiers easing into a specter of jagged claws reaching for the heavens. Two, maybe four helicopters circled the mushroom cloud like giant prehistoric vultures, their blades pounding out a beat that surged, faded and surged again in a primal cadence.

FINDING DEVO

Behind us, sirens screamed. Mountain and Bizco seemed to be taking a bead on a group of uniformed men about thirty yards away, the girls close behind. I followed their lead. Infernal dust the consistency of powdered milk stuck to my legs and had turned my teal-blue running shoes gray. Pebbles grew to stones, then rocks and blocks of concrete. White concrete. Blackened concrete. A lot of the concrete was blue. Some of it yellow. I trudged through a bit of red concrete and heard a ringing in my ears, a burst of tinnitus, then...nothing. Nothing but an underwater silence. A pasty yellow arm down at my feet blocked my next step. An arm severed below the shoulder. Why wasn't it bleeding from that pink fibrous tissue exposed above the bicep? For some reason I found it curious rather than revolting. It was a muscular arm, a man's arm, and looked as though it had been there for ages waiting to be discovered. A long lost appendage from an ancient marble sculpture. The fingers curved delicately around what appeared to be a baseball but was really a stone of some sort. A smooth white stone with blood where laces on a baseball would be. I stepped over the arm and found myself in a slow-motion silent movie. A muted three-dimensional horror flick. Ghosts drifted and stumbled about in a daze—a dozen or so figures covered in a mealy film, their faces grotesque masks streaked with sweat and blood. Darker figures had penetrated deeper into the ruins. Mexicans. Scores of local Mexicans crawled over cement boulders and crushed vehicles in search of survivors. Many wore official uniforms of one department or another; everyone intermixed, like assorted soccer clubs thrown together to take on a team from Planet Zero. They needed some coaching, which seemed to be left to a handful of men in orange hardhats organizing small teams of volunteers. Mountain and Ara were talking to one of them in what I assumed was the parking lot given all the smashed, partially buried cars around us. The smoky haze clung to my sunglasses; an underwater silence persisted, the sounds a muffled buzz inside my head. Bizco and Brenda stumbled over a heap of rubble up ahead. I experienced a moment of confusion and hesitated. If I were to find Johnny, I should begin on the coastal side of the Washington. His fishing boat would have been waiting for him at the pier. I veered left toward the south side of the ruins in search of a route to the coast. The rubble was difficult to navigate, like moving through glue. Just as I managed to gain some yardage something took hold of my shin. I looked down. A frail old woman sitting behind a car bumper had latched onto me. There was no car, just a bumper sticking straight up from a pile of gnarled debris. The woman had a death grip on my leg. A kinky halo of white hair angled out in puffy spokes around her head. Her broad factions appeared marbled, her brown eyes

215

red and listless. I peeled her cool, weathered hand from my shin, held it in mine and squatted next to her. Her lips were caramel colored. She licked them, said something. I couldn't hear a thing, not even my own breathing. I leaned in closer. There were spots on her hair. Black spots all over her white hair. Behind her ear was a fist-sized patch of crimson shag. A chopper flew over us and my ears cleared.

"My shoes," she said, "I can't go out without my shoes."

Her voice was as soft as a purring kitten's. I released her hand and removed my sunglasses to have a good look at her. She wasn't old at all, maybe mid-thirties, but looked as though she'd taken a nose dive into a vat of flour. A black woman in whiteface, her matted black afro glistening through a layer of ash and dust.

I lowered my bandanna. "You're injured," I said. "You have blood on your head."

"I can't go for a walk without my shoes," she stated plainly. "They're brand new."

She was seated on an irregular granite block that belonged on a jetty, or may have adorned a garden, and wore black shorts turned gray along with a gossamer blouse torn at the collar. The woman drew her knees up to her chest. Glass shards garnished the debris surrounding the bumper. She was barefoot but the blood on her head was the only sign of injury.

"Are you in pain?" I asked.

"It's going to rain and I need my shoes. Help me find my shoes."

I stood and looked around. Fumes invaded my nostrils— reminded me of a formaldehyde-soaked frog I dissected in a high school biology class. "Your shoes aren't here."

"Jessica has my shoes. She likes to wear my shoes. Makes her feel grown up."

"Why don't you get up and I'll help you find your shoes."

The woman smiled, her teeth brighter than the pancake that blanketed most everything. "Jessica thinks she's so smart. And she is. But that's what gets her into trouble sometimes."

I reached for her. "Let me help you up and we'll find your shoes."

The woman turned her head and shrank from me. I squatted next to her again. Suddenly her head spun back around and she viciously cried, "Jessica! Where's my baby!?! What have you done with Jessica!?! You've killed my baby!"

Her venomous shriek stunned me, felt like a powerful body blow. I lost my balance and tumbled back on my ass. She began sobbing then stopped, rested her chin between her knees and stared down at her feet. I blinked several times at her, amazed at how this frail creature had managed the strength of her violent outburst. I looked up at the dust-filled sky and drew a fetid breath. All at once, the universe had become a cacophony of sound: water from the fire trucks cascading off rubble; choppers and a wailing siren; a tumult of voices and shouts. I dropped my gaze to the bone-colored figure huddled before me. A living, breathing skeleton.

I stepped on my wayfarers when I got to my feet. Shattered them. *Bummer.* I left them in the rubble and stared about for my friends. They seemed to have disappeared. About twenty-five yards away a man in an orange hardhat stood with his back to me and spoke through a foghorn ordering everyone to stay clear of the building, the north tower's broad, devastated elevation. Two men in fatigues were with him, one with a German shepherd on a leash. Next to him was a familiar face. A middle-aged man talking to someone in street clothes but staring straight at me. I considered the injured woman again. She was partially hidden behind the bumper but I could see her take a deep breath. I had to get some help and took a couple steps toward the man with the foghorn, but that familiar staring face made me waver... I placed him: Fernando, from Pepe's taco stand last night, the fellow who confirmed there had been a police and federale raid. The guy he was talking to turned around. Manco's glasses blinked through the musty sunlight. He flipped me his solitary middle finger. Fernando said something into a handheld radio.

Fucking Manco. Should've put him in the hospital last night.

I decided it would be better to return the way I came and seek help at the emergency vehicles but checked on the woman first. This time I squatted several feet from her, on guard for another violent outburst. She still hugged her legs, her forehead resting on her knees. The blood behind her ear was coagulating into mud. I was about to tell her I'd be right back with help but swallowed my words as she raised her head and glared at me from the back of her skull with eyes of spent cinder. Blood trickled from the corner of her mouth. Black blood, from the liver.

A lugubrious voice escaped her lips like bubbles rising in a tar pit: "You'll never get away with it."

She closed her eyes and laid her cheek on her knees.

"Hey," I said, "don't sleep."

I scooted forward on my haunches and extended a tentative hand that grazed the crown of her head. She stared up at me, forehead contracted with steep stilted creases, her skeletal body shaking with the rage of pain; her eyeballs rolled up inside her head and froze into jaundiced nodes—ghoulish yellow marbles. I remained on my haunches, morbidly transfixed, my legs quivering as if straining to lift a great weight. Her head fell facedown upon her knees, but her posture didn't change. She just sat there, legs drawn up and arms wrapped around them, in sublime repose. I leaned forward on a knee and took her in my arms; she fell limp—her body light as a rag doll left to rot for decades in an abandoned attic. I wanted to scream at her, tell her to hang on, but my stomach dropped out from under me and my voice clogged in my throat. I listened at her gaping mouth for a breath of air, then felt for a pulse on her neck to confirm what I already knew. She was most certainly dead. The second dead body I'd ever seen that wasn't lying in state, and I hadn't touched the first (a neighbor's father committed suicide when I was ten. We found him in the garage, a bottle of whisky, the car running).

An odd feeling of grief and anguish swept over me, as though I'd lost a dear friend, even a family member. I couldn't understand it. I didn't even know her...

Do we grieve upon death because we sense our own? or do I grieve now because this is all so senseless?

Could I have saved her if I'd acted more decisively?

Guilt poked its insidious finger into my ribs. I whined involuntarily, thought about the woman's little girl, Jessica, dead...and Rosalita, and my baby girl...

The *crunch crunch crunch* of boots on gravel welled up behind me and a rigid jab of blunt steel between my shoulder blades stiffened my body.

"Súeltala y manos arriba." Release her and hands up.

My guilt and grief fell away like cool ashes, replaced by numbing fear. "Fuck," I murmured in English. Was I about to be shot for allowing this woman to die? I laid the body down and raised my hands.

"Levántate."

I rose and was ordered to turn around. A rifle pointed at my chest brandished by a private in fatigues. In Spanish I said, "The woman died before my eyes. There was nothing I could do."

Two army types attended the body. That left two policemen in nuisance masks and the raw-faced kid with the rifle. The cops patted me down, told me to lower my arms.

I said, "I tried to help her but—"

The three of them silenced me with a "Cállate!" (Shut up!). The two coppers grabbed me under my arms. I twisted my head around and caught a glimpse of Fernando as they hustled me over and around debris to a black and white squad car parked opposite the fire trucks.

I remembered Fernando's parting jab at me last night at Pepe's taco stand: "The police may want to talk to *you*, amigo."

FINDING DEVO

Then I remembered something else, but it was too late.

The cops spread me out against their car and rummaged through my pockets. One found money in a front pocket. The other pulled the bindle of cocaine from my right rear pocket.

They handcuffed me behind my back and spun me around. The army private trained his rifle on me as though I'd assassinated the president. The cop with the coke had put away his nuisance mask and sniffed at the drug like a piglet catching a whiff of carrion, releasing an audible squeal before securing the coke in a plastic bag. He belonged in Barnum and Bailey's Big Top, right between the bearded lady and Tom Thumb: the androgynous midget in the throes of a painful growth spurt. I gaped at him when he asked where I'd gotten the drugs, trying to look as dumb as I felt. I should never have said anything to them to begin with, in Spanish or any other language.

The cop came closer, asked again where I'd gotten the drugs. He had no eyebrows or hint of a beard, and his chin was but a thumb knuckle stuck beneath the wide fleshy mouth of a chimpanzee. The hairless chimp. His knotted high-bridge nose was out of place on that flat chimp face and had been broken a few times in the past, in fights with schoolmates who called him "Chimp". Chimp wore a wedding band thick as a brass knuckle and had slender, apparently harmless Indian-blooded hands. I'd soon change my appraisal of his hands. They were slender and dark but far from harmless. Chimp's balloon head twitched with impatience, teetering above his shoulders as though balanced on a bowling pin. A navy blue police cap kept his swelling pate from bursting like a balloon.

"Where is your identification?" His voice was raspy, cold and hard.

Chimp's soiled short sleeves draped down over his elbows. The belt around his pants had extra holes punched through it, the tail cut off short; he wore his pistol lower than an old-west gunslinger.

"Your identification!?!" he growled. Dress Chimp in spit-polish military brass and you'd have a furiously ugly Napoleon.

"Are you a terrorista?"

I said, "Terrorist? What?" in English and felt dumber than ever.

Chimp sneered at me, black eyes small and hostile. Shithead cop on a power trip. What the hell was he talking about? Me? a terrorist? *Stupid little fuck*. If not for their pistols and the punk with a rifle pointed at my gut, I coulda taken the three of 'em—Chimp, his chunky partner who was bigger than me but soft and fat, the straps of his nuisance mask embedded in his fat cheeks, and the pubescent army brat—with or without my hands cuffed. That's how I felt anyway.

Chimp gestured with his hand. The ferret-nosed private poked the muzzle of his rifle under my ear as Fat Cop opened the rear door and pushed me inside the squad car.

I saw myself in the rearview mirror as we pulled away. That infernal dust had turned my brown hair silver and partially camouflaged my black eye. I felt bad about the shirt Ara had lent me. It was a mess.

FAT Cop was driving, Chimp in the passenger seat. I sat alone in back.

"Set me free and I will give you five hundred dollars each," I said in deliberate, broken Spanish.

Chimp screeched, "Chinga tu puta madre!"

It was worth a try. I'd kept my Spanish broken because I wasn't sure if it was a good idea to let them know how well I spoke it.

The cops felt secure. Steel meshing separated us. They ignored me and I gave them nothing more to respond to. I'd smarted-off to cops from the backseat before. But that was long ago, in my own country, and under far different circumstances. Petty, drunken circumstances. Circumstances that assured bail despite my guilt or innocence. At the moment I wasn't sure of my guilt, innocence or bail (did they really think I was a terrorist or was I under arrest for drug possession?). How long was it wise to remain silent? Did I have the right to a phone call? When could I expect to see an attorney?

Static and voices were flying from the cop radio. A female voice broke through. Sounded like a standard advisory to be repeated throughout the day. Today's commercial flights into and out of Vallarta had been officially cancelled as of nine o'clock this morning (over an hour ago by my estimation). Chimp snatched up the microphone and asked about el comandante. She said el comandante was driving back to Vallarta from el DF. Chimp asked about the lieutenant. She said el teniente was due back at headquarters right now, "ahorita."

Chimp hung up the mike. "Híjole."

Fat Cop said, "Sí."

I wasn't sure what to make of this bit of news. Apparently, I'd be facing the lieutenant at police headquarters, a lieutenant who had taken over temporarily for el comandante. Vallarta was without its Police Comandante and the lieutenant was bound to have his hands full. I had no idea how this might work to my advantage...or disadvantage.

Chimp tried to make a call on his cell. He couldn't get through and cursed.

220

FINDING DEVO

We headed northeast on Francisco Villa Avenue. Fat Cop applied the gas but disengaged when a legion of vehicles blocked our passage. He stopped the car, stepped out and peered beyond the van in front of us. "Que desmadre," he said, his wide ass reared back behind the helm. "Hay un accidente." There was an accident up ahead. Chimp spit an order. Fat Cop doubled back to Medina Acencio Boulevard where we wallowed north through heavy traffic towards the marina. Southbound traffic marked for town was bumper to bumper. Fat Cop blasted the siren a few times as we listed between cars and trucks. Emergency vehicles commanded leeway. They barged through our northbound lanes going south as well as north. Busses were conspicuously absent (busses of all kinds are always up and running in Vallarta) and there was a shortage of police to direct traffic. How many cops remained at the police station to greet me?

To our right, despite the disaster we'd left behind at the Washington, the Plaza Caracol mall and Gigante supermarket were attracting business. My hotel, Casa Mexicana, was coming up on the left. I slid down in my seat and let the place pass with nary a glance. Was I afraid to be identified? Maybe. I didn't need any more surprises and maintained my low profile for the rest of the journey. Should I be identified it had to be on my terms, once I figured out what the hell those terms might be.

My head throbbed, my mouth and throat dry and dusty as smoke from a desert fire, and the handcuffs were too tight. Handcuffs are always too tight. One time, after a friendly brawl involving University of Oregon football players, my hands were eggplant purple when they finally removed the cuffs and tossed me into one of the drunk tanks. Thought I'd get gangrene. I was drunk and had mouthed off to the cops as they threw us into the paddywagon (we were having fun until they arrived).

I wasn't drunk now. Thanks to my early-morning adrenalin rush, I felt sharp. A little hung over but sharp. The gravity of my situation had forced me into a lucid state of mind and distracted me from my discomforts—the cat fur lining my mouth and throat, the bruisingly tight handcuffs, the dull thrumming at my temples.

Dumbshit Moron. How the hell could you forget about the coke in your pocket?

I closed my eyes and resolved to forget *all* my stupid errors and figure out some kind of strategy that would give me a fighting chance against these bastards.

THE mayor's dual-engine lancha docked down at the pier a kilometer or so from his house was one of the swiftest water crafts in Vallarta over a short distance. He advised the navy policing Banderas Bay that he would be putting it to use this morning to transport him and his wife to the Washington Hotel. Captain Muñoz directed him to land at the malecón. The smoke blanketing the coast at the Washington made landing at the hotel impossible.

Juan and Gloria stood by the Range Rover and reviewed strategy as Felipe readied the boat. The mayor's job was clear: to boost morale in the midst of disaster, coordinate and mobilize troops and reinforcements for the search and rescue effort at the Washington, and demonstrate leadership on and off camera. But how did Gloria plan on initiating a "preliminary investigation" into the "tragedy" as the governor had requested?

A short time ago, while alone in their kitchen up at the house, Gloria mentioned the terrorist rumor to her husband. Her words gushed forth, a confession aching to free her from guilt. She told him everything. She'd first heard the rumor from her friend, Immigration Inspector Sandra Villanueva, who in turn had heard it from Comandante Pasqual after receiving a passport from police to examine, a passport belonging to a jailed gangster who had started the rumor that precipitated the botched raid on that duplex Saturday night. By the time Gloria heard the rumor from Sandra, both Sandra and el comandante had dismissed it as a ploy employed by the gangster to distract police from focusing on other members of his gang who may have occupied that duplex.

"At the time," Gloria recounted, her eyes haunted, pleading for understanding, "the rumor really did seem farfetched. I mean, Arab terrorists...here? in Vallarta? How...? Is it possible...?" She dropped her head and put a hand to her heart. "I may have made a horrible, unforgivable mistake..."

Juan listened to his wife's story with a confused, empty expression and took her in his arms as she seemed to crumble before his eyes. He consoled her, told her that he wouldn't have believed the rumor either, the testimony of a gangster, that no one could have known the Washington would be hit, and that, as of yet, there was no way of determining whether or not Vallarta had been the victim of a terror attack or some kind of freak accident. "And if we are to find out what happened," he added delicately, "we cannot blame ourselves— burden ourselves with guilt."

Gloria dried her eyes on her husband's chest and met his anguished gaze with her own. Outside, Felipe's motorcycle roared up the driveway. Gloria gripped her husband's shoulders, a renewed, resolute fire in her eyes. "I *will* find out what happened," she said.

As Felipe fueled the lancha, Gloria determined that the first step in her preliminary investigation would be to get together with Sandra and Comandante Pasqual and discover all the particulars surrounding the rumor, examine all the evidence pertaining to the botched raid. Juan reminded his wife that el comandante was in el DF and offered to contact Lieutenant Benito Cuevas Romero, next in command and currently acting Comandante of the Police Department. Gloria assented. Benito was a very capable officer who'd likely been in on the raid and would have access to all the evidence she required. Juan's cell phone sounded. "Benito," he mouthed to his wife, and began pacing before the hood of their Range Rover as he listened to what Benito had to say. Felipe sparked up the lancha's motors. Juan rang off and met his wife's expectant gaze. "There has been an arrest at the Washington," he began...

39

CISEN Section Chief Alberto Matamoros (el jefe) had left his office door open. Garras strolled right on in. Senior Operative Alfredo Flores was seated before el jefe's desk. Both he and el jefe greeted Joaquín with a measured "qué pasa?" as he entered.

"My source in Vallarta has informed me that it was a probable terror attack," Garras said, blue eyes glancing off smoky images of the Washington Hotel on el jefe's computer screen.

El jefe stabbed out his cigarette. "Perpetrated by whom? Maoists? Drug cartels? Zapatistas?"

Garras frowned at el jefe's wry tone. "Zapatistas?" he said with a shake of his head. "I doubt—"

Senior Operative Flores intervened: "How about Islamistas?"

"Islamistas?" Garras shot Flores a disbelieving glare.

El jefe's tone hardened: "Looks like a possibility. CISEN Director Traficante just called and said as much. El Comandante of the Puerto Vallarta Police Department was summoned to el DF yesterday. He gave el director a briefing this morning. Apparently, testimony from a jailed gangster about Islamic terrorists operating in Vallarta was disregarded after a police raid carried out with the help of state federales turned up nothing this last Saturday."

SEVE VERDAD

Garras gripped the chair next to Flores. "*Islamic* terrorists? In Vallarta?... Foreign or domestic?"

"Unclear," said Flores. He crossed his arms, resolute, reserved jaw clenched. Like Garras, Flores was dressed in a gray cotton-blend suit left open at the collar. The similarities between the two men stopped there. As opposed to Joaquín's broad frame, heavy Basque cranium, thick black hair and clean-shaven Creole complexion, Flores had thinning salt-and-pepper hair, a robust mustache, slight build, and an elegant, high-boned Indian carriage. He admired Joaquín's talents but, like most at CISEN, remained on cordial rather than friendly terms with the imposing Chief Interrogator.

Garras sat down heavily. "Híjole. Islamic terrorists...in Vallarta? I—"

"Find it hard to believe?" El jefe balled his fists upon his desk. "So did Vallarta police. And so do I, quite frankly. We rarely find the motherfuckers outside of el DF and the country's border regions. Which is probably why the gangster's testimony was disregarded after that botched raid."

Joaquín's short conversation with Lieutenant Romero flashed across his mind. Was he in charge of the police department with el comandante out of town? Probably. Benito could handle the job, and had *all* he could possibly handle today. Nevertheless, Garras would see to it that the lieutenant found the time to fill him in on the particulars of this gangster's "testimony" and the ensuing botched raid. "Puta. And I assume this information went unreported to us by state federales because we no longer have a presence in Vallarta...? Pinches putos, too humiliated by a botched raid to report it to us here in Guadalajara."

"Jalisco federales will have their bullshit excuses," el jefe said. "And we do not require them to report every interrogation and raid conducted in the state." He lit another cigarette. Painful contempt riddled his smoke-scarred voice: "The government's priorities are all fucked up. Since this insane restructuring began last year we have seen Maoists blow up an oil pipeline, Islamists torch churches in Tepito...and puta madre drug cartels and gangsters continue to terrorize our citizens. But...if it turns out that a bomb went off in Vallarta..." el jefe jabbed his cigarette at the classified federale stills of the Washington's devastated north tower on his computer screen.

Senior Operative Flores fingered his mustache, his deep-set chestnut eyes narrowed on empty space...

Garras and el jefe narrowed their gazes on empty space as well, all thinking the same thing: If a bomb had exploded the Washington's north tower...

FINDING DEVO

This was a violent period in Mexico's history. The drug war had exacted a death toll unsurpassed in modern times. Not since the revolution a century ago had so much blood been shed. And as would be expected, tourism suffered. Canada and the USA had even issued advisories against travel to Mexico. It could be a dangerous place to visit. Few municipalities were untouched by the violence, yet most of Mexico remained relatively peaceful and, like Vallarta, far removed from the battles. Peak tourist seasons, like the current spring break, still meant that Vallarta's Washington Hotel was probably filled to near capacity. So if a bomb had destroyed the north tower of that hotel... Dios mío. Santa María madre de Dios... This was the deadliest single terror attack in Mexico's history, an atrocity the likes of which the country had never experienced before.

CISEN's job was to prevent such attacks, *any* such attacks. And they'd done so with admirable efficiency over the years. Terrorists—domestic and imported—were routinely arrested, jailed, tortured, and killed; heinous plots foiled. Failures occurred, naturally, as they always do. But even since restructuring began there had been some stirring successes: a Hamas splinter group was laid to waste by CISEN in the Mexico City barrio of Tepito as it prepared to bomb the presidential palace; an undercover CISEN operation led to the arrest of Zapatista sympathizers and Magonistas in Oaxaca City before they could torch the business district; another CISEN undercover operation led to the arrest of two Hezbollah militants suspected of forming ties with the Tijuana and Juárez drug cartels; and operatives had intercepted a Maoist and suspected bomber of that oil pipeline, Marcos Chamba, outside of Tikal, Guatemala, and smuggled him back into Mexico where he remained in custody.

The agency's successes were legion, yet CISEN received little publicity of any kind—good or bad. Its classified status precluded publicity. And when innocent civilians were caught up in CISEN dragnets—jailed, blackmailed or worse—the agency's abuse of power most always went undetected, unchallenged and unchecked. However, like the FBI and CIA, CISEN's existence and purpose were well known, certainly throughout Mexico. They were supposed to protect and defend the nation. An unforgivable intelligence failure like the one that may have precipitated a terrorist attack in Vallarta was bound to beg the media headline: Where was CISEN?

Where was CISEN? Being restructured and, with the kind of negative publicity a failure of this magnitude might bring, permanently disbanded. The future looked bleak, hopeless, especially against a capricious media and powerfully corrupt government, congress, judicial system, and Supreme Court.

225

SEVE VERDAD

Garras, Flores, and Jefe Alberto Matamoros joined in raging silence, watching their careers go up in flames.

El jefe snorted a decisive stream of smoke and nodded at Flores, a signal for him to practice his specialty: identify and attack the problem. Flores winced in consideration of the perplexing question. "The problem," he began slowly, "is that once something like this happens there is very little we can do until the smoke clears. We can surely determine if a bomb went off and try to find reliable witnesses, maybe even suspects. Officials at the scene are doing that right now. But in the immediate aftermath of a disaster like this, forensics is difficult, not just due to the danger—structural instability and blinding smoke—but because search and rescue take precedence."

Joaquín grunted, fierce blue eyes clouding over, luxuriating in anger, imagining his garras wrapped around the necks of those responsible for this massacre. Flores gave him a sideways, empathetic glance. Garras stuffed his hands in his jacket pockets, searching for his rubber ball.

Exasperation and disgust pinched el jefe's face, his regular, sanguine features flushed. "Híjole, Fredo," he said, "that is precisely why it is our job to prevent things like this from happening in the first place." He crushed his cigarette into the talavera ashtray on his desk. "A difficult thing to do when half the agency is out babysitting the fucking army, making sure it does its job...the United States of America's job! The gringos started this chinga su madre drug war nearly a century ago when they began enacting their drug laws and exporting them, spreading them across the continent and planet like the goddamn plague. Demand has done nothing but skyrocket ever since, and now México is paying the highest price of all in this corrupt fucking business." El jefe pawed at his pack of cigarettes on his desk. "Puta. Our resources are stretched to the limit. It was only a matter of time before something like this happened."

"We need a presence in Vallarta," said Operative Flores.

"Agreed." Joaquín's eyes steeled for action. "You never know what we might turn up and—" he held his thought and retrieved his buzzing cell phone at his belt.

El jefe directed a bitter smile at Flores. "Of course we need a presence in Vallarta," he said evenly. "Jalisco is our jurisdiction. But I remind you, Fredo, el director has informed me, informed *us*, that the Interior Ministry has ordered CISEN to let DF federales run the investigation. Puta madre burócratas y políticos. They already blame us for this catastrophe. Chingá ..."

226

Garras rose from his chair, turned his back and said, "No me digas," into his phone. He was getting somewhat excited about something, asking "what? when?" and...

Flores remained focused on el jefe: "Politicians and bureaucrats always find it easy to blame those working in the field for their own stupidity. It was their idea to restructure CISEN. Pinches cabrones."

Jefe Matamoros rolled his sleeves up another notch. "They are simply incapable of taking responsibility for their own screw ups, or rectifying them. Pen-*de*-jos." He shook a finger in the air, "But el director understands that CISEN will not stand down."

"We can have a team in Vallarta any time you order, Jefe," Flores said. "And local police as well as state federales will support us, but DF investigators—"

"Fuck the DF federales." El jefe rolled his sleeves up above his elbows, eyes holding on his Senior Operative. "El director and I are in complete agreement on that score. CISEN *will* assume control of this case. We are still the most powerful intelligence agency in the nation, the only intelligence agency with a national *and* international reach." He glanced up at the clock on his wall—nearly eleven o'clock already. "We will have a team in Vallarta this afternoon. And within twenty-four hours the investigation is ours. Entendido, Fredo?"

"Sí señor."

El jefe planted his elbows on his desk. "Begin with a small team. Prepare three of our men. I want them in Vallarta before the DF investigators arrive and—"

"I will be there when DF investigators arrive." Garras took an imperial stance before his superiors. "My source in Vallarta, Police Lieutenant Romero, has himself a prisoner—someone just arrested down at the Washington."

Flores said, "De veras? That was fast. A suspected terrorist?"

"Lieutenant Romero is on his way to police headquarters right now to interrogate him and has yet to speak to the arresting officer. But an army private who assisted in the arrest told the lieutenant that the suspect is a person of interest in the catastrophe at the Washington."

Jefe Matamoros didn't know if he was more taken aback by this startling news or his lead interrogator's authoritative posture. Garras did manage to get his way often enough. His unsurpassed skill as an interrogator and fearless soldier in the field gave him quite a bit of pull with his superiors. Joaquín's superiors, including CISEN Section Chief Alberto Matamoros, appreciated his skills. Yes they did. El jefe plainly recognized this as an opportunity for Garras to practice his specialty in the nascent stages of an investigation that was bound to gain monumental importance as the days and weeks rolled by.

The talents Garras possessed were indispensable and should be even more so right now.

El jefe relaxed in his chair for the first time today and allowed Garras a twisted grin. "That is good news Joaquín. The only good news we have had this entire jodida mañana. Looks like you will be going to Vallarta this afternoon to practice your skills. Flores will remain here and gather a team to join you tonight or tomorrow morning—once we receive official clearance from el director. And keep those DF federales in line. They may think they can take over this investigation but with you there they will be reminded of our power and influence. No one can keep CISEN out of an investigation of this magnitude, not for long."

40

WE slowed around some corners. I opened my eyes as the car pulled into a carport. Chimp and Fat Cop got out. My door opened and I was greeted by the barrel of another rifle, this one with a pug-nosed thug on the other end. Chimp ordered me out of the vehicle. I obeyed. Fat Cop pushed me in the back through an open glass door on the near side of the building. He pushed me again past dispatch and down a hallway. About half-way down, before the hall opened to a bright room of indiscernible dimensions, Chimp told me to stop. The rifle muzzle kneaded the small of my back as Chimp unlocked a door. A billy club I hadn't noticed before dangled down over his ass like a third leg. Fat Cop pushed me and followed inside, accompanied by the thug with the rifle. Chimp remained in the hall. I heard him lock the door behind us.

Fat Cop said, "Siéntate." He was in charge for the moment but didn't quite look up to the job. The disaster at the Washington had taken its toll on him. Sweat stood out against the layer of flab on his neck, his bovine face pinched to keep his protruding bloodshot eyes from squirting out their sockets. I took a seat on the near side of a gurney-shaped laminated table. Two empty wooden chairs in worn black vinyl taunted me from the other side. Fat Cop stood at his station to my right, Thug behind me to my left, rifle trained on my head.

The air smelled dank and antiseptic. I chanced a surreptitious glance around the room for blood stains missed during the last scrubbing. Immaculate, and about as accommodating as a gas chamber. The Chamber's twenty-foot square dimensions were suitable for boxing, professional wrestling, or plain ol' beatin' the crap out of someone. Its walls and ceiling were hospital white, the floor done in the same affectless marbled tile found in the rest of the building, with the exception of the holding tanks. I would find those floors done in grungy cement.

The walls were unadorned. Not even a two-way mirror to break the monotony. They probably had two-way mirrors at the Guadalajara and Mexico City police stations. I had no desire to find out. A lonely tin ashtray glittered on the table. Enough light refracted from the naked overhead bulb to perform surgery. That was most likely their plan—surgery of some sort or another.

I was perspiring again, as heavy now as at any time this morning. Surgery hadn't started yet so it seemed too early for this kind of sweat, but The Chamber had absolutely no ventilation.

They must bring a fan in here sometimes.

I tried to get the sweat dripping down my arms to lubricate the handcuffs behind my back. Fat cop knuckled my neck, told me to calm down. He didn't want me spoiling the fun by making Thug shoot me before the rest of the gang arrived to help him get his licks in.

What the hell is taking so long?

Shoes squeaked in the hall. A key in the lock. The door opened. Chimp entered and held the door with proper deference for a man I presumed to be the lieutenant I'd heard him mention on the cop-car radio. I didn't see any gold bars on his uniform or any other rank insignia but who the hell else could he be? Most the rest of the department was busy responding to a disaster at Vallarta's largest hotel. Chimp stood guard at the door. The lieutenant laid a pad of paper on the table and looked me over. He stripped off his thin jacket and draped it over a chair but didn't sit down. He just stood there, arms folded over his chest, studying me as a man might study a mediocre painting.

The lieutenant didn't holster his pistol at the hip like his underlings but had it secured in a shoulder holster. He was about my age, thirty-three, and about my height, but slender as a matador. Also unlike his underlings, he wore a tie, navy blue and loose under the collar. His black hair shined in the light and his olive smooth complexion promoted a heavy, impassive dark brow and big brown eyes. A thin scar under his jaw adorned his otherwise flawless features.

"Where did you get the cocaina?"

"Fala portuguêse?"

SEVE VERDAD

"You speak Spanish well enough." The lieutenant was soft spoken, as though he had infinite patience. He didn't even bat an eye at my Portuguese. I let him hear some more of it, along with a few Spanish words accompanied by a painful twist of my shoulders so he would understand my polite request to loosen my handcuffs.

I'd already spoken some Spanish to Chimp and Fat Cop, as well as English, but not much. My Anglo factions and fair complexion suggested I was North American yet they couldn't be certain. For all they knew, Brazilian Portuguese was my native tongue, and it was very unlikely these pigs spoke it. I was prepared to own up to my nationality but this early in the game there were three good reasons to keep them from knowing I was fluent in Spanish (or English, which any one of them might speak). First of all, playing dumb might buy me some time, force the lieutenant to get an interpreter before they kicked the shit outta me, someone who may not take to the sight of my blood staining The Chamber and offer protection. Secondly, whatever the charges against me, no matter what I said would probably make matters worse. And if, like Chimp, the lieutenant thought I was a terrorist, what good would denials do me against such an outrageous accusation? No good at all. So why not pretend I couldn't communicate in Spanish beyond an intelligible request for an attorney (and interpreter) anyhow? And finally, if they thought I didn't speak Spanish they might say something to one another I could use to advantage.

The lieutenant told Fat Cop to remove my handcuffs. Thug had his rifle ready and aimed, hoping I'd make a false move. I only massaged my wrists, and mopped sweat from my face with the bandanna around my neck.

"Now, let us begin again. Where did you get the cocaina?"

I certainly didn't want to tell them I'd gotten the drugs at Mountain's house and had a ready answer for this in the thin playbook I had prepared with my eyes closed in the cop car. But what I really wanted was not to say a damn thing—remain silent—like most everyone with half a brain knows we can do in America. Unfortunately, or fortunately, I wasn't under any kind of illusion that the rights I was familiar with in the United States applied in Mexico, despite the coming Mexican jurisprudence reforms I'd read about recently.

This was my first time ever arrested in a foreign country. A practical requirement for any writer with balls. Almost felt proud. But I had a sneaky hunch—certainty—that being arrested at a blood bath like the Washington Hotel wasn't exactly the same as getting tossed into a Mexican drunk tank after an evening of revelry and stupidness. I

230

still held out hope for a quick resolution to this crisis but, in short, I also knew—feared—my alleged crime(s) to be serious and my rights arcane, Napoleonic at best. And this was all the more reason to go with the play that would test the limits of my defense: "Quiero...uh... abogado."

Chimp slid over like a boxer and laid a left jab behind my right ear that had me hearing choppers again. I grimaced and drew a stinging breath between clenched teeth. The punch had caught me off guard but the answer to my question sure didn't. A definitive "No" to my request for an attorney. As I'd suspected, Mexican jurisprudence reforms were coming up right away, sometime *mañana*.

Presumed Guilty!

The lieutenant took a seat and calmly paused to light a cigarette with a golden lighter. "Paulo here is a fine conversationalist, do you not agree?" He laid the lighter on the table. "Perhaps you would rather continue this interview with him and his amigos. But I warn you, they do not have my patience."

"No com... No comprendo," I said, looking confused. Chimp took a step in my direction. A couple of Spanglish phrases from my playbook detained him. "Yo buy cocaina en Old Vallarta," I said quickly. "From plata vendor en la playa." Chimp sniggered, his long lip raised over decaying canines.

The lieutenant's readiness to have me beaten had forced my hand. As cops working a Mexican tourist town, they could communicate in Spanglish, and now they knew I could too.

Anyone arrested for drugs would figure the cops wanted to know where he got them, so my Spanglish didn't necessarily give away that I understood every word the lieutenant said. However, since I'd demonstrated I could speak Spanglish, switching back to Portuguese would be of no use at this point. Just as well. It was evident I had no right to an attorney and, as far as getting an interpreter...did they even care if I understood the questions being asked me as they beat me? Who the hell knew with these assholes...?

Spanglish still allowed me to play dumb though. Playing dumb suited me perfectly considering how I felt, and the strategy hadn't really been played yet. If I could convince them I didn't speak much Spanish they still might slip up and mention something to one another that I could use to my advantage, something that might leave them open to a counter-offensive I had devised in the playbook.

Playbook? That's exactly what I'd prepared, replete with the appropriate terminology: offense, defense, long bomb, ground game... I'd had time to come up with a game plan while handcuffed in the cop car. Game plan? Precisely. I had no experience with machinegun fire and tank maneuvers. This was war, and if you don't have experience with real warfare, try sports (in this case American football) to inspire your strategy...unless you wanna just give up. But was there any giving up to these pricks? What did I have to give up that would satisfy them?

The lieutenant snorted a steady stream of smoke and relaxed his arms on the table. "Cómo te llamas?"

Spanish 1. "Russell Martell." My true identity and profession were part of a ground game I'd rehearsed.

"Dónde está tu identificación?"

I had an answer for this as well. "Identification? Fue...uh... destroyed...en el Washington."

The lieutenant reposed in his chair, his Spanish phlegmatic, "You were staying at el Washington?"

"Uh...sí. Yo stay en el Washington." No way in hell I was gonna tell 'em the name of my hotel and hand over all my belongings.

The lieutenant waved his cigarette dispassionately. Chimp jump hooked me this time. Same knuckle, same spot. Put me on my knees. Thug gave me a kidney shot with the butt of his rifle for good measure. I rolled onto my back with a groan, sucking air like an asthmatic deposited on the sand by a twelve-foot close-out beach breaker. Fat Cop tried to pick me up by my shorts and bandanna. The bandanna slipped over my head, dropping the back of my skull to the floor. Now I heard singing hummingbirds—melodic birds with giant chopper wings pounding out painful waves of thunder between my ears. Fat Cop tried again—picked me up by my shorts and Ara's shirt. He tore Ara's shirt at the collar as he lifted me and sat me down on the chair.

"We have reason to believe you are not telling us the whole truth, Russell." The lieutenant pronounced my name with a pretty fair American-English accent. There was a soothing quality to his voice, like a doctor practicing bedside manners, though it didn't do much for the aches of torture in my head and kidneys. I remained doubled over in my seat, one arm hugging my torso, the other wrapped around the back of my skull. "Let me make a phone call," I croaked in English. "I can prove it." I struggled erect. "Soy periodista. A North American journalist... Aquí...para...business."

This bit of news got the lieutenant's attention. I knew it would. Journalists mean publicity and if the lieutenant was anything like most cops the world over, he took an interest in the publicity he received, good, bad, nefarious, or heroic. Naturally, he might kill me anyway, whether he believed I was really a journalist or not, but at least I'd given him pause, something more to think about, and given myself some field position. He raised his heavy eyebrows and those big brown eyes of his got even bigger. "En cúal línea aérea llegaste?"

I frowned ignorantly. "What?"

The lieutenant snuffed out his cigarette, his suspicious gaze piercing the smoke rising in the tin ashtray. "En qué...airline you fly?"

"Alaska. Last Thursday," I answered truthfully, and mulled over his Spanglish accent. Did he speak English better than he pretended to? Was *he* toying with *me*?

"Martell con," he held up two fingers, "doble L?"

"Two Ls. Yes."

The lieutenant made some notes on his pad. I hoped he was calculating a price. If not, I still had a long bomb to throw—a decent shot down field that wouldn't have done me any good at all compared to the Hail Mary I eventually threw. His next question, in pointed Spanish, knocked me right back on the defensive: "Does your business include murder, Señor Martell?"

My heart failed a beat as I repeated the word, "Homicidio?" Now I really was confused. Chimp had accused me of being a terrorist but... *The woman! He must be talking about the woman they found dead in my arms.* Panic formed a lump in my throat. I forced it up in a guttural spasm: "I didn't kill her. She died before my eyes!" My emotions were getting the best of me, my Spanish improving as desperation set in.

The lieutenant reached inside his jacket draped over the chair next to him and pulled out a plastic baggie along with a folded piece of paper. "See this?" he asked, Spanish steady as the baggie of cocaine suspended by his fingertips.

I nodded.

"This is your cocaina." He laid the baggie on the table. "Ahora, see this?" He unfolded the paper and showed it to me. The article that had served as a bindle. The picture of the dead guy at the marina.

I nodded.

"Can you tell me why you were in possession of cocaina *and* an article about a dead narcotraficante?"

Things were becoming clear, my expression clouding over. "Muerto? Dead? Who's dead?"

The lieutenant extended the picture of the dead guy. "*Él* está muerto, *dead.* Un narcotraficante muerto. Why you haf him *an' his* cocaina?"

My head felt like it was about to explode. The lieutenant couldn't possibly link the cocaine found in my pocket to the dead guy, could he? because it was wrapped in his photo? I might have gotten it in a million other places!

I quickly composed myself and gave him a vacuous stare. "Coincidence," I shrugged. "I had no idea quien...who he was."

The lieutenant stood, walked around the table, and raised his voice for the first time, his Latin tongue suave and menacing: "Coincidente?!?" He stuck the dead guy in front of my face. "Is it also a coincidence that the dead man in this photo was a known Iranian terrorist as well as a narcotraficante? Is it also a coincidence that you were found at the scene of an act of terrorism with his drugs wrapped in his picture?"

I hung my head, afraid, petrified that my face would reveal my complete and total understanding of his every word and nuance. Every mind-numbing syllable of his outlandish insinuation. Feigned ignorance was my last refuge and I clung to it like dying breaths.

Before I was arrested I remembered the terrorist rumor, and it had occurred to me that the disaster at the Washington might be an act of terrorism. But I hadn't revisited the dead guy discovered at the marina until I found myself handcuffed in a cop car.

I'd imagined that the dead guy might have been a drug dealer or gangster killed by terrorists, cops, or gangsters, but not that he was a terrorist himself... *An Iranian terrorist?!?* The possibility had never crossed my mind.

"Sé que comprendes, Russell." I know you understand.

I sure as hell did. Terrorists kill each other all the time, just like gangsters and drug dealers; connecting me to a dead terrorist not only implicated me in his murder but also in what must have been the *bombing* of the Washington Hotel... I fought a fierce desire to lash out in unmistakable Spanish, "Soy INOCENTE pinches pendejos! YOU are the corrupt guilty ones!" and kept my head down, my heart hammering in my throat. If I pissed them off too much they might just gut me right here in The Chamber and no one would be the wiser. What was left to do...? Stick to my ground game, for now. After all, while the lieutenant's tactics and murder accusation had me flustered, it was no surprise that he had, for all intents and purposes, accused me of terrorism. This was no time to abandon my game plan. I still had a long bomb to throw, and somewhere in the recesses of my mind a life-saving Hail Mary was being worked out.

I could feel the sweat burning through Ara's shirt as I raised my head and met the lieutenant's cool gaze—the confident gaze of a man who retained all the power. "No sé," I began in a conciliatory tone, "que you're talking about. Lucky to no morir yo, die myself. I heard the explosión from la playa y—" this time I saw Chimp coming and ducked; he adjusted his punch and nailed me between the shoulder

234

blades. His knuckles felt like chunks of tooled steel. I straightened up with a heavy grunt. Fat Cop slugged me in the liver.

"Shit," I groaned and doubled over in my seat again.

"You really are an egotistical hijo de puta, Russell," said the lieutenant. He strolled back to his chair and took a seat. I retched between my knees. A dry heave that resulted in a searing convulsion. The lieutenant clarified his insult: "Only an egotistical hijo de puta would kill a terrorist, steal his drugs, and then walk around town with the drugs wrapped in the dead man's photo as you brag about killing terrorists."

This about floored me (I was halfway there anyway). My head twitched in denial. *Brag about killing...? Where the hell did he get...?* Then I remembered. Those two shitheads I'd seen down at the Washington ruins. Manco and Fernando must have told the pigs all sorts of crap about me.

I recalled my encounter with Fernando at Pepe's taco stand and my snide response to his question about my black eye: *"I sliced up some Arab terrorists last night."*

Fuck if I'm not feeling stupider all the time.

I dragged myself upright with a few sharp, sunken moans.

"What else are you hiding, Russell?" the lieutenant said. His pleasant tone filled me with dread.

"Qué? What're you talking about? No hablo espa—"

"We shall see what else you are hiding, Russell," Chimp and Fat Cop approached me, "first beneath your shorts and then—"

"Wait, esperen!" I shook myself from the pigs, hands raised, seated and in full surrender. "Tranquilo," I said. "I'll do it."

The lieutenant assented, "Bien."

Chimp and Fat Cop backed off. I dropped my shorts in one easy motion and stepped out of them.

"No underwear, or socks," said the lieutenant. "How convenient. Ahora," he waved a finger up and down my body, "the shoes and shirt."

I kicked off my shoes and slipped off Ara's shirt. Then I carefully turned around and faced the lieutenant again. Chimp rummaged through my shoes and tossed them under the table.

"Muy bien, Russell," said the lieutenant. "Ahora, de rodillas."

"Rodi...?"

"On knees." The lieutenant's tight smile said that he didn't mind playing my little language games...since I didn't stand a chance against him anyway. I got to my knees. "De manos y rodillas," he ordered. On your hands and knees.

"Can I have some agua por favor?"

SEVE VERDAD

Chimp hissed, "Cállate." Seeing me naked and completely vulnerable excited him.

"Dije," said the lieutenant, "de *manos* y rodillas."

This was it. No more pretenses or language games. Only one option left. I quivered. From my nose to my toes I quivered. A body shiver I felt certain could propel my head right between the lieutenant's eyes and knock him dead. Problem was, Thug would shoot me in the back before I killed him... So I threw my Hail Mary instead, in perfect Spanish to be sure I was completely understood: "Why did you move the body of the dead *terrorista* to the marina, Lieutenant?"

Fat Cop slugged me between the shoulder blades (right where Chimp had socked me!). I fell to my chest. Chimp slapped my ass with what must have been his billy club, curdled my anus, kicked my ribs in, applied pressure to the sphincter, grunted like a hog nose-deep in carrion, drew his boot back once more...and the lieutenant said, "That will be sufficient, Paulo."

The lieutenant spoke up in the nick of time. I was prepared to suffer but not to the lengths of Chimp's nightstick. I gripped my ribs and sputtered a streak of agonized curses.

The lieutenant stood over me. His shoes had some of that infernal Washington dust around the soles, but the tops were shiny.

"Levántate, Russell," he said.

The pain in my ribs, back, and head made it tough to breathe let alone get up.

"Dije, de pie."

I answered with a tubercular cough and curled into a fetal position, the pain relentless. Thug flicked my ear with the nose of his rifle. The lieutenant nudged me with his foot. "Arriba, Russell."

As ordered, I crawled to my feet. Standing straight, I'd have looked the lieutenant straight in the eye, but settled on his tie.

"Siéntate, Russell."

I sat and slumped in the chair, arms hugging my body. Thug didn't lower his rifle for an instant. Chimp stood guard at the door, slapping his nightstick in his hand. He was proud of his billy club, its dents and scars.

"In the future you will address me as oficial or señor," said the lieutenant.

"Sí, oficial." Officer.

The lieutenant sat on the edge of the table and considered me once more. Through a throbbing yellow haze, I eyed him as well. The guy belonged in a soap opera. The handsome prick who breaks girls' hearts and makes them cry. He would've liked to make me cry, and scream and beg, but my question about him moving the dead body had piqued his interest enough to want to hear me talk rather than cry and scream.

And it was now clear that I could communicate with him perfectly. I spoke Spanish.

He shot a nod at my shorts. Fat Cop picked them up off the floor and tossed them to me. I put them on while seated.

"You must tell me how the body was moved, Russell," said the lieutenant.

His words were a salve for my wounds. I straightened my posture as sweet relief flowed through my veins, like a fist had just released my heart, my pulse. I could feel it, my pulse—strong and sure as my game plan, the playbook. Revisions to the playbook were ongoing but my Hail Mary had struck a nerve with these bastards, saved me from this brutal beating and kept me in the ballgame. It was a big gamble though. My knowledge that the body had been moved incriminated me. How would I know if I didn't have something to do with the guy's death? Well, I did know, strongly suspected anyhow, yet had absolutely nothing to do with killing him. And it wasn't like I'd confessed to the crime. Quite the contrary. My Hail Mary pointed the finger at *him*, the lieutenant. I accused *him* of moving the body and he wanted to know how the hell I knew the body had been moved, if I also knew *he* had killed that terrorist, and if anybody else knew as well. That's why he showed me some mercy. He wanted to hear all about it.

The lieutenant was trying to pin murder on me to absolve himself of the crime. Wasn't that it? And if my Hail Mary had given him the impression that I knew more about the crime than I really did, well, so be it! Muy bien. Excelente! I'd captured a modicum of momentum. The lieutenant thought I knew *how* the body was moved and, as a consequence, that *he* had moved the body after killing the terrorist. Now I had an advantage, a sliver of hope. Some field position! Bargaining power... And if the lieutenant really did think that I had killed that guy...? He still wanted all the details. A terrorist was dead, a bomb had gone off at the Washington, and another could be coming! Well, I'd give him something to consider all right. But first I pressed what little advantage I had with a request for the life sustenance I required most: "Agua, por favor. May I please have some water?"

My mouth and insides had been sucked dry by that infernal Washington dust and this beating I'd taken. The lieutenant leveled his chin at Chimp. It pleased me to watch that monkey obey me, even if it was through a two-bit soap star.

237

SEVE VERDAD

The lieutenant strolled around to his chair, sat down, and regarded me cynically, as though I'd asked permission to date his sister. Chimp was back with a Styrofoam cup of water. He sat it on the table beyond my reach. The lieutenant nodded his assent. I retrieved the cup, sat back down, and took several seconds to savor the water. "Más, por favor," I said and placed the cup back on the table.

The lieutenant tapped a pensive finger off his temple as I resumed my seat. "First—" he cut himself short at the sound of a subtle buzz. His phone. He retrieved what looked like a BlackBerry from his belt and stared at the screen, impassive dark brow furrowed in concentration, like he was thinking about three things at once.

More like a million things.

Lots of chaos around town right now. Maybe that's what caused him to commit an error with me.

Overall, the motherfucker simply wasn't prone to mistakes. Not here in The Chamber at any rate. Unflappable. That was my impression and I judged it to be dead-on accurate. Yet he may have committed an error. Just one. At the time, that tidbit of information he'd let slip about the dead guy at the marina being an Iranian terrorist may not have seemed like all that much, nothing more than a scare tactic to shock me into a confession. And it did shock me. But instead of "confessing," I focused on the dead man, someone I'd thought a lot about last night but had basically forgotten until I got arrested. Given the disaster at the Washington, the knowledge that the dead guy was a terrorist lent him a whole new significance. Anyone connected to his murder, including police (who I thought might have killed him anyway), could be tied to the slaughter, perhaps directly tied to it.

Somebody moved that body and the lieutenant wanted to know who, why, and how. Either that or, as my Hail Mary threatened to expose, *he*, the lieutenant, had moved the body himself and wanted to know what I had on him. Either I represented a valuable source of information to him or a threat. Due to his unshakable demeanor I couldn't tell which but felt fairly confident I represented both.

You'd think I would prefer being a valuable source of information to a threat. After all, people who feel threatened often act rashly, and any rash act on the lieutenant's part could result in my death...and a great deal of suffering. Yet whether I represented a genuine threat to him or not, I clearly understood that the sonofabitch was not beyond torturing me to get any valuable information I had anyway. So I really had nothing to lose and designed my Hail Mary as a threat, a thrust into the heart of the enemy. I had accused him of moving the body, el muerto. How could that not be a threat?!? That's why the play literally saved my ass! It turned the tables on him, caught him totally off guard with a sudden accusation well-grounded in two accurate assumptions: the body had been moved and whoever moved it could be tied to murder *and* terrorism—mass murder. Sure it was risky, possibly self-incriminating. But what choice did I have? These assholes were out to get me one way or another and I had to use every weapon at my disposal to defend myself. They fucked up big time leading up to the bombing of the Washington, starting with that botched raid. And it seemed entirely possible that they had also fucked up by killing that terrorist instead of interrogating him. So even if, like me, the lieutenant had nothing to do with the terrorist's death or moving the body, I intended to make him feel he could be fingered for it, just like he was doing to me.

I couldn't back down now. There was a chink in his armor, a flaw in his defenses I had to exploit or die.

The home team had me way overmatched and it was time to even up the score a bit, give myself some momentum going into halftime, assure myself a second half after...after what I assumed would be endless hours of confinement.

The lieutenant thumbed keys on his BlackBerry and left it on the table. Texting in time of crisis. "I assure you, Señor Martell," he said, his tone unaffected, "that your tricks and language games will get you nowhere. If you refuse to cooperate now, it will be more painful for you later. Now, how and why did you move the body?"

Later? The word infused me with confidence. It appeared that my strategy had bought me some time...that my strategy and the chaos in Vallarta had bought me some time.

I met the lieutenant's gaze unflinchingly. "I only know that the body was moved because *you* just confirmed it for me, señor," I said.

The lieutenant frowned. A small, darting frown tied to disdainful speculation in his eyes. "This is not a game, Russell."

"I realize that. And I still need more facts for my story about the dead terrorista found at the marina. But the first part was e-mailed yesterday and will be published tomorrow unless *I* say otherwise." I jabbed a thumb at my chest for emphasis.

"E-mail" is a great international term, right up there with "taxi" and "hotel". Everyone can get instant results with e-mail, and Chimp reacted instantly to my not-so-veiled threat, fidgeting on his feet like he had to take a piss. *Maybe* he *moved the body. When he fucks with me again I'll ask for his full name so I get it right in my coming story.*

The lieutenant pulled a cigarette from his breast pocket, lit it, reposed in his chair, and contemplated the ceiling.

"May I put on my shirt?"

The lieutenant assented, eyes on the ceiling. I decided right then to never wash Ara's shirt. It belonged under glass. My back and ribs moaned and cried as I slipped it on over my head.

"Where did you get your black eye?" The lieutenant seemed fixated on a blemish in the hospital-white ceiling. He jerked his head at me, "Eh?"

"My eye?" I brushed the bruise and underhanded my goatee, buying time to think of a reason for my black eye that would be less incriminating than taking a punch. "I got elbowed playing fútbol." I stuck out a chicken-wing elbow.

The lieutenant deadpanned me. "Americano?"

"Soccer."

He took a long drag off his cigarette and sat forward. "You will be booked under suspicion of murder," he said, "drug trafficking and terrorism."

A scorching cramp ballooned up through my stomach into my chest. I wanted to scream, tell him he was out of his Fucking Mind! that I didn't kill Anyone and never had!...that I wasn't a drug dealer and wanted a lawyer.

I licked sweat from my upper lip, and winced from a sudden pain shooting up my ass—a reminder of Chimp's nightstick. The lieutenant said, "Entendido?" Understood?

I shook my head, "No," and decided to run it straight up the gut, in international English and right between the lieutenant's soap-opera eyes: "Let's work this out financially, in cash, dollars."

The lieutenant narrowed his eyes on Chimp. I tightened up like a fightin' cock held fast on its mark. He fastened his eyes on me again. "I know you understand the charges against you, Russell."

No gain.

"I want a lawyer."

"You will be held for further questioning."

Thug's rifle barrel tickled my ear. The lieutenant said, "De pie." I stood. He remained seated. "Paulo will escort you to your quarters." Fat Cop handcuffed me behind my back.

"May I have my shoes?"

"You will be so charged," the lieutenant said.

To this day, filed away in my memory, I still have a picture of the lieutenant, leaning back in his chair, cigarette between his fingers, contemplating the ceiling, my running shoes under the table.

***

FINDING DEVO

A corridor bisected the cellblock. As you walked down the corridor from the cellblock door, three cells ran the length to the left, and three to the right. Cinderblock walls partitioned the cells. Two of the cells were occupied, both on the left-hand side—one by me at the end of the corridor, the other by four gringos up by the cellblock door. An empty cell separated us. My private cell provoked a burst of truculent jealousy in one of the gringos: "Hey! How come you got your own cell and there's four of us here in one?"

I called back, "How you know some gimp's not about to make me his sex slave in here?" How could he know? The walls and empty cell between us prevented us from seeing each other.

"Hey a-migo...me and my buddy, we been in here for ten, twelve hours at least. Some guys come, others go. But always from this cell. How come you're so motherfucking special?"

I had greeted the gringos in that first cell when the pigs escorted me into the cellblock, asked them if they got drunk enough last night. A haggard blond fellow snorted, "Not drunk enough to force the cops to draw their weapons." Thug had his rifle trained on me. Fat Cop gave me a shove down the corridor.

My cell was about six-feet wide and eight deep, quite a bit narrower than the others. All the cells were barred, naturally, and windowless. None of them had a bench or anything to sit or stretch out on, just the floor. At least my slab floor wasn't as filthy as the floor of the cell that held those gringos, and my walls weren't as scratched up with graffiti as the walls of the empty cell directly across from mine. "The Justice Fucked Me," wrote a previous guest to my quarters in Spanish. I shuddered, and swayed on my feet. Had he suffered the lengths of Chimp's nightstick?

"I must be dangerous," I announced. "Not your average drunk and brawling tourist."

"What'd you do? Kill somebody?"

I grumbled to myself, "I can't believe they think I did."

On our way to my "quarters", Chimp, Fat Cop and Thug stood me up against a wall in the processing room—the gateway to the cellblock—where a short fat chick in uniform snapped my mug shots. Then my cuffs were removed for fingerprints. She handed me a rag to clean the ink from my fingers and Fat Cop slapped the cuffs back on me. Thug never lowered his rifle.

I had my own cell because I was a dangerous man, too dangerous to throw in with the others. Hot anger singed my cheeks. Damn right I was dangerous. The abuse I'd suffered at the hands of these hijos de la chingada would make anyone dangerous.

241

SEVE VERDAD

The gringo in that first cell sounded like he was still running on last night's tequila: "Hey! Didja kill somebody or what?"

His husky insolence echoed through my eyeballs and out the hole punched between my shoulder blades. I brought my face up to the bars and clutched them like a hardened criminal. Up the corridor another pair of hands clutched bars, a blond forehead pinched between them.

"Haven't killed anyone yet," I said. "What time is it?"

"How the fuck should I know? They took my watch." A voice behind him mumbled something and he expounded on the topic: "It's gotta be noon or one o'clock, don't it? They gave us some grub at nine-thirty."

Not sure why I cared about the time. Natural curiosity I guess. I'd lost track of the time and wondered how much I had left. Would the cops be back at me before nightfall? Maybe not with all the chaos in town.

I engaged in a bit of light reading to take my mind off my troubles. Morose gray paint covered the cinderblock walls of the cells and provided a fine surface for scratching in personal messages or words of wisdom in Spanish and English. Besides the passages in my cell, I could make out a few on the far wall of the adjoining cell and several on the walls of the cell directly across from mine: "There is no place like here or home," "Judge me for who I am, not what I have become," and, "Save your own proper ass," were the most eloquent. "Fuck the pigs and their mothers" was a common visceral theme. Some sections of graffiti had been painted over and were ready for fresh prose. All you needed was half a brain and a stray chip of concrete or a sharp, sturdy fingernail. At the moment none of those items were at my disposal.

The floor was tepid under my feet and angled down to a drain in the near corner. A plastic bucket was there as well. I checked out the bucket—empty—and shuffled to the opposite corner of my cell. I gripped the bars and slowly lowered my rear onto the not-too-grimy cement floor. A sharp pang passed through my lower bowel. Felt like a thorn had fastened itself to my colon. *Exterior bruising... Sure it is. How the hell can a sphincter be* exteriorly *bruised?* I braced my ribs, eased back against the wall, and leered at the steel door to the cellblock.

Fucking Chimp.

I dropped my gaze and considered my trim toenails. Seemed like they were the only part of me that didn't hurt. My head throbbed with the ache of a thousand hangovers. I counted my ribs with my fingers and gasped upon reaching the bottom one. The pain was less than searing—not quite the intensity of hurt that accompanies a broken bone. Burning bile rose in my gullet. I hacked and spit at the drain. The shot fell three feet short. Couldn't even muster the strength to spit with authority.

The light was greasy. A discolored eight-foot florescent bulb along the wooden corridor ceiling. Tiny moths, or gnats, were sticking to it. They swarmed the bulb like flies buzzing a mangy mule's raw rump. Next to the light was some kind of darkened ventilation grating. It did little to relieve the humidity and simmering stench of urine and vomit. Most of the stink originated from that first cell. That's where the real horse flies were coming from. Those fat bloodsuckers sounded like hornets. I swatted at one with my open palm and missed, slapping my thigh after it bit me. There had to be a shit load of 'em down at the first cell, a plausible reason why my closet here at the end of the line inspired jealousy...

"If you didn't kill anyone, what the fuck ya doin' down there in solitary?"

"If I was in solitary I wouldn't have to listen to your stinkin' voice!"

I didn't have the energy to call him "asshole," or tell him he belonged in the crater beneath the Washington ruins.

There was no solitary. After all, I wasn't in prison, yet.

"You hear that sonic boom this morning? That's what it was, wasn't it? A real motherfucker! Like an earthquake!"

I ignored him. The morning's adrenalin rush had thoroughly dissipated. My tank was empty and this corner closet wasn't much of a pit stop. My stomach growled between my dented kidneys and sunken liver, a reminder that I hadn't eaten since last night. I ran a finger over the knot behind my ear. That was a mistake. Teams of bowlers began tossing strike after strike against the back of my skull. I stuck the heels of my hands in my eyes and massaged my head. The pain subsided some.

I could've used some food and water before a nap but didn't let those details stop me.

41

As a rule, Officer Paulo Pepino Revueltas (Chimp) never contacted Media Minister Lazarito Charlado from police headquarters. But with el comandante out of town, the lieutenant down at ground zero, and most the rest of the department either at the Washington or on traffic detail, why not make the call from right here in el comandante's office? No one would disturb him. He had a report to write up on the arrest he had made this morning and, for the time being, was in charge of everything at police headquarters—the cellblock, four officers on guard duty, and dispatch. He did use a calling card though, so there'd be no record of the phone call.

Lazarito always found time to take a call from his faithful snitch. Paulo's inside information didn't come cheap but was usually accurate. And he had picked the perfect moment to get in touch. The Media Minister sure could use a scoop. This was the bloodiest tragedy in the history of Vallarta, the entire state of Jalisco! Earth-shattering news. Lazarito's future depended upon nailing those responsible and bringing them to justice before...before he himself got nailed for corruption...obstruction of justice...conspiracy?!?

"Lo has visto?" Have you seen it? "Me estás chingando? Ni hay palabra..." Are you fucking kidding me? Words can't describe...

"An exploding sewer line did not cause *that*," said Chimp. "Then who the fuck did?" asked Lazarito. "Cartel gangsters? Maoistas? Anarquistas? Islamistas?"

"Tal vez islamistas," said Chimp.

"What makes you say that?"

"*Gringo* islamistas."

"Gringo...?" Lazarito hummed impatiently, "Get to the point Paulo. I assume this has something to do with the arrest police made this morning."

"So you heard."

"Híjole... Paulo, it is my job to know about such things."

"*I* made the arrest, Lazarito, of a suspected terrorist at ground zero. A gringo."

"That was fast work, Paulo, indeed it was. But if this gringo is a terrorist, why would he allow himself to be captured at the scene of the crime? I should think he would have escaped."

"Ego. He could not resist seeing his handiwork up close. Fucking cocky gringos. Always thinking they are too smart for the rest of us. But I have sources, witnesses and evidence to back up the arrest. Two sources at the Washington told me that last night they heard the suspect brag about killing terrorists in Vallarta—"

"*Killing terrorists*? How does that implicate—?"

"And I personally saw a dying woman accuse the gringo to his face of killing her baby. She accused him right there in the rubble. Her dying words—"

"She may have been delirious, Paulo. And was she speaking English?"

"Screaming English, yes... I understand enough English for that, Lazarito. Puta. I have to deal with gringos quite often in this town you know... And there is other evidence. Remember the dead man found at the marina I told you about?"

"How could I forget?"

"Pues, enough cocaine and cash were discovered on the body and in his car to conclude he was a drug dealer. And he has now been positively identified as an Iranian terrorist."

Lazarito couldn't contain his squealing surprise, "Really?!? Positively? An Iranian terrorist? My but that is astonishing news. Astonishing indeed."

Chimp gathered himself and lowered his voice: "Our gringo suspect may have killed him. Terrorists of all stripes often kill one another... Pinche arrogante. Que mentalidad...the pendejo had cocaine wrapped in a picture of the dead man, an article from La Estrella Nocturna. One of your favorite newspapers."

Lazarito let Paulo's last words pass without comment. He depended on editors of La Estrella Nocturna to stir the pot with information he leaked to them; Paulo correctly surmised as much, but there was no need to confirm or deny his innuendo. No need to give it any attention at all. What did merit the Media Minister's attention however were two fascinating revelations: the dead man was a terrorist and Paulo had arrested a suspected terrorist who may have killed him, a gringo terrorist in possession of cocaine conserved in a story Lazarito had outlined for the editors of La Estrella and embellished with a photo from his archives of a drunk passed out in the sand at a children's park in Guadalajara.

Lazarito's instincts—his spontaneous and all too natural desire to sensationalize a bit of news about a man found dead at the marina— had precipitated the identification of the victim as a murdered terrorist and aided in the capture of a suspect in the homicide who might also be a terrorist. And if terrorists were indeed responsible for the explosion at the Washington Hotel...

Incredible. This was the stuff of legend, divine proof that his talents for leaking information, manipulating rumors and managing the news were a sacred gift. And due to his gift, the story Lazarito required to bring the perpetrators of a heinous act of terror to justice and salvage and advance his career appeared to be coming together as rapidly as he had imagined.

Lazarito released a self-satisfying, whistling sigh. "Well, well, Paulo. Nicely done. I would not jump to the conclusion that this makes your gringo prisoner an Islamic terrorist however...unless you have evidence tying him to a specific terrorist organization?"

SEVE VERDAD

Chimp breathed into the phone. "No," he said. "Not yet."

"Nevertheless, Paulo, you may have nabbed a terrorist and the killer of a terrorist found dead at the marina all at once. We could use more evidence but, nicely done."

"I will have more evidence once we have a chance to interrogate the prisoner again. He...and..." Chimp skipped over his words. He wanted to emphasize the value of his prisoner by mentioning how he had incriminated himself during the interrogation when he talked of the dead man's body being moved—accused Lieutenant Romero of moving the body!—but he couldn't be sure the gringo had incriminated anyone.

Had the body been moved? Chimp hadn't a clue. His fieldwork generally consisted of graft and assisting in raids (including Saturday's humiliating botched raid), not murder investigations. Like most everyone in the department, he knew about the dead man found at the marina, but Chimp didn't know if the body had been moved or not, and it wasn't clear from the lieutenant's reaction to the prisoner's remarks if he knew either.

The interrogation of the gringo arrested at the Washington was classified. Lieutenant Romero made that clear before he left headquarters for the Washington and didn't say another word on the subject. As usual, very little could be deduced from his demeanor, yet Chimp felt reasonably certain he hadn't moved the body. If a police officer needed to move a dead body, why would he risk being seen moving it to a populated place like the marina? It didn't make sense, really didn't make sense for *anyone* to move a dead body to the marina. But if the body *was* moved, could the prisoner have known without having moved it himself? And why would the pinche gringo even suggest such a thing? To incriminate himself? No. To buy time. Like he had with his threat to publish a story. The puto was grasping at straws, implying he knew all about police blunders leading up to the bombing of the Washington, implying they would be publicized unless he, *Russell Martell*, prevented it. A clear attempt at extortion. Blackmail. Chimp almost admired the chingón...

That hijo de la chingada gringo terrorista was playing with fire and before long he'd have a nightstick up his culo.

Chimp quickly realized he had said enough to Lazarito. Snitching for him after an interrogation was tricky enough without the doubts raised by this maldito gringo. And should the Media Minister publicize information strictly traceable to the interrogation room, Lieutenant Romero would suspect he had a snitch on his hands. Given the gravity of the situation—the destruction at the Washington—the lieutenant was extra sensitive about this case. Chimp sensed his

246

trepidation when the prisoner told him he had e-mailed a draft of a story...a story that could expose police ineptitude and corruption and...

Chimp didn't know the full extent of police corruption but was always an eager participant. Business as usual. Would business as usual land him in prison this time? make him and the department scapegoats for what happened at the Washington Hotel?

Chimp couldn't wait to punish his prisoner. He'd see to it that there was nothing to fear from the egotistical, gutless chango and extract valuable information for Lazarito in the process. "...we are confident more witnesses will come forward."

"You should be proud of yourself, Paulo," Lazarito said. "Indeed you should. But you have left out a detail. A rather crucial one. What is the name of your suspect?"

Chimp hissed a chuckle and propped his feet up on el comandante's desk. The Media Minister was as predictable as a two-hundred-peso puta. "Lieutenant Romero is keeping it classified," said Chimp laconically, "confidential, for now. But you will have that detail when I receive payment. Sometime after I call you back this evening."

42

I hold out an empty cup. A pregnant woman with two grimy-faced kids in tow gives me a peso. I ask for water. She says fresh water costs too much.

A sudden cascade of water jerked me awake. Water dumped over my head and Ara's shirt. I gasped and shook my head in shock but remained seated, my back pressed against the wall.

Chimp cackled, "Agua para ti." He pushed the brim of his cap up off his hairless brow and exposed his decaying canines. Chimp had Manco's rodent eyes. A smaller rodent but no less malignant. I thought they might be related. He sauntered back up the corridor with a simian gait—bow legged and tottering from one side to the other. The water bucket hanging from his fingers dangled down around his ankles. It occurred to me that going to sleep could be a good strategy for receiving water.

Fat Cop met Chimp at the first cell. He called out two names. There was a cheer of relief, "Finally!" I drew my knees up and slumped over them, my forehead cushioned by my forearms. When would *my* relief come? When I forced Thug to shoot me? What the

247

hell had happened to me? *How* did it happen? Was there any way I could possibly save myself?

The steel door to the cellblock slammed shut. I thought about the two pricks who landed me in jail, Manco and the man Pepe had told me was chief of the Washington Hotel work crew, Fernando. They must have seen me tending to that dying woman at the Washington. Fernando was on the radio, probably in contact with cops, when Manco flipped me off. Both the sons a bitches were out to get me. I'd smarted off to both of them last night and now they were out to get me.

I sighed, "Shit," raised my head and stared unseeingly at the opposite wall. What dumb, rotten luck...although I had to admit, I sure could be a smartass. Nevertheless, what dumb, rotten luck. And that goddamn Chimp. Right off the bat his terrorist accusation threw me for a loop. Flabbergasted me. My capture was a feather in his cap. On our way to police headquarters my offer of a thousand dollars to set me free proved worthless...

Bribery might still work though, as an ancillary strategy in conjunction with some sort of offensive. *Yes, it just might...*

I reviewed my play-calling against the lieutenant. Should I have spoken up about the police raid instead of asking him why *he* had moved the dead body? Mentioning the raid, a *botched* raid, was in the playbook. Connecting the dead body to the raid (and police) was my long bomb. Asking the lieutenant why he had moved the body was a revised Hail Mary drawn up in sandlot dirt—on my knees and butt naked. It didn't tie the score but kept me in the ballgame. Got the lieutenant's attention and saved my ass, for the time being.

Many people knew about the raid. And the dead guy got a write-up in the paper. Mentioning the raid and its connection to the dead guy would not have gone deep enough. Might've just pissed 'em off more—backed me up against my own goal line and Chimp's nightstick instead of giving me some field to work with. But had my Hail Mary incriminated me? Maybe not. The pigs would be tearing me a new asshole in The Chamber right now if it had. My Hail Mary probably worked because the cops themselves moved the body for some corrupt reason, were afraid I knew why and how they moved it, and wanted to confirm my identity, see if I really was a journalist who might have e-mailed a story incriminating them—a story to be published tomorrow unless I prevented it. A story I'd be more than happy to guarantee would never be published if they set me free.

I'd hit a nerve, a real sore spot for the cops. And I had a good ground game. I really was a journalist here on business. The lieutenant could confirm as much through Immigration and Customs at the airport. I'd filled out the proper paperwork and left my Puebla address, just like always. Police could even check out my website, though with my black eye, goatee, and my hair covered in infernal Washington dust I wasn't so sure I looked like my picture... My hotel was booked separately from my flight, so when the lieutenant checked with Alaska Airlines he would find nothing on that score. Good. I didn't want the cops stealing all my gear at Casa Mexicana. And best of all, I really did have a story; the lieutenant just didn't know it hadn't been written yet.

But was this enough to prevent the pigs from subjecting me, a suspected *terrorista,* to further torture, or maybe even killing me and dumping my body...in the Washington ruins?

I'd told the lieutenant I was staying at the Washington. I didn't have a reservation but could've been staying with someone who did...

Was it a mistake to tell him I was lodged there?

A dark, loathsome swelling in my chest consumed me. I had committed one error on top of another...outfoxed myself. My game plan was flawed. Not only had I provided the lieutenant with the perfect location to dispose of my body—the Washington, my supposed hotel—but thanks to my offensive he thought I knew too much.

The lieutenant was privy to the truth. He knew the dead guy was connected to the raid. And since I said the body had been moved, I was connected...to everything—the dead guy (an Iranian terrorist), the raid, police foul-ups...even the terror attack itself!

Did the lieutenant really believe I was a terrorist? At the very least he believed I had a story. A story about police and federale incompetence that resulted in the bombing of the Washington Hotel. A story that made me a very dangerous man, perhaps a guilty man. I'd told the lieutenant that the first part of my story had already been e-mailed. If he didn't want to bargain for it, I was a dead man.

I'm exaggerating. He'll bargain. The game plan is solid...

My second guessing and self-doubt infused me with cold paranoia. I shivered, though it was quite warm on the cellblock. I swatted at a fly buzzing my nose and missed. Someone groaned and snored from the first cell up the corridor. He couldn't possibly know how good he had it compared to me. My legs tightened and flexed involuntarily, as if aching to run. With the pain in the rest of my body, I'd forgotten they'd been spared a beating. I made an effort to stand, if only to pace my cell. A stabbing white-hot light behind my eyes kept me seated in place against the wall. My breath shortened and burning bile rose in my gullet again. Nausea twisted my guts. I fell forward onto my hands and knees, crawled towards the bucket, and heaved just short of it, between the bucket and the drain. The nausea subsided...but now I had vomit to contend with. At least it was my own. I dunked spittle and snot directly into the bucket and fell back to my spot against the wall next to the bars. If more water was coming I might as well be in position, try to anticipate it and open my mouth the next time Chimp doused me.

Usually a strong puke like that brings relief. I felt worse. Sick of mind, body and soul. Dejected and stupid. I'd single handedly stunk up the joint. Blown the ballgame. The season. My life.

Single handedly?

Details. I needed details to figure out how I'd gotten myself into this mess, who all was involved, and what could possibly be done to save my life.

But I was too beat to concentrate

.

WATER woke me before I had a chance to dream.

"More water for you," said Chimp.

I lapped it from my lips and shirt collar.

"You will have fun tonight," he said, balloon head swelling gleefully beneath his cop cap.

I considered asking if his mother would be there, or maybe some cheerleaders, but sucked water from the collar of Ara's shirt instead.

Chimp banged his metal water bucket against the bars. Throbbing vibrations reverberated between my ears and stiffened me. The gong for round thirty-two. How many rounds did I have left? Something clicked behind my forehead, like a switch turned on and off and back on again in succession—my brain kicking into gear. Chimp banged his bucket against the bars once more. I dropped my head between my hands to protect my ears. The clicking in my head quickened and a strategy for escape materialized.

"El comandante is looking forward to meeting you," Chimp said. "He has special methods planned for captured terroristas."

I lifted my gaze to the heavens and began muttering like a nutcase. Portuguese mixed with English. Senseless gibberish.

"Fucking asesino. Would you like some food with your water, hijo de puta?" Chimp's tone had an icy rasp to it, like skates skidding across a frozen pond. I rocked back and forth and hummed a happy tune.

"You will need your strength for el comandante. You pinche—" The ice in Chimp's voice splintered and he hacked, spit a chunk on my head.

I dropped my head and murmured, "No hay. There isn't. Sí hay. Yes there is," over and over, my body rocking back and forth all the while. Chimp's pants were visible out the corner of my eye. He came close, knees between the bars. I spied his holstered gun. Chimp was curious, thought I might have something important to say. Curiosity would kill that chimpanzee.

He stepped back, sensing danger.

I sang softly, "Flores para los muertos." Flowers for the dead.

"Qué?" said Chimp.

In low, melancholy Spanish I sang, "Flowers for the dead, and then to eat." The words were sung once again and more gibberish escaped my mouth.

The cellblock door slammed shut. I looked up. Chimp was gone. I wiped his spittle from my temple with the sleeve of Ara's shirt.

Stupid superstitious bastard thought I was speaking tongues. One more second at the bars and I'd have killed the motherfucker right there, snapped that pencil neck of his like a year-old wishbone.

Insanity was added to the play book. "Crazy fucking gringo" wouldn't be a tough role to play if it came down to it.

Crazy fucking gringo. Like Manco called Devo.

Fat Cop entered the cellblock and retrieved the remaining two prisoners from the first cell. I expected some fanfare but heard only muted voices before the cellblock door slammed shut once more.

I thought about Devo, again. I'd thought about him briefly on the ride to the police station. After all, I had gotten the coke from him. At the time, his role in my capture seemed purely circumstantial. Through the cleansing clarity of insanity, I saw things differently.

Who said the body had been *dumped* at the marina? Devo.

Devo said the dead guy was supposed to die...and the cops didn't know who killed him.

Devo, with his sleight of hand, made sure I had the cocaine wrapped in a picture of the dead guy.

Devo the magician.

Devo the impressionist.

Devo the assassin? Devo the terrorist? Was it really such a leap? Didn't his knowledge that the body had been moved—"dumped at the marina"—incriminate *him*? Had he set me up, made me his fall guy?

How the hell could Devo know I would be down at the Washington primed to get busted? He knew I was a journalist, and if he also knew a bomb was to go off, he had to figure I'd head down there to get the story. Sure I was worried about Johnny, but I would have headed to the Washington anyway.

Shoulda given the coke to Johnny last night. How did Devo know I wouldn't?

I thought about Johnny. *He rarely misses a fishing trip.*

SEVE VERDAD

The subject of Johnny was too much. His fate was completely out of my hands.

A cockroach was by the drain munching my vomit. A smaller one crawled up the drain and skipped over to her partner. The sight of them didn't disgust me at all, no more than any other bug in the cellblock. A fly buzzed my ears and was gone before I could swat at it. I picked up my train of thought about Devo. Why would he set me up? What did he have to gain? How could he be sure I would react to events the way I did? Manco had never seen Devo before the party and was thoroughly intimidated by him. How could those two be connected? Where did Devo belong in the story?

Back to the story. Devo's part wasn't clear but I did uncover a classic Catch 22 that left me screwed no matter how you looked at it.

If the cops believed there was a story of mine to be published that incriminated them, wouldn't killing me look suspicious? Wouldn't they have to negotiate with me for it? Not necessarily. They could deny everything. Their shit always floats. And if they didn't believe I had a story to be published, well...I still knew too much... The game was rigged. All the charges against me would stick, if they wanted, or they could kill me, if they wanted.

I doubted anyone or any amount of money could save me.

43

WHEN Gloria and the mayor arrived at the Washington Hotel the sun was high in the sky; the veil of smoke and infernal dust that enveloped the disaster area seemed to blister and ooze under its increasing heat. Sirens, voices and cries boiled in their ears, acrid devastation penetrated their nuisance masks and singed their nostrils. Gloria stood with Juan as he conferred with the fire chief and a small rescue crew at the edge of the ruins, a sheen of grief across her brow. How could such a monstrous catastrophe have occurred? It was Gloria's job to initiate a preliminary investigation into that very question. And she knew precisely how and where to begin.

WINDOWS shattered behind security bars. Cracked display cases in the museum. Wooden chairs overturned in the dining hall. Pots and pans tossed on the kitchen floor. A broken vase and fallen portrait in one of the management offices. Gloria's precious arena had suffered the shockwaves from an explosion. Minor damage, nothing compared to the unmitigated disaster she'd seen at the Washington. Overall,

Arena Vallarta remained in good condition. Repairs would take no time at all.

The roundtable in the center of the dining hall would accommodate Gloria and three others this afternoon: Immigration Inspector Sandra Villanueva, Police Lieutenant Benito Cuevas Romero, and the police department's unofficial Investigative Analyst, a young man Gloria had met a few times in the past when he visited his father during the construction of Arena Vallarta, Pedro Santos.

Gloria had contacted both Lieutenant Benito Cuevas Romero and Sandra to inform them that, at the request of Governor Palacio, their presence was required at Arena Vallarta to begin a preliminary investigation into the cause of the disaster at the Washington Hotel. Benito's truncated briefing to her over the phone made it clear that Pedro's presence was required as well and she left it to him to see to it that the junior officer attended. Pedro had been examining evidence and reports that had a direct bearing on the investigation. The lieutenant quickly reviewed with Gloria two recent developments that also had a bearing on the investigation: the arrest of a gringo at ground zero this morning and the startling news that a man found dead at the marina this past Saturday had been identified as an Iranian terrorist.

Federal Immigration Inspector Sandra Villanueva also had a report ready on the dead man discovered at the marina and confirmed the lieutenant's findings to Gloria over the phone. Upon her arrival at Arena Vallarta, before she, Gloria, Pedro, and the lieutenant were even seated at the roundtable, Sandra laid into Benito with sharp accusatory questions: What details had he uncovered about the dead Iranian found at the marina? What else did he have on that gangster, *Paco*, arrested on Saturday? Were police guarding evidence that should be turned over to Immigration officials? "Given this morning's tragedy," she said, "it sure as hell looks like other foreign terrorists besides that dead man have visited Vallarta, and Immigration expects full cooperation from police. We cannot hope to discover who these people are if you withhold evidence as if this were an everyday turf battle between federal and local authorities." Sandra proffered Officer Santos a slice of her menacing hazel-brown glare. Pedro remained silent, taciturn and downcast, a demeanor he would maintain until the preliminary investigation was well underway. Lieutenant Romero lost some of his cool. In a scathing tone he reminded Sandra that police had reached out to Immigration for help Saturday evening and, if her department had been doing its job in the first place, the hijo de puta terrorista would not have gotten into the country at all. Sandra's head jerked as if she'd been slapped, her gaunt, Mayan features reddening. Gloria intervened, assured Sandra that all relevant evidence and information would be shared amongst *all* government departments, "starting right now," and quieted things down in a tearing rasp of existential purpose: "We are likely dealing with a terror attack and our very survival may depend on remaining calm and focused."

The dining hall fell silent; the four of them took their places at the roundtable.

LIEUTENANT Romero concluded his opening remarks with an analysis of the murder and how it pointed to a lone killer. Pedro nodded imperceptibly, Sandra pursed her lips thoughtfully, and Gloria requested a verdict: "Are you convinced of our prisoner's guilt, Lieutenant?"

"I am not convinced the suspect is guilty of terrorism, or murder," he replied. "But nor am I convinced of his innocence. Thus far, the evidence against him is circumstantial. And we know next to nothing about him. Does he have the background and training to have killed the Iranian terrorist in that fashion and commit an act of terror? We will investigate that as we verify his identity. But he knows too much about the terrorist's murder not to be involved somehow."

"Have you uncovered anything on the name he gave you?" Gloria asked.

"There is a North American journalist by the name of Russell Martell. After the interrogation, I took a couple of minutes to search for him on the Internet and found his website. The posted photo resembles our suspect but is inconclusive. We will have to match his fingerprints to be certain who he is."

"Have them faxed or e-mailed to my office," Sandra said. "I can forward them to Guadalajara and the United States for a match."

"Linda at police dispatch will be so advised."

Gloria said, "So to summarize what you have just told us, Lieutenant..." She reviewed her notes aloud, her tone patient and academic: "...evidence seems to suggest that a single assailant murdered the man found dead at the marina with his bare hands; a broken neck was the cause of death; the body was planted at the marina after the murder; the evidence found on the body was either planted or purposely left there for police to find; the man who was murdered has now been positively identified as an Iranian terrorist, which suggests he may have had something to do with what appears to have been a terror attack on the Washington; enough cocaine and money was recovered from the dead body and a Jeep registered to the terrorist's alias to conclude that he was also a narcotraficante; and our jailed suspect's connection to the murdered terrorist consists of cocaine found on him wrapped in an article about the victim, testimony from two witness who heard him speak of 'slicing up terrorists' last night, and the fact that he knew the body was moved to the marina after the murder took place."

"We have additional testimony," the lieutenant added forcefully. "Paulo, the arresting officer, is working on his report but I believe he witnessed a dying woman at ground zero accuse our suspect of killing her baby. She may have had some knowledge of our suspect's terrorist ties or seen him—"

"Has the baby been located?" Gloria interjected, pen raised. "And was anyone able to speak to the woman before she died, anyone besides our suspect?"

"No. She died on the spot. And it may be some time before we can tie her to anyone found dead or alive at the Washington..." Lieutenant Romero crossed his arms, dark brow reserved and unflinching.

Gloria laid her pen down and shifted her gaze around the table. Across the table, Pedro stared at his hands folded before him, lost in reflection. To her right, Sandra spoke up as she met Gloria's eyes. "We need more details," she said with a glance at the lieutenant opposite her, "most specifically, confirmation of the suspect's identity. But on the face of it, this all looks fairly incriminating."

"Yes it does," Gloria agreed, then demurred: "But *Mister Martell* might have obtained the cocaine anywhere. And was his bravado about 'slicing up terrorists' just that? innocent bravado? After all, the Iranian died from a broken neck and was not 'sliced up' or even bloodied. The witnesses to our prisoner's behavior last night need to be questioned again, as does anyone we can find who saw him this past weekend or knows him... Your conclusion that the body was moved appears sound, Lieutenant. I am at a loss to explain how a corpse could have been laying at the marina for an hour or more without being discovered. But could our suspect have known the body was moved without killing the victim and moving the body himself?... He, or *someone* may have killed the Iranian single handed as you suggest, but did accomplices help the killer move the body, accomplices also involved in bombing the Washington? Terrorists have been known to kill one another but, as of yet, we have no physical evidence linking our suspect to the murder; and even if he did kill the terrorist, does that make *him* one?"

"Not necessarily," the lieutenant said. "But if we match his fingerprints to unidentified prints found in the Jeep, we will have forensic evidence linking him to a terrorist."

"Fax or e-mail them to Sandra." Gloria faced the immigration inspector. "The police department needs all the help it can get, Sandra."

"Understood, señora. And I will check the airport Immigration database, or make a trip out there if necessary. If our suspect flew into Vallarta on Alaska, there will be a record of it, as well as a record of him passing through Immigration. And if he is a journalist here on business as he claims, he must have filled out the proper paperwork. That information should also be with Immigration at the airport."

"Very good, Sandra. But he may be claiming to be a man he is not, someone by the name of Russell Martell who he knows flew into town on Alaska—"

"A journalist he knows he resembles," the lieutenant interceded, "and may know personally or be related to, which is why we need to match his fingerprints to a name in order to verify who he is...or match a DNA sample to a name. He drank water from a cup I have in evidence and I will have blood drawn from him, but matching his fingerprints should prove more expedient than matching his DNA."

Sandra nodded her agreement. Gloria said, "Tell us about those passports, Sandra, and what you turned up on the dead Iranian terrorist."

"Bueno, señora."

Sandra's reference to Gloria as "señora" was a professional courtesy. They were actually well acquainted and enjoyed each other's company frequently. Both were in their early forties and, like Gloria, Sandra exercised a great deal of autonomy in her work, was greatly respected, and had a family of her own. Her husband wasn't Mayor but did own two restaurants in town. And Sandra found time to do much of his accounting work along with her duties as Immigration Inspector, duties generally limited to sorting through foreign work permits, immigration forms, and questionable tourist documents. This was not the first time suspected false passports had fallen into her hands but, given the circumstances, she knew all too well that they were the most critical documents she had ever examined.

Sandra had the same patina of infernal Washington dust on her clothes as Gloria, the lieutenant and Pedro had on theirs. All four of them were in blue turned varying shades of gray: the lieutenant in his uniform, Pedro in his jeans and pullover, Gloria in her jeans and denim shirt, and Sandra in her pants suit.

Their faces, hair and hands were relatively clean. Each had visited the bathroom upon arrival.

Sandra looped her auburn hair behind her ears and released a sigh heavy enough to drain some of her fatigue. "The three passports found on the dead man as well as the one belonging to the gangster arrested before Saturday's raid appear genuine," she said. "All are Venezuelan and current, but they are not biometric passports, which Venezuela began issuing in—"

Gloria interrupted, "Biometric...?"

"Something like 'smart-card' technology incorporated into phone and credit cards, Gloria. Radio Frequency Identification technology. Personal data, often including a photo and fingerprints, stored on a computer chip in the passport to verify the bearer's identity."

Pedro rocked his head in full understanding. Gloria said, "And the passports lack this technology?"

"Sí," Sandra said. "No technology is infallible, but it would have given me another avenue to authenticate the passports. They were supposedly issued after Venezuela started incorporating biometric technology into its passports, but despite Venezuelan *biometric requirements*, the country still regularly issues non-biometric passports. So it is no surprise that these four are not biometric." Sandra took a short sip of water and cleared her throat. "I was not able to find a record of them in my ID searches. This does not prove that they are forgeries but—" she narrowed her gaze on the lieutenant, "—since we now know that the dead terrorist is not the man identified in *his* passport..."

"We know that passport is false," he stated flatly.

"Which suggests the others might be false as well," Gloria said.

Thoughtful silence. Sandra slipped on the reading glasses dangling around her neck and thumbed through her thin folder on the table. "I was able to do a little research on the murder victim before our meeting here... Let me see... Our infamous dead man found at the marina is Abdul Ali Shar...Shar*ou*di."

Sandra referred to the computer printout of her ID search on Abdul Ali Sharoudi. The information had made a huge impact on her, an impact as large as the explosion that shook her office this morning. To Sandra's knowledge, no one of this man's infamy had ever even visited Vallarta before, much less been murdered here. The facts on him were astonishing and she couldn't help but add a dramatic flair to her voice as she reported them:

"Abdul Ali Sharoudi was a suspected member of the Iranian Revolutionary Guard captured in Iraq by United States and coalition forces in June of 2004. Political pressure forced his release from Guantánamo prison in Cuba and the Americans handed him over to authorities in Egypt where he faced charges stemming from his connections to the Muslim Brotherhood. Details are sketchy here but it appears that a firefight instigated by the Brotherhood sprang him from his jail keepers in Egypt four years ago." Sandra peered over her glasses and glanced about the table. "And Saturday he was found dead in Puerto Vallarta, México." She returned to her report. "Along with being a member of the Iranian Revolutionary Guard, Abdul was also a suspected moneyman for assorted terror groups, most notably Hamas and Hezbollah. He was a wanted man in Egypt until Mubarak was overthrown, remains wanted in the United States and Israel, and had been thought to only operate in the Middle East and Asia."

Sandra removed her reading glasses, eyebrows arched at Gloria. "United States authorities should be very interested to find that he was discovered murdered not too far south of their border, Gloria."

"As are we, Sandra. Lieutenant?"

"I think we can safely assume that all the passports are false. The one giving the Iranian an alias is clearly false and information I received this morning from my source in el DF indicates that the gangster's passport is false as well; and he may have been involved in smuggling terrorists across the northern border into the United States. So the two other passports found on the dead terrorist were probably intended for terrorists or gangsters still at large. I will provide you a fresh report on the gangster, *Paco*, tomorrow, señora."

"Very good, Lieutenant. And a copy for Immigration."

Lieutenant Romero allowed Sandra a courtesy nod. "Of course."

Gloria considered Enrique's son, Pedro, seated across the table from her. The few times she'd met him he'd struck her as an exceptionally bright, well-spoken young man with an agreeable, easy-going manner, his calm demeanor a refreshing contrast to Enrique's rather high energy. Right now he looked out of his league. Everyone seated at the table was an authority figure except him. Pedro's sheepish posture, wandering doe eyes and mussed curls lent him a school-boy innocence...innocence lost in the face of death. His pallor reflected dull disbelief and shock at what he'd seen at the Washington. Yet Gloria remained confident he could handle the pressure. *Cual el cuervo, tal su huevo*. The apple doesn't fall far from the tree, and Pedro was Enrique's son, a man who had handled the pressures and time constraints of building Arena Vallarta as well as could have possibly been expected.

"Pedro," Gloria said. "The lieutenant mentioned to me that you have been examining much of this evidence, including a computer disc found on the dead man. Tell us what you have come up with."

Pedro took a long sip of water and cleared his throat, the disc's clues, images and messages flashing through his mind—visions of severed heads...maps related to the spread of radical Islam in Latin America and throughout the world...Banderas Bay painted blood red

258

just before the Washington's north tower blew up... And that first message about an invasion and Mexico always arriving late for fiestas...an Islamist terror fiesta?!?

His examination of the disc last night should have alerted him to a coming attack. He'd been reminded of the terrorist rumor when he reviewed the police reports...why hadn't he given the rumor credence? especially since the disc called attention to radical Islam spreading throughout the Americas!...spreading like blood seeping from an open wound, flowing from a deep gash, gushing from a slit throat. He should have known what was coming. He should have pieced the puzzle together and personally alerted the police department! He should have personally contacted federales...tried repeatedly to contact the lieutenant...

Thus far, Pedro had kept his inner turmoil to himself, as he had when he called the lieutenant from his home office to inform him that the disc had targeted Banderas Bay just before the explosion this morning.

"Are you fucking kidding me?" Lieutenant Romero had responded into his phone with uncharacteristic hostility.

Pedro would have liked to reply to the lieutenant's outburst with a slice of his father's colorful language—"Why would I *motherfucking* kid about a thing like that?!?"—but resisted the urge and proceeded with a succinct report: the disc hadn't revealed anything of consequence since two minutes before the explosion but should be monitored at all times in case it did. Lieutenant Romero told Pedro to monitor the disc himself. "As soon as I can spare the manpower, an officer will relieve you," he said. "When he does, you are to brief him on his duties and report directly to me."

Pedro briefed the officer who arrived at his house to relieve him but didn't mention all the missed clues, the dots he'd failed to connect. Pedro still hadn't shared his burden with anyone and felt guilty as hell—all alone in purgatory awaiting his sentence to be handed down.

What an undreamable nightmare. He'd failed in his duties, and his failure contributed to the worst disaster imaginable! Yet Pedro's duties weren't over. Somehow he had to get a grip on his emotions and give an honest briefing to his superiors, even if it meant incriminating himself.

Pedro wiped his nervous palms on his pants and began slowly, skirting the edges of his investigation of the disc (and Gloria's eyes). "Pues..." he began, drawing out his words, "Whoever created the disc is very computer savvy, perhaps a computer expert. Its encryption and self-decryption are quite sophisticated... The disc seems to be programmed to reveal information on a timed schedule corresponding to specific dates and specific times, and I have come to the conclusion that it either includes an interior biometric clock of some sort to trigger and time its self-decryption or that it responds to an external signal somehow, perhaps via a biometric chip."

Gloria frowned, "Why...? I am not sure I follow."

"When I inserted the disc into my computer it asked for an access code, which means it is encrypted. Once you enter the code or password, most encrypted discs reveal their contents just like any DVD or compact disc that is not encoded. Without the code to an encrypted disc however, access is denied, and breaking a code can be very difficult if not impossible given modern encryption technology. My computer has yet to break the code. Nevertheless, the disc is revealing its contents anyway. But without the code you cannot skip around—fast-forward or reverse—in search of data. The disc only reveals what it wants you to see *when* it wants you to see it—on its own time schedule. And its self-decryption conforms to *real* time. The disc's program, its running time, is linked to our actual time and date." Pedro clasped his hands together on the table, white knuckled.

"I see," Gloria said, her brow wrinkled in thought. "Is the disc still active, revealing information?"

Pedro thrust his hands into his lap. "It looks that way, sí señora. An external hard drive is copying the disc's images, so we can view what it has revealed thus far. But we cannot fast-forward the disc itself, access data it has yet to reveal on its time schedule. And there is no way to be certain what will happen if we remove it from my computer, though it seems logical that it would adjust its self-decryption to the correct time and date when reinserted into a computer."

Pedro massaged the back of his neck and cleared his throat once again. His voice lacked its usual strength, like he was speaking into a paper bag; but he was holding his own and had a captivated audience.

He may have captivated his audience but Pedro could not have been more uncomfortable if he were being forced to confess to murder before a firing squad. His sense of guilt for not connecting the dots last night and anticipating this morning's attack weighed heavily upon him. He couldn't escape the heaving throes in his chest, his heart bounding about like a ship on the high seas. Pedro had the presence of mind to keep his nervous hands in his lap and out of sight for the most part, but found it agonizing to look anyone in the eye, especially Gloria, who was asking all the questions.

Gloria gave Pedro a quizzical stare. "This is all very interesting Pedro, but what information are we talking about? How are the disc's revelations relevant to our investigation?"

"The disc's last image before the explosion at the Washington is particularly relevant."

"How so?"

"Pues...after I inserted it into my home computer, the disc's interior timer or clock had it wait over twenty-four hours before it began revealing information—images, pictures, videos, maps...and words... But the disc did not target any specific city or geographic location to be hit until this morning when a map of México and North América appeared and...uh..." He hesitated and smoothed his hands over the table, then quickly forged ahead, afraid his hesitancy would expose his burden, "Banderas Bay turned red two minutes before the explosion."

Gloria blanched. "Are you suggesting...? Did you see Banderas Bay turn red, Pedro?"

"Not at the time, señora." Pedro swallowed the tremor in his voice. "But I viewed the copy later this morning on my father's computer and...according to the time on the copy, Banderas Bay turned red at 7:58 a.m."

Nervous shifting and stirring of bodies at the table. The lieutenant had heard this last detail from Pedro this morning but muttered restively anyhow. "Híjole," he said, and Sandra, "Santa María." Pedro drew a deep breath, his stomach lifting up around his throat. His conscience couldn't be cleared, not by the truth and certainly not by lying. He wasn't a good liar and now was no time to compound his errors with a lame attempt at protecting himself during an investigation into the deaths of hundreds of people. Certainly the most gruesome, harrowing, high-profile investigation he would ever have a hand in. He sipped his water, gulping audibly.

"What the..." Gloria stammered. "If... If I understand correctly...the disc knew what time it was and...that it was time to tell you *we* were the target?"

Sandra brought a hand to her throat. "Increíble."

"Sí," Pedro said, his voice tottery. "That is the gist of it. But even if I had seen the clue when it first came up, and understood what the disc was trying to say, it was too late to do anything about it and there was no way of knowing which part of the bay or Vallarta would be hit"—but I could have done something about it, he thought and lowered his gaze, if I had pieced the puzzle together last night and alerted police.

Gloria released a ghastly whisper, her pen slipping from her fingers, "Dios mío. If the disc predicted the attack then—"

The lieutenant intervened. "I have ordered the disc to be monitored at all times," he said, a note of triumphant forbearance in his voice. He retrieved the pager at his belt and set it on the table. "The officer monitoring the disc has orders to alert me if any more targets are painted red or if anything remotely threatening appears."

"And he is probably bored," Pedro added. "The disc remains stuck on one image or map most of the time."

"Stuck?" Gloria said.

Pedro wiped a trickle of sweat from his brow. "Sí señora. The images came at a fairly steady pace for a while last night. But according to the copy there was about a six-hour lull while I slept. And since the presumed attack this morning, it has only revealed a couple of inactive, nondescript maps. But..." Pedro let his voice trail off.

Gloria finished his thought: "That could change."

"Sí, señora. At any time."

"We should be viewing the disc and its copy right here right now in my office," Gloria intoned. "But I presume you have but one external hard drive recording the disc, and it needs to remain in place while the disc is running."

"I disconnected it to view the recording on my father's computer, señora, but could see the disc's current images on my computer and missed nothing."

"And you do not want to remove the disc from your computer for fear of disrupting its self-decryption."

"Sí señora. We can move the computer without disrupting the decryption process. I have it connected to a battery and surge protector. But I am not certain what to expect if I remove the disc."

"I understand, Pedro. And you also said that the disc's self-decryption may be tied to a biometric clock contained in the disc, or a chip receiving an external signal. I am not familiar with the intricacies of biometric technology but have you considered something simpler, like a time-delayed decryption...? or...if the disc is simply in synch with the date and time of your computer, or the time and date your computer retrieves from the Web?"

"I considered that, sí señora." Pedro's habitually roaming eyes averted Gloria's questioning stare. "Once I realized that the disc was predictive I disconnected my computer from the Internet and set its time back, and then forward eight hours, to see if the disc was in synch with it. But the adjustments had no effect on the disc's self-decryption." Pedro stared blankly at his glass of water. "Which makes sense," he shrugged. "If the disc were programmed to reveal itself according to the computer's time and date, anyone could gain complete access to it by simply adjusting the time and date of their computer." He glanced at the lieutenant. "The disc's programmer is too smart to allow the code to be circumvented so easily." Pedro tried looking Sandra in the eye and found her chin, a rather square one. "And as for a time-delayed decryption, a decryption programmed to begin twenty-four hours after an attempt to gain access...well... How could the author of the disc possibly know when I would attempt to gain access?" He raised his hands and shook his head in a gesture of incredulity. "I mean, Banderas Bay turned red *two minutes* before the explosion. There was no time to react." Pedro lowered his hands. "Timing like that is not simply coincidental."

"The timing of Banderas Bay turning red might have been coincidental if...or..." Gloria's voice faded as she pondered Pedro's general line of thinking.

Pedro shifted uneasily in his seat. "The disc was programmed to paint Banderas Bay as a target, señora," he said in a firm voice, resigned to his destiny. "So no matter how you look at it, the author of the disc knew an attack was imminent. And he made certain we did not receive this information with time to spare. The disc waited twenty-four hours before revealing its contents but I am convinced that, had we attempted to gain access to it a week ago, Banderas Bay still would have turned red at 7:58 this morning. The disc was never intended to give us sufficient warning" —or was it? he thought and paused abruptly. Pedro steeled himself against the relentless throes of guilt rising in his chest. If not for that terrorist rumor perhaps he couldn't have expected himself to anticipate the attack. But he did know about the rumor... He forced air from his lungs and quickly picked up where he left off, "—So I came to the conclusion that the disc must either have an interior clock or be receiving a signal, perhaps an Internet signal, to keep it in synch with our time and date, a clock or signal that prompts it to reveal specific information on a schedule that had it reveal a map targeting Banderas Bay just before the attack took place."

Pedro surveyed his captive audience: Sandra shaking her head in disbelief; the lieutenant stroking his chin, eyes narrowed; Gloria searching his face, speechless.

From the beginning of his briefing, Gloria noted the shock in Pedro's pallor. And, although articulate enough, he remained uneasy and shaken, his smooth adolescent features and voice quavering intermittently as he spoke. The devastation he had seen at the Washington might explain this, of course. The disaster had taken its toll on all of them and Pedro now found himself in the midst of an investigation into a presumed terror attack. He was taking on a lot of responsibility for one so young. Yet Gloria perceived something more in Pedro's demeanor, his skittish eyes and sheepish posture. A self-destructive emotion she'd been battling herself throughout this horrendous day. Guilt. Pedro likely feared he'd missed or not tied together clues the disc had revealed before the terrorists struck and, as a result, suffered self-recriminations, self-recriminations similar to the ones haunting Gloria about not giving the terrorist rumor its due attention. Pedro honestly believed he could have prevented the attack.

The young man was in a tough spot, and Gloria empathized with him. She really did. She had to. In many respects she felt the same way he did.

Pedro was an integral part of this investigation and needed to be handled with care. Gloria wanted a few more details from him before adjourning this meeting to examine the disc's revelations herself and didn't want him to get defensive or feel threatened. She sat forward in her chair, folded her hands on the table, and offered Pedro her best impersonation of a school teacher pleased with her pupil: "I can see you have given the disc a great deal of thought, Pedro. I am very impressed..."

Pedro looked up from his glass of water and held Gloria's gaze for the first time this afternoon. "Yes I have given it a lot of thought," he said stoically. "It has occupied most of my time the past twenty-four hours."

"I have to admit that your analysis appears sound," she proceeded. "And from what I gather, regardless of the timing of Banderas Bay turning red, the fact that the disc targeted Banderas Bay at all points the finger of blame at—"

"I know," Pedro interjected, his tone plaintive and harsh. "Señora," he added with chagrin. He balled his fists upon the table and met everyone's eyes as he confessed: "Whoever programmed the disc is very familiar with the dynamics and spread of radical Islam, here in the Américas and around the world. Its messages and images draw attention to it..." Pedro's voice caught, and he heard the anguished cries down at the Washington, saw the rubble and contorted faces, the horror and suffering. He felt completely alone, isolated within a tragedy he could not hope to comprehend. It was inconceivable. Unconscionable. He bowed his head as a lugubrious voice of submission arose from his diaphragm, remnants of his self-control: "I should have known..."

Pedro shaded his face with his hand. "*Rayos*," he cursed, his voice a pleading sob. "How could I have been so careless?"

Gloria leaned over the table and reached for him as if to save him from falling into an abyss. "Not you, Pedro," she said with a small cry. "*You* are *not* to blame. *Terroristas* are the guilty ones."

Pedro bit his lower lip and gripped the edge of the table. "Carajo," he cursed again, this time through clenched teeth. He pinched the bridge of his nose and shook his head. "I never... How do people conceive of doing such things?"

"Because they are bloodthirsty savages," Sandra said, her scathing words drowning the anguish in her voice.

Pedro pushed himself back from the table and raised his gaze to the ceiling, his eyes red-rimmed from stifled tears. The lieutenant spoke up, his commanding voice echoing in Pedro's ears: "You must not forget, Pedro, you...we can bring all hell down upon those sin madre terroristas."

Pedro drew a deep breath, as though preparing to perform a great athletic feat, and offered his superior officer a stalwart nod. "Sí señor," he said, and to Gloria, "I did not mean to lose control señora. Lo siento."

"No need to apologize," Gloria replied.

"We all feel the same way," Sandra said, "helpless because there was nothing we could do to prevent it, and guilty because we feel we could have prevented it."

"Yes we do," Gloria agreed. "And we must not dwell on those feelings. They are of no use to us right now." Gloria carefully regarded Pedro. He looked to have recovered somewhat, only a tad red-faced. "You said the disc draws attention to the spread of radical Islam here in the Américas."

"Sí señora."

"You and I are going to examine that disc's images, Pedro."

"Muy bien, señora."

"If we put our heads together, we may be able to discover who its author is."

"Sí, señora. Unlike the passports and drugs found on the Iranian, there were no fingerprints on the disc or its case. And the way it was secured to the inside of his leg... I think the disc in particular was a plant, and it may be the work of the assassin. Why he left it on the body with other evidence for police to find is unknown but—"

"The Iranian was probably murdered by a single assassin..." the lieutenant interposed coolly, careful not to sound defensive. He wanted to keep Pedro from stumbling into a sensitive subject: the possibility that the killer planned to frame police for the murder, a can of worms that could lead to speculation at the roundtable about the prisoner (a supposed journalist) threatening blackmail with a story to be published that incriminated police. If the gringo had a story, it might not only link police to the murder somehow but also expose police blunders and corruption leading up to the terror attack, expose police negligence as a contributing factor in the bombing of the Washington Hotel. Pedro didn't know about the prisoner's threat and the lieutenant intended to deal with this development in his own way, without interference from Gloria, the mayor, or anyone else, and with the help of his trusted ally, CISEN's Joaquín *Garras* de Jesús. "...a very efficient and ingenious killer. He left no forensic evidence tying anyone to the murder and was able to plant the body at the marina and escape without being witnessed. I would not be surprised at all if he is the author of the disc."

"The assassin may very well be the author of the disc," Gloria said. "But whoever the author is, that person knew an attack was coming and did nothing to prevent it."

"Which makes him a terrorist," said Lieutenant Romero.

"I should think so, Lieutenant. And if the assassin did not program the disc?"

Lieutenant Romero stared at Gloria with sleepy-eyed confidence. "If he planted it, he probably knows what is on it and who programmed it."

"Especially if he stole it to begin with," Pedro said. "Thieves generally know what it is they are stealing."

"He could have received the disc from someone and then acted on their orders," Sandra proffered. "In which case even if he planted the disc he may not have known what was on it."

"Anything is possible," the lieutenant retorted airily.

"It sure seems so in this case," Gloria said, "which does nothing to clarify the assassin's behavior." She glanced absently at her notes. "I suppose the disc was left on the body of a dead Iranian terrorist at the marina to make sure we got it, studied it as evidence related to the murder, and connected it to the Iranian terrorist. But to what end? Whether the assassin was acting on someone else's orders or not, that is one hell of a risk to take for no discernible reason. What could he or *anyone* have possibly gotten out of it? What is the motive? To make sure we connect the killer or *killers* to terrorists and, by extension, the attack on the Washington?"

Gloria searched each and every pair of eyes at the table. No one had an answer.

"I am not convinced of your lone assassin theory, Lieutenant," Gloria continued. "More than one person may have carried out the murder, though five killers would have certainly demolished and pulverized the victim. This was a very neat and quick murder, as you have interpreted from the preliminary autopsy report. Perhaps one assassin did kill the Iranian. And perhaps he acted on someone else's orders and has no idea what is on the disc. Yet, how ignorant is he? Are we to assume that someone capable of killing in this fashion, planting the body at the marina, and then escaping without being witnessed or leaving a trace of forensic evidence linking himself to the crime had no idea he had killed a terrorist? And if our suspect is the assassin, why would he suddenly expose himself to capture the way he did, at the scene of another crime he could be tied to? Did he really feel that invulnerable or is he just plain loco? Both? Or is he innocent?"

Pedro opened his mouth to speak but the lieutenant spoke first: "The man is in complete possession of his faculties. And if he is not the assassin I believe he will lead us to the assassin and, given the identity of the dead man and what we have learned about the disc, those responsible for the attack on the Washington."

Gloria leaned back in her chair, hands clasped at her waist. Sandra, Pedro, and Lieutenant Romero took her lead, losing themselves in moments of reflection. Through the dining hall's open doors, Gloria's office phone rang twice. A signal from the mayor to get in touch. Gloria and the others had turned off their cell phones to better concentrate on the issues at hand in this preliminary investigation into what appeared to be the bombing of the Washington Hotel.

"That maldito disc..." Gloria said distractedly. Her eyes met Pedro's. "...could paint another target at any time."

"Sí, señora."

Gloria slid her notepad and pen across the table to Pedro with an air of finality. "Write your cell number down for me. I know your address, though I have never had the pleasure of visiting your father or family at home. I shall meet you there. You and I will have a look at that disc's images right away, within the next hour or so. And Lieutenant?"

"Sí?"

"You have a photo, mug shots on file of our suspect?"

"Our computers at headquarters do. I will have dispatch e-mail them to Immigration." The lieutenant gave Sandra a courteous nod.

Pedro stood, said, "I will await your call, señora," and withdrew. Gloria told Sandra that her driver, Felipe, had a motorcycle. "He can give you a lift anywhere you need to go—your office, the airport—to get started on verifying the suspect's identity. That should help you beat traffic and you can pick up your car later."

"Good idea." Sandra gathered up her reports. The lieutenant retrieved his pager and stood from the table. Gloria said, "A couple more things before the two of you go." Sandra and the lieutenant paused attentively.

"Lieutenant. The mayor wants a briefing from you at the airport before federale investigators arrive from el DF."

"I know. I will have copies made of all police reports for him."

"I presume you will interrogate the prisoner again sometime after they arrive."

"Sí señora," he said, his tone as forbearing as Gloria's, calculated to conceal the expected arrival of his powerful ally, Garras, sometime this afternoon. Despite CISEN's political difficulties, the agency was bound to take over this investigation eventually. And in the interim, the mere presence of a CISEN man of Joaquín's status should provide Lieutenant Romero with all the leverage he needed to maintain control over any interrogation of the prisoner.

"The mayor and I will require full briefings and reports on all interrogations of the prisoner, Lieutenant. Until we have forensic evidence and reliable witnesses to the attack, *Russell Martell* may be our only link to the terrorists."

"I believe he is a link to the terrorists, señora. And he will tell us everything we need to know."

44

SNORING woke me up. My own. A fly buzzed my ears. I might have choked on it, flat on my back with my mouth wide open like I was.

I groaned onto my side. Cockroaches were throwing a vomit party at the bucket by the drain. Considering all the waste stinking up the cellblock they should've been larger, lengthened and fattened with human debris and excrement. Their figures conformed to their home base in the drain. Only a couple looked to be as long and fat as my thumb. I hacked and livened up the fiesta with an arching shot of bile. My kidneys ached. I curled up next to the bars and went back to sleep.

I dozed deep enough to forget my dreams. A fly bit my foot and woke me. I scooted back up against the wall. Two flies buzzed from my cell up the corridor to the smorgasbord in the first cell. Were the cops too shorthanded to hose it down? Or maybe someone new had been thrown in there. Might police have another suspect for my alleged crimes?

I called out, "Anybody home?!? Alguien está?!?"

No answer. Only the futile hum of the corridor vent in the ceiling beside the greasy florescent light bulb. After the worst tragedy in the history of Puerto Vallarta and the entire state of Jalisco, the worst tragedy the country had suffered since the Mexico City earthquake of 1985, an historical act of terror, I appeared to be the only one arrested.

Not a good sign. Maybe they really did think I was guilty, guilty of a crime I could not even conceive of much less execute. An inhuman slaughter masterminded by barbaric animals gathered in a cave somewhere, or perhaps around a table in a shack, or before a family hearth. How do you plan such things—the indiscriminate mass murder of innocents? What kind of twisted mentality does it take? The same mentality that leveled Dresden and dropped atomic bombs on Japan during World War II, a strategy designed to break the will of the enemy? Did such a strategy have a prayer of success outside of an all-out war in which millions upon millions were killed? Or was the terrorist mentality strictly base, focused on vengeance, power and hatred of "infidels"?

In the terrorist mind, all their victims are guilty.

Innocence has been lost forever.

I drew my knees up to my chest and dropped my head, a desperate wave of helplessness sweeping over me—fear and grief and pleading rage—similar to the feelings I had following 9/11.

I recalled my return flight from New York to Los Angeles four weeks or so after 9/11. The devastation at ground zero had shocked me just as much as those first images I'd seen on TV of planes flying into the towers. Nearly as shocking were the banal words uttered by a woman seated next to me on that flight back to Los Angeles. I had expressed to her something along the lines of how those who were capable of conceiving and executing such a senseless slaughter of innocents could only be dealt with in one way. She read the desolation in my bleary eyes, heard the pleading rage in my halting voice and said, in an offhand, careless tone, "Boy, that really affected you."

I wanted to shriek, "Of course it affected me! You! me! we're all the next targets! How could this despicable, bloodthirsty act of war not *affect* you?!?" But her lucid lack of empathy struck me dumb, speechless. Was she in shock or ignorant? Her intelligent blue eyes said neither. The 9/11 terror attacks were simply an inconceivable reality to her and had been transformed into nothing more than a disagreeable dream. Emotionally, and intellectually, she couldn't be burdened with their significance. The woman had no idea what it all meant and perhaps never would. But I felt I had a good idea what the attacks meant and somehow comprehended that my very survival depended on never forgetting the emotional burdens surrounding them.

If I had forgotten those emotions, those burdens over the years, they sure came rushing back now... I squeezed my eyes shut and longed for sleep to awaken me from this nightmare.

A Styrofoam cup of water stood outside my bars, a sandwich on a paper plate beside it. I stuck a hand through the bars to get at the sandwich. Not much of a meal. A jalapeño pepper and scrap of cheese between two slices of stale white bread. I left a slice of bread on the plate, broke the other slice over the pepper and cheese, and took a bite. My stomach lurched up against my sunken liver. It wasn't too bad though, the spikes of pain in my liver and kidneys I mean. The sandwich sucked. Tasted like something you'd pull out of a first-aid kit and slap on an open wound. I took another bite and chucked the rest out the bars. The water tasted good, once I convinced myself that the amoebas and parasites were hallucinations.

It appeared that my impression of a nut case had dissuaded Chimp from tormenting me for the time being. A fair amount of time must have passed since he last doused me. The sandwich indicated a three or four o'clock Mexican comida. Could the sandwich have arrived at six? What time was it? There was no way of telling, no window in my cell for the day or night to show through. I couldn't even keep a calendar if I wanted to, like POWs do in those war movies. I had absolutely no clue how long I'd been allowed to sleep or when the food arrived. But halftime had to be nearing an end. El comandante was bound to appear soon, probably with the lieutenant, Chimp and Fat Cop.

I assured myself there would be more arrests. At the very least for looting. Maybe even the terrorists themselves.

With all the bungling going on, they may never find the real killers... And with all the chaos, who knows what those pig coppers are up to right now?

I didn't see my own death but sure as hell sensed it. Death wasn't the worst of it. Everyone has to die. The pain would be the worst part. Dying in jail at the hands of these corrupt bastards would be as far from dying in your sleep as a sports writer is from becoming the next Shakespeare.

I recalled what I'd read about Cervantes taken prisoner; and Oscar Wilde's incarceration. Hadn't Shelley spent time behind bars? Maybe in the prison of his own mind and soul. Like Edgar Allen Poe.

I stared down the corridor to the door and its small square window. I half expected to see a face in the window, or a pair of eyes—someone taking an interest in their prisoner. Dull refracted light from the processing room glared back at me. If I moved away from the bars, a cop peering through that window wouldn't be able to see me. Would they think I'd escaped? or were they spying on me from a hidden camera? Where would they hide a camera in these barren walls and ceiling? or microphone? In the vent? My eyes flinched up to the grimy corridor vent next to the florescent light. What would they expect to see and hear? the pacings and mutterings of a guilty man?

The vent's feeble hum sputtered, gave me a start, like I'd caught my tormentors spying on me.

"I'm innocent you stupid bastards," I said in English. My echo ticked about the cellblock like pebbles tossed against a vacant window. I chuckled despite myself. The Chamber didn't even have a two-way mirror, how could I expect a hidden camera in here?

I really was in solitary now, the cellblock reserved for the lone suspect in the bombing of the Washington Hotel, my solitude a death knell. I shuddered against a sudden fit of panic. Did I have any hope at all? Would no one come to my aid and defense?

Famed existentialist Jean-Paul Sartre, a POW during World War II, and other prominent figures convinced the post-war French government to commute the sentence of Jean Genet. Genet, a talented writer as well as habitual thief and homosexual prostitute, managed to stay out of trouble thereafter... Western outrage over Alexander Solzhenitsyn's plight eventually got the political activist and prolific author released from the Russian gulag... Would anyone come to the rescue of a little-known American sports writer jailed and tortured unjustly in Mexico?

I felt the presence of kindred souls, writers who had been imprisoned throughout the centuries. There had to be thousands of them, millions, as though jail were a way to identify with the masses... Voltaire, for writings critical of the Church and State; Ken Kesey, jailed for possession of marijuana; and Henry David Thoreau, for protesting the Mexican-American war. O Henry began writing short stories in prison (for embezzlement? or was it extortion?). Neruda must have spent a night or two in jail for political activism. Cuban author and revolutionary José Martí was jailed for treason against Spain...

You're only a traitor until you win the revolution.

Dostoyevsky is one of my favorites. I read 'Crime and Punishment' three times...could write my own version of 'The Idiot', if I ever escaped this hell hole. Hard labor with Dostoyevsky in Siberia didn't seem too bad compared to Chimp's nightstick.

Cervantes is the romantic figure. He lost the use of a hand in battle and was taken prisoner by pirates for a number of years. Cervantes survived to become a literary giant.

Chimp and Manco fit right in with sixteenth-century pirates. The similarities between my destiny and that of Cervantes stopped right there. I didn't even care about my story anymore, and wouldn't live to write it if I did.

Wrong attitude, schmuck. Your story is the only thing that can save you.

The Roman philosopher/dramatist Seneca was accused of conspiracy and forced to take poison. The poet García Lorca was killed by Franco's Fascist Nationalist partisans during the Spanish civil war. And Daniel Pearl, a well-practiced but naive American journalist, was beheaded in Pakistan by Muslim fanatics.

My position couldn't be so desperate as compared to those four, could it?

I'm not guilty of murder or terrorism or drug trafficking, just possession and stupidity. But if I were guilty of everything, and the cops have probably sealed that verdict, what would I need to get off?

The answer tickled me like a feather dipping from your cap to your nose. It had always been there, but just out of sight. Now I saw it.

I needed a fall guy.

Devo.

My mind whirled. Why hadn't I thought of it before? Well, I wasn't accustomed to needing a fall guy. Liked to handle my own affairs. But this was the first time my affairs included charges of murder, terrorism and drug trafficking. Devo as fall guy made perfect sense. He'd given me the coke, the dead terrorist's coke according to the lieutenant, and may have actually killed the terrorist and moved the body. Why not? From what I'd seen of his tricks and imposing presence, Devo just might have been able to get away with it.

At Mountain's party, Devo demonstrated an uncommon interest in my "story"; my musings about why, where and how the dead guy was killed elicited revealing feedback from him. Devo said the dead guy was "intentionally murdered" and because the body was "dumped at the marina" the feds and police "couldn't take credit" for a kill made during the raid. His input dovetailed with my story, and Devo egged me on. "I'll bet you've come up with another angle on that dead guy you told me about," he challenged in the office as if to offer inspiration. But what he really wanted was to see how close I was getting to the truth! He knew the cops didn't kill the Iranian and move the body because *he* did!... Was Devo a terrorist, like the dead guy? Made sense. Terrorists kill each other all the time. Devo knew I would eventually come upon the truth and set me up!

But why? Why would Devo kill a fellow terrorist and dump the body at the marina? And why would he hang around and party at the cockfights after committing murder, and the next night at Mountain's place? Would an assassin and terrorist behave that way? What were his motives?

I didn't have the answers to these questions, didn't know anything for certain except that the cops needed a suspect. A suspect for the murder of a known terrorist and drug dealer found with his neck broken. A suspect who was himself a terrorist and could be implicated in the attack on the Washington. At this juncture, I was that suspect. But if I provided the cops with Devo, wouldn't that remove blame from me? wouldn't it put me in a much better position to rescue myself?

Maybe not. The cops could kill us both... And hadn't I seen Devo with the chief of police—el comandante—on Friday night? Sure! The night before the raid! El comandante and Devo at Ándale drinking and chattin' it up like old college roommates.

They were both out to get me from the start.

Devo, el comandante, Manco and Fernando. They're all out to get me.

I had demonstrated to the lieutenant that I knew too much yet, in reality, I didn't know nearly enough, maybe nothing at all. I could easily be wrong about Devo. Did it matter if I was wrong about him? Wouldn't he make a good fall guy anyway?

Shouldn't have said a goddamn thing to those pigs. Hard to do with a nightstick up your ass.

Once again all the second guessing and self-doubt was driving me nuts. Everyone suffers from second guessing and self-doubt, but try it in jail under my circumstances and see what it does to you.

I was good as dead. And Devo as fall guy was added to the playbook.

45

"THERE have been reports of a man arrested at the Washington Hotel this morning, Mayor Velázquez. Can you tell us who this man is and if he was arrested in connection with the disaster at the Washington?"

Lazarito turned up the volume to the 42-inch flat-screen TV across his office to better hear the mayor's reply. The two smaller TVs flanking it were muted—CNN en Español and FOX (in English)—, as was the one up on the wall behind him—TV Azteca.

He'd been waiting for this: AP reporter Leslie Hinot's interview with the mayor for Guadalajara's Channel 13 News, Juan's second televised interview within the last three hours or so. Sometime around one o'clock this afternoon Lazarito's man on the scene, Director of Guadalajara's Channel 13 News, Ignacio Mirador, had gotten the first shot at the mayor. Not much of a "shot" really, the questions scripted and answers prepared. And Leslie had the same scripted questions for the mayor, with two crucial exceptions: the question she'd just asked and a follow-up question. Questions Lazarito had personally instructed her to interject into the interview.

Leslie held her microphone steady under the mayor's chin. Juan paused in careful reflection. Lazarito scooted forward in his rather squeaky leather armchair and scrutinized the mayor's face, as well as the face of the man standing beside him, Lieutenant Romero, searching for a hint of subterfuge. The mayor scratched his cheek; Benito appeared to shift his weight a bit. Both men retained the swarthy equanimity of the Mexican Strongman—unflappable. Mayor Velázquez leveled an insipid gaze at the camera. "At this time," he said, "we have no comment on any alleged arrests. An investigation has been initiated into this tragic catastrophe and we shall keep the media informed as evidence comes to light."

Leslie spoke fluent Spanish with an Anglophone accent layered over it: "Are reports of an arrest made at the Washington this morning accurate?"

"No comment," said the mayor.

"Is it possible that the disaster at the Washington was not the result of an accident, an exploding gas or sewer line as has been reported?"

Lazarito smirked, "Muy bien." Leslie was sticking to her script, the script she promised to follow after he guaranteed her a leading role on television and first review of press releases in the coming days. As a Canadian and the only journalist in town with both AP and international press credentials, Leslie Hinot represented Lazarito's own personal link to the foreign media. She was sure to prove herself a most valuable resource as he spun this story to his advantage.

Mayor Velázquez nodded at Lieutenant Romero. "Todo es posible," said the lieutenant. Anything is possible.

Lazarito dimmed the volume and squeaked back in his chair, feet up off the carpet. "Valía la pena intentarlo," he sighed. It was worth a try. He slumped and leveled his gaze upon the laptop computer on his desk, the frozen, expressive image of a woman on You Tube. Lazarito had been scouring the Internet in search of a crucial detail he needed to advance his story and salvage his career: who was the gringo arrested at the Washington this morning? Lazarito's faithful snitch in the police department, Paulo, would deliver that information to him this evening, for a price, but he wasn't content to wait (or pay) if he might come upon information himself in a timely fashion. His first step in this effort was to search for a picture of the suspect. Beat photographers had presented him with photos and footage of a man arrested at ground zero but you couldn't even tell if he was gringo. Barricades and police had kept photographers at a distance; through the smoke and clutter of emergency vehicles and personnel, and with the arresting officers and a military man surrounding the suspect on the far side of a squad car, the photos and footage just couldn't be enhanced well enough on his computer to make out the suspect's face. Amateur unauthorized footage and stills were no better. Federales working at the behest of the president's Media and Communications Director had seized a bevy of cameras and cell phones from spectators and delivered them to The Bureau. Lazarito and his secretary, Esmeralda, got right to work on them. But try as they might, they could not find a single clear shot of the cabrón Paulo had arrested...

So Lazarito went online to see what he could discover.

You can get most anything you want online, and Lazarito found plenty to study about the Vallarta disaster, except a clear photo of the pinche gringo. There were grainy shots taken by spectators of an arrest made at the Washington and speculation as to who the man was (a hotel guest arrested for looting and possession of drugs? An innocent tourist getting railroaded? A belligerent drunk interfering with Search and Rescue? A suspected terrorist?) but he couldn't find a single name or definitive picture to go along with the hijo de puta. Lazarito's investigations online hadn't been a total loss, however. Even as he came up empty handed in his search for a picture or name of the man arrested this morning, he found it fascinating to see how the disaster played out on the Internet.

Precautions taken to prohibit unauthorized close-up footage or photos of the disaster curbed the number of horrifying images inundating the World Wide Web (distant shots and footage were less worrisome. They were shocking but fuzzy due to the smoke and commotion and didn't capture gory details). The images Lazarito encountered were unrevealing as to what had actually occurred at the Washington. It was evident that the north tower was in ruins but there was no way of determining how this could have possibly happened. Even better, everyone had an opinion. You Tube, Face Book, Twitter, Our Space, and Home Base were all abuzz. And bloggers were having a field day. A few nut cases spewed their hate—the North American capitalist-pig spring breakers in the imperialist Washington Hotel deserved their fate—but overall the tragedy seemed to have sent the entire world a-spin with giddy grief, outrage, and indecipherable chatter. Conjecture, supposition and outright fabrication were the norm, ad-hoc interviews with "survivors" emotional blather, inconclusive at best as to the cause of this unimaginable catastrophe. The only common thread was that there had been an explosion: a bomb was assembled and exploded in one of the hotel rooms; a gas line had ruptured and exploded; a delivery-truck bomb exploded the north tower; a bomb exploded in a tour bus as it pulled up to the hotel; and, finally, Lazarito's own contribution to the melee: a fuel leak had caused an explosion in a sewer-well beneath the hotel.

There was also speculation about a plane crashing into the hotel—a disabled plane, a plane that was shot down, or a plane deliberately flown into the Washington's north tower. Lazarito had thought of this possibility early on but his sources at the airport and nearby military base confirmed that no such incident had occurred.

Then there were the conspiracy theories. What would the Internet be without them? Everyone from the CIA to Mossad (Israeli Intelligence) and CISEN (Mexican Intelligence) was blamed for blowing the Washington...probably working in concert with Maoists, right-wing anti-immigration gringo militias, Zapatistas, anarchists, and/or drug cartels.

Muslim fanatics obsessed with killing all those North American tourists on spring break were also fingered on the Internet, the most plausible culprits to Lazarito's mind. The gringo arrested this morning appeared to be tied to an Iranian terrorist found dead at the marina.

The sheer volume of misinformation flooding the Internet gave Media Minister Charlado and Mexican censors the upper hand in the international (not to mention national) dissemination of this news story. Respectable international news outlets couldn't possibly weed through the incessant torrent of incomprehensible Internet chatter. Lazarito could see for himself on the televisions in his office that, for the most part, their only "reliable" sources were Mexican news casts and government spokesmen. Thus, just as Media and Communications Director Francisco Panza de León had predicted, the country and the world remained in the dark, for the time being, as to whether or not Mexico had been the victim of a terror attack or some kind of freak accident.

Yet the truth would come out eventually, and when it did...

A cold shiver creased Lazarito's flabby chest. He pictured himself before a judge trying to explain away his part in the corruption and blunders that led up to the bombing of Vallarta's largest hotel, obfuscating the bribe he'd received from el comandante to keep the botched raid out of the news and bury the report of the dead man found at the marina, repudiating accusations of extortion and

276

concealing evidence. In the face of such a barbaric slaughter, the judge would scoff at his defense. Lazarito heard himself deny that he was part of a conspiracy or had obstructed justice...pleading for mercy. His body went limp, overpowered by weakness and demonic despair. He stared down at the open duffle bag full of confiscated cameras and cell phones on the floor by his desk. If he didn't come up with a story that made him a big time player in identifying those responsible for the attack on the Washington, a story giving him leverage as a man to be dealt with on his own terms, he might have to sell those electronic devices to help make bail.

The Media and Communications Director must have plans to replace him. Someone higher up the political totem pole than Lazarito Charlado must be waiting in the wings for an appointment as the next Media Minister of Puerto Vallarta. A crony from el DF with direct ties to the president and his cabinet.

Whoever replaced Lazarito could wind up being his executioner, the bane of his existence capable of making his gravest fear, jail time, a reality.

Lazarito needed to break the case wide open, publish a story identifying the terrorists (that gringo arrested at ground zero as well as his accomplices), their methods, goals, motives and ideology. A story that would bring *all* the killers to justice. A story so earthshaking it would bury the trail of corruption leading to him and save his job...and keep him out of jail.

But in the meantime...

Media Minister Charlado reached for the cordless phone on his desk. He better have his wife come down to The Bureau and pick up this duffle bag full of cameras and cell phones, take it home and lock it in their safe, just in case...

46

CISEN Chief Interrogator and practiced throat ripper Joaquín 'Garras' de Jesús flew into Vallarta by helicopter from Guadalajara Monday afternoon, half an hour before three federale investigators from el DF landed in their jet with forensic and Search and Rescue teams.

Sam, Joaquín's pilot, had banked past the Washington and military choppers circling the scene, got close enough to taste the acrid stench and fuming destruction. Horrified curses escaped their lips. "Parece que fue una bomba," Sam barked over the roar of their chopper. Looks like it was a bomb. Garras spat, "Puta madre," and crushed his rubber ball from hand to hand.

Juan met the CISEN man at the airport, his trepidation at dealing with CISEN well concealed behind a staid leadership posture he'd perfected throughout the day. He had never dealt with CISEN before, never had a reason to. Despite a rise in gang-related crime over the past year or so, routine law enforcement was the norm in Vallarta. The town wasn't prone to high-profile kidnappings or murders, hadn't been overrun by drug cartels, wasn't a breeding ground for antigovernment subversives...nor had it ever suffered a terror attack of any kind until, perhaps, today.

Had Vallarta been the victim of a terror attack? DF federale investigators were due to arrive to help answer that very question. And the arrival of Joaquín de Jesús indicated that CISEN was prepared to enter into the investigation as well. The agency had a nasty reputation. CISEN's status as the nation's only national and international intelligence agency gave it seemingly unlimited power. Although only one operative had been deployed to Vallarta, Juan sensed it just might be a matter of time before CISEN took over the entire investigation into the disaster at the Washington Hotel.

Garras found Mayor Velázquez to be gracious and, as expected, haggard and red-eyed from the day's tragic events. The mayor confirmed essential information as they waited in the airport for the DF taskforce to arrive: yes it did appear that a bomb had exploded the Washington's north tower; yes there had been an arrest of a gangster and a botched raid on Saturday that may have a bearing on the case; and yes, a suspect had been taken into custody this morning. The mayor declined to comment on the gangster's testimony about Islamic terrorists in Vallarta however, insisting that they wait to review police reports and discuss particulars.

"After investigators from el DF arrive," he said, "and you all have a chance to view the destruction at the Washington firsthand, I will give a briefing and we can begin a formal investigation into this tragedy together."

Garras acquiesced to the mayor's wishes. Apparently, Mayor Juan Pacífico Velázquez wanted to keep control of the investigation himself, which was fine with Garras. It would help him hold those DF federales at bay until el jefe received clearance from el director to send in a CISEN team from Guadalajara to take over.

If Mayor Velázquez was aware of the power play about to take place under his nose, he showed no signs of it. "We are grateful for all the help we can get," the mayor told DF investigators and Joaquín as they left the airport for the Washington. Garras believed him, believed him grateful and, in accordance with CISEN's dossier on him, competent.

One of the few pleasures Garras had had today was watching the three DF federales frown and squirm as Mayor Velázquez introduced him to them at the airport. They wouldn't try to hoodwink the mayor into giving up control of the investigation to them with CISEN here. And they didn't. Not yet. A single CISEN man at the scene was enough to remind these pinches cabrones of the agency's power. They'd wait for reinforcements to arrive, perhaps their superiors, before attempting any outright takeover of the investigation, an attempt that was bound to fail. Garras remained supremely confident that CISEN would win out in any confrontation with DF federales. CISEN always did.

47

PEDRO paused the image on his father's computer screen, the same image he and Gloria had viewed twice already: a map of Mexico and North America, a copper-red swath extending from the southern border of Chiapas into the American heartland, Banderas Bay stained blood red.

The clock at the bottom read 7:58 a.m.

"Maldito seas," Gloria cursed. She glared across the office at Pedro's computer screen and the present images from the disc: two nondescript black and white maps—one of Asia, the other of the Middle East—that had remained unchanged since before her arrival well over an hour ago.

Pedro and Gloria were alone in the Santos household and had been examining police reports, the preliminary autopsy report of the dead Iranian, and the copy of the disc's images. Gloria stiffened in her seat, her voice sarcastic with a touch of disgust: "Whoever programmed the disc might be a computer expert but you certainly do not have to be one to examine its contents and understand that it predicted the attack on the Washington." She glanced at Pedro, sitting hunched into himself in the chair next to her, and echoed an opinion she had expressed nearly an hour ago: "No way in hell you or anyone else viewing the disc's contents could have known this prediction of an attack here in Vallarta was coming Pedro."

Gloria folded her hands into her lap. Pedro released a growling sigh. "Maybe not, señora," he said and leveled an empty gaze at his computer screen on his desk by the window opposite them. "That

279

maldito terrorist rumor is what has me flustered. Not just a rumor but testimony from the gangster, according to the interrogation report." He met Gloria's eyes. "I should have put it all together last night."

Gloria cringed at the thought of the rumor, the gangster's "testimony", still fighting her own self-recriminations over it. She stood and circled Enrique's desk. The lazy overhead fan stirred a sluggish breeze wafting in through the window and the air touched her like a desultory breath. Gloria wasn't one to confide in many people other than her husband but felt a need to relieve Pedro's burden. There was no harm in reminding him he was not the only one feeling guilty: "When the lieutenant mentioned the gangster's *testimony*—that so-called rumor—this afternoon in Arena Vallarta, what was the reaction of the others sitting at the table?"

Pedro gave her a questioning frown. "Señora?"

"The others being Sandra and me. Did we seem surprised to hear there had been talk of Arab, Islamic terrorists in Vallarta?"

"No. I assumed you had heard about it."

"I learned of the gangster's claims after Saturday's misguided raid. And what do you think my reaction was?"

"Well..." Pedro's frown softened into a reasoned smile. "You probably thought the gangster had lied to cover for other members in his gang. Like police and I did."

"We all found it hard to believe, Pedro." Gloria sat on the edge of the desk and looked down upon Pedro's calmed expression. "You were quite young at the time, Pedro," she said, her voice silky taught, "but may remember that, after the September-eleventh attacks in the United States, there were plenty of similar rumors circling around town for quite a while. Nothing ever came of them. And if there is one thing about Vallarta..."

"Cunden muchos rumores." Lots of rumors are spread.

"Exactamente." Gloria strengthened her posture. "We cannot use that as an excuse, of course, and we all feel responsible for what happened...for numerous reasons...but there is no use in dwelling on it. We have plenty of other things to think about," she glanced at the black and white maps on Pedro's computer screen, "starting with who programmed this disc? The same person who made sure it was left on a corpse at a place where we would find it?"

"If the disc was stolen and then planted on the body, probably not, señora. But I should think a thief would know what he stole, what was on the disc. On the other hand..." Pedro's voice trailed off. Gloria's question set in motion a long, familiar sequence of possible scenarios in his mind, each equally plausible.

FINDING DEVO

That same sequence of possible scenarios was flashing through Gloria's mind and she backtracked to get her bearings. "Much of the disc's contents are disturbing, to say the least..." she said, a sick ache rising in her stomach, "...in some cases horrifying. There is little doubt that its focus is the spread of Islamist terror and the evils of fanatic believers. And since it certainly seems to have predicted a terrorist attack here in Vallarta, it also points the finger of blame at Islamists. But should we jump to that conclusion?"

Pedro shook his head, "No. Last night I thought the disc might be some kind of ruse designed to distract my investigation into the murder of the man found dead at the marina. And that still might be the case. But it also could be a ruse intended to point the finger of blame at Islamists for bombing the Washington and away from the true culprits."

"The fact that the dead man turned out to be an Iranian terrorist also suggests that Islamists are behind an attack on the Washington, but..." Gloria paused and raised an intelligent brow, an invitation for Pedro to finish her thought.

"We still need more evidence," he said.

"Yes we do. The dead man could not have bombed the Washington or personally directed terrorists from the morgue. We have no concrete evidence that Islamists are behind a bombing of the Washington Hotel. However, I think we are safe in concluding that whoever programmed the disc is guilty of terrorism because they knew an attack was coming, did nothing to prevent it, and may have had a hand in it. The prediction of an attack here in Vallarta even seems like a reproach, spit in our eye because by then it was too late for us to do anything about it. But who programmed the disc? The killer or killers of that Iranian terrorist?"

"Perhaps, señora. But we may not know the answer to that question until we discover the assassin's motive for killing the Iranian and leaving the body and the disc for us to find at the marina."

"You believe we are dealing with a single assassin, like the lieutenant," Gloria stated flatly.

"You reviewed the reports on my desk with me, señora. The evidence is not overwhelming but it does seem entirely possible, even likely that a single man killed the Iranian with his bare hands."

"Do we have an assassin in jail right now, Pedro?"

"*Russell Martell* is a journalist," Pedro stressed casually, "like the lieutenant said. A sports writer. I pulled up his website before you got here. Whether or not our prisoner is that same man has yet to be determined."

"And even if he is a sports writer, he could also be the killer and a terrorist. After all, he knew the body had been moved."

Pedro swept his hands over his blue jeans. "He may be involved somehow. But I wonder how Lieutenant Romero got him to say such a thing? And it is possible that he knew the body was moved without having anything to do with the murder or moving the body."

"How?"

"That news story he had the cocaine wrapped in must contain information about when and where the body was found. He may even have been at the marina with other tourists when the dead man was discovered. And if he came upon the time of death somehow, he could have deduced that the body had been moved. It could not have been laying there at the marina for long without being discovered. Also, if he knew about the raid—"

"El comandante made sure the raid was kept out of the news."

Pedro said, "Really?" more statement than question. "That figures, since it was botched. But the suspect could have heard rumors about it and knew it occurred at or around the time the body was found. So he may have guessed that the man was killed at the raid and the body moved. If he is a journalist as he claims, his mind is accustomed to considering connections between events."

"But then... Are you suggesting he accused police of killing the man and moving the body?"

"Maybe. But he might have just let slip an assumption he had made about the case: the body was moved."

Gloria set her brow in a hard line. "If what you say about our suspect is true..."

Pedro finished her thought: "The real assassin is still at large, unless he died in the explosion this morning, which I doubt."

"Dios mío." Gloria's breath sawed in her throat. "Who the hell are we dealing with here? Is he Mexican? American? Black? White? Arab? Asian? Who are his accomplices?... Do we know anything specific about him at all?"

"Only that he is a very skilled and dangerous individual." Pedro narrowed his eyes on the frozen image on papi's computer screen. "Have we seen enough of the copy?"

Gloria nodded, "For now."

Pedro made some shifts and clicks on the keyboard and disconnected the external hard drive from its wiring for reconnection to his computer. Gloria retrieved her phone on the desk and checked her voicemail and text messages. She and Pedro had silenced their phones in response to several interruptions. Gloria shot off a quick text message to Sandra, then slid a chair over to Pedro's desk and idly watched him work, her thoughts occupied by a key question: "What do you think his motives are, Pedro?"

Pedro dusted off his hands and joined her before his computer screen. "The assassin or the author of the disc?"

"The assassin may have programmed the disc, stolen the disc, or received it from someone and acted on their orders. And he may have simply left the disc where it was on the body, though the absence of fingerprints on the disc and its case and the way it was secured to the dead man's leg point to a plant. So to simplify matters here, if we consider the assassin to be the author of the disc, what are his motives?"

"Overall, his behavior is a mystery to me, señora. You summed it up pretty well in Arena Vallarta this afternoon. The body was likely planted at the marina because it is a secure location where the dead man would not be robbed and we were sure to find him along with the disc and other evidence. And I suppose the assassin either planted or left the disc on the body of a dead terrorist so we would connect it to the terrorist and study the disc as evidence. If he had mailed it to us, we may not have had the patience to wait for the disc to decode itself and view its contents. But I have no idea why he wanted us to find the body with the disc and other evidence or why he killed the Iranian in the first place. Planting the body at the marina like that was an enormous risk, and the disc ties him to an act of terror. What did he get out of it? Did someone pay him an enormous amount of money to do it? If so, why? None of it makes sense."

Gloria regarded Pedro critically. "*Someone* made sure we got our hands on this disc, Pedro, and wants us to concentrate on it. Its importance cannot be denied since it predicted the attack on the Washington."

They sat forward in their chairs and stared at Pedro's computer monitor. "I wonder what the next message will be," Pedro said. "Those maps, maps of countries clear on the other side of the world, have not changed much at all."

Gloria sucked softly on her lower lip, cogitating, her eyes tilted up in her head. "You know, Pedro," she said, "there is one clue that might go to motive. The message that appeared last night after that last map of—"

Pedro's computer screen instantly produced a color map of South America. Gloria flinched. "—South América," she said.

Pedro's gaze hardened. "That looks something like it. And Venezuela began—" burnt-orange Venezuela started blinking.

"Blinking," said Gloria. She and Pedro exchanged darting, wary expressions. "A repetition?" Pedro ventured.

Gloria's eyes flickered with uncertainty. Was this a repetition? Was the disc about to reveal the message she had just referred to? If so, its timing was uncanny. "Power," she murmured, eyes steady on the computer monitor. She half expected the disc to respond with last night's message about power but the map remained the only image on the screen.

Pedro rounded out the refrain: "Use it or lose it to those who destroy you."

Gloria cocked her head at him. "Sounds more like advice than a threat. Yet, if we are to be destroyed if we do not use our power, well, then it sounds like a threat, a demand. And demands go to motive. But why would the author of the disc urge us to use our power or be destroyed? Why would he care to give us advice like that?"

Pedro hadn't thought much about this since the message appeared last night. "Hard to say," he said at length. "In retrospect, it seems like some kind of sign or omen of today's attack, and a warning of more attacks to come."

"Maybe. But telling us to use our power, what does that imply?"

"Pues...that we have not been using our power in some sense or another."

"Or not using it to our full capabilities..." Gloria intoned, "*Use it or lose it*," her expression expansive. "An old adage applicable to all kinds of power. Physical and intellectual." She smirked, thinking her next inference almost amusing: "And México always arrives late for fiestas... The author of this disc is scolding us, Pedro. He knew we would not be able to prevent today's attack and, like a professor, he is reprimanding us for not living up to our potential, for not recognizing the enemy and using our power to defend ourselves...for being late in attacking the enemy directly. And now we are suffering the consequences."

Pedro twisted up his face, like he'd caught a disagreeable odor. "If he wants us to defend ourselves, why not help us? Does it make sense for him to...?" He pursed his lips and tapped impatiently at his cheek. "So, if the assassin knew what was on the disc, he also knew an attack was imminent, but did he have a direct hand in it? or does he simply get some kind of sick pleasure out of scolding and lecturing us and watching us suffer? Both? And according to the disc, Islamic terror, radical Islam, is the enemy, but...how could we, México, have attacked...preemptively?"

"Who knows, Pedro? Any number of ways both at home and abroad I imagine. The important point is that it appears we are dealing with someone who has suggested, *demanded* we use our power more effectively or be destroyed. And his demands are what we need to focus on in order to discover his motives."

"But the demand resembles a riddle and is not clear, señora. Nor is it clear how to accommodate it. And if the demand is so important, why embed it in a disc full of other messages and images? There must be more to his motives than that."

"Agreed, Pedro. But power is a theme revealed by the disc and, when you think about it, is itself a motive..." Gloria counted the ways in the palm of her hand, "...for murder, war, rape, political corruption, you name it." She tilted her hand towards Pedro's computer screen, as though addressing the disc...and the assassin. "Power is the oldest motive in the book. And someone is always willing to commit heinous crimes to seize power from you as soon as you show weakness."

"But the assassin...the author of the disc...and..." Pedro paused in an effort to gather his thoughts. Gloria helped him along: "Terrorists, Pedro. We are dealing with terrorists."

"Sí, señora. But is power their motive? All they have done is injure us. How have they gained power?"

"Those pinches fanáticos find it more expedient to gain power by tearing others down rather than elevating themselves, or elevating *anything*. But why the assassin or the author of the disc would want to remind us that power is a motive and demand that we use our power is not at all clear."

Pedro laced his hands behind his head and fixed on the lone almond tree outside the office window, its leaves and branches dark against a low metallic sky. A cloudy, early dusk was beginning to settle over Vallarta. "So terror in and of itself empowers terrorists," he said.

Gloria replied in a sunken voice: "I am afraid often times it does." She flicked a trickle of perspiration from her temple and lifted her face to a vaporous breeze drifting in through the window. The draft of air hung in the office like heavy curtains instead of circulating out the open office door. Pedro sniffed at it. "Humid," he said and stood to adjust the knob on the wall behind his desk. The overhead fan accelerated a notch, its light fixture wobbling a bit. "Feels like rain."

Gloria drum rolled her fingers on the desk as Pedro took his seat. "One man's terrorist is another's freedom fighter," she said abstractedly.

"What was that, señora?"

"Another old adage, Pedro. And ultimately both terrorist and freedom fighter can be said to have the same motive: power. Why would the assassin want to remind us of the importance of power?"

"Why would he, the author of the disc, or *anyone* want to bother with *any* of this?" Pedro asked rhetorically. "What does he hope to gain by leaving us the disc, these messages and clues? And then he bombs the Washington? or allows it to be bombed?" Pedro slumped in his chair and massaged the fatigue from the back of his neck. "He really does seem deranged. But predicting the attack certainly forces us to focus on him. He must know we are taking what the disc has to say very seriously."

Gloria balled her fists upon the desk, resisting a wave of anger. She fixed on Pedro, her eyes sharp and red. "We better take him and the disc seriously," she said in a feral whisper. "The disc predicted one attack and may predict another."

Gloria's controlled rage was contagious and Pedro felt his own anger over the contemptible act of terror this morning grow hot in his chest. Yet he remained much more at ease now than earlier at their meeting in Arena Vallarta's dining hall, the anger simmering within him tempering the overwhelming guilt and grief he'd been struggling with. Pedro recognized his anger as an inspiring force, something he could harness to keep himself focused. And he was more focused now than he'd ever been in his life.

Pedro glared at the map on his computer screen with fierce, detached purpose. "Are you going to predict another attack?" he growled and looked a question at Gloria, "*spit in our eye again*? Is the assassin demonstrating his power, showing us how weak and incapable we are of stopping him? Or is he chastising us for being too weak to stop the terrorists? Is he actually responsible for bombing the Washington or did he just know it was going to happen? Is he trying to teach us a lesson? Is the disc some sort of elaborate, demented 'I told you so'?!?"

Gloria opened her mouth to speak but a sudden flash of light from the disc choked off her words.

48

JOAQUÍN Garras de Jesús couldn't remember when he'd last spent so much of one day pissed off, an entire morning and afternoon. His angry blood began simmering this morning when Lieutenant Romero telephoned him at CISEN headquarters with a report on what "sure as hell" looked like a terror attack on Puerto Vallarta's Washington Hotel. Then in el jefe's office, amidst speculation of Islamic terrorists in Vallarta and a "bomb" going off, Garras began luxuriating in anger, imagining his garras wrapped around the necks of those who might be responsible for such a barbaric massacre. Later this afternoon, Garras got a bird's-eye view of the destruction when Sam banked their helicopter past the Washington on their way to the Vallarta airport. "Looks like it was bomb," Sam said. Garras tempered his fury by breathing from his diaphragm through his nose and keeping his back straight—meditative self-control techniques that were part of his martial-arts training. Yet the ruinous sight and Sam's comment still elicited curses from him as he crushed his rubber ball from hand to hand... Joaquin's tour of the Washington with the mayor and federale investigators—Félix Sándovar, Edgar Barrera, and Tito Herrera— served to heat his angry blood once again, for all were in agreement: it sure as hell looked like a bomb had exploded the north tower of the hotel.

Was this a terror attack? Who might have perpetrated such a barbaric and cowardly slaughter of innocents? Mayor Juan Pacífico Velázquez convened a briefing in nearby Arena Vallarta to help answer those questions.

GARRAS and the DF federales intermittently perused copies of police reports as the mayor referred to his notes and debunked some of the explanations bandied about the media and World Wide Web for this morning's disaster: There was no sewer-well beneath the hotel that could have been flooded with fuel and caused an explosion; an exploding gas line would not have caused such extensive damage; and there were no visual remains, radar or video evidence, or credible reports of a plane crash blasting the Washington's north tower.

"Unless forthcoming forensic evidence suggests otherwise," added the mayor with unsteady aplomb, "it seems that the destruction at the Washington is the result of a bomb explosion. In essence, a terror attack."

The men about the table grumbled their agreement. Garras spoke up sharply yet without rancor: "It is my understanding that local authorities may have been forewarned about terrorists in Vallarta."

Juan had declined to comment when Joaquín questioned him at the airport about the terrorist rumor but didn't hesitate to answer now. This briefing required full disclosure of all facts surrounding the case. One by one he looked all four men in the eye and calmly informed them of this most embarrassing detail: "I am sorry to say that we were. As you will find in the reports, a couple of days ago an MS-13 gangster was arrested here in Vallarta. He is now in federal custody in el DF but, while under interrogation after his arrest, he spoke of

Islamist terrorists in Vallarta. His testimony precipitated a raid early Saturday evening on a duplex, but the raid produced no evidence whatsoever of terrorist activity. So the gangster's remarks were dismissed as a ploy..." A groan of regret wormed its way into Juan's voice. He took a sip of water and collected himself. "Given today's events, the gangster is once again a person of interest and is being treated as such by authorities in el DF."

Juan took another sip of water and cleared his throat. This had to be the most humiliating part of the case—testimony from a gangster dismissed as a baseless rumor after that botched raid when local authorities clearly should have continued to take it seriously. The immutable expressions around the table felt like a slap in his face, as though these men expected such valuable information from a gangster to go unheeded by inept local officials. Yet the mayor stood fast in his resolve to demonstrate leadership and forced a precise, composed note into his voice: "You will also find in your reports that a dead man was discovered at the marina on Saturday, murdered. He remained unidentified until this morning when fingerprint data revealed that he was a member of the Iranian Revolutionary Guard and a known terrorist moneyman."

This bit of news sparked curiosity; the men at the table began firing questions: Was there any connection between the dead Iranian and the gangster? Was the prisoner arrested this morning connected to the dead Iranian or the gangster? How was the Iranian killed? What was found on him?

The mayor raised his hands in a request for patience. "Everything is in the reports. Once you have a chance to review them thoroughly I am sure they will answer most all your questions. But we have one more thing to discuss before you do so. Our prisoner."

The commotion around the table died down. The mayor flipped through his notes as he related the circumstances surrounding the gringo's arrest—how he was accused of murder by a dying woman at ground zero and subsequently found to be in possession of cocaine neatly wrapped inside a folded picture of the dead man. "Cocaine was also found on the dead terrorist," pronounced the mayor in a tone worthy of a district attorney, "as well as in a Jeep registered to his alias." Juan paused to review another fact in his notes. "And the chief of the Washington work crew reported to the arresting officer that on Sunday night he heard the suspect speak of having killed a terrorist here in Vallarta. This suggests that the suspect may be a terrorist who killed a fellow terrorist or, at the very least, that he had knowledge of terrorist activity in Vallarta."

The federales grumbled derisively. Garras balled his fists but said nothing. Juan continued: "The suspect's identity has yet to be confirmed. He had no identification on him when arrested but did give a name while under interrogation: Russell Martell. The preliminary interrogation of the suspect was conducted by Lieutenant Benito Cuevas Romero of the Puerto Vallarta Police Department who has enlisted CISEN Lead Interrogator, Señor Joaquín de Jesús," Juan gestured in the CISEN man's direction, "to assist in further interrogations."

Federale Investigators Sándovar, Barrera, and Herrera voiced their objections to any special consideration given the CISEN man. The mayor checked the caller ID on his vibrating cell phone and excused himself to take the call. Garras clucked at the federales through a sneer. The mayor's swarthy complexion went pale. "A what?!?" he exclaimed into his phone, his eyes dancing about the dining hall as if expecting an intruder. "How bad?" Garras and the others regarded him with muted vigilance. Juan brought a hand to his forehead. "Stay there at headquarters, Lieutenant," he said. "We are on our way."

49

THE phone in the kitchen rang. Gloria and Pedro remained fixated on a point of light in the center of Pedro's dulled computer screen. "What happened?" Gloria said.

Pedro's voice quavered with anticipation: "Another message or image must be coming. We still have a number count at the bottom."

And there it was. Three words in white block lettering.

A twinge of uncertainty twisted Gloria's thoughts. She faced Pedro in search of reaffirmation: "This is the first time the disc has delivered a message in English?"

"Sí."

"How good is your English, Pedro?"

"Not very, señora. But I understand the first two words, 'Choose your...' "

Gloria stared unblinkingly at the message. "Motherfucker," she said.

"Qué?"

"Like 'puta madre' or 'chingada madre,' except in this sense he means 'cabrón' or 'chingón.' "

"Escoge tu cabrón?"

289

"Sí."

"How do you know?"

"Years of college in the United States."

"Is it some sort of idiom or refrain?"

"Not exactly, but..." Gloria remained transfixed on the message and silently mouthed the words, 'choose your motherfucker.' "This..." she said haltingly, "...goes to what we were speaking of... If one man's terrorist is another's freedom fighter, then it is just a matter of choosing your..."

"Cabrón."

Gloria's gaze flinched back to Pedro. "Sí." A chilling suspicion prickled her temples, like imagining a peeping Tom outside your window.

Pedro shrugged and blinked laconically at the message. "That seems an easy choice to make, especially for a woman. I cannot understand how women allow themselves to be subjugated like they are in those Islamic societies. They should—" Gloria gripped his shoulder, a raised finger stifling his words. Their eyes met and held in severe restraint. Pedro whispered, "Qué?"

Gloria rose from her chair, stepped over to the window, and stared outside. Dusk was darkening. The almond tree's pale trunk refracted light filtering out from the office. It was eerily quiet, only the soft whirl of the overhead fan interrupted the silence. Were they being spied upon? The disc had demonstrated uncanny timing all of a sudden, revealing a map and then a message related to their conversation.

"Pedro..." she said quietly as she turned to him. "Am I the only one fluent in English who has viewed the disc's contents?"

"Sí."

"In Arena Vallarta this afternoon, you said the disc might have an interior clock or be receiving a signal that controls its decryption."

"Is there another way to explain its behavior?"

Gloria slid into her chair next to him, took up Pedro's pen and notepad on the desk, and wrote out a couple of sentences for him: 'The disc appears to be revealing information that corresponds to our conversation. Have you searched this office for microphones?'

He shook his head no, doe eyes widening.

Gloria wrote something more: 'If the disc is receiving a signal, might it also be a bug?'

Pedro felt a little shiver run down his spine; an unnamed fear swept over him, the same feeling he had the previous evening when the disc first started revealing itself. Fear of the unknown, the unexplainable...the uncontrollable... Fear of the assassin... He took the pen from Gloria. 'Could be,' he wrote.

Gloria's pulse quickened in cadence with her racing mind. Why did the first and only message in English appear when she was privy to it, the only person fluent in English who had viewed the disc's images thus far? Did the author of the disc, or the assassin, know she was here? Was she being followed? spied upon? or did an eavesdropper simply recognize her voice, know who she was, that she spoke English, and flash the English phrase for her?

Pedro placed a clammy hand on Gloria's arm, jaw clenched, his breath halting. He came close and whispered, "If the disc is a receiver and transmitter, the assassin may be able to track its location."

Gloria felt a sudden current in her chest. She stood from the desk, nearly knocking her chair over. Pedro stood with her. Their eyes met in trembling fear. She signaled for him to follow her out of the office, away from the disc's prying ears, but when they made a move to exit, the door rattled...the front door to the house! Pedro's computer suddenly came alive with sound effects—a deep male voice coarse as sandpaper and menacing as the barrel of a gun pointed at your cranium:

"Al luchar contra los que desean la muerte tanto como tú deseas la vida, sólo hay una manera de vencerlos." When struggling against those who desire death as much as you desire life, there is only one way to beat them.

Pedro and Gloria locked onto each other in wide-eyed panic, suspended in space like a couple of flies in amber. The front door to the house was jarred open. Gloria leapt out of her skin, sprang to the office door and slammed it shut, her chest pressed against it to bar entry.

Another male voice sounded, from the living room: "Pedro!"

Pedro collapsed against the door next to Gloria and released a cry of relief. "Es mi hermano, señora," he said breathlessly. "Eduardo."

Gloria stood back from the door in deadened shock. Eduardo called out again, "Pedro?" and the disc chimed in: "Te acuerdas del cuento del Tío Tom? Pues, ahora tenemos las Tiitas Tomasinas!" Remember the story of Uncle Tom? Well, now we have Auntie Tomasinas!

Pedro opened his office door. What he saw momentarily stunned him. A ghostly figure covered in infernal dust. A figure resembling his brother Eduardo. After a second take, Pedro recognized his brother. A shrill feminine voice arose from his computer, in English:

"It is an honor to die for Allah, to rise up like our ancestors in jihad, the eternal path. To shed the blood of infidels, kufar. To be martyred and given new life in Paradise." Pedro captured his brother's darting eyes in his own. He took him by the arm and spirited him to the kitchen, away from the classified information coming alive on his computer.

A wave of dizziness passed through Gloria as she stumbled to her chair and took a seat before Pedro's computer monitor. Her eyes, moist with fright, scowled at the new image on the screen—a florescent cartoon caricature frozen in action, leaping in air, big adolescent eyes black and luminous. Its veil and long blue headscarf suggested this to be a girl. She wore blue pants, a mauve long-sleeve top, boots and gloves, and gripped a curved dagger overhead, poised to strike. The figure's eyes blinked languidly. "Two of my brothers have been martyred," she purred in English, "and my mother is proud. Now it is my turn."

A sudden bitterness twisted Gloria's mouth. "Your turn to do what, bitch?" she said.

The cartoon girl's eyes grew fierce, her menacing posture unchanged. The disc's deep sandpaper voice surfaced once more: "Sacrifice lives so Auntie Tomasinas may live in slavery."

Gloria felt her skin crawl, like snakes squirming beneath her flesh. Was the disc answering her? She went rigid at the sound of another voice: "Señora."

Gloria jerked her head to Pedro at the office door. "Sí?" she said, her even tone belying the angry anxiety shriveling her stomach.

"The mayor has been trying to contact you."

Gloria stood and reached for her blinking cell phone on Enrique's desk. "Qué pasa?"

Pedro kept his voice low and modulated: "There has been another explosion."

Gloria's blood rushed straight to her toes. "Qué?!?"

"A small one, señora. Close to the police station. No one was injured." His eyes alighted on his computer screen. "What...is that?"

Gloria swung her gaze around and stared in confusion at another image from the disc. A yellow smiley face against a pink background. In English, a child's tiny voice said, "And now a poem I learned in school today:

My bones are tempered blades of steel
wrapped in jihad, bombs, and zeal
I shall explode a kafir nest
Allah's will has been revealed."
Applause.

292

50

I spent at least another hour with my eyes closed, trying to meditate and clear my mind, or sleep. My bladder finally got the best of me. I'd been holding back from urinating for two reasons: the stabbing pain in my guts and head every time I moved, and an absurd idea that relieving my bladder would waste bodily fluid. The latter reason was no longer viable and the former would have to be dealt with. I had to go.

When I made a move to rise, the cockroaches loitering by the bucket scurried down the drain quicker than water skidding over a pipin' hot frying pan. Those suckers can really scoot. Wished I could join 'em. I got to my knees, gripped the bars, and steeled myself upright. Pain shot through my rectum, and the back of my skull folded around my head, forcing my face into the crook of my arm.

Fucking Chimp.

My ear boiled. The bone right behind my ear. I could feel it oozing and blistering and boiling, big as a golf ball.

Fucking Chimp.

Darts seared my temples, one right after the other. I practiced deep breathing techniques invented on the spot.

"You puss," I scolded myself.

That didn't do much good. So I raised my voice, nearly screamed: "Chingadostupidsonofahíjodeputabitchjodidobastardprick-whathefucksputamadrewrongwithyou!"

Alive, and well enough.

I shuffled to the drain, unzipped and squeezed my glutes together, waiting for my torqued ribs and warped internal organs to align themselves. Ready and set, I was curious as to how everything would function. Urine ached out upon a pair of antenna peaking up through the drain. It was a powerful stream, but the commotion it caused surprised me. A sound akin to a bass drum roll seemed to emanate from the drain. I imagined it was my piss flushing hundreds of cockroaches. Two elusive unidentified rusty bugs escaped the flood, six-stepping out of the drain and over to the bucket. Then the light went out.

"What the hell?" I said. Nothing but black silence answered; I just stood there, surrounded by darkness deeper than the deepest river at twilight, pretty badly banged up, my life on the line and my dick in my hand.

293

SEVE VERDAD

The good news was I hadn't pissed out my ass, felt any new searing pain, or seen any unusual colors in my urine before everything went dark. I zipped up and stepped toward the bars, reaching for them as I went.

I clutched the bars, my face between my hands, and waited for my eyes to adjust to the darkness. But the darkness remained absolute. There was no light to adjust to. The entire cellblock was a boundless void, a yawning bottomless grotto without beginning or end. Nothing shone through the small window in the door at the end of the corridor. Nothing shone at all, not a door, window or corridor. I blinked a couple of times—hard—and fluttered my eyelids. Livid emerald circles exploded into space; the golf ball behind my ear protested, sent a couple of darts flying... Now I saw some light...flittering fire flies performing dips and twirls. They danced within blackened billows and empty rapids. I felt disoriented, staggered back against the wall and lowered myself to the floor.

What was going on? Since the lights were out in the processing room as well as the cellblock, perhaps more time had passed than I thought and it was lights-out time. That didn't seem right though. The cops were gonna be back at me soon, weren't they?

It was a ploy. They were trying to break my spirit by leaving me alone in the dark with only my imagination to keep me company, didn't even want me entertained by bugs. They wanted me disoriented, lost in space and time.

That made sense.

I shut my eyes and felt comforted by the familiar darkness, a palpable obscurity that didn't appear absolute. With eyes closed the retina can play tricks, give a sense of proportion to darkness. I opened my eyes to test the difference. Sure seemed darker with my eyes open. Silent darkness. I heard breathing in the silence...my own. The hushed blackness made me sensitive to my own breathing. But there was something else. Another sound, or lack thereof. The feeble overhead ventilation had gone quiet.

Suffocate the prisoner in stench and obscurity.

That made sense as well.

I listened for something beyond darkness. Nothing. I shouted, "Gotta light?!?" My voice sank into oblivion, as a weighty stone skips upon water and disappears with a *kerplunk*. I waited. Did I hear something else? Yes. A faint chirping and rustling. Now gone. Had it come from behind the door? It must have. Nobody else was on the cellblock... Or was there?

Now I clearly heard something. A key in a door? A squeak of hinges. I got to my feet and readied myself to greet my tormentor. But

I still couldn't see a damn thing! Had the corridor door opened? Sounded like it but...why didn't they turn on a light? I pulled away from the bars.

Stay back... This could be it. A last chance to attack.

I kept my back against the wall, an arm's length from the bars, and let my eyes swim with the black currents up the corridor.

Years ago, on a night dissonant with the distant howl of coyotes, I was camping alone with nothing but redwoods to shield me. The woods were dyed almost as black as the cell block right now and a strange rustling sound brought me up in my sleeping bag. A feral growl from an animal I couldn't see shivered my bones; I held that position, on an elbow inside my sleeping bag, for the next half hour. Didn't move a muscle. Barely breathed.

That's how I was now in my cell, frozen solid, breathing slowed to a state of suspended animation. But I was standing, ready to defend myself, or attack.

Something was in the corridor. I could feel it. Why wasn't it making any noise? What was the purpose? It had to be my imagination. Then I heard something else. Fingers in a pocket...right beside me!

I wanted to fall to my knees, dodge a bullet, but remained frozen. The blackness ignited, and an eye appeared between the bars, large and brilliant as a block of ice beneath an ice pick. The eye blinked. Flame shimmered in the aquamarine iris. And I saw the hands. They were cupped and couched a match, steady beneath the eye.

"You asked for a light?" said Devo.

I thawed and released air from my lungs. "Wow. You scared the ever livin' crap outta me."

"Not sure I'm all to blame for that."

"What the hell are *you* doing here?"

Devo extinguished the match. My cell door opened with a clank. Instinctively, I scrambled for the bucket, the only item at my disposal that could serve as a weapon.

Plastic bucket. Crack it over his head and it'll cut good as steel.

"Let's go," I heard Devo say.

I stammered blindly, "Wha—what?"

"Would you rather stay? We don't have much time." He finger-nailed another match and turned his back on me. Rivulets of adrenalin coursed through my blood as I followed him down the corridor, my heart thumping in my ears. He eased the corridor door open. Across the processing room the hall was dark but a sliver of light filtered in from an office. A siren whooped from somewhere outside. Kinda close.

SEVE VERDAD

"Watch your step here," Devo said.

I glanced down at a crumpled figure on the floor. Mighta been Fat Cop. I stepped over him. We walked around two more bodies lying in a heap in the middle of the room and made for the office. Devo pushed the door open and closed it after us. A streetlamp shone through a broken window behind a desk. Night was falling outside. On the desk was a whorl of braided rope thick as a garden hose. Devo grabbed it. "Careful of glass," he said, eyes lowered at my bare feet. "I'm sure you don't need any more injuries."

The window had been shattered, then opened. Devo cleared a path for me with the soles of his shoes, tossed the rope through the window and anchored its hook beneath the windowsill.

"Been a while since I've repelled," I said.

Devo was out the window. I looked outside as he alighted on the sidewalk twenty or thirty feet below. The bars that had protected the window flopped from their moorings like a busted storm shutter. I took hold of the rope without thinking, stubbed a toe on the way down, and landed next to him. Devo snapped the rope overhead like a whip, freed the hook, and quickly coiled the rope under his arm. "Follow me," he said.

"Do I have a choice?"

He didn't answer. It was a serious question. Half a block around a corner we stopped alongside a late-model Jeep Wrangler. The windows and top were down.

"Get in."

I climbed aboard. Devo sparked the motor, turned on the headlights and ground the Jeep into gear. "Keep your head down till we cross the boulevard."

I slunk against the door and kept an eye on him. Devo slid the black bandanna off his head and tossed it in the back. A solid matching T-shirt tapered his torso and trimmed a sunken waist under dark belted blue jeans. His tan arms were thick and lithe, his chest deep and square. Devo looked older than he had the previous evening, nearly forty. Perhaps it was his beard. Last night he was clean shaven. Tonight brassy stubble ran ruggedly across his face and sinuous oxblood neck. Devo grinds nails with those whiskers, yanks screws from hinges with his teeth. He drove at a leisurely pace, obeying all traffic laws. An incredibly cool customer. He had moved quickly through the police station and out the window but never hurried. The guy was cooler than Joe Montana marshaling a winning touchdown drive, disciplined as Patton's troops taking Messina.

I was dumb-struck—had no idea what to make of him or my rescue. I felt profoundly grateful yet leery of more trouble. Not long ago I thought Devo might be a terrorist. Now he seemed a highly trained commando from a planet I had no desire to visit. He clearly had me at his mercy, if he wanted.

Devo reached into an ice chest on the backseat and handed me a bottled water. I stayed low and drank deeply. "Thanks," I said.

He stopped at a light and lit a cigar. "You can sit up if you like. We just crossed the boulevard."

I stayed put. "Those bodies back there...were they...?"

"Dead?"

"Yeah."

"No. No need to kill those stupid bastards. Never touch me."

Can anyone *touch you*?

We drove in silence for five or ten minutes, heading south, for the most part, as far as I could tell. I stayed low and sipped water. Devo stopped at a dim intersection, made a left and gained some speed. I sat up and found we were on Libramiento (Bypass Road), heading south around the eastern reaches of Vallarta. I groaned in pain and relief. Being in this Jeep with Devo was way preferable to Chimp's nightstick. I reached into the ice chest for an ice cube, pulled out a can of beer instead, and applied it to the golf ball behind my ear. The bitch stung like hell. I drew air through my teeth, "Fucking Chimp."

"Beat ya up good, huh?"

"A horse kicked the shit out of me worse once. Like to get a hold of those corrupt candy-ass bastards without their guns."

"Most assuredly." Devo gestured towards the backseat. "There's a sandwich back there for you. In a paper bag on the floor."

I located the sandwich. Tuna fish. Fresh, grilled tuna. I held the beer in place behind my ear with one hand and ate with the other. Soft sandwich, the tastiest I'd ever had. Chewing was painful. Sustenance and pain.

Sustenance and pain...sustenance and pain...

Felt like I was calling in an air raid.

"What time is it?" I asked.

" 'Bout eight-thirty or so."

Devo held the expression of a cabby making his eighth evening run to the airport. He wore no expression at all. And we were headed in the opposite direction from the airport.

"Thanks..." I said between careful bites. The back of my jaw felt like it had a screw impaled in it, "...for rescuing me."

"Don' mention it." Devo slowed for a speed bump.

SEVE VERDAD

About four bites remained of my sandwich. I closed my eyes and stuck my head into the wind. It wasn't a dream. I was free, and very much alive.

The golf ball had practically burned a hole through the beer can. I tossed the beer back into the ice chest, took a swig of water, and studied Devo's placid face in the moving shadows and street light. "How'd you know I was in so much trouble?" I said.

"Keep my eyes peeled and ears open."

"Guess I should try more of that... How the hell did you manage it? Single handed?"

"Appears so." He slowed for another speed bump.

"But how?"

"A little diversionary tactic. Didn't you hear?"

"Hear what? Didn't hear a thing."

"No?"

I thought for a moment. "Wait a sec. I was taking a leak and... Sounded like a drum or... What the..." My voice spiked, "You set off a bomb or somethin'?"

Devo pulled the cigar from his mouth and held it between his fingers on the wheel. A corona. Not too fat. His voice turned greasy, thuggish: "Don' wu-rry 'bout it. No buddy got huyt. Jus a ol' Buick meetin' its demeese... Big noise, bitta fiya. Unda da suycanstances, couldn' miss."

I thought about those elusive rusty bugs dancing away from my piss. "Then you cut the power. Pretty damn smart... And didn't kill anybody? ..." I took another bite of my sandwich. "I'd like to kill a few of those sadistic fucking pig coppers."

Devo jabbed me with a dull eye as he negotiated a well-illuminated curve leading to a tunnel. His mouth was rigid, forced in line. "Been enough killin' for one day, don't you think?"

He stuck the cigar back in his mouth and produced a couple of band aids. I scowled stupidly, like he was flippin' me the bird for no apparent reason.

"For your toe." He turned on the interior lights. "It's bleeding."

Indeed it was. The big toe on my right foot. It oozed blood onto the rubber floor mat. I devoured what remained of the sandwich, grabbed the band aids, and brought the injured appendage to my knee. Devo tossed me a clean rag from behind his seat. I moistened it with water and cleaned up the blood on my toe, revealing an impeccable, symmetrical wound. The dangling skin fit smartly back into place as I administered the band aids.

Devo down-shifted and swung a right for Old Vallarta.

"Where're we goin'?"

His cigar jumped from one corner of his mouth to the other. "A little business before I take you to your hideout. You know you're gonna have to hide for a while?"

"Sure. Whatever you say. Makes sense. Let's go to Casa Mexicana first."

"Your hotel?"

"Yeah."

"Cops don't know where you're staying?"

"No... Doubt it. Was my arrest publicized?"

Devo eyed me sideways. "An arrest at the Washington Hotel has not been confirmed or denied."

"So no one at Casa Mexican knows I've been arrested, or that I've escaped...yet. They'll give me another key to my room."

"And you want money."

"Passport too. Whatever I can grab. IDs, shoes, clothes, my phone and computer."

"Ballsy idea. Lots a cops in that vicinity. The boulevard is crawlin' with 'em. Has been since after the explosion this morning. And they're liable to shoot you on sight."

The golf ball quivered and tossed a dart. I brought a hand to the sudden pain behind my eyes. Devo flicked ashes from his cigar onto the passing road, slowed the Jeep to a pedestrian pace and made a right. "The cops have probably identified you by now," he said, "whether or not you told 'em your name. So your passport and IDs are useless to you."

"I gave 'em my name. Thought... Well... Sometimes I think too much."

"Or not enough about the right stuff."

"Yeah, like that coke you gave me. I got busted with it. And now those bastards think I'm a terrorist. Turns out that the dead guy we were talking about last night was a terrorist and drug dealer. And I had the coke wrapped in his picture."

Devo grunted, unaffected, as if everything I had to say to him was old news.

"You don't seem all that surprised or interested in what I'm telling you."

He took a leisurely left down an unfamiliar declivity. I noticed the sky, low and dark, ready to drizzle. The moon was hidden behind the clouds somewhere, trapped, as if it didn't exist at all. "Lots a blood on everyone's hands," Devo said. "Those corrupt coppers will try and wash some off on you." His dark profile chomped the cigar like a bull chewin' cud. He pulled the cigar from his mouth, spit out a piece, and scowled at the stub before chucking it. "You shoulda given the coke to Johnny."

Johnny's name brought a cry to my lips: "What about Johnny?!? Was he at the Washington this morning?"

Devo stopped abruptly at an intersection at the bottom of the hill and shot me a look hard enough to leave a bruise. "What about Johnny?" he said. He made a right towards the river. "Guess someone better advise him of your fuckup before the cops get their hands on him in their search for you…if he's not dead."

"Dead? Come on Devo. Don't mess with me."

Devo's tone turned gangsterish; sounded like James Cagney: "Hey pally, I don' know everthin'. I do know I saved your ass so don' go gettin' your panties all bunched up in there or I'll a saved it fer nuttin."

That shut me up for about four seconds. "What you save it for anyway?"

"You'll see."

"Where're we goin'?"

"You'll see."

"I don't need any more surprises."

"Too bad. Life's full of 'em. Might as well take advantage."

51

CHIMP slid his old Toyota Tercel in at the curb, cut the motor, and was about to get out and walk the block and a half to Lazarito's office when he received staggering news over his cell phone. At first he couldn't understand qué demonios the lieutenant was talking about. It had been a long, grueling day. A nightmare. And now…what? Another explosion? Just now!? Twenty minutes ago… Right down the street from…where? headquarters…?!? A car bomb…no injuries… And the prisoner has escaped!!!

Shivers ran across Chimp's shoulder blades, his breath coming in short gasps, like he was going into shock. He sank down in his car seat and closed his eyes in an effort to gain control of himself, his phone pressed tight against his ear. The lieutenant's voice was unrelenting, rattling inside his brain like peas in a drum. Said he'd seen the explosion firsthand as he was returning to headquarters, had felt the concussive blow from inside his police car…! "And where were you at the time, Paulo?"

Chimp's heart hammered in his chest, his tone fraught with honest confusion. Instinctively, defensively and rightly he reminded the lieutenant that he had given him relief, permission to go home for dinner and some rest before the next interrogation of the prisoner.

The lieutenant's response was scathing. A hell of a coincidence how the escape occurred while Paulo, the ranking officer at headquarters at the time, was on break. And obviously there would not be another interrogation of the suspect until they recaptured him! Deadly force was authorized... "This is unbelievable," the lieutenant hissed. "The gringo not only escaped but a power outage crashed the computers at headquarters and the mug shots we had on file of him appear to have been lost. And the mug-shot camera was stolen from el comandante's locked desk along with copies of the gringo's fingerprints. Who the hell was holding down the fort while I and most the rest of the department were busting our asses at ground zero with the fire department and Search and Rescue, Cantinflas?!? It is abundantly clear that you did not secure your post before abandoning it, Paulo."

Chimp was speechless. He had never heard Lieutenant Romero so enraged, couldn't even imagine an expression on his face to match his inflamed tone. After a moment of silence, the lieutenant seemed to regain his usual composure. "Evidently you do need some rest," he said evenly. "Stay at home until you receive further orders."

Click.

Chimp let this stunning turn of events sink in. The ensuing adrenalin rush instantly snapped him out of his initial shock. Now he was fuming mad. Fuming... That hijo de la chingada gringo he had arrested was one... Puta madre. Chinga su pinchísima puta madre! Who the hell did he think he was?

Bullets would stop the fucking gringo terrorista dead in his tracks.

The lieutenant hadn't offered many details into the prisoner's escape but the explosion indicated he had an accomplice. Did he have more than one accomplice? A network of terrorists doing his bidding? How many terrorists were running around town right under the department's nose?

Well, Chimp had a network too, and knew how to use it.

He would await further orders from the lieutenant, and he still had to meet with Lazarito... But now that he was back at square one with the prisoner, the escaped prisoner, it was time to call his cousin. Manco had led him to the suspect down at the Washington and just might lead him to the gringo again.

MEDIA Minister Lazarito Charlado tilted his melon noggin to the ceiling and released a dry wheezing whistle. "Well, well, Paulo. This development certainly sheds a different light on things, indeed it does."

Lazarito stared down placidly over his double chin at the small figure planted in the uncomfortable vinyl chair opposite his large mahogany desk. An ugly but indispensable figure. His faithful snitch, Paulo.

Paulo's head looked as though it would burst without that police cap tucked low on his forehead. His uniform, the fresh shirt he had donned, gave him no help, like dressing up a deformed pigmy. Lazarito wondered if Paulo's mother actually loved that face—a monkey's mug with a sow's snout attached to it. At least he didn't have to look at himself in the mirror while shaving every morning. The hairless jabalina. Lazarito had seen Paulo without his cap on and knew that his head, like his face (and the rest of his body, he imagined) was bald as a baby's behind. Paulo was balder than Lazarito himself would ever be...and uglier. But he sure was a dependable and loyal informant...as long as he was paid.

Chimp sneered and bared his decaying canines. "This may shed a different light on things, Lazarito, but my information is no less valuable."

"The escaped prisoner's name is sure to be released...along with his photo."

"They have all disappeared."

"Qué?"

"The mug shots we took of the prisoner, and his fingerprints."

A puffed expression of disbelief reddened Lazarito's face. He leaned forward, his deep armchair creaking, and stuck his feet on the carpet. "How did that happen?"

"A power outage at the time of the escape and explosion crashed the department's computers. It is unknown if his photos can be recovered. And the mug-shot camera as well as the suspect's fingerprints were stolen from el comandante's locked desk."

"And the suspect's identification card, driver's license, passport?"

"He had none when he was arrested, claimed they were lost at the Washington."

"He had a room at the Washington?"

"He claimed to during the interrogation."

"Híjole. So his name has not been verified?"

"Not to my knowledge."

The Media Minister scratched his balding pate as he digested Paulo's outlandish disclosures. "My, my," he said. "Our problems never seem to cease. A most unfortunate state of affairs, and embarrassing, for the department." Lazarito allowed his liquidy dark eyes to pool inside their heavy swags of flesh and rendered his sincerest (though not entirely heartfelt) empathy: "What a colossal tragedy. A disaster for all of us. And the Puerto Vallarta Police Department has dug itself into a tremendous hole. Lieutenant Romero is in quite a fix. Indeed he is." He shook his head with a *tisk tisk*. Like everyone else, the disaster at the Washington had shaken Lazarito to the core, but it had also reminded him of his divine duty to follow every lead and discover every culprit in this calamity. And at the moment, the Puerto Vallarta Police Department was in his crosshairs.

Media Minister Charlado solemnly reviewed the police department's sins out loud, thinking Paulo might add one or two to the list: "First a bungled raid accompanied by rumors of gangsters and terrorists running loose in Vallarta, rumors supported by the discovery of a murdered terrorist at the marina; then the failure to prevent what appears to have been a terror attack today at the Washington; and now the escape of the one and only suspect along with the disappearance of his mug shots and fingerprints...after a car bomb exploded outside police headquarters! The lieutenant must hope to God he recaptures his man before having to make a public statement."

Chimp shot Lazarito a hostile glare. "*I* plan to recapture him," he said.

Lazarito uttered a short whistling chuckle and leaned back in his rather squeaky leather armchair, feet off the carpet. "I am sure you do plan to recapture the prisoner, Paulo," he said, his head tilted back up to the ceiling, "or kill him."

Chimp didn't even attempt to disguise the cold hardness in his voice: "The lieutenant has authorized the use of deadly force."

The Media Minister appreciated that tidbit of information. He leveled a measured gaze at his faithful snitch. "The suspect clearly has accomplices, Paulo."

"So do we, Lazarito. He will not get far. There are still roadblocks on all routes heading out of Vallarta—to Melaque, Tepic and Guadalajara. He will not escape Vallarta alive and I do plan to recapture or kill him myself, even if I have to track him through the jungle." Chimp reposed in his chair and ran a knotted, Indian-blooded finger across his hairless brow where a thin perspiration had broken out. "My contacts led me to him in the first place and may do so again."

SEVE VERDAD

"I only pay for current, reliable information, Paulo, not predictions which may or may not prove reliable or valuable."

Chimp crossed his spindly legs, assuming his best imitation of a business man wielding the upper hand. "Considering the terror attack today, Lazarito, the information I already gave you this afternoon has to be the most valuable we have ever negotiated for... And I have more, will have more still... This is the biggest news story in the history of Vallarta...the entire state of Jalisco. Not since the 1985 México City earthquake—"

"Yes, Paulo. No doubt. But unless Lieutenant Romero recaptures his prisoner in short order, I expect he will have to enlist the media's help to provide publicity so the public may aid in the effort. What you offer now, the suspect's *alleged* name, is likely to be released soon, along with a sketch of him if no photos are available."

"But I offer you his name right now so you may try to verify it yourself right away."

The Media Minister squeaked forward in his chair and cut to the chase: "That is what I pay for, Paulo, to be first on the receiving end of breaking news. And the value of this scoop, including the information you provided this afternoon, I place at two thousand pesos."

"Five thousand, Lazarito, or five hundred *dollars*."

Lazarito retrieved ten two-hundred-peso bills from a drawer, added ten crisp one-hundred-peso bills from his breast pocket, and fanned them out on his desk. "Three thousand pesos."

Chimp got to his feet and reached for the money. Lazarito placed a hand over the bills. "The suspect's name, Paulo, por favor."

Chimp flared his nostrils, his snout quivering. "Russell Martell." He nabbed the money and began counting as he sat back down.

Lazarito nearly fell out of his chair, his liquidy eyes draining down his spine. He asked Paulo to repeat the name. Chimp lost count. "Russell Martell," he said.

Lazarito's rumpled eyebrows shot clear up to his scanty hairline. He remembered the name all too well, remembered the young man all too well, and on the spot pieced together a few details: Russell Martell, the uncredentialed supposed journalist at Arena Vallarta's dedication. Russell Martell, the gringo who, with unabashed impudence, had questioned him in public—right there in Arena Vallarta's central plaza—about the raid as if there were something to hide...some kind of cover-up! As if he, Russell Martell, had inside information and knew about the cover-up...

Did he have inside information because he was a terrorist who had escaped the raid? Would a terrorist care why the raid had not received publicity? Or was he really a journalist following up on a rumor? Both? Could he possibly be a journalist and a terrorist...*and* an assassin, the man who killed the Iranian found dead at the marina?

Lazarito recalled how, at Armando Montoya's party, Russell Martell intimated knowledge of his authority, the privileges he enjoyed in his exalted position as Media Minister. The liberties he took. And the way Señor Martell skirted his dialogue around the botched raid as though...as though issuing a threat! A threat to expose Lazarito's part in the cover-up...

Russell Martell knew an awful lot, too much...perhaps enough to expose police blunders as a contributing factor in a terror attack this morning and implicate the Media Minister in a cover-up of those blunders...

Corruption, police blunders...the kinds of things journalists dig for...

Was *Mister* Martell's egotistical banter a deception? Was he really a journalist?

If nothing else, Russell Martell's knowledge made him a dangerous man...but an assassin and terrorist?!?

Chimp folded the pesos into his pocket and caught Lazarito staring blankly at his desktop. "The name mean something to you, Lazarito?"

Lazarito pushed himself back from his desk and immediately regained his composure, replete with affable smile and twinkling eyes. "No Paulo, not at all. But I do expect an exclusive briefing from you should you recapture this gringo terrorista...and any cohorts he may have. An exclusive *interview*. Indeed I do." Lazarito paused, and quickly decided to offer honest inspiration—a bounty of sorts: "I will add another three...five thousand pesos to the sum you just received and make you a famous man when you have his head on a stick, Paulo."

"An exclusive like that will definitely be worth over five hundred dollars, Lazarito. A thousand...or more."

"We shall see, Paulo. Indeed we will."

52

DEVO parked and insisted I accompany him. He wasn't sure how long he'd be. I resisted: "What the hell kinda surprise is this? an appearance in a public place?" Devo chuckled, told me it was the best place to hide, for now. I'd blend right in. "Everyone looks the same around Vallarta tonight," he said, "like hell." Then he remarked on the paucity of windows in El Cabezón. I wouldn't be seen from outside. And a beer was in order. Now was the time to get one. I reminded him that there was Modelo in the ice chest. He reminded me that El Cabezón had Dos Equis Lager on tap.

So that was it. How could I argue with the guy?...after his performance? He wasn't gonna break me outta jail and then get me busted in Big Head, was he? And a Dos Equis Lager on tap did sound good.

I slouched behind Devo as we entered. The backside of two dust-filled shirts shimmered at the bar. At an adjacent table, a tableau of three gloomy men sipped beer through pallid masticating faces. Devo stopped short, put a hand on my shoulder, and pointed me to a booth on the exterior wall. I let my breath clog in my throat so I wouldn't cry out, and my knees buckled, like I'd been struck by a blow. Johnny was seated there, talking with Brenda.

In an instant I was standing at his side. "Been lookin' for you," I said gruffly. He stared up at me with a foppish grin. I sat next to him, wrapped an arm around his shoulders and squeezed him tight enough to leave me breathless. Johnny clapped me on my chest. "Easy does it Russ," he said. "I survived the day. Don't crush me now."

I released him with a pat on the back and sighed happily, "Sonofabitch. Catch any fish?"

He smirked sheepishly. "Must've overslept."

Brenda said, "Thought we might have to visit you in jail."

Johnny and Brenda's clothes were filled with chalky dirt and dust, like they had spent the day sliding head first into home plate. Johnny's tousled hair looked like a faded clown's wig, and he was wearing jeans. I rarely see him in long pants when we're keeping warm south of the border. Brenda had taken the time to beat ash and dust from the UDLA Aztecas cap on her head but the school colors were now pink and turquoise instead of orange and green. Both of them must have washed up some in the bathroom. Their faces were clean. Brenda folded her hands on the table. They were nicked and scratched, her fingernails chipped and tarnished. Long sleeves protected her arms.

"They ain't made a jail yet that can hold me," I joked and placed a hand over hers. Brenda's eyes were red and unsmiling, her hands cold as Oregon coastal waters. She gave my hand a tight squeeze and took a sip of water.

"How much it cost ya?" Johnny asked.

"Too much," I answered with a shabby shake of my head. If they thought I'd bribed my way out of jail, that was fine with me. I wasn't quite sure how to explain my escape anyhow. I stared around the tavern for Devo. He was at the bar.

Johnny drank from his beer mug. "Ya got off easy," he said. "Kickin' back in jail, leaving the heavy lifting to us." He glanced at Brenda. Her gaze was unseeing and about as accommodating as a stone fence.

"Sorry," I said with an eye to Brenda; the horrid destruction and suffering at the Washington attenuated her features. "I wanted to help out down there but, well... None of my plans panned out today."

A shadow of Brenda's smile crossed her face. Up until that moment, I thought she might be in shock. Johnny said, "You don't know the half of it, Russ. Miguel and I got lucky last night and I don't mean laid." He finished his beer to slow himself down. "We tried to get into the girls' room. Damn lucky we failed." Johnny blinked; his pink eyes moistened as he bit his upper lip.

He'd lost me. "You mean Gail's room? Your date at the party?"

"Yeah Gail's room. The adjoining rooms she and her three girlfriends from the University of Texas shared. The rooms that used to be right in the center of the Washington's north tower..."

"Christ." I leaned back and ran the heels of my hands over my temples. The golf ball vibrated and throbbed. Johnny was seated to my left and couldn't see the swelling behind my ear.

Brenda's melodic voice sounded like broken piano strings: "Nobody knows for certain...what happened to them."

"That's because Gail and her friends are buried under Mount Saint Helens." Johnny drew a wretched breath. Looked as though he might scream, or cry. "Can't fucking believe it..."

"Heavy equipment arrived from Guadalajara," Brenda continued, "but can't be used much yet...might crush survivors."

"Help arrived from the States as well," Devo said. He sat a tray on the table replete with a pitcher of beer, mugs, four shots of tequila, and a plate of limes and salt. He poured the beer, slid in next to Brenda, and raised a shot of tequila.

The three of us knocked back tequila. Brenda had a sip of beer. We fell into silence, the day's black events hanging over our heads like a bleeding mushroom cloud.

A waitress came over with a tray of silverware, chips, salsa, tortillas, and a plate of dorado and carne asada. I excused myself to the restroom.

Boy was I filthy. Would've liked to take a sponge bath right there in the restroom. Settled for using a paper towel to clean the grime from my arms, legs, feet and hands. Then I scrubbed my face, gave my hair a quick rinse, and blew my nose. The golf ball shuddered and my ears popped, relieving pressure from my head as though I'd equalized while scuba diving. I poked a finger into my right ear thinking some blood may have been released from the golf ball. Nothing. But I wanted blood, Chimp's blood...Fat Cop's and the lieutenant's.

I took hold of the sink with both hands; raging energy coiled up inside me, rage set to spring into violent action. Right then and there I determined that fight was preferable to flight. I'd rip each and every one of those gutless pig pricks the new asshole they were gonna rip me.

"Don't I wish," I murmured with a penetrating glare into my eyes reflected in the mirror. My reflection reminded me that I'd better cool it: *Cops are liable to shoot you on sight... Chimp and Fat Cop could even walk in on me right now...or—*

I stared about the bathroom. Once again I had that feeling of being watched, like in my jail cell. That same paranoid feeling. No one else occupied the bathroom, yet the feeling deepened—a sense of being held captive, at the mercy of my tormentors. I looked up at the small vent in the ceiling...listened to its whirr...and imagined a camera planted inside. It was an irrational thought but I couldn't help myself. My circumstances had changed so drastically as to be irrational, unbelievable... Identical? Was I now Devo's prisoner instead of the cops'?

Devo was in control—of me and my circumstances. Was Devo for real? Definitely. What were his motives? Did he know I was ready to give him up back there in my cell? Why did he tell me Johnny might be dead? Because he didn't want me thinking straight? It couldn't have been to give me a pleasant surprise...

Hell of a way to surprise a guy—tellin' me one of my closest buddies might be dead when he knew damn well he was alive...didn't he? Why did Devo rescue me? What the hell does he want from me?

Could Devo be trusted? I couldn't be certain. Was it worth the risk to trust him, leave myself at his mercy? I barely knew the guy and given his performance tonight, the way he broke me outta jail and left crumpled bodies in his wake, he might be more dangerous than the Vallarta police and federales combined.

By the time I sat back down next to Johnny, I'd convinced myself that my assessment of Devo was not an exaggeration. That didn't stop my stomach from growling at the sight and smell of the food though. But for that tuna fish sandwich I'd eaten in Devo's Jeep I hadn't had any sustenance all day.

I made a carne asada taco and a comment about the charming Vallarta police. Brenda toyed with a slice of dorado, said Vallarta police were always charming, as long as you paid. Johnny squeezed lime onto a dorado taco, said I had plenty of money. Devo watched us and was well into his second or third beer before I launched into my second taco—dorado and carne asada, with salsa casera.

"Where's Mountain?" I asked.

"That guy's a livin', breathin' ten-ton tractor," Johnny said. "Could use a thousand Mountains down at the Washington right now."

Brenda dabbed her mouth with a napkin. "Armando's still at the Washington with Bizco."

"Bet he can move some rock," I said. "What about his friend he was worried about...? Leslie...?"

"She was in the south tower," Johnny said. "Pretty shook up. Mountain was happy to see her."

"Ara?"

"Ara got sick," Brenda said, "had to go home. I'm on my way to see her right now."

Our eyes held and a note of whimsical affection entered my voice: "Thanks for coming."

Brenda's eyes smiled at me. "We were wondering where you were when Devo told us what happened."

"Really? When was that?" I looked at Devo. Did he wink at me?

"About noon," he said and refilled our beers. I made a mental note to ask Johnny what Devo had said "happened." Devo aimed a toneless voice at me: "Russell's gonna disappear for a while."

I said, "Uh, that's right," and dripped salsa from a chip to the table. The crow's feet at Devo's left eye crinkled. I was sure he winked at me this time.

"Not a bad idea," said Brenda. "Things are crazy around here. Ara and I hope to leave for Guadalajara tomorrow." She took hold of her beer but didn't drink from it. "I better go and see how she's doing."

Devo rose from the table to let Brenda out of the booth. I asked her if she still had my room key.

"Up at the house."

"Can you give it to Johnny, please?"

"Sure." She glanced at Johnny. "Come on up to the house and I'll give it to you."

"He'll be up there shortly," I said with a nod at Johnny's questioning frown.

Devo gave Brenda his hand as she stood, and asked her if she had money for a cab. Brenda said she preferred to walk.

"Looks like rain out there," he said.

I stood and dusted off my...Ara's shirt. "Tell Ara I might have to keep the shirt. It's such a mess and—"

Brenda's small chuckle interrupted me. "Everyone and everything's a mess. Keep it. She'll understand." We exchanged pecks on the cheek. Devo accompanied her to the exit. There was some blood high on the seat of her pants. At least I imagined it was blood— *the blood of a victim or survivor?*

A lump formed in my throat when Brenda looked back and said, "Cíao." When would I see her again?

I resumed my place next to Johnny, my voice imperative: "You need to do me a big favor, Johnny. But don't take any unnecessary risks. If something doesn't look right, abort."

"Sounds like my specialty. Whaddaya got in mind? A midnight harvest and transport?"

"Just as risky. Maybe more so. I need you to get into my room and grab some of my gear. The cops don't know where I was staying. But they might find out soon. You have to go right away."

"Cops don't know where you're staying...? What? Are they still after you?"

"Most likely," Devo said. He sat down across from us. "Martell doesn't need another run-in with 'em."

I aimed a sharp whisper at Johnny: "Just get the key from Brenda. Room 1163. Stuff what you can into my backpack—shoes and clothes, laptop, phone, and my passport pouch. The pouch is the most important. It's in the safe in the closet and contains money and credit cards."

I was about to tell Johnny the combination but considered Devo's presence. Was it wise to reveal much to him? At this point he knew my room number but there was no reason to say the safe's combination out loud when it made sense to write it out for Johnny anyway. "I'll write the combo down for you," I said and made a move to get a pencil from the waitress. Devo offered me a pencil. It simply appeared in his hand as if from nowhere. I accepted it with a cockeyed "thanks" and minor show of surprise. Johnny chewed on his beer. He hadn't noticed Devo's sleight of hand, wasn't concerned about the guy at all, but I sure was. Devo was the wild card in my predicament.

I wrote the safe's combination and my room number on a napkin, then added my Mom's and my Dad's phone numbers. My parents are divorced and I told Johnny to leave a message with at least one of them, tell them I was okay, working a scoop about the terror attack, and would be in touch soon.

"Nobody's sure it was a terror attack," Johnny said.

I felt the blood rush to my face; the golf ball quivered, adding an edge to my tone: "It was a terror attack. Believe me. The cops are pretty damn sure of that. And from what I can gather, fanatical

310

Muslims are behind it. A dead Iranian terrorist is connected somehow."

"Really?" Johnny pondered this revelation, beer clutched between his hands. "Sure heard a lot of rumors at the Washington about a plane crash or a bomb but the cops, federales and firemen never said anything about a terror attack. Most people seem to think a sewer line flooded with fuel exploded and—"

"They probably don't wanna talk about a terror attack in public," I intervened, "until they gather more evidence. But I'm telling' ya—"

"Your folks will ask questions."

"Tell 'em I'm doing investigative work on the *disaster*, helping rescue teams. You don't need to get into details. Just tell 'em I'll be in touch. Call them first, from a pay phone, before doing anything else. Leave a message if they don't answer..."

Johnny downed the last shot of tequila without lime or grimace. "Jeez, the cops really got ya on the run, huh? What the hell happened?"

"Nothin' that won't be resolved after a short while," Devo said.

Devo's confidence was contagious, made me leery. How far could I trust him? Who the hell was he? Was he setting me up for another fall? Had he set me up for the first one? Was he using me as some kind of patsy? He had sprung me from jail but it wasn't like we were part of the same gang, the same crime family. And just like a gangster on the run, now that I was free I planned to stay that way through my own cunning and with the help of those I held in strictest confidence, such as Johnny...and maybe Mountain, if I needed him and could contact him.

Johnny challenged Devo in a low growl, as if sensing my anxiety: "Nothin' that won't be resolved in a short while? What the fuck does that mean?" He shot me a scornful look, like I'd insulted him. "What the hell's goin' on? I thought you were picked up for questioning after finding a dead body."

"He was," Devo said. I saw a cigar in his mouth but it was actually his middle finger, tapping lightly at those narrow wolfish lips. "Then I had to help him escape. You never know what those shithead coppers are capable of."

Johnny's eyes grew wide and luminous. "Escape?" He planted his forearms on the table, his voice a near whisper, "A jailbreak? Wow..." His gaze flickered between me and Devo. "Tell me about it."

"No time," said Devo.

"Aw shucks, Russ. Ya gotta write about it then." Johnny sounded like a kid asking about the big gift-wrapped box under the Christmas tree.

311

"So you'll grab my gear for me?" I said.

"Sure." Johnny straightened his posture. "Anything to be part of *that* story. But we're gonna hafta work out some details."

Devo got up and swaggered towards the bar. I faced Johnny. "The details can wait. First you need to know more about what you're getting into."

"Shoot."

"Those sadistic pigs accused me of terrorism and drug trafficking. They found some coke on me."

Johnny blanched, appraised me for a few seconds, and chuckled humorlessly... "Jeez Russ. Your stories get better all the time."

"Let's hope so. This one ain't finished yet. Does Devo or anyone from the party know where you're staying?"

"I don't think so. No. Not really a place to brag about. Think I mentioned it to Miguel at the end of the evening. We were gonna share a cab but were headed in opposite directions."

Devo had disappeared. Had he stepped outside? Maybe in the bathroom. I grabbed Johnny's elbow by the gills and laid my forehead against his. "Let's go."

I was out the door. It had begun to drizzle. Johnny tugged on my shirt. "What about Devo?"

As I suspected, Devo was nowhere in sight. He'd probably gone to the head. A cab stopped before my raised hand. I hustled Johnny into the backseat, sat beside him and gave the cabby directions to Mountain's house.

"Devo can take care of the check," I said, "and himself. Got any money?"

"Five, six hundred pesos. My god what happened to your head?"

I put a finger to my lips. "Got a phone card?"

"Tapped it out."

Johnny bought a phone card at a liquor store while I pretended I wasn't hiding in the cab. When he got back I told the cabby to find a pay phone. He did, but the corner was pretty well lit. Johnny made the call to my mom for me. The two minutes he spent on the line seemed like an hour.

As the cabby pulled away from the curb Johnny handed me the napkin with all those numbers on it and put his arm around me. "Be careful," he said, "and I love you. Love, Mom." He didn't kiss me.

Johnny had told Mom I was busy with rescue crews, which was true. But the one I needed to rescue was myself.

MONDAY evening, after his faithful snitch, Paulo, had left The Bureau, Media Minister Lazarito Charlado sat at his desk in front of his laptop computer and scoured the Internet for information on Russell Martell. Dirt on Russell Martell. The criminal record of Russell Martell. The sordid past of Russell Martell.

But first he had to discover who Russell Martell was, which wasn't too difficult since a North American journalist by that name had his own website. The photo resembled the gringo Lazarito had met except he was clean-faced, without a goatee or black eye... He examined the cocky white smile, the stylish wave to his hair, the accommodating oval face, and recognized something lurking behind his veracious eyes—fearless insolence. This was the same man who had questioned him at Armando Montoya's party and Arena Vallarta.

Russell Martell had attended college in the States and abroad, was fluent in English, Spanish, and Portuguese, and had become an itinerant journalist of minor repute employed by an international sports magazine based in Seattle, Washington. This didn't discount that he was also a terrorist, of course. Terrorists often lead double lives.

Lazarito broadened his investigation to include public records and a criminal search. Russell Martell was six feet tall, one hundred and ninety-five pounds, and widowed. He had married right here in Vallarta, to a local girl. Rosa Alma de Levante. She died in childbirth at Hospital Santa María, Guadalajara. Suspicious? Lazarito thought so. The mortality rate of child-bearing women in Mexico was high compared to more developed nations but childbirth resulting in the death of both mother and child was not a common occurrence. Might Russell Martell have played a hand in his own wife and child's death? The possibility fit Lazarito's developing theory of the gringo as an extortionist, assassin and terrorist.

On the other hand...

Lazarito retrieved his cell phone and texted Paulo. Police were probably questioning Rosa's family right now. His faithful snitch better keep him apprized.

The criminal record of Russell Martell: arrested for drunk and disorderly conduct on two occasions. Once when he was eighteen years old, and again ten years ago, at twenty-three. Shortly thereafter, Russell Martell was charged with assault of a bar patron. The charges were dropped. Self-defense. Nothing else in his *recorded* past suggested a propensity towards violence, but the propensity was clearly there. Did this man have the makings of a terrorist? He must, Lazarito thought. After all, his escape from jail demonstrated guilt.

What about his talent as a writer? Was he any good? Lazarito pulled up a story of his about deep-sea fishing off the coast of Costa Rica and began reading. Russell Martell appeared to be a fairly decent writer, perhaps talented. The discovery sickened Lazarito. He slumped in his chair. If the pinche gringo had a story to tell that incriminated him, he could probably tell it well enough to have the Media Minister of Puerto Vallarta arrested.

Lazarito hung his head and mulled over the fix he was in. A horrible jam. No longer would a big time story making him a big time player in bringing terrorists to justice be enough to salvage his career. Now he needed the head of a terrorist on a stick. The head of a terrorist who knew too much and how to tell it if he wasn't silenced. Russell Martell's head.

Yesterday Russell Martell came off as a cocky gringo journalist who appeared to have made some accurate assumptions about Lazarito's role in covering up police blunders. At the time, this was disconcerting, even worrisome. Publicized stories about the corruption of government officials commonly initiated a modicum of pretended public outrage from politicians, outrage smoothed over with a few payoffs. The gringo had startled Lazarito but didn't represent a dangerous threat. If Señor Martell had proved too meddlesome, Lazarito would have consorted with police to have him arrested, and then deported back to his country where he'd have had the opportunity to report his banal story to a disinterested public in the United States.

Now, however, the gringo represented something entirely different. Russell Martell was a thoroughly dangerous man. His audacious escape demonstrated knowledge of guilt, guilt of murder and terrorism. And he did appear to be a journalist. A journalist with an incriminating story to tell. A story about corruption, concealing evidence, and obstruction of justice—crimes that precipitated the bombing of the Washington Hotel. A story that could destroy Lazarito's career and his life.

Lazarito lifted his black gaze to the muted televisions across his office, the disparate images filling jagged spaces in his mind. The mere thought of incarceration set him on edge with nervous chest pangs, his heart thumping and innards churning, as if he'd already been found guilty, though he hadn't even been accused of anything yet.

Throwing Russell Martell in jail would not be good enough. He needed to be silenced. And the hijo de puta had just escaped from jail anyway!...which could be a blessing. Now he might be killed, permanently silenced in the manhunt for him.

Paulo was right. The chances were slim that the gringo would escape Vallarta alive. But what if he didn't escape Vallarta and survived in custody, survived to tell his story to federales and have it leaked to the Media and Communications Director...and the international media?

Lazarito hoisted himself out of his leather chair, waddled over to a window and opened it. Fresh air to clear his mind... Sticky, humid air...exceedingly odd weather for this time of year, weather dominated by a misty drizzle that seemed to reveal bits and pieces of a vague sky... His mind cycled over and over his possible options. As long as he remained Media Minister of Puerto Vallarta, he could squelch any testimony from the gringo that might be leaked to the media. But how long would Russell Martell remain in Vallarta if he were recaptured? Not long. He'd be transferred to Guadalajara or el DF and guarded under maximum security, beyond Lazarito's reach and influence.

The only option was to stay the course and come up with a story, but on a grander scale. Russell Martell was a terrorist, a brutal killer of innocents. It shouldn't be too difficult to come up with an earth-shattering story that would overshadow anything *El Gringo Terrorista* had to say, focus attention on his crimes and paint him as a liar as well as a mass murderer.

Media Minister Charlado didn't generally write for the papers or media websites anymore. He might occasionally scribe an editorial for the Vallarta Diaro or a Guadalajara newspaper or two, and as Media Minister he determined the content of the news coming out of Vallarta, but his days as a reporter were long gone. Nowadays when he had a scoop, Lazarito outlined his take on it and handed it over to any one of a number of reporters in Vallarta or Guadalajara, or, as circumstances dictated, simply leaked the story to the appropriate media outlet. However, now he envisioned himself writing a story of international import for the Vallarta Diario. A story about El Gringo Terrorista, Russell Martell, who brought death and destruction down upon Puerto Vallarta. Russell Martell's motive for his act of terror was unclear, but Lazarito would discover one (was Señor Martell a Muslim fanatic linked to the death of that Iranian terrorist and obsessed with killing North American infidels in the Washington Hotel? Or maybe a racist right-wing anti-immigration fanatic who struck Mexico for political reasons, perhaps because of unfettered Mexican immigration into the USA? Was he a 21st century Timothy McVeigh who murdered his own countrymen in the Washington Hotel for supporting Mexico with tourist dollars...?).

SEVE VERDAD

Lazarito brought a pensive hand to his chin and recovered a few lost threads of his thoughts. Señor Martell was at Armando Montoya's party. This was key. It meant that if he didn't personally know Armando Montoya he certainly arrived with someone who did, someone who might lead Lazarito to him... And the gringo seemed at ease at the party, at least he did in the living room where they had their second encounter of the day...gregarious, talking as if amongst friends, and unafraid of taking jabs at Lazarito himself...almost like he was showing off, trying to impress...

Lazarito drew a sanguine breath. Things were coming clear within this odd evening mist. Brenda was with them in the living room. Brenda...Valencia. The only woman in their group. Lazarito's heart bunny hopped at the thought of her. That was one sexy mamacita. Smart too. He couldn't blame Señor Martell for trying to impress her. Well, Lazarito would soon make his own impression upon the sultry wench. He had the perfect reason to contact her. She was associated with the suspect. As Lazarito withdrew from the group, he had overheard Brenda refer to a story the gringo had written—*"Pretty good Russell..."*

Lazarito slid the window shut, hitched up his slacks, and waddled over to his desk to make a phone call. He would find out all about this Brenda...

The fax machine came to life in his secretary's office, its distinct whirl and hum breaking the silence in The Bureau. Lazarito retrieved the reading glasses on his desk and waddled into his secretary's office.

The moment he laid eyes on the fax he was filled with such anxious surprise he had to have a seat at his secretary's desk to steady himself. If The Bureau's walls had come tumbling down upon him, Lazarito couldn't have been more stupefied. He laid the fax flat on the desk, slapped on his reading glasses, and flicked on the desk lamp. The florescent overhead lighting wasn't sufficient. Media Minister Charlado wanted to study this astonishing tip carefully, make sure there was no mistake.

Who could have sent this?!? He quickly perused the pages. Two pages. Nothing identified the sender. He checked the caller ID on his fax machine. Blocked. An anonymous fax containing an astonishing tip. Astonishing information. Lazarito had never received anything quite like it before, certainly not gratis. He had just paid Paulo three thousand pesos for much less! Of course if Paulo ended up killing El Gringo Terrorista it would be worth it.

The fax didn't have a cover page so the first thing that had caught his eye was the photo. Lazarito recognized the oval face, the symmetrical Anglo features, the thick brown hair and amused green eyes. The wide neck and muscular jaw. The full mouth. It was Russell Martell all right. The photo looked similar to the one on his website. And beneath the photo, in large black block lettering, were the words **SE BUSCA**. (Wanted.)

Lazarito read and reread the charges—Russell Martell's alleged criminal history—in wide-eyed detail, nodding intermittently with a squealing "hummm." Increíble! He was very impressed. Impressed with himself most of all. He had intuited some of this. The fax provided missing pieces to the story germinating in Lazarito's brain. An earth-shattering story that would save his career and perhaps elevate him into the highest echelons of political power...if he publicized it before someone else did.

Had this information been sent to someone else? He waddled back into his office, fax and reading glasses in hand, and glanced about at his television screens. Might this picture of Russell Martell appear at any moment along with commentary on the charges mentioned in the fax? Had police received the fax?

Lazarito made for his desk, retrieved the remote, and punched the volume to the large flat-screen TV opposite him. A live report from Stadium Sport Park across the street from ground zero. Lights were being dismantled for use on the ruins...

He had to publish right away, before someone else could take credit for the story. Before the Media and Communications Director arrived tomorrow.

Lazarito took a seat at his desk and made a few clicks and shifts on his computer. The screen flashed to a blank page, cursor blinking, set to receive prose. His hands froze on the keypad as he considered another option: Should he have Guadalajara's channel 13 news publicize it all right now? What about his promise to Gloria not to mention anything about a terror attack for twenty-four hours? did the prisoner's escape alter their agreement? Should he contact Gloria before doing anything? or maybe Paulo, to find out if the fax had been received at police headquarters...?

Just get started on the story right away, he told himself, and see to it that it's on the front page of tomorrow's edition of the Vallarta Diario. Twenty-four hours will have passed by then...almost...and I will have adhered to my agreement with Gloria...practically...

But could he have confidence in the source of the fax? Lazarito had intuited some of its information but had encountered nothing online to support these allegations.

He needed independent support for the information. Lazarito scrutinized the short paragraph at the end. It stated that Russell Martell had a room at Casa Mexicana and might be expected to return there now that he had escaped from jail after his attack on the Washington. Whoever sent the fax must be very well informed. Not many knew there was a suspect at all for the bombing of the Washington let alone an escaped prisoner named Russell Martell.

And Paulo said that the gringo had claimed to be staying at the Washington.

Lazarito found the number for Casa Mexicana online. If reception confirmed that Russell Martell was staying there, that would lend credence to the other information contained in the fax. As he reached for his landline phone, his cell phone sounded right beside it. A slice of mariachi music. He answered with a terse, "Diga."

Lazarito recognized the sketchy voice of authority on the other end of the line, a voice he hadn't heard in a couple of days, and immediately modulated his tone: "Señor Comandante. A pleasure to hear your voice again, though I wish it were under better circumstances."

"So do I Lazarito. Puta madre. I am on my way back to Vallarta to resume my duties right now."

"I heard about your sudden leave of absence, Comandante. Most unfortunate. We have been in dire straits since your departure. Where are you now? Have you been brought up to date?"

"Just north of Vallarta—fifteen minutes from headquarters. What a fucking disaster. And the mayor has just informed me that the one and only suspect has escaped! I am sure you, Lazarito, with all your sources, are also aware of this."

"Interesting you should mention that, Héctor. I believe we can be of assistance to one another on that particular issue."

"Have you spoken to Lieutenant Romero?"

"Not recently, no. It appears that the lieutenant, given his precarious and, how shall we say...embarrassing position, is not willing to avail himself of the media just yet."

"Pinche puto. Tell me what you have, Lazarito, and we can work out the details later. I know I still owe you for postponing that story on the raid but I need something to go on before I get to headquarters, something on the escaped prisoner."

Lazarito digressed coyly: "Like his name?"

Héctor raised his voice a notch: "I already know his name, Lazarito. And so do you I wager. Híjole. But the mayor told me that nobody at headquarters seems to know much if anything else about him."

Lazarito hummed agreeably, "Is that so...?" El comandante had just confirmed that the fax had not been received at police headquarters.

318

"They know very little, Lazarito, aside from the fact that he is a supposed journalist."

Lazarito fingered the fax on his desk. "I would not count on journalism as his principal profession, Héctor. But I do believe I have a lead into his whereabouts that just might interest you."

54

GLORIA greeted the girls at police dispatch and charged down the hall, the heels of her boots sparking the tile floor. The hall opened up into the spacious, brightly lit processing room where she stopped short and fixed on her husband perched upon the booking counter, a team of men (and Sandra) seated before him. Juan was in full spate:

"...laid out two of our men here," the mayor extended a hand to the center of his team, "another just beyond the cell block door here," hand pointed off to the right, "sprung our prisoner and spirited him back through el comandante's office," a gesture dead ahead, "where copies of the suspect's fingerprints and the mug-shot camera were stolen from the locked desk; then, we assume, they repelled out the window."

Gloria stepped to the open office door to her left and looked inside. But for the shattered window, nothing looked amiss or disturbed—ashtray, computer monitor, notepad and lonely pen stand on the desk, bookshelves in order against the wall. She entered and examined the desk drawers...all closed, without a sign of forced entry. "Amazing," she muttered and peered out the window, nearly a ten-meter drop, "Increíble." The steel security bars looked to have been melted from their moorings at one end on the exterior wall, pried loose at the other. They hung uselessly by their two remaining anchors, bent and mangled.

Gloria returned to the processing room and glanced about the pitifully angry faces staring up at her husband, unfamiliar faces aside from her friend, Immigration Inspector Sandra Villanueva, still in her dust-filled blue pantsuit, and Lieutenant Romero: eight uniformed police officers, including the lieutenant, and four suits—three blue and one gray—sullied from rummaging around the Washington ruins, all tieless (Gloria assumed they were the DF federale investigators and the CISEN man her husband had told her were due in town this afternoon)... The mayor's jeans were soiled, but he wore a clean brown button-down shirt.

SEVE VERDAD

Mayor Juan Pacífico Velázquez acknowledged his wife with a nod in her direction. "It is fortunate," he said, eyes directed at his troops, "that no one was injured by what appears to have been a car bomb." Juan dropped his gaze to the front row. "Minor injuries were sustained by the felled officers here in the processing room however, and none of you remembers seeing a damn thing?"

Three uniforms seated in front stirred uncomfortably, shook their heads and grumbled, "No, híjole," "Puta, no," and "Ching, no."

"Apparently there was a blackout..." the mayor deadpanned his wife, offering a touch of irony that belied the gravity of the situation, "...a power surge and outage which, along with the car bomb, seems to have facilitated the prisoner's escape. The power outage also crashed our computers, leaving us without our suspect's downloaded mug shots. And now," he returned his gaze to the front row, "you all suffer from stiff necks and headaches."

Nervous shifting and grumbles here and there, the three officers in question insisting they were fine.

Juan pointed off to his right. "And the cellblock door was closed when you approached it during the blackout, Officer Contreras?"

"Sí."

"So you had separated yourself from the other two officers and were attacked from behind after they were felled."

"Parece que sí." Seems so. "I think I heard something, but before I could even turn and shine my light behind me..." Officer Contreras grimaced with chagrin and massaged the back of his neck.

"I see." The mayor kept his disdain well hidden behind a serene veneer, an actor's aplomb. He had already played the heavy when he upbraided the lieutenant for what he considered a lapse in duty—allowing the prisoner to escape—and needn't risk alienating Officer Contreras or the other two officers who had been overpowered by playing the role once again. Between the botched raid, the unforgivable massacre at the Washington this morning, and the suspect's escape, the Puerto Vallarta Police Department had been severely humiliated. If he treated these men too harshly there might be a drop in morale which, in spite of it all, remained high. None were giving up. Far from it. All were chomping at the bit to recapture or kill Russell Martell (the mayor supported the lieutenant's authorization of deadly force as a last resort). The attack on the Washington was an attack on each and every one of them and their natural, justified, and appropriate reaction was to fight back, strike some blows for their side. There was still opportunity for the police department to regain at least a measure of prestige, if everyone worked together.

Gloria said, "Evidently, Señor Martell's accomplices are highly trained. This was a well-conceived and executed plan of escape."

Everyone's attention shifted to the woman flanking them. Gloria stood at the perimeter of the processing room, leather bag draped over a shoulder, her narrow umber eyes surveying the troops before her with respect. Her dusty clothes indicated she had spent her share of time down at ground zero, but her face and golden locks had a luster to them, like her voice. Subtly captivating.

Garras fixed his fiery blue eyes on this woman of sublime authority; Gloria held his gaze without a hint of submission. Garras knew who she was, had reviewed CISEN's dossier on her in Guadalajara before leaving for Vallarta, and wasn't surprised to find her here given her influence in the mayor's career. "His escape demonstrates knowledge of guilt," he said brusquely. "We discussed this before your arrival, señora. The car bomb, power outage, and the window broken from the outside all point to accomplices, well-trained accomplices who were prepared to break him out of jail, and perhaps anyone else in their terrorist gang we might have gotten our hands on."

Gloria knitted her brow and shook her head in bitter disbelief. Garras turned his attention to the group as a whole. "Given the scenario the mayor and I have just reviewed, we have to consider the possibility of at least two or more accomplices."

Everyone confirmed this last observation with assenting grunts and words, except the lieutenant.

Lieutenant Benito Cuevas Romero, a man Garras had come to know over the years as a talented, level-headed officer, was uncharacteristically sullen, still stewing over the upbraiding the mayor had given him for allowing the prisoner to escape. Garras would have liked to come to his defense but knew it wasn't his place to do so. And the lieutenant had been in charge. The buck stopped with him. Yet Garras felt that the mayor was going overboard to protect his own ass and passing the buck himself. As Mayor of a town in a state of emergency, Señor Velázquez should have seen to it himself that police headquarters was better secured.

How *did* the lieutenant let the prisoner escape? Well, he told the mayor he was returning to headquarters from ground zero when it happened. The car bomb went off before his eyes! The man who was in charge at headquarters at the time, Officer Paulo Pepino Revueltas, had been granted relief but had evidently left his post without securing it adequately and...etcetera, etcetera.

When the mayor had finished with Lieutenant Romero, Garras took Benito aside and told him that the pinche ranking officer at headquarters who had left his post without securing it should have his throat ripped out. The lieutenant agreed.

Juan slid off of the booking counter and pointed over heads to Gloria. "This is my wife, Gloria, for those of you who do not know. Anything new on that disc, Gloria?"

"Nothing that might help in recapturing Russell Martell. The disc's contents can be better monitored and examined here, where we can work in shifts. So Pedro and Officer Mendoza will deliver it and Pedro's computer to headquarters shortly."

The mayor extended a hand toward Garras and the federale investigators. "From left to right these men in blue are Federale Investigators Herrera, Barrera, and Sándovar, along with the man in gray at the end, CISEN's Joaquín de Jesús. We are also expecting Comandante Pasqual to join us at any moment."

The investigators gave Gloria courtesy nods. She said, "Un placer." and considered the CISEN man. His thick carnivorous lips, broad imperial nose, and wide, creased brow advanced an expression of perpetual impatience with the incompetence of local officials. And his eyes were a blue of such vitality Gloria doubted their authenticity. She didn't doubt the authenticity of the man however. He just struck her as violently aggressive and wondered how this would affect his judgment in what should be a dispassionate investigation. As for the federale investigators, they were nondescript men of regular features— dark eyes and complexion, black hair. Clean shaven, like the CISEN man. The three of them together couldn't match the CISEN man's energy or intensity. Next to him they looked like junior-league footballers awaiting a chance to take the field.

Gloria knew that everyone in Mexico, aside from high-powered políticos and judges, was junior league compared to CISEN.

The mayor retrieved a sheet of paper from the booking counter and passed it forward. "We have some good news, Gloria," he said. "Sandra has matched our suspect's fingerprints and verified his identity. His name and photo have been faxed to the Media and Communications Center in el DF and will soon be broadcasted all over the nation and the world." Juan raised a triumphant finger. "And all roadblocks leading out of Vallarta have copies of this flier along with a current description of Russell Martell provided by Lieutenant Romero."

"Current description?" Gloria accepted the flier from Sandra and wrinkled her nose at it. "Where are his mug shots?"

Juan opened his mouth to reply but Sandra intervened: "I never received an e-mail of his mug shots."

Gloria's eyes flashed at Lieutenant Romero. "I thought—"

"I instructed Lula to e-mail them," said the lieutenant. "But somehow they were..." He searched Sandra's face for help. She obliged and finished his sentence: "Lost in transmission."

Sandra added a sharp note of dismay to her voice as she met Gloria's befuddled gaze. "There have been some strange happenings in cyberspace today."

Gloria said, "Really?" more statement than question.

"Apparently, it all started with some glitches at the television transmission station here in Vallarta this morning. Computer links were compromised and unauthorized video footage was transmitted on national television without the knowledge of censors at the Media and Communications Center in el DF."

"A bizarre striptease," Juan said, "by women in burkas that has also infected the Internet." Wry chuckles rippled through the room. "Someone has a peculiar sense of humor."

Sandra cocked her head at the mayor. "I believe there is more to it than that, señor," she said, eyes back on Gloria. "I received mug shots but, as it turned out, of a drug dealer arrested in Vallarta last year, not of Russell Martell, though Lula insists she sent me the correct photos. Computer data here at headquarters may have been compromised before the blackout. Computer files at Immigration and the airport have been compromised—data either lost completely or jumbled and indecipherable."

"A virus?"

"I would think so, Gloria. Makes you wonder how we ever got along without computers. I was finally able to match the suspect's faxed fingerprints though, not to any found in the Jeep but he is in fact Russell Martell, a North American journalist who was married to a local Vallarta girl. She died in childbirth last year. At Santa María Hospital, Guadalajara. The baby died as well. Immigration officers accompanied police to her parent's house here in Vallarta and found them at home. They both insist that Russell Martell must be innocent and have no idea where he is."

"Or *who* he *really* is," the lieutenant clarified, "—a terrorist."

Sandra nodded noncommittally.

Gloria felt herself distracted as she stared at the flier in her hand, the picture of Russell Martell. Was he the assassin? A terrorist? The author of the disc? Might he be behind these computer malfunctions? "So Russell Martell does not look like this right now?" she said to no one in particular.

"He had facial hair and a black eye when I interrogated him," Lieutenant Romero huffed derisively, "Russell Martell uses that photo for his website. Looks like a publicity shot."

SEVE VERDAD

"A publicity shot for putos," grumbled an officer in the front row. The remark elicited short laughter from the men seated around him.

"Cálmense muchachos," said the mayor. "We do not need to underestimate this man again. If you laugh now it may be at your own expense." The mayor's team grew quiet. "Our sketch artist is in Acapulco, Gloria. But one should be arriving from Tepic this evening. Lieutenant Romero and the arresting officer will be called upon to help him construct an accurate current image of Russell Martell." The mayor paced the length of the booking counter. "Publicly, Señor Martell is wanted for drug trafficking and arson related to the disaster at the Washington. He is considered armed and dangerous. As of yet, however, and I have discussed this with our Media Minister, there is still to be no mention of a bomb going off or terrorists at large. Is that understood?" Concordant nods and vocal agreement all around. "There is no need to cause panic when we have barely begun an investigation and have not come to any positive conclusions about what the hell happened at the Washington today."

Federale Investigator Sándovar spoke up: "From what I understand, Russell Martell's capture was not made public, so his escape need not be. It is enough that the public and law enforcement know he is at large."

"Hopefully we will recapture him tonight," said Investigator Barrera, "and then tomorrow we can decide how to play it in the media."

"Agreed," said the mayor. "I have instructed our Media Minister to only publicize that our suspect, Russell Martell, is at large and that he may have accomplices, and not to mention anything about his arrest or escape...yet."

An onerous bellow from the CISEN man cut through the chatter: "We need to recapture him quickly and round up his accomplices." Garras stared around the room, captivating the eyes of most everyone. "The longer we delay, the more time he has to put distance between himself and Vallarta. And in order to recapture him quickly, we need reliable information as to his whereabouts. Getting the word out about this man will help, but nothing can replace legwork. We have leads to follow. I recommend we revisit his dead-wife's family, and find the two men who witnessed him with that dying woman at ground zero. Any one of them may then provide us with another source of information. You never know where a valuable source may come from and—"

Suddenly a new voice entered the fray. A theatrical response to the CISEN man's directives. "Your source has arrived," said Héctor Diamante Pasqual.

Garras swiveled his head around at the disheveled man entering the processing room. The mayor stepped forward to greet Héctor. "Comandante. A pleasure to have you back. We need all the help we can get."

El comandante shook the mayor's hand with solemn words of condolence: "I cannot begin to express my grief and sorrow upon hearing the news this morning."

Garras needed some clarification: "You know where the suspect is holed up, Comandante?"

Héctor replied expansively in an effort to reassert his authority as Comandante of the Puerto Vallarta Police Department. "No," he said. "But I do have a lead on him, a place to start looking for clues as to his whereabouts. The name of his hotel here in Vallarta..."

55

CHIMP came away from his meeting with Lazarito richer in pesos and seeing dollar signs. Dollar signs within the misty evening drizzle, dollar signs stamped on every traffic signal and tail light on the way back to his apartment. The Media Minister's offer of a bounty for the head of Russell Martell infused him with wistful greed to accompany his aching desire for vengeance.

Vengeance, the hard and immediate lust for blood, Russell Martell's blood, boiled the blood coursing through Chimp's veins. Vengeance for the blood the gringo terrorista had shed at the Washington. Vengeance for his infuriating escape from jail... And the lieutenant blamed *him* for the prisoner's escape! told him to stay at home, practically relieved him from duty! Chingá!

Chimp was bound and determined to redeem himself; delusions of grandeur filled his bulbous head at the prospect of redemption, swamped his primitive brain. When he had that terrorist's head on a stick, when vengeance was his, not only would he collect Lazarito's bounty but the Media Minister would make him famous, a media star. Wealth, fame, and power were his for the taking.

Chimp parked at his apartment complex and pounded the steering wheel. He needed to get back on duty right away. His cousin, Manco, had a lead for him, was waiting to guide him to a house where the gringo was seen last night and might very well return to meet his girlfriend...maybe hide out.

He imagined himself blasting Russell Martell's head away, catching him off guard and...BLAM! gringo terrorista brains splattered across the morning news. But that maldito terrorista was a dangerous hijo de puta and had accomplices, more than a girlfriend to shelter and protect him. Chimp wanted to be the one to blow his brains out but couldn't deny he needed backup. Armed and trained backup. Backup Manco was not capable of giving him. Chimp needed police backup and wished to God he could get back on duty and get it.

His cell phone sounded and Chimp's wish was granted, from a most unexpected source: el comandante. Back in town and taking over for the lieutenant.

"Get back on duty right away, Paulo. The lieutenant was way out of line to relieve you. We need every man right now."

"Sí Comandante. Gracias Comandante."

"The suspect may have returned to his room at Casa Mexicana after his escape and I am gathering a team to raid it. I expect you at headquarters immediately."

Chimp's pulse quickened, his response constricted in his throat. He didn't want to disobey el comandante, couldn't disobey el comandante, but he just had to take advantage of this opportunity to follow his own designs, follow his own lead on the terrorist. And the best way to do that was to simply come right out and say so: "I also have a lead into the suspect's whereabouts, señor."

"Really? And what is that?"

"A house where he was seen last night, señor."

"Your source?"

"One of the men who led me to him at ground zero, señor. And I also understand that the gringo may have family here in Vallarta, family by marriage—"

"Los Levante. Police have followed up on that lead, Paulo. Nothing has come of it yet. But what is this about a house the gringo was seen at last night?"

"All I need is a squad car and a partner, señor, to do surveillance and—"

"Where are you now?"

"My apartment, señor."

"Bueno. We need to follow every lead. Officer Contreras will pick you up shortly. And keep me posted. If you locate the suspect contact me right away before doing anything. We cannot afford any more foul-ups. Por Dios, we have had enough."

56

BRENDA climbed the steep winding stairs leading to the villas overlooking the bay as if they were part of her workout routine, which they were when she was in Vallarta. She often jogged along Playa de los Muertos, then took the steps one or two at a time up to the highway, picked them up again on the other side, and continued clear on up to Armando's house without breaking stride. Naturally, if she wasn't working out she liked to pause here and there to enjoy the view, face the ocean breeze wafting inland like a pleasant melody and take a breather. Not tonight though. There couldn't possibly be anything pleasing about the view tonight, unless you enjoyed reliving the pain and suffering of others. Brenda had spent the entire day helping tend the injured at ground zero. Why look back for the open wound scarring Vallarta's coastline? Better to keep her legs pumping and lose herself in exercise.

Yet she did look back. Why? Curiosity perhaps, and fatigue. An uncommon tightness cramping her back and legs gave her pause, a sharp reminder that the day's traumas had pushed her to the limit. A grueling, miserable day. The most vile day of her life. Brenda's breathing labored as she crested the steps, heavy with intimate, surreal burdens. Incomprehensible burdens. Unreal burdens. Were they unreal? Could she wish the day away like a waking dream? Had it all been a barbarous, unconscionable nightmare?

The view from her perch above Vallarta reaffirmed the brutal truth. A low drizzly sky dulled the city lights and, north of the malecón, a deathly hole blackened the coastline. A smoky hole that gobbled up the artificial light shining upon it. A hole as deep and acute as the hole in the pit of her stomach.

"Sickening," she said in English and turned her back on the cruel, depressing sight.

Brenda strode through the vaporous drizzle towards the meager light of a streetlamp and the trail that snaked amongst the woods to Armando's place. The air was warm and thick yet she felt chilled, as though battling a fever in a cold sweat. She thought the weather eerie, unseasonable and haunting. Appropriate for her morbid state of mind. How many dead bodies had she seen today, really seen and recognized as dead? Amidst the chaos and destruction everything seemed a blur. It was hard to place a number on it. About a dozen, she imagined. It wasn't like they were piled one on top of the other like you might see in a war movie. Most of the dead were still buried beneath the rubble...along with survivors, and those who would soon be dead... Had she seen more than a dozen dead today? Probably, especially counting those in critical condition, at death's door, like the two bodies in that demolished car Bizco discovered this morning.

Bizco had dragged her to the car by the end of his leash and let out a flurry of pitched barks, as if he'd treed a wild animal. Brenda spied a motionless body inside the car as Armando, alerted by Bizco's alarm, joined them. A plateau of rubble and debris partially interred the vehicle, completely covered the rear end and tapered down around the windows on each side. The smashed roof was exposed, and two enormous concrete boulders encased the car's hood. Between the boulders, behind the shattered windshield, a body was visible.

Armando instantly came up with a method to free the victim. The necessary tool was close at hand—a warped steel crossbeam lying on the ground just off the car's front bumper. He hoisted it overhead, wedged it between the massive blocks of concrete encasing the vehicle's frontend, anchored his feet at the wheel-well and, using the beam as a lever, tumbled one of the boulders off and away from the vehicle. An astounding feat of strength that took all of ten seconds for him to accomplish.

Brenda was flabbergasted, as were two firemen who arrived at the scene to offer assistance only to find themselves gasping and gaping behind their protective visors at Mountain's Herculean performance. The man had handled a thick two-meter solid-steel beam like a baton and a concrete boulder the size of a minivan like a child's building block.

Two bodies were recovered from the wreckage. A man and a woman, each bleeding profusely from deep gashes in their heads where the roof had caved in on them. The firemen pronounced them alive but they sure looked dead. The sight of them forced Brenda to retreat within a sudden wave of nausea. She strangled a couple of dry heaves, cursing herself for her weakness. She didn't get sick again at ground zero.

Brenda stepped up onto the darkened trail leading to Armando La Montaña Montoya's house, lightened her pace, and slowly converged with her opaque surroundings—the silhouettes and vapid spaces. She knew this path well, a fairly even grade—not too tricky, unless you tried to sprint it in pitched darkness. Brenda took her time and let her eyes adjust to the ghostly light filtering through the woods from neighboring houses. She had chosen this route instead of the lighted street, not because it was a shortcut to Armando's place, but because she felt the need to sheathe herself in obscurity and hide from the day's cruelties... Or was it a macabre instinct? a selfless desire to share a hint of the darkness few would escape alive inside the blackened tomb that was once the Washington Hotel...?

At times during the day, Brenda felt numbed to the carnage as she helped tend the wounded, as if viewing herself from above, watching herself react in a crisis—a nightmare. The only thing to do was act and react. There hadn't been an opportunity to internalize everything like she was right now. She caught a whiff of blood and came to a stop to shake the swoon from her head. She'd never considered blood to have a particular smell beyond that of a butcher shop or the occasional fish she gutted. But now blood's visceral scent meshed with the acrid chalky stench of destruction, that infernal dust she'd been toiling in the past ten hours. She could still smell it on her clothes and body.

Brenda stared through the chain-link fence bordering Armando's property, up the clearing to the house. The lights were on and she could make out the deck. The place didn't look like much from down here. A cute home nestled in the woods. A deceiving perspective. It was a good sized house, plenty big enough to raise a family. Her sister's new home. Ara and Armando's new home.

This should be a time for rejoicing in the union of a young couple and the birth of a family. A celebration of love. Instead it was a time for grief, sorrow and pain. Just like...like when she was to be married.

Brenda's heart sank into that hole in the pit of her stomach. Her next breath brought a moan of throbbing despair, and nausea. The noxious stench of death overtook her and she let loose with a violent retch, her vomit spilling through the chain-link fence. She fell to her knees and sobbed, her soul awash in memories of her dead lover. Her murdered fiancé.

Ricardo had been flashing in and out of her thoughts throughout the day and was now vivid in her mind's eye. His taciturn, thoughtful expression gave way to an easy, disarming smile, his chiseled jaw, stern brow and rugged exterior a decoy to set her up for his charms and sharp wit. Brenda had fallen for those charms almost immediately...love at first sight. And he fell for her too, unafraid to reveal his vulnerabilities and willing to give of himself completely when he asked her, his mariposa, to marry him.

Their engagement was short, senselessly and brutally ended when AA Flight 3356 crashed into the ocean.

Ricky's death plunged Brenda into a ghastly depression. An endless drone of confusion and agony. In an instant, her dreams had been shattered and with them life's meaning. She wandered aimlessly through life...like a child huddled in the woods, hiding in a thicket as war raged and stole from her her most precious gifts.

Like so many under similar circumstances, Brenda not only survived but came back strong. She was hitting her stride in life again when today, once more, terror struck her down. Right here in Vallarta she was reliving the nightmare.

She choked back her hot tears, popped to her feet and clutched the fence bordering Armando's property as though encaged, held prisoner by the ruthless killers responsible for her torment. Were the same bastards who killed Ricardo responsible for today's carnage? Were the heathen scum destroying her life again? She didn't doubt it. The possibility had crossed her mind several times today but she'd kept it to herself amidst all the speculation and rumors flying about. Yet now, at this point in the evening, it all made sense. Her life, and perhaps her death, were inextricably linked to terrorists. Evidence had been slowly coming to light that Islamic fanatics had downed her fiancé's plane and now, it seemed to her, the same sick, bloodthirsty terrorists who had killed him were responsible for the carnage at the Washington.

Like Ricky's plane, the Washington had been full of American tourists, a natural target for the fanatical Muslim beasts; and the animals were proud of their work. You could see and hear it in their rhetoric over the years, since well before the 9/11 attacks in the United States or her fiancé's death. Brenda could hear them calling for the death of infidels, the fervent cheers and righteous bullshit, the religiously fanatic crowds spewing hatred... She saw the fisted fascist salutes, the flag burnings, and the veiled, subjugated women joining the frenzy as if they had something to gain by the sufferings of others, as if they could hope to gain anything at all in their backward, pathetic societies.

All at once, weakness was not an option. Brenda set her jaw and steeled herself with a tug on the brim of her cap. She wouldn't let these inhuman, subhuman barbarians get the best of her again. She refused to be that child huddled in the woods. Brenda vowed right then and there to fight back. She had the strength to do so, and knew where to turn to find the means.

57

THE cabby and I were parked two blocks and around a corner from Mountain's house, below a Spanish-style villa and across from the globular light of a streetlamp. The misty drizzle reminded me more of Monterey, California, than Vallarta, except it was warm. I had my window down, as did the cabby. He was under the impression that Johnny had gone to fetch his girlfriend in the villa but Johnny was really off to retrieve my room key and Mountain's cell number.

I'd told Johnny to be cool and quick, but not to hurry. Johnny strolled around the corner like a man checking out babes on the beach.

The cabby and I had exchanged little more than a handful of words since he picked me and Johnny up. He didn't speak English. That's what he told me at any rate. Just enough to get the tourists around, like most cabbies in Vallarta. Right away I made it clear that my Spanish was fluent and I was sick of that sickening news on the radio, "The same sickening news everyone has heard all day," I said with grieving angst, honest emotion to mask the motive behind my complaint. The last thing I needed was to have to knock the cabby out and jack his car after hearing my name and description announced over the airwaves. He turned the car radio off and, other than my directions to him, silence dominated the mood inside the cab. Grim silence. The cabby didn't seem to think twice about keeping the radio off, like he'd been sickened enough by the day's news himself. Good thing for him.

He'd yet to look me over but I'd sized him up some: over the hill at fifty or so, well fed. Kept his family well fed. I could knock him out in the blink of an eye. In fact, he looked to be half out right now, shoulders stooped and head listing. A long, brutal day...

It didn't appear that Johnny and I had made much of an impression on him. Devo was right. Everyone looked the same around Vallarta tonight, through the cabby's eyes and tens of thousands of others. How precarious was my position? It figured to be pretty damn precarious. Had my jailbreak made news yet? Was *Russell Martell* wanted for terrorism in connection with an attack on the Washington Hotel? The answers to both those questions had to be yes, didn't they? And what about the cabby? Wouldn't he have heard about me, recognized me from a description on the radio? A sharp tingle of suspicion ran down my spine. Might he have signaled for help on his cell phone without me noticing? pressed an emergency button or something...? He'd contacted dispatch on the way up here—on speaker. Could Johnny and I be walking into a trap? I balled my fist and fixed on the gray at his temples. *One clean shot and lights out...*

The cabby extended a lethargic hand to his rearview mirror and grazed the image of the Virgen de Guadeloupe dangling below it. Then he brought his fingertips to his lips and crossed himself before hanging his head in silent prayer. The simple gesture pacified me...and offered an opening to test him, see how much he knew. "Que disastre," I sighed sadly. "A terrible, horrible tragedy."

SEVE VERDAD

The back of his head rocked lazily from one side to the other before stabilizing, as though on a spring. "A terrible tragedy for everyone," he said.

I leaned forward in a show of empathy. He continued: "Many turistas were killed. Estadounidense turistas. Hundreds. Your paisanos, no?"

I averted his eyes in the rearview mirror. "There must have been victims from other countries as well," I said and reclined. "From México, your paisanos."

The cabby glanced over his shoulder at me, then stared vacantly out the front windshield, his voice small: "Two taxis from the Washington have been missing since this morning."

"Friends of yours?"

"I know them."

"Lo siento mucho." I'm very sorry.

"*Rayos*. The only thing to do about it is work." The cabby raised his voice slightly, "Especially now. Transportation is difficult. Taxis are needed..." He stiffened and crossed his arms over his chest in a show of quiet resolve.

Silence was appropriate and welcome. This cabby didn't appear to be on the lookout for a wanted man. So far, I'd been lucky. Some cabs in Vallarta include a CB radio. This one didn't. If he were to receive news about an escaped prisoner, it would come over the car radio or his cell phone in its cradle on the dash. The car radio remained off so that left his phone. I had to be ready to strike if it sounded or he reached for it... What if he reached for it while he was driving? And even if he got a description of Russell Martell, would he match it to me, know I was him? Could I take the chance he wouldn't? My toes bunched on the floor mat, my fingers digging into the seat. Should I just go ahead and knock this guy out now and jack his car? or would that be a rash act...*another* rash act?

I'd taken a rash gamble jumping into this cab with Johnny in the first place. Did it without thinking much. Just followed my instincts, instincts that told me it was time to take control of my destiny. I had a bit of time to think things through now though...and boy was I disgusted with my improvised plan. What the hell was I thinkin'?!? Sure I'd been smart enough to keep the name of my hotel from the lieutenant. And, on the face of it, it seemed reasonable to salvage my IDs, electronics and cash before the cops got to them. Then I could hoof it north, catch a bus or two to Tepic and keep right on going until I reached the border. But the cops had my mug shots and fingerprints and had probably verified my identity by now. My name and face must be all over TV news casts and the Internet—*Se Busca: El Gringo*

Terrorista! Wouldn't someone at Casa Mexicana have called police to inform them that the infamous Russell Martell had booked a room in their hotel? Wouldn't cops be waiting for me if I returned there?!?

According to Devo, my arrest "had not been confirmed or denied." So if I had attempted a return to my room immediately after my escape, I might have gotten away with recovering my belongings. Reception at Casa Mexicana wouldn't have recognized me as anyone other than a guest who had misplaced his room key. But too much time had passed at this point. Any attempt to return to my room was clearly suicide. My escape had to be big news. Employees at Casa Mexicana must be on the lookout for me, cops ready to raid my room.

What the hell was I doing?!? Johnny and I shouldn't even be here right now! For what? My room key? Mountain's cell number? I'd love to contact Mountain but, could he help me? And what use was my room key? I couldn't risk going back to my hotel now!

Or could I? As long as Johnny delivered my key to me and I didn't have to expose myself at reception to request a spare, surely I could backside Casa Mexicana from the coast and scout out the hotel to make sure all was clear before attempting to get into my room.

I brought a chastening fist to my forehead and cursed myself— my stupidity and indecision, and for asking Johnny to help me before I'd thought this through. I dropped my head as though in silent prayer, so as not to alert the cabby to my violent turmoil. He stirred but said nothing.

I always knew Johnny had balls. Then again, he knew I had some solid cojones as well. Helped him with an emergency midnight harvest and transport once.

Where's that fine line between bravery and stupidity?

What good are balls when your mission is doomed to begin with? Yet Johnny took me at my word and was willing to take risks for me...

Johnny's loyalty made me feel grateful and ashamed all at once.

The cabby's cell phone rang, gave me a start. I drew my fist back, my breath high against the rising pulse in my throat. Was this it? word of my escape to all Vallarta cabbies? He reached out and pressed speaker. Dispatch said something about him going to pick up a fare in Gaviotas after he dropped his passengers. He rang off abruptly with a "bueno" and slouched in the driver's seat. "Work will never end tonight," he said.

I dropped my fist into the palm of my hand and held it there, rigid and restrained. This guy had no idea how close he'd come to getting clobbered. My entire body felt electrified, poised for both fight and flight, like I could drive this cab through a hail of bullets and speed on into the night in flames forever...pain be damned...

Pain. Aches and pains. The food and drink in El Cabezón and this new adrenalin rush had masked them but they were sure to return in force. The morning after was bound to hurt worse than four quarters of tackle football and a millennium hangover combined.

Don't think about tomorrow's game! You've got another half left tonight!

More like another fifteen rounds. All things considered, I felt strong. Like a boxer who fights harder at the sight of his own blood, the beating I'd taken steeled my determination.

Sadistic fucking Chimp.

"Pain in the ass" had acquired new meaning for me. But that damn golf ball was my weakest spot. It had taken root in my skull—planted and unplayable. The only relief I'd get was when the bitch oozed out my ear, or was iced.

The cabby started up the car and turned on his headlights. Johnny had rounded the corner.

58

CHIMP, Fat Cop, and Manco were sitting in a late model black and white Pontiac parked across the street from Mountain's place, about a block away. A large walnut tree, its branches drooping in the liquid night air, buffered their position against the curb.

Manco scratched his armpit creasing his stump, pulled the cigarette from his lips, and snorted a steady stream of smoke. "You still have not told me how it happened, Paulo," he said. "This has to be the first escape ever from the Vallarta jail."

Chimp lit a cigarette and flicked the extinguished match out his passenger seat window. "I was at home at the time. On authorized break. But Officer Contreras was there." Chimp sniggered, "Tell cousin Manco what you saw of the jailbreak, Raúl."

Fat Cop stiffened behind the steering wheel, irked at his partner's caustic jab to his wounded pride. Paulo knew damn well what he saw of the jailbreak. Not a whole hell of a lot since he'd been knocked unconscious for the first time in his life. "Classified," he said. "And you know that Paulo. We should not even be discussing the escape."

Manco squealed from the backseat, "Yehee, *classified.*"

Chimp smirked agreeably. "Cousin Manco knows there was an escape, Raúl," he said. "We are here to recapture Russell Martell. He only wants a little information about the escape in return for the information he gives us about the gringo."

334

"And money," said Manco. "Do not forget the money."

Chimp's smirk dissolved on his face. He reached into his pocket for a two-hundred-peso note and passed it to his cousin. "If we catch him here, I will double that."

"Your escaped prisoner or his girlfriend could show up at any time," Manco replied quickly, "and might be in the house right now. The lights have been on since we got here."

Chimp scrutinized the house through plumes of cigarette smoke. "No movement inside. But he might be hiding in there with his terrorist friends."

"I never said that terrorists would hole up here," Manco said. "Only that Russell Martell might show up. He was at a party here last night, and his girlfriend is staying here so—"

Fat Cop cut him off: "Maybe she is a terrorist too."

Manco sucked his cigarette down and chucked it out the window. "Look," he said, "if she shows up, nab her. Her name is Brenda. Pinche puta. Streaked hair. Good looking. Nice curves. She might know where he is. And if that gringo shows up, you can nab or kill him. And he might be in there with her right now. But believe me, I know for a fact that the house is not a terrorist hideout or base of operations."

"Go knock on the door yourself," Chimp said, "and have a look around. You were at the party last night. You know the owner of the house, no?"

"Sure. Give me a hundred dollars and you have a deal. But whether I knock on the door or you knock on the door, the result will be the same if your man is not there. Once he finds out I paid the place a visit, he will never show up. We locked horns at the party last night. And he saw me at the Washington, probably knows I witnessed that dying woman accuse him of murder and figures I tipped you off about him. And if he is in the house and sees me, he will be alerted to the danger and is liable to escape out the back, down the hillside and over the fence."

Fat Cop released a low growl: "If no one shows within the hour..."

Chimp finished his thought, "We will call for backup and raid the place."

"Good idea," Manco agreed eagerly, though he had no intention of hanging around to see the show. He pawed absently at the car keys in his front pocket. His rented Monte Carlo was parked in Old Vallarta. Manco had work to do tonight. Big plans.

For Manco, what happened at the Washington was more destiny than disaster, more justice than barbarism, and it was time to seize the moment, take advantage of the chaos and confusion. Russell Martell had taken advantage of it with his daring jailbreak. Now it was his turn.

When his cousin told him over the phone that the prisoner had escaped, Manco couldn't believe it, his initial response: "Someone was paid off."

"Not this time," Paulo replied. "He had accomplices. And we are now fairly certain that the disaster at the Washington was the result of a terror attack. He is our only suspect and no one wanted to see him escape, not for any amount of money."

"A terror attack?" Manco said. "No kidding. So those terrorist rumors are true." Manco sounded pensive but in reality was genuinely moved by the audacity of such an attack. Too bad it hadn't occurred in the USA, the cradle of capitalist debauchery and neoliberal imperialism, the evils impoverishing third-world lands. But a gringo playhouse like the Washington Hotel here in Vallarta was almost as good. Better, actually. After all, Manco was here in Vallarta, and the attack, while a disaster for most everyone, represented opportunity to him. How and why it happened vaguely interested him; what mattered most was the resulting chaos. That's what provided him an opening to carry out his own nefarious plot, as did law enforcement's preoccupation with Russell Martell.

Did Russell Martell blow the Washington? Manco had his doubts but once again it didn't matter. To his mind, Russell Martell was guilty anyhow. The gringo represented all he despised about estadounidenses—self-righteous, self-indulgent, sarcastic, and ignorant of the pain and suffering he and his paisanos were responsible for the world over. What did he compare La Raza to at the party last night? Aryan Nations? And what did he call the Aztecas? original hijos de la chingada? It was immaterial whether or not Russell Martell actually blew the Washington. By definition the imperialist gringo was a terrorist.

Amazing how he'd escaped from jail. Manco almost admired him for that. But he wouldn't get far. Police were bound to recapture or kill the cocky chingón without further help from him. And he didn't have time to give police more help anyway, couldn't spend much more time at all sitting here in a squad car thinking about Señor Martell; Manco's cohort, Javier, the Cora Zapatista, was expecting him in El Pitillal in an hour or so. Manco would not be available for his cousin the rest of the evening, so he might as well squeeze what money he could out of him now.

Manco fingered his wispy mustache. "I still think he will show up here sooner or later," he said, "if he is not in the house right now. But if for some reason I am wrong, I have another tip for you."

Chimp laid his dark rodent eyes upon those of his cousin. Manco's eyes loomed large behind his glasses and Chimp knew exactly what they signified. "How much?" he said.

"Just another two hundred pesos. But if it pans out..."

Chimp counted out the money and gave it to him. "I will take care of you if the tip proves worthy."

Manco folded the bills into his pocket. "A source of mine told me today that one of Señor Martell's friends is staying at El Marciano Hotel. Johnny Miles."

"Neels?" Chimp was making a note, cigarette clenched between his teeth.

"*Miles*," Manco said. "Como *milla*, with an M."

"Description?"

"Gringo. A bit taller than me. Slender, brown hair and eyes. Drunk last night. You should not have any trouble with him at all."

Fat Cop issued a sharp whisper: "Someone just climbed up from behind that hedge on the left."

"Looks nice," said Chimp. "Is she...?"

"Could be." Manco opened his door to leave. "You better go get her. Adiós."

59

JOHNNY motioned me out of the cab. He draped a fraternal arm over my shoulder as I closed the door behind me. "Pigs up ahead."

I bucked up against him. "What?"

"A black and white parked down the street."

I steadied my eyes on his unflinching expression. "No shit."

Johnny let his arm drop from my shoulder. His eyes were aglow with heightened perception, his tone dull and composed. "Didn't even try to get into the house," he said. "Spotted 'em just in time. Always on the lookout you know. Part of my training."

"Good job. What're they doin'?"

"Just sittin' there across the street from Mountain's place. A block or so away. I crept through some woods to have a closer peek at 'em. Three in the car. Two in front. One in back."

I chuckled at Johnny's impulses. Spotting the car wasn't enough for him. He also had to play guerrilla warfare.

"Either they're scopin' Montoya's place," he said, "or some corrupt shit's goin' down. Drugs, payoffs. The guy in back usually has cuffs on, don't he?"

"Been there myself."

"So have I. This one was smokin' a cig."

"Let's get the hell outta here."

I told the cabby to head for Libramiento the way we came, to drive by "another friend's house." He pulled a U turn.

"Were the lights on in the house?"

"Oh yeah." Johnny spread his wings over the back of the car seat and relaxed his agile middleweight frame, taking satisfaction in the bit of excitement he'd just experienced. Cops don't rattle him. Not much does. Johnny is battle-hardened and was proud of his perfectly executed impromptu reconnaissance mission. "Everything looked cool." He eyed the cabby and leaned into me, his voice a decided whisper. "No tellin' what's up but if it's something serious you'd think I'd a spotted an unmarked car as well. But I didn't." He wrapped his arms around his torso and ran a hand over a scabbing surface wound on his elbow. "Under the circumstances though, I decided to abort the mission."

"Right. Excellent job."

I patted him on the back and told the cabby to forget our other friend's house and take us directly over Libramiento to the library.

"Biblioteca?" Johnny repeated. "Why the library?"

"On the way to your place."

"So you're not gonna..."

I shook my head slowly. "Without my key, I can't..." I squeezed my eyes shut and massaged my temples. My indecision was driving me nuts; I could feel my teeth grind as I tried to think things through again. Was making an appearance at reception for a key to my room worth the risk? I sure could use my cash and... "Just gimme all your money," I said at last, "and I'm outta town."

Johnny chewed on his upper lip. "*All* my money?"

"Cúanto eh a Tepic?" I said to the cabby.

He braked abruptly at the highway. "Tepic?"

"Sí, Tepic."

"500 dólares."

"Qué?!?"

"500 dólares." He crossed the highway and eased down into Old Vallarta.

"I thought you were working because you are needed. Five hundred is way too much."

"The highway to Tepic is very slow," said the cabby. "There are roadblocks. Roadblocks on the way to Melaque and Las Palmas also."

"Roadblocks?" I shrunk into the backseat and digested this. Of course there were roadblocks. Terrorists were on the loose! Russell Martell was on the loose.

On the run headlong into a roadblock. Brilliant.

I wasn't thinking straight, yet straight enough to ask a pressing question: "Are there any roadblocks around town?"

"There were," said the cabby, "but the streets are all open now, except the boulevard in front of the Washington."

That was a relief. At least I was safe in the cab, for now.

"When will you be able to drive to Tepic directly, without roadblocks?"

The cabby accelerated up to Libramiento. "Who knows?" he said. "Tomorrow maybe."

I considered playing the innocent tourist and asking why there were roadblocks (were they looking for someone? someone connected to the explosion at the Washington this morning?) but there was no point in it. I had all the information I needed and had said enough. The wind fell from my sails. I couldn't escape town tonight.

Johnny asked what was going on. I translated as if commenting on the weather. Threw in a comment about the weather, this odd Monterey mist. Johnny understood completely and recommended we go to his place "to get a game plan."

"We need one," I said.

60

BRENDA'S moment of weakness down on the darkened trail had forced her to pool her energy; her deliberate strides strengthened as she progressed up the grade. The trail crested at the end of a long tall hedge to her left. The hedge skirted Armando's front lawn and butted up to the sidewalk and a streetlamp. A gauze of mist veiled the light from the streetlamp. Brenda rounded the hedge and lamppost and angled over the lawn towards the illuminated entry to the house. The grass was slick underfoot. She slipped on the slight incline, regained her footing, then froze in the high beams of an approaching vehicle. The car hopped the shallow curb and skidded to a stop below her, its right front and rear tires on the sidewalk. A black and white police car. "Qué diablos?" she mouthed, more curious than startled. Brenda had been working with police down at the Washington all day and wondered if these officers might need assistance of some sort.

The front doors popped open. A short ugly creature in uniform emerged from the near passenger door. "Un momento por favor, señorita," he said in a pitched, stilted voice. He stepped onto the lawn and paused a few meters short of her. "We have a couple of questions for you."

Brenda couldn't place his face—sow or monkey? Sow she determined. She could smell it. Putrid swine. A broad-shouldered police officer with an equally broad waistline had jumped out of the driver's side of the vehicle. He circled the rear end of the car, strode up onto the lawn and planted himself between her and the entry to the house about ten meters away. "Are you Brenda?" he asked huskily, his lips stretched in a vague smile.

A sudden gout of fear throbbed in Brenda's chest. She was abruptly aware that she'd been boxed in—the house to her back, the hedge to her right, the squad car and ugly runt just below her, and a brute to her left. She retreated a step and sturdied her UDLA billcap, like a ballplayer readying herself at the plate. "What do you want?"

The ugly one advanced. "You are Brenda?"

Brenda thrust out a hand. "Stop right there!" He halted. The front door to the house popped opened. Ara stepped out the door, black hair in tassels over the shoulders of her white robe. "Brenda? Qué pasa?"

"No sé."

The big one swung his gaze from Ara back to Brenda. "So you *are* Brenda," he said.

"Russell Martell's woman," the short ugly one breathed. He advanced another step.

"Get off our property!" Brenda barked, the name *Russell Martell* issuing a lump in her throat. What did this have to do with Russell? Had he been picked up for questioning again? Was he in danger or— Brenda quickly realized that *she* was the one in danger. There was no mistaking the menacing look in these men's eyes, menacing and lascivious under the brims of their blue cop hats. Like a couple of teenage delinquents about to graduate from robbery to rape. The backs of her legs quivered. If these bastards got their hands on her—

"This is *your* house?" the ugly one said.

Ara yelled from the front door, "*My* house! Get off my property!"

Ara's outburst seemed to distract the ugly pig. Brenda made a break for it, certain she'd be quick enough to circle the hedge and lose these beasts in the woods on the darkened trail. No way they could catch her. Nobody could. But she had made a critical miscalculation, a critical misjudgment. That short ugly swine wasn't a sow but a monkey. A leaping lemur! What a reach! What a grip! Even so, she'd nearly escaped. He only had her by the ankle, one handed and laid out on his belly. But that was enough to plant her flat on her face. She heard her sister scream and slam the door shut. "Ara," she gasped as she kicked and struggled for air. Brenda's fall had knocked the wind out of her. She gagged on soppy turf, her free right leg striking empty space, flailing for the head of the animal gripping her ankle. She contorted her torso and crashed the heel of her sneaker down on his arm. He let loose with a wicked groan, "Puta," and released her. "Fucking prick!" she screamed in English. Brenda gathered herself for a quick sprint, but it was too late. The big one had a hold of her— picked her right up kicking and screeching, his arms crushing her breasts as he carried her toward the squad car. Her heels found a soft spot between his legs; he adjusted his grip with a growl, "We have a real wildcat on our hands, Paulo."

Chimp cackled salaciously, "*Wildcat.*"

Brenda gained some traction on the edge of the sidewalk and managed to twist her body around. She cuffed the fat cop's ears and sent his hat flying, clawed his face and kneed him in the gut. She heard the air rush out his lungs, but he was still strong enough to plow her through the open car door. Brenda's head glanced off the steering wheel as he collapsed on top of her, their bodies draped over the two front seats. Her cap blinded her for a second, an agonizing second of crushing darkness beneath a man twice her size. A yawning cavern opened up inside her. Fear and black death. She felt she might be finished. Brenda shook her cap from her face and, within her desperation, perceived an advantage, instinctively sensed her advantage: the big fat cop sprawled on top of her, his head buried in her armpit, was sucking air and snorting like a wounded fighting bull primed to be slayed. She wrenched her left arm around his head and repeatedly rabbit punched the base of his skull with her right fist. He took a wild swing at her, his right arm careening harmlessly off the steering wheel, and snorted a painful curse. Brenda released his head and the moment he pushed himself off of her to give himself room to strike, she had her heels planted between his ribs.

Chimp poked his head in the car expecting to see a wildcat subdued beneath his burly partner. Instead he got an eyeful of his partner's wide ass piling into his chest with enough force to topple a building. They both tumbled over the lawn. Fat Cop was splayed out on his back, but Chimp wound up on his feet. Didn't even lose his hat. Brenda swung her legs out of the car. He blocked her escape, arms spread. "Resisting arrest, señorita? Now you will spend many nights in jail."

Tears of rage sprang into Brenda's eyes and dissolved within a startled cry as a baseball whizzed by the ugly monkey's head and skipped off the car's roof. Ara yelled at him from across the lawn: "Get off my property! Leave her alone! My husband—"

Fat Cop scrambled to his feet and charged her. Ara yelped, "Chingá!" raced back into the house and bolted the door behind her.

Chimp had felt the air from the baseball singe his ear, heard it whistle by his head like a bullet, and instantly ducked as a matter of reflex, yet he kept his prey—the wildcat—in his sights. Brenda was on her feet. Chimp shuffled to his left, towards the rear of the car in an effort to pin her against the open passenger door. Brenda knew this game and easily juked him. She feinted in the direction he was moving, got him to commit, and high-stepped out of reach towards the hedge and darkened trail. Once again, however, she'd made a critical miscalculation. The big cop blindsided her, knocked her senseless with a bone-crunching tackle.

Brenda lay on her back, breast heaving, ocean-green eyes rolling about her head. Fat Cop and Chimp hovered over her, hands on knees, breathing heavily. Chimp retreated to the car and opened the rear door. "Toss her in." Fat Cop gathered her in his arms and stretched her out on the bench seat, flat on her back. "Handcuff her." Fat Cop stepped back, reached for the cuffs at his waist, and noticed he was missing something. "My pistol," he said. "Where...?"

Chimp spat, "Under the car. Pinche cabrón. Did you have the thumb break secured?" Chimp patted the pistol snapped securely inside the holster below his waist. "Get your gun. I will take care of la señorita."

Fat Cop knelt by the open passenger door for a look under the car. Chimp pulled off Brenda's shoes and leaned through the backdoor of the vehicle for a close look at his prisoner, dark rodent eyes aglitter. Neither he nor his partner noticed the truck that had slid in at the curb about twenty yards behind them. A big king-cab truck with a very large man at the wheel.

Brenda's somnolent oval expression shone with the pearl of youth, her cheeks and neck flushed from her passionate struggle. A lecherous grin spread across Chimp's face at the sight of his helpless victim, a grin that never finished itself. Before he knew it a violent tug at the seat of his pants sent him flying into space, howling and squealing in the heavy evening air like a thousand tortured pigs, "EEYAOOoooooow...!" Fat Cop, his chest wedged under the car and legs akimbo over the sidewalk, was startled by the sound. Had the wildcat come to life and kicked his partner in the nuts? He made a final reach for his pistol but, before he could nab it, a mighty yank on his gun belt swept him out from under the vehicle with such dispatch he completely lost his bearings, as if he were back in the processing room during the blackout, shaking the cobwebs from his head as he regained consciousness.

Mountain looked down upon him with the dull rage of a giant struggling not to vent his fury lest he destroy everything in sight. He gripped the fat cop by the scruff of the neck and lifted him off the grass. "Hijo de puta," he began and was interrupted by Ara's alarm from the front door: "The little one has a gun!"

Armando La Montaña Montoya handled Fat Cop like a crash-test dummy thrown into the ring with him. A flimsy rag doll. He tossed him into the air by the armpits, caught him against his chest, and shielded himself behind his body. Mountain pressed his chin against the back of the fat cop's neck and eyed the little runt with the gun. Apparently, the hedge had broken his fall, he didn't even lose his hat. He teetered on the edge of Mountain's property, pistol raised.

"Get back in the house Ara," Mountain said. He heard her slam the door.

Fat cap gasped, "I ca-n-n-ot br-eathe."

"Let him go!" Chimp screeched. "Let him go or you die."

"Go ahead and shoot," Mountain challenged levelly. "After you kill your partner you are the next to go."

Chimp sneered and advanced a couple of steps. Fat Cop let loose with an agonizing howl, "Nooooooooooo!" His chest felt like it was being flattened beneath a tank. The blood-curdling cry stopped Chimp in his tracks. "What the hell do you want?" Mountain growled. "Do you have a warrant?"

Chimp fidgeted on his feet. This wasn't what he expected at all. Why didn't cousin Manco tell him this house was occupied by a mountainous beast? Even if he had a clean shot at him it wouldn't stop him. Multiple shots might not stop him, unless he landed one through his partner's eye and into his head. Like shooting a rhinoceros. "We have reason to believe—"

"Reason to believe is not enough!" Mountain sustained Fat Cop with one arm and brought a meat-cleaver paw to his throat. Fat Cop gasped and choked, his tongue squirting out his mouth. "Drop your gun or your friend dies. And you will be next, I promise."

Chimp took a step back. Fat Cop retched, "Arghhhh!" his tongue flapping about like a speed bag pummeled by a champion. "Drop it!" Mountain roared. Chimp tossed his gun.

"Now back away." Chimp obeyed.

Brenda stirred and sat up in the backseat of the squad car. Mountain yelled out, "Sergio?!?" His nephew popped his head up from inside the truck. "Sí?"

"Get over here and help Aunt Brenda out of this car and into the house. And let Bizco out."

Brenda massaged the back of her neck and stared blankly at her shoes on the sidewalk. Ara called out to her from the front door, "Ven Brenda! Rápido!"

"Bizco too," Mountain said. Ara clapped her hands and called Bizco. He rumbled up to her.

Brenda planted her feet on the curb, her mind clearing within a vision of that fat pig's eyes scratched out. Mountain sensed her fury. "Get in the house, Brenda," he ordered without so much as a glance at her. "I will handle this. Get her into the house, Sergio, pronto!"

Brenda grabbed her shoes and Sergio hustled her into the house.

Mountain fixed flat brown eyes on the ugly little runt standing on his lawn. Somehow he had hung on to his hat but he could see he had quite the potato head under it; stick that head in the oven and it would blow if you didn't poke extra holes in it. He briefly visualized himself beating these assholes to a pulp. It was a gratifying vision but, unfortunately, a sound beating might make matters worse. He knew why they were here. A call from Devo was responsible for his timely arrival. The best way to assure that more police would not show up tonight was through a different course of action.

Mountain slowly backed his way to his front door. "The two of you will be charged with trespassing, false arrest, and menacing," he said to the ugly runt. He removed his hand from the fat officer's throat. Fat Cop coughed and convulsed, his breath constricted by the massive forearm wrapped around his ribs. Mountain ripped the badge from his chest. "I am going to give the mayor this badge number and see to it that you are so charged. And I warn you, if you ever try anything like this again you will not escape here with your lives."

Chimp watched in amazement at the ease with which the big man sent his partner sliding along the wet grass on his back towards the squad car. When he looked up, the mountainous beast was gone.

61

LIBRAMIENTO was closed northbound just before the boulevard, three blocks northeast of the Washington. Cars weren't being searched but traffic was stop and go as our cabby approached Francisco Villa

Avenue, the only northern route open to non-emergency vehicles. Devo had spoken the truth. There were lots of cops. I felt like Poe's purloined letter—hidden right before their eyes. Fortunately, the police were all busy directing traffic or driving from one place to another. I didn't see any federales or army. They must have been concentrated at the Washington ruins and the roadblocks heading out of town.

I directed the cabby through some side streets and acted disappointed when "David's" car wasn't parked in front of a dimly lit house. Johnny and I got out anyway, "to wait for him." Johnny paid the fare. The cabby mechanically went on his way.

"Good job," Johnny said.

"What?"

"Keepin' the cabby in the dark about my hotel. Guess that lump behind your ear hasn't infected your brain yet."

We were ideally positioned—five blocks or so from El Marciano Hotel on a quiet residential road with just enough streetlamps to keep me from stubbing another toe.

The drizzle was steady. All that smoke from the disaster may have had something to do with the mist and drizzle. This time of year it might shower (especially up in the mountains) but was mostly clear. I couldn't remember seeing Vallarta so misty. We began walking, unaffected.

"Cops got your shoes?"

"Yep."

"Bastards."

"Yep."

"Got tough with ya too, huh?"

"Motherfuckers. Unless you want a lump to match mine, or worse, better stay way out in front of me. We don't need to be seen entering the hotel together or walking together. Devo said they're liable to shoot me on sight."

"Really? Guess I better stay outta the crossfire."

"First gimme all your money, in case I have to make a break for it."

Johnny reached into his pocket and handed me a wad of bills. "Crime doesn't pay."

"Pays somebody." I stuffed the money into my pocket. Down the street, headlights crawled toward us. I slowed my pace and moved directly behind Johnny.

"You using me as a human shield?" he said.

"If they don't see me they won't shoot." The headlights turned east—inland, to our right. I skipped over a hole in the sidewalk. I was no stranger to going barefoot, my feet were pretty tough. As a teenager

345

the soles of my feet were tougher'n tanned bull's hide. Right now they needed a good scrubbing. *I* needed a good scrubbing. A shower would feel good.

"Why'd we ditch Devo?"

"Don't need 'im anymore."

We were quiet for a short time. "What's your room number?" I said. "Gotta plan?"

We stopped and huddled up for the play. Johnny called it: "Two-seventy-two. Straight past the garden, up the stairs and make a left. Take the key. It'll get you in." Johnny gave me the key. A regular house key dangling from a clamshell marked **El Marciano**. "I'll tell her I misplaced my key at a friend's house, get a spare, and head straight for my room. Just push the buzzer, hold the key up in front of the bars so she can see it, and she'll let you in like a regular guest."

"What if—"

"If she hassles you, which she won't, just tell her you're my buddy and found my key. Then you can have her come get me and we'll pay for you to stay the night."

"Any night-time security?"

"A guy arrives at about midnight. Maybe twelve thirty. At least he did last year. I got in late the last couple of nights so I'm not sure when he came on duty." Johnny checked his watch. "Probably won't show for an hour or so. The ol' lady will be at the desk. Sometimes a girl or one of her sons stays late. Her husband takes over in the morning. He should be in bed by now. Don't worry. Piece a cake."

"Piece a cake," I repeated levelly, "but I'm ready to ditch the key and make a break for it at the first sign of cops."

"Check."

"What if the old lady recognizes me from a news flash? We gotta assume I'm a wanted man."

"The lobby doesn't have a TV but..." Johnny pondered this for a few seconds. "If she recognizes you, she won't let you in, that's for sure. I'll give you five minutes. If you don't show, I'll meet you down the alley between the hotel and the grocery store and give you more money for a quick getaway. But I really think the key will get you in without a problem."

"How much more money you got?"

"Five hundred hidden in my room. Five in a strong box behind reception. Should I get the money in the strong box right away?"

"No. The five in your room will be enough." I clapped him on the back. "Don't talk to strangers." We chuckled grimly. Johnny gripped my bicep. "You're halfway home buddy. We'll figure it out. See ya in a few."

ENRIQUE Santos, the robust, burly voiced union leader of the Vallarta chapter of Obreros Unidos, had been managing men and equipment all day Monday and he thought he'd heard every rumor under the smoky, dusty sun concerning the disaster, every rumor permeating this sticky, grimy, drizzly evening. But this had to be biggest *jalada* yet. And he had first heard it on the radio!

He didn't care if it came with a government stamp of approval or had been blessed by the church. It couldn't be true! Absurd on the face of it.

Enrique considered calling the mayor about it but opted for his son Pedro instead. He was on the police force, and Pedro had told him he was working the investigation into this insane bloodbath. "What the hell is going on over there at police headquarters?!?" he exclaimed into his phone. "Have you people lost your minds? I know this man! The idea is preposterous!"

Pedro was aghast. Not at his father's tone. He was accustomed to his energetic outbursts and didn't take it personally. The poignant irony of papi's revelation was what floored him. Everyone was looking for leads into Russell Martell's whereabouts. The mayor had seen to it that his name and face were publicized, and el comandante was organizing a team to raid the suspect's hotel room (a raid that would not include Pedro)... And now it turns out that his father knows Russell Martell?!? Increíble.

Enrique got even hotter under the collar when Pedro asked him if he knew where Russell Martell was. "Are you fucking kidding me?!?" he bellowed. "Not only are police after the wrong man but now you think he has been working with me and rescue crews here at ground zero all day? I have no idea where the hell he is. But I will tell you and anyone else who cares to listen that you are after the wrong man!"

Pedro agreed to let his father voice his opinion to both him and Gloria in person in Arena Vallarta's dining hall shortly after 11 p.m. that evening, thirty minutes before police gathered to raid Russell Martell's room at Casa Mexicana.

***

"I have known the man for years," Enrique said. "Long enough to judge his character."

"Is he a good friend?" said Gloria.

"We are fairly close, sure. I met his wife before she died. She was born right here in Vallarta. And he has been to my house, played with my daughter, met my wife! I have talked with him, spent time with the man, gone fishing with him, drank beer and smoked cigars with him, watched sports with him..."

"How well did you know his wife?"

"Not very. I only met her a few times before she died in child birth. The baby was lost as well. A horrible tragedy. Russell was crestfallen. Not the same man... He mourned with her family here in Vallarta for nearly two weeks afterwards..." Enrique paused and set his jaw against a sudden tightness in his throat. "Russell Martell is not an arsonist, Gloria, or a terrorist. He is a journalist! A sports writer for God's sake. I have read his stuff in magazines!"

"We never said he was actually wanted for terrorism only—"

"Come on, Gloria. News on the radio says he is wanted for arson in connection with the disaster. That sounds like terrorism to me, especially considering the destruction at the Washington."

"When was the last time you saw Russell Martell?"

"We watched the fight together at Rudy's Sports Bar on Friday night, and then I saw him briefly there again the following evening, Saturday."

"Why has Pedro never met him?"

"Russell has only been to my house once. Pedro was not there. No one was home but me, my wife, and Angélica. When I see Russell, it is usually after work or on weekends. Ask anyone in Rudy's Sports Bar in Old Vallarta. They know him."

Pedro sat close to his father and believed every word he said. Pedro had his own doubts about Russell Martell's guilt, had shared them with Gloria during their examination of the disc, and wanted to back up what his father was saying but...there was one problem. And Gloria expressed it: "How do you explain his escape from jail, Enrique? We are sure he had accomplices. That looks pretty incriminating to me."

"For all I know he paid off police. News on the radio says he is also wanted for drugs so perhaps there was a payoff. There usually is when drugs are involved."

"Do you know Russell to take or deal drugs?"

"Deal? No. He drinks, Gloria...told me once that marijuana is a good cure for hangovers. But I do not give a damn if the man does marijuana, cocaine, opium or anything else. He is not a terrorist."

"Have you any idea where he might get his drugs?" As soon as she asked the question Gloria flushed with embarrassment at Enrique's

348

injured scowl, afraid she had just insulted one of the most honorable men she knew.

"Do you think I am hiding something, Gloria?"

"Of course not."

"I came here voluntarily, Gloria."

"I understand, Enrique. Forgive me. We told you about *Mister* Martell's escape from jail because it has a bearing on your claim that he is innocent, and so do these questions. Please bear with me and try not to take them personally."

"I suppose that depends on what the next question is, Gloria."

Gloria stiffened her resolve and adopted a new line of questioning in her even, friendly tone: "Have you ever talked politics with Russell, Enrique?"

Enrique slouched in his chair and crossed his formidable forearms below his chest. Though never exactly the picture of calm, Enrique had managed to keep himself collected and poised throughout this horrific day. He always performed admirably under pressure and was not about to lose his cool now, but this was getting ridiculous. Politics? Did Gloria honestly believe Russell had confided some kind of radical political ideology to him?

First thing Enrique did upon arrival was wash up in the bathroom and help himself to a shot of tequila and a beer from the bar. Much deserved and rejuvenating. He stared at the empty Corona bottle on the table, his jaw slackened, burly voice tamed, his scarred, boxer's brow weary. "Sometimes we talk politics," he said. "Just harmless banter..." Enrique's face brightened. He smiled past Gloria as though remembering a pleasant dream. "I remember once Russell said, 'Nothing ever changes in México so it makes sense for Mexicans to continue to blame América for it.' " He looked directly at Gloria and laughed. "That was a good one."

Gloria had to smile. "Not bad."

Pedro said, "That should have come from a Mexican."

"Or, uh...what was it...?" Enrique scratched his head. He had a couple more of Russell's refrains on the tip of his tongue and wanted to express them properly: " 'There are lots of problems with América and the worst of them are the chingones planning to take her place when she falls.' And, 'Imprison markets and you will only have to set the bastards free again.' " Enrique shrugged and smirked. "You know. Simple things that are humorous because they ring true. Guess that is why he writes. But I have never heard him get real political, no."

"Has he ever expressed radical views sympathetic to terrorists—"

"No."

"—or struck you as religiously fanatic or anti-religion?"

"Russell can be fanatical about sports, Gloria. That is his job. Sometimes it bores him and he thinks about writing on other subjects but I have never known him to be radical or fanatical in a religious, anti-religious, or any other sense at all."

"Has the subject of terrorism ever come up between the two of you?"

Enrique shook his head. "The man is not a terrorist."

Gloria wasn't giving in. She was thinking about the disc and needed to know if Russell Martell's mindset fit its revelations, if he could have had something to do with the disc's creation. "What about *Islamic* terror? What does he think of that?"

Enrique paused, his eyes red and narrow. "*Islamic* terror, Gloria? Are we talking about radical *Islamists* now? This conversation has taken quite a turn all of a sudden."

"We are only trying to cover every possibility, Enrique. Bear with me, please."

Enrique sighed heavily. He was beginning to wonder if this was an interview or an interrogation. Yet he also felt a responsibility to his friend Russell. If their positions were reversed, Russell would defend him. And there was nothing to defend anyhow! Russell had never said anything to him on these subjects that he felt ashamed of or needed to hide.

So he came right out and told Gloria what he remembered Russell saying about Islamic terror:

"Russell once said that the test of a terrorist State is to piss on its holy book. In the USA, piss on the Bible and it will end up in the New York Museum of Modern Art. Piss on the Koran in most any Muslim country and you are beheaded or stoned to death... Which do *you* think is the terrorist State, Gloria?"

"The answer to that question is clear," she said. "And I am sure Mister Martell knows it is." Gloria wasn't exactly fond of Russell Martell's satiric bent but she didn't find his refrains offensive or self-incriminating either.

"All I know, Gloria," Enrique said, "is that you have fingered the wrong man. It is possible he knows something about what may have happened at the Washington today. Russell is a journalist and could have information about this whole affair that will interest you. But there is absolutely no way he is a terrorist, arsonist or anything of the kind. He could not and would not be involved in such things. It is not in his nature."

Gloria folded her hands upon the table and shifted her gaze between father and son. Few people in Vallarta had gained her respect more than Enrique, the foreman of her beloved Arena Vallarta project.

And in the last seven hours or so her estimation of Pedro as an exceptionally intelligent and composed young man had grown considerably.

"Pedro," she said.

"Sí señora."

"Your father's last statement. We addressed something like it not long ago."

"Sí señora."

"And?"

"I do not know about the suspect's nature, señora. But my father's opinion of him supports my suspicion that he is not the assassin. And according to Sandra's report, Russell Martell does not fit the profile of the assassin. He does not have the training or—"

"Assassin?" Enrique interrupted, a rhetorical crack to his voice. "You mean terrorist."

"Enrique." Gloria silently cursed herself. She was fatigued and had committed a fundamental error, or allowed Pedro to. As a matter of course, Enrique needed to be informed of the suspect's arrest and escape because these facts went directly to his testimony about Russell Martell's innocence. But as a rule, potential witnesses should never be privy to the particulars of an investigation. And Enrique was on the verge of knowing more than he needed to know.

Enrique shot her a questioning frown. "Sí, Gloria?"

"Enrique... I am going to visit Rudy's Sports Bar tonight and ask about Señor Russell Martell. And I thank you for your help. Your testimony has been valuable and I expect to talk with you further about our suspect. I also expect you not to speak of this interview to anyone. But at this juncture," her gaze drifted between father and son once again, "Pedro and I need to discuss this matter in private."

Enrique cocked his head mulishly at Gloria, like she'd just offered a deal he had to refuse. He had a question or two of his own he wanted answered now, like, what was this about an assassin? Pedro's sharp, reasoned tone reminded him that now was not the time to assert himself: "Police business, papi."

He stared critically at his son and saw himself, his tenacity, and a level of patient intelligence he admired yet rarely attained.

Enrique relented with a proud, affectionate smile. "I understand. Police business." He draped an arm around his son. "But I remind both of you that if you are after terrorists they are getting away while you waste time searching for Russell."

JOHNNY pressed forward, had gained twenty-five yards on me. Five seconds later his silhouette made a right and disappeared. El Marciano was across the street, two blocks from the corner. A pedestrian stepped off the curb heading west toward the boulevard; two cars passed him going the same direction. My road was tranquil but every step brought a new assessment of possible hiding places and escape routes. A vehicle squealed behind me and I jumped onto an overgrown lawn, ready to hop the fence next to the house. The car passed me by.

I'd stayed at El Marciano once years ago. It was a clean cheap dive in those days. Since they fixed it up, the hotel had become reasonably inexpensive and fairly popular. Amazing what an investment in bathrooms and televisions can do for a hotel. I recalled the alley that separated El Marciano from the small family grocery store Johnny had mentioned. A dirt alley lined in shrubbery and backyard fences. Hop a fence or two or three and you might be able to vanish, for a while.

I crossed the street. Headlights burned up the road. I ducked between a tree and the jutting grocery-store wall. A box of discarded vegetables were at my feet and something like a tomato squished between my toes. I watched the nondescript car pass. Another vehicle approached, this one from the boulevard. I peeled remnants of a peach from my foot. The vehicle slowed perceptibly. A black and white police car. My breathing grew shallow and I went rigid, pulse racing. The car drew past me alongside El Marciano Hotel. I could see the driver clearly in the low light. Fat Cop. He parked, opened his door and said something back over his shoulder.

Chimp got out from the other side, muttered, and marched around the frontend of the car. Fat Cop spoke up a little louder: "Seguro? Sin apoyo?" Sure? Without back-up?

Chimp spit on the sidewalk. "Chingao. Let them look all over for the cocksucker. Manco is *my* snitch. I deserve to kill the fucking hijo de puta myself, if he is here."

Chimp's tone oozed angry humiliation. Was he one of those cops Devo knocked out when he sprung me from jail? Did he think Johnny had sprung me? And how did Manco get the name of Johnny's hotel? Did Chimp and Fat Cop expect to find me holed up here with him? Evidently so. And Johnny was about to pay for my "crimes" and stupid mistakes!

Fat Cop got out of the car. Chimp punched the buzzer, said, "Policía," and whispered something to Fat Cop. They both unsnapped the thumb brake around their pistols. Fat Cop swung the bars open and led the way inside.

A worldly force sprang from the earth beneath my feet, surged through my body and sprouted out the top of my head. White-hot, forged rage. I'd been plenty angry before in my life, but this was an entirely new feeling. The rage of mass destruction. It would have to be tempered, like an assassin's blade. The pigs were out for blood. My blood. And I was out for theirs. Rescuing Johnny was a good way to get it. They had guns, but I might have the advantage. Not only had I not been seen but Chimp was overconfident, bereft of fear—too angry to be afraid, or cautious.

Problem was, rage had made *me* unthinkingly fearless, a risky condition that leaves one vulnerable to mistakes...mistakes Chimp was making at this very moment: he had failed to clear his perimeter and left his rear open to attack.

Do boxers utilize rage to harness fear or fear to harness rage?

Either way, I needed a dose of good ol' recognizable fear to get me thinkin' straight.

Fear of death didn't work, made me wanna torch the hotel and drive a car bomb into the police station. Fear of God, His retribution (wrath) reminded me of the terror attack and infused me with a desire to annihilate Allah. Fear for Johnny, of failing him, did the trick. That was enough to kick my brain into gear. Jumping into that cab without thinking might have been a stupid move but I'd been lucky, up to now. This was an opportunity to be good. Damn good. I was ready and willing to walk that fine line between stupidity and bravery. Stupidity because, instead of running, which could save my ass, I was about to do something extremely dangerous that I'd never remotely attempted before; failure would bring disaster. And bravery...because it needed to be done. *Who knows what they'll do to Johnny?!?* Success would bring freedom, keep us alive.

The trick was to think, but not too much. Cobblestones littered the alley. I only needed one heavy stone the size of my fist that could be slipped into the pocket of my cargo shorts. It felt just right when I picked it up.

I'm goin' in.

I stared through the bars guarding the open door at the entry. A mere twenty yards would bring me to the foot of the stairs. That was Chimp disappearing at the top of them...

I heard voices down the alley beside the hotel.

Witnesses will have to be killed. The idea was exhilarating. I had the mindset of a killer, a composed, thinking killer. I rang the buzzer, smiled, and held up the key.

SEVE VERDAD

A woman appeared at the open door and buzzed the bars open. I said, "Buenas noches," but didn't see her.

She said, "No tan buenas." Not so good. I passed by her without another word. "Is your room upstairs?" she asked. "Wait...before you go up the stairs..."

Pipe down puta or you're dead.

To my right the mangy garden had been spruced up with a birdbath and mangy flowering bushes. Straight ahead the stairway shone like the backside of a carrousel pony. It briefly occurred to me that maybe I wasn't attempting something so foreign after all. I'd never attacked armed cops before but I certainly had been in my share of scuffles. Cracked a whiskey bottle over an offensive tackle's head once. If I caught Chimp and Fat Cop in the right position, instinct alone could carry me to victory.

I took the steps two at a time, grateful for my bare feet. They didn't make a sound. I stopped at the head of the stairs, pulled the stone from my pocket, and peered down the hallway.

In sports, talk about "being in the zone" is common place. The talk is common place, but it's far from a common place to be. Quarterbacks describe plays unfolding in slow motion, how every receiver was wide open. Basketball players see the ball in the net before they shoot it. For golfers, greens lead to holes large as basketball hoops. Baseball sluggers see the ball big as a grapefruit. To baseball pitchers, a target the size of a flea can't be missed.

Matadors become one with the bull in a graceful dance of death.

My zone was somewhere between the matador and Beethoven. It certainly wasn't that of an accountant, surgeon or poet. As I stepped into the hall my head rang with the horns and strings of Beethoven's fifth: *Dah Dah Dah Daaah. Dah Dah Dah Daaaaah...*

Timing was key. Decent timing might be good enough but, with a little luck, perfect timing was possible. I softened the symphony in my brain and located Johnny's room: five doors down on the left. The door had been left ajar. Voices and grunts filtered out into the hall, swirled over me in cadence with my strides, respiration, level pulse, and Beethoven. There was a sparkling simplicity to everything, clarity of sound and sight, like fly fishing the river at sunrise. I paused at the door and could hear the soft whirl of an overhead fan, taste its air on my lips. I faintly considered gentling the door open...but it had been left ajar for a purpose...my timing *was* perfect. Fat Cop's wide ass was visible. I took immediate advantage. With the stone in my left hand I pushed the door with my right, took two quick stealthy steps and struck. My attack made all the noise of an osprey snatching a salmon, and had the impact of an Indy 500 car wreck.

FINDING DEVO

The scene did not unfold, it just was. A still life demolished. Chimp and Fat Cop had Johnny facedown on the bed; Chimp a shade to the right with a knee imbedded in the small of Johnny's back, Fat Cop a shade to the left, both hands gripping Johnny's legs. Their backs were to me and Johnny wasn't struggling in the least, which served to accentuate the vulnerability of my prey. The instant before my blows came raining down the cops were, for all intents and purposes, motionless, poised to receive justice. My stone struck the base of Fat Cop's skull with enough force to crush a coconut and adhered to my hand. The battle plan was streamlined. My right fist, a formidable but by no means indestructible weapon, would not have to be used. The stone had worked with such alacrity and finality (Fat Cop crumpled off the end of the bed like a bull impaled with a flawless estocada) that all I had to do was extend the natural arc of my swing to hook it into Chimp's face.

Chimp never saw the blow coming. He barely had time to look up from the handcuffs he fumbled before I had the stone planted where his nose used to be. It was a bloody mess. I'd forgotten how bloody noses can be, and his had to be as bloody as they get. The blow squashed his nose like a grape beneath my heel, painting his entire face crimson and splattering blood up in the air, down on the floor, around the walls, and onto my face, neck, arms, legs...and Ara's shirt. Chimp's oversized skull crashed to the solid vinyl floor. I stood over my conquest like a victorious gladiator. That nose needed to be flattened or removed to better match his chimp face. The only thing that would actually improve Chimp's looks was death itself.

I knelt next to his hat and placed my right hand around that pencil neck of his, getting a feel for how easy it would be to kill him, relishing the feeling of power over the fucking prick son of a bitch who tried to sodomize me with his nightstick. But Chimp was out and my rage subsided, a bit. *I'll wait till he's conscious to kill him. It'll feel better that way, for me. Make him look his executioner in the face.* Something took hold of my arm.

"Don't kill him," Johnny said.

I dropped the stone. Johnny stared at me as though I was a four-eyed fish, or a six-legged horse.

"Oh...right," I said. "Mission's not accomplished yet. Pack up your shit." I jumped to the door. A couple was having a heated argument in a room down the hall. The woman sounded drunk, screamed she'd leave right now if there was somewhere to go. I locked the door shut and checked out Fat Cop. A prize pig taking a siesta. My stone had caught more neck than skull. The side of his neck. Any higher on the head and it would have killed him. I stripped him of his

355

gun belt, shoes, and shirt, put them in a pile with his hat, and dragged him into the bathroom. He had deep scratches on his face and neck. Looked like he'd gotten into a fight with a lynx. Chimp groaned back in the room so I saved his life by taking his head in my hands and banging it on the floor to quiet him down. I appreciated the sight—his head without his cop hat on. He was totally hairless: The Hairless Sodomite Chimp. Now, with his nose caved and bottom teeth protruding through his lower lip, he was the Bloody Hairless Pekinese. I gave him the same treatment as Fat Cop but left his shoes on and planted his nightstick down the seat of his pants.

I returned to the bed to retrieve Chimp's handcuffs. Johnny was seated on the floor next to the closet gripping his ankle. "Shit Johnny, what's wrong?"

Johnny rolled his socks down and placed his feet together. His right ankle was red and swelling. "The little shit stomped me. I didn't even resist and he stomped my ankle." Johnny was in a state of disbelief. Calm, measured, disbelief.

"Can you walk?"

"A little. I dunno."

Johnny had packed some of his stuff. I pulled a pair of shorts and two shirts from the closet.

"I'll pack my shit," he said.

"Just helpin'. We gotta go."

I returned to the bathroom with Chimp's cuffs, removed Fat Cop's cuffs from his belt, and cuffed both cops to the plumbing under the sink. Then I rifled through their pockets, stomped their cell phones with the heel of my foot, chucked the handcuff keys into the toilet, and flushed 'em down...after taking a piss. I washed up as best I could in the sink, the near end of the sink to avoid tripping over the pig coppers on the floor, and toweled off. I was pretty damn satisfied with my reflection in the mirror—one badass motherfucker. There was no stoppin' me. The blood-stained towel in the blood-stained sink looked good too, as did the blood on Ara's shirt—matched its soiled color. I grabbed Johnny's shaving kit and toothbrush.

"This all you got in the bathroom?" I tossed his kit and toothbrush onto the bed, along with his passport I'd retrieved from Chimp's back pocket.

"Yeah." Johnny didn't look up from his pack.

"Don't forget your passport."

Johnny said, "What? Oh yeah," as though he'd laid it on the bed himself.

I said, "They had it comin'," in hopes of some acknowledgment. There was none. Once again I considered killing Chimp, desiring more

356

blood after the appetizer I'd tasted. Fear of wasting time got me thinking again. I sat on the edge of the bed and tried on Fat Cop's shoes. They were too small, irritated my stubbed toe. "Shit."

"Now what?" Johnny was kneeling at the foot of the bed, his backpack ready to go.

"Nothin'. Thought I'd get some shoes outta this deal."

Johnny struck me—backhanded my chest. "Shoes?!?" His fingers got snagged in the collar of Ara's shirt, where Fat cop had torn it in the interrogation Chamber. I heard the tear rip and enlarge as he carelessly shook his hand free. Something snapped in my brain at the sound. The golf ball threw a dart, infused me with rage. "Shoes?!?" Johnny repeated. "Forget about—"

I took a fist full of Johnny's shirt, tossed him down on the bed, and pressed my forearm across his neck. He was instantly faceless, an electric pastel swirl of milky white and red and brown, sans center or substance. Time came to an abrupt halt. Somewhere in the mass of radiant paint was a recognizable figure. I fastened my eyes to it and eased the pressure on Johnny's throat so he wouldn't pass out before hearing the undeniable truth:

"I just saved your fucking ass," I hissed. "But I may have come here to kill someone...save myself instead of you." I released him. He gasped, rolled to his stomach and vomited over the edge of the bed. "And if I kill a sadistic prick pig for his shoes, what the fuck do you care? 'specially when I save your hide in the process."

"Russell," he coughed. "Just thought..." he hacked and spit, "we shouldn't waste time."

I handed him the bottled water sticking out the top of his backpack. "You're flustered," I said. "But we do have to go. Clean that blood from your neck."

Johnny swished water around in his mouth, spit it out on the floor, swished more water and shot a stream at the closet door. "Thanks."

"For what?"

Johnny took a gulp of water, made like he was gonna puke again, coughed instead and blew his nose into the bed sheet. "For saving me. That was unbelievable. How did you...? What's happened to you?"

Except for my blurred exceedingly sharp vision, my tranquil racing pulse, my fogged impeccably clear mind, and my numb ultra-sensitive body, I didn't understand what the hell he was talking about.

"We gotta go," I said.

"I don't think I can walk."

"You won't have to. Not far anyway. We got wheels."

I moistened the bed sheet with some water and helped Johnny clean Chimp's blood from his neck and hair. Then I synched Fat Cop's holster around my waist and put on his hat and shirt. Left the shirt untucked to hide the gun. Not a bad fit.

Johnny said he didn't want Chimp's "cop stuff." I told him he was gonna need the hat and shirt and stuffed them into his backpack. It made no sense to leave Chimp his Beretta to shoot me with so I checked the safety and wedged it under my gun belt. The stone was already holstered in the side pocket of my cargo shorts.

I said, "Wonder if I should gag the motherfuckers."

"They'll be out for a while. Let's get the fuck outta here."

I entered the bathroom. They were breathing. And somehow I had miraculously saved Chimp's life once again, this time by leaving him on his side instead of face-up where he surely would have choked to death on his own blood, the blood pooling around his cheek beneath a cuffed arm.

Am I going to regret not killing them?

"Lights out." I flicked off the light and closed the bathroom door.

JOHNNY'S pack was on my back, his left arm draped over my shoulders. Anyone who spied us better not ask any questions or think twice about more walking wounded today. If they did I'd shoot 'em, shoot up the whole fucking hotel. Johnny groaned painfully going down the stairs. I hustled him to reception. He rang the bell. I sat his pack down and hopscotched to the bars at the entrance. A car passed the hotel. The street was clear. The police car, dirty from the day's activities, looked good to go, just like me, but less abused, I hoped.

At reception, the old lady and her old man were telling Johnny he'd have to wait until tomorrow to get into the strong box. I was at Johnny's side in a flash and slammed Chimp's gun on the counter. "Give me the key to the entrance and his paperwork, room 272."

The woman drew a tremulous breath. Her old man wheezed. A sixtyish little brown-faced couple, she with puffy reddish hair and he beetle-browed with the puffy face of interrupted sleep. She exhaled and squinted at me. I tore the phone from the wall. "Ahora mismo!" Right now!

She yelped, quickly sorted through some files, and handed me the paperwork with a trembling hand. Her husband put an arm around her. I had no time to feel sorry for them and politely asked for the entrance key again. She gave it to me. I asked where the hell the computer was. She said they didn't have one yet.

I scanned the paperwork. "Seventy-five bucks a night... Spring-break rates... Box 542. You fill out anything else?"

Johnny said, "No. Let's get into my box. I got five hundred bucks in there."

I folded the paperwork into my back pocket. "You get all your money outta your room?"

"Yeah."

"Two-twenty-five for three nights, plus damages. Let these nice folks here keep the five hundred in your box. You still have cash, credit cards. And I just got reimbursed for a slice of my troubles. Corrupt bastards had plenty of money on 'em—" voices echoed from beyond the garden. I jumped out into the foyer, Chimp's gun at my side. "Back to your rooms!"

A male voice surged from the other side of the birdbath: "We need something to eat!"

I yelled, "Back to your rooms! No one leaves tonight!"

His figure appeared to the left of the birdbath. I skipped behind one of the mangy bushes to hide my shorts, flashed the gun at him and made sure he got a good look at my cop shirt and hat. He beat a hasty retreat. My hand gripped Chimp's Beretta like that of a seasoned killer. I double checked the safety and glanced back at reception. The clock on the wall read 11:45.

I found a cell phone in the room behind reception, smashed it, and told the old couple I'd torch the hotel if they didn't stay put in there for the next hour. The door didn't lock from the outside but the threat might've bought us an extra fifteen minutes or so. As we left, I used my stone to break the key off in the lock to the barred entry.

64

LIEUTENANT Benito Cuevas Romero swept the facade of Casa Mexicana with his binoculars, refocused on the target area, and spoke into his handheld radio. "Yes I have the room spotted, Comandante. The light remains on, as our reconnaissance team reported. Over."

"No mistake? The light is on?"

"Sí. The privacy curtains are drawn but the opaque curtains are open. And the balcony is clear. Over."

"Have you seen any shadows, signs of movement inside the room as reported earlier? Over."

"Not yet...wait. I just saw a shadow pass by the window, Comandante. And again. Someone is in there."

SEVE VERDAD

The lieutenant was hunkered down on the beach with a police sergeant from Tepic—another extra hand in from out of town to assist in any way possible. El comandante had assured Lieutenant Romero that Sargento Bolívar was as good as his resume: an experienced bodyguard and crack shot with a rifle, the Remington 700P he was scoping the hotel with right now.

As spotter, the lieutenant conferred with Bolívar to verify that his sharpshooter had the right room in his sights—center of the hotel one floor from the top. Seventy meters or so away. The only room in that sector with a light on. All neighboring rooms had been evacuated.

Three more teams of two police officers each—a marksman and spotter—were similarly hunkered down along the beach. One of those spotters manned a searchlight to illuminate the balcony when he received the order. And four teams of police—three each—had cordoned off the beach at either end of Casa Mexicana as well as the pool area so innocents would not get caught in the crossfire should this raid come down to a firefight.

"We will win a firefight," said the mayor as el comandante left headquarters for Casa Mexicana, "but what if a bomb is in there?"

"What do you suggest we do?" said CISEN Lead Interrogator Joaquín de Jesús, "wait for it to go off?"

There wasn't much debate over the issue. They needed to move fast and maintain the element of surprise.

El comandante was careful not to disrupt the hotel by storming it with his troops. They moved quickly in thin ranks, two-by-two up separate stairwells to the eleventh floor.

Down by the water's edge, ambient light radiating from the hotel floated through the warm mist like weighty gas, falling well short of the officers lying in wait above the tide on the steep sand. The lieutenant spied more than a few pensive silhouettes standing out on balconies. They may have known something was up but were well removed from the target area. The only way those figures would see or hear anything at all was if there was a firefight...or worse.

On the eleventh floor of Casa Mexicana, el comandante had gathered a team of ten men including himself: Joaquín de Jesús, the three federale agents from el DF, and five uniformed Vallarta police, all clad in body armor and helmets and armed to kill.

El comandante relayed the latest: the lieutenant had glimpsed shadows in the room. One or more persons were likely in there, possibly their suspect. "Beach teams stand by," he said into his radio and gave the signal to his men.

FINDING DEVO

Garras moved into position to one side of room 1163, his .44 held at a forty-five degree angle from the floor, a 9mm holstered at his hip. The federales opposite him gripped fully automatic Glocks; Vallarta police were armed with standard issue Berettas. El comandante brought up the rear, behind Garras, 9mm in one hand, his handheld radio in the other.

Hernando Talla, a big expansive officer, took point. He was one of the three men who had been incapacitated during the prisoner's escape and relished his position, expecting a slice of revenge. His field partner, Diego, was to simply slide the card key through the lock, turn the handle, and get the hell out of the way of the battering ram manned by the two officers behind him. (The card key would open the door but the security latch would likely be in place on the other side.)

Butterflies fluttered in el comandante's chest. He really needed this one. He and the department had suffered one debacle after another the past few days, culminating in the inconceivable attack on the Washington this morning and the escape of Russell Martell this evening; he could not afford to screw up another raid. Overall he remained confident though, and sensed that this might be his finest hour. He had the manpower, firepower, and a sound strategy, including the element of surprise...but hadn't he had all that going for him for Saturday's botched raid as well?

Everyone had some butterflies. This was a big moment. If terrorists were in there you could wind up a hero, dead, or both. Sure you were confident, wouldn't be trying it otherwise. But even the federales felt flutters twittering their trigger fingers. Not Garras though. He relished opportunities like this and didn't feel a butterfly's breath in his chest. Supremely confident, although he did have his misgivings.

Thus far, local law enforcement had not shown themselves to be up to snuff and Garras had his doubts as to whether or not they could perform well now. And the federales were out for glory, desperate to upstage him, the CISEN man. This was bound to make them prone to mistakes. But, as Garras guarded the rear, any resistance should be softened up for him, and his shots always rang true. The raid would be a success...unless their man or men were not inside this room. In that case the raid would be a tactical, if not unmitigated failure.

Garras thought this entirely possible. He had read a copy of the police report on Saturday's botched raid. El comandante had acted precipitously on what amounted to faulty information wrested from that jailed gangster "Paco". He might be making a similar mistake now.

SEVE VERDAD

Garras hoped this raid yielded someone to be interrogated, someone he could practice his specialty on, or resulted in the death of terrorists; but whether it did or not he knew there were bound to be enough loose ends left dangling to require CISEN's intervention. An Iranian terrorist had been found dead at the marina! a sure indication of foreign complicity in the Washington massacre. CISEN, with its international reach, would have to be employed to conduct this investigation sooner rather than later.

El comandante pressed his radio to his lips. "Spot the balcony."

Diego slid the card through the lock, turned the handle and scooted aside as the battering ram crushed the door open. Hernando Talla and the federales led the way inside and announced their presence in stentorian voices—a cacophony of baritone bluster intended to intimidate whoever was in the room into disarming before shots were fired. It seemed to do the trick. No shots were fired. Hernando busted into the bathroom on his right and waved the others through. But the bathroom, bedroom, balcony and closet were already cleared. The place was empty.

El comandante planted himself in the bedroom amidst a din of frustrated curses and raised his voice into his radio. "I thought you said you saw shadows, someone up here, Lieutenant!"

"I did, señor." The lieutenant seemed to choke on his words, "I...I have no idea what else it could have been. Over."

"There is not a soul in here! The room is empty!"

"Completely empty," said Garras. He stood at the closet examining the wall safe. "Including the closet and..." Garras eased the safe open with a pencil so el comandante could see for himself, "the safe."

"And the bed has not been slept in," observed Investigator Herrera. "Freshly made. At reception they said maid service was sporadic today due to all the chaos. This room was not cleaned or requested to be cleaned. When was the last time our infamous Señor Martell slept here?"

"Lieutenant?"

The lieutenant's voice crackled over el comandante's radio, "Sí?"

"Get those men off the beach and down to headquarters. I shall meet you there shortly. Over and out."

The balcony went dark. El comandante ordered his five uniformed officers to grab the battering ram and return to headquarters. This time Hernando led the way *out* the door, without the stentorian bluster. The only words at all from him and the other officers were mumbles of "hijo de la chingada," "puta madre," and, "me lleva."

FINDING DEVO

Federale Investigator Sándovar was on his knees peering under the bed. "Find anything, Sándovar?" said el comandante.

Sándovar got to his feet, a look of puzzled exasperation on his face. "Even if he did not sleep here last night, if the suspect returned here after his escape to gather his belongings he must have been in quite a hurry. Clothes, trash, some kind of clue should have been left behind. But the way things look around here he left before the last cleaning yesterday. And if that is the case, why was the room booked until Saturday? And why did he leave without checking out? His American Express voucher is still at reception."

Garras exited the bathroom. "Bathroom is clean and dry," he said, "towels neat, unused. And the trashcan is empty. It looks as though the chingón packed up and left this room sometime yesterday, well before his arrest this morning. The bed has not been slept in...the maid may have swept away any forensic evidence yesterday."

Investigator Barrera closed the last of the dresser drawers he was searching. "The night manager said she saw him Saturday night. He probably vacated the room Sunday sometime to prepare for the attack this morning. And maybe he skipped checkout to cover his ass in case we came looking for him, so we would think he was still here."

"It still may be possible to discover forensic evidence he left behind," Sándovar said, "at the very least fingerprints... We need to know precisely when maid service last cleaned this room, what time they cleaned it and what, if anything, they saw or found in here. And as of right now this room cannot be touched by maid service or anyone else until we have a chance to go over it thoroughly. I recommend we get someone up here from hotel security to board this door up right away."

"Agreed," said el comandante. "And we need to interview the maids."

Garras leaned back against the bedroom wall, hands stuffed in his pockets, arms bowed, looking muscle bound. His body armor broadened his frame, adding breadth, an extra dimension to his wide reach and wrestler's physique. His helmet was extra-large to accommodate his thick cranium; the holstered .44 bulging from underneath his left shoulder added extra muscle, muscle Garras still hoped to exercise this evening. He regarded el comandante and the three federale investigators cynically, his eyes blue stripes under charcoal eyebrows. "Our suspect is two steps ahead of us," he said evenly. "If we do not recapture or kill him within the next twelve to eighteen hours we may not have another chance for quite some time. And if he has already found his way out of Vallarta...well, then he is a hundred kilometers or more ahead of us by now."

"What are you suggesting?" said el comandante.

Garras pulled his cell phone from its case at his belt. "That we work all night to catch this man. And that we get some real professional help here. CISEN will have to take this case over right away. I shall inform my section chief that further delays are unacceptable and insist that a team be flown out here immediately."

"That will have to be cleared through el DF," said Investigator Barrera. "CISEN has no authority here."

Investigator Sándovar shot the CISEN man an angry glance. "*We* shall decide when to take over the investigation, not CISEN."

"CISEN was ordered to stand down on this one," said Investigator Herrera. "And—"

Garras hissed, "No one tells CISEN to stand down, especially when national security is at stake. And from what I have seen and read about this case, the national security of México is most definitely at stake here." Garras shifted his penetrating glare to el comandante. "Your people should have informed CISEN immediately when it was discovered that the dead man found at the marina was an Iranian terrorist. This case has an international scope and that was a dereliction of duty. As are two botched raids in three days." Garras trapped the federale investigators in his fierce stare, "Botched raids carried out with the help of *pinches federales*."

Garras stepped off the wall, el comandante and the three federales in a row before him. They had no defense, nothing to say, and just stood there mute, as though the CISEN man had his garras at their throats ready to squeeze should they utter a sound. And he did have them by the throats. They knew it. This case had CISEN written all over it.

Investigators Barrera and Herrera pushed their helmets off their foreheads and looked thoughtfully at Sándovar. None of them had ever heard of Joaquín de Jesús before today, but that was not surprising. CISEN wasn't exactly in the habit of fraternizing with DF federale agents. Even as CISEN restructured to integrate into the army in its war against gangsters and drug cartels the agency remained an enigma. An all-powerful, all-seeing phantom. You knew the beast was around somewhere but tried not to think much about it because there was nothing on earth you could do to thwart its power anyway, not without someone from the highest levels of government to run interference for you. No investigator, be it a state or DF federale or private eye, knew exactly when CISEN, with its national and international reach, was going to exercise its jurisdiction over a case until the agency up and took it from you...

Federale investigators Sándovar, Herrera, and Barrera had obtained backing from DF government officials. Whether or not this would be enough to thwart CISEN remained to be seen.

Sándovar wasn't ready to throw in the towel. "Under the circumstances," he said, "I will have to confer with our superiors in el DF right away. However, until we receive orders to the contrary, this investigation is still being run by local authorities until we take it over." Sándovar turned to el comandante. "We shall meet you at police headquarters, señor, to map out our next course of action."

The three federale investigators marched out of the room single file, Sándovar at the lead. Up until now Garras wasn't sure who was leading that team of federale putos. Not that it mattered. Sándovar was nothing to him. A peon. Junior league.

Garras removed his helmet, had a seat on the bed, and began punching numbers on his cell phone. Tremors rippled down the backs of Héctor's legs. Finding himself alone with the CISEN man after yet another humiliating botched raid filled him with a desperate sense of urgency. CISEN was about to take over this case, would they insist that the Comandante of the Puerto Vallarta Police Department be replaced? Héctor had to do something to ingratiate himself to Señor de Jesús. His career depended on it.

"Señor de Jesús..." he began haltingly, "I want you to know that the Puerto Vallarta Police Department will do everything in its power to assist CISEN. I—"

"I thought you were going to talk to hotel security about boarding up this room."

"Sí, señor. Right away."

Héctor Diamante Pasqual found some spring to his step as he exited the room. He couldn't allow himself to get discouraged. There must be a way to redeem himself. CISEN would soon exercise its authority, yet Héctor knew that the agency wasn't beyond utilizing any and every resource at its disposal to aid in an investigation, including local police and federales, as long as CISEN was the *mandamás*—big shot, the one giving the orders. He had to make sure he put himself in a position to aid CISEN and work with them. If he played his cards right, he may yet have a hand in the recapture or death of Russell Martell. He had to! It was the one sure way to salvage his reputation and career. And he wasn't beyond kissing CISEN ass to do it.

GARRAS remained seated on the bed, all alone now in room 1163, waiting patiently for his section chief to pick up. But for some reason he couldn't get through. No voice mail, nothing. Just ringing and ringing and ringing.

Odd. He spoke to him only an hour and a half ago.

Garras tried again. His section chief picked up right away, his voice smoky and gruff, and a bit peeved: "What news have you now, Joaquín? Another escape or bombing? Is Vallarta about to be overrun by terrorists and gangsters?"

"Maybe, Jefe. The raid on the escaped prisoner's room turned up absolutely nothing. Local law enforcement and DF federales are bungling this case as we speak. I recommend you helicopter a team out here right away to exercise some authority and—"

El jefe cut him off, "Helicopter? In this weather?"

"What weather, Jefe?" Garras glanced out the open sliding glass door. "Just a bit of mist and drizzle. There is no wind or—"

"Take a look outside, hombre. We have near hurricane conditions here in Guadalajara. Are you sure Vallarta is not suffering the same?"

Garras stood from the bed, strolled out onto the balcony and glanced about. Agitated ocean waters sounded through the mist and drizzle. "The weather is rare for this time of year, Jefe, but far from hurricane conditions. If a helicopter is impossible perhaps our jet can make the run. Fill it with as many men as we can and—"

"Are you telling me the sky is not opening up out there? I have it on my computer screen right now. Vallarta is in the midst of a torrential storm."

Garras leaned out over the rail to have a look up at the sky beyond the balcony above, befuddled. Qué diablos was el jefe talking about? The sky was dark, sure, and this mist, eerie but...a storm, hurricane? "Sorry, Jefe. You are mistaken. We are not suffering a storm here. Only this strange drizzly mist... Jefe? Are you there, Jefe? Can you hear me?" The line went dead. Garras stared at his phone. What was that all about? Hurricane conditions? in Guadalajara?

Garras planted his elbows on the railing and tried his section chief's number again. A hot wind kicked up off the ocean, gave him an inexplicable chill. This weather *was* strange, but a hurricane?

He waited for his section chief's phone to ring. It didn't ring, but Garras heard his smoky voice. A low, sanguine breath that set the hair on the back of his neck on end.

"There is a storm, Garras," said the smoky voice. A sonorous whisper far removed yet directly behind the cell phone Garras had pressed to his ear. "And I am the hurricane."

Garras didn't even attempt to reach for his .44. It was too late for that. An intruder was upon him! A killer. Only an experienced assassin could have put him off his guard like this, set him up for an ambush, an assault from the rear. A cunning assassin who left him with nothing but a flash of instinct to defend himself. He tried to thrust an elbow back and strike a debilitating blow before wheeling around and attacking, ripping a throat or throwing a punch, but it was too late for that as well. The CISEN man was instantly immobilized, unable to breathe, unable to even turn his head! Something had a hold of his throat, a powerful, steeled grip! a monstrous, unshakable claw ripping and tearing at his larynx and crushing the vertebrae in his neck... Had his neck been snapped?!? Was that why he couldn't move?!?

"I cannot afford to have CISEN around just yet, Garras," said the voice. A new voice. A toneless, emotionless voice. The last voice Joaquín Garras de Jesús would ever hear. "Poetic justice, Garras. You lived by the garra and now you die by the garra."

Garras couldn't move, but his killer had no trouble at all manipulating him—hanging him off the balcony, ripping his throat out with two violent shakes of his claw, and letting him silently fall eleven stories where the corpse of Joaquín Garras de Jesús was planted deep within the flowering red hibiscus bordering Casa Mexicana's koi pond.

65

JOHNNY'S mood went from ebullient to sober in no time at all. As we took off in the cop car he called me a hero. "A *goddamn* hero!" he hollered, "like an army commando rescuing a hostage!" His voice fulminated with unrestrained emotion, like we'd just pulled off a bank heist, or won a championship ballgame. He clapped me on the shoulder. "When we get back to the States I'm gonna pin a medal on you."

"Thanks. But how the hell we gonna get back to the States?"

My question quieted him. I pulled down a darkened side street and slowed the car. Johnny set his jaw. "Two choices," he said. "Try to escape Vallarta now or hide out somewhere until—"

"Devo told me he had a place for me to hide out," I interjected in a flat voice to disguise my chagrin. Given how my attempt to gain control of my destiny had nearly led to disaster, I shouldn't have left Devo in the first place. "We gotta find him..."

"CHRIST Russ, do you really need to attract attention?"

SEVE VERDAD

I flipped off the siren and flashing lights. They were the last pieces of equipment to be tested and had only been on for a second or two. "Just making sure I know how they work. We might need 'em."

Our police car was a late-model Pontiac with automatic transmission, decent brakes and acceleration, fog lamps, functioning high and low beams, adjustable windshield wipers (they remained on low for the time being), air conditioning, and a half-tank of gas. Johnny was seated next to me in Chimp's hat and blood-stained shirt, his foot up on the dash to relieve pressure from his ankle. He had a badge on his chest. The shirt I was wearing, Fat Cop's, had a hole in it where the badge should be. I'd probably lost the badge in Johnny's room.

I tested the car's acceleration again and braked. Johnny reached for the CB radio and turned up the volume. "You hear that?"

"Sure did."

Crackling voices on the CB were reporting action along the boulevard. Johnny didn't understand the Spanish but did recognize the words "Casa Mexicana."

I could feel his eyes boring into me as I drove. "Something's happening at your hotel," he said.

"You surprised?"

"We'd a been busted there."

"And nearly got busted at your hotel. But we didn't." I lowered the CB's volume. The static grated on my nerves, though the CB could prove invaluable as it provided information about what the cops were up to.

I'd turned off the car's AM radio a minute ago, after hearing my name and description and that I was wanted for arson related to the "disaster" at the Washington. Russell Martell was armed and dangerous and thought to have accomplices. I didn't hear anything about a jailbreak or that I was wanted for *bombing* the Washington, but listening to that crap and translating it for Johnny cluttered my mind and made me wanna scream, so I kept the radio off. An ironic truth to the report wasn't lost on Johnny however: I *was* armed and dangerous and *he* was my accomplice.

I made a leisurely left. "If we hear your hotel's name over the CB," I said, "then we're in big trouble. Once police visit Hotel Marciano and find Chimp and Fat Cop they'll know we jacked this car and search like hell for it."

"Chimp?"

"You got his hat and shirt on. The little shit who stomped your ankle. Gave me this lump," I flicked my earlobe at him, "the golf ball

368

behind my ear. He busted me at the Washington and tried to fuck me with his nightstick at police headquarters."

"He did huh?" Johnny snorted, "Chimp and Fat Cop. Sounds like a charming couple. Hope this plan works out better than the last one so I don't hafta meet the rest of the gang." He sank down in his seat and crossed his arms, a dry, hectic look on his face.

Our "plan" was to find Devo, our only option. Roadblocks prevented our escape from Vallarta and we wouldn't last long in the woods or a suburban deathtrap. I had severe doubts about Devo and his motives, but there was nowhere else to turn. He'd rescued me once tonight and might be able to do so again. The best place to start looking for him was where we left him, in El Cabezón. I was driving slowly, trying to feel my way back to Libramiento and the route Devo had taken to avoid cops after breaking me out of jail.

Johnny grumbled, "How in the hell did those pigs know about my hotel?"

"Manco," I said and swung a leisurely right.

"What?"

"Carlos. You met him at the party, didn't you? The guy with one arm."

"Yeah, I remember that guy... So?"

"Manco's connected to Chimp. I heard Chimp mention him to Fat Cop before they entered your hotel."

Johnny scowled. "Chimp...and Manco...and Fat Cop. Whatever you say, Russ."

Our road doubled back toward Hotel Marciano. I cursed, "Damn. We don't have time to dick around looking for a safe route. We're gonna have to go for that traffic jam at Francisco Villa and Libramiento—Bypass Road."

"The way the taxi brought us."

"Yeah."

"A few cops around there."

"I know. When we see an opening we gotta go for it."

I was taking it nice and easy, as if trying to avoid the inevitable, but felt we would make it, just didn't know how much to rush things.

Johnny said, "I never told Manco anything 'cept my name."

"First and last?"

"I don't fucking remember...what the—"

"I know, Johnny. Shit. Sorry. Manco could've gotten our full names at the party, or who knows where else. Don't matter. But Miguel, the guy you and Gail left the party with last night, he knew where you were staying, right?"

"Yeah."

"Manco's a devious prick. I'll be damned if I can keep up with the fucking hijo de puta. He knows we're buddies. He must have spoken with Miguel sometime today and given the name of your hotel to Chimp. I doubt Miguel knows what a shithead Manco is but..."

Johnny craned his neck at me. "You've gotta be kidding. Why the hell would Manco do that?!? Any of this?!? Did he also have Chimp bust you down at the Washington?"

"Maybe. Saw him there."

"Why would a guy like that be involved with Mountain or *anyone* you hang out with?"

"Rosalita's friends were, are the ones I generally hang with." I shot Johnny a pitiful glance. "You know that. Mountain's a good buddy but I didn't know many people at his party, least of all Manco... Manco's family is old friends with Mountain's, that's what Brenda said at the party anyway. And Mountain'll be plenty pissed when he finds out about all this. But Manco... I butted heads with him last night. The guy's a punk asshole with some heavy stones to grind."

That's all I said on the subject but my suspicions about Manco's motives ran much deeper. Deeper than the crater at the bottom of the Washington ruins.

Johnny held his head in his hands. He was borderline totally, inconsolably, irrevocably pissed-off, ready to lose control at any moment 'cause he had no control anyway. His injured ankle had a lot to do with it, along with my insights into Manco's treachery. I'm sure my foray into half-bridled insanity back in his hotel room had Johnny on edge as well. The depth of our predicament suddenly overwhelmed me. I stopped the car, eyes holding on the empty street before us. "Story gettin' any better yet?" I said.

He replied with a snort. A friendly snort, more throat than diaphragm.

I waited.

Johnny said, "That's what I get for hangin' with you."

"Get your foot off the dash. Start acting like a cop."

"Show some respect for the law."

I eased my foot on the gas. "We *are* the law."

"Better be."

66

MEDIA Minister Lazarito Charlado muted one TV and turned up the volume to another—the latest news about Russell Martell. Same as the last news broadcast about him. Same fresh-faced photo, same alleged crimes: arson related to the disaster at the Washington and drug trafficking. Considered armed and dangerous. Nothing new. Nothing related to the astonishing fax Lazarito had received earlier this evening here at The Bureau. Lazarito locked the fax in his desk, a self-satisfied smile curling his lips. It appeared that whoever sent him the communiqué was his own personal source, and a knowledgeable one. El comandante had called Lazarito back over an hour ago to confirm a key piece of information contained in the fax—the name of Russell Martell's hotel.

Once he received that confirmation, Lazarito lent credence to other information contained in the fax and whipped together a sensational story on El Gringo Terrorista for publication in tomorrow's edition of the Vallarta Diario. His sources, glossed over as "knowledgeable" and "intimate," were the anonymous fax, his own insights derived from his personal encounters with the egotistical Gringo Terrorista, and information provided him by his faithful snitch, Paulo. The result was but a few columns of prose, yet the words spoke volumes. Succinct and to the point, the article was sure to leave the reader begging for more, national and international media outlets begging for more, Lazarito's most important audience, the Mexican pueblo, begging for more. And he would give them more, for a price. A price to be paid not only in money but status and power.

He had e-mailed the story for publication over half an hour ago. If el comandante called to inform him that Russell Martell was killed or captured tonight, perhaps during the raid on his hotel room, it would not diminish the story's impact. Lazarito knew that rumors of a bomb going off at the Washington would not die but be corroborated, as would the rumors of terrorists here in Vallarta—a terrorist *conspiracy* here in Vallarta. His story in the Vallarta Diario tomorrow was designed and destined to begin bringing the truth to the people, a truth he would continue to expound upon and hammer home in the media in the days and weeks to come.

Lazarito dimmed the TV's volume, reclined in his rather squeaky leather armchair, and felt his fatigue ebb as he closed his eyes. For most of the day and into the night, it looked as though his career might be another casualty of the day's devastation and carnage. Yet somehow he had managed to snatch personal victory from disastrous anguish and defeat, a personal victory that would make him a big player in the pursuit, capture and/or death of the perpetrators of a heinous crime...or *crimes.* Who knew what acts of barbarism these terrorists had committed in the past? and what crimes they planned for the future...? With Lazarito Charlado on the job to expose these monsters, Mexico and the world could rest easier. Lazarito could rest easier. In fact, he already was resting easier, reposed in a dreamlike state. A broad smile lifted his fleshy cheeks. He envisioned himself a towering figure, a majestic figure, a hero to be dealt with on his own terms—the man who broke the case of the bombing of the Washington wide open.

Then he received a startling phone call that set him on edge again, literally floored him, and reminded the Media Minister that he hadn't snatched victory from disastrous defeat just yet.

LAZARITO reached for his cordless phone. "Media Minister Charlado," he answered, noting the *restricted number* message on his caller ID, as well as the time—midnight.

"Señor Charlado?" cooed a meek feminine voice Lazarito couldn't place.

"Sí...? To whom am I speaking?"

"Araceli, Señor Charlado. We met at the dedication of Arena Vallarta and then at my party last night. My fiancé's party, Armando Montoya."

"Yes, of course," he said slowly and braced himself over his desk as though preparing to arm wrestle. Russell Martell was at that party. "Araceli..." Lazarito had been on a roll the last couple of hours tonight and sensed a reality check coming his way, "...to what do I owe this unexpected pleasure?"

"I suppose it is unexpected. I am sorry."

"Not at all, Araceli." Lazarito also sensed opportunity. This might be a first: an interview with someone who knew the suspect. After his faithful snitch, Paulo, had informed him that *Russell Martell* was the name of the escaped prisoner, he'd planned on hunting down guests from Armando Montoya's party who may have known him. Was Araceli about to save him the trouble? Or maybe she would cause him trouble. Did she know he had met Russell Martell, spoken with him at her party? Had Russell Martell said something to her about the botched raid? the cover-up? "How can I be of assistance?" he said politely.

"I hope you understand, Señor Charlado, that, considering its content and with all the confusion today, I thought it prudent not to attach my name to the fax I sent you. And I wanted to make this personal call to make sure you received it."

Lazarito took a sharp gulp of air to keep himself together. He never would have guessed...but he had only received one anonymous fax... "Which fax are you referring to, Araceli? Did it have someone else's name on the cover page?"

"No. There was no cover page. And your office was the only place I sent it. It was a fax pertaining to a certain guest at my house last night. I am not sure if you met him but his name is all over the news now."

Lazarito's voice cracked. He cleared his throat. "Momentito Araceli," he said, his voice cracking again, "let me see if I can locate it." Media Minister Charlado muffled the phone against his ponderous belly and took a few moments to calm his racing mind.

Now he knew the source of the anonymous fax. This was something of a relief. As a rule, a journalist should always know where his information comes from. Moreover, although Lazarito had only just met her yesterday, Araceli did not in the least strike him as some crackpot out to publicize outlandish claims. It appeared that, once again, his instincts were right on the money. He'd made the right decision in using the fax as a source for his story in the Vallarta Diario.

But Araceli presented a problem. A problem he'd been somewhat prepared for but didn't expect to have to deal with tonight. A problem that brought back all his fears of disgrace, humiliation...and incarceration.

Russell Martell knew about the cover-up of the botched raid and Lazarito was in no hurry to divulge that he had met him. If the maldito gringo had said anything to anybody about the cover-up, wrote anything...if and when it came to light that Russell Martell knew of the cover-up, or that Lazarito knew he knew...

Lazarito hoped to God the hijo de puta was killed tonight.

If only he had refused el comandante's bribe just this once and published that story on the raid, seen to it that police and federales were held accountable, the public alerted to the possible threat, this whole nightmare might have been averted—the carnage at the Washington and the charges of corruption and concealing evidence shadowing him like the sins of his fathers...the sins of Mexico. The sins of the Aztecs. The sins of Cortez.

Charges of corruption and concealing evidence might be the least of Lazarito's worries. If one of those DF political cronies out for his job discovered he had met Russell Martell, that the Media Minister knew Russell Martell was aware of the cover-up, he just might have his culo fried for obstruction of justice as well, complicity in...accessory to...an act of terror...

Guilty by association...a real possibility the rare times cases of corruption were prosecuted in Mexico.

SEVE VERDAD

Right from the start Lazarito knew Russell Martell was no good but there was no way on earth he could have known the man was a terrorist. And he hadn't exactly withheld or concealed evidence, certainly nothing that would have identified Russell Martell as a terrorist. Yet in the heat of battle for his position as Media Minister (not to mention his reputation and freedom) that probably wouldn't matter and he didn't need to lend ammunition to his enemies by revealing to anybody that he knew El Gringo Terrorista. Not to Araceli or anyone else... Not yet anyway. Not just before his power was solidified with his sensational story in tomorrow's paper!

Araceli wasn't sure if he had met Russell Martell. A good sign. Hopefully the gringo hadn't communicated his take on the botched raid and ensuing cover-up to her or anyone of consequence and was a dead man before he did.

He had already lied about this once. When his faithful snitch, Paulo, asked him if the name *Russell Martell* meant anything to him Lazarito said "not at all." That was a trivial lie though. Names are often forgotten. And at present, the photo of Russell Martell on the news was sufficiently distinct from the man he had met yesterday and the case still so fresh that he had plausible deniability should the mayor or anyone else in a position of power suddenly find out he had met Russell Martell. He could simply say he didn't *remember* having met him. Claiming a lapse in memory is always a reliable, if only temporary defense.

It would be a great relief if Russell Martell were killed tonight. Outstanding news. But he may have already communicated his knowledge of the cover-up to someone, and the first place to begin that search was with those who had attended Armando Montoya's party. Lazarito planned to interview everyone from the party he could possibly contact. He had to before some gung-ho journalist did and exposed his sins to the world.

Lazarito wished he could kill Russell Martell himself, shoot him dead. Shoot him in the back of the head with the pistol stashed in his dresser at home. Kill him before he spilled his guts about the cover-up. Kill him before...someone reminded the Media Minister of Puerto Vallarta that he had indeed met Russell Martell. It was only a matter of time before someone did. He'd been seen with him at Armando Montoya's party. And right now, at this very moment, Araceli was curious if he had met him. Lazarito couldn't lie to her and say he never met Russell Martell. Should someone from the party tell her they saw him speaking with him he might lose her confidence...or worse.

Getting caught in a lie like that was a sure sign of having something to hide. Russell Martell had demonstrated he knew about the cover-up of the botched raid, so Lazarito did have something to hide with respect to him, but there was no sense in risking exposure by lying to Araceli about having met him... And in the long run, did it really matter? Did it really matter that he had met Russell Martell at the party? that the cocky cabrón had introduced himself to him in front of witnesses? In and of itself, no. Fear of the cover-up of the botched raid coming to light was what horrified Lazarito. Many people must have known or met Russell Martell at the party. Had the mayor been in the right spot at the right time he might have met him (Lazarito was certain he hadn't. The mayor had given no indication that he had and was most always with the Media Minister during the party or within his line of vision amongst the guests).

Did Lazarito have to remain defensive about having met Russell Martell? At this juncture, he realized there was no use in it. Subterfuge is often more dangerous than the truth when the subterfuge is apt to be discovered. It just made the truth appear more incriminating, or damning lies look like the truth. And opportunities were at hand right now. Foremost, an opportunity to garner information from Araceli. An opportunity to take advantage of, not squander by assuming a defensive posture.

Lazarito reminded himself to have confidence. After his earthshaking story broke tomorrow he would solidify his position of power. Any accusations against him were destined to be killed and buried by the truth (no way he could have known Russell Martell was a terrorist!) or spun beyond recognition by his own indomitable guile (by hook or crook he would see to it that any charges implicating him of corruption never gained traction in the media or anywhere else). Now was the time to use his guile. The perfect time. Araceli was on the other end of the phone to help him *remember* Russell Martell...

Araceli represented a source, a valuable source. She needn't know how valuable she was of course. She'd find much of the information contained in her fax on tomorrow's front page but that didn't necessarily mean it came from her. Yet Lazarito knew how valuable she was. Araceli needed to be treated with care, at the very least because she had not requested anything in return for her information...yet.

Would she ask for something in return for her information? Maybe not. Perhaps she merely acted out of the goodness of her heart, a desire to see justice done. How much did she know? Enough to understand that Media Minister Lazarito Charlado was the only man worthy of receiving her fax, the only man worthy of publicizing the information she had to share. Araceli knew enough to realize that the media can shine the light of truth on the guilty and see to it that justice is done. She knew enough to...be milked for more information. Important information Lazarito had intended to get before he had received her fax...information on the connection between Russell Martell and that sexy mamacita at the party, Brenda.

If anyone else at the party knew about the cover-up it just might be Brenda.

Lazarito was back in his element. He'd treat Araceli with care but essentially the same as anybody else—with half-truths and deception until he got what he wanted.

Media Minister Charlado brought the phone to his ear and rustled some papers on his desk for effect. "Araceli?"

"Sí?"

"So sorry for the short delay. I have the fax in my hand right now. Most informative, indeed it is. But was this man really at your party last night?"

"Sí señor. Naturally I had no idea at the time that he was...was planning..." Araceli's voice faded. Lazarito thought he heard her sniffle.

"I understand, Araceli. Of course you had no idea. But you did send me the fax so—"

"Sometimes it is impossible to know what to believe. So many rumors. But after what happened this morning I just had to get the word out about this man and knew you could publicize it."

"I see. May I ask why you did not go to police with your information?"

Araceli whimpered, "Oh I beg you not to tell them I sent you the fax. They may try to implicate me in this...this..."

Lazarito soothed Araceli's pleas in a gentle, paternal tone. "I understand," he said. "You have my assurance of complete confidentiality, Araceli. It was most wise and brave of you to send the fax to me, indeed it was... Let me take this opportunity to thank you for your information. I am sure it will be most useful."

"But my information is not on the news...only his picture and that he is wanted for drug trafficking, and arson related to—"

"Have patience, Araceli." Lazarito clucked at the irony. If not for his own patience and the promise he'd made to wait at least twenty-four hours before implicating terrorists in today's catastrophe, Araceli would have found much of the information contained in her fax reported in the media by now. "The day has been most trying, Araceli," he added, "chaotic. But I assure you that the information in your fax is and will be useful, if anything to corroborate other sources of information at my disposal."

Araceli sniffled again, audibly this time. "I thought maybe you remembered him..."

"Now that you mention it...let me take a closer look at your fax here." Lazarito relaxed in his deep leather armchair and stared at his open palm, imagining the fax (judiciously secured in his locked desk) in his empty hand. "This photo is similar to the one on television and the Internet... I have no idea where those came from. Naturally, I cannot take credit for all the media releases. Impossible to do that. And everyone has their hands full today. I am sure you understand."

"I think so, Señor Charlado. But I thought my fax would be of special importance."

Lazarito hiccupped lugubriously, his feet lifting off the carpet as he reclined in his chair. "It *is* of special importance, Araceli. I assure you it is. And thanks to you I do indeed remember this man from your party. It had not occurred to me before but... Yes. He does seem familiar... Did he...? I must say he looked quite a bit different last night. He had facial hair, and a black eye?"

"That was him. The man in the fax."

"My, my. But at the risk of sounding impertinent, why was such a notorious character at your party?"

"Do you remember seeing him with anyone there?"

"I believe so. He was chatting with a young woman, a woman I met briefly. Her name was..." Lazarito wheezed in feigned reflection. "It seems her name escapes me at the moment..."

"Probably my sister," said Araceli. "Brenda."

"Ahh yes, Brenda. Your sister? Really...I had no idea. Did he arrive with her?"

"No. But their relationship...it..."

"Yes?"

"I believe we should talk about this in person, Señor Charlado."

"Most certainly, Araceli. How about tomorrow morning, in my office?"

"I think not. But I will call you there around eleven. Then we can meet somewhere and..."

"Yes?"

"I may have more information for you."

Lazarito squeaked back further in his chair and prompted Araceli with a lilting hum. "Might you give me a hint, my dear? Surprises after a catastrophe such as the one we suffered today can be most disconcerting."

Araceli hesitated. Her tone gained a sharp, secretive inflection: "For now I can only say that it has to do with something you may already know, something about a police raid this evening."

SEVE VERDAD

Lazarito cringed in shock at the word "raid", disturbing his equilibrium. His chair released an onerous creak, teetered backward, and landed him flat on his back, phone pressed to his ear, pudgy knees pointed at the ceiling. It was all he could do to keep from tumbling out of his chair, making a racket and alerting Araceli to the fact that he'd been literally floored by her knowledge of a raid (thank God she was talking about tonight's raid on Russell Martell's room and not Saturday's botched raid...wasn't she?). But as things stood now, or as he lay there now, Araceli was none the wiser and Lazarito, ever the great improviser, didn't even attempt to get up. He was fine where he was and, without demurring, released a provocative "hummm...?" a squeal of disbelief, and added, "Raid? My but you are full of surprises. What is this about a raid?"

"The raid on..." Araceli lowered her voice to a near whisper, "...on Señor Martell's room tonight turned up nothing. Absolutely nothing."

Lazarito contemplated the ceiling (he had nowhere else to look) and quickly decided to risk being more frank with Araceli than he had originally intended: "Fascinating, Araceli. I had no idea the raid had concluded yet. I must say you have piqued my interest once again. You are a most intriguing individual. May I ask where you get your information?"

"The same place you do, Señor Charlado."

"And where is that?"

"I have my sources."

67

WE were stuck in southbound traffic on Francisco Villa, the two-lane avenue leading to Libramiento Highway, Old Vallarta, El Cabezón and Devo—our last resort.

A white police pickup straddled the sidewalk up ahead off to my right, its headlights illuminating the cop directing traffic. You could usually get to and from the coastal boulevard via Libramiento but that route was closed to all but emergency vehicles. Traffic converged on the intersection from three directions and waited to be waved through south, onto Libramiento, or north, onto Francisco Villa. We were stopped behind fifteen cars or so, waiting our turn to head south on Libramiento. To my left, northbound vehicles waved through the intersection passed us by in a smooth, mostly orderly fashion. There was no room for me to make a break for it. I needed to make that break before we were recognized as a couple of gringos driving around in a Mexican police car—Russell Martell and an accomplice who'd bludgeoned two cops and jacked their car.

I kept the windshield wipers on low. They swept the mist from our windshield every ten seconds or so. The damp weather worked to our advantage. Ambient light was dulled, the full moon completely obscured. But myriad headlights pierced the darkness and broke up the shadows in our car. If anyone should get a good look at us, try to talk to us (especially a real cop), we were busted. Every second brought us closer to discovery.

We were buckled into our seats, windows rolled up, the AC on medium. Static and nondescript voices emanated from the CB radio. Fat Cop's hat sat low on my head, gave me the sensation of peering out from beneath a punch bowl...or crash helmet. Johnny sensed we were running out of time: "Gonna hafta punch it soon."

"Punch it where? The intersection is completely blocked."

"Don't think it's a good idea to pull right up to it. That cop directing traffic is liable to try and say hello to us—his fellow police officers."

Oncoming traffic to my left thinned some. I inched our car over but there still wasn't enough space to make a move. My only other option was to hit the siren and overhead lights, hop to my right, slice past that police pickup straddling the curb, and make tracks through the closed section of Libramiento to the boulevard, like police reacting to an emergency call. But I could only take the boulevard north, the opposite direction I wanted to go. If I took it south, I'd end up stuck in a death trap—the Washington Hotel.

What would Devo do in this situation? He never hurries.

Johnny said, "We could punch it to the right."

My heart hammered in my chest but I kept my cool. We still had time to be patient. "We might have to."

I stared at the police pickup straddling the curb and mulled over the option. A uniform emerged from the passenger side of the vehicle. I imagined taking him out in the effort, pummeling him with my bumper, dragging him under the car and wiping the pavement with him. The golf ball behind my ear quivered and ached, egging me on. Our line of cars began moving. We slowly advanced.

The uniform strolled into the intersection. The cop directing traffic held both hands up, stopped the flow of vehicles from all three directions, and turned to talk to him, leaving a hole in the intersection I could barrel through for some broken-field running.

"This is your chance," Johnny said.

I gritted my teeth. "Soon as this last car passes."

379

SEVE VERDAD

Without a steady flow of vehicles waved through the intersection northbound, Francisco Villa's northbound lane was about to clear. I considered flashing our overhead blue and red lights (would they attract too much attention?) and blasting the siren (the signal for cops to follow?!?), and waited patiently for the last in a line of cars to pass me on my left.

"Get ready to peel out," Johnny said.

As the last car passed I hopped into the northbound lane and punched it. At the intersection, the car to my right lurched forward and stopped short as we popped through the hole, cut left and broke free onto Libramiento with a tad of burnin' rubber.

"You got it! Go baby...go!" Johnny's cheers resounded in the punch bowl, in harmony with my heart pounding out the Oregon Duck fight song between my ears.

Eighty kilometers per hour and climbing... Fifty, sixty mph.

The golf ball felt ready to explode and tossed a dart that blinded me for an instant. My legs were shaking but I kept the pedal to the metal, flipped on those flashin' lights and made the siren scream. A string of cars going our direction moved over for us. Beyond them my lanes were blocked by two pairs of tail lights; a train of headlights hugged the center of the road...

Goddamn third-world drivers. Probably think I'm delivering a pizza.

I slowed and blasted my high beams and fog lamps. The tail lights swerved to the right. I punched it again and immediately slammed on the brakes for a speed bump that jarred the car and got us airborne. My head banged against the ceiling. Johnny cursed. "Hold on," I said and got the car back up to speed, flying. *Pretty good pick up.*

I turned up the windshield wipers. "How we doin' back there?" Johnny had unbuckled himself to keep watch through the rear window. "Lookin' good," he said. "Way to bust loose. If they're followin' they got a late start."

I eased off the gas. We were going uphill but the road had begun to serpentine and I race cars about as often as bombs explode Vallarta hotels. The four-lane highway narrowed to two lanes. There wasn't much room for error. One waver and I'd end up plastered on the rocky embankment to my right or in a head-on collision to my left. Traffic was yielding from both directions but the curves were getting tighter and you can't yield to something you can't see. I turned off my fog lamps and dimmed the high beams.

Even if I don't waver the other guy might kill me.

A woman's voice cut through the muffled static and chatter on the CB radio. I braked and screeched around some curves. You're supposed to brake *before* the curves but they snuck up on me. The car got squirrelly on the wet pavement. I kept my feet free of the pedals and let the grade steady our vehicle. Then I hit the gas and passed five, six more cars pulling over for us.

Johnny buckled himself back into his seat. "Still lookin' good back there," he said. "Just try not to kill us."

Sounded like he was telling me not to overcook the meat on the grill. His life was in my hands and he wasn't about to make matters worse by panicking or complaining about my driving.

More curves up ahead, blind curves, but I was ready for them and applied the brakes in plenty of time. Thought I braked in plenty of time. Nearly rear ended a blind and deaf slowpoke. A blind and deaf slowpoke doin' fifty. He beat it onto the shoulder.

The voice on the CB radio was calling car 92, asking its destination. A straightaway leading to a tunnel allowed for more gas. Didn't look at the speedometer but we had to be doin' eighty. A pickup and two taxis got the hell outta our way. Three pair of headlights flew out the tunnel and streaked by like double-barreled shotgun blasts: *Wham! Wham! Wham!*

Johnny said, "Jeezus...some people have no respect for the law."

We blew through the tunnel. The radio's voice said, "Paulo, a dónde vas?" Paulo, where are you going? I turned off the siren and took my foot off the gas. "They're calling us," I said.

"Really? How do you know?"

"Chimp is Paulo. She's calling Paulo."

"Ignore her. Wait. String 'em along. Can you string 'em along?"

"Wish I had Devo's knack for voices. I'll tell her...I know." I snatched the CB mike, raised my voice half an octave, added a rasp, and clicked the button in succession as I spoke to give the impression that the radio was not working properly. I braked for a few narrow speed bumps. She asked me to repeat myself. "Rumbo al Hotel Rosalinda," I said and hung up the mike. Headed for Hotel Rosalinda.

"Entendido. Fuera," she said. Understood. Out.

"Hotel Rosalinda?" said Johnny.

"Keep 'em on the other side of the malecón."

"Would we be going this way to get to the Rosalinda?"

"Maybe. Who knows? The way the roads are... Don't confuse me."

Libramiento declined into Old Vallarta. I turned off the flashing lights, made a tranquil right, and dimmed the windshield wipers. It was a relief to go slow and let the car drive itself through the darkened streets. We lowered our windows.

Johnny said, "That was a rush." He put his foot back up on the dash.

"No kidding. Wanna drive?"

"You're doin' a great job. But if I could move my accelerator foot I'd give it a try."

"Think it's broken?"

"Can't be. I dunno. Maybe. Fucker hurts. If it was broken it'd hurt more, wouldn't it?"

"Maybe."

"Think we'll find Devo at Big Head?"

"After what we been through to get here we better," I said. "El Cabezón was the last place we saw him and I'm not sure where else to look. If he's not there someone might know where he went. Just pray we don't run into any more cops between here and there. If we stick to these side streets we should be okay." I snapped my head around and got my bearings. "I know where we are."

"Me too. It's where we're headed that has me worried."

"El Cabezón, or where we end up?"

"If we end up anywhere but the States we're in big trouble... You'll be goin' inside El Cabezón?"

"Guess so. I'd send you but you can't walk."

I stopped at a stop sign. A Toyota slowed at the sight of our police car. I swung a left at the River Cuale. Big Head was three blocks down and to the left a block and a half. I took the left and saw Devo's car exactly as he had parked it after breaking me outta jail.

"There's his car," I said.

"Which one?"

"The black Jeep Wrangler on the right."

We pulled up next to the Jeep. The driver's door popped open revealing a familiar figure reclined in the seat.

Johnny poked his head out his window. "Wanna go for a ride?" he said.

"Think my wheels might attract less attention," Devo replied dryly. He looked as though he'd been snoozing before we showed up, or meditating. The sight of him filled me with relief, relief tempered by a sense of dread. Could I trust him? I didn't have a choice. He'd rescued me once and I had to take the gamble he could do it again. Devo stretched and dropped a leg out his car door. "You guys havin' fun? Didn't stay out very late."

FINDING DEVO

Johnny unbuckled, tore off Chimp's hat and shirt, opened the door, and tossed his backpack out onto the street. "Help me out. I can't walk too well."

Devo helped Johnny and his backpack into the backseat of his Jeep. Then he shut the passenger door to my squad car and pierced me with steely eyes. "Park the car by the river, Martell. Lose the cop getup, and hustle back."

"Back in a flash."

"And Martell?"

"Yeah?"

"Stash the guns under the seat with the car keys. Make sure the car is locked up tight."

I glanced down at the holster bulging beneath my cop shirt. "You sure? About the guns?"

Devo sharpened the steel in his eyes.

"Whatever you say. I'll be right back."

I killed the engine beneath a couple of droopy-leafed trees by the riverbank, wrapped Fat Cop's gun belt around his holstered pistol and Chimp's Beretta, and stuffed the bundle under the seat along with the car keys. It wouldn't fit. I forced it. Chimp's gun popped loose, slid down the foot-well accompanied by the tinkling keys. "Damn." I switched on the interior light and ducked down to retrieve the gun and keys. Something caught my eye. Something poking out from under the seat. Letters, initials on a cap: UDLA. Familiar letters on a faded old Universidad de las Américas cap. I retrieved the cap and brought it up into the light. It wasn't faded or old, just dusty and abused. The infernal Washington dust ingraining the cap also looked familiar, as did the long strands of hair dangling from the Velcro strap at the back. I stared at the cap in horrid fascination. A woman had been wearing it recently. A woman who had innocently attached herself to me and was now in danger. A woman I had put in danger.

My stomach knotted up, thoroughly sickening me. *First I put Johnny in jeopardy and now...*

I imagined her in the clutches of dirty bastard coppers, at the mercy of the lieutenant. A breathless quiver in my chest constricted my throat, paralyzed me with panic and fear. Fear for myself, fear for those around me, fear for Brenda.

RUSSELL Martell was innocent. That's what they told Gloria in Rudy's Sports Bar—the proprietor, Rudy, as well as three solitary patrons, Nacho, Sancho, and Alfonso, who also knew the suspect. Rudy had seen and spoken to Señor Martell right here as recently as Saturday evening. "Russell" had been "in good spirits, drinking and chatting" with a gringo named "Johnny." Gloria jotted down a description of Johnny. Nacho, Sancho, and Alfonso had watched Friday Night Fights on TV here with Russell and Enrique Santos.

Nacho, Sancho, and Alfonso were callused men, wizened beyond their thirty some odd years, creased of cheek and brow. Looked as if they could still go more than a few rounds though, even at this late hour and after thirty some odd beers. Rudy had several issues of New World Sports en Español on hand to show Gloria. Each contained a story by Russell Martell, four with his looping signature below the byline. He grudgingly let her borrow one of the signed issues—a possible aid in her investigation—after she signed a promissory note to return it in the same condition she received it. Nacho, Sancho, and Alfonso added their signatures to the note as witnesses. Rudy wasn't taking any chances. Russell Martell's signature on one of his stories had to be worth decent money right now, given his sudden fame and infamy, and just might become a collector's item one day.

Not exactly Gloria's type of establishment, Rudy's. Bare tables, a couple of dining rooms and a bar. Kitchen in the back. Three flat-screen televisions and a jukebox, all dark and silent. Yellowing florescent lighting. A faint odor of stale beer and cigars. Gloria imagined the joint was often noisy and filled with drunks and half drunks, rough customers—malendrines—, as well as stray tourists, stalwart working men like Enrique Santos, and a gaggle of hookers. It was bleak tonight though. Everyone and every place was bleak tonight. Gloria had never been inside Rudy's before or met the owner, but Rudy wasn't in the least bit apprehensive about meeting the mayor's wife or expressing himself honestly in response to her queries. "The pinche policía," he scoffed as he prepared to close up shop for the night, "will find who is responsible for the Washington when they get their heads out of their culos and take a good look at the puta madre corruptos in the mirror."

Grim chuckles from Nacho, Sancho, and Alfonso, their stubbled faces hovering over cervezas at the bar. Gloria almost chuckled too. She thought the comment contained more than a grain of truth.

FINDING DEVO
* * *

THE Range Rover beat a steady tattoo over the cobblestone streets, Felipe at the helm, Gloria in the backseat speaking to her husband on the phone.

The mayor was at his wits end. "That maldito gringo is making fools out of us, Gloria," he fumed. "Fools! The raid on his hotel room at Casa Mexicana turned up nothing and I just received word that a man fitting his description attacked and nearly killed two police officers at another hotel, El Marciano, a few kilometers from Casa Mexicana."

"Are the officers okay?"

"Both officers were found unconscious but not critical. We assume they were following a lead. And before they arrived at El Marciano they were seen at Armando Montoya's house."

"Armando Montoya's? Why...?"

Juan paused to modulate his tone. This was an embarrassing detail—police invading Armando Montoya's property on their own initiative. Armando had proven himself an exceptionally honorable man, especially over the last twenty-four hours or so. Juan and his wife were well aware of his heroics at ground zero and most grateful that the popular athlete had agreed to wrestle at Arena Vallarta. Armando deserved to be treated with utmost respect yet had been downright disrespected.

"I talked with Héctor..." Juan began haltingly, "...questioned el comandante fairly thoroughly about it... He gave the go-ahead for them to act on their own initiative and..."

"Out with it, Juan."

"El comandante thinks that the officers in question probably went to Armando's house to inquire about Russell Martell before casing another location—El Marciano. He gave them the go-ahead to act on their own initiative after one of the officers told him that Russell Martell was seen 'at a house last night,' evidently, Armando's house." Juan lowered his voice surreptitiously, "It seems that Señor Martell was at Armando's party."

Juan heard his wife suck in her breath. "Really?" she said. "Pues, if Armando knows or remembers he was at his party then I am sure he will assist police any way he can."

"I agree. Armando would never aid and abet a criminal. But..."

"Yes Juan? What happened?"

"Armando gave me a personal call, to my cell phone. He had to kick the officers off his property and was not at all happy about it. Furious in fact. They did not have a warrant and, apparently, accosted a guest out on his front lawn, someone he considers a member of his family. His future sister-in-law."

"Dios mío." Gloria wanted to scream but controlled herself with a grunting, haughty laugh: "Ja! Pinches estúpidos. Armando probably could have killed them both before they ever had a chance to make it to El Marciano." Police blunders and miscues over the past few days were laughable, if they weren't so serious, and Gloria got serious: "This is intolerable, Juan. We cannot have police harassing private citizens at home on their own initiative. Especially Armando Montoya."

"I know, I know! I will make a point of paying Armando a visit tomorrow, or perhaps tonight at ground zero, in hopes of smoothing things over with him. He threatened to press charges and—"

"Press charges? You better hold el comandante responsible for this, Juan."

"I will, believe me. But..."

"But what, Juan?"

Juan cleared his throat. "CISEN may be tougher to control," he said pointedly. "The last time el comandante spoke to Joaquín de Jesús he was calling his section chief to insist that a team of CISEN operatives be flown into Vallarta immediately. We suspect he is at the airport awaiting their arrival right now."

"We cannot have CISEN trampling the rights of private citizens either, Juan."

"Agreed. They will most likely gather here at police headquarters and I will do everything in my power to prevent them from invading Armando's or anyone else's property without due cause. But in the meantime Russell Martell is still at large and a massive manhunt will have to be undertaken to recapture or kill him."

Gloria thought about Enrique, the patrons in Rudy's Sports Bar, and Rudy himself. All convinced of Russell Martell's innocence. And Pedro had his doubts about his guilt as well. Should she bring up the possibility of the gringo's innocence? Gloria discarded the idea, for the time being. Thanks to his daring escape from jail, Russell Martell had already been tried and convicted of all charges by police, federales, CISEN...and the mayor. And Gloria had to admit that his jailbreak indicated guilt of *something.*

"Juan," she said blandly, her fatigue sounding, "deal with the manhunt, CISEN, and Armando Montoya. You can do it and it is your responsibility. But what about that disc? I assume someone is monitoring it there at headquarters."

"At all times, Gloria. Pedro is due here at any moment to bring the last of our computers back on line and check on the disc. And

Federale Investigator Barrera used some sort of spectrum analyzer to determine if the disc is a bug."

"And?"

"He thinks it might be a bug but his measurements were inconclusive. The disc may be interfering with his electronics somehow. A close physical examination of the disc would probably settle the issue but Barrera does not want to remove it from Pedro's computer and disrupt its decryption."

Gloria cursed the disc under her breath. "Felipe will deliver me there directly, Juan. I believe I have come up with a strategy that will help us determine whether or not that disc is a bug."

69

DEVO set off for "a pit stop" in the suburbs up the Rio Cuale before taking us to our hideout. Johnny was horizontal in the backseat of the Jeep, his bare right foot planted atop his backpack where two icy beers smothered his injured ankle. In his left hand he held what I assumed was Brenda's UDLA Aztecas cap I'd found in that police car.

"Gotta admit the hat looks familiar," he said. "But I don't see how you can be jumpin' to conclusions at a time like this, Russ. It's no time to panic."

I was sitting low in the passenger seat, icing the golf ball with a beer, Johnny's Oakland A's baseball cap tucked down on my forehead. "Who the hell's panicking?" I said. "If I was panicked I'd be shootin' up the police station with those pistols I had, tryin' to rescue her and probably getting myself killed in the process."

"Why doncha just go down there and nuke 'em with some cobblestones?" Johnny tossed the UDLA cap onto my lap. "You shoulda seen Russ in action at my hotel, Devo. He made a bloody mess."

"You told him already," I said. "More interested in Brenda right now."

"Didn't finish tellin' 'im. Didn't tell 'im how bloody it was. And it sure was bloody, Devo, lemme tell ya. Russ, he bludgeoned those two sonsabitches with a cobblestone, a cobblestone! and left 'em out cold in the bathroom like a couple a clubbed marlin. Incredible."

Devo swung a left onto Libramiento and accelerated. "Good job, Martell," he said. Sounded like he was giving me an offhand compliment for writing a comprehensible letter to the editor.

"Like to go back to El Marciano and interrogate those pigs," I said. "Find out about Brenda... You got a cell, Devo?"

"You wanna call Brenda?"

"Got her number?"

"Can't say as I do." He down shifted and took a hard right off Libramiento down to the Cuale River. The rutted cobblestone street rattled the car.

"Mountain then," I said, "or his house. You know his number, don't ya?"

Devo said, "Yeah," and shook his head negatively. "None of us should make any calls, not with you around, Martell. Calls are traceable and you're a wanted man. The most wanted man in Mexico, the entire continent. Your face and name are all over the news and World Wide Web. Authorities here haven't come right out and accused you of terrorism yet, but that's what they want you for."

"Figured that." I eyed him suspiciously. "So why you helpin' me?"

Devo kept his eyes on the road. " 'Cause you're innocent."

"How do you know?"

Johnny blurted out, "Don't be an ass, Russ... The same way any of us know you're innocent. You wouldn't wanna call Mountain if you suspected he thought you were guilty, would ya? Jeez. You want me to go up against the cops again to prove my feelings on the subject? Just thank Devo for Christ sake."

"Thanks, Devo."

"Don' mention it."

Johnny grumbled, "Shit. After what we been through there ain't no amount of testifyin' from *anybody's* gonna save us now."

Devo coasted onto a bridge over the Rio Cuale. We'd just cruised the tail end of the suburb Buenos Aries, headed for another Vallarta suburb, Paso Ancho. Mexico. Authentic Mexico, without the abject poverty that riddles so much of the country. A poor village by North American standards but immeasurably rich by most all standards—rich tropical forest, friendly local population. On the north side of the river, a towering volcanic eminence girders Paso Ancho. It resembles a granite glacier formation and, in the rainy season (summer), becomes a waterfall. This time of year there'd be no waterfall and even if there were, we couldn't see it at night through this exceedingly odd misty drizzle.

Devo eased onto the dirt road on the other side of the bridge and negotiated several bumps, taking it slow and easy. "You don't seem very concerned about Brenda, Devo," I observed.

He shot me an indifferent glance. "Think I'm with Johnny on this one, Martell."

"Relax, will ya Russ?" Johnny removed a beer from his ankle, cracked it, and hoisted himself up to have a sip. "Just think of the timing." A bit of beer splashed onto his shirt. "How could those pigs have had time to snatch Brenda after she left us at Big Head, deliver her to headquarters, and get to my place to try and arrest us by eleven?"

"More like eleven thirty."

"Whatever. Still ain't likely."

"You saw that cop car up at Mountain's, Johnny. Maybe that was them and they grabbed her up there before she got to the house. And maybe they never took her to headquarters. Maybe they just beat her, roughed her up in the car where she lost her hat. That damned Manco probably told the pigs she was seen with me last night and—"

Devo intervened: "Manco? The punk from the party. Wouldn't surprise me if he told the cops you were at Montoya's last night."

I studied Devo's impassive profile. "That so? You did seem to know somethin' about him at the party. Tweaked him and his pals pretty good out on the deck."

"Had my eye on the little shit."

"Why's that?"

"Same reason you did."

Devo had me stumped for a second but I remembered: "Oh. *Viva la raza.*"

"That, and I saw him bully Gail. Guy's a prick."

I pictured Gail dancing at the party, recalled her blameless blue eyes, and heard her vivacious southern belle accent. "Poor Gail," I said with a sigh that seemed to drain my lungs. "And her friends..."

Johnny took a long, lingering drink from his beer. "Poor Gail," he echoed, his eyes rounded with sadness. "Buried under all that rubble... Unbelievable. First time I ever felt lucky not to get lucky. She shoulda come to my place."

Johnny was so pained by the thought of Gail he completely missed the humor in his own words. Devo and I snickered though. I pushed Gail from my mind and took a fix on our surroundings, what little I could see in the sullen light cast by the Jeep's headlights and a few lonely streetlamps. An artisan store, clothing store, a tavern. Single-family dwellings built from cinderblock. During the day men worked with mortar, women managed households, kids played barefoot in the street and swam the river. The street was abandoned now. Cars were parked here and there but there wasn't a soul in sight. Would it soon be overrun by police on a manhunt for Russell Martell?

"How far we goin' upriver?" I said.

Devo braked for a rut in the road. "Not far. A few more blocks. Up over this hill here."

"Cops are bound to search these neighborhoods all along the Rio Cuale."

"Yep. They will." Devo accelerated up the grade. "We won't be stayin' long."

Devo parked before an isolated cinderblock structure with a pitched metal roof. Johnny asked about his pack. Devo told him to leave it. I helped Johnny to the front door while Devo grabbed a daypack from the cargo box behind the backseat.

Devo switched on the light. A bare bulb hanging from a cord above our heads. The place was furnished with a crude wooden table, matching chair, and three straw mats in the middle of the dirt floor. An ocean breeze wafted up from the river and circulated through the barred screen windows. The place was perfect for a last stand, if we had a cache of weapons.

"Nice fort," I said. "Got rocket launchers?"

Devo sat his pack on the table. "Make yourselves comfortable," he said, indicating the floor mats.

Johnny and I eased ourselves down on the mats. I'd left the UDLA cap in the car but couldn't get Brenda out of my mind: "What about those hairs dangling from the back of the hat?"

"What about 'em?" Johnny said.

"Looked like they came from a woman to me."

Johnny took an exasperated breath. "Look, Russ. In the squad car you said one of the cops mentioned Manco on their way into my hotel."

"He did but—"

"You didn't hear them mention Brenda, did you?"

"No but—"

"You're thinkin' too much, and not very straight." Johnny leaned back on his hands and slung his right leg over a knee to keep his ankle elevated. "That lump behind your ear has you all fucked up."

"That bitch has gotta sting." Devo almost sounded sympathetic. He unzipped his daypack and took a seat at the table, facing us.

"That fat-pig's face was all scratched up," I said. "Maybe it was Brenda who gave him those scratches."

"What're ya gonna do, Martell?" Devo asked. "Report her disappearance to police?"

"I can't just do nothing."

FINDING DEVO

Devo drew a black metal case from his daypack. "Why the hell not? Sometimes nothing is the best thing to do. And at the moment, it's the *only* thing for you to do."

"Nothing?"

"Nothing. You and Johnny just rest up a bit, let me do some leg work here." Devo worked the combination to his metal case. I shifted my position, sat cross-legged and folded my arms under my chest. Just the thought of doing nothing for Brenda filled me with shame, a guilt reminiscent of how I felt when Rosalita died, except I really was helpless then. She died while I was en route to meet her and her folks at the hospital in Guadalajara and, though it was no consolation at the time, there really was nothing to be done from an altitude of thirty thousand feet. I still beat myself up thinking I should have flown into Vallarta at least a week earlier to be with her and possibly save her. I should have anticipated every eventuality, including a difficult, deadly difficult premature delivery, and taken her to Guadalajara myself for the best possible care at the slightest sign of trouble, *before* any sign of trouble! I was too late. Agonizingly late... Was I too late again? I wasn't helpless right now so what the hell was my excuse?!? I imagined making off with Devo's Jeep, kidnapping a cop (the lieutenant) and holding him hostage in exchange for Brenda...or torturing the lieutenant until he spilled his guts about her, told me where to find her. Or why not just break into that cop car I hijacked, drive back to Johnny's hotel, grab those guns stashed under the seat, bust into the hotel and Johnny's room, and pistol whip Chimp and Fat Cop till they fessed-up about Brenda?

"She might be in real danger," I said. "Her life could be at stake."

Devo opened his metal case and stiffened, his deep chest expanding beneath his black T-shirt. A spotless shirt. That struck me, finally. Most everyone I'd seen since my arrest this morning had at least some sign of that infernal Washington dust on them, or was outright filthy dirty, like me and Johnny. But not Devo. He was clean. Clean when he rescued me from jail, clean in El Cabezón, clean right now. He was a tad damp from the humid drizzle though, the sticky evening...and his eyes were lit, cobalt blue, brilliant contrasts to the thick brassy stubble covering his face and the layered hanks of sandy-brown hair draped over his head. A well-groomed pirate. A swashbuckler of fortune.

Devo flicked his hair aside and let both eyes drill me. "*Her* life might be at stake?" he said evenly. "You better take some stock in yourself, Martell, recognize the enemy or *you're* the dead one."

"Which enemy are you referring to?" My sardonic query carried an unintended implication I tried to disguise behind a wry smile.

391

Devo's eyes glazed over in a forbearing shade of aquamarine. "Not me, Martell. If I wanted you dead, you would be."

That seemed true enough.

"Never said you were the enemy," I parried defensively. I may not have said as much but the thought sure as hell had occurred to me.

"Russ knows you're not the enemy, Devo," Johnny said.

Devo dismissed Johnny's comment with a toss of his head, like he knew I'd be crazy not to have some misgivings about him. "The cops and federales who are after you are the enemy, that right Martell?"

I snorted. "Damn straight."

"And after they kill you, they'll nuke LA."

I screwed up my face at Devo's serious expression. "What? Wouldn't go that far."

"But you do know who *would* nuke LA, doncha Martell. Another enemy. An enemy far more dangerous than the cops and federales after your sorry ass. The enemy who struck the Washington today. The enemy the cops reminded you of when they let slip that the dead man found at the marina was an Iranian terrorist."

Devo's knowing smile gave me the uneasy feeling of seeing myself through his eyes, and I heard his next words before they escaped his lips: "You've known *that* enemy for quite some time, Martell. Your op-ed piece in memory of 9/11 made it clear."

All at once my thoughts contracted; I froze up inside, like he'd revealed some deep dark secret I'd been harboring.

Johnny's voice seemed a distant echo: "Op-ed piece?...about 9/11? That have something to do with the Islamos Russ said blew the Washington back in El Cabezón?"

Devo was right. I did know the enemy that blew the Washington, had written about them. And he'd mentioned my op-ed piece before, last night, when I first met him in the game room at Mountain's party. Was that what had attracted him to me from the start? a lucid, satiric flurry written in disillusion and anger in anticipation of the third anniversary of 9/11? A unique departure from my mundane sports-centered prose? A brief foray into the morass of our time?

"I call 'em as I see 'em," I said in a guarded tone.

"Right," Devo replied. "I believe you titled the piece *Make the Call*."

"Make the call?" Johnny said. "What, a penalty? A play? An out? How come you never sent me a copy of that one, Russ?"

"It wasn't about sports."

"Oh. Right. The Islamos then."

"The key term," Devo said, "was *Islamisalaamis*."

Johnny wrinkled his nose at the term. "Islami...salamis? What the hell is that?"

"Islami-*sala-a-mis*" Devo clarified. "As in *salaam*. Peace be with you..."

"As I blow myself up in your buildings, markets, mosques, and churches," I appended.

Devo paraphrased from 'Make the Call': "*Islamofascist* is a derogatory term. It provokes violence."

"Hostile language must be censored," I said. "We need to be politically correct, for the good of society at large... In football, the *long bomb* is out. Let's call it the *skyline*."

Devo sighed with excessive emotion, "Soothing imagery."

Johnny looked as though he'd just taken a sip of sour milk. "What the hell're you guys talkin' about?"

" '*Iconoclastic disaster* has an appeasing ring to it and dissuades the militancy propagated by the term *terror attack*.' " My voice had acquired a lyrical timbre. Like most people, I can't help but enjoy quoting myself on occasion: "And 'beheadings aren't Islamic justice but *cultural population control*.' "

Devo assented with an ironical laugh, "*Most* effective at controlling populations... And *stealing* a base?" he prompted.

"Gives kids the wrong impression," I said. "*Singing* a base is more appropriate. And *foul* ball is no good. Sounds like it stinks. Might offend somebody. *Lemon* ball is preferable."

Johnny said, "Huh? Sounds like a buncha bull is what it sounds like. *Lemon ball? Singing a base?* Can't understand the game at all when you use words like that."

Devo's thin smile deepened. "Exactly the point. Calls like that aren't very inspiring, are they Johnny?"

"Inspiring? Only losers would get inspiration from that kinda horseshit."

"That about sums it up," I said.

Devo challenged Johnny: "And if you can't name the enemy, Johnny? know him for what he is? What happens then?"

"Suppose he kicks the shit outta ya, or kills ya."

Devo flashed me a toothy grin. "You should've e-mailed the piece to him, Martell. Sounds like he understands perfectly."

"It woulda bored him."

"You shoulda let me edit it from what I've heard so far," Johnny said.

Devo released a deep molasses chuckle. "I'll find you a copy, Johnny," he said. "You'll get a kick out of it after the two of you get outta this mess." He slackened in his chair, his good humor subdued.

393

"I thought the piece excellent, Martell, and prescient, given the increasingly insidious nature of politically correct speech. But we'll discuss your talents in more depth some other time."

He retrieved a small but unusually thick laptop computer from his metal case, opened it up, and sat back while it booted.

Johnny said, "Whatcha got there Devo?" His expression held an eager spirit all of a sudden.

"An advantage," said Devo.

Devo typed on his computer and made some clicks and shifts. I got up to have a look at the screen but was overcome by lightheadedness, a dizzy spell that sat me right back down on the mat. Then the overhead bulb went out.

Johnny and I shuddered, "What the hell...?" and were instantly transfixed by Devo. His predatory eyes and leaden grin glowed in the artificial light of his computer screen; his rakish voice hummed in our ears: "We have contact."

70

TRAFFIC had thinned quite a bit by 1:00 a.m. Tuesday but Manco wasn't taking any chances on the road. He and Javier were carrying cargo that could land them in jail for years and years if police stopped them and searched the car.

The intersection of Francisco Villa Avenue and Libramiento was the trouble spot and Manco knew precisely how to avoid it. He had driven all around these side streets between Vallarta and the suburb of El Pitillal three times since this afternoon and had his route nailed down. Barring an accident or some other unforeseen mishap, they shouldn't have any close encounters with police on their way into Vallarta.

There was little chance of an accident, not one caused by Manco at any rate. Javier had as much confidence in Manco's driving as his own, as long as the car had an automatic transmission. His one-armed partner had demonstrated admirable dexterity behind the wheel of a stick shift in the past—left foot on the clutch, right foot off the accelerator, right leg up to control the steering wheel, right hand down to shift gears, foot off the clutch, right hand back up to the steering wheel, right leg back down and foot on the gas; but Manco was more comfortable driving an automatic. And for the job at hand, the car also needed a decent sized trunk to store materiel and munitions.

FINDING DEVO

The black Chevy Monte Carlo Pati rented for Manco before she left for Guadalajara this afternoon fit the bill, and he wasted little time in acquiring the supplies necessary for his diabolical plan, ingenious in its timing and simplicity.

Fill twenty-four twelve-ounce Coca Cola bottles with gasoline and a quantity of sawdust, dangle a shorn rag out the mouths of each for a fuse, cork and seal with duct tape, and you have a case of Molotov cocktails. Not complicated, but you do need a place to assemble them. And well before sunset, as the sun descended behind the macabre graphite glow of a sinking sky, the Zapatista and the anarchist had readied their bombs west of the Vallarta suburb El Pitillal, amongst the wooded, unpopulated banks of the Pitillal River...

They each took a knee in the weeds and stony dirt and bent to their work—Manco stabilizing the bottles on the ground one at a time as Javier judiciously filled them with the incendiary mixture of sawdust and gasoline.

"These were very effective in Oaxaca last year," Manco said, referring to the uprisings in support of the teachers-union strike that ended up requiring the intervention of the Mexican army.

"Never had the pleasure of using them," said Javier, "but how difficult can it be?"

"Not difficult at all. Light the fuse and throw it. Then say a Huichol prayer for your brother Germán and..."

"Fuck the tobacco plantations," they said in unison.

Javier's brother, Germán, did not die working the pesticide poisoned tobacco plantations like their father. He died fighting for his rights, something Javier admired and determined to emulate...

The government managed to pacify a great majority of Javier's people—the Huichol and Cora—by issuing tighter controls on the use of pesticides and meting out treatment and monetary compensation to victims of pesticide poisoning. But the dispute over territorial rights had never been resolved. Ejidos (reservations) granted to indigenous populations by the government remained a mere pittance compared to their claims on the land. As a result, some Cora and Huichol grew rebellious and opted to join armed conflict. Germán Menticlaro, Javier's eldest brother, had made such a decision. Five years ago he left his home in Tepic and traveled south through the states of Jalisco and Michoacán to Guerrero where he joined the Popular Revolutionary Army (EPR). He never returned. Javier claimed his body in Acapulco, Guerrero, a year and a half later. Government-backed paramilitaries had killed him and twenty-four other EPR members (two of whom were also Cora) on the outskirts of Agua Caliente. Germán and his comrades had planned a takeover of thermoelectric plants, banks, and government offices; they were holed up at a ranch with arms and explosives when paramilitaries came for them.

Germán Menticlaro's death came on the heels of the well-publicized killings of five unarmed Indian (Mayan) campesinos in Mexico's southernmost state, Chiapas. Zapatistas who were reportedly fomenting violence but were in fact unarmed and killed in cold blood. Paramilitaries had been responsible for that massacre also and Javier, now a knotty-muscled twenty year old with an untamed spirit and a few knife fights under his belt, soon came to the conclusion that one paramilitary group was just like another and synonymous with oppression and the government itself.

After delivering his brother's body to his bereaved mother and family in Tepic, Javier returned to Guerrero to exact his revenge. He joined EPR members in two ambushes on police personnel. Javier made his bones in Guerrero, slitting the throat of a police officer in the first ambush and killing two more with an assault rifle in the second.

Javier sustained an entry and exit bullet wound through his left shoulder in the second ambush. A badge of honor. A scar he wore with pride along with the silver streak below his chest he had received at eighteen in a knife fight when demonstrations in Guadalajara during a Día de la Raza parade (Day of the *Race*, Columbus Day in the US) turned ugly.

Javier preferred the knife. It required him to get close to his adversary. Close and personal, like his grievances.

Unlike his brother, Javier never entirely took to the EPR. As a strictly Maoist organization, it didn't appear to have the best interests of indigenous Mexicans at heart. So Javier returned to Tepic a couple of years ago. Shortly thereafter, Zapatistas from Chiapas passed through town to express solidarity with the Cora and Huichol and recruit followers for their forthcoming May Day march in Mexico City.

The Zapatistas had not fully mobilized militarily since 1994. By the 21st century, the largely indigenous insurrection seemed to have fizzled, though the Zapatistas had managed to carve out their own territory of self-rule in southern Mexico. As the drug war irrupted into a full-fledged conflagration, the Zapatistas made a resurgence with demonstrations that castigated the Mexican and United States governments for *inventing* drug laws and instigating an artificial war that had slaughtered tens of thousands nationwide and primarily benefited corrupt elites. The theme echoed those of other demonstrations popping up around the country, demonstrations that had begun to resonate with Mexicans in general, whatever their political sympathies.

FINDING DEVO

Javier's political sympathies remained communist and, when Chiapas Zapatistas visited Tepic, he quickly surmised that they had taken advantage of the drug war to advance an anti-government, communist ideology. Unlike the Maoist EPR however, the Zapatistas represented an indigenous Mexican movement. Javier was smitten, not just because he felt a natural kinship to a communist indigenous movement but because the Zapatistas actually had an *army* of their own.

If the Zapatistas could carve out their own territory with an army, why not the Cora and Huichol?

Over the past couple of years, Javier had taken it upon himself to inspire the Cora and Huichol to embrace the Zapatista creed. He achieved less than moderate success. All too often he was reminded that Jalisco and Nyarit were a long, long way from Chiapas, their indigenous populations not nearly as isolated from the federal government and its headquarters in el DF as the Zapatistas. An armed indigenous insurrection had little to no hope of success in this part of Mexico...

Javier comprehended the vulnerability of his people. Their geographic location alone made negotiations with the federal government preferable to armed conflict. Yet the government had become interminably embroiled in a drug war that only served to benefit many of the same corrupt corporate and political elites responsible for subjugating indigenous populations in the first place. He couldn't help but believe that, once these elites suffered direct, debilitating blows, the government charged with protecting them would be revealed as a paper tiger and his people would find the courage to forge an alliance with the Zapatistas and fight.

And tonight was the night for Javier to personally strike one of those blows.

As night fell upon the Zapatista and the anarchist, they had their Molotov cocktails scrupulously stashed in the woods for later retrieval. Javier expressed his admiration for the plan: "The Zapatistas have an army in Chiapas but we do not need one."

"Chaos is the key," replied Manco. "Erase the people's faith in government with chaos and we can bring down empires. The destruction at the Washington has given us an opening. An incredible stroke of luck we cannot afford to waste."

"Maybe those who blew the Washington have the same ideas about chaos."

"Maybe," said Manco. "We cannot hope to match that spectacle, but we can take advantage of it, cause more destruction, fear, uncertainty and chaos."

Around 1:00 a.m. Tuesday, as Manco adroitly negotiated the misty side streets through the barrio of Valentín Gómez on his way to Libramiento and their target, Javier raised this subject again: "So, more chaos is our strategy for fucking the tobacco plantations..."

"Chaos achieved by the destruction of a symbolic landmark," Manco expounded, "a symbol of corporate power and capitalist injustice, just like the Washington."

"I like the strategy. But by its nature, chaos can cause things to go wrong."

"Not for us. And certainly not tonight. Chaos is our friend. Because of the chaos already in play our target has been left unprotected. At least it was an hour or so ago when I last staked it out."

"But if something should go wrong, Manco, I am not afraid to shed some blood to set it right."

Manco stopped the Chevy Monte Carlo beneath the veiled light of a streetlamp at the intersection of Héroes de la Patria and Libramiento. He locked onto Javier—the Zapatista's stormy black eyes filled with a bland fire. Javier's dark, dour expression made clear that he had shed his share of blood for the cause; more than many. More than Manco.

"Your scars prove you are not afraid," Manco said. "That is why providence has brought us together. And we shall be triumphant."

71

THE first thing Gloria noticed when she entered el comandante's office was the boarded-up window behind Pedro, the window through which Russell Martell had escaped. The second thing she noticed was the computer screen Pedro swiveled around on the desk. "No change, señora," he said with an air of professionalism. "The map looks just as it did forty minutes ago when Federale Investigator Barrera first saw the target painted." Pedro motioned to el comandante's computer monitor on the right-hand corner of the desk, "He was reviewing a copy of the disc's contents on el comandante's computer when Kabul turned red on my monitor."

Gloria approached for a closer look at the map of Asia, the Middle East and northern Africa on Pedro's computer screen. "And Señor Barrera confirmed the prediction of a terror attack in Kabul," she stated in a flat voice. Pedro had called her with the news ten minutes ago.

"Sí señora. There are reports of the bombing on the Internet. The disc targeted Kabul approximately five minutes before the attack occurred... The Taliban drove a car bomb into a girls school," he added with some emotion.

"A girls school..." Gloria pinched her eyes shut. "...jodidos animales."

Pedro was somewhat taken aback by Gloria's vulgarity but agreed completely that these people were fucking animals. "De acuerdo, señora," he said.

Gloria felt her cheeks getting hot, a hard twist of rage in her stomach. "Predicting terror attacks in a place like Kabul is not nearly as difficult as predicting one here in Vallarta," she said. "You can pick most any day of the week and predict Muslim fanatics blowing themselves and each other up in the Middle East, Asia, and Africa." She glared at the red dot targeting Kabul. "I assume there is no mistake. Señor Barrera certainly seems competent."

"He knows quite a bit about encryption technology and—" Pedro cut himself short in response to Gloria's raised finger. Their eyes met in succinct understanding...

DF Federale Investigator Barrera was examining a crime scene at El Marciano Hotel with the other DF federale investigators and Vallarta police. Pedro had also discussed this with Gloria over the phone, as well as Señor Barrera's inconclusive attempt to detect a bug within the disc. Gloria signaled Pedro to follow her out of the office. They needed to review something else they had briefly discussed over the phone: Gloria's strategy on how to discover if the disc was indeed a bug.

TWO tiny spots of red appeared on Pedro's computer screen as they took their places at el comandante's desk. "Istanbul and Baghdad," Gloria said.

"Shall I check for news reports, señora?"

"Probably too early for any reports, Pedro." Gloria pointed at her prepared script on the desk before them, the signal to begin their subterfuge.

Was the disc a bug, a transmitter and receiver? Was someone listening to them and manipulating the disc's images? Given the disc's behavior, it seemed entirely possible, and the script Gloria had prepared was designed to help confirm this possibility. The script was pure invention. It had nothing to do with any investigation or what the disc was currently revealing. So if Gloria and Pedro's baseless dialogue elicited a related response from the disc, then there would be little doubt that someone was listening in and manipulating the disc's images... And whoever was listening just might get careless and offer clues as to their identity.

Pedro nodded forcefully. Gloria said, "Red in Somalia and Yemen now as well."

Pedro responded on cue: "And Istanbul. Looks like multiple coordinated attacks coming."

Gloria cocked her head at Pedro. They'd just invented three targets to go with the newly painted ones in Istanbul and Baghdad, and Pedro had another line to add to his last. He read it aloud from Gloria's script with one eye on his computer screen: "The disc is getting bolder in its predictions. Can it possibly always be right?"

"Whoever programmed it is not infallible," Gloria replied, "and neither are those who killed the Iranian found dead at the marina."

"Have our investigations turned up more clues into the murder, señora?" Pedro said, sounding more hopeful than he felt.

"The coroner has informed me that hair and fibers have been discovered on the dead Iranian found at the marina. Hair that might yield DNA, and fibers that could indicate the dead man's location when he was killed or just prior to his death, or as his body was being moved."

"That is promising, señora."

"Yes it is," said Gloria. "And CISEN has a dossier on the dead Iranian terrorist. He had known ties to the EPR."

If someone was listening, they figured to be involved in the murder of the Iranian terrorist and the attack on the Washington. Gloria and Pedro's initial machinations were designed to raise doubt in the eavesdropper's mind about the reliability of the images the disc presented and the assassin's modus operandi when he killed the Iranian. Would the attempt result in a hasty response of some kind from the disc, perhaps a message corresponding to Gloria and Pedro's dialogue? They'd have to wait and see. And their current gambit, a play on ideology connecting the dead Iranian to a Maoist terror organization, could elicit some kind of response from the disc as well, if an eavesdropper was controlling its images.

Pedro raised his voice theatrically: "The EPR?!? The Popular Revolutionary Army? The Maoists who blew up the oil pipelines in Veracruz?"

"Sí. It appears a communist may have turned on a radical Islamist and killed him at the Vallarta marina."

"Turned on him, señora?"

"It happens. Pancho Villa turned on Carranza. Hitler turned on Stalin. Muslims turned on the Americans after the Soviets were run out of Afghanistan. If the EPR and Islamists have found a common enemy—" Gloria stopped short. Pedro's computer screen had gone blank.

Pedro and Gloria eyed each other apprehensively. Two sentences in white block lettering illuminated the screen, one on top of the other. The first in Spanish, the other in English.

Pedro read the first message out loud: " 'El enemigo de tu enemigo no es tu amigo, y tus enemigos se unen en contra tuya.' "

(The enemy of your enemy is not your friend, and your enemies unite against you.)

Gloria read the second message to herself, the minute hairs along her forearms shifting as she relived the chilling possibility that this phrase in *English* was specifically meant for her: Despite their rhetoric and behavior, you remain disbelieving and impotent in the face of the enemy, even as they strike you personally, in your own house.

"What does it mean, señora?" Pedro said, "the message in English?"Gloria ran a hand across her face and scowled at Pedro's computer screen. "A reference to the...the Washington...?" she said, her tone plaintive, almost pleading. "Or is it...?" She got to her feet, anxiety issuing a knot between her shoulder blades. Instinctively, she knew she was on the verge of panic. Was her home in danger? Her children? And what "rhetoric" was the assassin talking about?

Gloria grew pale, and Pedro felt the blood rush from his own face as he tried to get a look into her frightened, skittish eyes. "Qué, señora?"

Gloria gasped and bit the back of her hand. She had attempted to fluster the eavesdropper (the assassin?!?) and he'd turned the tables on her...or was this his plan all along? He must have known that, after today's calamity, paranoia could strike anyone viewing the disc's contents.

She clenched her jaw and forced a calm note into her voice: "It appears to be a threat, Pedro. A personal one."

72

DEVO had reversed himself at the table, his back to us, so Johnny and I could see the computer screen from our positions on the straw mats on the dirt floor. There wasn't much to look at, just a road map of Vallarta. Black lines against a white background. A dozen or so street names. Four labeled landmarks: the airport, the marina, the Washington, and Arena Vallarta. The screen was small, twelve inches or so, but the map vivid in our darkened fort. I sat cross-legged at the foot of Devo's chair, off to his right, and could clearly read the names of the streets and landmarks. Johnny was behind me, off to my right, leaning back on his hands, his injured ankle slung over a knee.

"You see something I don't, Devo?" I asked. At that instant a little flashing red dot came into view about three-quarters the way down the right side of the screen.

Johnny said, "What's that?"

The red dot slowly progressed south-west on the map. "Devo's tracking someone," I guessed. "You plant a GPS tracking device on a car Devo?"

Devo's eye twinkled blue in the scattered glow of his computer screen as he made some shifts and clicks on the keypad. A small yellow sign, a thin figure-eight—an infinity sign I hadn't noticed before—lit up above the keypad in the left-hand corner.

Johnny sat up and looked over my shoulder. "What's that yellow light above the keypad?"

Devo tapped a finger off his right ear and paused, as if... "You listening in too, Devo?" I said. "You have a bug in the car?"

Devo pressed a couple of keys simultaneously. "Not the car," he murmured. The screen flashed to a page of computer language, a machine code of some sort. Wild looking hieroglyphics. He squinted at it for several seconds and clicked on something. The road map reappeared.

"You read that shit?"

Devo ignored me, lost in thought.

"What is this?" Johnny asked half in jest, "some kinda game with real people in the program?"

"If it's a game, Devo's got it fixed. He's tracking a car in one location and has a bug planted in another."

"But how is he listening in? You have a mike in your ear or something Devo? Can we have a look at it?"

"Not a mike, Johnny," I said. "Must be a receiver of some kind."

"Whatever, Russ. Just tryin' to get a handle on Devo's toys." Johnny grumbled a curse at his ankle as he leaned back on his hands and elevated it over a knee. "That yellow figure-eight help you listen in Devo...?"

Devo released a small chuckle, eyes steady on his computer screen. He typed, clicked, and typed some more. The flashing red dot on the map had come to a stop on some side street intersecting with Libramiento.

Devo reclined in his seat. "It's called a facilitator," he said, "that yellow infinity sign, the device glowing there in the corner above the keypad. It broadens and amplifies my reception. It also has various other functions we don't have time to get into right now."

"Your reception...?" I mused. "The computer's reception or...do you actually have a receiver in your ear?"

"The facilitator helps my timing," Devo said shortly. "And right now, it's just about time for us to go." He made a few more shifts and clicks with an air of finality.

A familiar fear entered my brain, creeping anxiety. Devo's contrivances with his computer had awakened all the misgivings I had about him. He rose from his chair. I slid back on my butt to give him some room. "What the hell's going on here, Devo?" My breath sawed in my throat, my tone harsh with suspicion. "Who are you tracking? Why are you tracking them? And who are you listening to?"

Shadowy light played off his expression, his mouth twisted in a purposeful half-grin. "You'll find out when the time comes, Martell. A lotta shit's gone down today and I don't blame you for not trustin' me completely. We just met yesterday. But I did rescue you from jail and as things stand right now you have two choices: stay here and try to hide until police and federales find you, or come with me and save your ass."

"Russ shoulda never left you after you broke him outta jail," Johnny said. He'd never harbored the doubts I had about Devo.

I snapped my head around to him. "Easy for you to say Johnny. You didn't see his performance at police headquarters." I stared back up at Devo. "Who the hell could get away with that? Who are you? What do you want from me?"

Devo crossed his arms and tapped a foot with feigned impatience. "Which is it gonna be, Martell?"

"We're goin' with you Devo," Johnny chirped. "We got nowhere else to go. Russ is just paranoid."

My eyes widened on Johnny, my voice short of a screech: "That's 'cause everyone's trying to kill me!"

"Not everyone, Martell."

I searched Devo's shadowy scowl, a pitiless scowl, like he didn't give a shit if I lived or died at this point. Somehow this was reassuring. I had no idea what he had in store for me but he wasn't trying to kill me. He'd let the cops and feds kill me if I insisted, but he wasn't the one trying to kill me.

"Guess I got no choice but to go with you," I said.

Johnny guffawed, "Ha! No kidding," and scooted up next to me. "How 'bout showin' us that mike in your ear before we go, Devo?"

Devo made a sympathetic noise. "You're insatiable, Johnny," he said.

"Yeah, hungry. Russ made me puke in my hotel room not long ago. A good portion of that food and beer we had at Big Head."

Devo paused, then swept a hand over us as if to salaam. "Ask the facilitator, and it shall provide."

The computer screen glimmered golden just then, its light playing about our darkened fort like a sunset reflected off the ocean. Something appeared in Devo's hand. A disc. No. A hockey puck? A tin of tobacco? He stuck it in front of my nose. "Take it."

I showed it to Johnny. He was disappointed: "Shoe polish? Can't eat shoe polish."

Devo swung his chair around and had a seat before us. "No, guess you can't. Lemme see that." I gave the tin back to him. Devo fisted it, brushed his hands together, and the tin was gone; the naked overhead bulb flashed on, flooding our fort with light and giving Johnny and me a start. Devo tossed Johnny an apple.

"Cool." Johnny took an eager bite. "The apple makes this trick better than the ones you showed me playin' Ping-Pong at the party last night."

"Devo showed you tricks while playin' Ping-Pong?" I said archly.

Johnny gurgled a mouthful. "Swallowed...the ball."

"Swallowed...? the Ping-Pong ball?"

"Drank it right down with beer, smacked his lips, and spit it up again."

I deadpanned Devo. "What else ya got?"

Johnny said, "Let's see the mike."

Devo took a deep breath and held it, cheeks all puffed, his nostrils flared to twice their normal size. Looked like a hairy blowfish. Then he jarred his head to one side with the heel of his left hand, forced air from his lungs, and out popped...something, a silver something, from his right ear into his right hand.

"Very good," he said without a hint of irony. "Wondered if I'd ever get this thing out." He extended his open palm and showed it to us.

"Quartz battery?" I wondered aloud. It looked like one. Size of a dime. Thick as a couple of nickels stuck together.

"Johnny's *mike*," Devo said. "Its base must be lodged in my head somewhere." He held the "mike" up between his fingers and tilted his head, his body canted upon the chair, and dropped it a good eighteen inches directly into his left ear. I said, "Good shot," then recoiled as Devo doubled over and choked, gasped and retched, his head between his knees. He took hold of his knees, steadied himself, and with great effort pushed his torso vertical, face contorted and heated, aquamarine

404

eyes rolling about...then...dry heaves—really goin' at it, wriggling in his chair like an eel. Johnny gasped, "What the...?" I made a move to help, give Devo a slap on the back, when he suddenly froze, his left arm outstretched to detain me.

He hacked and spit the mike out into his hand. "Damn. Missed."

A moment of silence as Devo weaved spittle between his fingers. Johnny tittered. Devo wiped his hand on his pants, took a breath and tried again, his face pinched in severe concentration.

He got that mike to fall clear through his head three times in a row, both directions, in one ear and out the other, smooth, without a hitch, canting on each attempt to let gravity work for him. But on his fourth attempt the mike "got snagged" in his septum and he had to free it out his mouth with a firm jolt to the back of his head. Then he gulped it down and said, "Enough games."

That shoe polish came in handy before we left the fort. Along with a little makeup it helped give me a darkened, Latin look. The games never end with Devo. Just a matter of how serious they get.

73

THE damp weather and late hour thinned the morose crowds teaming behind barricades and hazard tape at the Washington. Field lights disassembled from Stadium Sport Park and hastily erected on makeshift scaffoldings illuminated the disaster area. The low growl of generators used to power the lighting reverberated in the swampy evening air. Meanwhile, visibility in the trenches at ground zero was as bad as any time that day. The north tower's inland expanse had been all but obliterated in the explosive catastrophe this morning, but the day's initial offshore breeze had swept much of the attending dusty ash and smoke seaside, up and out of the disaster area. By afternoon however, the wind shifted, and it continued to blow onshore. The north tower's remaining walls acted as a windbreak and, within the looming, cratered structure, smoke lingered and festered, some of it rising like waves of heat off a desert floor, a great bulk of it discharged in mass as jet streams of water were fired from fire trucks upon smoldering cauldrons of rubble. The misty drizzle kept the ash down but also gave the smoke some body. A primordial fog resulted throughout much of the ruins. This hampered visibility for spectators and rescue workers alike. To make matters worse for Search and Rescue, the footing had become slick and ever more treacherous due to the moisture—the otherworldly mist that had fallen over Vallarta like an ague.

Search and Rescue was further hampered when its most formidable asset—Armando Montoya—took a spill.

Mountain knew how to take a fall, on the football field as well as in the wrestling ring. He'd taken much worse falls than this mere slip and trip. Yet as he popped to his feet he realized that something out of the ordinary had happened this time. He hissed a curse against the short stab of pain in his midsection, a curse punctuated by a startled groan at the sight of his own blood. Concrete and gnarled rebar had shredded his T-shirt and sliced a nasty, abrasive gash in his abdomen the shape of Baja California. He widened the tear in his shirt and stared at his wound in puzzled dismay, as though examining an inexplicable dent in his truck: how the hell did this happen?!? Two men from his Search and Rescue team took him by the arms. "Vámanos, Montoya," one of them said. "You need a medic."

"Give him a medal," said the other. He raised his respirator to his forehead. "Your work here is done, Montaña."

Mountain acquiesced with a snarling frown. After a few steps he stopped short, tore off his respirator and spun around. "Bizco!" he called out abruptly, "Bizco!"

A teammate gripped his bicep. "Get to a medic, Montoya. I will find Bizco."

Mountain glanced at him over his shoulder, unseeing, and stared down at his wound once again, the blood staining his belt. "Bueno," he assented with a snort of disgust at his clumsiness. "Find my puppy. He could not have gone far."

ENRIQUE Santos dumped a load of debris and rubble at a makeshift quarry yard just north of the Washington, drove back to the northeastern expanse of the ruins, and parked the dump truck off the front bumper of his Dodge pickup. He slammed the door shut with finality as he hopped out. This was it for him. Beat tired, filthy dirty, and done for the day. A grizzly, horrific day. He paused at the door to his Dodge and stared starkly at the illuminated fog veiling ground zero. What a suffocating hell hole, he thought. Enrique flicked on the headlamp strapped to his helmet and, with the stolid resolve of an athlete wrapping up his daily workout, set off for the emergency vehicles parked along the outskirts of what used to be the Washington's parking lot. He might as well check on the status of the rescue effort before retiring.

A welling commotion from somewhere off to his right detained him...raised voices and the trample of boots over rubble...a distant cry of "Bizco!" Enrique swung his head around to the sound and was confronted by a vision so startling the earth seemed to fall away beneath him. His heart jumped against his ribs as he stumbled backwards, his eyes fixed on an inhuman apparition lumbering towards him like Satan's own sentry; the muscled, crimson hindquarters, the yellow-rimmed, beastly eyes staring...God only knew where!...right back at him from within a blood-red head the size of an anvil. Enrique heard someone call out "Bizco!" once again; a flash of recognition seared his temples, held him in place as the animal sat before him, a leash hanging carelessly from the spiked collar adorning his neck.

Enrique wedged his heart from his ribs with a barking grunt. "B-Bizco," he sputtered. "You scared the puta madre hell out of me. Thought you were the devil himself."

Bizco cocked his head, eyes suddenly doleful, crossed upon Enrique's tortuous expression, his droopy jowl and wrinkled brow offering a semblance of bemused sorrow at the traumas suffered by his human friends.

Enrique remembered Bizco, had met him and Armando Montoya in passing this afternoon. Their heroics were quickly becoming legendary. He approached and examined Bizco's bloodied snout, ran a hand over his crimson pelt. "Qué demonios...?" he wondered out loud at the blood coming off on his hands and clothes. "Are you injured or—" Bizco abruptly stood and circled Enrique with a playful yelp. A clear demonstration that he was uninjured.

Two rescue workers Enrique vaguely recognized joined him, panting as though they had come running from a great distance, respirators dangling below their necks. One of them took a knee next to Bizco and draped an arm over his back. "Good boy, Bizco," he gasped. His partner rested his hands on his knees, his breathing hard and fast. "Híjole," he spat and shot Enrique a sharp, desperate glance. "We need men and equipment. Lighting too."

Enrique felt a sudden burst of energy rise in his chest, as though getting his second and third winds in the late rounds of a grueling fight. "What the—" he began. The man kneeling beside Bizco answered his question before he could get it out. "Bizco discovered a tomb on the west side of the ruins," he said, "a narrow cave clear around the northern wall." He stood, Bizco's leash in hand. "We think there are survivors down there."

DEVO handed me the passport. "Repeat it one more time," he said. "Then read it from the passport."

"In Spanish or Portuguese?"

"English this time, if you like."

"Esteban Enrique Bellán, from Caracas, Venezuela. Born on November ninth, 1977... Second trip to Mexico. And I've also been to Brazil, was born there. They're the only stamps in the passport. You had to go back a ways for that name, Devo."

Devo closed the gap between our Jeep and the car in front of us. We were fourth in line at the roadblock, heading south, out of town. "Guess I shouldn't be surprised you recognize the name," he said, "given your profession... Johnny?"

"John Brodie, from San Francisco. Hall of famer."

"*College* Football Hall of Fame," Devo said. "Bay Area as well. And you're not *that* John Brodie. Just play it straight, Johnny. You both remember an address to give in case asked?"

I gave him one on Avenida Simón Bolívar, Caracas. Johnny recited an address in Knob Hill, San Francisco.

I opened the passport and scrutinized the photo. "My picture looks like it coulda been today's mug shot."

"It is, Esteban, with a little doctoring to match your makeup— shoe-polished hair and beard and camouflaged black eye."

"Too bad this isn't a US passport. Sure could use one to get back in the States."

"A US passport might make them take a second and third look at you. And you can get into the States without a passport. It's done all the time."

I read the data in the passport and studied the photo again. The picture looked more than a little like Russell Martell to me. "How the hell you manage to doctor my photo?"

"Play your part and everything will come clear soon enough, Esteban." Devo eased the car forward.

"How come I didn't get a passport like him?" Johnny felt slighted.

"You don't need one. The hotel voucher I have in John Brodie's name will get you through the roadblock. And like I told you before, Johnny, if they ask you for a birth date, which they probably won't, give 'em one of your sister's." Devo retrieved my false passport and blinked at us. "You guys wanna meet the mayor's wife?"

Johnny popped his head up from his horizontal position in the backseat of the Jeep, "Really?" I shrank in the front and said, "No."

"There she goes," Devo said. A silver Range Rover followed by a white police pickup passed right by Devo's open window and pulled up to the roadblock. Both vehicles were summarily waved through.

"Guess it must be somebody important." I sounded unconvinced but if Devo said it was her it probably was. "You sure that was her—the mayor's wife?"

"Where she goin'?" said Johnny.

"Gloria," said Devo, "is headed home. But she'll come a streakin' back before she gets there."

"How do you know?"

"Guess we'll see if I do, Esteban." Devo casually stuck his elbow out the window. We were next in line.

75

IT was nearly 1:30 a.m., not late at all by Vallarta's partying standards. Yet the malecón was nearly deserted. And so were surrounding streets. The action was due north along the coast, at the Washington. A horrifying spectacle but it attracted a crowd.

And there was to be one other hotspot lit up in Vallarta tonight. The anarchist and the Zapatista would see to it.

The black Chevy Monte Carlo traveled north at a leisurely pace, from Old Vallarta along Morelos, past the malecón a block to the left, and jogged over to Peru. Then it made a left on Uruguay toward the sea, a good eight to ten blocks south of the Washington.

Manco backtracked south, paralleled the coast on the boulevard to Avenida México, made another left, backtracked again, and parked the car in the shadow between two streetlamps one block inland from the target they had just circled. He and Javier peered out the rear window of the Monte Carlo and surveyed the backside of Arena Vallarta in cold, calculated anticipation.

"Unprotected," said Javier. "And just enough light to see what we are doing."

Manco pushed his glasses up the bridge of his nose. "The windows are barred," he said, "but, from what I saw this afternoon, most all within our reach were broken by the shockwaves from the explosion this morning. A huge advantage. Just light the fuse with your lighter and throw the bomb straight through the bars. Remember,

409

we are handling incendiary devices, not actual bombs. You have to throw them hard enough to break the bottles for them to work."

"Entendido."

"Try to aim between the bars. The Coke bottles should fit. But even if you miss, with most the windows already shattered..."

"The place will go up in a ball of flame."

Manco's voice fluttered with nervous excitement. "Yes it will," he said.

Javier hoisted the case of Molotov cocktails from the trunk and walked in lockstep behind Manco towards the arena. The plan was simple. Javier would leave eight firebombs with Manco on the near (inland) side of Arena Vallarta, the section they were approaching right now. Several windows were broken along that wall and Manco would begin the assault as soon as Javier disappeared around the front-end of the arena. Javier had the advantage of being two-handed, so he could attack in sequence, with greater speed than Manco, circle the arena and meet up with him at the rear for a final assault (if firebombs remained) before making their escape.

Javier stared at the backside of the arena dead ahead. "Not much to be done from the rear," he murmured. "Just those four windows above the garage doors."

"We can shatter any remaining firebombs against plaster if we have to."

"Too bad we cannot get inside."

Manco made a move to cross the street and felt Javier tug at his shirt. "Car coming," said Javier. The two of them ducked back into an alley.

"A truck," whispered Manco. "Qué diablos?"

"Híjole. Backing right up to the garages."

Manco removed his glasses and wiped the mist from the lenses. "How many in the truck?"

Javier narrowed his hard gaze on the pickup as it parked in the misty light cast by flood lamps high on Arena Vallarta's rear wall. "Only one. A man."

Manco slapped his glasses on and glared at the vehicle with sinister anxiety, weighing his options. He was not to be denied. If circumstances beyond his control resulted in the death of this intruder, so be it. "What the fuck is he doing here? Who is he?"

A stout, sturdy figure emerged from the truck jangling a key chain. Authoritative air. Balanced, athletic gait.

The natural curl to Javier's lip spread into a malevolent grin. He recognized this man, as well as the opportunity he represented, an opportunity for the Zapatista to crush a nemesis and leave him for dead once he served his purpose. "Enrique Santos," he breathed out in a low growl. "You remember him from the meeting here Saturday night. And he is going to let us into the arena."

Javier flexed the tendons in his neck like a fighting cock and let cold hate soothe the fire in his belly. He opened up the case of firebombs. "Grab a six pack," he told Manco. "I will leave the rest by the arena after crossing the street. Give me one minute and Enrique Santos will be dead inside that garage."

"You sure? On your own?"

"This man is mine. And I can sneak up on him better alone, finish him before he knows I am there."

Javier crossed the street in smooth, stealthy strides, set the Molotov cocktails down next to the arena, and pulled his switchblade from his pocket.

ENRIQUE had no time to waste. Search and Rescue were acting on the assumption that survivors were trapped in the narrow cave Bizco discovered and men as well as equipment were being deployed to the area at this very moment. The cave had been created by an avalanche and the possibility of another avalanche occurring at that same spot made this an exceptionally dangerous operation. Inside Arena Vallarta's garage Enrique had access to the item needed to power lights and illuminate the danger zone at the isolated cave: a portable 3KW generator on wheels that could be lifted by two men over rubble to the farthest expanse of the Washington's devastated north tower.

He backed up to the rear of the arena and parked, his mind reviewing a mental check list. The generator was new, had only been used a half-dozen times or so during the construction of Arena Vallarta. They'd have no problems with it at the Washington but he better check the oil before moving it. He should also bring along his stout two-liter gas can. It could be filled when he returned to ground zero and easily carried over rough terrain. Enrique hopped out of his truck and made for the standard door between the two four-car garage doors. He'd have to move some things around in the left-hand side of the garage to get to the generator and then clear a path in order to wheel it into his truck. He unlocked the door, opened it, and flipped on the overhead florescent lights. Fairly well organized in here. He'd wait until he had the 3KW in position before opening the electric garage door and lowering the ramp under the bed of his truck. The generator was a little heavy for one man to handle but he could manage as long as he only had to roll it on its wheels and not fully lift it on his own. Enrique moved a table and a few chairs, slid the table saw aside, and spied the gas can just beyond the forklift. The 3KW was opposite the forklift, up against the wall next to a boxed 42" flat-screen television he had ordered installed today along with that oblong bathroom mirror standing off to the side. This morning's disaster delayed his furnishing the arena with those two items. He skirted the forklift and caught a glimpse of himself in the mirror. A bloody, filthy mess. Enrique looked down at his pants. Most all that blood must have come from Bizco's pelt. For the most part, Enrique had been managing dump trucks throughout the day; he hadn't spent enough time with victims of the blast to get this bloody, so it must be from Bizco and the dead bodies he discovered. The *survivors* he discovered? *Survivors*, Enrique thought. Bizco may have found survivors in need of rescue down in that cave. There was no time to lose and he chided himself for his short mental diversion. As he started for the generator, something else caught his eye in the mirror—a shadowy, silent figure directly behind him, and the glint of a blade.

Enrique heard the knife cleave air and slice his shirt as he dove behind the forklift, felt the sting across his back as he rolled to his feet, his gas can and an oil rag in hand. His attacker was quick, had circled the forklift like a cat and assumed a knife fighter's pose, feet spread, knees bent, knife hand—his right—slightly extended. Blood thudded in Enrique's temples at the sight of the familiar angry glare and lean-faced visage. "Javier," he sneered, his tongue lathering the name with contempt. He tightened his grip on the handle of his gas can, and considered making a break for the door but knew that furniture and the table saw blocked his way behind him, as did a heavy metal desk to his left and the forklift to his right. One false, tangled step in retreat and the Zapatista would surely kill him. Enrique thrust the gas can at Javier's knife—a lashing left jab that missed its mark but got his quarry to backup. He whipped the oil rag around his right hand. Thin protection against a knife but at least it was something.

Javier snarled a dangerous smile. He tossed his knife from one hand to the other and back again, his lithe, muscled physique standing out beneath his black T-shirt. "Pinche puto," he said. "You will not escape your precious arena alive."

Enrique flexed his jaw, teeth grinding. "A coward who strikes and misses when his man's back is turned is the one who dies you stupid naco." He assumed a boxer's stance, his brawler's stance—low crouch, left fist (his gas can) and foot forward, right fist tucked under his chin. In his heyday as a journeyman prizefighter, Enrique's plodding style belied surprising foot and hand speed that often caught rivals off guard. He won his share of fights against similarly suited brawlers, but a majority of his victories were against opponents who were certain they could outbox him—dance and dodge, stick and move—only to find themselves stunned by his quick feet and hands and helpless in a corner as he pummeled them mercilessly. Naturally, he'd never had to face a knife in the ring. Yet along with his boxing instincts, Enrique also retained the street skills of a young tough from the barrios of Guadalajara. More than a few scrapes he'd gotten into as a youth involved knives. In or out of the ring, Enrique had never killed anybody, but he sure tasted that killer instinct now. He could smell the blood trickling down his back, viscous and raw, as if dripping from his brow. He needed to end this fight right away, demolish his adversary or die.

Perspiration had popped out on Javier's brow and he could hear his heart hammering in his ears. He held no illusions about intimidating Enrique. With or without a knife, he could not expect to simply scare and overpower him. That's why he'd hoped to stab him in the back before he had a chance to defend himself. The lost opportunity changed everything. Javier knew his enemy, understood Enrique as more than just a lackey for cooperate interests destroying Mexico, its lands and indigenous populations. Raised in Guadalajara, the man had been a street thug before beginning his boxing career. He was no stranger to knives. And as a former professional boxer, Enrique's fists were registered lethal weapons. Not much if anything intimidated him. Age may have slowed his reflexes but Enrique kept himself fit and, at forty-six, over twenty years Javier's senior, he was far from a feeble old man. Without his knife and in close quarters like this—*a ring*—deep down inside Javier doubted he would stand much of a chance against him.

But Javier had his knife, and one other thing going for him: desperation. He had to take Enrique down, kill him or he and Manco would be busted for attempting to firebomb Arena Vallarta and thrown in jail for a very long time.

Enrique double jabbed with his gas can, aiming for the knife rather than the head or body. Javier stood his ground but was not quick enough with the knife. It clanged uselessly against the empty can. He slashed air and retreated a step. Enrique snorted a smirk. This kid would be no match for him at all without a weapon. He plodded forward but before he could get off another double jab Javier beat him to the punch, switched knife hands and jabbed left handed, nearly cutting Enrique's chest. Enrique backed up and bounced on his toes. Javier had demonstrated some ring savvy. Not only did he switch knife hands and adapt his stance to slip the gas can, he jabbed instead of slashing. This kept him balanced and greatly improved his accuracy. He better not underestimate the Zapatista.

For a fleeting instant, Enrique wished he had a knife as well, or a club (not to mention a gun), rather than his meager defenses—an empty gas can for a left and an oily cloth wrapped around his right.

Javier sensed his advantage and maintained the knife in his left hand to better clear and counter the gas can in Enrique's left. But he wasn't about to underestimate Enrique either. The cabrón could knock him out with one crisp punch to the jaw. Javier jabbed again, a slick thrust intended to debilitate the right hand cocked under Enrique's chin poised to deliver a knockout blow. The tip of the blade nicked his elbow and was gone just as the gas can hooked for Javier's arm. Javier gained confidence; there was no way the old man could match his speed. And something else raised his confidence, sent an electric surge of adrenalin coursing through his veins. Manco had slunk into the garage, a firebomb in hand. If Javier managed to back his adversary up close to the table saw, Manco should be in position to crack him over the head with the bottle.

CARLOS *El Manco* Mansalva couldn't win in hand-to-hand combat against a skilled opponent if he had six hands, much less the solitary hand appending his remaining arm. Even in the days when he had two hands and arms his slight build and small stature weren't exactly suited to the activity. Manco was acutely aware of this fact and, as he dedicated his devious mind to incitement to riot, he often dreamed of an opportunity to bloody himself for the cause, shed the blood of adversaries and pick up a scar or two, like the badges of honor Javier had acquired over the years. So when he furtively approached the garage and heard the clamor filtering out the open door—the clang of metal against metal and the shuffling of feet—he leapt to one side of the door as if jolted out of bed by a startling noise, as if shocked from a dream into the reality of that very dream. Evidently, Javier had not killed Enrique Santos yet and might be in need of assistance. Could this be Manco's chance to prove himself in battle? Could he help Javier kill this intruder? He sat his six pack of firebombs aside, gripped one of them by the neck, and peeked inside the door, his breath stilled and halting. A short stab of panic in his chest caused him to recoil, his back flat against the exterior doorframe. His brief glimpse had revealed his partner's trouble. Manco didn't know much about union leader Enrique Santos but he clearly was not dead as Javier had predicted. Far from it. The man had a gas can to shield himself from Javier's knife and maintained a menacing, dauntless stance despite a long, slicing wound across his back. And any attempt Manco might make to attack from the rear and crack Enrique Santos over the head with a Molotov cocktail was blocked by equipment and furniture. He couldn't sneak up on him which, for good reason, had been Javier's intention. Señor Santos exhibited the form of a dangerous individual. Manco's look at him may have been brief but it spoke volumes. His dauntless boxer's pose struck him as that of an experienced fighter relishing the opportunity to practice his skills. Manco steeled himself. Retreat was out of the question, certainly for Javier and, by extension, him. They had come too far, past the point of no return. An act of cowardice would only lead to disaster, inevitable capture by police and imprisonment. He and Javier had to kill Enrique Santos and bring this operation to a glorious conclusion, or die trying. Should he just brazenly enter the fray? walk in with the six pack of firebombs and begin hurling them at Enrique? He indulged the image, even imagined igniting the bombs as he threw them in sequence, as if two-handed, but discarded the idea as rash and impulsive. Igniting bombs was out of the question. He'd kill his partner in a firestorm and maybe himself as well. And besides, he couldn't carry the bottles and throw them as if two-handed anyway...and even if he could he didn't have confidence in the accuracy of his throwing arm. Unless he was lucky enough to nail Señor Santos in the head, the act was just as liable to distract and endanger Javier as Enrique... He had but one option: use one of his disadvantages to advantage. His slight frame, a disadvantage when it came to brawling, was very well suited to concealment. Maybe he could position himself for a surprise attack and crack the bottle over Enrique's head.

Manco gripped his firebomb like a club, the coke bottle thick and weighty in his hand. He peeked in the door to make sure Enrique Santos still had his back to him, and made his move.

INSTINCTIVELY, Enrique chanced a quick glance over his shoulder. Did the Zapatista have an ally? perhaps a gang with him? He thought this entirely possible but didn't see anyone. He better take care of business before he was outnumbered. The old prizefighter shrewdly noted Javier's cockiness—his eyes, loose and dark, glittering with unrestrained energy. A cockiness that, in the past, had left boxers on the canvass at his feet. And the Zapatista had committed a critical error towards the end of their last parry, an error he would not get away with again. Enrique dropped his defenses, played possum for an instant, and drew Javier into his snare. The Zapatista jabbed. This time Enrique feinted a left hook towards the knife hand; Javier pulled up in defense, off balance and wide open for a thundering right.

SEVE VERDAD

It must have been a perfect punch because Javier never saw it coming. And Enrique, a scrappy brawler rather than knockout artist, had never landed a better one. When his right fist landed square on the boney point of Javier's chin, the old prizefighter could feel the power clear down to his toes. Javier's eyes rolled up in his head. He fell straight back, paralyzed, his entire body rigid, toppling in slow motion. His head careened off a corner of the portable 3KW generator and he landed on his back, legs stiff and twitching.

Enrique picked up Javier's knife and headed straight for the open door. He had to lockout any accomplices the Zapatista might have. But accomplices to what? Why was Javier here to begin with? Just by chance? Dumb luck? Or did he have a plan...a plan to destroy Arena Vallarta? And if he had accomplices, why didn't they come to his aid? Had Javier, in his bloodlust to ambush his nemesis from behind, been separated from his amigos...?

Enrique needed backup and absently felt for his cell phone at his belt with his knife hand. He'd call Alejandro, and have Pedro get police over here.

He gripped the door and took a surreptitious look outside. Nothing but his truck parked in the misty light cast by flood lamps high on the arena's exterior wall. He folded the knife into his pocket and felt a pinprick of apprehension at the base of his skull as he locked himself inside the garage, an inkling that he'd overlooked a valuable clue in the empty evening mist. Then everything went black.

Enrique Santos, a fighter who had withstood as much and more than he gave in the ring without ever getting knocked out, slumped to his knees, sustained himself for a moment with his hands, and crumpled to the floor.

Manco hovered over his victim, astounded by his conquest. He nudged the union leader with his foot, got no reaction, and stared vacantly at the blood oozing through the firebomb's gasoline and sawdust composite near the top of Enrique's head. In a flash of panicked lucidity, he visualized another lifeless body. Manco rushed across the garage to his partner. "Javier," he said and kneeled next to him. "Me oyes?" Can you hear me? Blood pooled around Javier's ear. Manco gripped his shoulder and searched his ashen, slumbering face for life. "Javier," he repeated and raised his voice against a sharp twist of desperation in his stomach, "Me oyes Javier?!?" He listened at Javier's nose for a breath of air and heard him breathing, but also heard something else. A throaty moan from behind. Manco stood and stared across the garage towards the locked door, rodent eyes large as saucers behind his glasses. That hijo de puta Enrique Santos was stirring! on his elbows and shaking the cobwebs from his head! Manco

416

looked about frantically for a weapon, a hammer or wrench, something to crack over his head again. The brute might be upon him in a matter of seconds! His eyes lit upon the gas can by the forklift. He snatched it and scrambled for the door. Enrique was on his hands and knees. Manco slammed the gas can down upon his skull again and again, his muscles screaming in bottomless black rage with every blow.

Manco slumped beside his motionless victim and sucked air. Was Enrique Santos dead? Was this his first kill in the name of the cause? his first kill in his life? "Era hora," he muttered. About time. About time he got his hands bloody—his *hand* bloody. Manco stumbled towards Javier, then straightened himself and took a few seconds to appreciate the scene. It was strangely inspiring. Two men lay dead, or near death, each suffering the just rewards of their respective causes. As a capitalist sympathizer, Enrique Santos deserved his fate. And Javier? He was dead to the world and Manco couldn't move him, try and save him. Not one handed and with any hope of a clean escape. Too much incriminating evidence was scattered about, and someone was bound to miss Señor Santos eventually, probably sooner rather than later. He must have come here on an errand of some sort. Someone would come looking for him. What was there to do? Escape right now? Abandon the glorious plan? But...what about all the incriminating evidence? the shattered incendiary bomb, the blood, the two lifeless bodies?... Manco couldn't leave Javier at the mercy of police. He wouldn't survive encaged, behind bars. And when tortured he might even talk, rat out his anarchist accomplice. No, Manco couldn't abandon the operation now; especially since, at this point, he was *inside* the arena. The firebombing of Arena Vallarta could be carried out with greater effectiveness and alacrity than the planned attack on its perimeter. Furthermore, it would destroy all the incriminating evidence: the shattered incendiary bomb, *all* the bombs, the blood, and the bodies of Javier Menticlaro and Enrique Santos.

Javier deserved his fate as well... It would be an honorable fate, an honorable death, once Manco brought their mission to its glorious conclusion.

76

COMANDANTE Héctor Diamante Pasqual slouched over the booking counter in the processing room, telephone pressed to his ear. "Very good, Hernando," he said. "We are conducting a strategy session right now and a team will be organized to join your men there." He hung up the phone in its cradle and was about to address the troops seated before him—six uniformed Vallarta police officers, including Lieutenant Romero, and the three DF federales—when the mayor entered from the hall. "Have they spoken yet?" Héctor asked him.

Juan shook his head restively, "Not much." He paused and addressed the room as a whole: "Officers Revueltas and Contreras will remain under observation in the hospital for the next couple of days. Perhaps tomorrow they will be able to tell us exactly what the hell happened at Hotel Marciano this evening."

The mayor's pronouncement elicited a throng of afflicted comments—uneasy chatter rising within clouds of smoke and coffee in the processing room. All were aware that the department had suffered two casualties tonight but the reminder brought curses to their lips. Talk of justice and revenge for this brutal attack on police officers. Juan raised his voice to the men: "Their injuries do not appear life threatening. And I share your sentiments, caballeros. Justice will be done. As you all know, two gringos made off with their squad car, and one of them fits the description of Russell Martell."

Lieutenant Romero about chewed off the end of his cigarette at the mention of Russell Martell's name... How did the chingón do it? First an attack on the Washington, then a jailbreak, then a disappearing act in his hotel room, and now...two officers bludgeoned at El Marciano Hotel, all in one day! like he'd been doing chores and checking them off his list.

Lieutenant Romero had seen shadows behind those curtains in that hotel room. Someone was in there...had to be! Yet...qué demonios pasó? Next thing he knew el comandante furiously reported that the room was empty. Empty?!? Impossible!... Time and time again Russell Martell had demonstrated an uncanny ability to humiliate him and the entire police force.

Humiliate...? It was much worse than that. And much worse than the gringo's threat to publish a story implicating police in the murder of a terrorist. A story that might expose police blunders and corruption as contributing factors in the deadliest terror attack ever carried out on Mexican soil. Russell Martell was a terrorist, had killed multitudes and continued to escape justice, continued to evade police and get away with murder. And given the way he continued to get away with murder, what was to stop him from killing whomever he wanted, including Lieutenant Benito Cuevas Romero of the Puerto Vallarta Police Department?

418

FINDING DEVO

Russell Martell had to be stopped. And the only way to stop a terrorist this *tramposo* and dangerous was to kill him before he killed you.

El comandante said, "The squad car has been located in Old Vallarta, parked north of Insurgentes on the banks of the Rio Cuale. Officer Talla —"

The phone on the booking counter rang, interrupting him. He answered it as Lieutenant Romero spoke up: "The gringo may have ditched the car for another."

Federale Investigator Sándovar stood from his chair to speak, but before he could utter a sound, el comandante gained everyone's attention with a hushed exclamation into the telephone: "Fire?!?"

77

AT the roadblock some kid in fatigues, a couple of stripes on his sleeve and an automatic weapon slung over his shoulder, asked us for identification like a bouncer with a beef. Devo handed him the documents—two passports and Johnny's (John Brodie's) voucher for Hotel La Joya de Mismaloya. The kid looked at the passports, then shined his flashlight on us and asked Johnny where his passport was. Devo said he didn't speak Spanish and that his passport was at the hotel in Mismaloya. He asked Devo to step out of the car. Devo did so, and showed him the laptop in his daypack. Johnny sat up in his seat. He stayed put while I got out to allow another kid in fatigues access to the car. I surreptitiously surveyed the four other *federales* manning the roadblock, hands behind my back, cool as can be. Could've easily puked from nervousness but was cool as can be. Haggard (wasn't everybody today?) but acquiescent. Sweatin' bullets (*'cause of the mist and humidity,* I told myself, ignoring my churning guts). I dabbed the sweat from my face with the tail of Johnny's collared shirt Devo had told me to wear. A few stitches had popped when I put it on and I'd left it unbuttoned. Kept Johnny's A's cap pushed up off my forehead some. I had nothing to hide; just an innocent tourist. Stayed out from under the streetlamp off the Jeep's rear bumper though... I took a calming breath and stared at my filthy bare feet on the pavement. Did Johnny's hotel voucher mean I would get to take a bath in a luxury hotel tonight? Or would I end up back in The Chamber with a nightstick up my culo? I stuffed my hands into my pockets, the golf ball behind my ear thumping in cadence to my hammering heart. The kid talking to Devo took another look at me over the Jeep's roof. I

419

met his gaze. He asked me where in Venezuela I was born. I told him I was born in São Paulo, Brazil—a clever ruse devised by Devo to distract from any North American accent they might detect in my Spanish. And should I be tested I spoke Portuguese fairly fluently. (Devo had tested my Portuguese himself, said he'd read my bio on my website and knew I spoke it but had me practice with him anyway.) Devo said something to the kid. I imagined he slipped him some cash but it was just that—my imagination. The soldier searching the Jeep reared out of the car and Devo and I were motioned back in.

The kid took another look at Johnny, mentioned there was another roadblock before Melaque, and sent us on our way with a "conduzca con cuidado." Drive carefully.

78

CURSES and cries of disbelief filled the processing room. Juan approached the booking counter, his voice a whispering roar. "How bad?"

El comandante stood from the counter. "The fire department is en route."

Lieutenant Romero joined them. El comandante's voice acquired an urgent hiss: "A maldito fire just might light a fire in the bellies of vandals and arsonists, and activists still in town who were frustrated by all the security at the dedication. You both remember what happened after Hurricane Kenna. We may be faced with far greater troubles this time."

Muted eye contact between the mayor and his two senior police officers. Searching eyes...as though taking a moment to internalize the implications of a far-off explosion. They remembered Hurricane Kenna. The initial solidarity exhibited by the populace in the face of that disaster fractured as the days passed. Looting and vandalism became growing problems. This was not surprising at the time (disasters do inevitably provide opportunities for lawlessness) and it would be no surprise if similar problems were to arise in the wake of the disaster at the Washington. But a fire at Arena Vallarta less than twenty-four hours after an explosion at Vallarta's largest hotel suggested that Vallarta may have already begun to slip into lawlessness.

"Híjole," said Mayor Velázquez. Furious desperation registered in his face. "We already have the deadliest disaster in the history of Jalisco on our hands."

"And not a natural one," the lieutenant reminded him. "We have to consider the possibility that Russell Martell is behind this fire as well."

Commotion reigned in the processing room. Federale Investigator Sándovar stepped into the conversation at the booking counter, his voice low and modulated; yet within his brown eyes lurked the stiff-necked pride of a general ready to pull rank, bust some heads. "Panic, fear, and chaos are the goals of terrorists," he said. "And without decisive action, we just might be faced with it. All of it. For days and days."

The lieutenant glimpsed Officer Posada poking his head out of el comandante's office across the processing room. He raised his voice, "Anything on that disc Mariano?"

"Nada. Qué pasa?"

The processing room echoed with the answer to his question.

The mayor turned to his troops and lifted his voice above the din. "Cálmense caballeros," he said, "cálmense." The commotion dimmed. "Now is the time for cool heads to prevail. Especially amongst government officials."

Police headquarters was immediately abandoned to dispatch and a security detail. Everyone else was off to the fire, except the lieutenant. Mayor Velázquez ordered him to ground zero. "Manage the crowd and the troops, Lieutenant," he said, "and await further orders."

THE boulevard remained impassable at the Washington so the mayor and el comandante led a police caravan over Libramiento to the fire, el comandante at the helm of their squad car. The mayor called his wife and reported the latest news to her. Gloria could not believe what she was hearing. "A fire?" she said, her voice piquing, "at Arena Vallarta?!? How...what the hell are you talking about?!?"

Juan responded defensively, his voice quavering, "From...what the fire department has reported...it sounds like it might be a bad one."

Gloria whispered a shriek into her phone: "If this city is not under siege it sure as hell seems like it, Juan. And you better make sure everyone under your command starts acting like it is or things are going to get even worse!"

Click.

There was a book to follow, procedures mapped out for disasters such as hurricanes and earthquakes. And terror attacks. There was a procedure to follow for a foreign invasion of Banderas Bay as well. Hell, there was a procedure for most any eventuality. Procedures that included, under extreme circumstances, lockdowns and curfews.

SEVE VERDAD

The mayor discussed the book with el comandante on their way to the fire. A tense conversation but not heated. Only one issue to decide—whether or not to follow the safest most secure course of action: a lockdown between the Washington and Arena Vallarta and a curfew for the entire city.

El comandante reminded the mayor that a military curfew had never been imposed in Vallarta before. This wasn't Chiapas or Oaxaca, hotbeds of activism and rebel activity, or Culiacán, Tijuana, Nogales, Nuevo Laredo, Ciudad Juarez and so much of the northern border region where gangsters and drug cartels were in open warfare with the federal government (not to mention US border patrols). Curfews and lockdowns weren't such a rarity in those places.

The mayor cursed. "And this is Puerto Vallarta," he said.

"Sí," replied el comandante.

The mayor looked out the window, northwest, over and beyond the Rio Cuale, every breath issuing a greater tightness in his chest. "There it is..." he said grimly, a wavering flicker in his eye. A tiny glare. It hardly seemed possible but there it was. His beloved arena. On the verge of destruction.

"Sí," said el comandante. "A toda madre."

Mayor Velázquez spied el comandante sideways, his voice hard and foreboding: "Vallarta may very well be under attack, Héctor. And if we do declare a lockdown and curfew, it will make these disasters more difficult to explain away as accidental...even if, by some improbable circumstance, they are."

Comandante Pasqual shuddered, the last few days flashing through his mind like his last days on earth. Police foul-ups, payoffs, corruption. Death, destruction. A finger of blame at the department. His career in the balance. The mayor knew the score. El comandante could feel his eyes boring into him, needling his conscience.

There was only one answer to give him. The answer of a police chief. Commander of the Puerto Vallarta Police Department. Héctor huffed, "Chinga Lazarito. We have to do what is best for Vallarta and deal with the publicity as it comes."

As they dropped down into Old Vallarta and backtracked north, the mayor continued to flip a coin in his head over imposing a curfew and lockdown. The glow, and then the blaze came into view northeast of the malecón. It was all el comandante could do to keep from driving off the road. "Santísima madre de Dios."

"Dios mío," Juan said solemnly. "Looks like the gates of hell."

DEVO slipped the Jeep into gear and stoically steered us on our way, south, towards Mismaloya.

"We gonna use that hotel voucher in Mismaloya?" I asked, "or we gotta face another roadblock?"

"No more roadblocks tonight."

"Thank Christ," said Johnny. He repositioned himself in the backseat and propped his ankle up on his backpack.

Devo's daypack was at my feet; he thrust his hand inside, pulled Ara's shirt from it and stuffed it into my belly like a football. Nearly knocked the wind outta me. "Your intimate connection to Brenda," he said.

"You mean—" I was gonna say Ara, since it was her shirt, but quickly realized he might be right. I'd become awfully attached to Ara's Plaza de Toros Guadalajara shirt, not just because it bore the scars of my harrowing journey and belonged under glass, it also represented an intimate connection to "...both Brenda and her sister, Ara," I said.

Devo nodded imperceptibly. I folded my keepsake and sat on it. Devo drove with all the urgency of a tour guide way ahead of schedule. If not for the meddlesome mist and drizzle, he'd have pointed out landmarks and scenic vistas. Johnny fished a few beers out of the ice chest and applied a couple to his ankle. "You can give me my money back now Russ, since you got plenty from the cops and we're outta town."

I handed Johnny the wad of bills he'd given me on our way to his hotel. "And here's two hundred pesos for trashing your room. Might as well pay for my stay." I flipped him a couple hundred peso notes and reached into the ice chest for a beer to apply to the golf ball.

Devo eyed the thick roll of bills in my right hand. "Ripped off the cops, huh?"

I stuffed the roll into my pocket. "Just took back the thousand pesos or so they stole when they arrested me, plus some compensation." The golf ball sizzled against the cold beer can. I drew a stinging breath between my teeth. "Not nearly enough compensation."

"Oh he got his compensation." Johnny popped a Modelo and took a slug. "Shoulda seen how he left those bastards."

"Been better off lettin' 'em bust your ass," I shot back.

"Didn't say I wasn't grateful."

"Did it more for myself than you think. Those pricks were out to get me. Still are. They want me dead. Dead, dead. Probably should've killed 'em."

"No," Devo said. "You did right. You let 'em see you?"

"The owners at reception saw me. Maybe a guest or two. Chimp, the little shit mighta seen me...if he remembers. Whadda's it matter? They know it was me, will blame me for it anyway. But what I don't get is...?" I paused in careful reflection. There were so many things I didn't understand about my circumstances I'd suddenly forgotten which I wanted to talk about.

"Ye-es?" Devo drew out the word like a concierge, ready to answer any question.

"How the hell you weren't seen at police headquarters? In the cop car, I heard my description on the radio but there was no description of my supposed accomplices. And those cops who raided Johnny's room manhandled him like *he* was my partner in crime, the man who sprung me from jail."

Johnny was fascinated by my insight. "Nobody saw you guys escape?" he said. "I mean...didn't you have to tie anybody up? You kill 'em instead? No, you couldn't a done that or they'd of...uh..." He took a couple thoughtful swigs of beer.

"The cops at El Marciano were out for blood, Martell," Devo said, "and careless."

"Yeah they were. I thought about that at the time. But how did you—"

"Same way you did at El Marciano. You sized up the situation and took care of business."

"Sure as hell did," Johnny said. He guzzled beer. We fell silent.

The curves in the road and the drone of the car engine offered a familiar comfort zone, as though I was back on vacation. Let someone else drive and when you wake up, you're in a new place. Devo allowed a car to pass from behind. Not one had passed from the other direction, going north into Vallarta. My gaze attached itself to the red taillights until they disappeared around a bend. I felt myself drifting within our headlight beams, between holes in the misty drizzle, hypnotized by visions of a soft bed and room service. Johnny snored. I checked him out—All City Johnny Miles, on his back, laid out. Hat over his face. Knows how to ice himself down. His legs were crossed and elevated atop his backpack, icy beers wedged about his ankle. I removed my beer from the golf ball, laid my head back on the headrest and closed my eyes.

Devo said, "There goes Gloria."

FINDING DEVO

I opened my eyes in time to see headlights streak by going the opposite direction. "No shit. Where's she headed in such a hurry?"

Devo turned on the radio. "Guess it won't clutter your mind too much to hear some news, now that we're outta town."

The man on the radio said that this catastrophe might not turn out to be deadly. No one was thought to be inside the arena, "But do you really think that *two* catastrophes within less than twenty-four hours of one another are a coincidence Comandante Pasqual?"

"We cannot say as of yet," said el comandante. "One, perhaps both, may have been accidental."

The first voice grew strident, his Spanish rapid: "Is Russell Martell a suspect for this fire here at Arena Vallarta, he and any accomplices? He is already wanted in connection with the explosion at the Washington which, you have to admit, señor, does not look like it was the result of a ruptured gas line or kids playing with matches."

"We are not ruling anything out. But at this juncture speculation gets us nowhere. We ask that the public remain calm and stay off the streets. More facts are needed before reaching any conclusions and..." I lowered the volume, my insides turning to ice, a quiver curling my mouth.

The radio murmured that the fire would be contained, but the arena was likely to be completely destroyed...

Devo was unmoved: "I suppose you do have accomplices. Just not for the crimes they think you committed." He switched the radio off. "After what happened at Johnny's hotel, it's just a matter of time before they place you guys together."

I shook my head in frustration and disbelief. "Vallarta's under attack and they're blaming *me* for it? Goddamn idiots..." I ran a beleaguered hand through my hair. Johnny's cap tumbled carelessly off my shoulder. "And in the meantime the real terrorists are getting away."

Johnny snorted in his sleep, blissfully oblivious...or was he mocking me?...*real terrorists?*

The words struck an alarming chord in my brain... Devo knew a news flash was coming! knew the arena had gone up in flames! knew before Gloria found out about it... And how could he have known unless he was involved, and had accomplices himself?!?

Terrorist accomplices he's in contact with...via the receiver in his ear?!?

Whether or not Devo really had a receiver hidden in his ear, the guy had to be connected somehow. He knew too much, way too much. I was stunned, past numb, and shaded my suspecting, fearful eyes from him with a hand.

Once again that familiar fear possessed me. Fear of Devo, what he was capable of. Fear for my life, if I left him, if I stayed. Fear heating me up, urging action. But what the hell was there to do? Sock Devo and jack his Jeep? The guy could probably squash me like a gnat. Who was I seated next to? And what did he want from me?

A guttural voice penetrated my brain like a nail through my ear: "I surmised it, Martell."

"What?" I shuddered and faced him.

"The fire." Devo stared back at me, an opaque eye blanketed in darkness, the other a scintilla of blue reflected in the pale light of the Jeep's dash. He brought his eyes back to the road, his profile a stern silhouette.

"B-but how?" I stammered.

"You saw the culprits on my computer screen up at the fort. That little red dot we were tracking on the map. Manco the anarchist and his Zapatista friend."

"Manco?!?" My eyes rolled around in my head... "And a *Zapatista?* Who? Was he at the party with Manco?"

"No."

I blew out a contemptuous breath. "Manco," I hissed and shot Devo a blistering glare. "If you knew what they were up to, why didn't you stop them? Why bother tracking them if you're not gonna stop them?"

Devo slowed for a coming curve. "Can't control everything," he said tonelessly. "And the fire at the arena works to our advantage, stretches resources that might otherwise be used to search for you."

"You almost make it sound like you planned the fire."

"Like I said, I *surmised* as much."

Johnny stirred, groaned beneath his fedora. I released a moan that mimicked him. "Christ almighty...does the death and destruction ever end?"

"Lotta destructive forces in the world." Devo coasted around a bend in the road. "More than just *Islamisalaamis*. If you recall, drugs and corrupt coppers played a major role in your bust and incarceration today, not to mention the beating you took."

"How could I forget?" I said in a haughty tone Devo seemed to ignore. "Drugs were just another excuse for them to torture and destroy me."

"What do you make of that?"

I let loose a silent, contemplative breath. "Not sure what to make of it. Suppose in some sense I was nearly another victim of the drug war today."

426

Devo tilted his head to that. "The drug war has resulted in Vietnam *Redux*," he advanced, "especially along the southern US border, though far too many refuse to look at it that way."

"Vietnam Redux?" I blinked stupidly at him. "What does that have to do with me?"

"Everything's interconnected. And you're the infamous *Russell Martell*. I'm afraid you have no choice but to accept your destiny in this violent world and fight to save your life."

"I *have* been fighting... What the hell kinda destiny you talkin' about?"

"It's still being written."

"Still being written? By whom?"

Devo responded with silence, eyes on the road. I stared at him for a few long seconds. When I looked away he said, "It's a perpetual battle."

My stomach contracted with a jolt, thrusting my heart up around my throat. A classic big-game choke. *Perpetual battle?* All I wanted was for this nightmare to end and get back home! Did Devo expect me to continue to perform in this cutthroat game? a game of life and death?!? It was painfully obvious that I had nowhere near his ability or training. I had no business competing under this kind of pressure, no experience.

I tried to think of something to say to hide my fear and give me an out...and the truth came tumbling out: "Hey man, this ain't exactly my bag, you know? I got lucky with those cops in Johnny's room, particularly in my timing. And I made a mess. A bloody mess. You moved in and out of that police station like some kinda disease. Wish I had your talents, I honestly do. But I'm not cut out for that kinda shit."

Devo looked me over with a small smile. "Surprised yourself up in Johnny's room tonight, huh?"

"Guess so. Relied on instinct mostly."

"Your performance went beyond instinct, Martell." Devo allowed me an approving nod. "You did good tonight. But you're right. This type of action might not be your thing. However, that doesn't mean you can't contribute. Every warrior has his place, even if it's with a pen instead of a sword."

A pen instead of a sword? Devo swung a left. "Hey, where you goin'?" Instead of heading for the beach and hotel off to our right, Devo had turned onto the dirt road that led to the village of Mismaloya.

"You didn't think we were gonna get caught in a luxury hotel, did you?"

"Well, yeah. Uh, no. I mean... That voucher. I thought maybe..." I didn't see how the village would be any safer than the hotel. It could easily be more dangerous.

Devo clung to the high ground at a fork in the road and shifted into four-wheel drive. "Don't worry," he said, "We're not going down to the village."

"How far we headed up the Mismaloya River? La Arcadia?"

"Further. How'er you on horseback?"

"Like it fine, when the sun's out. If we're doin' this, why didn't we just take a boat to Quimixto or Yelapa or...somethin'?"

"Bay's a bust. Swimmin' with navy and cops. Relax. Stick with me and you'll have a bed in an hour or so."

"Hard to relax when you change the plan on me."

"Plan's not changed. If somethin' were to go wrong, best you know as little as possible. And you shoulda figured we weren't going to La Joya de Mismaloya. The hotel would be about as safe for you right now as Casa Mexicana."

Devo's concern for my safety gave me pause. "Why are you doing this?" I said.

"Doin' what?"

"Helping us."

"You mean, what's in it for me?"

"Yeah."

"What do *you* think?"

Under my breath I mused, "What do I think...?" *I think you're a fool for helping me? I think this is all a game to you? I think I'm lucky you're around? I think everyone, including you, is out to get me? I think I should have stayed home?* "Haven't a clue," I said at last, and stared out my window. *I think it's gonna rain.*

I heard a mild beep in my ear, a common sort of ringing that converted into a prosaic nasal voice: "The day's lessons haven't sunk in yet, eh m'boy?" Devo's W.C. Fields impression was so precise I was surprised to find him behind the wheel instead of W.C. himself. He drew out his words, his nasal tone theatrically inflected, "Ahh ye-es. The kid needs more clues. Na-tur-ally. A vic*tim*...of circumstance. Consequence *of*...lack of experience. What a nuisance." Devo's hawkish nose grew bulbous, his face distorted. I blinked several times and brought him back into focus. He downshifted over bumps in the road and reverted to even-key Devo. "My motives certainly have nothing to do with your good looks," he said with an imperative wink, as though I needed reassurance that *he* was driving the Jeep and not a dead, drunk comedian. "Might have something to do with your wit, if you channel it in the right direction. Ask yourself what's in it for the enemy and you'll find what's in it for me."

I gaped at him, and heard my jaw pop below the golf ball as I snapped my mouth shut. My inner ear tingled. I felt strangely disoriented and stared back at Johnny, to get my bearings, see if he was still onboard. His hat was pinned to his face, as though it would fly away without his arm draped over it. The Jeep rocked and lurched, jarred my sunken liver and dented kidneys. I hugged my bruised ribs.

"You need some rest, Martell."

I gave Devo a look of shabby indifference, as if he'd just told me my hair was brown or that two plus two equals four. "So after a good night's sleep your intentions will come clear and all this insanity will make sense?"

"Possibly. All I can tell you right now is that you're a tool. A means to an end. And that end means more than mere survival."

I slumped and massaged a dull pain behind my eyes. Devo's cryptic responses to my queries were fatiguing, wearing me out. I couldn't get a straight answer out of the guy.

I reassessed him for the umpteenth time since I met him at Mountain's party and was vaguely mollified. Thus far he'd sprung me from jail, through a roadblock and out of Vallarta. Pretty damn impressive, to say the least. It appeared likely he would get me a bed for the night. I took a deep breath, reclined, and watched the drizzle turn to rain. The road from Mismaloya to La Arcadia has a tendency to flood during the rainy season, which was months away as I figured it. But figurin' had little to do with my last eighteen hours or so, unless terror attacks, drug busts, sadistic cops, jailbreaks and a one-man cavalry named Devo were requisite to your daily *rutina*.

A huge dip in the road pitched us starboard. Johnny grumbled, "Can't you guys take it easy?"

I said, "Won't be stayin' at a luxury hotel tonight."

"Figures," he said. Johnny rolled onto his side, face covered by his fedora. One of his beers rolled to the floor. I stuck it into the ice chest with mine. He snorted, snored, snorted, and grumbled, "Fucking ankle."

Gentle rain became a drumming downpour, but the road wasn't sloppy, just bumpy. Too bumpy to sleep. Johnny couldn't have been able to do much more than rest his eyelids, which was a good idea.

ACROSS the street from what used to be the Washington parking lot, upwards of two hundred spectators braved a burgeoning tropical rain to view the deadliest catastrophe in the history of the Mexican state of Jalisco. And each and every one of them knew that yet another catastrophic spectacle was unfolding this evening. Word couldn't have traveled faster in a cathedral; they could see it with their own eyes on the sullen city-block horizon—first an inexplicable luminescence, now a hellish glow ascending in the black sky. Arena Vallarta was on fire.

Lieutenant Benito Cuevas Romero stood in the middle of the rock-ribbed street, well beyond the generators and lights used to illuminate the Washington ruins. He glared at the surreal corona mounting to the south—Arena Vallarta—and then surveyed the throngs of people opposite him beneath the feeble glow of streetlamps. An uneasy crowd, splintering and teaming in restless confusion behind barricades and hazard tape manned by police and military personnel, their afflicted grumblings surging like a rising tide. The fire had yet to cause outright panic. Arena Vallarta was a good ten to twelve blocks away...and it wasn't like people were trapped inside. The place should be empty. Chances of the blaze spreading were remote given the wet weather and rapid response of fire fighters who'd spent the last eighteen hours or so on active duty. Most of the spectators appeared ghoulishly torn between taking in the destruction before their eyes here at the Washington or going to see the fire firsthand.

Benito was joined by Lieutenant Tabio from the military camp located on the outskirts of the Vallarta airport. "No one is running around screaming *fire*," said Lieutenant Tabio, his voice raw from shouting orders for most of the day and night. "But that crowd is getting edgy and our men exasperated with shrugging off their questions about arson." Like Lieutenant Romero, Lieutenant Tabio had donned plastic raingear. His protuberant eyes and nose peered out from beneath his unstrapped helmet where a couple of gold bars shone through the grime. "At the request of the fire department," he added, "I have ordered men to the arena to help with crowd control."

Lieutenant Romero cursed, "Puta," his face clouding over in dull anger. "Before that maldito fire broke out it seemed we finally had plenty of manpower here." He spit in disgust and answered his cell phone.

Mayor Velázquez sounded a million miles away, an echo from deep within an endless chasm of sounds enveloping both of them: cascading water, the hum of generators, distant sirens, drowning voices. Lieutenant Romero raised his voice, said he couldn't hear him. The mayor's tone sharpened. Lieutenant Romero was instantly overcome with anxiety and relief all at once. Anxiety because something was about to be done that had never been attempted in Vallarta before. And relief...because it needed to be done. The only sure way to prevent further catastrophe.

There was to be a lockdown between the Washington and Arena Vallarta, and a curfew implemented from the Rio Pitillal on through Playa de los Muertos. "The first order of business for you, Benito," said the mayor, "is to disperse that crowd over there—get everyone to return to their hotels and homes as calmly and orderly as possible. Make sure things do not get out of hand."

Lieutenant Romero relayed the order to Lieutenant Tabio. "A good idea," they both agreed. "We have to exercise our authority and maintain control of the city," said Lieutenant Romero. "But enforce the order delicately so as not to cause alarm."

Easier said than done. As soon as authorities wielding foghorns announced that it was time for everyone to return to their domiciles, the rising tide of murmurs from the crowd grew into swells of distress: Why? We have a right to stay. We're not guilty of anything! Find the terrorists!... Has the government lost control of the city? The fire must be a case of arson! First the Washington, now the arena, what's next?!?

Lieutenant Romero understood the irony of the situation. The actions of authorities were triggering the very unrest they hoped to prevent. He damned himself for having little alternative and even less insight into the idiosyncrasies of human nature. Instinctively, the lieutenant had suspected that the spectators would become unruly when ordered to return home no matter how delicately they were handled. But intellectually he could not figure exactly why, how bad it would get, or if there was any way to prevent it under the circumstances.

There was no changing course. Vallarta was in a state of emergency and the decision to disperse the crowd had already been made. The only decision to make. Discontent buzzed through the masses like an electrical current, producing shouts of protest and demands for the head of Russell Martell and all his sin madre terrorista amigos.

Thankfully, there wasn't a stampede. More like organized chaos. Some shouldered their way through the throngs but most departed the scene frigidly—stubborn but also perplexed and angered by orders to return home, as though they'd planned on spending the night. No one attempted to approach ground zero, but the crowed retreated in every other direction and, despite warnings against visiting the arena, a good portion of those heading south marched defiantly, their resolute strides suggesting they planned to do exactly that.

Within the multitudes, a smattering of Vallarta's dirty underbelly lingered, those without much if any home to return to. Destitute adolescents and men. Tiny women in rags clutching their young. They were as tattered and forlorn as the Washington ruins and had been taking advantage of the spectacle to beg and sell gum.

Lieutenant Romero got back in touch with the mayor. "The crowd has become agitated, señor," he said. "They are dispersing but many look to be making for the fire instead of home."

"Have police assist military units ordered to lockdown streets between the Washington and Arena Vallarta, Lieutenant. Any officers we can spare. I will make the necessary pleas for calm over the airways and into the streets themselves and officially announce a curfew."

"Muy bien, señor."

"And avoid violence at all costs. Por Dios we have had enough."

The lieutenant made for Officer Sánchez standing at the south end of police barricades cajoling the crowd through a foghorn. He'd have him organize a team to help with the lockdown. But someone got to Sánchez before he did. Two men. Rescue workers by the looks of their helmets and overalls. They spoke to Sánchez in a demonstrative fashion, pleading hands raised in urgency, as though they had yet another emergency for police to respond to. The lieutenant quickened his pace. Sánchez swung around and pointed him out to the men. "Qué pasa?" said Lieutenant Romero as he approached, his tone betraying onerous apprehension—what the hell could have possibly gone wrong now?

"We have lost a man," said the shorter of the two rescue workers. He mopped the moisture from his face with the collar of his shirt and clarified himself, "Enrique Santos."

Lieutenant Romero frowned dumbly. "What do you mean *lost* him?"

The taller rescue worker pushed his helmet off his forehead, his eyes leveled on the lieutenant's. "Last we saw of him he was off to pick up a generator at Arena Vallarta," he said. "He should have returned some time ago and is not answering his cellular phone."

"Have you—"

The shorter one cut the lieutenant off, anticipating his question: "We just came from the arena and drove by his house. His truck is nowhere to be found."

"Enrique Santos?" the lieutenant said, his tone emphatic.

"Sí," the men chorused.

Lieutenant Romero sighed heavily, "Híjole." Any man gone missing was a concern but Enrique Santos was Pedro's father and merited special attention. He retrieved a pencil and notepad from beneath his raingear. "I am sure he will show up soon but give me his phone number for police dispatch and a description of his truck so they can get the word out. And when he does show up, be sure to inform police immediately."

81

DEVO'S Jeep rocked and creaked like a horse buggy over the dirt road up to La Arcadia, but I managed to rest my eyes. I opened them when the ride leveled out. As I'd suspected, we had arrived at the restaurant's smooth circular parking lot. I rolled my window down some and checked out La Arcadia's looming silhouette off to our right.

La Arcadia is a three-tiered restaurant overlooking the Mismaloya River surrounded by mountains of untamed mangroves, parota trees, plantains, birds of paradise—all manner of jungle flora and fauna. It attracts its share of tourists but closes at 7 p.m., three or four hours after the traditional Mexican comida. Aside from an exceptional swimming hole and gastronomy specializing in mariscos, La Arcadia's claim to fame is its location for the blockbuster action flick 'Hunted'. The charred fuselage of a Cessna used in the movie is perched on a pedestal to one side of the entrance to remind tourists of this notable distinction. The dirt road leading from the town of Mismaloya to La Arcadia ends at a barbwire chain-link fence skirting the far end of the restaurant's parking lot. I figured we would walk through the restaurant, cross the foot bridge, and mount our horses on the other side of the river. There's a trail there I was familiar with but had never followed for more than a mile on foot. I'd figured wrong.

Devo pulled directly up to the locked gate in the fence, cut the engine and headlights, and told us to "Relax for a minute or two." He exited and took off around the back of the Jeep towards a light on the far side of the restaurant.

Johnny sat up, his voice groggy with interrupted sleep. "What's up?"

"Like I said a while ago, no luxury hotel tonight."

"And like *I* said," he retorted sardonically, "figures."

"Arena Vallarta was...is being destroyed by fire as we speak."

"What?" Johnny looked as though I'd thrown cold water on his face. The whites of his eyes shined in the dark. "You gotta be kiddin' me. When'd you hear about that?"

"It was on the radio when you were snoozin' back there."

"Holy shit. How'd it happen? Anybody hurt?"

"No reports of casualties. How'd it happen...?" I tucked my lips between my teeth and considered the question. Devo's convenient explanation about Manco and a Zapatista setting the blaze didn't sit well with me. Not sure why. Probably because Devo himself didn't sit well with me. The guy was an enigma, his motives shady at best. "Who knows how it happened?" I shrugged. "Arson, probably. But they'll blame it on me. Heard 'em say as much on the radio."

"Did ya? Wow. So they're bound to blame me as well...eventually."

"Devo said that you and I will be linked sooner or later."

"After what went down in my hotel, that's an easy call." Johnny ran a disparaging hand through his mane. "A fire at Arena Vallarta? Damn. Unbelievable. Is Vallarta under attack or what?"

"Looks that way, don't it?"

"Sure as hell does. First the Washington and now the arena. Never thought anything like this could happen in Vallarta, *any* place you'd ever find *me*." Johnny slouched and shook his head. "So what's in store?"

"Horses."

"Horses?" Johnny grimaced. "Don't think I can ride with this ankle."

"Let's see." I turned on the interior light. Johnny raised his foot and gingerly set it up on the side of the driver's seat. The ankle was red and bigger than when I'd seen it in his hotel room. "Can you move it? How inflamed is it?"

Johnny bent his toes, flexed his ankle, and put the back of his hand to it. "Feels pretty warm. Hurts like hell. You think it's broken?"

"Christ, Johnny. If it is we're gonna have to get you to a doctor, soon. We'll ice the hell out of it and see if the swelling goes down tomorrow. Devo must have ice where we're goin'. We still have some in the ice chest... Might just be a real bad sprain. It's not like there are protruding bones. You hear or feel it crack? or did it just buckle?"

"Both. I'd a rolled with it, but the big guy had a hold of me."

"Sonofabitch."

"Glad they didn't shoot me."

"If they had caught me in there with you they would have."

Something rustled outside my door. A figure in a hooded poncho was standing there with two horses. Devo. A hooded fellow with a

434

flashlight was unlocking the gate. The horses were brown, maybe red. I couldn't see too well in the dark and drizzly rain. One horse was much bigger than the other and had saddlebags. Devo pulled a bundle out of a saddlebag, opened the car door and handed it to me. "Put these on."

I gave one of the ponchos to Johnny. "Not even gonna try to put on my shoe," he said.

"Stick it in your pack. Two horses. You'll be doublin'."

I got out of the car. A gust of wind blew Ara's shirt from my hand. I shook a splatter of mud from it and hung it at my hip underneath the poncho. A patch of sky was faintly illuminated above distant mountains. The full moon battled the storm, shedding what light it could. At the gate, Devo looked up from the guy with the flashlight, told me to grab Johnny's pack. He wrapped the pack in a poncho, handed me a headlamp, and secured the pack atop the smaller horse's rump. I fastened the lamp around my head and shined it on Johnny. He didn't look so hot. Pain etched his face. He told me to get the fucking light out of his eyes.

Devo and I lifted Johnny onto a blanket behind the big horse's saddle. I yanked a thorn from my foot and mounted the smaller horse. My saddle was about as comfy as a hotplate—set my bruised butt on fire. I cursed Chimp, dismounted, and shortened the stirrups to set myself high in the saddle. Johnny asked Devo about the ice chest. He said to leave it, we'd have plenty of beer and ice. The fellow with the flashlight came over to have a word with Devo. He pulled back his hood and I could see he wasn't a fellow but a young Mexican woman. She barely came up to Devo's chest. Devo leaned over, whispered in her ear and pecked her on the forehead. Then he mounted the big horse, careful not to disturb Johnny.

"Don't be afraid to take hold of my waist to steady yourself," he said. Johnny did so. The Mexican girl shut the gate behind us.

Devo focused his headlamp on the trail and told me to keep mine on his big horse's rump. "The light's more for you than your horse," he said, "but it'll help keep the animal in line. She's used to following on his ass."

I patted my horse's neck. "What's her name?"

"Lucha. This one here's El Cid. They know their way around so don't do anything more than hang on to the reins and saddle horn."

It rained and drizzled all at once—raindrops falling through the steady drizzle. The wind picked up, had to snap the collar of my hood to keep it over my head. A drum roll and a flash in the sky. I anticipated a clap of thunder that didn't report. Lucha kept her nose on El Cid's tail as we strolled up to a ridge and down into the woods.

Both horses were red but Lucha's mane had some blond in it that wasn't evident in El Cid's tail. Johnny flexed his leg to elevate his ankle. I asked him how he was doing. He said he could use some drugs. Devo said he'd give him something when we arrived.

"Arrive where?" Johnny said.

"Your beds."

That satisfied us.

The wind grew wicked, howling and shrieking through the forest like an insane witch frustrated by her inability to corral us. Rain fell from the canopy in flurries, pelting my poncho and tumbling over my calves and feet. I imagined we could be washed away at any moment and saw my lifeless body being dragged from the river the next day, identified as that of a terrorist. Mom and Dad united in their fight to clear my name. Oh how distraught they'd be! From under my hood, the headlamp shone on El Cid's muscled hindquarters. His thick tail would pull me to safety in a flood.

We bore left at a fork in the trail and trudged uphill. The woods remained dense, allowing for frequent brushes with tree limbs, mangroves, and high-reaching ferns. After about twenty minutes or so, the trail leveled off abreast a long brick wall crowned with glass shards set in cement. The wind abated. A lull in the storm was at hand, punctuated by the stalwart clip-clop of our horses' hooves. The forest sagged from the unseasonable downpour, enveloping us in an evergreen blanket. For the first time in quite a while I felt safe, as though welcomed home, the day's traumas shadows of a different world, touching me without meaning. I relaxed for a moment and bounced in the saddle. A thorny pain pierced my rectum. I stiffened, leaned over the saddle horn and cursed Chimp. His bloody Pekinese mug flashed before my eyes. I resisted apparitions—wounded ghosts, a dead woman draped over my arm—and a wave of angry paranoia and dull despair. I bolstered my position in the saddle and managed to recapture the feeling of security, not expecting it to last.

A large rough-sawn wooden gate encased in eight-foot wrought-iron spears appeared in the brick wall. The spears could puncture corrugated steel, skewer flesh and bone. Devo dismounted. A padlock the size of my fist secured the two sides of the gate. Devo unlocked it with a key from his pocket and swung the gate open. He led El Cid through by the reins. Lucha followed. I wanted to comment on the gate, the wall, the weather, but was unwilling to break the unspoken spell that had come over us. Devo shut the gate, mounted up, and led us over a sheared lawn. We passed a jacaranda with pale purple blooms on our left and a giant ceiba to our right. Dead ahead was a thatch-roofed cabin the size of a two-car garage. As we got closer, I could see it was made of brick with a window on either side of a door.

"Hemos llegado," Devo said. We have arrived.

82

THE smoke had texture, the viscous consistency of water. Pedro swam through it, cleaved the gray chalkiness with his hands and sent it swirling about him. He could feel the sting in his lungs and eyes and held his breath. A door. There had to be a door at hand, a way to escape. He remembered seeing one, didn't he? Pedro reached out blindly in a frantic search for something, anything solid to ground himself, provide a sense of direction—remind him which way was up, down, backwards, and forwards. He cried out, "Help! Someone help me!" but his voice lacked strength, his words constricted. The smoke splintered, parted as if answering his call. Pedro sucked in a harsh breath and gripped the door handle. It wouldn't budge. He pounded on the door and screamed, "Let me out! Someone let me out of here!" The door popped open. His father stood before him, his expression serene, as if he'd just come home from a relaxing Sunday afternoon on the beach. "Stop your screaming, mijo," he said. "This is no time to panic."

"But the smoke, papi. The smoke is choking me."

"Do not be afraid, Pedro. I am always with you." Enrique pointed off his son's shoulder, his shadow-filled eyes darkening his features. "You must go back and face it, Pedro."

"But..."

Papi's voice hardened, "You can do it, mijo. You have to."

Pedro retreated numbly. The door swung past his nose and slammed shut. "Papi!" he cried, pounding on the door. "Papi! Come back papi!" Sickly smoke besieged him. Pedro gagged. Chimes went off in his head, bells...an alarm? Had someone sounded an alarm? Pedro fell to his knees. "Help me," he whimpered.

The bells grew louder and a voice—papi's voice?—intoned, "They bury us alive."

Pedro bolted up on the living room couch, hungry for air and cold with sweat. He reached for his cell phone on the coffee table. The bells chiming his ears fell silent. "Sí?"

"Sorry to wake you, Pedro," said Lieutenant Romero, his tone patient and strict. "But your assistance is required."

Pedro shook remnants of his nightmare from his head. "Qué pasa, señor?"

"A fire has broken out at Arena Vallarta."

Pedro swung his legs off the couch. "Qué?!?" He flipped on the lamp. "A fire? How bad?"

"Bad enough to probably destroy the place. This rain should help keep it from spreading though. The glow from the blaze is visible here at ground zero."

"You are at ground zero?"

"Managing troops again, Pedro."

"How did the fire start? Has anybody been hurt?"

"As far as we know, the arena is empty. We cannot be certain it was arson but, all things considered, Russell Martell and his accomplices are prime suspects."

Pedro slouched, elbows on his knees, a million thoughts racing through his brain, a million questions. "What are your orders, señor?"

"We are short on manpower again, Pedro, and need you at headquarters to monitor that disc."

Ese pinche maldito disc, thought Pedro... Might this fire have something to do with that last English message it revealed? What was it...? you ignore the enemy even as they strike you in your own house? Gloria's translation of the phrase was succinct but Pedro found her interpretation of its meaning specious. Her dash home to protect her family seemed an overreaction. He didn't say as much but did mention that "it would be out of character" for the assassin to attack her home and family. "Too personal and impulsive," he said. "The man has a grander plan."

It might have been prudent to send a squad car up to her house but la señora was determined to go as well. And who was Pedro, a mere junior officer in the police department, to question her decision, her fear?

Yet was she on the right track? Her family wasn't trapped in Arena Vallarta but it was as precious to her as her house, her home.

"I will leave for headquarters right away, señor," Pedro said. In fact, he was already dressed and ready to go, having fallen asleep on the couch fully clothed. "Have you heard from Señora Velázquez?"

The lieutenant told Pedro that Gloria was most likely at the arena. "And Pedro?"

"Sí?"

"Have you heard from your father?"

"My father?"

"Has he called or come home tonight, Pedro?"

"I fell asleep here on the living room couch some time ago, señor, and have not heard him come in."

"Police just drove by your house and did not see his truck parked outside."

"Then he must still be at ground zero."

Murmurs on the lieutenant's end, like he'd covered his phone to speak to someone else. Pedro caught a whiff of acrid smoke, an inkling of the nightmare from which he'd just awoken. Yes, he had heard from papi recently, in that suffocating nightmare. The lieutenant was back on the line: "Pedro?"

"Sí?"

"Leave a note for your father before going to headquarters. We believe his phone has gone dead and are unable to contact him. Have him call me or dispatch when he gets home."

Pedro raised his voice against an anxious pang in his chest. "He is not there?"

"At around one thirty a.m. he left to pick up a generator at Arena Vallarta but his truck is nowhere to be found, and neither is he. Not at the arena or here at the Washington. He was probably delayed picking up supplies at another location and will show up soon. Just leave him that note and get down to headquarters. I will call you back within the hour."

83

WE helped Johnny into the cabin. He shook us off, hopped over the concrete floor to the double bed, stripped off his poncho and made himself comfortable with the pillows—one under his head and one to elevate his right foot. Devo kneeled next to the bed, his headlamp shining on Johnny's lower extremities. "Let's have a look."

"Can't miss it," Johnny said.

"Right about that. Lift your leg...straight out. Good." Devo hiked up the pant leg and placed his left hand under Johnny's right calf.

"What're you doin'?"

"Relax your leg... That ankle's good'n inflamed. Move your foot."

Johnny moved his foot slightly and flexed his toes.

"I'm going to touch your ankle. You tell me where it hurts. Okay?"

"It hurts all over."

"I know. I'll touch lightly. Ready?"

439

"I guess."

Devo palpated the top and sides of the ankle. "That hurt," said Johnny. "And that."

He laid Johnny's ankle down on the pillow and pointed his headlamp straight up. "Turn off your light, Martell." I did so.

Devo rose from the bedside and faced me; a penlight appeared in his right hand, its light beam glancing off my cheek. "Hold still for a moment, Martell; and keep your eyes open." He stood close, within a foot or so, and focused a narrow beam into my right eye, then the left. Devo turned off the penlight and flipped his headlamp down so it shined over my head. "Turn on your light so you can see... Point it up out of my eyes. That's good." He held up two fingers. "How many?"

"Two. Now three. Five. One."

"Follow my finger. Eyes only...good...good...okay. What day is it?"

"Monday. Early Tuesday morning."

"When did you arrive in Vallarta?"

"Four, five days ago."

"You vomit in jail?"

"Yep."

"Nauseous now?"

"No."

"How's your neck feel?"

"Fine."

"I'm gonna touch you. Just relax your head."

Devo placed his hands on either side of my jaw, turned my head in both directions, and gently tilted it from one side to the other. "That hurt at all?"

"No. A little. But only from that damn golf ball behind my ear, where Chimp socked me a couple times."

"You're head hurt anywhere else?"

"At the back. One a those pigs dropped my head on the floor when they were interrogating me."

"Hurt bad when you touch it?"

"Nothin' like the golf ball."

"Okay. Turn your head. Let's see how ugly it's gotten."

I thought Devo might touch my ear, bend it some to get a better look at the golf ball, but he only shined his headlamp behind it. "Looks li-ike that chunk a sausage's been a bilyn too la-ong," he drawled. "But it hasn't gotten any worse since I last saw it outside of El Cabezón. Little bastard used the point of his knuckle, or a ring. Good spot to use it." Devo turned from me and stepped over to the

440

table a couple yards from the front door. "Would've examined you guys earlier but there was nothing to do for you until we got here."

"That it?" Johnny was surprised his exam wasn't longer and more painful. He rolled onto his side and blinked at Devo's back as if the doctor had told him he'd be out for the season. Johnny's never out for the season.

Two ice chests and a large box were under the table. Devo squatted and opened an ice chest. The table was wooden, not quite as long as a picnic table. A lantern, clock, a couple of flashlights and folded towels sat on top of it, along with a laptop computer. Behind the table were two wooden chairs, the front door and two windows. A door and two windows also broke up the back wall. All four windows in the cabin were screened, without glass. A refined smell of teak oil came from the table and chairs. They were of dark wood and appeared in good condition. The aroma reminded me of a pleasure cruise I'd taken years ago on a thirty-foot wooden sailboat. The memory was pleasant but shortly after my cruise the boat was wrecked on a reef by a rogue wave and subsequently salvaged for timber. Devo, the swashbuckler, fit right in with my recollections.

He returned to the bed with a couple of cold compresses and bottled water. "The ankle doesn't look good but I doubt it's broken. Keep this on it. And this one's for the lump on your head." Devo handed us each a cold compress and a pint of bottled water. Johnny and I dutifully applied the compresses to our respective injuries. "There're two more compresses in the chest; you can switch as you need them. I'll be right back."

Devo shut the front door behind him. Outside, the wind and rain were gaining strength again. I pulled off my poncho, dropped it on the floor next to Johnny's, and sat on the edge of the bed. Ara's shirt protected my hand from the cold compress behind my ear. I pointed my headlamp across the floor at a sheeted futon. My bed for the evening, I assumed. Johnny muttered, "What a character."

I kept my voice down, below the raucous storm: "You don't know the half of it."

"The party was the first time I had more than a beer with the guy."

"Let's hope he's right about your ankle."

"Seems awful sure of himself. 'Course, I never thought he lacked confidence."

"What's that you said about him Saturday night, in Rudy's before the cockfights...? Well, let me tell ya, Johnny, he ain't no regular guy. He can do a lot more than pound some booze and bullshit about sports, chicks and politics...or slice and dice some dumbshit canary out in Mendocino County. Much, much more."

"Yeah. You'll have to—" Johnny broke off his thought as the front door opened. My headlamp shined on Devo, his on me. He'd stripped off his poncho and had Johnny's backpack slung over a shoulder. He placed the pack at the foot of the bed and pulled two pill bottles from a pouch in his hand. "You both can take a Vicodin for the pain, and an anti-inflammatory, the long thick pill. There's food in the box and ice chests under the table to take with the anti-inflammatory. Water, juice and soda as well. You can have a beer but should probably leave the hard stuff alone if you take the drugs." Devo handed us the pills. "I'd offer sleeping pills but you guys can't afford to be too groggy in the morning. And Martell can't take one anyway 'cause of the bump on his head. Might have a concussion." He stuffed the pill pouch into his pocket.

"I slept some in jail."

"Or passed out." Devo stepped over to the table, struck a match and lit the propane lantern. The lantern did a decent job of lighting up the cabin but there wasn't much more to see: a mosquito net tied up about six feet above Johnny's bed, a pillow in sight just beyond my futon, a household broom in the far corner, and a section of carpet rolled up against the brick wall next to a trashcan. Devo turned off his headlamp and grabbed the alarm clock and flashlights from the table. "You got 3:30 a.m. Johnny?"

Johnny checked his watch. "Just about."

Devo wound the alarm clock as he drifted over to the futon. The man never wastes a movement. Like Brenda on the dance floor, smooth; except Devo has a tangible military bearing that matches his voice, until he does those impersonations or plays a character he's invented. But he is smooth. Smooth as a python's belly. Smooth as a razor blade, a bullet, a warhead.

Devo set a flashlight and the alarm clock down at the head of the futon and scrutinized me and Johnny, hands on hips. "It's set to wake you at five thirty, Martell. You might wanna set it once more for seven or eight before snoozing again. A concussion can kill you, put you to sleep permanently. And you'll be pretty damn sore in the morning, all over, so it'll be tempting to simply pass out. Try not to. You should be all right though. The eyes are reacting pretty good."

"You splittin'?" I said.

"Be back tomorrow before noon." He picked up the ponchos and hung them on the wooden door pegs on the backdoor. They'd left a puddle on the concrete floor; I was going to apologize for it but Devo kept talking: "Don't think you'll need the mosquito net, Johnny.

Rarely much of a problem this time of year. Remember to turn off the lantern. We have a couple more propane canisters for it but they can go fast. Matches are on the table." Devo stood over us and tossed a flashlight onto Johnny's bed. "If you want to use the candles set them on the concrete floor. And don't fool with the laptop tonight. It's set to boot-up automatically tomorrow morning if you wanna check it out... I'll take your headlamp, Martell. Flashlights'll last a while."

I stuffed the pills into my pocket and handed him the headlamp. "Where'd you find this place?"

"Belongs to an acquaintance. Have a look around in the morning. Out back you'll find an outhouse and a shower, soap. We pipe water in from upriver. Towels on the table here. That shoe polish in your hair and beard will stick for a while, Martell. Let it."

I said, "Thought there wouldn't be any luxury hotels tonight."

The comment elicited a wry smile from Devo. "Not a bad place to hang out. It'll cost ya."

"Can't wait to pay. Must have needed a team of mules for the brick and concrete."

"*Teams*—two-and four-legged."

"Place got a name?" If it didn't I'd give it one.

"Finca Torodea. Or just Torodea."

I got up from the bed, put the compress in my left hand and extended my right. He shook it. "Thanks," I said.

"Yeah, thanks a lot," Johnny rejoined.

Devo nodded, turned from us, and walked out the door without another word.

Johnny palmed his pills into his mouth and chugged some water. "Aren't you gonna take yours?"

"Maybe. I'll wait and see if he's poisoned you."

"Huh? Oh. Forgot how paranoid you are."

I walked over to the near window and stared outside. Both horses were gone. Devo had vanished into the rain.

Book III

Camacho

Never let your sense of morals get in the way of doing what's right.

Isaac Asimov

We are dismayed when we find that even disaster cannot cure us of our faults.

Marquis de Vauvenargues

LIEUTENANT Benito Cuevas Romero acknowledged the three officers standing guard outside police headquarters and ambled past dispatch with a brusque greeting for the girls working the counter. The day's grueling events were taking their toll on him. His desire for Russell Martell's blood hadn't diminished but a wretched fatigue had set in after well over twenty hours without a wink of sleep. Was Russell Martell finally getting some rest? Had he found a secure spot to gather his strength? Or was he on drugs, cocaine and methamphetamine to keep him going? Was he plotting or carrying out another attack right now? still going strong after bludgeoning two police officers and setting fire to Arena Vallarta?

And Enrique Santos. Was Russell Martell responsible for his disappearance?

The lieutenant resolved to get some shuteye on a cot here at headquarters, then maybe take some caffeine pills with his coffee to get himself going again. He had to keep going, couldn't truly rest until Russell Martell was dead. Would he be able to sleep at all? Perhaps not, and certainly not before examining that disc's new message with Pedro.

He entered el comandante's office and found the young junior officer pacing nervously behind the desk, hands thrust in his pockets. "Any word on my father, señor?" Pedro asked, his eyes wild as his unkempt curls.

"Not yet, Pedro." The lieutenant stripped off his thin raincoat and hung it and his hat on the coat tree in the corner.

Pedro's damp boots squeaked over the tiled floor as he rounded the desk. "Request permission to initiate my own search for him, señor. My motorbike can cover a lot of ground quickly and—"

"Vallarta," Lieutenant Romero interposed in a forbearing tone, "is in a state of emergency, Pedro. Resources are stretched to the limit. Police, federales, the fire department, and the military are all occupied at the Washington, Arena Vallarta, roadblocks, and with enforcing the lockdown and curfew. And el comandante is spearheading a manhunt for Russell Martell along the Rio Cuale, where Hernando Talla's team discovered the squad car the gringo is presumed to have hijacked. But a printout of your father's driver's license, a description of his truck, and the truck's license plate number are circulating amongst our troops, Pedro. No has forgotten him."

Pedro stood with skittish poise, doe eyes pleading. Lieutenant Romero placed a hand on his shoulder. "I understand your concerns,

Pedro," he said. "But this disc is at the core of our troubles and we have to concentrate on this new message you reported before I grant your request." The lieutenant circled the desk and sat down heavily in el comandante's chair, eyes focused on the message on the computer screen: ¿Quién se ha ganado el poder? Sigue la publicidad y corrupción.

(Who has gained power? Follow the publicity and corruption.)

Pedro shuffled around the desk to have a look over the lieutenant's shoulder. "A riddle, Pedro?" said Lieutenant Romero. "Or is it a hint, coaching of some kind?"

"You can never tell with this thing," Pedro replied slowly, his mind on his missing father. "Sometimes it seems like the disc is just playing an elaborate mind game."

"A treacherous mind game. I have been briefed on its contents and—" the lieutenant cut himself off before mentioning that the disc might be a bug. Everyone in the department had been warned to watch what they said when in the same room as the disc. If it was indeed a bug, there was no need to let on that they suspected as much. "—its idiosyncrasies. But has the disc constructed phrases like this before, with a question and a clue to the answer?"

"Not exactly, señor. Not like this, no." Pedro stiffened. There it was again, that gnawing feeling inside his chest. A fluttering, irregular strength to his heartbeat. A twinge of panic. He had to get the hell out of here and find papi. He smoothed his voice, afraid he might scream. "But power was mentioned once before," he said. "Sunday night. In reference to México, I think."

"México? the entire country?"

"Señora Velázquez took it a step further, suggested it was a reference to power in general, the world over. But in this case..." Pedro released a desperate sigh. This maldito disc was making his life more and more miserable by the second. Papi was missing and he hadn't the time to mess with its capricious messages and veiled threats. His entire relationship with the puto was like something out of a novel he read once: you find yourself hitched to an emotionally disturbed woman— full of threats and indecipherable insanity. Life becomes unbearable... If only he could just kill the bitch—

"In this case, what?" said the lieutenant.

Pedro cleared his throat and forced a thoughtful tone from his lungs: "Hard to say. Sounds rather personal, like it refers to a specific person."

Pedro circled the desk and began pacing again. The lieutenant frowned, his eyes narrowed into thin slits. "Dios mío," he said. "Follow corruption and it can lead you most anywhere, especially in this country. But what is this about publicity? Has a powerful and important person been arrested for corruption that we should know about, someone forced to give up power to another?"

"Perhaps. Maybe we should scour the newspapers and the Web." Pedro couldn't think of another answer to give him. What he really wanted was to, once again, request permission to go look for papi. Where the hell could he be? Why hadn't he called? How long had he been missing? since leaving for Arena Vallarta from the Washington? Over two hours now!

Lieutenant Romero lifted his head to Pedro. The kid was distracted, looking off into space, doe eyes keen, jaw locked—ready to fight, or fly out of here to ground zero and Arena Vallarta in search of his father. He couldn't expect Pedro to concentrate on the disc under these circumstances. The lieutenant reached for the pack of cigarettes in his breast pocket. "You are dismissed, Pedro."

The alacrity with which the order was given caught Pedro off guard. He stared at the lieutenant as though offered a substantial bonus for a job well done. The lieutenant gave him an affirmative nod. Pedro held his gaze, gratitude welling up inside. "Gracias, señor," he said.

The lieutenant pointed a cigarette at the blank computer screen on el comandante's desk opposite Pedro's. "I will review the copy of the disc on el comandante's computer, Pedro. And expect a call from me or dispatch if a new clue pops up on yours."

"Sí señor." He turned to leave.

"And Pedro..."

"Sí?" Pedro retrieved his raingear from the coat tree.

"Pick up a newspaper or two when they come out this morning. See if there is some kind of publicity related to this latest clue. I will check the Internet. And let me know when you find your father."

85

A mean buzzing in my ears woke me up. The same annoying buzz all old-fashioned alarm clocks make. I shut the damn thing off and released an angry curse as the Dallas Cowboy defensive line crashed down upon me. I knew it was the Dallas Cowboys because the blue stars on their helmets were pasted to my eyes. That pissed me off too. I can't stand the Cowboys. My hand felt for the flashlight. The light cut through the stars but did nothing to relieve the ton of knees and elbows thumping my entire body and plastering me to my futon. I'd have passed out under the pileup but a sudden pressure in my lower bowel was about to force a trip to the outhouse and another reminder of Chimp's nightstick. The prospect increased my fury.

"God. Damn. Motherfuckers!" A titanic effort sat me up. A comet streaked across the room and disintegrated above Johnny's bed. Johnny groaned and resumed normal respiration. Devo's pills weren't poison, past expiration, or anything of the sort. I pulled the pills from my pocket and took them with the water by my futon.

It was a laborious trip to the outhouse, pain in places that never hurt before, that shouldn't hurt, but bloodless, as far as I could determine. As per Devo's instructions, I reset the alarm for eight o'clock. Then I crawled into bed with an apple and a fresh cold compress to apply to the golf ball.

Small bites from the apple were the recommended dosage. Chewing produced an audible click at the jaw below the golf ball and opening wide for big bites offered all the satisfaction of a root canal. Rising for a soft plantain was out of the question. I hadn't the strength to challenge the Cowboys again. I managed to eat nearly half the apple before falling asleep to claps of thunder.

86

JUAN and Gloria leaned on each other in the drifting haze of a smoky false dawn. The rain had stopped and they slumped together on a bench at the far end of Arena Vallarta's ash-filled plaza, mesmerized by the dying fire's morose sulfur flames.

Gloria coughed weakly. "I never felt so helpless," she said. Her hair was matted and blackened and hung from her scalp like strands of knitted yarn.

"Like fighting a voracious monster." Juan pawed absently at his soaked, soot-filled clothes. From the moment he arrived at the arena with el comandante, the fire struck him as a living, breathing beast, its million flaming tongues lapping at a luminous stormy sky, consuming all in its path. "If not for the rain, the fire department would probably not have it contained yet."

Gloria stared at the fire trucks around the arena, the streams of water pounding innumerable hotspots within the smoldering expanse and crumbling framework of her dream—Arena Vallarta. "We cannot let them get the best of us, Juan," she said. An emptiness welled in her chest, the essence of self-doubt and defeat. She felt naked, stripped of her defenses, and shivered as though frightened by her own words.

452

Juan draped an arm around his wife. "We need to clean up and gather our strength."

They fell silent. Both of them understood that rest would be impossible, like trying to sleep through an air raid. Their senses were swamped in sirens, smoke, blood and destruction...all the sights, sounds and odors that had dominated their lives the last twenty hours or so.

"Sí," said Gloria. "Vamos a casa."

They stood as one, of a single mind and purpose. Only by working together could they gain the strength to overcome the forces destroying their lives and Vallarta.

Pedro Santos was at the Range Rover talking with their driver, Felipe, across the street from the arena. Gloria took him aside. Yes they'd heard about his father she said, but he had not been missing long and was bound to turn up safe and sound. He may have just suffered some car trouble...and might be at the Washington or home right now. Pedro recoiled, unwilling to let Gloria distract him from his all-important mission. "Not at home," he said. "Or at the Washington." Pedro wasn't all there, restless as a spooked colt. Though not yet twenty-three, his face held the numb, withered expression of a man twice his age resolved to overcome a string of personal tragedies. Gloria's respect for him deepened into maternal affection, her empathy nearly drowning out her own sorrows and worries. She rested a tender hand on his shoulder and told him he needed some sleep, that it was dangerous to zip around town on his motorbike in his condition. Pedro shrugged her off. He'd be fine. He put his helmet on and mounted his bike. Gloria asked him about the disc.

"Lieutenant Romero should be monitoring it," he said as he flipped up his visor. "Or another officer. And another clue popped up..."

87

THE clouds parted with the first watery light of morning and by 7:30 a.m. Tuesday, as the black Huey helicopter descended into Puerto Vallarta, only a handful of scattered thunderheads floated about in the skittish breeze. The weather had lifted from the low land, yet the bay bellowed with hostile swells, and forested mountain peaks shrouded in stormy gloom brooded over the foul coastal scenery—Arena Vallarta's charred skeleton and the wretched remains of the Washington's north tower.

SEVE VERDAD

Comandante Héctor Diamante Pasqual stood at attention on the airport tarmac, teetering as though balanced over an abyss. In a few short days his career and reputation had been damaged as badly as Vallarta itself. He'd personally presided over two botched raids that had precipitated two unimaginable catastrophes. How could he possibly recover from such tragedy and disgrace? Héctor felt himself on his last legs professionally, physically, and mentally. He wavered at attention, struggling to keep from taking that final fall into oblivion and defeat. He'd stared into the abyss now and again this morning and found his own haggard visage, his own pleading gray eyes staring back at him; so neither protocol nor good manners forced his current posture. It was either stand at attention or tumble into the abyss. Collapse from fatigue and grief. Collapse under pressure. Collapse and lose everything.

He must stand at attention and prepare to be condemned, or granted a reprieve...by CISEN. Mexican Intelligence. The powerful all-seeing phantom.

Beyond the sonic thumping of rotor blades, el comandante stalwartly greeted the four CISEN men as they loaded luggage into the police van and climbed aboard. Terse introductions. A word here and there of condolence. And then off to police headquarters.

Nobody looked forward to coming under CISEN's thumb, not the mayor, Vallarta police, or federale investigators, despite needing every bit of help they could possibly get from all quarters for the beleaguered city. It was like being forced to hand over your sick child to an unknown doctor in the emergency ward. She may need the care but that doesn't mean you are relieved or pleased to hand her over, particularly when you have to do everything the doctor says. Agree or disagree. No second opinions. Like it or not. El comandante was as leery of CISEN as anyone else. But he also recognized that the agency offered an ultimate opportunity for him to survive this insane ordeal and redeem himself. This was his last gasp, his one and only remaining opportunity to overcome the abominable streak of police foul-ups that had plagued him these past few days. If he could assist these men, prove his worth and help bring Russell Martell and his accomplices to justice, his position as Comandante of the Puerto Vallarta Police Department might be salvageable.

El comandante summoned the inner strength available to most all who are at the end of their rope and managed a professional, gracious bearing in the presence of CISEN. Nine hours ago he was working with CISEN Lead Interrogator Joaquín de Jesús in preparation for the raid on Russell Martell's room, his first personal contact with the agency. He knew full well that everyone treads lightly around CISEN,

454

but Héctor intended to do much more than tread lightly now. That's why he was driving this van with four CISEN operatives onboard. That's why he volunteered to relieve the mayor of this unhappy task. That's why he was so willing to swallow his pride and subordinate himself to the powers that be.

In short, Héctor Diamante Pasqual was prepared and anxious to kiss CISEN ass.

The four CISEN men were all similarly attired. Dark tailored suits. Shirts white and crisp, left open at the collar. Reflective sunglasses not unlike the ones Héctor wore. Senior CISEN Operative Alfredo Flores was in the passenger seat. A slight, dapper man about Héctor's age—mid-forties—with slick salt-and-pepper hair and a robust mustache that accentuated his high cheekbones. Flores asked Comandante Pasqual if he had brought police reports to review. Something dark crossed his face when Héctor informed him that the reports were waiting for them at police headquarters.

"We will be there in no time at all," added el comandante agreeably. "Not much traffic this morning."

In the backseat, Operative Blanco stonily mentioned that they had noticed the absence of traffic when they flew in.

Héctor choked back a nervous quiver in his voice. "Traffic was horrible yesterday," he said. "But we have taken steps to remedy that problem, and any other possible complications with the general public. Last night we implemented a curfew and—"

"So I understand," Flores interrupted. His voice was toneless. A man with a job to do. "Your mayor spoke with our section chief early this morning." Flores surveyed the streets, the pedestrians and vehicles. "We expect a full and complete briefing as soon as possible."

Héctor wiped trickles of sweat from his brow. He had to ingratiate himself to this man, give him every opportunity to take him under his wing. "We are under tremendous stress and pressure here, señor, and in desperate need of your assistance, any assistance. And I want to give you my personal assurance that I will be at your disposal. We, the department, have—"

"When was the last time you got some sleep, Comandante?" Senior Operative Flores ran his eyes over the graying stubble covering el comandante's weary face, the worry lines creasing his brow. CISEN had a dossier on him, as well as most all ranking police officers in the country. This one was no more corrupt than any other (corruption was to be expected. The rule throughout Mexico) but, given the events of the past few days, it also appeared he was inept. And the man looked like hell, notwithstanding the circumstances. El comandante had taken the time to slip on a fresh polyester shirt, clean up his face and hands, comb his hair, and wipe down his shoes. But his trousers were sooty and his "fresh" shirt already rumpled and spotted with sticky perspiration. And there was an odd odor to him. Or was it the van? Perhaps Vallarta itself. Like burning chemicals. Flores could only imagine the pair of beet-red eyes behind el comandante's sunglasses.

"Sleep, señor?" Héctor hadn't slept since Sunday night, after he was whisked off to Mexico City to be debriefed about that gangster Paco and Saturday's botched raid. He certainly wasn't going to mention that. "No time for sleep," he said. "Plenty of coffee at headquarters."

Two of the CISEN men in back lit up cigarettes. Flores adjusted the air conditioner and cracked his window. Héctor slowed for a red light and ran it.

"Our first order of business," said Flores, "is to find CISEN Operative Joaquín de Jesús. No one has been able to reach him. He should have contacted us at least six hours ago."

El comandante nodded restively. He knew what was coming. No avoiding it. When he volunteered to pick up CISEN at the airport he prepared to face it—the inevitable questions and insinuations. Might as well get them over with. He was either going to sink or swim with these men. Flores plunged him into the swamp headfirst: "I understand you were the last to see him, Comandante."

"Sí, señor. That we know of. Two officers returned to the hotel room early this morning where I last saw Señor de Jesús, and there was no sign of him anywhere in the hotel. And the last time I spoke with him he was calling your section chief."

"Why did you wait until this morning to look for him?"

"We had no idea he was missing, señor. We assumed he was working on his own initiative and—"

"You were occupied with other matters."

"Sí, señor."

Héctor swallowed the lump in his throat. He had no reason to feel guilty for the disappearance of Señor de Jesús. No reason at all. But, with all the screw ups lately...would another finger of blame be pointed at him? from CISEN?!?

Naturally he'd thought of this possibility already and had considered getting lost for a while rather than risk facing it so soon. But there was nowhere to hide and Héctor came to the conclusion that it was best to meet the issue head on, sooner rather than later. Besides, he really had nothing to do with the disappearance of Joaquín de Jesús, nothing beyond being the last person to see him...and talk with him.

Thinking you can meet and discuss an issue head on with CISEN and actually doing it are two completely distinct propositions. And,

456

now that el comandante found himself in the midst of the phantom, its devious power enveloping him like a fatal disease, the danger was crystallized. Much more than his career was at stake here. A chill ran up Héctor's back at the thought of being subjected to a CISEN interrogation.

Comandante Héctor Diamante Pasqual prayed to God for the safe return of Joaquín de Jesús.

Flores said, "Our section chief never received that call you refer to."

"Sí señor. So I was told, by Mayor Velázquez."

"You are sure Joaquín made that call?"

"That is what Señor de Jesús said he was doing at the time, señor."

"Did you hear him speak to our section chief?"

"No, señor. I left the room to have a word with hotel security."

"Casa Mexicana Hotel. About ten minutes south of here."

"Sí, señor."

Flores resisted an urge to have el comandante detour directly to the hotel, and another to continue questioning him here in the van. They'd be at police headquarters shortly. Best to wait for the briefing and peruse the reports before jumping into any investigation. Always best to do that. And there were two other pressing issues to consider in conjunction with the briefing. First, where was Media Minister Lazarito Charlado? Aside from el comandante, this was the other man Flores wanted to question personally. Where the hell did he get his information on this Russell Martell? CISEN didn't have a dossier on the gringo but, according to Joaquín's short reports over the phone before his disappearance last night and the story Señor Charlado splashed all over the news this morning about *El Gringo Terrorista*, they damn well better start one. And second, Flores was to gather all the intelligence and evidence he could and prepare the ground for CISEN to take over the investigation into the explosion at the Washington, and perhaps the Arena Vallarta fire as well. The agency hadn't received official clearance from el DF yet, but that wouldn't stop them. They'd get it.

88

OFFICER Hernando Talla paused in mid-stride on the concrete path, eyes focused on something across Casa Mexicana's koi pond, his brow furrowed in vague suspicion. Diego glanced up at his expansive partner and followed the point of his gaze. A hummingbird danced along the breadth of the blooming hibiscus garden and darted away. "See something?"

"Not sure."

They were in search of clues into the disappearance of Joaquín de Jesús and had surveyed the pond and surrounding plant life about twenty minutes ago. Nothing out of the ordinary. Nothing to catch the eye along the water's shallow bottom. No sign of tracks or trampled foliage on the other side. But something held Hernando's attention now. He extended a hand and, as one's eye is drawn to a flaw in a painting, traced a minute line along the tall outcroppings of the dense vegetation opposite them. "Where are the flowers in the middle of the hibiscus?" he asked his partner. "It almost looks like a hole there in the center."

Diego pushed the brim of his cap off his forehead and focused on the subtle distortion in the flowering greenery. He swept his gaze up the hotel's façade. Russell Martell's room was on the eleventh floor. "If something were there...we should have seen it from the balcony."

"Maybe," Hernando said as he kicked off his boots. "And maybe not." He took off his socks and rolled his pant legs up above his knees.

Officer Hernando Talla waded into the pond with a mild splash, scattering koi. As he reached the opposite bank, he noticed a distinct indentation in the center of the hibiscus produced by crisscrossing shoots and freshly broken stems. He stared up at the enormity of the hotel and let his eyes fall back down upon the hibiscus. The brush was thick and high. Around the damaged area the lean of tall flowers sagging from last night's downpour draped the indentation. This might explain why it wasn't seen from Russell Martell's balcony. He cocked a calculating brow at the hotel, a good ten meters distant. No one could jump or toss a body that far yet *something* looked to have fallen from the sky and landed here. Had someone thrown a suitcase from their balcony? a chair? With an absent shrug and grunt Hernando stepped up onto the bank, his feet sinking in grassy mud. He parted the vegetation with his hands and ducked into the garden.

Diego drew close to the pond as his partner disappeared into the dense flora. A sudden succession of shrill whistles—an alarm from Hernando's police whistle!—propelled him into the water, gun drawn. The hibiscus rustled wildly. Diego slipped on the mossy bottom and righted himself. Hernando appeared on the bank before him, hands on knees, sucking air as if he had just scaled a mountain. Diego froze. "Qué pasa?" he croaked, transfixed by his partner's pale expression, grimacing eyes and tortured mouth.

FINDING DEVO

A member of their team echoed the question from the bank behind Diego: "Qué pasa?"

Hernando convulsed as though about to vomit. "We need a forensics team," he gasped. "I have found Señor de Jesús."

89

GLORIA looked damn good. How did she do it? Lazarito knew she must have been up all night. Lord knows, he was. A few winks of sleep and then...fire! At Gloria's precious arena! Lazarito managed the news from his condominium, viewed the spectacle on television, and never did get much shuteye. But Gloria... First the Washington and then the fire... What was her secret? In the face of multiple catastrophes she looked to have had a full-night's sleep, showered, and then dressed for a picnic. Blue jeans. A no-frills green button-down blouse. Glossy lips and thin makeup. The woman appeared ready to wrestle her kids on the beach...

Or bust him in the chops right here in The Bureau.

Gloria slapped a copy of the Vallarta Diario down on his office desk. "What kind of trash is this, Lazarito?" she said, a vulgar middle finger pointed at the photo of Russell Martell. "Do you realize what you have done? Not only did you break our agreement but these outlandish accusations—"

"The agreement," Lazarito intervened, a haughty index finger pointed upward, "was to wait *one day* before publicizing anything on a probable terror attack. I—"

"Twenty-four hours, Lazarito. And I will not split hairs with you. You knew damn well that any publicity of this nature had to be cleared with me, with me and Governor Palacio." Gloria balled her fist upon the headline:

Se Busca
¡El Gringo Terrorista!

"This is way over the top, even for you. Publicity like this whips up emotions and may provide enough of a distraction to allow the perpetrators of heinous, barbaric crimes to escape."

Lazarito raised a rumpled eyebrow. "Are you suggesting that Russell Martell is innocent?"

"His innocence or guilt is not the issue." Gloria paused and lifted her glare to the TV up on the wall behind Lazarito, its muted image—

459

news casters who were no doubt lending credence to the Media Minister's story. "Your job," she continued, eyes back on the Media Minister, "was and is simply to get the word out about Russell Martell. He is *wanted*, not *guilty* as you have charged him..." Gloria paced the length of Lazarito's desk. "A gringo terrorist with ties to Mossad? A Jew implicated in an attempt to bomb the Mexican Senate Chambers? A North American anti-immigration fanatic who explodes the Washington to strike a blow against his spineless countrymen and México all at once?" She planted herself opposite him, hands on hips. "Have you any proof at all to back yourself up on this? What are your sources?"

"I am under no obligation to reveal my sources."

"You are to me, Lazarito. This is precisely why Governor Palacio reminded me to keep a tight leash on you. The investigation is ongoing and wild stories like this inhibit our ability to gather facts and find reliable witnesses." Gloria stared into Lazarito's fleshy eyes. "I recommended you for this job," she stated flatly, "and can have you fired this instant. What are your sources for the story?"

Lazarito puffed his cheeks, a slow smile gathering on his face. Gloria's indignation was to be expected and would be of great concern if he didn't have the upper hand... But he did have the upper hand, and knew exactly how to wield it.

"My sources are my privilege," he hummed. "And if you want me fired, at this juncture I suggest you speak with the president's Media and Communications Director rather than the governor, señora. Señor Panza de León is fascinated by my story and is due in my office this afternoon for a briefing."

Lazarito's reference to the Media and Communications Director gave Gloria a pang. She'd never met the man but knew that the president and members of his cabinet were due in town this afternoon to survey the destruction Vallarta had suffered... Now that she thought about it, Señor de León was bound to be "fascinated" by Media Minister Charlado's story...but...would he also react favorably to it and encourage Lazarito? She had her doubts, yet Lazarito's innuendo was clear. Her voice picked up a cutting edge in response:

"Are you threatening to go over the governor's head? That seems a risky proposition, Lazarito. Do you honestly believe that the Media and Communications Director will disregard Governor Palacio's recommendations?"

Lazarito shrugged carelessly and retrieved the TV remote on his desk. "Under the circumstances, señora," he said, "Governor Palacio will likely find himself obligated to follow the director's lead. Señor de León understands that the press is also required to investigate and considers my story invaluable. If we are to bring *El Gringo Terrorista* to justice, we need the help of the Mexican pueblo who, thanks to me, is now galvanized." Lazarito pressed a couple of buttons on the remote. The sound of media filled his office, in English:

"The rally began just after nine o'clock this morning and now numbers in the hundreds here at Guadalajara's famous zócalo, the birthplace of tequila and mariachi music. But today the atmosphere is not so festive..."

Gloria stared up at the TV on the wall behind Lazarito. "That woman..."

"Leslie Hinot." Lazarito sat the remote on his desk and squeaked back in his leather chair, his amused gaze skipping over the identical TV images against the wall opposite him, behind Gloria. "A Canadian with the Associated Press."

Gloria refocused on the TV above and behind Lazarito, trying to place the woman with the microphone. Leslie stood before a mass of people, many holding signs and banners. The most prominent read, 'Diga No a la Invasión Estadounidense' (Say No to the United States Invasion), and 'Los EEUU, EL Estado Terrorista' (The USA, THE Terrorist State). Myriad chants could be heard in the background. The camera zoomed in on Leslie Hinot. Suddenly Gloria knew exactly where she'd seen her before. "That woman covered the Arena Vallarta fire," she said.

Lazarito fingered his double chin. "Ignacio flew her to Guadalajara this morning in the network's helicopter. Leslie is a fine addition to my team in these difficult times. Indeed she is."

Leslie Hinot reached for someone off to her right. Gloria cringed at the introduction of Pati Redondo, her smug plump face and priggish big brown eyes. Leslie translated for the camera as her interview with Pati progressed: "What is it you hope to bring to the world's attention with this rally, Pati?"

Pati waved to someone off camera and spoke in a solemn voice laced with venom:

"Yesterday's terrorist attack in Vallarta was a culmination of centuries of North American and European imperialism and conquest in our nation. We are gathered here today to remind the world that México stands with all nations against the United States—the government of the United States of North América—and its illegal wars against impoverished peoples under the guise of a War on Terror." Pati paused for Leslie's translation; cheers rose behind her. "And as this rally spreads across México and into other countries where a kinship to our suffering is felt, it is our hope that the United

461

States of North América shall finally be recognized as the terrorist nation that it is and be brought to justice."

Leslie brushed a blond wisp of hair from her face, her voice gaining strength. "Are you suggesting that the USA is directly responsible for the attack on the Washington?"

"At the very least it is a natural consequence of North American policy and transgressions. And as we all know, a gringo Jew is the prime suspect..."

Gloria snatched up the remote and turned off the TV behind Lazarito. "Enough of this crap," she said in English. Leslie Hinot's voice resonated from the other TVs across the office. Gloria tossed the remote back onto the desk. "And turn off those others as well. I am not here to view a circus with you."

Lazarito muted the news cast. "I thought you might be interested in how I have managed to rally our pueblo," he smirked.

Gloria's eyes bored into him. "Pati Redondo is a fool, Lazarito."

"Perhaps. But a useful fool."

"México stands with all nations against the United States? You call that useful? I suppose you and Pati wish to put México in league with nations harboring and supporting al Qaeda, the Taliban, and Hezbollah. Was that your intention as well, Lazarito?"

"My intentions are no different than those of any responsible journalist."

"Is that so? Well, *Señor Periodista*, an Iranian terrorist was found dead at the marina here in Vallarta two days ago." Gloria rested her hands on the desk and leaned into the Media Minister. "Convenient how you left him out of your article this morning, your exposé worthy of a trash tabloid."

Lazarito perked up in his chair. He sensed an opening to question Gloria about her own investigation. "Have you any proof directly linking the dead terrorist to Russell Martell? Is Russell Martell a suspect in his death?"

"So you knew about the dead man, that he was a terrorist."

"It is my job to know about such things, señora." Lazarito relaxed in his chair, hands tented upon his ponderous belly. "Indeed it is. And I may include the Iranian in a follow-up article."

"A follow-up article?" Gloria said, arms crossed. "Let me guess: Russell Martell ambushed and brutalized a Muslim in a crazed effort to incite a religious war in México... Are you preparing to bestow the mantle of victimhood on Islamic terrorists?"

"I should think not. Certainly not at this juncture. I only go where the story leads."

FINDING DEVO

Gloria snorted, "Seems to me the story goes where *you* lead *it,* Lazarito."

Media Minister Charlado dismissed the comment with a toss of his head. "As you wish." To his mind there was no difference between the two when you have the truth on your side; Gloria's feelings on the subject were immaterial. His story was gaining a life of its own, momentum enough to thrust him into the upper echelons of power. Lazarito's afternoon briefing to the Media and Communications Director was to be his first professional as well as personal contact with the highest levels of government. He anticipated a stirring endorsement from Francisco Panza de León, especially with an ace in the hole like Araceli.

He must meet with Araceli before the briefing, make sure he had another story, more information at hand when needed. Araceli was due to call soon and he'd instructed his secretary, Esmeralda, to buzz him twice when she did. A most valuable source, Araceli. Her promised meeting with him today tantalized Lazarito with a whirlwind of thrilling possibilities. Further insights into Russell Martell's crimes, maybe even clues into his whereabouts were in the offing.

The day's coming attractions weren't without a pitfall however. Gloria represented a minor intrusion easily overcome by Lazarito's growing popularity and influence but there was one hitch to his plans that set him on edge. Esmeralda had given him an unexpected message this morning upon his arrival at The Bureau a short time ago, and it was needling him like a nervous twitch. CISEN was in town. An Alfredo Flores said he would be dropping by to visit the Media Minister. Lazarito was well aware that CISEN did not make social calls. Like Gloria, this Flores was probably after his sources for his story.

Lazarito's story had made him a popular figure all right, a man to be reckoned with. And while he had no desire to lock horns with the powerful intelligence agency, he certainly wasn't going to simply relinquish the upper hand by spilling his guts to CISEN, not when he was on the verge of garnering more information and insuring his position of power, his future. Fortunately, although Lazarito hadn't exactly planned for this contingency, his tactics did provide him with a solution to his dilemma. If he could pit CISEN against the Media and Communications Director—a member of the president's cabinet and apparent ally—Señor Flores might find himself obligated not to interfere with Media Minister Charlado's duties. Lazarito would then be able to meet with Araceli without CISEN at his throat.

Gloria had begun pacing again, arms folded, lost in thought. "So," she said at last, "for some reason you decided to print your

463

irresponsible theories and ignore the fact that yesterday's events may have been the result of an Islamist plot."

"My sources pointed in another direction—to an extremely plausible and, I might add, evocative truth." Lazarito leaned forward in his chair and planted his feet on the carpet. "Besides, if Islamic terrorists bombed the Washington and set fire to the arena, why have they not claimed responsibility? They most always do."

"There is no evidence that the two events are directly related, Lazarito. And not much time has passed for anyone to claim responsibility. But now, thanks to you, maybe no one will. The USA is a principle target of radical Islam and, if Islamic terrorists are guilty of bombing the Washington, I am sure they are pleased to have Americans blamed for the carnage. You even provided them with an extra bonus. The implication of a *Jewish-American* conspiracy."

"You sound more and more convinced that Islamists are to blame. Is there something you are not telling me? Is Russell Martell a follower of radical Islam?"

"There is not enough evidence to reach *any* conclusions yet, Lazarito. Can you possibly understand that? And whipping up emotions like you have only hinders unbiased investigations."

Lazarito looked at Gloria from beneath lowered eyelids, like she was a naïve school girl. "As I mentioned," he said, his tone unnervingly composed, "the press is free to investigate as well. Freedom of the press is a wonderful thing. Indispensable. We both know the Washington was bombed and by definition that is an act of terror. And I am convinced that the light of truth I have shined on the tragedy will lead to the capture or death of the perpetrators."

Gloria looped her locks behind her ears and searched his unflappable, bulbous expression. Lazarito was a pompous ass but, out of respect for her family's political ties, he had always been someone she could deal with and control. This careless, obstinate attitude towards her was way out of character for him. What the hell was he up to? Was he really willing to risk his career on this outlandish story of his? And if so, why now? Why the hurry? Even if he had reliable sources, why couldn't he wait for an official investigation to uncover more facts, concrete evidence to support (or refute) his claims? She stared about his office as if it contained a missing clue to his behavior; the answer came to her in a flash of insight. The last time she was in The Bureau, the Media Minister had just accepted a bribe from el comandante. A bribe to cover up Saturday's botched raid... The bribe demonstrated that Lazarito knew some very dangerous individuals might have escaped the raid and be at large in Vallarta, yet he had willfully participated in the cover-up anyway...

FINDING DEVO

Gloria glared at the Media Minister, a renewed fire in her eyes. "You treacherous hijo de puta," she sneered. "You invented and embellished this story of yours to protect your own ass, to insulate yourself from charges of corruption for covering up Saturday's botched raid. A cover-up which quieted that terrorist rumor and may have aided the perpetrators of yesterday's attack. You believe that, as the Mexican pueblo laps up your mierda, your career will be furthered, power solidified, and your corruption forgotten."

The color ebbed from Lazarito's face as he attempted to mask his surprise at Gloria's astute deduction behind an injured tone: "That is an outrageous accusation. My sources are most reliable. I refuse to sacrifice the integrity of my position or dignify your statement with even another word on the subject."

Gloria offered Lazarito feigned applause, her tone laced with condescension. "Bravo, Señor Media Minister," she said. "Bravo. First you tout freedom of the press and now the integrity of your position." Gloria shook her head in disgust. "If anything, your actions have shown both to be an illusion. Your position is not one of integrity because your press poisons public opinion to your particular vision. As a result, the press is not free at all but merely a medium for you to seize power, power that will prove all our freedoms illusory should your transgressions allow the enemy time to destroy each and every one of us outright."

Lazarito snuffed blandly, as if she'd just recited a juvenile poem. "Your hyperbole does not justify censorship, señora," he said.

"Censorship is your department," she shot back. "Part and parcel of our *free press*."

"As Media Minister, indeed it is my department."

"Not for long, Lazarito."

"We shall see, señora. And as for illusions, pues, we live in a land of illusions, illusions which are most effective when they take this form, do you not agree?" He reached for his remote and clicked without lifting it from his desk. Leslie Hinot's voice singed Gloria's ears: "Numbers are growing here at the zócalo, as are cries for justice and Russell Martell's head..."

Gloria resisted a seething desire to slap Lazarito. She and her husband already had a plan in the works on how to deal with him, a plan that would not be furthered by allowing herself to lose control. Best to leave now rather than waste time with him. Gloria retrieved her bag on the vinyl chair. Lazarito's desk phone buzzed. Gloria paused. Lazarito cocked his head. The single buzz meant Esmeralda did not have Araceli on the line. He hit the intercom button. "Sí?"

"Señor Flores is here to see you, Señor Charlado. From CISEN."

AN Indian head was in the window. An Indian of indiscernible age with amused dark eyes, a hooked nose, and long silver-streaked black hair. He stared at me through the near front window. I squeezed my eyes shut and refocused. He was gone. A dream? I rolled off my futon and made for the door, my head floating through a hazy pain. Devo's drugs had begun to work their magic, reduced the Cowboy defensive line to a single wrestler knuckling a few sensitive pressure points. I poked my head out the front door. No Indian. I headed for the rear of the cabin for a look out the back window. No Indian. Odd...like he'd appeared just for me, sent out vibes to wake me and make eye contact before vanishing. Was it a dream? No. I'd seen him, could still picture him; the vision might have been frightening but for the Indian's expression of passive levity, as though observing children at play. Did he find my presence here amusing? I found *his* presence disconcerting. Devo didn't mention we'd have company.

Johnny snored and grumbled in his sleep. I opened the backdoor. A generous blue sky welcomed me along with a green-ribbon field garnished with coconut trees and flowering jacaranda. Vaporous forest scents rose to the hard light. Fifty yards or so down field was another cabin. Beyond the cabin, lumpy menacing clouds hunkered down around the surrounding hills like surly uninvited guests bloated with booze. The Indian was nowhere in sight. I considered the outdoor shower off to my right, about twenty feet from the outhouse. A shower could wait. *Where the hell is that Indian?*

Not only where, but who? His sanguine expression remained imprinted on my mind. As I walked along the grass toward the other cabin, it struck me that he might be the caretaker of Finca Torodea. The lawn was well kempt, shorn and raked.

The brick cabin across the lawn was twice the size of ours and sported a pizza-sized satellite dish on the roof along with two solar panels. I circled the cabin. Around the other side an awning and raised wooden porch trimmed in red blooming bougainvillea ran its length. Coconuts were piled in a heap next to a chopping block a few paces from the porch steps. Two mules were grazing out where the grass was left to grow long, about fifteen yards from the outhouse and shower, next to an open-ended horse stall. I saw a decent-sized generator in the horse stall, and a lawn mower.

A two-wheeled mule cart was parked by the cabin. Finca Torodea was well supplied. On the porch, the awning sheltered a barbecue, bag of coal, coiled extension cords, a jug of motor oil, and a five-liter can of gas. A small Honda generator sat against the cabin wall next to a rake, broom, and trashcan.

Did the Indian live here? Perhaps he wasn't the caretaker but the owner of Finca Torodea.

This cabin had a TV and stereo. I could see them in the living room through a screened window. Links to the outside world...and news about the fugitive Russell Martell. The golf ball behind my ear tingled. Was I ready to see my face on the news or was it better to remain in the dark?

No way I could remain in the dark. I had to find out what was going on...how many people I had killed, the extent of the death and destruction I had wrought.

I approached the door. It had been left unlatched and popped open when I knocked. "Hay alguien en casa?" I said. No answer. I took a tentative step inside. A kitchen and two bedroom doors were off to my left. I stepped off the wooden floor onto the carpet laid out in the living room. "Anybody home?" I said in English. Silence. The cabin had the feel of a frat house deserted for spring break. A few empty beer cans littered the coffee table, and the air smelled musty and vacant. Chairs and a small dining table stood at one end next to the porch door, a pedestal fan, desk and chair against the wall at the opposite end. In the middle was a recliner beside a brick-red sofa facing the entertainment center.

Neither the TV nor stereo worked. No power. I made for a lamp in the corner to see if its outlet was getting power and was ensnared by my reflection in a mirror on the wall. A small mirror the size and shape of a porthole. I stared at the face reflected in the cloistered light. The guy staring back at me didn't look much like any photo ID of mine, or even the man I saw in the mirror in Mountain's bedroom Sunday night. I recognized my black eye but last night's makeup lingered, most notably the shoe polish blackening my hair and beard. I sneered wild eyed. Impressive. *That's one rough SOB.*

Russell Martell. The Fugitive. Slayer of cops and innocents. The scourge of Vallarta. Hide your women folk and children 'cause he's on the loose.

Thought the fancy might give me a chuckle but it only made me dizzy. Sick even. Sick and desperate. I glanced away from my reflection, as if to escape an identity that was not mine...to remind myself who I really was—an innocent man falsely accused. How could this be happening? No way I was a terrorist or a killer, yet...I certainly would kill to save my life, had almost killed those two pigs last night.

Kill or be killed.

Would it come down to that? I looked at myself in the mirror again. Were those the eyes of a killer?

The subtle sound of a sharpened blade sliding across steel gave me a start. I swung my head around. "Qué...?" I said, and heard it again, in succession this time. The *snip snip* of sheers coming from somewhere—the far end of the cabin?—like a gardener trimming a hedge. I paused to listen. *Snip snip snip.* Was the Indian outside doing some work? or was the noise coming from one of the bedrooms? I made for the far bedroom door.

Snip snip. I knocked on the door. No answer. "Alguien está?" I said and slowly opened the door. *Snip snip snip.* The room was empty, and darker than I expected, the lone window above the bed shaded by curtains. I gentled the door all the way open. A sliver of backlight over my shoulder played off an image to the left of the window. Two images. My breath caught as I recoiled. Was it? Could it be...? My face!

Once again I stared at myself, this time not in a mirror. The images captivated me...creepy yet alluring, like seeing your own ghost. They were truer renditions than my reflection in the mirror but, what were they doing here, stuck to the brick wall like wanted posters? Two enlarged photos of my face—full face and profile...in each my scowl was masked by an exasperated smirk, as if my presence before the camera was absurd beyond belief, the most ridiculous, outrageous...perilous position I'd ever found myself in.

My mug shots. They had to be copies of my mug shots from when I was arrested yesterday.

I was transfixed, so transfixed that, as I approached the photos, I failed to notice I was not alone.

Snip snip. I wheeled around at the sound. The Indian stood at the door, a backlit silhouette, sheers in hand. An ancient warrior come for his retribution. He pointed his sheers off to my left. My eyes followed the gesture to the bed and the outline of a prone figure beneath a sleeping bag.

"Russell Martell," said the Indian, "meet Russell Martell."

<h2 style="text-align:center">91</h2>

PEDRO picked at the hole in his jeans. His knee was bloodied from a skid-out he took on his motorbike this morning. He'd popped right up after the mishap, continued his search for papi and didn't notice the abrasion until he got home. He lifted his desolate gaze to his elder brother, Alejandro, seated across from him and younger brother Eduardo at the dining table. "I searched all over," Pedro said despairingly. "From the Washington south, past the roadblock and into Conchas Chinas, while you and Lalo searched the northern neighborhoods."

His big brother planted his bricklayer forearms on the table. "Buenos Aires?" he queried, "Paso Ancho? Las Peñas y—"

"*Todas partes,*" Pedro reiterated. *Everywhere.*

Eduardo bounced his knee and wrung his hands. "We have to do something," he implored.

"We *are* doing something, Lalo." Alejandro drew a patient breath, "Planning action." Eduardo had started out composed enough when the two of them first teamed up in Alejandro's truck to search for papi and his truck a few hours ago. But since then he had begun to fall apart, his repetitive whiney voice and nervous hands a hindrance to clear thinking. Alejandro fixed Pedro with their father's tan eyes. "We have canvassed neighborhoods," he said, "contacted family members and friends, businesses and business associates, and searched all over town. Ma and Uncle Ramiro's team are still searching around town for papi and his truck. Now is the time to expand our northern perimeter, as Uncle Ramiro suggested, push deeper into the northern suburbs. They are heavily populated and more extensive than those to the south."

Pedro massaged the back of his neck. "We could redeploy to the Washington and Arena Vallarta, try again to find someone who may have seen him or his truck last night or this morning."

"Uncle Ramiro has taken over for us at the disaster areas and downtown," Alejandro reminded him. "And federales continue to canvass the neighborhoods around both the arena and the Washington in search of witnesses. Papi may even be a potential witness to arson, if he ever made it to Arena Vallarta last night. Police dispatch will call if there are any new leads into his whereabouts, as will Search and Rescue and my men managing the dump trucks at the Washington. And if there are any clues to be found at Arena Vallarta, such as a missing generator papi might have picked up last night or something, we may not know for quite some time. The remains are still smoking hot."

"There has to be something else to go on." Eduardo set his desperate, pleading eyes on Pedro. "Are you sure you are not overlooking a clue, Pedro? Maybe papi's disappearance has something to do with the bombing of the Washington, or the fire. Maybe he was kidnapped by terrorists or—"

SEVE VERDAD

Alejandro clanked his empty coffee cup on the table, his voice piqued: "Cálmate, Lalo. No sense in jumping to unsubstantiated conclusions. Whatever might have happened to papi, we need to continue to search for him and his truck. Puerto Vallarta is not a gigantic metropolis. We can search Vallarta and enlist more friends to help us." He lowered his voice and directed it at Pedro. "Now, as I was saying, we should expand our northern perimeter..."

Pedro remained attentive to his older brother; Alejandro's bearing inspired teamwork and kept them focused. But something clicked in his brain with Eduardo's plea, sent his mind reeling through his last sleepless hours like he had lived them in a fog only the clarity of hindsight could penetrate. Had he overlooked something? Maybe so. Pedro muttered the clue to himself as if recalling a forgotten poem: "Quién se ha ganado el poder? Sigue la publicidad y corrupción." Who has gained power? Follow the publicity and corruption.

Eduardo quietly responded, "He *does* remember something."

Alejandro cocked his head, distracted but hopeful. "What was that, Pedro?"

"For some reason I forgot," Pedro said, a sharp note of self-reproach entering his voice. "I mean I think it occurred to me before but..." Pedro gritted his teeth, angry with himself for overlooking a possible lead into papi's whereabouts. He pointed out a copy of the Vallarta Diario on the table. "I bought that paper this morning, looked it over and then forgot about it. Puta..."

Alejandro retrieved the paper. "This? What the hell does this paper have to do with papi?"

"Good question." Pedro took the Diario from his brother, spread it out on the table and began perusing its pages. "Did I miss something?" he wondered aloud, his thoughts coalescing. Should he violate police regulations and disclose a piece of a classified investigation to his brothers? the riddle the disc presented early this morning? That maldito disc! Its contents were related to terrorism...and might his father's disappearance be as well? Papi had disappeared in the midst of enormous destruction; he may have been a victim of terrorism either at the Washington or Arena Vallarta. Didn't that make the disc's revelations relevant to *this* investigation...?

His father's life could depend on unraveling the riddle. Pedro chided himself for even debating whether or not to enlist his brothers' help. Of course he needed their help. Police were undermanned and there was no time to lose!

"What could you have missed that will help us find papi?" Alejandro said. "Something unrelated to the big stories about the Washington and Russell Martell?"

Pedro shook his head imperceptibly and flipped back to the front page: a smoky image of the Washington's pulverized north tower and attending article. Russell Martell occupied the bottom quarter of the page—his photo and a story titled,

Se Busca
¡El Gringo Terrorista!

"Police received a tip early this morning," Pedro began slowly. "There is reason to believe that someone in the news has gained power as a direct result of the destruction Vallarta has suffered, someone who is also tied to corruption." Pedro lifted his eyes to Alejandro. "We received the tip after the fire at the arena, not long after papi's disappearance."

"So you think there might be a connection between the fire, the tip, and papi's disappearance?"

"Maybe."

Alejandro mused, "Someone in the news has gained power?" He leaned back in his chair. "Russell Martell is getting most all the publicity, and whether he is guilty or not—"

"Do you have reason to believe he is innocent?" Pedro interrupted archly.

Alejandro shrugged, "Only papi's word. I was in a dump truck with him last night when news about the gringo *Russell Martell* broke over the radio and he about threw a fit. You know how he can get. First he turned up the volume to make sure there was no mistake, then started cursing at the radio. Cursing police, the mayor. Not quite yelling but spitting mad...glaring right at the radio, telling it how he knew Russell, how there was no way he could have had anything to do with a fire and explosion at the Washington." Alejandro mugged his father's fury: " 'Are they accusing him of terrorism?!? Pendejos! No fucking way!' "

Eduardo cracked a smile. "You sound just like him. Better than when you told me the story this morning."

"Papi said he was going to talk to you about him, Pedro."

Pedro gave Alejandro an affirmative nod. "He did. And expressed those same feelings about him, more or less."

"If papi says Russell Martell is innocent, that is enough for me."

"Me too," Eduardo said.

Alejandro crossed his arms and got back on point: "But innocent or guilty, how has Russell Martell gained power? Seems to me the man is on the verge of losing everything."

"But if he escapes," Eduardo ventured, "maybe he and his fellow terroristas gain power. And even if he is captured or killed, maybe they win by having killed so many and—"

Pedro cut him off: "I thought you agreed he is innocent."

"I do..." Eduardo's knee began bouncing again "...if papi is so sure he is innocent... What are you looking for in the paper then, Pedro? Do *you* think Russell Martell is guilty? or responsible for papi's disappearance?"

"We cannot rule anything out..." Pedro paused, and quickly decided to be candid with his brothers, "...but I doubt it." He flipped through the paper. "The tip probably refers to someone else, someone tied to publicity *and corruption*... Where is the corruption?"

Alejandro placed a hand over the newspaper. "Everywhere," he said. He folded the Vallarta Diario back to the front page and fingered the article beside the photo of Russell Martell. "Especially here. You think papi would befriend the man described in this article, defend him? No way!" Alejandro set his jaw. He'd come to an indisputable conclusion. "Papi is a great judge of character," he began again, his voice modulated, "has to be with all the men he manages. This hijo de puta Lazarito Charlado printed a pack of lies about Russell Martell. And why?" he tilted a hand at Pedro. "To give *himself* publicity, further his career and enhance his power, you can bet on that." He shifted his gaze between his brothers. "Either one of you heard of him?"

"No," Eduardo said.

Pedro's eyes wandered. "The name rings a bell," he said. "Wonder where he gets his information." Pedro leveled his wandering eyes on Alejandro. "My investigations of Russell Martell turned up none of that trash. Nothing even close."

"So police are not a source for Señor Charlado's story?"

Pedro stared unflinchingly at his older brother. "Anything is possible, Alejandro. But not to my knowledge. No."

Alejandro folded his hands on the table, his tone measured: "After the last election, Lazarito Charlado was appointed Media Minister of Vallarta by Governor Palacio. He mostly works behind the scenes, manages propaganda, the media and publicity, coordinating with counterparts in Guadalajara and throughout the state. And, as I worked very closely with papi in the construction of Arena Vallarta, I can tell you that he was instrumental in publicizing its dedication."

"You ever meet him?" Pedro asked.

"Met him during the construction of Arena Vallarta. He dropped by the arena several times when the mayor and his wife were there. Papi knows him, filled me in some about him. Lazarito has an office,

The Bureau, off of Francisco Villa. Papi says he is a friendly, gregarious, hijo de la chingada. A real chingón. If anyone wants to pick up some dirt on somebody in this town, or cover their ass...if anybody needs any kind of publicity, good or bad, about *anything*, or is looking to stifle publicity, they go to him. The man has always had power, the power of the media."

"And with power comes corruption," Pedro said, echoing a well-known truism.

"Especially in México," Alejandro rejoined. "You should not be surprised, Pedro, if your comandante has paid him off more than a few times."

The three brothers exchanged muted glances, reading each other's thoughts.

"Corruption," said Eduardo.

Pedro responded deliberately, as if swearing out an indictment against the Media Minister: "Power and publicity. This Lazarito Charlado has it all. But does that mean he knows what happened to papi?"

"Papi's disappearance has been reported on the radio and television," Alejandro said, "so I would think the Media Minister knows he is missing. But there is no reason to believe he actually knows where he is."

"Maybe we should talk to him and find out if he knows where papi is," Eduardo suggested, his words coming rapidly. "Papi's disappearance could be tied to terrorism; and the tip police received, that sounds like it is tied to terrorism too so that means—" Eduardo stifled himself to let his thoughts catch up with his tongue.

Alejandro got the gist of his little brother's logic and shot Pedro a clarifying question: "Is the source for that tip to police linked to terrorism, Pedro?"

"Sí... But the source is more like a piece of evidence rather than a person who can be questioned or interrogated."

"Not sure I understand."

Eduardo blurted out, "The Media Minister is tied to terrorism!"

Pedro and Alejandro stared at Eduardo's emphatic expression with unblinking comprehension.

"At the very least," Pedro said thoughtfully, "it is possible that Lazarito's source or *sources* for his story this morning are linked to terrorism."

"They also seem unreliable," Alejandro said, "or untruthful."

"And misleading," Pedro added, "perhaps purposefully misleading so as to focus attention on Russell Martell instead of the guilty parties. But the source for the tip police received..." Pedro considered the source for a moment, the disc. Its revelations sure were cryptic at times, to say the least...but its predictions had been accurate, "...has proved very reliable in many respects. And since the tip appears to suggest that Media Minister Charlado is somehow linked to terrorists—"

Eduardo interjected: "Like papi's disappearance."

"His disappearance *may be* tied to terrorism," Alejandro emphasized.

"We should find out where Señor Charlado gets his information," Pedro concluded imperatively. "It is possible that his sources know something about papi's disappearance."

"Possible," Alejandro said, "But..."

Pedro finished his thought, "Not altogether probable."

"How probable is it that we will stumble across papi's truck?" Eduardo clasped his hands prayerfully upon the table. "We need to do something besides drive around looking for papi and his truck like we are *lost.*"

Alejandro raised his voice in reproach: "There are still plenty of neighborhoods we have yet to search, Lalo. We are not lost." He dropped his gaze to the Vallarta Diario, the headline by Russell Martell's photo, and looked up with a commanding nod for both his brothers. "We need to follow every lead and it appears that Señor Charlado presents one, perhaps a vital one. However, from what I understand about the media as well as the Media Minister, he will not simply divulge his sources to us. So we will have to come up with a shrewd strategy to discover them." Alejandro met Pedro's expectant doe eyes.

"I can follow him on my motorbike," Pedro said. "Maybe he will lead me to them."

Alejandro's voice gained an authoritative note of finality: "We can pull up a photo of Lazarito Charlado on the Internet, Pedro, and I will give you a physical description of him. With one call to his office I should be able to find out if he is in or when he is due to arrive. You stake him out. Follow him wherever he goes, see who he talks to. And stay in contact with me while Lalo and I hunt for papi's truck."

92

IN all his years at CISEN, Senior Operative Alfredo Flores had never seen anything like what he saw at Casa Mexicana this morning. He could not get it out of his mind. A sight so horrifying he knew it would stick with him for the rest of his life. Yet the lingering vision of a dead man with his jugular splayed and laid open like a marlin with its gills ripped out its throat was only part of what disturbed him. What he found most disconcerting and frightening was that someone had been able to overpower and brutalize a CISEN man of Joaquín's talents and experience with such apparent ease, without leaving so much as a trace of evidence behind (other than the dead body) or signs of a struggle. Who could get away with that? Russell Martell? the man who had reserved the room in which Garras was last seen alive? the man Lazarito Charlado had dubbed "El Gringo Terrorista"?

Señor Charlado had made some startling claims in the Vallarta Diario today which, if true, indicated that he knew an awful lot about Russell Martell. Might his profile of him and/or his accomplices implicate El Gringo Terrorista in such a flawlessly executed, brutally inconceivable murder? And where did the Media Minister get his information on Russell Martell?

Flores had every intention of getting the answers to those questions.

When Flores left the crime scene at Casa Mexicana to a forensics team and his CISEN men, he remained shocked and horrified at the manner in which Garras had been killed. When he arrived at The Bureau, he mostly felt a burning desire for revenge. Garras had had few real friends in CISEN and Flores did not count himself among them. But Garras was something of a legend and his loss was a loss for everyone in the agency. A loss to be avenged...investigated without prejudice but with an eye to the prime suspect: Russell Martell.

Media Minister Charlado greeted Flores at the door to his office with a solemn handshake and pleasantry: "Señor Flores. I do wish we could have met under more agreeable circumstances."

"If the circumstances were agreeable," Flores replied bluntly, "I would not be here." He turned his attention to the woman of sublime elegance and command standing before the Media Minister's desk. A face he instantly recognized. CISEN had a dossier on her and her entire family. Los Infante. Ranchers rich in agave. Gloria the eldest of five children. Fiercely independent. Savvy and well educated. A natural leader. Mentor, wife and confidant of Mayor Juan Pacífico Velázquez. Inspiration behind Arena Vallarta. Prefers working behind the scenes...etcetera. Governor Palacio had requested she begin a preliminary investigation into the disaster at the Washington Hotel; a reasonable request given its immediacy, Gloria's capabilities, and her access to local sources of information and intelligence.

What did she know about Russell Martell?

SEVE VERDAD

He approached and tipped his head to her. "And you must be Señora Infante Velázquez," he said cordially. "I understand that you have begun an informal investigation into yesterday's tragic events."

"CISEN is well informed," Gloria said, her gracious smile belying her choleric anger at Lazarito's insolent treatment of her this morning. Was she about to receive more of the same from this CISEN man? His genteel manner and voice were that of a waiter at a high-class restaurant, but she felt a twinge of apprehension as she met his secretive brown eyes. The glint of white around his iris lent a pitiless sheen to his stare, a shine, like a predatory animal peering out from within a cave. A beast with intellect. A chilling combination. His interest in her "informal investigation" was to be expected. CISEN's job was to take over investigations... Juan had told her that CISEN reinforcements had arrived. What wasn't expected however was this CISEN man's sudden appearance here at The Bureau. Was he here to question her or Lazarito? Both? Gloria had absolutely no intention of sharing information with him in front of Lazarito. Who knew what kind of devious spin the Media Minister would put on what she divulged?

Lazarito waddled back to his desk. "I imagine that CISEN is always well informed," he said affably and took his seat. The CISEN man's interest in Gloria's investigation titillated his instincts. Was this an opportunity to squeeze information from her? Perhaps this meeting could be used to advantage. "How may we be of assistance to CISEN, Señor Flores?"

Flores set his leather briefcase down at the foot of the desk and spoke in an easy, matter-of-fact tone: "Before you can be of assistance, Señor Charlado, I think you should be brought up to date on the latest development. Yesterday's tragedies have claimed yet another victim, a man whose whereabouts were unknown until a short time ago. CISEN Lead Interrogator Joaquín de Jesús was found dead at Casa Mexicana Hotel this morning."

Lazarito went rigid behind his desk, his mouth flaccid, as though the words didn't register, which they didn't. A CISEN man was in town yesterday? Why hadn't his faithful snitch Paulo informed him of this?

Gloria blanched, an unconscious hand reaching for the chair by her side. "Dios mío," she said and took a seat, her shoulder bag cradled in her lap. "How did it happen?"

Flores proffered her an inscrutable glance. "How did it happen?" he repeated deliberately, as if prepared to give a lecture on the subject. "When I left Casa Mexicana fifteen minutes ago, my men and I were shaking our heads over that very question. They are conducting an investigation into what appears to have been a murder. Thus far, the only conclusions we have reached are that there are no signs of a struggle where the body was found or in the room where Joaquín was last seen alive on the eleventh floor of the hotel—Russell Martell's room, to be precise... And the manner in which he was killed is unfathomable, especially given his training and skill."

"What manner is that?" Lazarito had latched onto the story. All he needed were a few details to own it.

Flores stared dully at the Media Minister, his eager tone. "The best we can determine," he said, "is that Joaquín had his throat ripped out by a wild animal and was then dropped, sent flying from an altitude sufficient enough to bury him from view on impact in the hibiscus bordering Casa Mexicana's koi pond."

Gloria looked a question at him, her gaze steady. "A wild animal? You have got to be kidding."

"I am afraid not, señora. Of course it is possible that the wild animal to which I refer is a human being. Do either of you know of anyone in particular, Russell Martell perhaps, who may have the training and strength to manhandle a skilled CISEN operative in such a fashion as to literally rip his throat out and hurl him from an eleventh floor balcony without leaving a trace?"

Gloria shuddered and winced at the imagery; she absently pawed at her cell phone in her pocket, a reflex to call her husband with the news. It vibrated at her touch. She retrieved it. A text message from Juan. Gloria retreated into herself to read it.

Lazarito sank into his deep leather chair, rumpled brow raised and cheeks puffed. Flores puzzled over the expression. Lazarito resembled an overripe pumpkin. "Does Russell Martell strike you as a man who could accomplish such a feat, Señor Charlado?"

Lazarito chortled, "I thought him capable of most anything but...this? I really—"

"Where do you get your information on him, Lazarito?"

"I would like to know that myself." Gloria stood from her chair. She would have liked nothing more than to assist Flores in questioning Lazarito, if she could trust him not to turn the tables on her before the Media Minister. "But I am afraid I must be going."

"One moment, if you please, señora."

Gloria paused at the CISEN man's disarming smile. "Sí?"

"You have not answered my question."

"And what was that?"

"Does Russell Martell strike you as a man capable of killing a trained CISEN operative in that fashion?"

Sharp suspicion creased Gloria's chest. Flores was already turning the tables on her. "Frankly, no," she said with a glance at her watch. "Now if that is all, I—"

"And the dead terrorist found at the marina, señora?"

She spied the CISEN man sideways, and could feel Lazarito's impertinent stare boring into her. "What about him?"

"Do you believe Russell Martell capable of killing him in *that* fashion? breaking a man's neck, arm, and ankle?"

"Anything is possible." Gloria dipped into her bag for a business card and presented it to Flores—a courtesy to postpone the inevitable. "Call me for a briefing of my preliminary investigation."

"You can count on it, señora."

Gloria was out the door. Lazarito mused, "When that story broke about the dead man found at the marina, I had my doubts about his death being accidental."

Flores smirked impatiently. "Where do you get your information on Russell Martell, Lazarito?"

"My sources are privileged—protected, señor. I believe I have that right. Indeed I do."

"Yes you do have that right, if you wish to spend time in jail. But I think you can be reasoned with. I understand you are scheduled to give a briefing to the president's Media and Communications Director later this afternoon, Señor Francisco Panza de León."

Lazarito felt the plump curve of his cheek twitch nervously just below the eye... He shouldn't be surprised at CISEN's intelligence of his forthcoming meeting with the Media and Communications Director but, nevertheless, was startled when confronted with it. Was this man Flores in communication with Señor de León? If so, his hopes of pitting one against the other to buy himself time to meet with Araceli without CISEN at his throat were dwindling fast. His connections to the highest levels of government may not provide him with any protection at all against the all-seeing, all-powerful phantom.

Flores let a stinging silence linger in the room as he awaited a response from the Media Minister.

Lazarito cleared his throat. "Sí señor," he said. "I am indeed scheduled for a meeting with the Media and Communications Director this afternoon."

"And I am sure you are aware that he will ask you this same question about your sources."

"He did not mention that when we spoke on the phone this morning."

FINDING DEVO

"The Media and Communications Director is not so indiscrete as to speak of such matters over the phone. But I assure you the issue is paramount."

Lazarito shifted uneasily in his chair. He was beginning to perspire through his shirt and ran a finger around the collar as if to loosen it, though he wasn't wearing a tie and the collar was unbuttoned. Flores regarded him as if viewing an uncommon species of fish washed up on the shore. Up until now, Lazarito Charlado had been an insignificant footnote in CISEN files. A bit player unworthy of a dossier. Yet in the last twenty-four hours Puerto Vallarta's Media Minister had demonstrated an uncanny ability to manipulate the media and was on the verge of capturing the imagination of the entire nation with an astounding story about the prime suspect in the deadliest terror attack in Mexico's history (and the man who may have murdered Joaquín de Jesús). How much of his story in this morning's Vallarta Diario was based in fact remained to be seen. In all likelihood the Washington had indeed been bombed, so the cornerstone of Lazarito's story appeared sound: terrorists were to blame for the carnage. But if the principal suspect, Russell Martell, was a gringo fanatic with ties to Mossad (Israeli Intelligence) as Lazarito claimed, CISEN knew nothing about it. Russell Martell had escaped from jail and could very well be a terrorist, but CISEN didn't know much about him at all other than what they had gleaned from his website. Apparently, "El Gringo Terrorista" was also an itinerant sports journalist from Oregon. That didn't mean Lazarito was wrong about him, of course. The Media Minister might have reliable sources CISEN was not privy to, sources that prompted him to tie Russell Martell to another terrorist plot in his story...a foiled plot to blow up the Main Senate Chambers building in Mexico City six years ago.

At the time, implications of a Jewish conspiracy were picked up by the media, as Lazarito's story accurately recounted. Beyond that, the Media Minister's claims were questionable, but they did force CISEN to revisit their sting operation. CISEN, never given to publicity anyhow, had been especially circumspect with the details of the case because, although they were successful in thwarting the attack, the operation was a tactical failure. All but one of the conspirators escaped, and he killed himself with a bullet to the brain. His identity was never verified and documents found at the scene tying him to Mossad proved to be forgeries. Yet the terrorist's Barak pistol was Israeli as were the recovered explosives. Through diplomatic and intelligence channels, Israel convincingly disavowed any involvement, and subsequent CISEN investigations pointed to Hezbollah in Tepito as the probable culprit. But agency raids in that Mexico City barrio didn't uncover any hard evidence of an Islamist conspiracy. The case went cold. Dead cold. In effect, Lazarito's story about "El Gringo Terrorista" opened an old wound for CISEN. Was the prime suspect in the bombing of the Washington, Russell Martell, really a fanatic gringo with ties to Mossad? or were Hezbollah and/or other Islamic terror groups attempting to frame Israel and Jews as CISEN had suspected six years ago? Was the attack on the Washington related to the foiled plot to bomb the Senate Chambers building? What did Media Minister Charlado actually know and how did he know it?

"The issue is paramount?" Lazarito said, as if repeating the CISEN man's words weakened their meaning.

Flores smiled menacingly. "I assure you."

A spasm of dread washed over Lazarito's concentration and filled him with confusion. It seemed Flores was acting in concert with the Media and Communications Director...or...was he bluffing? Did he need to bluff? Wasn't it likely he'd be in touch with members of the president's cabinet? Had he ever stood a chance against CISEN?

Though confused, Lazarito remained lucid enough to realize that, if he wasn't careful, his story might land him in jail as Flores had threatened instead of saving him from it.

Lazarito gathered his strength for a last stand, a final effort to free himself from CISEN's unyielding clutches. He had to call the bluff, if that was what it was, find out if Flores really was in communication with Señor de León. He reached for his cell phone on his desk and sputtered, "Perhaps I...I think I shall call the Media and Communications Director. He knows that...when we meet I will have all the information he requires."

Flores saw an opening and seized upon it like a high-priced attorney cross examining a star witness. "Is that so?" he said, circling the desk. Flores stood right next to the Media Minister. Lazarito had to crank his head all the way back to face up to him. "Are you expecting more information from your source before our meeting with *Francisco*, Lazarito? If so, I suggest you make arrangements to meet with your source personally. We would both benefit from such an encounter."

As if on cue, the Media Minister's intercom buzzed, twice. Esmeralda had Araceli on the line. Lazarito visibly flinched and stared at the phone, its blinking light, his plump cheek twitching in sequence to the rapid drum beat of his heart.

Once again the intercom buzzed twice. Flores said, "You better take that call, Minister Charlado. And pretend I am not here."

LIEUTENANT Benito Cuevas Romero was parked in his Cutlass about two blocks up the street from The Bureau. He had arrived just in time to see Flores enter the building. Was another CISEN operative lurking about these side streets somewhere? If they discovered him, CISEN could spoil his efforts to monitor Lazarito's movements.

Lieutenant Romero hacked and spit out his window, "Que vengan." Let them come, putos. Fucking CISEN. Who could trust a government agency with that much power? Even if he worked with them, nothing was to stop them from hanging him for incompetence, corruption...even murder of that terrorist found dead at the marina. If they interfered with his efforts right now to case Lazarito he'd offer his help, as if that had been his intention all along. But no way he was going to join hands with the devil of his own accord, appear at Flores' side up in Lazarito's office like he could trust CISEN to treat him fairly. Fuck them. If they wanted him let them come right now. Otherwise, he'd work on his own initiative, and CISEN could go to hell. Hijos de la rechingada puta madre.

Lieutenant Romero popped a caffeine pill, chased it with coffee dregs, and lit a cigarette. Prepared to battle tedium. Surveillance was always like this, a struggle against boredom until, suddenly, action. Or perhaps nothing at all. You could never tell. And it was best done with a partner, an extra pair of eyes. But in this case he had to go it alone. If el comandante weren't occupied with CISEN at Casa Mexicana, the lieutenant might have confided in him. And Pedro, well, he was too concerned with his father's disappearance to bring along and, in any case, had very little field experience... It was best to go it alone. Should the lieutenant have an opportunity to confront and question the Media Minister, Lazarito might let the recriminations fly...chastise him for allowing Russell Martell to escape and who knew what other real or imagined sin or crime? No sense in exposing a partner to that kind of confrontation.

Lazarito was a devious hijo de puta. Lieutenant Romero had a hunch he planted that story in La Estrella Nocturna about the dead man found with his neck broken. The attending photo didn't quite match the crime scene. Why would Lazarito plant that story and photo? For his own devious purposes. Who knew with Lazarito?

Lazarito had never exactly threatened the lieutenant before but that didn't mean he couldn't or wouldn't.

How much of a threat did Lazarito present? A threat commensurate with the enormity of the events of these past few days.

SEVE VERDAD

Lieutenant Romero removed his sunglasses and let his gaze sink into the target area, the last sixty hours or so of his life fulminating within a corrosive sense of failure: Saturday's botched raid; the ensuing cover-up (facilitated by none other than Media Minister Lazarito Charlado); the dead terrorist found at the marina; the devastation at the Washington; Russell Martell's escape from jail; the police fiascos at Casa Mexicana and Hotel Marciano last night; the Arena Vallarta fire; and Garras' lifeless body discovered this morning at Casa Mexicana, his throat ripped to shreds. Lieutenant Romero hadn't seen the body but the hair on his neck curled when Officer Talla related the gruesome discovery to him over the phone.

Lieutenant Romero flexed his knuckles around the steering wheel. Failure, humiliation, unmitigated disaster...that about summed up these last two and a half days or so. There was plenty of blame to go around of course, and Lazarito Charlado knew it. He always kept himself well informed. As Vallarta's Media Minister he had to. The cabrón probably had enough damning evidence compiled against Vallarta police (replete with rumor and innuendo) to implicate and convict every officer in the force of corruption, incompetence, obstruction of justice...accessory to murder...maybe even mass murder; who knew with Lazarito?!? No one was more guilty than Russell Martell, but if the Media Minister had intimate knowledge of *El Gringo Terrorista* and a certain story the gringo had to tell implicating police in the murder of a terrorist found dead at the marina, and if Lazarito's sources for his astonishing article published in the Vallarta Diario this morning were still talking, well...then Lazarito had loads of ammunition. Lieutenant Romero could be exposed to threats and accusations grave enough to land him in jail.

Lazarito might not be as dangerous as El Gringo Terrorista but he wasn't beyond destroying others to protect his own corrupt culo and advance his career.

Where the hell did Lazarito get his information on Russell Martell? It wasn't that the lieutenant found his revelations in this morning's news hard to believe. To a large degree they made sense, yet...who were his sources? Was the Media Minister in contact with terrorists?

The lieutenant renewed his fix on the sidewalk in front of the entrance to The Bureau's stairwell. A few pedestrians. Parked cars lined the street... "Follow the publicity and corruption," he muttered. The disc seemed to have incriminated the Media Minister so...maybe he was tied to terrorists somehow.

Would Lazarito lead him to Russell Martell? That's what he was here to find out.

Russell Martell... The mere thought of him infused the lieutenant with beguiling, indomitable anger. El Gringo Terrorista seemed capable of anything—terror attacks, jailbreaks, casting shadows in one place while bludgeoning armed police officers in another; arson...barehanded murders. How did he do it? The man had accomplices. *Someone* sprang him from jail...the same man he was seen with at El Marciano Hotel? Yet with all this destruction and mayhem...was a gang of terrorists running loose in Vallarta?

They would all have to be killed.

Or did he want Russell Martell alive? Yes, for a while. Make him suffer, vomit his guts, give up all and everything he knew. Everything about the dead terrorist found at the marina...and that disc. Everything about the Washington and Arena Vallarta. Everything about that story incriminating police he claimed to have e-mailed.

And Garras. How did he manage to take down one of CISEN's fiercest operatives with such apparent ease? The lieutenant squeezed his arm down over his shoulder holster—the pistol beneath his dress shirt. He may have no choice but to kill Russell Martell before Russell Martell killed him.

Lieutenant Romero flicked his cigarette out his window and slumped in his seat, luxuriating in willful rage, his gaze drifting in and out of focus. He sat up, suddenly alert. Someone had exited The Bureau. A feminine figure. Trim blond. Authoritative strides. Heading his way. Was it...? He cursed and shrank down in his seat in the hopes of avoiding detection. Gloria. She must have arrived before Flores, before—

A knock on his Oldsmobile's rear window struck him like a blow to the kidneys, straightened him right up and swung his head around. "Puta," he mouthed. The mayor opened the rear door with a "buenos días, Teniente." Affable, accommodating eyes. Fresh blue slacks, striped tie and neat short-sleeve button-down. Dressed for the camera. Juan took a seat in the back and shut the door. "We thought it best to join forces with you rather than follow your car, Lieutenant. You are prepared to tail Lazarito?"

The lieutenant stifled another curse. "Sí señor."

Gloria opened the passenger door. "Always on the job, eh Lieutenant?" She sat her bag down in the foot-well and took her place next to Benito. "Waiting for someone, Benito?"

Lieutenant Romero felt his cheeks flush. "Uh...evidently." He'd been on the lookout for a CISEN operative casing The Bureau, was even prepared to offer his assistance should they interfere with him. But Gloria and the mayor had caught him completely off guard. Juan had beat him to the punch. The mayor must have arrived to back up

Gloria and do his own surveillance before the lieutenant got here. Or maybe he dropped Gloria off and hung around...

A thin, triumphant smile creased Gloria's lips. "Three pair of eyes are better than one or two when doing surveillance."

Lieutenant Romero smoothed his pinstriped shirt and sat up with military poise. "Thought it best to operate on my own initiative," he said, "since el comandante and the mayor were kind enough to give me some relief this morning."

Juan chuckled carelessly. "Everyone is entitled to a bit of relief, Lieutenant, especially with the pressure we are all under. But most use it to go home and get some rest. And it appears you did make it home to change out of uniform and clean up but, may I ask what possessed you to stakeout our Media Minister instead of getting some sleep?"

Lieutenant Romero and the mayor spied each other through the rearview mirror. The lieutenant said, "I might ask you the same question, señor."

"The mayor and I do not have the luxury of relief," Gloria said. The lieutenant glimpsed his reflection in her wraparound sunglasses. Gloria looked prepared to take a motorcycle ride. Blue jeans, blouse, all-terrain sneakers. He caught a mild whiff of jasmine—her perfume. Both she and the mayor seemed potently alert. He idly wondered what they had taken this morning besides a shower and extra cups of coffee to keep themselves going.

Lieutenant Romero acquiesced with an approving smile: "Perhaps we are all too weary to rest, señora... And Lazarito?"

Gloria settled back in her seat, eyes focused dead ahead. The street was quiet; a dozen or so parked cars and a handful of pedestrians. When Lazarito left The Bureau he'd be easy to spot. "Our Media Minister probably wishes he had stayed home in bed," she said. "I left him with a CISEN man. Alfredo Flores." She half glanced at her husband. Upon leaving The Bureau, on her way down the stairwell, she'd called and told him that CISEN had arrived but had not mentioned the man's name.

Juan loosened his tie, and his tongue. The solemn dignity and strength he reserved for the camera easily gave way to a tone of energetic verve: "Benito is familiar with our friends from CISEN, Gloria. You must have recognized Alfredo when he entered The Bureau, Lieutenant. A pity I missed CISEN's arrival at police headquarters this morning but I was busy with public relations and strengthening the morale of our brave troops working under the most trying of circumstances in the trenches at the Washington and Arena Vallarta. But you were with CISEN at headquarters when I called early this morning, Lieutenant... How did that briefing with them go?"

"The gist of it, señor, is that it is just a matter of time before CISEN takes over the investigations into the bombing of the Washington and the fire at Arena Vallarta."

"No doubt," said Gloria. "But that has not stopped you, stopped *us* from working on our own initiative, Lieutenant. And I am sure you have your eye on the big prize—Russell Martell. What makes you think Señor Charlado will lead us to him? Was it that story of his in the Diario this morning or have you another clue to go on?"

Gloria perused Benito's face for a hint of deception. Would he claim to only be interested in Lazarito's sources for his story or had he connected the disc's last clue to Lazarito? the clue Pedro had relayed to her in the ash-filled false dawn at Arena Vallarta. A clue—riddle—which, once Gloria and the mayor saw Lazarito's story splashed all over the news, seemed to incriminate Vallarta's Media Minister and suggest that his sources were linked to terrorism...and perhaps Russell Martell, or the author of the disc.

Lieutenant Romero responded with unwavering calm: "Who has gained power?"

"*Indeed,*" Juan puffed, a finger to his mustache. "Who has gained power?"

Gloria rounded out the disc's riddle: "Follow the corruption and publicity. Is that the disc's latest clue, Lieutenant?"

"As far as I know. Officer Andrade and a CISEN man were monitoring it when I left headquarters. And last I spoke to Pedro, around six thirty this morning when he called again asking about his father, he said he had mentioned the clue to you, Gloria. But really, the clue or...uh, riddle made little sense until I read Lazarito's article in the paper."

Gloria swallowed the distress in her throat. Poor Pedro. Enrique had to turn up soon, had to! But she couldn't think of that now. She had to remain focused on... "Pinche Lazarito. We are all aware of his power and lack of scruples. The connection between him and the disc's riddle is plain now that, apparently, our Media Minister's story about *El Gringo Terrorista* has galvanized the Mexican pueblo and garnered him even more power."

"The riddle also suggests that Lazarito's sources may be tied to terrorism," the lieutenant added with deductive aplomb. "After all, the riddle points to him, and the disc itself is tied to terrorism."

"Did you share your insights with CISEN, Lieutenant?" Gloria inquired.

The lieutenant let a hint of injury crack his voice: "I hope you are kidding, señora. These deductions go well beyond a briefing. CISEN can make their own deductions. Unlike us though, they may not be fully aware of Lazarito's corruption and *lack of scruples*. And regardless of the disc's riddle, I am sure CISEN is very interested in Lazarito's sources for his story."

"Flores most certainly is," Gloria said. "But I wonder when or if he will get them."

"Lazarito had to know his story would focus attention on him," Juan said. "But that attention is liable to give him much more grief than he bargained for, especially from CISEN."

They fell silent, all eyes on the entrance to The Bureau, though there was plenty more to talk about. The lieutenant wondered if the mayor and Gloria had heard about Garras; Gloria thought about the guilt or innocence of Russell Martell; and the mayor flashed on two bludgeoned police officers who were now conscious in the hospital but couldn't remember a damn thing, barely remembered their own names. How did Russell Martell—? Juan took a look out the rear window, a lingering, apprehensive look. "Híjole," he said. "It suddenly occurred to me... The three of us in here like this...we could be vulnerable—"

Gloria and the lieutenant spoke up in unison: "There he is."

Juan stuck his head between them, eyes searching out the front windshield. "Accompanied by our CISEN man?"

Gloria watched carefully as Lazarito nodded up at the dapper Flores before leading him down the sidewalk. "Yes," she said. "Señor Flores has attached himself to Lazarito. It appears we are now obliged to follow our Media Minister *and* the CISEN man, Lieutenant."

"El comandante reserved two cars for CISEN," the lieutenant said. "A gray Chrysler Le Baron and black Ford Expedition. But...looks like they are going to take Lazarito's Volkswagen Jetta."

"Stay some distance behind," the mayor ordered evenly. "But careful not to lose them. This Flores is probably very adept at spotting a tail. And keep on the lookout for the Le Baron and Expedition. Flores probably has backup."

Lieutenant Romero slapped on his sunglasses. "Entendido."

Juan relaxed, arms spread over the backseat. "If CISEN tries to detain us let me handle it. We have the right to conduct our own investigation...pinches cabrones."

94

IF and when I ever face a jury for my crimes, I know how I will plead. Convince a jury you acted in self-defense, in defense of friends or family, or even in defense of a stranger, and you can get away with murder, kill with impunity...kill anybody without facing legal retribution. The use of deadly force is transformed from murder into a moral and honorable act via the kill or be killed rationale: kill in order to save yourself; kill or others will die including, quite possibly, yourself; kill to avoid further bloodshed; kill now or multitudes will die later.

And when it comes right down to it, this is the most poignant justification for war. Leaders might be driven by a blood lust for power and revenge (or perhaps the venerable ethics of liberty, equality, and justice) but the rally cry to war reaches its peak when nations, cultures, tribes, individuals fervently believe that their way of life, their very existence is threatened by another. If bombs haven't yet exploded your neighborhoods, they will! The enemy has a face, a name. It doesn't matter if the reasoning is sound, whether your life, your family, your country, culture and god are really in peril. Maybe they are, maybe they're not. The victor will be judge and jury on that score and point his finger at the aggressor—the guilty party. But what does matter, what is most compelling in this ultimate act of taking life, is that you *feel* as though a knife is at your throat. You are convinced that your life and all you care for depends on the death of another. You are ready for war. Killing isn't murder; it's your moral and legal obligation.

And I was at war. *We* were at war. That's how I justified my accessory to murder at any rate, to myself and to Johnny. Naturally, it wasn't murder but an act of self-defense—the killing of a blood-thirsty Islamo terrorist who would just as soon behead me as look at me. Camacho, my new found Indian confidant, said as much and I believed him...willfully believed him...

Our victim's name was "Russell Martell"—my double. "Formerly Ahmed Mehri Fayed," Camacho said when he pointed him out to me with his shears in the shadowy light of that cabin bedroom. "An Islamist who helped mastermind the terror attack on the Washington."

I'd been so startled and captivated by my mug shots up on the wall I hadn't noticed the inert form in the bed, all but his head covered by a sleeping bag. Yet another rendition of my face. A wondrous rendition with an implicit secret to render.

It didn't take a genius to figure out what was up. I mean hell, a terrorist, made up to match my photos on the wall, was out cold in the bed. A Russell Martell look-alike, alive but dead to the world—peaceful, dour, drugged. What could possibly be his purpose? to appear at parties and hustle chicks in my stead? I didn't need much prompting from Camacho to understand that this man was my fall guy and that his head was gonna have to be blown off.

"Russell Martell has to die," Camacho said in deliberate Spanish, "in order to save your life."

He bared his teeth at my enlightened expression, his missing eyetooth a lost fang. Aggressive hooked nose. Yet there was something assuasive about him. His youthful, accommodating voice, perhaps, but mostly his eyes—darker than shadows but with a glimmering smile in the iris. Camacho introduced himself. We shared a conspiratorial stare as I shook his spidery, diminutive hand. He was a short fellow but well put together. A man accustomed to outdoor work. He wore black draw-string pants and a tan tank top; his huarache sandals seemed molded to his feet. I had a million questions for him but didn't know where to begin. I thought about Devo, naturally, and wondered about the particulars of the plot. Evidently, the plot had been hatched by Devo and Camacho, and perhaps others; a deep sense of gratitude and relief welled up inside me. Whatever their motives, these guys were going through a lot of trouble to save my life. So the first natural question was, "What can I do to help?"

Camacho sat his shears down at the foot of the bed and pulled the sleeping bag off my double. "Help me move this *rechingado terrorista* into the mule cart outside and ready him for transport."

He gripped my double's torso under the arms. I took the legs and we lifted him from the bed. My double was in dark polyester slacks, barefoot and shirtless. A thick band of gauze wrapped his chest.

"This Islamist pig would slit your throat for being Jewish," Camacho said.

"I am not Jewish...or of any religious faith."

"He would slit your throat for that then."

Reasonable. Actually, it sounded totally unreasonable, yet all too probable given the horrors I'd seen at the Washington, horrors perpetrated by fanatical Islamisalaamis like my fall guy; not to mention the horrors I'd experienced at the hands of sadistic fucking coppers. This mass murderer needed to be killed to prevent more bloodshed and save my life. I felt awash in clarity of purpose, the singular confidence of having but one course of action, similar to when I climbed those stairs at Johnny's hotel to clobber Chimp and Fat Cop, and afterwards, as we pressed our escape in their squad car. Except here, with Camacho, my senses weren't keened to every possible threat, and my heart wasn't pounding out an anxious rhythm in my chest but fluttering with exhilaration. Instead of the constraints of imminent death, a fear that my next move could be my last, it was all I could do to stave off the rush of sheer elation (overconfidence can always destroy you. I wasn't out of the woods yet). Victory was about to be snatched from defeat, life from death. I was walking on air, my mind celebrating a comeback. I would reinvent myself upon my return to the States: Russell Martell, the sports journalist victimized by evil terror and Mexican injustice, becomes the Thomas Paine of the war against radical Islam...radical Islam and sadistic third-world police...sadistic fucking police *everywhere!*

Fucking Chimp...and the lieutenant.

We laid Ahmed in the mule cart. I imagined he was Chimp...Fat Cop...the lieutenant—*Blow all their heads off*—and took a lingering look at the Islamisalaami—the seamless puttied nose and tawny tint to his hair and shallow goatee. The rakish bruise under the eye. The late morning heat shimmering over his makeup...

A resentful curl to his lip.

All at once, his insolent smirk possessed me, sucked me in and spit me out, triggering an inexplicable sense of vertigo. My head contracted into my stomach, like I was going up in a high-speed elevator, and I found myself suspended in air, looking down upon Russell Martell—my own corpse.

I wavered, swayed on my feet, then widened my stance and braced my resolve. "Not quite as tall as me," I observed.

Camacho snickered disarmingly. "Witnesses identifying him as Russell Martell will not see him standing. A stimulant will bring him to in the front seat of a pickup just before a blast sends him to meet his pig putas in the inferno."

Sobering details. "And where will I be?"

"Far from the scene making a clean getaway, if you follow Devo's instructions."

"A getaway to where? the States? Home?"

"Safety." Camacho cocked an eyebrow at me. "Do you prefer los federales y policía?"

"No," I replied quickly. I still had my doubts about Devo and his motives, and Camacho's motives as well—why were they helping me? what did they want from me? who the hell were they?—but, who the hell cared at this point?!? I'd been sprung from jail, spirited away to a hideout, given drugs for my pain and a bed for the night, and now a plan for a "clean getaway" was staring me in the face... Did I prefer los federales y policía? No fuckin' way!

Camacho's eyes, his aggressive hooked nose and angled jaw all grinned at me. I grinned back, my nerves steeled. "Pig putas in the inferno?" I clucked.

We chuckled righteously, like soldiers sharing a crude joke in the latrine.

SEVE VERDAD

A familiar tittering voice swung my head around: "You guys kill someone already?"

Johnny was at the far end of the cabin, leaning over a wooden chair he employed as a walker, his hair curled in moisture. He'd managed to clean himself up before hobbling over here from the other cabin. Shirtless, Johnny wore knee-length blue and white basketball shorts and a single sneaker; his slender muscles flexed painfully as he limped up to the mule cart. He took a look inside and quietly blurted, "Oh my god. Is he really...?"

"Dead?" I prompted. "Not yet."

Like I said, it didn't take a genius to figure out what was up. Johnny's head twitched from side to side, his eyes shifting between my two faces. Comparing, computing. I shot him a cocky smirk; his dumbfounded expression immediately transformed into one of blinking comprehension.

"Kill a terrorist," I said pragmatically, "save my life. Couldn't ask for a better deal."

Johnny recoiled and began hemmin' and hawin', gripping and twisting his chair into the ground, his tongue contorted with the angst of a man forced to confess to a crime he didn't commit: "How do you know he's a terrorist?"

"Camacho says so," I said. "Which means Devo says so."

"Devo says so," Johnny repeated sourly. He gave Camacho a quick once over, as if to dismiss the Indian as Devo's collaborator, and asked me how we were gonna do it. "Blow him up in front of witnesses," I answered. "Give him the same treatment he and his kind give everyone else." Johnny looked horrified and insisted we couldn't just kill the guy. "Let's turn him in," he said.

I blinked at him stupidly, like he'd uttered an incomprehensible joke. "Like hell we'll turn him in," I retorted. "Turn yourself in. This man's good as dead."

"But that disguise won't work. We'll get busted."

I snorted a laugh, "Busted? You're worried about getting busted?!?" Johnny had risked jail time for far less in his marijuana business. "This operation is worth more than a million tons of weed. It'll save our lives. And Devo's not gonna get us busted, not after all he's done for us." I fixed him with an unyielding stare. "Gotta go with it Johnny. No choice."

"But he probably has a family, a wife, kids...a dog..."

"A dog?" I said scornfully. "Are you outta your cotton pickin' mind?"

Camacho eased himself into the conversation, in Spanish: "Muslims—Islamists—do not keep dogs." He had his foot atop a

490

wheel to the cart, arms rested on a knee, a look of passive levity on his face, like watching children at play. "Dogs and pigs are the lowest of creatures in Islam. Islamists keep many wives but no dogs."

Camacho's Spanish was precise but held a peculiar accent, a halting hiss I attributed to the influence of an Indian dialect. I idly wondered how much English he spoke or understood and leapt at the opportunity to needle Johnny with an embellished translation of his words:

"Camacho says Islamos don't keep dogs, Johnny. Lots of wives so they've no need for dogs. How do ya like that?" My wild, mocking eyes skewered him. "Dogs are against their religion, and so are you. And they'll have you enslaved and killed like a dog once shariah law is implemented."

Johnny scowled at me crookedly. "You're crazed," he said. "Crazier now than when you clobbered those pigs in my hotel."

"And you're lucky I did clobber 'em."

"Sure. But this guy—"

I interrupted in a menacing tone: "It's kill or be killed, Johnny. My life is at stake, and so is yours. Puss out and we'll end up dead."

Johnny was momentarily dazed. He looked down distractedly upon Ahmed. "He's bleeding through his bandage," he said. "Why the hell bother dressing that wound in his chest if you're just gonna kill him?"

Camacho's Spanish was bland, unaffected: "Because we need him alive, for now."

Johnny frowned at Camacho's Spanish. In English I asked Camacho if he spoke English. He replied with a small shrug. Johnny shook his head blackly over his chair and limped away. His knowledge of the crime (as he saw it) made him an accessory. Worry lines wrinkled his brow, aging his boyish factions.

I wasn't about to let his guilt infect me. I saw things differently. Much differently! But Johnny's concern for our victim did set me thinking: "What about innocent bystanders, Camacho? Will anyone else be hurt by the blast?"

"The vest our sin madre terrorista will be wearing is rigged to *implode* instead of explode." Camacho offered me a firm nod, "A consideration to humanity. Little will be left of him and he will be the only casualty."

I muttered, *"Implode...?"* Camacho blinked languidly at me, like I must have understood what he was talking about...and in a couple of heartbeats, I did. Unlike the *exploding* bombs fanatical Islamists like Ahmed strap to everyone from their own children to mental cases, abused women and the religiously insane, this *imploding* bomb was

491

not designed to kill as many as possible but only... "*Russell Martell*," I reaffirmed, "will be the only casualty?"

Camacho sharpened his gaze upon me. "Sí."

Incredible. I wanted to hear all about the scheme: how did an imploding vest work exactly? where would "Russell Martell" meet his end? who were the witnesses that would identify him? and... "Do we have something more than this disguise to fool police and witnesses? Have you a false passport for him, something to plant in the pickup that will identify this guy as Russell Martell?"

A shrewd smile creased Camacho's lips. "I have told you all you need to know, for now," he said. "Just follow Devo's instructions."

"We will," I assured him with conviction. I stared back at Johnny, sitting in his chair, his ankle elevated on the chopping block at the foot of the porch, arms crossed mulishly. He looked to be stewing over an unjust sentence handed down by the judge, pondering an assault on his jail keepers. I drew close to him, squatted by his side, and let the silky voice of reason try to bring him around: "Do you have another solution? The longer I'm at large, *we're* at large, and the longer we remain stuck here, the more deadly our position becomes."

Johnny stared at me abruptly, and hesitated for a second to dull his irritation. "Maybe if we turn him in we'll get off. We can't just—"

"Turn him in? That's just plumb loco, hombre. Those cops'll blast us new assholes. Take my word for it. I faced 'em twice yesterday and I'll be damned if I'm gonna risk facin' 'em again today, or ever again, 'less I'm sure of killin' 'em."

"Devo said he'd be back before noon. Let's wait for him. See what he says." Johnny shot a furtive glance at Camacho. "Doncha think Devo woulda mentioned this Indian last night if we were expected to be his accomplices?"

"Maybe." I twisted my head around at Camacho. He was covering my double with a ratty brown blanket, dedicating himself to the winning game plan as if the *real* Russell Martell could be left out of it. "And maybe not."

Johnny's expression turned bitter, accusatory.

"Look," I said. "We gotta forget our mistakes and screw-ups—"

"*Our* mistakes and screw-ups?"

"*Any and all* mistakes and screw-ups. We can't dwell on them when there's a job to do, a way outta this mess." I took a knee. "Listen. There's not gonna be a big explosion. The terrorist is the only one who's gonna get it. Witnesses will identify me inside a pickup but he'll end up fried beyond recognition. So federales and cops are liable to think I was killed for days, weeks even, at least until they get results from a DNA test. This is our chance to make a clean getaway. Now's not the time to choke."

Johnny snorted at the word "choke". He took a fix on his ankle, hideously swollen and banded in pink and purple. Lumpy and deformed. Johnny knows how to nurse an injury but, unlike me (broken ribs, torn hamstring), had never been laid up for an extended period. Johnny's blessed with a pliable body and the lithe, muscular legs of a track athlete—800 meter man or long jumper—that rarely if ever let him down. But now, just when he needed his legs most, to run for his life and stay ahead of the law, he had an overripe mango for a right ankle.

Johnny's nostrils dilated, broadening the gentle arc of his nose; the corners of his eyes and mouth twitched with resentment. He stared at me, and his expression seemed to soften. "Last night I called you a hero," he said.

The memory elicited a smile from me. "This is war, a time for heroes." I stood from him. "Goddamn coppers nearly killed both of us yesterday. And terrorists would've killed you at the Washington had you showed for your fishing trip or spent the morning doing Gail in her room. Might not get so lucky next time."

Johnny bristled. "Look Russ, I'll do whatever it takes to save us. But don't gimme that crap about not bein' so lucky next time. The chances of me seeing another disaster like the one yesterday are slim to none."

A word lathered on my tongue, *"Disaster?* It was a terror attack and you know it, Johnny."

"Whatever. Still never happen anywheres near me again."

"Oh, that's a good one. Brilliant. *Never happen anywhere near me. It's a statistical rarity!* Americans on the mainland shoulda used that logic after Pearl Harbor in 1941. One hell of an excuse for complacency and cowardice."

"You at Washington yesterday?"

Johnny started at the polite, uncomfortable question. Camacho's broken English. Johnny crossed his injured ankle over a knee and placed a protective hand over it. "Yeah," he said. "We both were. Missed the explosion though, luckily."

Camacho had a seat on the porch steps and looped his silver-streaked hair behind his ears. "That nothing. Much worse come soon in your country."

I shifted my weight from foot to foot. Johnny gulped so loud I heard him. Somehow Camacho's easy demeanor added veracity to his auguring words. If I had said the same, Johnny probably would've brushed me off with a snide remark about fear mongering, how only pussies succumb to it or something. But coming from a mild-mannered stranger, and an Indian no less, lent the prediction an exotic truth, like reading Confucius or the Talmud. Johnny's semblance immediately altered, assuming a palsied, stricken cast. Ashen. I was overcome by a foreboding chill—images of wounded ghosts in bloodied masks...their tormented cries. The chalky, putrid stench of death and desolation. Camacho's words rang true, were self-evident in my view given the nature of the enemy. Yet the certainty he brought to them was frightening, terrifying... I wished he wasn't telling the truth.

"How do you know?" I said to him, noting that his grim prediction hadn't altered his expression—the smiling glint in his dark eyes.

"Conozco el enemigo...I know enemy, study them. Speak language."

"You speak their language? What? Arabic?"

"And Farsi." Camacho stood off the porch steps, knitted his fingers and stretched his arms overhead with a reach well beyond a man of his small frame. I heard his knuckles crack and saw that he was double-jointed at both the elbows and wrists, his hands and arms forming warped V-shapes that pained my testicles to look at. He brought his arms to his sides with sinewy grace, disciplined blood pumping the vascular cords standing out against a thin layer of skin. I was reminded of his backlit silhouette when he entered the bedroom in the cabin, shears in hand, an ancient warrior come for his retribution. Viscerally, I comprehended that Camacho's pleasant, unassuming demeanor and diminutive size were not to be taken for granted. He looked to be in terrific shape, body fat of a flyweight prizefighter—three percent, thereabouts. His tank top revealed a hard and corded physique. And he was, evidently, a highly trusted confidant of Devo's, a man who had demonstrated some amazing skills... What Camacho lacked in size he made up for in stature, strength and agility. Knowledge. He was not a man to be trifled with.

Johnny must have sensed the same thing and modulated his tone in a show of respect: "Where in Mexico are you from, Camacho?"

"Tepito. Born in Lebanon."

Johnny arched his eyebrows. "The Middle East?"

"Sí."

Camacho's hardened gaze stifled the gaggle of questions forming in my brain. My voice cracked and, before I could utter another sound, he answered my most pressing query, in brusque Spanish, his first hint of impatience. "The enemy will likely strike your country by the winter solstice," he said with a glance at the mules grazing out beyond the horse stall. "Now, we must prepare the mules so I can deliver this puta madre terrorista to his destiny."

95

PEDRO down shifted and kicked up gravel as he skid to a stop along the backside of the Pemex gas station below the road to Mismaloya and Melaque—La Carretera a Barra de Navidad. He flipped up the tinted visor to his helmet and spied the target car waiting at the roadblock fifty meters away—a red Volkswagen Jetta with Media Minister Lazarito Charlado at the helm and that mystery man who'd visited The Bureau this morning in the passenger seat. Pedro had seen the mystery man park his gray Chrysler Le Baron down the street from The Bureau, double back on foot, and get buzzed in. Was he a source for Lazarito's story this morning? Did the two of them hold the key to papi's whereabouts? If not, they could be headed for a rendezvous with someone somewhere who might. And there was another car to think about. Lieutenant Romero's brown Cutlass to the rear of the line. He had the mayor and Gloria with him. Lazarito and his partner would not recognize Pedro on his motorbike but they would. This was Pedro's first stakeout and tail and it was shaping up to be a tricky one—tail a car tailing the target car. There didn't appear to be yet another tail but one thing was certain: the Media Minister had attracted a lot of attention with his story this morning.

Pedro considered joining forces with those in the Cutlass, calling Gloria and making his presence known. But no. Then he'd have to follow their orders. Lieutenant Romero, Gloria, and the mayor were most likely after Lazarito's sources for his story, and Pedro was after more than that. He had to find papi. What if they ordered him to stand down at a crucial moment, when an informant appeared who he wanted to tail? He couldn't afford to take that chance.

Random vehicles were being searched at the roadblock for arms and suspicious incendiary materials (and Russell Martell hidden in a trunk); drivers and passengers without identification were given special attention. Overall, traffic moved along in an orderly fashion. The Media Minister's car probably wouldn't be searched, and everyone in Lieutenant Romero's car had the authority to pass through the roadblock without delay. When the time was right, Pedro would shoot to the front of the line on his motorbike and present his police identification, which would get him waved on through as well.

SEVE VERDAD

He removed a glove, retrieved his cell phone at his belt, and texted his brother Alejandro: *sur hacia mismal.*

South towards Mismaloya.

AFTER about five minutes on the winding road, Pedro had a stroke of luck. A black Ford Expedition exited Dreams Hotel and kept a good pace four cars behind the lieutenant's. The SUV's bulk provided excellent cover and he tucked himself behind it. Every now and then he caught a glimpse of the lieutenant's Cutlass, and even the Media Minister's red Volkswagen sedan rounding bends in the distance. Pedro's Honda 250 could catch Lazarito in no time on this narrow twisting highway. If Pedro didn't have that Cutlass—Lieutenant Romero, Gloria and the mayor—to contend with, he would close the gap. What he needed now was for the Lieutenant to get a flat tire, or have a breakdown... Pedro indulged the fantasy, imagined himself executing a one-man sting operation. He'd sneak up on the Media Minister when he reached his destination and confront him and his informants...speak casually with them on the beach, and when they refused to share their information, he'd manhandle the frumpy Media Minister, stick his gun to his head and demand that they divulge where Enrique Santos was. If they still refused, Pedro would start shooting, blow out kneecaps and elbows until they begged for mercy and gave up everything they knew about his father's disappearance...the Arena Vallarta fire...the Washington...and Russell Martell.

That's the way Mike Hammer would handle it if *his* father's life were at stake, wouldn't he? So why not Pedro Santos?

Pedro eased off the gas. His speed seemed to increase in proportion to his aggression; the last thing he needed was to rear end that SUV and dump his bike, maybe fly over the shoreline cliffs to his right or die in a head-on collision to his left. Pedro rolled his shoulders, loosened up a bit and cooled his young blood. He knew his limitations. He wasn't cut out for violence and brutality. Best to attack this case more like Sherlock Holmes than Mike Hammer, kind of like Belascorán Shayne. This furious sense of urgency cluttered his mind and was bound to leave him prone to mistakes if he didn't contain it. Besides, the Media Minister and his sources might not know anything at all about papi's disappearance. Pedro reminded himself that his job was simply to gather information and keep his big brother informed, so they could coordinate their efforts if and when action needed to be taken.

But what might that action entail?

Pedro was a decent shot with his Glock, practiced with it once or twice a month. Kept it clean and locked in its case. But he rarely if ever got any fieldwork; if he had to draw his gun today, pull it from its holster at the small of his back, it would be the first time with the intention of using it against another human being. Big trouble if he had to do that. You don't brandish a weapon unless you're willing to use it. Pedro was willing, but also determined to only draw his pistol as a last resort—his ultimate defense. It would mean that Lazarito had led him into danger, to a dangerous informant or, perhaps, to Russell Martell or even the assassin himself.

Papi didn't believe Russell Martell to be a terrorist "or anything of the kind." Yet the gringo had to be considered armed and dangerous. *Someone* had sprung him from jail...and someone blew the Washington...and someone, it seemed, had set Arena Vallarta ablaze. There were an awful lot of *someones* around bent on murder and mayhem and it sure looked like Russell Martell was linked to them somehow. And one of those someones could be an informant for the Media Minister. It was entirely possible that Pedro would find himself in need of a weapon.

He settled into the rhythm of the ride, the revs of his motorbike and the curves in the road. Pedro kept his eyes on the road—the SUV in front of him and the Lieutenant's Cutlass coming into view every now and then up ahead—but he also took care to regularly glance through his mirrors, just in case another tail appeared—one of the mayor's cars...or maybe an unmarked police car or pickup...or...

A gray sedan a few cars back. Pedro swerved as he looked through his mirror again. A car resembling the Chrysler Le Baron Lazarito's mystery guest had arrived in at The Bureau was back there. Might the mystery man also have a mystery partner, someone charged with guarding the Media Minister's rear?

Pedro battled nervous tension—a fidgety tightness in his legs and back. He felt boxed in, like he was driving the target vehicle others were homing in on. He needed to protect himself. As the ocean to his right faded from view behind the northern expanse of Hotel La Joya de Mismaloya, its condos and apartments, Pedro came up with a plan of action. The main body of the hotel and its parking lot were coming up on his right, down this grade, about sixty meters away. He'd simply pull into the parking lot and let that gray car pass. If it was the Le Baron, he'd tail it, if not he could quickly make up the distance lost on his bike and tuck himself back behind this SUV again.

The Ford Expedition in front of him slowed. Pedro drifted to the right for a look past it. What he saw was so startling he forgot he was driving. A brake light flashed in his eye. The Ford he was following came to an abrupt stop. Pedro slammed on his brakes and leaned into a shuddering, sideways skid. He righted himself inches from the Ford's bumper. He leaned over his bike and stared around the SUV in absorbed fascination at the truck about to cross the street from the hotel's parking lot. Was it? Could it be? Papi's truck! That was papi's three-quarter-ton Dodge pickup! He recognized the color—black turned dirty gray from yesterday's work—as well as the mag wheels, and the tool chest exposed above the bed. A woman, or was that a boy in a black billcap and sunglasses behind the wheel? What was he, she doing with papi's truck?!? The lieutenant's Cutlass made a right and pulled past papi's truck into the parking lot. Lazarito must have pulled in as well. Did the lieutenant miss papi's truck? Wasn't he on the lookout for it? Maybe he didn't recognize the truck, filthy as it was. Pedro gunned his motor and fish-tailed the rear end of his bike to spin out from the stalled SUV blocking his way. Before he could gain traction the SUV lurched backwards, clipped his bike, and sent him sprawling on the pavement.

His gloved hands broke his fall. Pedro popped to his feet, his curses reverberating inside his helmet. Across the street, papi's truck eased onto the dirt road towards the pueblo of Mismaloya. Pedro might have been able to make a break for it, take a running leap into the bed of the truck, pull his pistol, and commandeer the vehicle, but a car obstructed him. That gray Le Baron had nosed up to the SUV. Pedro glimpsed the driver's reflective sunglasses and mean mouth. He scrambled for his bike. Through a panicked frenzy he heard impatient traffic horns and the passenger door to the SUV open. Pedro furiously calculated an escape route, righted his bike, and found he had nowhere to go. An iron grip around his arm and the blunt thrust of steel—the barrel of a gun to his back—froze him in place.

"Has venido suficiente lejos, hombre," said a raspy voice. You have come far enough.

***

ENRIQUE'S truck may have been filthy dirty—covered in that infernal Washington dust and grime—but the main reason the lieutenant, Gloria and the mayor missed seeing it was the poignant, gruesome discussion they were having as they tailed Lazarito. A discussion about a ripped throat.

"According to Officer Hernando Talla," said Lieutenant Romero, "the body was buried from view in the hibiscus garden, like it had been hurled from a balcony or the roof of the hotel. Or dropped from an aircraft. He said it resembled something out of a horror movie.

498

Joaquín was nearly decapitated, his throat shredded by what appeared to be a wild animal."

Gloria's stomach turned at the imagery. "Our CISEN man, Alfredo Flores, described something similar in Lazarito's office."

Juan's voice spiked, "And there were no signs of a struggle?" A shadow of fear flickered across his mien. This was the first he'd heard about what had to be the most shocking single murder in the history of Vallarta, all the more shocking because the victim was a highly trained CISEN operative. If Joaquín could be killed without a struggle, what was to protect any of them from a similar fate?

"No signs of a struggle...no." The lieutenant glanced at the black SUV coming into view again through his rearview mirror. "As I mentioned, Hernando was at a loss to explain it. But he did say that those DF federales as well as CISEN had arrived at Casa Mexicana this morning. They may have uncovered some clues by now. If that black SUV behind us is the same car el comandante reserved for CISEN, we may have an opportunity to ask them."

Gloria said, "Lazarito is turning into La Joya's parking lot."

"I see him," replied the lieutenant.

Juan stared out the rear window at the black SUV. "Do you think CISEN is tailing us?... Looks like the SUV has come to a stop."

"Sí," said the lieutenant.

Gloria shuddered, the image of a dead man's shredded throat invading her mind's eye. Juan shifted uneasily in his seat, that same image in his own mind's eye, and forced a note of calm into his shaken tone: "If El Gringo Terrorista is responsible for Joaquín's death, he must be a highly trained killer."

Lieutenant Romero veered for the far end of the hotel's parking lot, to keep some distance between them and Lazarito's sedan. Gloria glanced at her husband and shook her head imperceptibly, mildly miffed at Juan's employment of the words "Gringo Terrorista." The question of Russell Martell's guilt or innocence had been something of a sore spot between them since they were finally able to put their heads together at home this morning. Juan was all but convinced he was guilty of terrorism, arson, the murder of the Iranian, and the attack on the two police officers at Hotel Marciano, and couldn't understand why Gloria remained so guarded on the subject. Gloria wasn't entirely certain herself, beyond the reasonable doubts Pedro and Enrique had expressed, as well as Sandra, once she came up with her profile of Russell Martell. And when Gloria remarked that the perpetrator of the attack on the Washington would not be so stupid as to risk exposure and arrest at the scene of his own crime, it rang hollow with Juan. After all, Russell Martell had escaped from jail. He was still at large and, since his escape, two officers had been bludgeoned nearly to death and Arena Vallarta burned to the ground. The proprietors of Hotel Marciano didn't recognize Russell Martell from his photo but had given police a description of him that more or less matched the lieutenant's and proved useful for an artist's rendition of the gringo. Ultimately, Juan couldn't help but agree with Gloria's argument to "leave no stone unturned and not jump to conclusions." Yet his usage of the term "Gringo Terrorista" indicated that the death of CISEN's Joaquín de Jesús had him jumping to conclusions once again.

Lieutenant Romero backed his Cutlass into a parking spot under a tree by the riverbank. Lazarito's car was parked about twenty meters from the entrance to the hotel, forty meters or so away from them.

"They are not getting out of the car," Gloria observed.

The lieutenant reached for the pack of cigarettes in his breast pocket. "Patience. They may be waiting for someone."

"Interesting," Juan mused, "how Russell Martell has not used a firearm. And neither did his accomplices who sprang him from jail. We cannot count on that remaining the case, of course. And indications are that he used some sort of weapon to bludgeon Paulo and Raúl in Hotel Marciano. Unfortunately, neither remembers a damn thing."

Gloria bit her tongue, unwilling to relive the question of Russell Martell's guilt or innocence with her husband here in Benito's car. So she swerved the subject: "Sandra has yet to turn up anything on the man staying in that room at El Marciano; the name given police by the proprietor was John Milas."

"Russell Martell is a smart hijo de puta," said Juan. "I give him that. He removed his friend's file from the records so we cannot yet verify if John Milas is the correct name."

The lieutenant snorted an angry stream of smoke out his window. They'd already discussed the police fiasco at Hotel Marciano while on the road, as well as Russell Martell's audacity and intelligence. The subjects were grating on him... The mere idea of two armed police officers getting physically overwhelmed in a hotel room like that infuriated him. Yet the memory of how the mayor dressed him down for Russell Martell's jailbreak when Paulo was the one in charge at police headquarters at the time mitigated his fury, allowed for idle musings about Paulo's facial injuries improving his looks. They certainly couldn't hurt.

Lieutenant Romero rolled his jaw, heavy rancor hanging on his features. That Gringo Terrorista wasn't as smart as he thought and would meet his end at the point of a gun, the lieutenant's gun.

An ocean breeze coaxed its way into the car. Gloria faced it through her open window. "How long are Lazarito and our CISEN man just going to sit there?" she wondered out loud.

Juan leaned in from the backseat. "They must be awaiting further instructions—a phone call or something. Maybe one of us should circle around to the beach, enter the hotel and—" He was going to suggest "stakeout the lobby" but halted in mid-sentence to cast a wary eye at a gray Le Baron coasting through the parking lot, heading their way. The driver accelerated a tad and came to a stop just off the lieutenant's front bumper.

Gloria muttered, "Qué diablos?"

Lieutenant Romero dropped his cigarette out the window. "CISEN," he said. "Señor Tórrez. I met him at headquarters this morning."

"Let me handle this," said Juan, a twinge of anger quickening his pulse. "CISEN has no authority over us."

Gloria shook her head, a sigh of resignation escaping her lungs. "They may or may not have authority over us, Juan. But stay cool. At the very least we will have to work with them now."

Señor Tórrez stepped out of the car and strolled up to the Lieutenant's Cutlass. A stocky fellow with a short, sloping forehead, shiny black hair, a flat nose, and thick pylon forearms bulging out the rolled-up sleeves of his dress shirt. Juan judged him to be just shy of thirty years old, though the reflective sunglasses hiding his eyes made it difficult to tell. A CISEN enforcer perhaps, on his way up the ranks.

Tórrez stood before Juan's open window and extended a stubby-fingered hand. "Señor Velázquez?" he said, his oily voice dripping with feigned respect.

"Sí?" Juan gave the hand a quick shake, mindful that this youngster's air of superiority was part and parcel of the CISEN mentality.

"A pleasure to meet you, Señor Mayor. Rodrigo Tórrez, CISEN." Tórrez recognized Lieutenant Romero with a nodded "Teniente" and extended his stubby fingers once again, this time to Gloria. "And you must be Señora Infante Velázquez."

Gloria gripped the hand firmly enough to sense its solid contours. "What can we do for you?"

Tórrez sucked his beefy lips between his teeth, pulled a wallet from his front pocket and flipped it open. "Does this man work for you?"

Juan accepted the wallet. He frowned at the Puerto Vallarta Police ID and badge, passed the wallet to Gloria, and shot Tórrez an authoritative glare. "What is this all about?"

Tórrez answered the mayor's question tight mouthed: "I believe you already know what most of this is about, señor. But for now, we just want to confirm that Pedro Santos is a member of the police department."

Lieutenant Romero looked up from the wallet in Gloria's hand and grunted under his breath. "He is."

Gloria grit her teeth, determined to follow her own advice about keeping cool. "Since you have his wallet, I assume you have him in custody, Señor Tórrez?"

"At the moment," said Tórrez, "he is sitting peacefully inside our SUV a kilometer or so from here. Just outside of Mismaloya. Handcuffed but peaceful. The young man was on the verge of interfering with a CISEN investigation."

The lieutenant mumbled, "Híjole," and Juan, "Dios mío."

Gloria choked down a throe of anger. "You will release him at once."

"I am afraid not, señora," Tórrez said, his tone subtly patronizing. "But I am authorized to invite you," he swept his gaze over the three of them, "all of you to join Pedro and us in our SUV. As you can see, CISEN has this operation totally under control, and we plan to keep it that way."

96

"**WONDER** how much life the battery has," I said.

Johnny helped himself to a slice of smoked dorado off the paper plate at his side. "Devo programmed the computer to boot automatically, so I'm sure he'll be back before the battery dies."

We were back in our cabin. Johnny was in bed, his head propped up on a couple of pillows, injured ankle wrapped in a cold compress and elevated on another, his left knee drawn up to support the laptop computer angled over his waist. I had a good view of the Toshiba's 14-inch screen from my chair off his shoulder. "Sharp picture," I said. "But what is this, a geography lesson?"

The computer screen was divided into three panels—Mexico on the left, British Columbia on the right, and the USA in the middle. "If Devo's got a plan to kill your double, he has more on his mind than geography."

"Not just my double, Johnny, but a terrorist. I think Devo knows exactly who the terrorists are who blew the Washington and we're about to kill one of them."

Johnny appraised me with a cynical scowl. "That's convenient," he said, "since you're all for killing the guy. But you ever stop and really think about what it means if Devo knows *who the terrorists are?*"

"The *full* implication? I think so. Devo mighta known the attack on the Washington was coming."

"So why the hell didn't he stop it?"

"I'm not sure."

Johnny huffed, "You're not sure? That's just great, Russ. Tell me you've thought about this more than that."

"Look, I know where you're goin' with this. But if Devo was a bloodthirsty terrorist we'd be dead, or I would be. I don't know who he is or what motivates him but just because he knows who the terrorists are doesn't necessarily make him one."

"We don't know much about him, I'll grant you that." Johnny clicked on British Columbia. The computer revealed a map of Vancouver and English Bay in the upper left-hand corner. Three other panels contained photos of hotels, the names and locations clearly notated. "Always wanted to go to Whistler" Johnny said. "Look at those mountains." He clicked on the Pan Pacific Hotel. A denied-entry box popped up. "Shit. That's the fourth time."

"Really?"

"Yeah. But when I clicked on a blue tongue marked *don't visit me*, it opened."

"Don't visit me?"

"Yeah."

"So you visited." I helped myself to some dorado.

"We're in the icon right now."

"I see... Interesting. Maybe you flunked a test."

"A test?"

I shrugged and took a slug of water. "To see how trustworthy we are. You opened an icon that said *don't visit me.*"

Johnny rolled his eyes at me. "Yeah, right. A test. Devo already thinks we're trustworthy enough to spring you from jail and spirit us both through a roadblock and outta Vallarta to this ranch. And now it looks like he's got a plan to kill your double to keep the cops off our trail."

I shook my head in awe. "Incredible. Heard about those kind of guys, you know?"

Johnny clicked back to the three maps. "What? Like Special-Ops or somethin'?"

"Yeah... A Special-Ops Magician. A Delta-Force Wizard. You've seen some of his magic tricks, but he does impressions and impersonations too. Noticed the different accents he uses? His Spanish and Portuguese are flawless. Probably speaks several languages fluently. The Multilingual Navy-Seal Illusionist...or somethin'."

"Good one, Russ." Johnny clicked on Mexico. The map filled the screen. "But why the hell would a guy like that give a shit about us? It's not like we're good friends or family."

"Last night he said my place as a warrior would be with a pen instead of a sword."

Johnny had the arrow on the screen pointed at Puerto Vallarta. He paused and smirked at me. "A warrior...with a pen?"

"To help fight the Islamisalaamis and destructive forces in a violent world."

"Destructive forces in a violent world?" Johnny screwed up his face, like the words were incoherent gibberish. "When did Devo say that?"

"While you were snoozin' in the back of the Jeep last night."

"You're gonna be a warrior with a pen? So what the hell does that make me? an accident along for the ride?"

"You had an accident, but I don't think you *are* an accident. He had that paperwork prepared for us to pass through the roadblock. And looks like he had this cabin here ready for two."

Johnny ran the back of his hand over the sparse stubble trimming his jaw. "You know," he said, "having that paperwork to show those federales at the roadblock last night was smooth. And he's got access to this ranch. The guy's well prepared, that's for sure...but for what?"

"We gotta stick with him. Besides, where else we gonna turn?"

"Dunno. But he left us this computer for some reason. Maybe it'll give us a clue as to what the hell he expects from us." Johnny clicked on Puerto Vallarta. The screen divided into four panels. "There's the Washington."

"I see it," I said. "Before the attack."

"Before the attack." Johnny was now apparently convinced that the Washington had been bombed.

"And the Holiday Inn," I added, "Marriot, Alta Sierra."

He clicked the Washington. It shimmered like a 3-D holograph. A shiver singed the back of my neck. Johnny was agog, spaniel eyes wide as shot glasses. "What the hell is this, Russ?"

I slid off my chair and kneeled next to his bed. "Looks like Middle Eastern writing. Arabic or Farsi. Scroll down."

Johnny scrolled to a map of the streets leading to the Washington; more writing, and a floor plan of the hotel. He lowered his voice, "This Devo's computer?"

"Funny how we don't know for sure."

The heavy sound of hooves lifted our gazes to the front door. I jumped to my feet and looked out the window. "Devo," I said.

97

Cᴵˢᴱᴺ Senior Operative Alfredo Flores could think of only one reason why Araceli had not told Lazarito to make sure he was alone when he met her at Restaurante La Flor de Mismaloya. "Naïveté," he said. "The girl has little idea of the position she has put herself in by offering you information on Russell Martell."

Lazarito eased his Volkswagen sedan onto the dirt road leading to the village of Mismaloya. "Indeed. As I recall, from our brief encounters, she is the picture of innocence."

"But we cannot assume she is a fool." Flores grunted sharply, "Araceli must have seen your story this morning and recognized her fax to you as a primary source...though we may assume she is not entirely aware of the stir you have caused in law enforcement and intelligence circles."

A wry smile played over Lazarito's fleshy face as he veered down towards the pueblito. "Apparently, she has little confidence in our bungling police force. The girl must hope that by imparting information to me," Lazarito gave Flores a respectful nod, "competent people will take over the case and capture or kill El Gringo Terrorista."

Flores stared out his window down at the river snaking into view through the mangroves, mulling over his strategy to take Araceli into custody as a material witness to the crimes of Russell Martell. "Araceli could be more sagacious than she lets on. She may not have mentioned anything of the sort to you over the phone but perhaps she expects you to bring along someone like me to the meeting, and might bring along someone herself, or have them waiting in the wings."

Lazarito wheezed nervously as he rounded a rutted bend in the road. Flores gestured up ahead, to a wide circular pull-out across the street from Hotel Iguana on the outskirts of town. "Pull up under that tree on the right," he ordered, "behind the SUV."

Lazarito stopped astride the rear end of the black Ford Expedition parked between a gray Le Baron and a motorbike. Flores fingered the Media Minister's shirt, directly below the bug he was wearing under his collar. "I will be listening," Flores said. "And watching. When the time is right, expect me to join you...and Araceli."

The Media Minister sucked beads of sweat from his upper lip. "I hope you are not planning any violence. I am sure Araceli will cooperate with CISEN."

"CISEN," Flores said quietly, "always acts in accordance with the circumstances."

98

I stepped outside and called out to Devo: "How's Brenda?!?"

Devo gathered the reins. El Cid reared up with a whinny and cantered, Lucha close behind. "If I knew, I wouldn't tell you."

Devo was decked out in hiking boots, jeans, sunglasses and a black cowboy hat. The sleeves to his gray denim shirt were cut off at the shoulder. A Buck knife was holstered at his leather belt, a rifle at El Cid's flank. He seemed a mile high up there in that saddle. An American Tall Tale. Paul Bunyan's wayward cousin. He dismounted, a scintilla of green flashing from behind his shades. "Forget about Brenda. You got other things to think about, Martell. And should something go wrong, it's best that you know as little as possible about *anyone's* whereabouts."

"What could go wrong?"

"Very few plans work to perfection. But they can still work, if you're prepared." He slung the reins around the hitching post and tended to the backpack behind the saddle. Lucha nuzzled El Cid's rump. I patted the white star on the stud's nose. I hadn't gotten a good look at El Cid last night. A magnificent animal. Powerfully muscled, like something Michelangelo carved on. His red coat held a polished sheen, groomed for paparazzi. The horse was ready for the Derby. Sleek, strong and supple. He chomped at the bit, stomped, and raised his head from my hand. I considered the rifle, the stock end sticking out from its holster behind the saddle bags. "What're we huntin' today?"

Devo shouldered the backpack, his expression inscrutable. "Anything we like."

I followed him into the cabin. Devo said "mornin' " to Johnny lying on the bed and took a seat at the table. He dipped into his pack. "These yours, Martell?" He tossed me my swim trunks.

"Yeah."

"These yours too?" He held out the socks and shirt I'd also left at Mountain's.

"Sure are. Thanks." I tossed my clothes onto my futon. Johnny said, "Got my buds in your pack there?"

Devo pulled off his sunglasses and wrinkled his brow at him. "Your buds?"

"Had to ditch 'em last night. When we made off with that cop car."

Devo laid his shades on the table. He looked younger today, about my age, though his beard was nearly full, lending him a sage aspect well beyond my years. He pushed his hat off his forehead. "Sorry Johnny," he said. "I'm not quite that good." Devo gestured for the laptop on Johnny's bed. "You guys find something to keep yourselves occupied on that computer?"

I retrieved the computer and sat it on the table. Johnny said, "Sure did." He propped himself up on an elbow. "And we're not so sure we liked what we saw on that thing."

A southern drawl seeped into Devo's voice: "Ya ain't seen nothin' yet, compadre."

Johnny and I eyed each other, and I said what we were thinking: "Is that computer full of terror targets or what, Devo?"

Devo opened the laptop, his aquamarine eyes amused. *"Full of terror targets?* You make it sound like a piñata or somethin'. Try again. You know more about this computer than you think."

"Really? Like what?"

"Who it belongs to."

I frowned. "I'll give you a hint," he said. "It doesn't belong to me or your double we're about to fry." Devo made some shifts and clicks on the keypad and slid the laptop around so Johnny and I could see the screen. "Recognize anyone in this picture?"

I examined the image: a fiery protest. American flags raised in flames by hooded figures in black. A smattering of painted faces and misshapen masks. A colorful backdrop of green and pink balloons. A large sign with the red words *War Fucks* emblazoned on it.

Johnny dropped his head down on his pillow. "No one could recognize a soul in that mob," he said.

Devo's eyes glazed over in a tawny sheen. "Un-huh. But you do know a few of those characters." He turned the computer from us. "One in particular I'm interested in: Billy Lopper."

"Billy Lopper?" I stared at Johnny. "Haven't I hearda him?"

Johnny's face grew taught. "Yeah. He's a grower. Sorta. Don't see him a whole lot anymore since he...uh...lost touch with Mother Nature."

He shifted his gaze between me and Devo, like he knew we both understood. Johnny had always made it clear to me that the cultivation of marijuana wasn't just about money or the *outlaw cowboy* thrill of it all. Not for him. "Corrupt government and corporate despots" were responsible for making marijuana illegal in the first place and if he had his way it would be *re-legalized*, which set him apart from smugglers and many growers who supported drug and marijuana prohibition to keep their profits up. Above all Johnny saw himself as a caretaker of the timeless union between Mother Nature and "The Mother Herb"— an herb with profound medicinal as well as industrial properties. "Mother Nature and her herbs are next to godliness," he'd often expound. This was "the grower's covenant." One visit to Johnny's magnificent blooming garden reaching for a full harvest moon made me a believer.

Evidently, Billy Lopper had broken the covenant, disrespected Mother Nature. I wasn't sure how (perhaps by ripping off someone's plants or straying from the cultivation of herbs and polluting the land with crystal-meth poisons) but Johnny's blighted expression made clear that he had. "You met him once or twice, Russ," he said. "In Santa Cruz." Johnny's eyes darted to Devo. "What the hell does Billy have to do with us? And how do *you* know him?"

"Billy and I have never met," Devo said. "But I do know quite a bit about him. Northern California's pot-farming community isn't exactly cloistered." Devo folded his hands on the table, like an executive, and added a singsong quality to his voice: "Managed to let Billy think he learned a little about me when I was there..."

"Like that story about you growin' dope on government land?" Johnny said incisively. "How the feds ripped you off?"

"Anything else?" Devo asked.

"You escaped," Johnny added, and eyed me. "Also heard you didn't give anyone up but had to fillet a pigeon, a canary bird."

"Is that story true, Devo?" I said, my tone neutral, like a good reporter's.

"It only has to be believable to have its intended impact."

I blew out a hard breath. "What impact? What the hell is this all about?"

Devo removed his hat. "Billy and his pals will avoid me like the plague." He dropped his hat upon his backpack.

Johnny and I nodded at one another as if to confirm a suspicion we'd always had. Devo made some more clicks and shifts on the keypad as he spoke: "The ulterior motives of activists like Billy are intertwined with those of other radicals, like your double we're about to fry, Martell." He showed us the computer screen again. This time I did recognize someone, not Billy Lopper but someone else. A graying long-haired professor. He stood tall on stage behind a podium, his block-like head and righteous jaw angled squarely over broad shoulders. He was flanked by followers in black and extended a fist towards dozens, perhaps hundreds of onlookers.

"Billy is motivated by the most unsophisticated of ideals," Devo said. "Anarchy."

Johnny was somber, as if burying the neighbor's dog. " 'Fraid so," he muttered at the computer screen. "He's more involved with those nuts every time I see him."

"Can you see Billy, Johnny?" Devo reached around the laptop and clicked without looking at the screen. The picture zoomed in on the row of figures behind and to the left of the professor. "How 'bout now?"

"Yeah that's him," Johnny said shortly, as if loath to identify a friend in a police lineup.

"Which?" I asked him.

"Right there in the middle. In black. Well, they're all in black... The black T-shirt with that upside down peace sign on it. Uh...long dark hair, scraggly beard..."

"Guess he looks familiar," I said. "But I definitely recognize that professor. He called the victims of 9/11 Brown Shirts. And he was in Pakistan a couple of weeks later, railing against America. If the US was half as fascist as he says, he'd be dead. Professor—"

"Dead," Devo interjected. "A good name for him. Professor Dead."

I was about to ask him what he meant by that but Johnny raised his voice. "Whaddaya mean *half* as fascist?" he flared. He propped himself back up on an elbow and spit his words at me like I'd pissed in his mouth or somethin': "We got more people in jail in the US than any country on earth, most of 'em for consensual, *victimless* crimes, drugs an' shit."

"Land of the free and the home of the incarcerated," Devo advanced agreeably.

Johnny remained focused on me and didn't acknowledge Devo's twist on the American national anthem. "Fascist American politicians invented drug laws to repo money and property...and people," he growled, "make us slaves to the State. Can't *legally* take my property if I rape and kill someone but they can if I grow herb on it...and without any *due process* at all... Everyone in jail for drugs is a political prisoner. Don' tell me who the fuckin' fascists are. I battle them daily."

Devo grinned, "A freedom fighter."

"You'd be shot for growin' dope in China, Johnny," I said dryly.

SEVE VERDAD

"That's a good one, Russ. Compare America to the commies—they're no different from fascists anyway. And we shoot and kill growers in the States too. Sheriffs shot three in the back in the Douglas County woods just over six months ago. Fascist pigs."

I blanched at the news. Devo raised his hands in a gesture for calm. "You'll get your shot at *Fascist America*, Johnny."

"I fight my battles my way. Not lookin' for a *shot* at nobody."

Devo chuckled, "Don't worry. You won't have to pull the trigger."

"Don't hafta pull the trigger to be an accessory to murder."

"Or a hero," Devo said.

I scratched an incoherent itch at the base of my skull. "What does this have to do with killing my double?"

"We'll get to that and be outta here by noon."

Johnny regarded Devo from beneath lowered eyelids, a pained look of resignation on his face. "What the hell you want from me, Devo?"

Devo's eyes acquired a hypnotic shade of green—metallic, like water pouring over mossy stones in a swift stream. "Just be yourself," he said, "then act in manners contrary to your nature. Part of infiltrate and doublecross."

Johnny screwed up his face. "Infiltrate and double-cross?"

"An old trick anarchists are mostly incapable of practicing." Devo eyeballed me. "The Islamisalaami enemy has mastered the art form though—pretend to assimilate into a culture as you secretly plan its destruction."

He reposed in his chair and spread his hands, as if offering a gift. "At this moment in time we find ourselves at a nexus where destructive forces in a violent world are all feeding off each other and propagating greater violence. And within these destructive forces, strong and weak alliances are formed." Devo leveled a cobalt stare at Johnny. "You'll find anarchists in that mix of destructive forces—comprendes, Johnny?"

Johnny flinched, his eyes tilted up in his head, cogitating.

"Yeah," he said finally. "I comprendo." Johnny sat up abruptly and planted his feet on the floor. "You're sayin' Billy connects me somehow to that Islamo you're fryin' today. And for gettin' me outta Mexico I'm supposta help you out back in the States...like maybe prepare for that attack Camacho said is comin' by infiltratin' and double-crossin' anarchists...whatever that means."

"Keeping tabs," Devo said. "And reporting."

FINDING DEVO

Johnny flashed me a terse smile and measured his words: "I'm havin' a hard time figuring who the scariest motherfucker is, Devo. The policía, Islamos, federales, anarchists, or *you.*"

Devo's visage grew rawboned, his eyes the color of burning gas, a yellow flame igniting the pupil. He rose from behind the table and unfolded his frame with deliberate care, as if his head would bust through the ceiling if he didn't control himself. I held my breath and shrank in my chair, my insides inching up against my ribs. The man looked seven-feet tall! Johnny retreated onto his back as Devo extended a jagged finger at him. "Right you are Johnny," he said, his voice a sonorous tide. "There are motherfuckers on all sides. Always been that way."

Devo rubbed his chin in a gesture of careful consideration, and rested his rear on the edge of the table.

"Genghis Kahn is one of my favorites," he said. The fire had gone from his eyes, replaced by a scholarly glow. "Can't think of a greater motherfucker." He cocked a brow at me. "Can you Martell?"

I felt an anxious twinge in my chest, like he was giving me a pop quiz I'd better not fail. "Greater—" I said haltingly. "Never heard him described quite that way. The guy was a terror though."

"To the West, he was the scourge of the earth. Black Death himself." Devo fixed on Johnny, his slack-jawed expression. "But Genghis was the greatest *hero* on earth to Mongols. Can you name a few similar characters, Johnny? Alexander the Great perhaps? Caesar? Napoleon?"

Johnny cleared his throat. "Heard of 'em," he croaked, and searched my face as if to ask, "Where the hell is Devo going with this?"

I had a good idea where this was going and aimed a tight smile at Devo. "Heroes and villains all."

Devo seemed to relax a notch. "And the Muslim evisceration and conquest of ancient Christian lands in the Middle East and North Africa?" he said, "the spread of Islam by force of arms throughout the Iberian Peninsula? the sacking of Jerusalem?"

"Terrifying to native inhabitants but—"

"Heroic to Muslims," Johnny interposed keenly.

"*Allah's will,*" Devo rejoined. "And Allah's will begat the crusades. Were Christian crusaders terrorists or avenging heroes?" Devo dropped his gaze, as though reflecting upon his own life.

I wondered how far he was willing to advance this theme: "Are you suggesting that 9/11 may have been a heroic historic step towards Islamic redemption and world domination rather than an act of terror?"

SEVE VERDAD

"Take your pick," he shrugged. "According to Professor Dead and a whole slew of others living right here in the West, America had it coming because America itself is a terrorist State."

Devo stood off the table and looked us over. "Thanks to the Islamisalaami motherfucker, destructive forces in a violent world were on display at the Washington yesterday. And that was but a taste of things to come." He circled the table and took his seat. "There are indeed motherfuckers on all sides," he stated flatly. "And today you both have an opportunity to choose *your* motherfucker."

A gentle breeze wafted through the windows and open door behind Devo. Johnny propped himself back up on an elbow to greet it, his brow set in a dauntless line. "But how do we know which motherfucker *you* are, Devo?" he said. "You've got a computer loaded with the floor plan of the Washington and a bunch of Arabic scribbling. Looks pretty incriminating to me."

Devo closed the laptop. "Who does this computer belong to, Martell?"

"Considering all that Middle Eastern writing we saw and the floor plan of the Washington, a terrorist."

"Which terrorist?"

"If it doesn't belong to my double we're about to fry, then..." My voice faded. I showed Devo the top of my head and considered my bare feet. The answer to his question was right there. I'd gotten the necessary information when my shoes were taken from me in The Chamber down at police headquarters. I stared at Johnny, his spaniel eyes questioning: how the hell can *you* possibly know who the computer belongs to? So I reminded him:

"Aside from my double, the only terrorist I've any personal knowledge of around here is the dead Iranian found at the marina on Saturday." I could feel Devo's eyes needling me, coaxing the obvious conclusion from me, a conclusion I had reached once before, while in my jail cell. My stomach clenched as the words came tumbling out, "Devo must have killed him."

Johnny's face went blank. The words didn't register for him. I stared at Devo, his passive expression, and felt encouraged. Nothing I said threatened him in any way. "You broke his neck," I advanced, "and made off with this computer."

Johnny gasped, "No shit."

Devo tilted his head to that and said nothing.

I glanced at Johnny for help. My next conclusion was something we'd touched on earlier, before Devo arrived this morning. But Johnny was stuck on Devo, regarding him as though he'd never seen him before, with both respect and fear, like a quarterback might size up a

512

ferocious new linebacker on the practice field—we better keep *that* man on *our* team.

Devo's eyes smiled at me knowingly. "Go ahead and tell us more, Martell," he said, a hint of irony seeping into his voice. "Don't worry. I won't take it personally."

"Well... I'm not sure if the computer exactly incriminates you but...it seems to contain information that you might have been able to use to prevent the bombing."

Devo proffered me an exasperated smirk. "You're missing the larger picture. After all," he showed me his open palms, "here we are."

"The reason I'm missing the larger picture is because I don't know what the hell you're about."

"What does the enemy want, Martell?"

"What do you mean?"

"You asked me why I was helping you guys out, remember? in the car last night?"

"Yeah..." I rifled through my memory, momentarily stumped. "You said...uh...well, can't remember exactly. If I find out what the enemy wants, I'll know what you want?"

"That's right. So what does the enemy want?"

"Power," Johnny interceded. "Just like all motherfuckers."

I started at Johnny's cocksure tone. "We're supposed to give Devo power? His motive for helping us is power? Seems to me he's got plenty of power as it is." I looked askance at Devo. A tingle of doubt tickled my temples. "Don't you Devo?"

Devo smiled, the same carefree smile I'd seen on Camacho's face. "Maybe," he said. "But that doesn't mean I can't lose it...in life as well as death."

I slouched into a question mark. "Lose it to whom? Islamisalaamis?"

"No one's immune to an attack like the one we saw yesterday, Martell. But we can battle the destructive forces that cause them."

I straightened my posture. "Do you have a network or something doing battle against Islamisalaamis and *destructive forces in a violent world?* a network you expect Johnny and me to join?"

Devo looked at me unblinking, like a crushing handshake. "Let's just say that if you and Johnny perform well for me today, you'll find it's in your best interests to do so later on as well."

My heart skipped a few beats, but my voice was steady: "Is that a threat?"

Devo chuckled mirthlessly. "A portrait, Martell," he said, slipping into a gangsterish, Jersey tone. "Jus' da waee tings woykes, da waee tings izz." He dipped his chin. "We have a common enemy. More than one."

"You make it sound like a mutually advantageous relationship."

Devo's eyes grew dark and lethargic, as though peering out from behind violet membranes.

A tenuous tremble crossed my shoulders; I shook off a spooky feeling. Devo seemed to brighten in response, his voice dull and matter-of-fact: "If a team isn't greater than the sum of its parts, it's not worth organizing."

Johnny mumbled, "Shit," like he didn't really mean it.

My emotions were viscous, thick yet fluid—oil and water. I couldn't get a grip on them. Helplessness was there, a feeling that my life was not my own, but also a growing resolve. What choice did Johnny and I have? If we were to get home we had to stick it out with Devo and risk whatever hold he might have over us later.

In order to stick it out with Devo however, I needed some reassurance, answers to some questions. One of those questions had been needling me since I first met him at Mountain's party: "Who are you, Devo? Who could possibly get away with all this?"

"Get away with what?" he said blandly.

"Most everything you've done the last couple of days."

"At the moment, I'm the man with your life in his hands."

"I know but—" *The Multi-lingual Navy-Seal Illusionist.* "You work for the government?"

My question produced a deep belly laugh from him. "What the hell you talkin' about?" he chortled. "You're a marked man, hombre...a ruthless terrorist. *El Gringo Terrorista.*"

"El Gringo Terrorista?"

"That's right. *El Gringo Terrorista.* It's all over the papers and TV. The most wanted man in the hemisphere. If CISEN or the CIA catches up with you you'll know, or be dead before you know it."

Cold fear fluttered through my chest. If Devo could save me from CISEN and the CIA, it didn't matter *who* he was. But what did he want in return? Johnny stirred uneasily in his bed. "Anything about me in the news this morning?"

"Not yet, Johnny. But that could change at any time. Follow my instructions and you'll be all right."

I shot Devo a sidelong glance. "Instructions that include infiltrating and double-crossing anarchists." My voice grew harsh with suspicion. "But what do you expect from me?"

Devo folded his hands on the table and gave me a critical look. "A cartoonist," he said, "who is also an exceptional photographer, will be in contact with you, to help you along. You *will* be available when the time is right."

"A cartoonist? You want me writing for the funny papers? or maybe composing captions to sketches of horned pigs in headscarves and turbans?"

Devo nodded thoughtfully, "If you like. But prose is more your style I think."

Johnny said, "Sketches of horned pigs in headscarves and turbans?"

Devo winked at him. "Russell Martell's idea of dehumanizing the enemy. A common practice in times of war." He scrutinized me. "Not bad, Martell. 'Human rights is a western concept inadmissible in Islam,' to quote Ayatollah Khomeini, so why not dehumanize Islamisalaamis? They certainly provide plenty of materiel in that regard."

Something dark crossed his mien, his eyes gray and flat, like stones. "But the destructive forces at work in this violent world consist of much more than Islamisalaamis. On our way up here last night, we touched on that subject as well, Martell. The cartoonist you're to meet will educate you further on the larger picture and help sharpen your prose. And maybe you'll also compose captions to sketches of horned pigs in headscarves and turbans as you suggest..." Devo smoothed his hands over the table. "It's a risky job, riskier than Johnny's. Islamos, and others, will probably put a price on your head. Writers and artists often run that risk. But you'll be protected. I'll see to it."

I stood from my chair with a small groan, "Christ," and turned my back on him. A grim anticipation of the future—the immediate and not so distant—had invaded my spirit. I slunk to the back window behind Johnny's bed as if to glimpse a simpler life that might be mine. The shower was out there. It might not make me feel like a new man but I sure could use one. Johnny said, "You'll see to it, huh Devo? Makin' it sound awful simple. But first you gotta get us outta here."

"Guess I'll have to come up with a pen name," I mused out the window.

"More like an alias," Devo said. I turned from the window. A pair of old canvas sneakers landed at my feet with a thump. "Might be a bit big for you, Martell. Got 'em from a neighbor, taller than you but not quite as burly."

Johnny said, "Got any more Vicodin, Devo? Sure could use some."

"Sure. And we'll have to wrap that ankle. You'll be ridin' solo this time."

A small pang creased my chest. There were only two horses. Why would *I* be riding double? Johnny was the one with the injured ankle. *He* rode double last night... "Why—?"

Devo quickly cut me off. "You'll be *hiking solo*, Martell," he said. "Through the woods upriver till your double is dead."

99

A coastal breeze refreshed the occupants in the Ford Expedition parked in the shade a kilometer or so west of the pueblo Mismaloya. Windows and the front doors had been left open to allow for ventilation. CISEN Senior Operative Alfredo Flores took his place in the passenger seat and swiveled the chair around. He smiled briefly at the four unfriendly faces in the back—Pedro and the lieutenant seated forward of the cargo bay, Gloria and Juan just forward of them.

Flores greeted the mayor first, "A pleasure, Señor Mayor," he said, "though I hoped we would meet in more comfortable quarters. Senior Operative Alfredo Flores, CISEN."

Juan shook his hand cordially but didn't bother hiding the dismay in his voice. "I expect a complete briefing of your operation, Señor Flores," he said. "We all do."

Flores wrinkled his brow at Tórrez beside him in the driver's seat. Tórrez put a hand to his earpiece and pointed a pencil at the GPS map before the dash. "Rivera is in position across the street," he said, the tip of his pencil moving between red dots. "Lazarito is pulling up to the restaurant. Still awaiting word from Blanco. On the map, he looks to be in position."

Flores removed his sunglasses and offered Juan an imperative gaze. "You will be allowed pertinent information, Señor Mayor." Flores nodded to the other occupants in the vehicle. "Señora Infante Velázquez," he said, "Lieutenant Romero," and with a subtle chuckle added, "and you must be Pedro Santos, our errant detective. So sorry we had to handcuff you, Señor Santos, but as you had inserted yourself into the midst of a CISEN operation we were obligated to discover your intentions and who you were."

Pedro massaged his liberated wrists, doe eyes narrow and defiant. "The Señor Santos I am concerned with," he said with forced calm, "is my father, Enrique Santos. He has been missing since last night and, like I told those thugs of yours who apprehended me, I spotted his truck en route to Mismaloya, or perhaps up to La Arcadia."

516

"Entendido," said Tórrez into the mike clipped under his collar. He leaned towards Flores, his voice low: "Blanco is in position by the restaurant. Lazarito has taken a seat at a table in the open air. And Blanco has spotted the truck Officer Santos refers to—a black Dodge pickup parked across the street. He has not approached the vehicle but it appears empty."

"Tell both Blanco and Rivera to await orders from me before approaching the truck. We cannot risk alerting whoever parked it there to our presence."

Tórrez muttered this into his mike. Gloria said, "Interesting coincidence." Pedro's tone grew harsh with urgency: "I told those guys, Señor Flores, to be on the lookout for a young woman or boy in a dark billcap. He, or she was driving my father's truck when I saw it."

Flores retrieved the handheld computer at his belt. "Rest assured, Officer Santos," he said, "that my men will not miss a thing." Flores pressed a button on his computer and passed it forward. "Do any of you recognize either of the two young women on this screen?"

A curious look of recognition passed over Juan's face as he accepted the handheld computer from Flores. "My wife and I met Araceli Valencia," he handed the computer to Gloria, "at the dedication of Arena Vallarta on Sunday." Juan held Flores' penetrating stare. "And I met her again that evening, Sunday, along with her sister Brenda, the other girl named on the screen, at a party given by Araceli's fiancé, Armando Montoya."

"Neither one of you have had any other contact with them?"

The mayor said, "No," and Gloria, "None whatsoever. And I have never met Brenda." She passed the computer to Pedro. He scrutinized the screen along with the lieutenant. Flores studied the faces of the two Vallarta police officers for any sign of recognition or deception. Lieutenant Romero shook his head, told Flores he'd never seen either woman before.

Flores said, "Recognize either of them, Officer Santos?"

"Neither looks familiar." He passed the computer forward.

Flores retrieved his computer from Gloria. "What do any of you know about Araceli's fiancé, Armando Montoya?"

"He is a highly respected member of the community," Juan said through clenched teeth. Last night Armando was understandably furious at the intrusion he had suffered at the hands of Vallarta police and there was no reason to subject him to an unexpected visit from CISEN. "What are your intentions, Flores?" Juan asked quickly. "If you wish to speak with Armando I insist you let me arrange the meeting."

SEVE VERDAD

"I am sure, Señor Flores," Gloria added with an acquiescent smile, "that Armando Montoya will be happy to cooperate with CISEN in any way possible. But for now I believe it is time you briefed us on this operation."

Lieutenant Romero raised his voice: "Agreed. We know about Joaquín's murder, Señor Flores. Your men refused to talk much about it to us but I assume CISEN is responding, that more operatives have arrived in Vallarta."

"I believe," said Flores laconically, "that a team of operatives is currently being briefed by your Comandante and our federale friends at police headquarters."

The lieutenant pressed what he saw as an advantage: "It is clear you need our help, all the help you can get. So I suggest we stop wasting time and that you disclose the details of this operation here in Mismaloya and what you expect from us."

Flores glanced at his partner in the driver's seat. Tórrez raised a finger to his ear piece and shook his head imperceptibly, a signal that nothing of consequence was happening with Lazarito.

"What I expect," rejoined Flores, his deep-set eyes boring into the lieutenant, "is to capture or kill Russell Martell. And you, Lieutenant, can help us identify him should that opportunity arise."

Flores reached behind his chair, produced a crisp sheet of paper, and passed it to Gloria. "The latest rendition of Russell Martell," he said. "According to Lieutenant Romero and the proprietors of Hotel Marciano, Russell Martell looks somewhat different than his publicized photo. A bruised right eye is his distinguishing feature. Have the three of you ever met someone resembling this artist's rendition of him?"

Pedro and the lieutenant leaned forward in their seats to have a look. Juan said, "Gloria and I saw that sketch on television this morning and neither of us have ever seen him before."

"Pedro?" Flores asked. "Does that man look familiar to you?"

"No. And neither did his picture in the paper."

Flores relaxed his gaze over the four of them. "Your Media Minister," he said, "Señor Lazarito Charlado, has admitted to seeing Russell Martell at that party Sunday night, to me and, apparently, in a phone conversation with Araceli Valencia last night."

Pedro nearly leapt from his seat at the news. He fired a string of questions at the CISEN man: "Does Lazarito actually *know* Russell Martell? Did Armando Montoya *invite* Russell Martell to his party? And what about Brenda Valencia? How do you know she is acquainted with Russell Martell? Did Lazarito see him with her at the party? Or did Araceli tell Lazarito her sister knew him?"

518

Flores cocked his head as though faced with an unexpected dilemma. He shot Pedro an eyeball to eyeball glare, challenging him to present further problems. The kid's leading questions gave Flores the feeling that, despite being outranked by everyone in the car, his emotional quest to find his father might cause him to act impulsively, once again on his own initiative and without regard to interfering with a CISEN investigation.

Pedro's gun, wallet, and cell phone would remain locked in the trunk of the Le Baron; Flores would have Tórrez pay the young man special attention.

"We should not jump to conclusions with regards to Armando," said Juan, as much to Flores as Pedro. "There were many guests at his party. If he met Russell Martell it could have been in passing and he may not remember."

Gloria furrowed her brow in thought. She, Juan, and Lieutenant Romero had suspected that Russell Martell was at that party. After all, police had followed a lead to Armando's house last night. Yet Flores' confirmation that the gringo had not only attended the party but been seen by Lazarito raised questions about Armando Montoya as well as Lazarito. Was it possible that Armando actually *invited* Russell Martell to his party? Gloria dismissed the idea. If Armando knew anything at all about Russell Martell, he would have certainly informed police. As Juan had mentioned to Gloria last night: there was no way Armando Montoya would aid and abet a "criminal."

Gloria eyed Flores dubiously, "Did our Media Minister actually meet Russell Martell, Señor Flores?"

"He recalled seeing him at the party," Flores replied.

"He admitted this to you this morning?" the mayor clarified, "and to Araceli last night?"

"Sí." Flores paused. Gloria proffered her husband a speculative stare. Lieutenant Romero asked the question formulating in their minds: "Was Araceli Lazarito's source for his story?"

"Apparently," Flores said. "One of them at any rate. Apart from Lieutenant Romero, of all the people who may have come into contact with Russell Martell or might be friendly with him, Lazarito and Araceli are the ones currently within our reach. We expect them to meet at any time now... And we are not jumping to conclusions with respect to Armando Montoya, Señor Mayor," he added curtly, mindful not to impart too much information, information about the fax Araceli had sent the Media Minister and the possibility that Armando, her fiancé, knew about it. These four were gathered here for a specific purpose and Flores refused to get sidetracked—hoodwinked into breaking agency regulations by giving a full briefing of a CISEN investigation to outsiders without due cause. "Everyone at Armando Montoya's party is a person of interest, including Señor Montoya. They all had an opportunity to come into contact with Russell Martell."

Juan brought a pensive hand to his chin and caught Gloria's eye. They were on the same page: if Araceli was a source for Lazarito's story, might Armando Montoya know something about Russell Martell as well?

Like Flores, Pedro refused to get sidetracked. Lazarito, Araceli, Russell Martell...any one of them might lead him to papi. "Did Araceli specifically contact Lazarito last night to give him information about Russell Martell, Señor Flores?" he said, his eyes every bit as penetrating as the CISEN man's, "or was there another—"

Flores interrupted, his voice unnaturally piqued: "This is not a briefing, Officer Santos, or an interrogation." He folded his hands in his lap, regained his composure, and surveyed the unfriendly faces once more. "If a briefing is to be given by CISEN, it will be at a time and place of our choosing."

Pedro crossed his arms, resentful, sullen anger darkening his brow. Coming under CISEN's thumb like this wouldn't be nearly so bad if he could call or text Alejandro, have his brothers search papi's truck for clues into his whereabouts, scour Mismaloya for him, or follow the road to La Arcadia and search the woods if need be. But these puta madre CISEN güeyes had confiscated his cell phone and, when Gloria, the mayor and the lieutenant arrived, had insisted that they turn theirs off. Pedro glanced sideways at Lieutenant Romero's phone holstered at his belt and forcefully resisted an urge to snatch it.

The lieutenant said, "If Lazarito can identify Russell Martell, Señor Flores, why do you need me?"

"An extra pair of eyes to physically identify Russell Martell might be needed should he show up here in Mismaloya. And you have met the man, interrogated him.

"I will fit you with a receiver and audio transmitter, Lieutenant. An earpiece and microphone programmed for five-way communication between you, me, and my operatives. Then you will accompany me and station yourself across the street from Restaurante La Flor de Mismaloya where Operative Rivera will advise you."

Flores raised his eyebrows at Tórrez. "Nothing yet," said Tórrez.

Flores continued, "The rest of you are to remain here until further notice. Any attempt to exit this vehicle and approach Mismaloya will subject you to federal charges of interfering with a CISEN investigation. Araceli has yet to arrive but, whatever the results of her meeting with Lazarito, it is likely that all of you will prove useful, helpful in this investigation once we have persons of interest in our custody and available for questioning."

100

I let the forest take me down a foot path to where the river flattened out along a stony beach—an unusually wide section of the Mismaloya that looked shallow enough to cross without getting your chest wet. I'd hiked up the Mismaloya River before but never this far and always on the other side, the south side, the most memorable time over a year ago with Rosalita.

Dulce Rosalita.

That was the first time we made love in the woods. Rosalita must have been pregnant by then. We came to that conclusion not long afterwards, though at the time it should have been clear. Everything about her suggested new life. Stripped down to her white bikini, she had that delicious fertile glow about her, her nubile figure ripening like a plum before it falls to earth. I could still taste the biting press of her swollen lips on mine, feel her nails clawing my back and scalp, the electric passion binding our naked bodies, the mixing of our silky sweat. I still felt it, all of it, from my head to my toes, and trembled, like we trembled in each other's arms after our lovemaking, as though clinging to our last breaths of life...

I shook off the memory. Now was not the time to lose myself in the past or I might be taking my last breaths soon enough.

White gulls flapped over the water, skipped along the opposite bank of the river, their catcalls taunting me: where the hell are *you* going, gringo?

"Home," I murmured.

Not directly, however. In order to get home I had to follow Devo's instructions, which were simple enough but had separated me from Johnny and left me on my own, hiking upriver.

"We have to keep you far removed from your double, Martell." Devo had told me. "And should something go wrong, if you're captured, it's best that you don't know anything—where Johnny and I are headed, who's to guide you out of here, or how you're going to get back to the States."

We were beneath the twisted branches of the giant ceiba towering between the cabin and the gate to Finca Torodea. On foot and with me alongside, Devo led El Cid out from under the ceiba towards the gate. Johnny brought up the rear atop Lucha. "Think of this as

521

preparation for a fishing trip, Martell," Devo advised. "Stay cool and just do what you do before you drift your boat downriver. Pretend you're planning to fish the Mismaloya."

I frowned skeptically, unsure if Devo was needling me, trying to inspire me, or giving me a false sense of security by lending my mission a benign familiarity.

"Just head upriver, Russ," Johnny said. "Gotta scout upriver before drifting down it."

"Exactamente," said Devo. "Scout upriver until your guide appears."

"At least give me a gun," I entreated, "to defend myself. You have that rifle holsterd on El Cid's rump, but I'm the hunted one."

A hint of irony colored Devo's response: "If you have to use a gun, Martell, you're sure to be outgunned, and as good as dead anyway."

"Thanks for the vote of confidence. How 'bout a cyanide capsule? Biting down on that'll keep 'em from capturing me alive."

"If you have to die, Martell, attack with that knife in your daypack. Your pursuers are convinced you're a killer and will shoot to kill."

I snorted derisively, "That's comforting."

Johnny said, "Hell of a way to go down fighting, Devo." We paused at the gate. "Why not give him a gun just in case, so he can take a pig down with him?"

Panic pierced my heart like an ice needle. I winced at Johnny. "Or just use a cobblestone, Russ," he added through a grim smile. "Worked last time."

I aimed a composed glare at Devo. "How will I know my guide when I see him?"

"You'll know. Just scout upriver. Don't try to follow me and Johnny downriver or you'll crash and burn."

"My greasy makeup won't fool him?" I half-jested. Devo had touched up the shoe polish in my hair and beard and camouflaged my bruised eye again "to keep up appearances."

"No."

Johnny swung his right leg up over Lucha's neck, kicked his left foot free of its stirrup, and stuck a one-footed landing by my side, hand on my shoulder. "You want me to go with you, Russ?" He put some weight on his right foot, the ankle wrapped thick beneath an athletic sock, and made a lame attempt at bolstering his stance. I gripped his torso to give him a boost back onto Lucha. "Get your ass back up there."

FINDING DEVO

Johnny bumped his forehead against mine—a tacit football head-butt to fire me up. I helped him back into the saddle.

"You're on your own, Martell," Devo said.

I faced him. "For how long?"

"For now." His curt tone said the subject was closed.

After exiting the gate, I reached up to Johnny. Our hands met, thumbs looped. "I'll e-mail you back in the States," were his parting words.

As I gazed across the water, a paradox in Devo's instructions struck me. From what I knew of the Mismaloya River, most sections were too shallow and narrow to drift, though the water level was high for this time of year due to last night's unseasonable downpour. Storm clouds continued to surge, smothering the mountainous forests far above. I removed Johnny's A's cap and fingered sweat through my hair, careful to avoid the golf ball. The heat was becoming oppressive. The water tempted me, sparkling green under the sun. Suddenly I realized that standing out in the sun wasn't the smartest thing to do. Someone might see me, recognize me. But didn't someone have to see me if they were to be my guide?

I hiked upriver for a spell and paused in the shade beside a boulder, next to broken water and a deep swirling pool. A fishing hole. The water sure looked enticing, crystalline and cool... I stripped off the daypack Devo had given me, along with my shirt, and fished out the bottled water stuffed in the pack with my filthy shorts, Ara's shirt, bagged food (which also contained some Vicodin), and the pocketknife. Devo had also stuck a pen and writing tablet in there. *A warrior with the pen.* I preferred the knife, retrieved it, and examined the three-inch blade. It could pare an apple, gut a fish...or slice a throat if need be.

I chugged some water, stuffed it back into my pack with my shirt, and set off upriver again, the knife tucked in the front pocket of my swim trunks.

I kept close to the river but on several occasions had to vector left and thread thick forest, uphill over broken paths to get around water and impassable sheer rock. My pace was confident and steady, stubbornly steady, the exercise a purpose all its own.

The river was a natural compass. No way I could get lost. It ran down to the coast (civilization) and up into wilderness. I lost the trail every now and then because there wasn't much of a trail to speak of, but never lost the river.

The woods guided me down to the river again, to a symphony of falling water. A log jam had created an inviting waterfall—a six-foot cascade tumbling into a fishing hole. There was a spot for me just off the river bank, a cubby hole within the ferns under a hardwood tree. I took a break, ate sparsely—a slice of glazed beef and a handful of nuts—and indulged the doubts beginning to wash over me. Where was my guide? Who was he and how was he going to get me back to the States? How much farther did I have to scout upriver before he found me? What if he didn't find me? or if something happened to him and he was unable to reach me?... I couldn't continue upriver. There was nothing but endless rainforest. Would I have to hike back downriver, skirt Mismaloya and head for the highway in search of a bus or cab? My filthy shorts in the daypack contained enough money for a long bus ride to the border but I didn't have a passport. Could I escape without help? I was sure to be recognized as the *real* Russell Martell, wasn't I? Would I have to spend the night in the woods? regroup for a mad dash tomorrow? escape after news of Russell Martell's death had spread, offering me a modicum of cover? But how would I know if the plan to kill my double succeeded? If my guide didn't show, would that mean it had failed?

My survival depended on a million variables, each and every one of them beyond my control. And thinking about them ate away at my confidence, replacing it with creeping anxiety.

Devo told me to stay cool. Easy for him to say. I'm *the hunted one.*

I closed my eyes and took a dozen or so halting breaths, deep breaths...counting them silently until my respiration came unwavering. I opened my eyes and internalized the tranquility of my surroundings. My home is located on acres of wooded land in the Great Pacific Northwest; tropical woods are just as appealing and powerful, more so in many respects, once you get past the humidity. The humidity could be beat with a plunge into the water though...and so could the hot anxiety threatening to suffocate me...

101

ONCE again Lazarito Charlado was working overtime, trying to figure out how he could regain the upper hand, save his career and stay out of jail. And once again he could think of only one sure way to secure his salvation: Russell Martell had to die before he spilled his guts to CISEN or anyone else. With Russell Martell dead, Lazarito was reasonably certain he could hold CISEN and that chingón Flores at bay with partial truths and deception. But if the maldito Gringo Terrorista was captured, any story he had to tell about the cover-up of the botched raid and meeting the Media Minister on *two* separate occasions—the dedication of Arena Vallarta as well as Armando Montoya's party—would be increasingly difficult if not impossible to spin, especially with CISEN in charge of the prisoner. Lazarito was already under the agency's thumb; when Russell Martell told his story to CISEN, how long would it be before the Media Minister of Puerto Vallarta found himself subject to a CISEN interrogation?

Lazarito prayed to God that Araceli knew where to find Russell Martell, and that El Gringo Terrorista was armed and prepared to die in a last stand. A CISEN-led ambush on Russell Martell's hideout seemed the only chance he had of seeing *Mister* Martell dead.

Lazarito stabbed the corner of his quesadilla with his fork. He didn't have much of an appetite. His mental gymnastics had tied his stomach in knots. He shifted his ponderous girth, sipped beer in the parasol shade and scanned the overgrown empty lots across the dirt road. CISEN was out there somewhere, hidden amongst the trees or behind a cinderblock wall...and maybe here at the restaurant as well. Two innocuous looking couples occupied nearby tables, but a CISEN man might be inside La Flor de Mismaloya, keeping tabs on the Media Minister. He glanced at his watch, the fourth or fifth time he'd done so in the last fifteen minutes. Nearly 12:30 now. What was keeping Araceli?

A light-hearted commotion off to his left distracted him. Giggling children at the taco stand. The cook, a pear-shaped man with a clownish round face, wide grin, and eyebrows arched clear up to his hairline, was entertaining three young boys. Lazarito took a few seconds to appreciate the youngsters' innocence, the carefree youth so very far removed from his troubles.

One of the boys said, "Put it on again, Señor Pepe." The others chimed, "Sí!"

Lazarito noticed something in the cook's (Pepe's) hand, a colorful piece of cloth. Pepe twirled it on a finger, draped it over his head, and pulled it down over his face.

A mask. The cook was wearing a sparkling red mask with thin golden stripes. "I am Masked Apocalypse," he snarled, arms spread wide. The boys screeched and laughed, the biggest—oldest—answering, "And I am Gorila Two Face," his hands clawed overhead.

Lazarito took another stab at his food. He'd never been much of a wrestling fan but sure wished that the scheduled match between Masked Apocalypse and Armando *La Montaña* Montoya hadn't gone up in smoke with the disasters at the Washington and Arena Vallarta yesterday. Had his entire life gone up in smoke yesterday? Maybe. Just a couple of short days ago Lazarito had no idea how good he had it, or how bad things could get.

***

AHMED Mehri Fayed, bodyguard for Masked Apocalypse, master of knives and explosives, author of unspeakable crimes, lay inert in the cab of Enrique's truck across the street from La Flor de Mismaloya, flat on his back, in a state of semi-consciousness, his first brush with consciousness of any sort the past twenty-four hours. This wasn't the peaceful consciousness between wakefulness and slumber however, the kind that rolls you over comfortably in bed and eases you back to sleep. Ahmed was trapped in a paralyzing consciousness, the kind that sets you twitching within a horrifying nightmare, struggling to shake yourself awake.

He'd had similar nightmarish visions before, but they hadn't paralyzed him with fear. Visions of his ancestors butchered by medieval Crusaders and apostates from the religion of Islam. Visions of fathers and grandfathers, mothers and grandmothers, brothers and sisters slaughtered by contemporary Crusaders and apostates: Palestinian refugees cut down in Jordan; martyrs killed in Iraq, Afghanistan, Pakistan, Palestine, Bangladesh, the Sudan and beyond. Blood to be sanctified in Paradise and, eventually, with Ahmed's death, his own blood as well. A martyr's death awaited Ahmed. And with his martyr's death would come assurance of eternal salvation for visiting death and destruction upon apostates and the infidel West corrupting the lands of Allah and His prophet, Muhammad; Muslim lands destined to encompass the earth.

Ahmed Mehri Fayed had dipped his awakened hands again and again in glorious blood in defense of those lands, without fear but vengeful joy in meting out justice to the enemies of Islam—heretic invaders and corrupters of the faith. So the blood, pooling now under his cheek, wasn't what petrified him and made this a horrifying nightmare. What made this a horrifying nightmare was a vision of the giant with flaming eyes, his octopus hand wrapped around Ahmed's neck and face, locking his head in place and forcing him to view the unthinkable, the terrifyingly unfathomable: the contorted, severed head of Muhammad himself, his beard matted and crimson, his grimace foul with the stench of defeat.

How could this be?!? How could the most virtuous and perfect of men suffer such a sacrilegious indignity? What did it mean? Was all lost? Was this the true fate of the Prophet and his followers? NO! It

526

couldn't be! This had to be a lie, a trick perpetrated on him by Satan—the giant with flaming eyes. This must be a test of his faith.

In his waking nightmare, Ahmed prayed for strength: "Islam is the answer and jihad is the way." He begged Allah to forgive his weakness and provide a sign, something to reinforce his faith.

His prayers were answered. A voice from somewhere inside his brain yet beyond Ahmed's dream answered him. A clear, soothing voice, in Arabic, the blessed language of Allah: "Seek Masked Apocalypse and you shall be saved."

Ahmed mouthed the words "Masked Apocalypse," smacked his lips through a sickening sweetness invading his palate, and blinked his eyes open.

***

BEYOND Enrique's truck and up a gentle slope at the far end of a vacant lot, CISEN's "extra pair of eyes", Lieutenant Benito Cuevas Romero, was in position, cloaked by dense undergrowth. His mission: be on the lookout for Russell Martell.

Before he came under CISEN's thumb, Lieutenant Romero wasn't certain whether he wanted Russell Martell dead or alive, whether he wanted to force El Gringo Terrorista to vomit his guts, give up all he knew, possessed and cherished before killing him, or kill him on the spot with a bullet to the brain and immediately squelch any incriminating story he might tell. But now that CISEN was taking charge and Flores heading up any interrogation of Russell Martell should he be captured, the lieutenant had but one option: shoot Russell Martell dead on sight once he got the opportunity. He could not be allowed to live to tell his tale to CISEN.

If he got the opportunity, he couldn't hesitate. If he hesitated, he might end up like Garras. Did Garras hesitate when he had the chance? Did he ever have a chance?

A spasm of fear splintered Lieutenant Romero's concentration. He released his palm-sized binoculars and let them dangle at his chest, his hand jumping to the gun holstered beneath his shirt. The lieutenant pivoted and peeked around the cinderblock wall guarding his rear. Nothing but the overgrown road and a couple of shacks nestled up in the woods. He swallowed thickly. His senses were keen but he could not escape the feeling that he was missing something, like *he* was the one being spied upon, hunted.

He leaned into his thicket, his hiding place buffered by a trompeta tree, and resumed his position, CISEN-issue binoculars in hand. It was imperative to keep his wits about him, remain calm and alert. The odds of Russell Martell exposing himself here in Mismaloya while Lazarito rendezvoused with Araceli might be slim, but Lieutenant Romero clearly understood this operation's intrinsic danger: El Gringo Terrorista could strike at any time and when you least expected it.

CISEN preferred to take Russell Martell alive so he could be interrogated. Flores had mentioned this just before he and the lieutenant abandoned the Ford Expedition for their brief walk to stakeout Restaurante La Flor de Mismaloya. Russell Martell was considered armed and extremely dangerous, so Flores made certain that Lieutenant Romero remained armed, though he did relieve him of his cell phone as a precaution against "any possible electronic interference" with the earpiece and mike the lieutenant would be wearing. Lieutenant Romero knew Flores really wanted his phone to prevent him from calling for police backup and muddling CISEN's operation. But he acquiesced without complaint, as though perfectly willing to subordinate himself to CISEN. The lieutenant's disdain for the agency and the power it wielded was acute but he had no trouble hiding his feelings. All he needed was his gun to accomplish his goals, and this operation just might provide him with an opportunity to use it.

Too bad he didn't have a rifle along with his pistol, to extend his range. Through his binoculars, he took a bead on Lazarito toying with his food, some seventy meters distant. An impossible shot with a pistol should Russell Martell appear. It was just as well he didn't have a rifle though. Whether or not El Gringo Terrorista was armed with anything more than his bare hands, any claim Lieutenant Romero made of self-defense would most likely depend on being in close proximity to him.

Lieutenant Romero panned to Enrique Santos' truck across the street from the restaurant, its dirty hood and clean windshield. The truck was the wild card in this game. He and Flores had briefly discussed the implications during their walk into Mismaloya. Enrique had apparently been en route to Arena Vallarta when he disappeared and, if Russell Martell and/or any accomplices (the person in the dark billcap Pedro saw driving the truck?) were responsible for the fire, they might have abducted or killed Enrique, made off with his truck, and driven it here today for some reason.

"Do not approach the truck or the restaurant, Lieutenant," Flores had instructed him. "If those responsible for the truck's appearance here in Mismaloya suspect that we have the area under surveillance they will get spooked and we may never get another chance to capture and question them. And report any suspicious persons who approach the truck or restaurant, specifically Russell Martell."

Lieutenant Romero was prepared to do more than that. Should he spot accomplices with Russell Martell, perhaps as they approached from a distance, he would not hesitate to abandon his post and kill them along with El Gringo Terrorista, though he had to admit that seriously wounding at least one accomplice might be preferable to killing him, or her. *Someone* needed to be kept alive to interrogate.

He shifted his attention from the truck back to Lazarito, then swept his binoculars up along the sidewalk, over a few pedestrians, an artisan store, lavandería, snack shop, and a cervecería. The lieutenant surveyed the empty dirt road, drifted back down to the truck and...his heart leaped against his ribs at the sight of movement in the truck, right behind the steering wheel. Was someone in the cab of Enrique's truck?!? The voice of CISEN Operative Rivera, stationed in the lot adjacent to him, crackled in Lieutenant Romero's ear. Something out of the ordinary was happening at the taco stand next to the restaurant. "Do you see the man in the mask, Lieutenant?" But the crackling voice didn't register or, if it did, Lieutenant Romero was too stunned to answer. He remained transfixed on the man in the truck, his face visible now through the windshield. A sight so unexpected he didn't dare take his eyes off of it or move a muscle for fear it would disappear as suddenly as it had appeared. Was it...could it be? He refocused his binoculars on the pale, glazed face, the fine goatee, the pleading, searching eyes, one of them...blackened! The lieutenant pressed his binoculars against his eyes hard enough to leave bruises. That was Russell Martell! He had been hiding in the truck this whole time, right under their noses!

Russell Martell turned his face from view. Another voice crackled in the lieutenant's ear. Operative Blanco, stationed at the restaurant. "Someone is in the truck. Lieutenant Romero! Can you identify the man in the truck?"

The lieutenant's voice grated in his throat, "I think—" was all he could manage before a brilliant flash of light blinded him.

***

THE man in the mask stepped out from behind the taco stand and pounded his chest in mock challenge to the boys. "Masked Apocalypse takes no prisoners!" The boys squealed and huddled together at a stool. The oldest faced the challenge and pounded his chest with cartoonish bravery: "Gorila Two Face has no fear!"

Lazarito sipped beer and looked on in befuddled amusement. This cook was really taking his role seriously. He might be putting on a show for the kids but if the performance continued much longer, or louder, it would become quite an annoyance.

The man in the mask turned from the boys and faced the street, arms outstretched as though preparing to give a long lost friend a giant bear hug. He let loose with a stentorian growl, "*I am* Masked Apocalypse!" The boys responded with gleeful cries behind him. He froze, hands extended, suddenly petrified, like he'd seen a ghost. Lazarito thought he noticed his lips quivering through a hole in the mask, and felt the blood drain from his face upon hearing him exclaim his next words, outlandish words he never could have expected to hear: "And *that* is Russell Martell!"

Lazarito's stupefied gaze followed his gesture to the truck across the street. His beer glass slipped from his hand and shattered on the ground, but he took no notice of this for there before him, plain as day, was Russell Martell, hands spread against the driver's window, mouth and eyes screaming silently, calling out to...to Masked Apocalypse?

The next thing he knew, Lazarito was flat on his ass. It wasn't the force of the blast that put him there but his shuddering terror and surprise at the explosion. One second he was staring in stark, fearful disbelief at the face behind the window, the face of the man he wanted dead, and in the blink of an eye both the face and window were shattered within a flash of light, an empty red mass, and BANG! like a gun going off. He could still hear the noise, the shot, ringing in his head like early morning church bells, and the cries and gasps of the couples seated near him.

Flames were consuming the cab of the truck. A man came running out of the restaurant with a fire extinguisher, blew past Lazarito, crossed the street and attacked the flames, engulfing the cab in billows of white powder.

There was a hand on Lazarito's back. A heavy square face looked down upon him from behind reflective sunglasses. "I am Operative Blanco, CISEN," said the taught mouth. "Are you injured?"

Lazarito focused on the pulsing vein at the man's temple. "I...I am not sure."

"Did you see the man in the truck?"

"Sí. Russell Martell."

The mouth twitched, "You are certain?"

Lazarito's chest heaved. He coughed and wheezed, "Sí. It was him."

Blanco said, "Stay where you are. I will be back," and strode off for the truck.

***

530

INSIDE the Ford Expedition, Gloria, Juan, and Pedro all exchanged startled looks and stared out the windows. Gloria squeezed against her husband's shoulder for a look out the side window; Pedro got to his knees to see out the rear windows. Operative Tórrez opened the driver's door and searched the empty dirt road towards town, speaking rapidly into the mike at his collar.

"That sounded like a gun," Pedro said.

"Or firecracker," answered Juan, and Gloria, "Or a car backfiring."

Pedro's pulse quickened as panic inched its way through his chest. Papi's truck was spotted in town and if that was a gunshot... He spied Tórrez just outside the driver's door. The CISEN man's back was turned. Pedro saw his chance. The remaining doors to the SUV were locked but most of the windows were open, the passenger window all the way down. He drew a stealthy breath. Without a word to Gloria or Juan (who were still looking out their window), Pedro crept out of his seat, slipped past them, made for the front of the vehicle and, like the agile young man he was, vaulted himself clear out the passenger window feet first, landing in one fell swoop beside his Honda motorbike. His hand instantly found the hide-a-key under the gas tank.

Pedro's helmet flew off the back of his seat and bounced about behind the Ford Expedition like a soccer ball as he sped off. Tórrez arrived at a sprint, gave the helmet a swift kick and shook his fist at Pedro in a cloud of dust. Gloria and Juan shared an astonished chuckle at the display. The CISEN man seemed reduced to an enraged bully teased by the slippery class clown.

Juan gasped with admiration, "Que cojones!" and added that he'd probably do the same were he in the young man's shoes. "Pedro is determined to find his father. If he needs to be defended against federal charges of interfering with a CISEN investigation I will offer my services gratis."

"You might have to, Juan," Gloria said, her eyes trained on the CISEN man. "But Tórrez looks to have forgotten him already."

Juan raised a curious brow as he observed Tórrez through the rear windows. The CISEN man's demeanor had completely changed— from enraged bully to pacing academic immersed in the intricacies of a great dilemma. Tórrez put a hand to his earpiece as he walked in a broad circle behind the SUV. He intermittently muttered into his mike, his head alternately shaking and nodding, his face wearing a thick-furrowed expression of stupefied angst.

"I wonder..." Gloria's voice trailed off.

Juan finished her thought, "What happened?" He made an instinctive move for the open driver's door but stopped in mid-seat. A rigidly composed Tórrez loped by his window and took his place behind the wheel. He turned to his passengers and gave them the news straight out, his voice toneless: "There was an explosion in Enrique's truck. Witnesses identified the man in the cab as Russell Martell, and he is dead."

***

LAZARITO stared about in utter confusion, his heart pounding his chest like a fist on a door. Qué demonios had just happened? Did Russell Martell blow himself up or had someone tossed a grenade? No, it couldn't have been a grenade. Lazarito was no expert when it came to explosives but whatever it was that happened didn't rise to the damage a grenade would cause. The truck, what he could make out of it through a white fog and black smoke, was still in one piece. And the sound—he heard it again in his head, a single shot, BANG!—was wholly inconsistent with the thunder one associates with powerful explosives. Two women stood at the entrance to the restaurant in near embrace, wearing expressions of shock rather than anguish. People were beginning to congregate along the street. From what Lazarito could gather, no one but Russell Martell had been injured. The cook, who had been closest to the blast, had clearly not suffered any injury. He had removed his mask and wielded a fire extinguisher—retrieved, apparently, from his taco stand. He worked feverishly with the man from the restaurant to snuff out the sputtering flames. The boys stood before the taco stand, the oldest cajoling the other two to follow him across the street for a closer look. Lazarito, flat on his ass, was the only person felled by the blast.

He took stock in himself, moved his pudgy feet and legs, and massaged his arms. All there. No pain. But when he planted his right hand on the ground to leverage himself onto a knee the pain came, sliced through the heel of his hand clear up to his shoulder. Lazarito cursed, jerked his hand up as from a hot stove, and bounced back down on his butt. He stared incomprehensively at the crimson liquid oozing out a gash below his thumb and dumbly watched it drip to the ground, staining the broken beer glass at his side.

"You are wounded."

Lazarito's melon head listed within a wave of nausea. He looked up at Flores and searched his impervious face for a bit of sympathy. "Sí," he swooned. "I believe I am."

532

FINDING DEVO
***

PEDRO exploded over the bumps and ruts in the road, dust burning in his wake thick as the smoke he saw belching from the vehicle parked across the street from Restaurante La Flor de Mismaloya. He eased off the gas and internalized the sight of it, his heart thumping in his ears. No flames that he could see. The fire must have been put out by the two men emptying their fire extinguishers into...into the cab...the cab of a pickup truck. The truck CISEN had located! Papi's truck! Pedro hit the gas, popped a wheelie, and raced at a high-pitched roar towards the truck. He slammed on the brakes, sent his Honda into a shuddering sideways drift that left him on his feet and his bike on the ground not two car lengths from his father's Dodge pickup. "Papi!" he screamed.

Lieutenant Romero intercepted him at a rush, his face flushed, breathing accelerated, as though he'd come running from some distance. He grabbed Pedro by the shoulders, his fingers digging in. "Your father is not in the truck!" he declared in a great voice. "Cálmate Pedro."

Pedro stared at him vacantly, like the lieutenant had spoken a language he'd never heard before. "Qué? Where is he?"

"Your guess is as good as mine." The lieutenant released him. "But it does appear that our search for Russell Martell has ended."

Pedro blinked his wide doe eyes over papi's truck. The smoke was clearing little by little. He recognized CISEN Operatives Blanco and Rivera, the two men from the Ford Expedition who'd taken him into custody. They stood by the driver's door to the truck gesticulating with a man in a cook's apron holding a fire extinguisher. Pedro felt the earth move under him, the confusion and panic settling and contracting. He took a dust-filled breath. "You saw Russell Martell in the truck, señor?" he said, his voice a dry rasp.

Lieutenant Romero nodded. "And Operative Blanco just told me that Lazarito did as well."

"What happened?"

"Hard to say. It looked like a small explosion of some kind."

Pedro took a step forward. The lieutenant detained him with a hand on his chest and a low, commanding voice. "Follow me, Pedro. Stay close, out of CISEN's way, jodidos chingones."

They watched from the middle of the street. The cook had stripped off his apron; operatives Blanco and Rivera were draping it over the driver's door and through the shattered window to protect their hands as they worked to open the door.

Blanco spat, "Híjole. Not much is left of him inside there."

533

SEVE VERDAD

"Jale!" ordered Rivera. Pull!

A sickening stench invaded Pedro's nostrils—charred flesh and blood, and gunpowder mixed with a spurious, noxious odor of burning rubber and plastics. He vaguely noticed other people gathering around and pressed forward to one side of the cook. The door to the truck popped open, releasing tufts of residual smoke. The cook jumped back with a "madre de Dios" and covered his nose and mouth with his hand. Blanco and Rivera shrank from the vehicle, feet crunching bloodied glass, each with his face buried in the crook of his arm. Pedro lowered himself below the smoke to see past them, straining to see a recognizable shape, a tangible form within the blackened cab. And he did see something, though it wasn't exactly recognizable: scorched, disconnected legs contorted in the foot-well and a torso in what remained of the seat—a mutilated, grotesque torso cauterized into a lumpy smoldering mass, like a decapitated hog left to burn deep in a barbecue pit.

Knots formed in Pedro's throat and stomach. Whirling voices buzzed his ears. From behind he heard the lieutenant say, "Not even his own mother could identify Russell Martell now."

The nausea came quickly. Pedro turned from the scene, retreated onto a knee and vomited. "Puta," he cursed, and convulsed with a violent retch.

Lieutenant Romero placed a hand on his shoulder. "You okay, Pedro?"

Pedro blew stinging bile from his nose onto the road and steeled himself. "Sí," he said. The lieutenant helped him to his feet.

"Was Russell Martell the man in that truck?" a child's voice said.

Pedro and the lieutenant stared down blankly upon a curious brown face and short crop of black hair. "Sí," Lieutenant Romero assured the boy stiffly. "Russell Martell."

Pedro looked into the boy's bright inquisitive eyes. He seemed oddly unmoved by all the commotion. "Did you see the man in the truck?" Pedro asked him.

"Sí."

"Did you see him park the truck here?"

The boy shook his head. "No. Not him."

"Who then? Who parked it here?"

The boy shrugged, his inquisitive eyes searching, and stared off to his right. Pedro and the lieutenant followed the point of his gaze and spied someone, a dark, diminutive figure standing next to a red motorcycle, arms crossed, two or three blocks up the road. They studied the figure—male in a tank top, short and trim, long hair, angular Indian features. The Indian slapped on his sunglasses, mounted his motorcycle and sped off up the road towards La Arcadia.

Lieutenant Romero narrowed his gaze on the boy. "Was the Indian driving the truck, hijo?" he said.

The boy looked over his shoulder at his friends by the taco stand. Pedro took him by the shoulders. "The Indian," he said. "Did you see the Indian driving the truck?"

The boy whimpered, frightened by Pedro's sudden change in manner and tone. "Quizás. Quíen sabe?" Maybe. Who knows? He squirmed from Pedro's grasp and scampered away, past the taco stand towards the river, his two friends in tow. Pedro made a dash for his motorbike, the lieutenant hot on his heels. Lieutenant Romero hesitated while Pedro righted his bike, then gripped his bicep and the handle bars before he could hop on it. Pedro responded to him with eyes wild as an animal's, "Do not try to stop me, señor."

The lieutenant loosened his grip, the stern lines in his face slipping into a partial smile. "On the contrary, Pedro," he said flatly, his smile turning vengeful. If that Indian knew anything at all about Russell Martell's last days on earth, he wanted the first shot at him. "Chinga Flores and CISEN. I am going with you."

Pedro and Lieutenant Romero tore off on Pedro's motorbike, their dust still hanging in the air when Operative Tórrez pulled up in the Ford Expedition with Gloria and Juan.

102

THE log jam at the cascade broke the river and forced a long shallow rapid over rounded pale rocks along the far end of the fishing hole. A large boulder buffered the falls on my side. I shouldered my pack and skirted the boulder. Not a soul in sight on either side of the river. Where was my guide? Sweat dripped from my nose like water from a leaky faucet. The heat and humidity were formidable yet...was I also on the verge of panic? Why? Instinctively, I felt there was no reason to panic—*my guide could show anytime now... Anytime*—and then I hit upon the principal source of my anxiety: I had no clue how long or how far I was supposed to scout upriver. "Just do what you do before you drift your boat downriver," Devo had instructed plainly, which was about the same as telling me to "study the river and enjoy the hike."

SEVE VERDAD

Devo probably didn't tell me how long or how far to scout upriver because he wasn't sure himself. Yet he'd also instructed me to "stay cool," and that's precisely what I intended to do.

Directly behind the cascade the draw of current was imperceptible, the water's smooth apron leading to the falls glassy. I stripped, jumped in naked, and was instantly rejuvenated, the effect more invigorating than a cool rush of mountain air.

April in Vallarta brings warm ocean currents. But the rivers stay cool, not cold but refreshing. My cool dip cut right through the heat and humidity, soothed my anxious nerves and allowed a moment's respite.

This section of the river was chest high at its deepest with a sandy bottom. My injured ribs and kidneys squawked and cried when I tried to swim so I drifted on my back for a spell instead. And I submerged a few times, twice with my eyes open. It's another world underwater—light hazy green inside the river. The environment shielded me from my land-born plights and dilemmas, if only for a short time.

There was a fresh coolness to the hot day now. I felt it while standing in the middle of the river, spliced by the forest's mid-day shadow. The south side of the river remained bathed in sun. A faint incline of flat cobbles blended to a narrow beach along the bank, and there was plenty of room for back casting if you were fly fishing. The north side of the river where I'd left my gear had none of those qualities.

If I was drifting in my boat I'd land on the beach.

I retrieved my gear, crossed the river, landed on the narrow beach, and laid on the sand in the sun with Johnny's cap over my face until dry.

Did I feel better? I thought so. My anxiety seemed to have abated some. But I quickly realized I had another problem: I couldn't move. I tried but as soon as I flexed my muscles in an effort to get up, the Cowboy defensive line pummeled me again. The golf ball, my dented kidneys, bruised rectum, my entire body shuddered and throbbed in painful rebellion.

Devo's pills had worn off.

Fucking Chimp...and the lieutenant...and Fat Cop...and...

I eased onto my side, dipped into my pack for a Vicodin, downed it with a slug of water and collapsed onto my back with Johnny's cap over my face.

PEDRO and Lieutenant Romero didn't see the Indian's motorcycle again until they reached the end of the dirt road at La Arcadia. The Indian was nowhere to be seen but they recognized his red Honda 750 parked adjacent to the restaurant at the edge of the parking lot. Pedro cruised past the motorcycle and they surveyed the restaurant for signs of someone inside. Razor-wire gates sealed the entrance. "The place looks empty," the lieutenant observed. Pedro circled the vacant parking lot. Lieutenant Romero swept a finger over the unmarked terrain. "Last night's rain prepared the ground for fresh tracks," he said. "It appears that the Indian's Honda is the only vehicle to visit La Arcadia today."

Pedro parked by the Indian's motorcycle above the fence line. They dismounted. "He probably breached this fence somewhere," the lieutenant said. He stepped down into the brush to walk the fence line. Pedro made a move to follow, then stared back at the three-tiered restaurant. La Arcadia should be open, serving *lunch* and preparing the traditional Mexican comida. They must have taken the day off due to yesterday's catastrophes. But the restaurant had to have a phone inside and Pedro needed to call Alejandro, inform him that he was following a possible lead into the whereabouts of their father—an Indian who may have been driving papi's truck.

A sharp whistle swung his head around. Lieutenant Romero waved him over from behind a bush.

The lieutenant had found a hole in the fence. Neat cuts creasing bent chain links. A hole big enough for a man to squeeze through. Dry brush and bramble had been trampled on the other side of the fence. "He must have gone this way," the lieutenant said, "and then picked up the trail on the other side of the river."

Pedro followed him through the fence and upriver to the foot of the waterfall below La Arcadia's swimming hole. He looked up at the restaurant, the metal overhead doors barring entry. "I should call my brother," he said quietly. "But La Arcadia is locked up."

Lieutenant Romero glanced up at the restaurant. Pedro had mentioned his need to call Alejandro once already, on their way up here from Mismaloya. CISEN had both of their phones.

"We can break into the restaurant later," the lieutenant said, "if we have to. First we need to see if we can pick up that Indian's trail." No way was he going to sacrifice finding the Indian to make a phone call. He had to question him before anyone else had a chance to... Yet if the Indian was indeed involved in the death of Russell Martell, he might have accomplices; the lieutenant and Pedro could very well find themselves in need of backup. Lieutenant Romero absently pawed at the wire in his pocket—the receiver/transmitter Flores had fitted him with. He'd stripped it off and forgotten about it until now. The thing was only good for communication with CISEN and he had no desire to communicate with them, not at present at any rate. He'd try to in an emergency but doubted the wire had much range... Should he and Pedro find themselves in need of backup they might have to use La Arcadia's phone.

Pedro gave the lieutenant a firm, concordant nod. Breaking into La Arcadia would take time and they had no time to lose. Papi's life could be at stake! He eased himself atop a boulder and peered over the wooden footbridge that crossed the swimming hole to the trail on the south side of the river. Pedro cast his eyes and ears into the woods. That Indian was up there somewhere, and maybe papi as well.

"I will take point, Pedro." Lieutenant Romero was right beside him, his Glock drawn.

Pedro followed him over the footbridge. They each took a knee on the other side to examine some impressions in the dirt. "Only one set of footprints," the lieutenant said.

"Going upriver," answered Pedro.

"They look fresh. The earth has dried here but, after all that rain last night—"

"They must be fresh."

Their eyes locked in succinct understanding. They were on the right track and unified in their purpose.

The trail was well traveled but less than ideal for tracking someone through dense forest. The prints frequently disappeared within the gnarled protruding roots and rounded rocks embedded in gravelly dirt. Pedro and the lieutenant proceeded cautiously, senses heightened, sensitive to any noise or movement in the woods. Lieutenant Romero led the way, Glock in hand. He halted on the smooth crest of an incline and pointed out their prey's tracks with his gun. The tracks disappeared down the trail towards the river. Pedro extended a quiet finger to the river and swept it along the trail rising back into the forest about twenty meters up ahead, indicating the route the Indian must have taken upriver. The lieutenant gestured to a rocky ledge off to their right and whispered into Pedro's ear. "Best to keep to the high ground," he said. "Stay here while I scout the trail beyond this ridge. If the trail is clear," he turned his cheek and released a sharp birdsong whistle, "I will whistle for you to head for those boulders down below." He pointed down to a rocky prominence that broke the riverbank and forced the trail up into the woods. "Then you go down for a look upriver, a view unobstructed by these woods. See if you spot the Indian...or anyone else."

Pedro watched Lieutenant Romero's slender figure proceed along the tricky embankment, impressed by his sure footedness and stealth as he utilized the high ground and trees for cover, gun hand poised. The man moved like a cat, graceful and strong, which somehow surprised Pedro. He had to remind himself that the lieutenant, while second in command in the department, was not much older than his brother, Alejandro, and, since he kept himself fit and lithe, why shouldn't he be athletic? Pedro felt fortunate that the lieutenant had insisted on coming along. He couldn't ask for a better partner. The lieutenant slipped, causing a minor noise and land slide, but Pedro's heart had barely skipped a beat before he vanished into thick foliage without missing another step.

Presently, Pedro heard his whistle. He took the gentle slope down to the river and stopped in the shade a few meters short of the tall boulders breaking the riverbank. The boulders extended into the river, blocking his view upriver. He glanced up the trail. Lieutenant Romero raised a hand from behind a tree and signaled for him to have a look upriver. Pedro stepped into the sun. The river dazzled, its undulating waters lancing splintered light into his eyes. He scrambled over to where the boulders forced a shallow bending rapid, took purchase on a mossy log and leaned into the jutting rock. He searched for a toehold or crevice to help leverage himself up for a look over the shelf, but the surface was too smooth for him to gain traction. Pedro jumped from the log onto the riverbank, slipped off his shoes and socks, rolled up his pant legs, and waded into the water, the rocky bottom flat and cool under his feet. He peeked around the boulder upriver, his knee just short of the lazy rapid, and shaded his eyes with a hand.

Pedro ducked back behind the boulder abruptly, his breath short. Was the river—the sunlight bounding off water like myriad flashbulbs—playing tricks on him? He took another look around the boulder, both hands cupped over his eyes. This time he kept his head in place for several seconds and concentrated on the protruding bend in the river about eighty meters away. A small, rounded silhouette came into focus, huddled at the water's edge, dipping its hands into the river and splashing water over its head. The silhouette lengthened into the shape of a diminutive man. Pedro recognized the clothing—tank top, loose fitting pants—and watched him walk around the bend into the woods...

The Indian. It had to be the Indian. Pedro leapt from the water, threw on his shoes, stuffed his socks in a back pocket and dashed up the trail quick as a jackrabbit chased by a hound. But when he crested the hill the lieutenant was nowhere in sight. Pedro stopped short, his heart a pounding sledge hammer in his solar plexus about knocking the wind out of him. He continued along the trail searching frantically for the lieutenant, and spun around at a sudden whistle in his ear. Lieutenant Romero stepped down from the undergrowth just above him, gun at the ready, his eyes shrewd black dots—the eyes of a killer standing out against the thin veil of concern on his face. "Qué te pasa, Pedro?"

"I saw him." Pedro gulped down the high-pitched panic in his voice and grimaced apologetically, hands on knees to catch his breath. His mad dash had put the lieutenant on the defensive—dug in and ready to shoot to kill. Pedro chided himself. He needn't have raced up the trail as though chased by a wild animal.

The lieutenant joined him on the trail. His dress shirt was unbuttoned and hung loosely about his waist and sweat-marked T-shirt, exposing the holster below his chest. He told Pedro to calm down.

"Tranquilízate, Pedro," he said with a hand on his back. He asked who it was he saw, thinking that, given his fervid state, Pedro might have seen his father being spirited away by kidnappers.

Pedro straightened himself before the lieutenant's impassioned expression. "I saw the Indian upriver, señor," he said breathlessly. "Eighty meters or so upriver."

Lieutenant Romero holstered his pistol. "You are certain it was the Indian, the same man we saw in Mismaloya?"

"I cannot be positively certain, señor. But it sure looked like him, same build and clothing. And he is heading east, upriver."

"Alone?"

"He looked to be."

Lieutenant Romero set off on the trail. "Vámanos," he said.

104

THE cellblock is overgrown with twisted vines and tree branches. The vines grow before my eyes, extend through the bars and encircle me. Night falls. Fibrous tentacles snake through my body and smother my face.

I bolted upright. "Sonuvabitch," I said and brought a hand to the searing pain in my back. A high-pitched racket assaulted my ears. I stared across the water into the forest in search of its source. Sounded like macaws, or monkeys. A rapid clicking noise followed. An alien

540

sound I attributed to squirrels harvesting nuts or something. I dressed on the sand—put on my swim trunks, socks and shoes—and took a short breather in response to my aching pains. A Herculean effort brought me to my feet. I hadn't napped long. The sun remained high in the sky. I surveyed my surroundings. The wilderness had taken on a foreboding aspect, like I was trapped in a haunted house. My eyes searched upriver, both sides of the river. Despite last night's downpour and the storm clouds smothering the mountaintops, the Mismaloya remained narrow and easily traversed. If my guide was around, I'd see him no matter which side of the river he was on, and he'd see me as well, as long as we both stuck to the river. What if he didn't show? Would I have to spend the night in the woods? I didn't like that idea. I'd just find myself in the same predicament tomorrow. If my guide didn't show, I'd hike down to the highway under the cover of darkness and make my escape—catch a cab or bus to Melaque on my way to Guadalajara and the border.

A tacky numbness had invaded my palate. The Vicodin was poised to work its magic. I stuck the bottled water and Johnny's cap into my daypack and set off upriver. The river narrowed considerably up ahead and disappeared into the woods about seventy yards distant. I paused to survey my surroundings once again. The rocky terrain behind my little beach girded a bluff covered in jungle fauna. A path rounded the bluff. A path downriver. Was that the trail I should take if I was left without a guide? What kind of condition was it in? I hoped it was in better condition than the one I'd taken to get here, which basically amounted to no trail at all. You could break your neck hiking terrain like that at night.

I was at a crossroads. Had I traveled far enough upriver? too far? How far back downriver should I go?

Just far enough to check out the condition of the trail...might even find my guide waiting for me...

I needed to familiarize myself with a route downriver in case I was left without a guide. I had to be prepared to act should I find myself abandoned in the jungle.

The old Converse sneakers Devo had given me were ragged but highly functional. I felt myself getting into a rhythm as I rounded the bluff.

105

WORD of a car bomb killing Russell Martell in Mismaloya spread faster than rumors in a sorority house and reached Hotel La Joya de Mismaloya on the beach across the highway in no time at all. Sullen tourists at the hotel were still reeling from yesterday's horrific events in Vallarta and the news inspired a morbid curiosity that seemed to lift their spirits. El Gringo Terrorista is dead? Right here in Mismaloya? Wow! Let's grab a beer and check it out! By the time the smoke cleared from the explosion, tourists were converging on the scene with neighborhood locals as if attending a macabre pep rally. Mayor Juan Pacífico Velázquez had already ordered reinforcements to Mismaloya. When the first emergency vehicle arrived—a fire truck responding to initial reports of a fire—the mayor put the men to work on crowd and traffic control. Juan had had plenty of practice delegating responsibility the past couple of days and slipped into his role without much if any prompting from Flores and CISEN. Technically, the sleepy village lay outside his jurisdiction, but the only troops Mismaloya's self-appointed "mayor", Bernardino Aguas Tlaxtopel, had experience managing were the customers who frequented his cervecería. He threw what support he could muster behind Juan. Within thirty to forty minutes after the death of El Gringo Terrorista, as the sun settled into its interminably hot afternoon arc, a square-block perimeter had been cordoned off around Restaurante La Flor de Mismaloya and the dirt road leading into and out of the village closed to all but emergency vehicles.

Meanwhile, three additional CISEN operatives had arrived. They examined the Dodge pickup truck and the gruesome sight inside its cab. *Someone* had died in there but there was no telling who it was. Across the street at La Flor de Mismaloya, Flores and Operative Rivera had canvassed everyone in the restaurant on that question, taken down their names, and released all but the two most reliable witnesses to the car bomb and *Russell Martell's* death: Media Minister Lazarito Charlado and the cook at the taco stand, José (Pepe) López.

Gloria slowly paced the restaurant's patio, her attention split between the men gathered around Lazarito seated at one table and Operative Tórrez at another manning a laptop computer and handheld radio. She paused for a look over Tórrez's shoulder at the map on the computer screen. There had been little change in the position of the blinking red dot. Lieutenant Romero, another witness who had identified Russell Martell in the pickup, was being tracked via his wire. He remained out of range for radio contact. Pedro was with him and they looked to be meandering about La Arcadia, most likely following a lead into the whereabouts of Pedro's father and the owner of the pickup truck, Enrique Santos.

Pedro and Lieutenant Romero's mad dash up the road towards La Arcadia hadn't gone unnoticed. But since CISEN had its hands full here in Mismaloya, Flores decided on the spot to pool his resources and let the two errant officers go ahead and work on their own initiative, for now.

Lazarito Charlado slumped in his chair, his wounded hand wrapped in a rag, his frumpy shirt soaked in cold perspiration. He had passed out at the sight of his own blood. Mostly revived now, his vision glazed over as he watched the CISEN men across the street inspect the gutted pickup containing the charred remains of Russell Martell.

CISEN Operative Blanco was on his knees by Lazarito's table rifling through a backpack discovered in the large tool chest in the bed of the pickup. He'd found a money belt in the pack that contained documents and credit cards belonging to Russell Martell; Flores and Operative Rivera examined them as they stood beside Lazarito.

"Do you recognize this man, Lazarito?"

Lazarito stared at the open passport Flores held under his nose. A beguiled expression of recognition suffused his wan features. "Not exactly." He wheezed a fat man's exhausted sigh. "Looks similar to the publicized photo of Russell Martell. But when I saw him at Montoya's party on Sunday he had facial hair and a black eye, like he did when I saw him in that truck."

"And you, señor?" Flores held the passport photo up to the pear-shaped cook standing opposite the Media Minister. Pepe answered without hesitation: "I have seen that man before at my taco stand in Puerto Vallarta. Russell Martell. And like Señor Lazarito said, on Sunday night he had facial hair and a black eye, as he did today when I saw him in the truck."

Operative Rivera tilted his head at Pepe. "And yesterday you did not report to police that you had seen Russell Martell this past weekend because...?" he prompted in an effort to get the cook to repeat the story he'd already given CISEN, to make sure there was no mistake, and that Pepe wasn't hiding something.

"I was asleep when news about Russell Martell broke last night." Pepe's tone betrayed a hint of impatience at being detained like this. "I left my name with police dispatch this morning when I saw his picture in the paper and a sketch of him on television. He visited my taco stand on Friday, Saturday, and Sunday evenings."

Rivera was about to prod the cook further, ask him how well he knew Russell Martell, when Operative Blanco declared, "A laptop." He held it up in his gloved hand. "A Macintosh laptop. It was tucked inside a pocket at the bottom of the backpack."

"Have Operative Valenzuela examine it," Flores said. Blanco left the laptop in the backpack and withdrew.

"May I, Señor Flores?" Gloria stood beside the senior operative, handkerchief extended. Unlike Flores, she wasn't wearing latex gloves. He handed her the passport and glanced at the truck across the street. Federale Investigator Sándovar and CISEN Operative Cienfuegos were taking pictures of the human remains inside the cab. Blanco circled the rear of the vehicle to have a word with Operative Valenzuela. "Evidence seems to suggest," Flores began, a thoughtful hand to his chin, "that the victim in the truck is Russell Martell." He steadied his gaze on Operative Rivera. "But as the body is burned beyond recognition—"

"We will have to wait for results of a DNA test to be certain," Gloria interposed. She raised her eyes from the passport in her hand. Flores nodded sharply. "And we still have another witness to question," he said and shot Tórrez an inquisitive stare.

"Lieutenant Romero looks to be on his way back to Mismaloya," Tórrez intoned. He spun his laptop around for all to see. "His signal indicates that he and Officer Santos are back on the motorbike and heading west at a steady speed along the road," he added. "Downriver in our direction."

106

LIEUTENANT Romero allowed Pedro to lead the way upriver for a spell as they picked up the pace in pursuit of the Indian. Pedro walked with a singular purpose, fists balled and strides steady. He had one thing on his mind: find his father. Sighting the Indian had heightened his sense of urgency and expectation of success. Pedro sensed his prey and could not allow him to get away. Lieutenant Romero appreciated Pedro's resolve and forged ahead with equally strong strides in an effort to gain ground on the Indian.

The lieutenant observed sheer rock up ahead. It buffered the river and cut the trail at a blind corner. He pierced the air with a short whistle. Pedro wheeled around, his face flushed and eyes expectant. The lieutenant put a hand to his pistol holstered beneath his shirt and paused beside Pedro for a look up the blind trail. "Take care here," he whispered. He drew his gun and motioned for Pedro to keep behind him. Lieutenant Romero peered around the rock cutting the trail and visibly relaxed into a straightened posture. Pedro joined him at his side. The lieutenant pointed his pistol upriver. "Follow the river to that bluff up there," he said. "I am right behind you."

Pedro set off again, a little slower this time, torn between the need to "take care" and a relentless determination to question that Indian. Did he park papi's truck across the street from La Flor de Mismaloya? What did he know about papi's disappearance? Did he have anything to do with Russell Martell's death or the attack on the Washington? Lieutenant Romero followed a few steps behind, similarly preoccupied. Yet his determination to find and question the Indian was tempered by his experience and a sharpened sense of awareness. If the Indian had accomplices, there might be clues around indicating how many they were. Footprints or— He spotted a clue off to their left and whistled for Pedro. The lieutenant stepped down off the trail. Pedro joined him at the water's edge. "What do you make of that, Pedro?" he said, pistol aimed at the ground.

Pedro wrinkled his brow in careful consideration, then shot a finger at the horse tracks and pile of manure as if they sullied his own front lawn. "More than one horse made those tracks," he said.

"And where did they come from?"

Pedro's head twitched. "Since there are no horse tracks on our trail, they must have come from the river, or the other side of the river."

Lieutenant Romero pawed at the pack of cigarettes in his pants pocket. He sure could use one but the smoke and odor might give him and Pedro away as easily as raised voices. He leaned back against a tree and swept his gaze over the wide perimeter of impressions in the sandy dirt. "Enough tracks there for a guided tour on horseback... Maybe they came down from the mountains southeast of here— Chico's Paradise and El Rio Tuito."

Pedro studied the ground. Were the Indian's accomplices riding these horses? Might they know where papi was? Were they with papi? Did they have him tied up atop one of the horses? He squatted and refocused on a number of prints, his gaze narrowed in concentration. "Take a look at this, señor."

Lieutenant Romero holstered his pistol and squatted next to him. "That is a good-sized dog," he said.

Pedro nodded, "Only a few prints. The animal must have gone into the water after making them."

"And come from the water." The lieutenant gave Pedro a pat on the back and stood over him. "What else can we deduce from these clues, without spending much more time on them?"

Pedro rose from his squat, eyes fixed on the dog tracks. "If we assume the dog is with the horses, then we can also assume that foreign tourists were not riding the horses." He glanced up at the lieutenant. "Foreigners do not generally bring their dogs here on vacation, much less a dog this large. So these tracks could belong to those aiding the Indian."

"Perhaps..." Lieutenant Romero proffered Pedro a dry smirk. "But take another look at the evidence. What can you tell me about that pile of mierda?"

Pedro swatted a fly from his nose. "Fairly fresh, señor."

"That manure," said the lieutenant, "has been in this shade here since the horse left it and—"

"It has begun to dry, señor."

"Exactamente."

"And since I saw the Indian about twenty minutes or so ago..."

"That Indian is either awfully late in meeting those horses or they have nothing to do with one another."

"We better go find out which it is." Pedro took a few steps up onto the trail and turned around. "Vámanos?"

Lieutenant Romero lowered his gaze, as if experiencing a moment of indecision. "Pedro?" he said.

"Sí?"

The lieutenant looked him in the eye, his black eyebrows a question mark over his face. "We have only seen a single set of footprints but...there may be innocent hikers and tourists up here as well as that Indian."

"Sí, señor. And maybe they have seen the Indian or whoever is riding those horses."

"Maybe."

Lieutenant Romero joined him on the trail, his expression renewed and resolute. "On the other hand," he said, "that Indian appears to be escaping to somewhere and we could be outnumbered when we find him. If that is the case, be prepared to retreat back to La Arcadia."

Pedro kept step behind him. "I will be careful, señor, ready for anything."

AT Restaurante La Flor de Mismaloya, Pepe López had been excused with the understanding that, as a witness to the death of a man he identified as Russell Martell, he would make himself available to CISEN should they call on him. CISEN Operative Agustín Moreno Valenzuela, a thirty-year-old heavyset man with a creased brow and keen hazel-brown eyes, had joined Lazarito at his table. Flores stood behind him and nodded affirmatively at the image on the laptop computer discovered in "Russell Martell's" backpack. "I believe the Media Minister will recognize that," he said.

Operative Valenzuela spun the computer around so Media Minister Charlado could view the screen. Lazarito sucked in a sharp breath. Gloria drew near the table for a closer look. "What is it?" she said, her eyes skipping over the lines of print below a photo of Russell Martell.

"A copy of the fax our Media Minister received last night," Flores replied. He paused to retrieve his phone buzzing at his belt. "Give them a demonstration of what else you discovered, Valenzuela." Flores retreated to answer his phone.

Valenzuela took hold of the computer with his gloved hands and connected a small hand-held microphone to it. He made a couple of clicks, placed his thumb on a dial beneath the touchpad, and brought the mike to his lips. "Recognize this voice, Lazarito?" he cooed, a wry smile playing across his face.

Lazarito felt the hair on his neck stand on end. "Híjole," he gasped.

Operative Tórrez, monitoring Lieutenant Romero's movements on a laptop at the adjacent table, released a provocative chuckle. "You sound like a college girl, Agustín," he said.

Lazarito's face crimsoned.

"Whose voice is it?" Gloria asked him.

Valenzuela added a sultry note to his tone: "I have...*information* for you, Señor Charlado."

Lazarito clutched his injured hand over his ponderous girth. Tórrez snickered.

Flores resumed his position behind Valenzuela. "Does that sound something like the person you spoke to on the phone last night and this morning, Señor Charlado?"

Lazarito gulped audibly. "Pues...it could be."

Gloria looked a question at Flores, her mouth slightly agape. "A voice synthesizer, señora," he said.

"*Modulator* or *changer,* to be more precise," Valenzuela clarified.

"It appears," Flores said, "that someone, Russell Martell perhaps, lured our Media Minister to Mismaloya with an impression of Araceli Valencia over the phone last night and this morning."

Gloria shook her head incredulously. "But why?"

"Unclear," Flores said. "But he also managed to lure *us* here. We all may have been his targets, as was, it seems, a murdered man discovered by CISEN and state federales in an office building in El Pitillal about five minutes ago, the last place from where this computer received an Internet signal."

Lazarito puffed his cheeks as he absorbed this astounding news. "Has the dead man been identified?" Gloria said.

Flores shook his head, "Not yet... He was found with a knife sunk into his chest."

Gloria pulled a chair out from the table and sat down heavily. Valenzuela tilted his head up to Flores. "How long has the man been dead, señor?"

"Unknown," Flores said.

"So he may have sent the fax to Media Minister Charlado."

"And was then killed for it."

Gloria lifted her gaze to Flores. "Whose computer is this, Russell Martell's or the dead man's?"

"Russell Martell's," Lazarito said. He raised a rumpled brow at Flores. Gloria frowned at Lazarito's smug tone. What kind of spin was the Media Minister preparing to put on this story?

"The murdered man may have double-crossed Russell Martell," Flores advanced. "But the computer..." his voice trailed off.

"I should be able to discover who it belongs to," Valenzuela said, "but it might take some time."

"It seems to me," Lazarito hummed, "that this whole affair here today is the result of a ruse perpetrated by Russell Martell in an effort to silence me."

Flores cocked his head at Lazarito, like he'd thought of that. "Maybe," he said, "and to commit mass murder. A ruse that exploded in Russell Martell's face."

Operative Blanco approached from the truck across the street and addressed Flores. "The bomb may have misfired," he said. "An unusual devise in that we have not discovered much shrapnel. And considering the condition of the remains, the victim might have been wearing an explosives-laden vest. His head was literally blown off."

"Are you suggesting he was on a suicide-bombing mission?" Flores asked reasonably.

"Maybe," Blanco shrugged. "Or maybe he planned to plant the vest somewhere and make his escape."

Flores glanced down at Valenzuela, and shifted his gaze between Blanco and Tórrez. "We have a lot of forensic work to do," he said.

108

THE Vicodin had begun to work its magic. After five minutes or so on the trail downriver my stride had gone from laborious and painful to loose and smooth, my muscles supple under a sheen of perspiration. Amazing how that stuff works, especially once you get your blood flowing with a little exercise. The pain from my injuries was still present but severely diluted—a twinge and tingling ache every now and then but never acute; my limbs felt light, as if tempered by an aluminum alloy instead of dense bone. The drug didn't just numb my pains but seemed to stimulate healthy muscles as well. Between my rejuvenating swim, the Vicodin, and this short warm-up, I felt as strong as I did before my arrest and the beating those pig coppers gave me.

Gimme a shot of adrenalin along with a dose of anger and fear, and I could better my performance in Johnny's hotel room—kill that fucking lieutenant along with all *the sadistic chimps and fat cops in the department.*

The fantasy galvanized me. I spent a small time entertaining it, inhaling that cocksucker Lieutenant's nicotine breath as my hands gripped his neck, and watching those soap-opera eyes of his bulge out their sockets as I strangled the life from him with my bare hands. Bludgeoning the lieutenant with a cobblestone was an appealing vision as well of course (I'd had some success with that weapon), as was slitting his throat and blowing up the motherfucking police station. What he and his pig buddies did to me was beyond the pale, humiliating, agonizing, intolerable and illegal. They violated my human rights, my entire being! They deserved a fate worse than death and, if I hadn't done some quick thinking in The Chamber to buy time, they'd have seen to it that I suffered a similar fate...

And if not for Devo, I'd have been at their mercy.

The memory of Devo's heroics reminded me of my limitations and snapped me back to the here and now, slowed me down—my mind and body. It wasn't like I'd been walking fast, purposely keeping a quicker pace than I had upriver, but there's nothing like a well-traveled trail to improve your speed, and this trail on the south side of

549

the river was much better defined than the one on the north side east of Finca Torodea. Plus, aside from a handful of inclines, it was downhill, and would continue downhill with intermittent inclines until La Arcadia, until the coast, actually.

It suddenly occurred to me that I'd probably covered some distance back downriver. The trail was in good condition, good enough to hike in moonlight tonight if I had to. Yet Devo's instructions were to scout *upriver* to encounter my guide.

I took a decline down to a pleasant soft shoulder in the riverbank and a familiar, nondescript section of the Mismaloya. I looked up and downriver. Not a soul in sight... Had I passed my starting point on the other side in such a short period of time? Unlikely but tough to tell for certain. The river was narrow here and, as I recalled, considerably wider at my starting point. I took in the forest around me: mangroves, a smattering of old hardwood trees—almond, walnut...and a giant parota, the kind canoes are carved out of. Orchids and bromeliads adorned overhanging branches, and vines twisted around tree trunks like mammoth boas constricting their prey. Gnarled roots bulked above ground on the trail producing useful steps, if you didn't trip, and sunlight penetrated the canopy above, falling in patches over lush undergrowth.

Bounding hand-sized white butterflies, and smaller purple ones, were the bugs I noticed. I'd had decent luck with bugs lately, suffered only a couple bites since my experience with them in jail.

I shook off the memory of jail, a burning desire to vent my vengeance on those puta madre pigs, and skipped onto the trail and up the hill.

Scout upriver.

PEDRO and the lieutenant proceeded deliberately—on the lookout for more tracks, sensitive to any noise in the woods, Lieutenant Romero at point, his gun in hand. Whenever the trail fell to the river and disappeared back up into the woods, the lieutenant scouted ahead on the high ground and signaled for Pedro with a short whistle indicating all clear.

Thirst became an issue. Pedro was the first to mention it, his low murmur grazing the lieutenant's ears: "I wonder if that Indian is as thirsty as we are."

The lieutenant stopped short, a finger pressed to his lips, eyes fixed beyond a hill rising from the river. Pedro followed the point of his gaze, and felt a tremor in his chest at the sign of movement in the wood; the lieutenant felt a tremor too, in his forearm as he thumbed the oiled safety on his gun.

SOMETHING odd happened to me after I gained the brow of the hill and pressed on back up the trail. It might have been the drugs and the hasty exertion employed when starting back uphill, but mostly I attribute it to that damn golf ball behind my ear. My vision clouded, the world whirling away in a misty fog, and my ears popped as though equalizing to a great height. My head felt swollen and light, like it was filled with helium, yet too numb and heavy for my neck to support. I tripped, caught myself against an unidentified species of tree and took a breather, the humid air tired in my lungs.

Nice head rush.

And that's what it was, more or less, stronger than when Johnny slipped me a joint laced with hash about a year ago but shorter lived. Yet instead of the melting relaxation one feels with weed or wine, dull fatigue overcame me, as though I'd been writing and reading for hours on end without a break.

Two screaming papagayos jolted my head upward in time to catch their colors in flight through fanned leaves. *Papagayos?*

Must have escaped from the zoo or something. No wild papagayos around these parts...or macaws. Thought I heard macaws from my little beach. Monkeys too...monkeys?

The only wild monkeys around here were the kind that walked upright, like Chimp.

Pigs walk upright too.

The idea set the ridges on my stomach aquiver, tickled me. I hugged the tree to keep from losing myself in laughter.

But why not lose yourself in laughter? Laughter's good for you, isn't it?

So I went ahead and giggled a little, but the sound frightened me and I immediately stopped, like someone had slapped my face to sober me up. A good scare—fright—can do that to you, sober you right up. And the reason my giggle frightened me was because this was no time to lose myself in laughter. I hadn't exactly strayed from my mission but the position in which I currently found myself could be dangerous.

If cops are looking for me up here, they'll likely start on this side of the river, on this well-traveled trail.

I pushed myself from the tree, took a deep breath, and dusted off my bare chest. All there, mind and vision clear. I turned to step back onto the trail. Once again something detained me. A rapid knock on wood, the kind woodpeckers make. In and of itself, the noise wasn't so strange. Woodpeckers are around most everywhere. But he seemed rather close and distracted me for a moment; my eyes searched for him, ears perked. And with ears perked, I heard another sound, down the trail below, a murmuring, "Ching. No es el indio."

I pivoted and jumped behind the tree, nearly hugging it again, my heart a steady gallop against its rough bark. Had someone just said that *I* wasn't the Indian or was he speaking of someone else? I pressed into the tree, became one with it to keep myself hidden. But was there a need to hide? Could I hide? and from whom? Beads of sweat skied down the back of my neck. A gnawing feeling inside my chest told me to chance a peek around my tree. An array of branches and leaves and fauna blocked my vision but I spotted them. Couldn't make out their faces but there were two of them. Two men. First one...then the other followed his lead. They stuck to the trees and fauna bordering the trail rising from the riverbank as though expecting an ambush. One of them, the first, held a gun.

No one else was around so I must have been the one who wasn't "el indio"—the Indian.

Would my guide be looking for an "indio"? Did I have two guides instead of one? Would one of my guides be brandishing a pistol as if prepared to shoot me instead of greet me?... The answers to those questions seemed a definitive *no*.

Fear pooled inside me, cold as snow melt. I stilled my breath, Devo's voice echoing in my ears along with my galloping heart: "And should something go wrong, if you're captured..."

Should I run? Wouldn't that be a sure sign of guilt and impel the man with the gun to shoot at me? How could I outrun bullets? And they were looking for an Indian, not Russell Martell. Russell Martell should be dead by now, shouldn't he? Would these two recognize me if I just acted like a tourist out for a hike?

I chanced one more peek, just as the one in a pinstriped shirt and gripping the gun disappeared from view behind dense foliage below the hill's crest. I decided right then and there that running was out of the question. These guys weren't looking for me, but if I ran they just might shoot first and ask questions later. And hiding was a bad idea. They'd already spotted me; if I suddenly disappeared it would raise their suspicions as much as running would. So I really only had two options: walk past them going downriver or continue upriver, my back to them and that gun.

I snatched the pocketknife from my pocket, opened its blade, and slipped it back into my pocket tip first for easy retrieval. Then I stepped onto the trail casual as a man out for an afternoon stroll, my stomach doing reckless backflips. Sweat poured from me like I was in the middle of a marathon. Devo had instructed me to scout upriver and that's where I headed. If they called out to me, I'd probably have to face them, talk to them. Or should I just keep right on walking, ignore them, force them to catch up to me if they wanted to talk?

With that gun, they can force me to do whatever they want.

A young voice surged behind me, quietly raised, as if a loud voice might unduly scare me: "Oiga, señor. Le podemos hablar?" Can we speak to you?

I ignored him, but I couldn't ignore Devo, the sonorous oracle inside my head: "If you have to die, Martell, attack with that knife..."

My mouth had gone completely dry, parched. I gulped down a sticky metallic thickness, my heart pulsing in my throat, frosty fear chilling my chest. I stayed the course, anticipating a louder voice from behind, one I'd have to react to unless I was deaf. None came. Did they not want to raise their voices? Evidently not. They must have been hesitant about causing a commotion in the woods and alerting that Indian they were after.

Indian...Camacho?

If these guys were after Camacho, the game might be up no matter what I did at this point. Had the plot to kill my double failed? Or maybe it succeeded but Camacho had been seen at the scene of the crime and unwittingly led these two straight to me. Was there any chance in hell they were after someone completely unconnected to Russell Martell, the most wanted man in Mexico?

An assumption like that could be my last. I focused on the trail, ever conscious that if they discovered my identity they'd surely capture or kill me.

My legs moved automatically down a gentle slope. Halfway down I heard him behind me—his quickened footfall—and then his voice soft as a whisper in my ear: "Oiga, señor. Nos puede asistir?" Can you assist us?

I stopped at the foot of the slope and looked over my shoulder. A young man with a boy's face made a beeline for me at a half-trot and planted himself on a smooth rock a few steps above me. He wore a printed shirt and jeans. I faced him, expecting his partner in the pinstriped shirt to appear over his shoulder at any second, gun in hand.

I'm half naked, so they may think I'm unarmed. Maybe I can catch them off guard.

There was no escape. I had to assume the worst or pay the ultimate price. Somewhere in the recesses of my mind an image took shape of me chatting with these guys, offering assistance, fooling them into thinking they'd stumbled upon an innocent tourist. But even if that were possible, how long would the subterfuge last? And how could I continue my mission with these sonsabitches prowling around?

No, there was no escape, no alternative.

Steel yourself for battle.

Much like my experience with Chimp and Fat Cop in Johnny's hotel room, timing was key. Those pigs never saw me coming— literally never saw me coming—and couldn't have been more vulnerable if I had caught them with their pants down in the middle of a rape. And this doe-eyed kid standing before me now, while looking straight at me, wouldn't see me coming either. I felt an aching twitch in my gut as my muscles prepared for attack, and carefully smiled. I could overpower this youngster in the blink of an eye, put the knife to his throat and use him as a human shield against that gun. But first I needed to wait for the man with the gun, to see my enemy, make sure I knew where he was, maybe even shake his hand before jabbing my knife into his throat. The kid shifted his weight, anxious hands clasped at his waist, his expression bereft of recognition, bottomless dark eyes liquid and overflowing, like he'd seen enough of life's horrors these past days to last a lifetime. I judged him to be eighteen to twenty-one or two—too young to die but he just might have to. I was too young to die as well.

Russell Martell speaks Spanish. "I'm sorry," I said. "I don't speak Spanish. Uh...no...hablo español."

The kid frowned and blinked as if racking his brain for English words to communicate. He didn't recognize me. But that was no guarantee that the guy with the gun wouldn't. I slipped off my daypack and stooped to set it by my feet. As I anticipated, the other guy appeared right then and I made sure that the kid's figure hid my face from view when he did.

WHEN they first saw movement in the wood, Lieutenant Romero and Pedro Santos froze for long seconds, as though their vision could burn through the trees and foliage and reveal who was there. The movement had been but a color shift accompanied by a muffled sound of feet on dry brush and pebbles, like someone had stumbled off the trail. The lieutenant calculated that he had but two options: approach slowly from the tricky, exceptionally sheer high ground, or make a quiet dash down the trail to the river to see if he could get a better view back up into the forest. He signaled to a small embankment off the shoulder of the river; he and Pedro took off for its cover.

Someone was up there, stepping back from a tree as though he'd just urinated off the trail. They couldn't make him out clearly through the vegetation but they both saw that he was male, and white, his daypack small against his broad bare back; probably a gringo tourist. Their nerves, keyed for the hunt, wound in tight anticipation of corralling the Indian, sagged perceptibly. They sighed in concert as though preparing to take a break. Pedro's voice sawed through his disabused breath: "Ching, no es el indio."

Lieutenant Romero stiffened at the sound of Pedro's voice, his instincts suddenly awakened. Now was not the time to get careless. The man up there could just be a tourist, but maybe he wasn't. Maybe he was tied to the Indian somehow. And maybe he wasn't alone. The lieutenant clutched Pedro's arm, pulled him close to the embankment with a "shhh" and whispered, "Looks like only one man up there, a gringo tourist, but we cannot be certain who he is or if he is alone."

Pedro blinked up into the woods and squinted, his brow and nose wrinkled and disconcerted. "I think...where did he go?"

The lieutenant mouthed, "Puta," and tensed his muscles against an urge to chase after the gringo. The man might have seen the Indian, or be associated with him; he didn't want to lose him, or expose himself to danger in an effort to approach him. "He may have heard you, Pedro," he said, his voice a forceful whisper. "We cannot let him escape. Follow when I give you the signal from behind that big Parota."

The lieutenant scurried over the embankment, took cover behind the parota tree, and signaled to Pedro. They paused together in the silent wood, then repeated the procedure three times up the hill until they gained the brow. A hiker walked calmly along the trail, his back to them. Lieutenant Romero hesitated. "He is alone and appears unarmed," he whispered.

Pedro responded in a whisper: "We need to talk to him. Maybe he has seen the Indian."

The lieutenant flipped the safety on his pistol, holstered it, and buttoned a couple of shirt buttons to hide it. "Go ahead and get his attention. But keep your voice down."

Pedro took several quickened steps to lessen the distance between him and the hiker. "Oiga señor. Le podemos hablar?"

The man strolled around a bend in the trail as though lost in thought, oblivious to everything but his own exercise. Pedro glanced back at the lieutenant. The lieutenant waved him forward, then hastened his pace when he saw Pedro round the bend and sink down a declination in the trail. Watching Pedro slip from view like that raised his heartbeat high in his chest. This might be a big mistake. What if that hiker was leading them into a trap? The lieutenant drew his pistol in mid-stride, heard Pedro ask the man if he could assist them, and felt his tension dissipate at the sheepish response. The guy didn't speak Spanish and had apologized for it in English like a solicitous gringo caught without his dictionary. Lieutenant Romero relaxed his pace, gun hand behind his back, and glimpsed the stooped flank of the man below Pedro. "We look for Indian," the lieutenant said. He extended his left hand as though patting the head of a child. "A shorr' Indian man."

Pedro cocked an eyebrow over his shoulder, surprise curling the corner of his mouth. He'd never heard the lieutenant string words together in English before. The lieutenant seemed to anticipate Pedro's surprise with a rare affected twinkle in his eye and a wink. But the wink never finished itself. Color drained from the lieutenant's face as the wink froze—eyelid shut. His other eye, his left, widened in black astonishment, utter amazement and horror, like he had two distinct faces: one dozing off and the other living a nightmare, *reliving* a nightmare risen from the dead. The lieutenant looked stunned, his handsome face distorted and ugly, as though he'd been struck a paralyzing blow; and in the instant it took him to find himself whole again, in the second it took the lieutenant to come to his senses and brandish his gun, in that moment when Pedro recognized the danger reflected in his deformed visage, it was too late. A steel arm closed around Pedro's neck and lifted him off the ground like he was made of straw. He felt the sharp prick of a knife below his right ear, hot breath on his cheek, and heard the menacing, desperate voice of death:

"Suelta el arma, Teniente, o el niño muere." Drop the gun, Lieutenant, or the kid dies.

I had been dreaming of killing him, tasted relished anger, smelled his tobacco breath, saw my hands around his neck and those soap-opera eyes of his bulging from their sockets as I strangled the life from him. Fear, anger and adrenalin, I'd told myself, were all I needed to match and better my performance in Johnny's hotel room. Well, once again, I had all three surging through me, full throttle. And because I'd been dreaming of killing him and was steeled for battle, when I saw the lieutenant standing up the slope behind that kid my reaction came as naturally as a big leaguer crushing a hanging curveball over the fence, naturally as a linebacker blindsiding a quarterback, as quickly and easily as smashing a venomous spider under foot. There was no hesitation, I mean *none.* It didn't matter that I'd never held a knife to someone's throat before. Could you crush a black widow without practice? I certainly knew how to get a man in a choke hold, men much larger than this wispy runt, so what was the problem if my right hand held a knife? There was none. I didn't even have to think about it, was smart enough not to think at all, just live the dream.

The kid gurgled over the crook of my arm, like he might say something if he could only breathe. I loosened my grip a smidgen, didn't want him dying on me while I still needed him alive. Once again I told the lieutenant to drop his gun or the niño would die, sharper this time so there would be no doubt. And at that moment I really did feel I could kill the kid. Trouble was, it was the lieutenant who I wanted dead, and he knew it.

His gun wavered a little, like he was taking my demand under consideration. I kept my head buried behind the kid's, my chin knuckled against his neck, but could see the lieutenant out of my right eye, feel his glare upon me hotter than a blistering sun. He steadied his gun and said, "Russell Martell. I thought you were dead, burning in hell."

"Thought I might be too. Turned out I was still in México, waiting for you."

The kid gasped and whimpered. My knife scratched a blood line behind his ear. The lieutenant leveled the barrel of his gun between the kid's eyes. "Lo siento, Pedro," he said. I'm sorry.

Unbelievable. The motherfucker was actually willing to kill us both! The kid, Pedro, meant nothing to him compared to having my head on a stick. I dropped the knife and lifted Pedro by the hitch of his pants, my left hand clutching his hair. The only thing left to do was rush the man, use Pedro as a shield, maybe even throw him at the lieutenant, launch him into the gun and attack.

Pedro screamed, "NononoNo!" his arms flailing, his feet running on air. My strength seemed superhuman, like those stories you hear about—people able to lift a car off a loved one in the heat of tragedy. And I had to outweigh the kid by forty or fifty pounds. Even if I wasn't in a life and death struggle, amped on adrenalin and numb on Vicodin and lusting for the lieutenant's blood, I could handle this kid Pedro as easily as wrestling my sister.

It was an uphill battle though, the lieutenant and his gun about five yards up the slope. It took me a second to gain some traction, and in that second a shot came, BANG! like a blow to my chest. I slipped on the incline, regained my footing, and seized up at the sight of the lieutenant, Pedro's limp body extended before me like a shield. The lieutenant stood rigid, his hands fisted crimson at his chest. I spied his gun on the ground and jerked my gaze back up to him. Our eyes met and held. He hissed between his teeth, offering final resistance, defiance. He seemed frozen in space and time, like a statue, and then tumbled like a statue from its pedestal, sideways, his shoulder landing on the trail above me with a thud, malicious brown eyes fixed on me.

My mind reeled. What on earth had just happened? Misfire? Had the gun exploded in his hand? I laid Pedro on his back and stood over the lieutenant's twitching body, my legs shaking as though made of rubber. His hands gripped the neck of a pointed shaft at his chest, his expression contorted and flushed, as if he were straining to lift a massive weight. Then, all at once, he relaxed. His soap-opera eyes rolled up in his head and I could hear the life, his last breaths exit his lungs like bubbles blown through a straw. Blood pooled beneath him inexorably. My eyes flashed to the wrought-iron rod protruding from his back.

The lieutenant had been impaled by a spear.

"Is the boy all right?"

If my legs hadn't been made of rubber, I'd have jumped clear outta my skin at Camacho's sudden appearance. "What the hell?" I said in English.

Camacho strode past the lieutenant's body like he wasn't there and kneeled next to Pedro. "We want this chico alive and well," he said in his precise Spanish. Pedro's face was spangled in blood. Camacho cradled his head. "You have water in your daypack?"

I retrieved the water and handed it to Camacho in a quavering hand. Camacho's eyes smiled at me, though his face looked stern, his lips pinched reproachfully under his aggressive hooked nose. A professor disappointed in the performance of a prize pupil.

"Scared, Russell?" he said. "You should be. The lieutenant was a dead man walking, but Pedro nearly got killed because you did not follow instructions. You need to go back upriver right away and find your guide. Our timing is still good."

Camacho placed a capful of water to Pedro's lips. The kid coughed, blinked open his large doe eyes, and looked up at Camacho as though lost in an unfathomable dream. Pedro clamped his eyes shut, his brow whitening with the effort, and refocused on Camacho. Camacho sat the kid up, their backs to the lieutenant's corpse. He wrapped an arm around Pedro, held him tight, as if expecting him to try and escape.

Pedro struggled weakly. "What happened? Who are you?"

"Call me Camacho, Pedro. I will be your guide for the next couple of days."

RAFAEL, a young junior police officer with dark tousled hair and the face of a choir boy, gave Media Minister Lazarito Charlado a ride to La Joya de Mismaloya to have his hand treated by the hotel's medic. They took the back way out of Mismaloya, a circular route to avoid the growing number of spectators teaming behind police barricades on the west side of town. Rafael produced his police ID at a roadblock on the dirt road and was summarily waved through. Lazarito sat in the passenger seat of his Volkswagen, injured right hand wrapped in a bloodied rag and raised to his chest, cell phone pressed to his ear. But for a mild headache and his throbbing hand, he had fully recovered, felt as good as he had all day...better than he had in days in fact. The bane of his existence, the man who had unleashed unspeakable horror on his beloved adopted home town of Puerto Vallarta, the mass murderer who threatened to destroy his career, his life, El Gringo Terrorista, Russell Martell, was dead! had died before his eyes! What a story!

And Lazarito told his story to the Managing Editor of the Vallarta Diario.

"I am a firsthand eyewitness, Arturo," he said into his phone. "Quote me, Media Minister Lazarito Charlado. Russell Martell, El Gringo Terrorista, is dead."

Arturo told Lazarito that reporters and a television crew were having trouble getting into Mismaloya. "Is there an accident somewhere?"

"Roadblocks," Lazarito said. "Vehicles are being searched and drivers questioned. Russell Martell's accomplices may be lurking about."

"There are reports of a car bomb killing El Gringo Terrorista."

Lazarito described the sequence of events, how he "and six other witnesses" spotted Russell Martell in a truck parked across the street from Restaurante La Flor de Mismaloya just before the bomb went off, how the concussive force of the blast had blown the Media Minister from his chair and knocked him out, and how he'd suffered an injury to his arm and hand from flying shrapnel. "I am on my way to have my wounds treated at La Joya de Mismaloya Hotel," Lazarito concluded.

"Was anyone else injured or killed?"

"No."

"Was it a device rigged to the vehicle or—"

"A bomb inside the truck, apparently."

SEVE VERDAD

"Suicide? Murder? Or did the bomb go off accidentally?"

Lazarito paused. A story was germinating in his head that he was tempted to try out on Arturo: how he had had forced Russell Martell into an act of desperation. How El Gringo Terrorista had come to Mismaloya to kill his nemesis, Media Minister Lazarito Charlado, and in his haste had found death himself. How Lazarito had anticipated Russell Martell's every move and...

Anticipated his every move? Best to wait a while before telling this story. Russell Martell was dead but who knew the extent of his crimes?

"At this juncture," Lazarito said, "authorities at the scene believe the bomb went off accidentally. The gringo probably planned to explode it in the restaurant, or perhaps La Joya de Mismaloya Hotel."

"What do you mean you *saw him in a parked truck*, Lazarito? Did you see him park the truck or get into the truck?

"He must have gotten into the truck before I spotted him. Details will be forthcoming, Arturo. I shall contact you after my wounds are treated. Lazarito Charlado is on the case. And I will be prepared to give the president's Media and Communications Director a full briefing upon my return to Vallarta."

An officer directing traffic at a roadblock waved Rafael across the highway. Rafael could hear Arturo's excited voice emanating from the Media Minister's cell phone as he crossed the street and pulled into the hotel's parking lot. Lazarito shook his head impatiently, as though unable or unwilling to answer the questions shot at him. "Russell Martell's belongings and passport were found in a steel tool chest in the bed of the truck, Arturo," the Media Minister said with a lingering glance at Rafael. "And I saw him as clearly as I see this handsome young man driving my car right now."

Rafael parked at the entrance to the hotel, got out, and rounded the car to open the Media Minister's door for him. "I will send you some photos as soon as possible," Lazarito said to Arturo and abruptly rang off.

Rafael offered Media Minister Charlado a helping hand out of the vehicle. "I heard federale investigators discussing the possibility that Russell Martell was murdered," he said with a nonchalant lift of his young eyebrows.

Lazarito hiccoughed, "Is that so?" He accepted the young man's hand and hoisted himself out of his seat. "I must say, there is plenty of speculation. Indeed there is." Lazarito surveyed Rafael's face—dimpled chin, rounded cherubic mouth, golden-brown eyes. The picture of innocence. "Where are you from, mijo?" Lazarito asked.

"Vallarta. I joined the force three weeks ago."

Media Minister Charlado ran his gaze over the kid's neat uniform. He fished a fifty-peso note from his pocket and extended it to him. "Gracias for the ride, Rafael. This is for your troubles."

Rafael raised his hands in sheepish protest. "No trouble at all, señor. Part of my job."

"And a fine job you are doing, mijo." Lazarito stuffed the note into the kid's breast pocket. "The police deserve all the support we can give them."

Rafael shrugged and dropped his chin. "Gracias señor," he said.

Lazarito squeezed his injured right hand to his chest and patted Rafael on the back with his left. "Take my car back to Mismaloya," he suggested lightly. He guided the young man back around to the driver's side of his Jetta. "We cannot have you neglect your duties while I receive treatment. I am sure your partners and those federales appreciate your assistance."

"But how will you...when shall I return for you?"

Lazarito's eyes glittered piously within heavy swags of flesh. "Give me your cell phone number, Rafael. I will be in contact..."

They exchanged phone numbers.

As Rafael pulled away in Lazarito's car, he punched some numbers on his cell phone.

"Diga," said the voice on the other end of the line.

"I have just dropped him off, Señor Flores," Rafael reported, "and expect him to remain in contact with me..."

110

I had some time to think during my hike back upriver. Couldn't help myself, although that's what set me downriver to begin with and nearly got me killed. Thinking too much. Thinking about the plot to kill my double, speculating about what to do if left without a guide. Two things I didn't have to think about this time upriver.

When Camacho told me to head back upriver, that our timing was "still good", I didn't respond immediately. He and Pedro were huddled below the lieutenant's impaled corpse, and Camacho caught me lingering, saw the million questions forming on my tongue, the shock and awe in my expression, and shot me a glare that set my soul on fire. "Upriver," he commanded. "Your guide is waiting for you."

I shouldered my pack and made tracks.

My guide was waiting for me. Outstanding news. Did that mean the plot to kill my double had succeeded? In and of itself, no. But I didn't need Camacho to confirm as much. The lieutenant had already done so. As I held my knife to Pedro's jugular, the lieutenant made it clear that he thought I was dead, "burning in hell."

The plot to kill my double must have succeeded. "Russell Martell" was dead.

My confidence returned in force. I'd have a guide and Russell Martell was dead. Amazing. Everything seemed to be going as planned despite my foul-up...

Heading downriver like I did would have been a worthwhile detour if *I* had been the one to kill the lieutenant instead of Camacho. I was lucky Camacho killed him though. After all, the lieutenant had a gun, and me in his sights.

Was my guide armed to kill? Might there be another intruder in these woods who would have to die? My strides quickened, my vision acute and amplified to take in the river, woods and the trail all at once. I had to find my guide...my bodyguard, or I might end up like the lieutenant. The dead lieutenant. What did Camacho plan on doing with his body? leave it there for wild animals and vultures to feed on and police and tourists to find? Did Camacho have an accomplice? another member of Devo's *team*? someone who would bury the body? And what about that kid Pedro? What was his relationship to the lieutenant? If he was a fellow police officer, why wasn't he armed?... Camacho was probably "el indio" the lieutenant and Pedro were after and had lured them upriver. Why did he lure them upriver?... So he could kidnap Pedro; the sadistic prick lieutenant was a "dead man walking". But how did Camacho plan to keep Pedro under wing, under his control, and why did he want to?

"We want this chico alive and well," Camacho had said, as if Pedro were a key player in his and Devo's master plan. Who the hell was Pedro? Would I be seeing him again in the role Devo had scripted for me?

Maybe Pedro would assist the cartoonist I was supposed to meet eventually, write captions to sketches of horned pigs in headscarves and turbans.

Sorry Pedro. I never really intended to kill you like that sadistic puta madre lieutenant did.

I didn't mean to do a lot of things—put Pedro in danger, myself in danger, Johnny in danger...Brenda...

Brenda.

Boy did I feel low all of a sudden. Lower than a worm in the bottom of the ocean. My pace slackened. What a heel I was. It's one thing to put yourself in danger but why screw up everyone else's life as well?

FINDING DEVO

The sun snapped me out of my stupor. I circled a bluff about thirty yards from the river, the sun hot on my face and chest. Shadows blanketed this section of the river, where I'd taken my swim, and had encroached on my little beach. I stopped short at the edge of the bluff. Someone was sitting on my beach. Rounded shoulders, the back of a head. A silhouette partially obscured by the shallow embankment. I stepped out from the bluff and scanned the rocky terrain. No one else in sight.

Could this be my guide, the person I've been searching for? or another intruder? An innocent hiker could turn out to be an intruder if I'm recognized as Russell Martell.

I approached with stealth, to check this guy out before he had a chance to check me out. Rocks and cobbles ground under my feet; the river and waterfall would drown the noise on my beach. The silhouette's profile sharpened. I could make out the clothing, *her* yellow bikini top and black billcap, hair twisted up underneath. She stirred, stretched out her legs and leaned back on her hands. I hesitated and admired those legs—cinnamon-brown legs a shade darker than her tan shorts. Balletic legs. Shapely and trim. Smooth and strong. A dancer's legs... *Brenda!*

There was no mistaking those legs. I'd admired them plenty at Mountain's party, even got my hands on them. My heart leapt and sang; a sudden electric rush released my guilt-bound spirit. I didn't have to rescue Brenda from my pursuers, my foul-ups and rash actions. She was right here!...to rescue...*me?* I choked on a cry for joy. "Brenda," I said, my voice a pleading drum roll.

She reacted as to an unfamiliar bird song, swiveled her head around just enough to see me, her eyes shaded by sunglasses. It was Brenda all right—her oval face and button nose...gentle chin and rich lips. I pressed forward at a trot, shrugged off my daypack and planted myself on my knees in the sand next to her. "Russell," she said and flashed me that smile—a beautiful morning every day. "Just the man I wanted to see and—"

I silenced her with a kiss on her lips. "Kiss," I said.

Brenda licked her lips. "That too."

I embraced her with a hug so powerful it brought tears to my eyes. "I was worried about you," I said.

"I've been thinking about you too, Russell. You're coming to Guadalajara with me."

I pulled back from her. "You're my guide?"

Her hair tickled my shoulders as she shook off her cap. "I suppose you could put it that way." She caressed my head and leaned into me, her mouth salty and sweet—a spice I couldn't quite identify. I

563

ran my hands over her back. We melded, filled all the time and space that had been separating us.

She removed her sunglasses and searched my face.

"Recognize me?" I grinned.

"I like your hair better natural brown."

"It's only shoe polish. It's greasy but we can wash it out." I sat close to her in the sand. "This is the best surprise I could've hoped for. Got any others?"

Brenda twisted her mouth and winked at me. "A few," she said. "Secrets really. Secrets to share if you promise not to tell."

My eyes danced over the yellow bikini top hugging her delectable bust line. "I promise."

She reached for her daypack by her side, retrieved a small rectangular box, and extended it to me. "This should help explain a few things."

The box was thin and black. I took it. "You can open the box," she said, "but can't keep what's inside."

I lifted the lid to the box. A silver wristwatch was inside, laid out on a thin sheet of gauze. A man's wristwatch, square-faced and jeweled. It was strangely discolored, the crystal cracked. The watch had stopped at 11:45. I said, "Looks like it was a beautiful watch."

"Yes it was. Have a closer look."

I removed the watch. It appeared to have been scorched in several places. Bluish discolorations were evident along the plated band and around the clock. I turned it over in the palm of my hand. An inscription in English was on the back. My eyes swelled as I read it aloud: " 'To my love with all my love, always. Your Mariposa.' "

I swallowed thickly, eyes raised to her. Brenda's lips trembled, a soft wrinkle creasing her brow. I tried to soothe her hurt as best I could: "Mariposa. He chose the right pet name for you, Brenda. You're as light as butterfly wings on the dance floor."

Brenda sighed and blinked away a tear, her melodic voice saddened. "Remember what I told you about him at Armando's party?"

I secured the watch in its box and returned it to her. "You said he died in that plane crash in Peru, in that terror attack. And then...well—" my voice cracked. "You said we have something in common. You know...with respect to Rosalita's death."

Brenda slipped the box into her pack and hugged her knees. "We have something else in common now too, Russell."

Brenda and I have quite a bit in common besides our dead lovers: common languages, book smarts, a love for athletics and music. But she was referring to something else. "Devo," I said.

"Yes. Devo."

"When did you meet him?"

"A year or so ago. Through Armando." Brenda gazed out over the river. "Armando met Devo through a mutual friend," she said, "a gallero from Nyarit. Devo hooked up with Armando in Guadalajara about a year ago and that's when Ara and I met him."

"So what's his angle? I mean, why—"

"Devo gave me the watch."

I blanched. My eyes must've been as big as saucers, though my voice remained level: "Wow. Devo...when—"

"Last night. Actually, Devo gave the watch to Ara to give to me."

"Didn't that flip you out?"

"Sorta." Brenda shrugged, "But not so much, since it came from Devo. He knew Richard, my fiancé. We discussed his death a few times. We both understand that the enemy who killed Ricardo is our common enemy. All of us...*infidels* have a common enemy."

I frowned stubbornly. Brenda hadn't answered my question. "But what's his angle?" I repeated, my tone reserved. "Does he have some kind of network or—"

Brenda cut me off with a hand on my knee that sent a tingle up the inside of my thigh. "Have faith, infidel," she clucked with a touch of irony. "When Devo finds you, or you find him, it's not just by chance. Everything will come clear soon enough. But first you're coming with me to Guadalajara."

I opened my mouth to speak; Brenda placed her fingers over my lips to quiet me. She turned my head. "That greasy makeup under your eye is running," she said, "and...Dios mío! That's a nasty lump behind your ear." Brenda ran her hand over my chest. "And you have a bruise under your ribs. You get those when the police took you in for questioning?"

Her coconut oil fragrance had me salivating. "It's all much better, thanks to Devo."

"Thanks to Devo, huh?"

Our eyes embraced. "And thanks to you."

She reached around my neck. My pulse came alive, but before our lips met she suddenly recoiled, released a frightening cry, her expression frozen in shock at a vision over my shoulder. I wheeled around and sucked in a strangled breath at a pair of beastly eyes.

Brenda gasped, "Bizco. Tan sigiloso eres." You're so sneaky.

"Bizco," I shuddered with relief...felt like an old friend had greeted me with a shot to the solar plexus.

Bizco rested his chest on the cobbled bank above us, a prodigious nose-distance away, ears perked, head cocked, eyes crossed on Brenda's breast. He belonged in a cartoon.

"You lucky dog, Bizco," I said. "How many gorgeous women do you see?"

He licked his chops and panted. Brenda sniggered, "Bizco sees and smells plenty of everything."

I stood and looked over him towards the bluff. "If you're here, Bizco, your Dad can't be far."

Brenda's voice sharpened: "You have more bruises on your back, Russell! What happened to you?"

"You guessed it. Those charming Vallarta cops." I searched the landscape upriver. Three horses were strolling our way in the near distance, the solitary rider as thick as the horse beneath him. Armando La Montaña Montoya. Bizco took off for him.

Brenda curled her legs under her rear. "Armando's coming?" she said, more statement than question.

"Be here in a minute or two."

She patted the sand. "Then we still have a moment alone."

111

ACROSS the street from La Flor de Mismaloya, a tow truck had arrived to haul Enrique's pickup to Vallarta along with the headless, immolated cadaver inside. CISEN and federale investigators had determined that there was no way to peel Russell Martell's remains from the charred cab of the truck for transport in a separate vehicle, not without destroying and contaminating evidence. So the entire *desmadre* had to be transported to the morgue and lab in Puerto Vallarta for a thorough forensic examination.

Senior CISEN Operative Alfredo Flores would keep abreast of the forensic examination yet, for the moment, he found himself detained at La Flor de Mismaloya. He stared over Operative Tórrez's shoulder and grumbled at the laptop computer screen on the table, "Qué demonios are they up to? Joy riding?"

Operatives Blanco and Rivera stood to his left, Gloria to his right, all fixed upon the flashing red dot on the screen—the signal from Lieutenant Romero's wire. "What is this?" Blanco questioned. "The fourth time they have stopped along the road?"

"Fifth," said Tórrez.

Rivera shook his head disdainfully. "Pinche Vallarta policía. They have no idea where the fuck they are going or what they are doing."

Tórrez pointed a pencil at the flashing dot and traced a line along the map. "They know enough to stay between these two points," he said. "Just south of La Arcadia and about seven kilometers north of Mismaloya. Back and forth."

"Pinche Vallarta policía," Rivera repeated. "Romero probably stuffed his wire into his pocket and forgot about it. He has no desire to communicate with us."

"Claro," Blanco agreed. "He thinks he is on to something. Some sort of clue into the death of El Gringo Terrorista. A clue he wants to follow up on himself, without CISEN—"

"Lieutenant Romero," Gloria intervened subtly, "is with Officer Pedro Santos." All eyes were upon her, as if she had uttered an undiscovered truth. "And Pedro," she proceeded, "will not rest until he finds his father."

Flores glared at Enrique's pickup being hoisted by the tow truck across the street. "Enough speculation," he said abruptly. "Tórrez?"

Operative Tórrez craned his head up from the computer screen. "Sí señor?"

"Blanco and Rivera will accompany you in the Ford. Find the lieutenant and see what the hell he and Officer Santos are up to. And call me immediately with a report."

Gloria retrieved her bag and headed for the Ford as if Flores had given her the order. CISEN would not be allowed to manhandle Pedro again. She'd see to it.

112

THE police pickup blew through Old Vallarta with its siren screaming and red and blue lights flashing. Not an unusual occurrence in Puerto Vallarta these last couple of days. Cars cleared out of its way automatically; pedestrians barely batted an eye at yet another emergency vehicle tearing through town.

Mayor Juan Pacífico Velázquez sat in the passenger seat reviewing the script he was rewriting in his head, and getting into character for his first meeting with the highest levels of the Mexican government. Presidente Cárdenas de Ortega and members of his cabinet were due to arrive at the airport shortly in Presidential Transport 02 for a tour of Vallarta's disaster areas and a briefing from the mayor, a briefing that would include an astounding development: the death of Russell Martell.

Was Russell Martell's death accidental? Murder? Suicide? Preventable? Inevitable? Juan didn't know and neither did Gloria, CISEN, or anyone else. Hell, until they had the results of a DNA test, the corpse couldn't even be positively identified.

"Do not dwell on the negative," Gloria admonished before Juan left Mismaloya. "There are witnesses to Russell Martell's death and his belongings were found in the bed of the truck. Lord knows we have suffered enough. Put a positive spin on our efforts for the president and worry about the details when you preside over a full and thorough briefing this evening. The death of Russell Martell may not be reason to celebrate, but this is your moment to shine, Juan."

Gloria was right. He had to rise to the occasion, look upon this as an opportunity to make a positive impression on the president. Everyone else would have their chance to do the same during the full briefing. "Everyone" was bound to include federales, Immigration Inspector Sandra Villanueva, Gloria, and CISEN, as well as el comandante and Lieutenant Romero. Maybe even Officer Pedro Santos. The reason Gloria stayed behind in Mismaloya rather than accompany him to the airport was to find Pedro and protect him from further abuse at the hands of CISEN. "I cannot allow CISEN to mistreat Pedro again," she had told her husband back in Mismaloya, a shadow of guilt hardening her features. "The young man is indispensable and only guilty of trying to find his father."

The police pickup accelerated onto Libramiento. Juan thought about Pedro's father and wondered where he could be. Enrique was just as indispensable as his son Pedro.

113

COMANDANTE Héctor Diamante Pasqual had done everything in his power to ingratiate himself to Senior Operative Alfredo Flores and CISEN. He picked up operatives at the airport, saw to it that they had vehicles at their disposal, and had been tireless in his briefings to them at police headquarters. And what were the rewards for his efforts? Had he been supported in his position as Comandante? granted a participatory role in their investigations? No. Nothing of the sort. He'd hoped to be allowed to work alongside CISEN in the field and aid in the recapture or death of Russell Martell, redeem himself for the raids he had botched. But instead he'd received nothing but rebuffs and

568

loathsome orders from CISEN to man his station. Where was Héctor when news of Russell Martell's death was reported to police dispatch? Where was he confined while the mayor made his way from Mismaloya to the airport to meet Presidente Cárdenas de Ortega and members of his cabinet? Where would he have to stay put as Juan gave the president a tour of the disasters at the Washington and Arena Vallarta? Where else but in his office at police headquarters monitoring this maldito disc!!!

El comandante paced his office and stepped to his open door for a languid glance down the hallway to the entrance of police headquarters. Headquarters had been abandoned to three officers standing guard outside, the girls at dispatch, and him. He could not have felt more isolated if he were in solitary confinement. Héctor spat a curse, returned to his chair behind his desk, and settled his dreary eyes upon the disc's latest unchanging image: a tedious geographical map of Mexico in brown and gray.

The importance of the disc could not be denied. Not only did it predict the attack on the Washington but appeared to have predicted the Arena Vallarta fire as well. The disc had to be monitored but, what a thankless chore! There were lives to be saved at the Washington, the president was coming to town, and here he sat, the Comandante of the Puerto Vallarta Police Department, staring at a meaningless map...

The image of Mexico faded, replaced by a geographical map of Alaska. It said so in black block lettering across inconsequential shades of gray and brown: ALASKA. Several cities and towns were labeled. Pinche puto. This was a new one. Alaska. Alaska hadn't appeared before, not solo like this. It was as if the disc was reminding him of its importance, that it still held untold secrets: keep your eye on me because you never know what will pop up...

Héctor felt his mustache begin to sweat. Significant revelations might still come from the disc. Maybe a painted target...in Mexico? That was the biggest fear, another painted target in Mexico. But maybe a painted target across the border—al norte—wouldn't be so bad. Far enough away to present little if any direct threat to him or his paisanos yet close enough to bring him plenty of attention here at headquarters. That would be ideal! Presidente Cárdenes de Ortega, members of his cabinet, and the mayor would come running to police headquarters to check it out. Phone calls of international import pertaining to the security of the United States and Mexico would be made from this office... Then the president would require a briefing. A full briefing conducted by Comandante Héctor Diamante Pasqual himself at police headquarters instead of one dominated by the mayor at Dreams or some other swanky hotel.

He'd have to put the best spin possible on police blunders, of course. No doubt about it, errors had been committed...by everyone. Yet, El Gringo Terrorista was dead, wasn't he? Blown to bits in a truck. Héctor had few details to this astonishing turn of events but the pressure brought to bear on Russell Martell by police and government authorities had to be a contributing factor in his demise. If police were to be blamed for contributing to El Gringo Terrorista's reign of terror, shouldn't they receive some credit for his death as well?

The map of Alaska blinked and expanded its scope to include British Columbia and northwest American states. Color was added to its features. No red targets...yet... Another attack had to be coming somewhere. Perhaps in British Columbia, Washington state, or Oregon. He needed to prepare himself for just such an eventuality. Héctor visualized his briefing to the president and members of his cabinet. If he managed to get in the president's good graces, his career would skyrocket! He could run for mayor, or governor, or...

Héctor's gaze drifted from the computer screen. He reclined in his chair, unconscionably inspired by the fancy...

114

MOUNTAIN heard a chopper but I wasn't so sure. Sounded like low rumbling thunder from the storm clouds up over the adjacent ridge. He insisted that the sound came from below and some distance behind us, "Over the Mismaloya River. The echo can play tricks on your ears."

Mountain, Brenda and I had put quite a bit of distance between us and the Mismaloya. About three hours on horseback, all uphill through the jungle at a fairly grueling pace. Bizco brought up the rear, for the most part. And Ara, I'd been informed, was to meet us in Guadalajara.

"That chopper after you or me?" I chided Mountain in English.

"Dey don' know who deyz afta. An youz dead, buddy."

"After they run a DNA test on my fried double, they'll know I'm not dead."

"No dey won'," Mountain said gruffly. "Youz dead an' *contaminated.*"

"Contaminated? What? How?"

"How the hell do I know?" he replied in Spanish. "Injections and explosive solvents. Just be thankful you do not *look* dead and contaminated."

FINDING DEVO

Down on my little beach, before we began our trek for Chico's Paradise, Montoya told me I looked great for a dead guy.

"Feel great," I said, "now that I have you and Brenda with me."

Mountain wore Levis, a sleeveless blue denim shirt, sunglasses and a Miami Dolphins billcap. Scratches and scabs—grotesque tattoos—scarred his pylon arms and meat cleaver hands, a result of his work as a human bulldozer down at the Washington. There was no time for pleasantries. We weren't exactly running late but Mountain did mention that we'd have gotten an earlier start had I kept hiking upriver to meet him and Brenda. Brenda had hiked back downriver in the hopes of coming across me. I wanted to apologize for the delay, make an excuse about getting distracted and numb on Vicodin and running into a Vallarta Police Lieutenant, but could see he wasn't interested. Not now at any rate. Mountain took the lead on his horse like a seasoned cavalry soldier, a major leading his troops in retreat. The only thing to do was keep his pace.

Chico's Paradise is a restaurant nestled in the mountains on the Tuito River southeast of Mismaloya. Numerous swimming holes and rock slides play along the river and the scenery is typical tropical paradise. The restaurant and river were just about completely blanketed in shade when we arrived, the sun in descent upon a mountain ridge. Not many cars in the parking lot. An old man wearing a straw sombrero and an affable, wizened expression relieved us of our horses. We piled into Mountain's King Cab truck like war-weary travelers and headed on down the road towards the coast.

"**Y**OUZ cumfable, buddy?"

"Yeah. She's comfy." My head was in Brenda's lap. I'd gotten horizontal in the back of the cab of Mountain's truck after we hit the coastal road for Melaque and Guadalajara.

Brenda caressed the hair at my temple. "Keep your head down Esteban," she said coyly. "Let Bizco do the talking."

Bizco was in the passenger seat, his prodigious nose out the window. Brenda had my passport in her daypack...Esteban Enrique Bellán's passport. A Brazilian version of the Venezuelan passport Devo had used for me at the roadblock last night.

Mountain had a tortuous detour mapped out around Melaque that should skirt any roadblock on our way to Guadalajara, but there was always a chance of running into cops. He'd already honked and waved at a police pickup when we dropped down onto the highway from Chico's Paradise. They'd responded with a cheer for "BIZCO!"

SEVE VERDAD

Letting Bizco do the talking wasn't a bad idea. His heroics at the Washington were legendary from what Mountain and Brenda had told me, not to mention that cheer from police. But I still had my doubts. "Bizco might be a hero," I said. "But if he or any of us have to do *any talking*, we may be in serious trouble."

Mountain's Spanish sounded like gravel sliding down a chute: "El Gringo Terrorista está muerto, *buddy*. And even though la policía y los federales are still looking for his accomplices, pues..." Mountain looked over his shoulder and winked at Brenda, "...everyone knows Brenda and I are not killers...or terroristas."

Brenda tittered, "Could anyone even imagine I'm a killer?"

"Guess that's something you and I don't have in common, Brenda," I said. "*Everyone* thinks I'm a killer...and a terrorist."

Brenda patted my shoulder. "No they don't, Esteban," she retorted reassuringly. "No they don't."

I slid a hand under Brenda's leg and closed my eyes. Between the three of them—Brenda, Mountain, and Bizco—the King Cab reeked of dauntless equanimity. And Brenda is the perfect pillow. I napped. Brenda stirred to get something from her daypack but otherwise didn't disturb me. When I awoke she was asleep, head back, her hair framing an angelic countenance. I sat up. The sun had set but dusk hadn't darkened yet; Montoya had begun an arduous climb through the mountainous roads leading to Guadalajara. Brenda's lips parted and her brow twitched somnolently. I couldn't resist those lips and leaned in to kiss them, but was distracted by an odd image, a face staring up at me from a sketch pad left open at Brenda's side. A bearded pig face with fangs, its headdress draped behind pointy little horns.

THE END

ACKNOWLEDGEMENTS

A very deep thank you to my mother for her years of comments and edits on this writing journey, to my stepfather for his edits and comments and my sister for her comments and art work.

ABOUT THE AUTHOR

SEVE VERDAD was born in Southern California and educated in the USA as well as abroad. He has resided in Latin America, the Great Pacific Northwest, and California. Currently, his whereabouts are unknown. He is wanted for prohibition crimes not unlike some of those described in his fiction and has published his works, in part, to bring attention to his plight and the plight of countless others like him.

www.ingramcontent.com/pod-product-compliance
Lightning Source LLC
Chambersburg PA
CBHW051928020726
47501CB00001B/31